The Three Sunrises

KRISTEN HARTMAN

Beach Reader Books
Fort Myers, FL

This is a work of fiction. The events and characters described herein are imaginary and are not intended to refer to specific places or living persons. The opinions expressed in this manuscript are solely the opinions of the author and do not represent the opinions or thoughts of the publisher. The author has represented and warranted full ownership and/or legal right to publish all the materials in this book.

Cover Illustration by Fanqi Zeng, 2013, based on the original design by Kristen Hartman.
Author Photo by Joan Burke

Beach Reader Books
http://www.beachreaderbooks.com

ISBN: 978-0-578-07081-0

PRINTED IN THE UNITED STATES OF AMERICA

ACKNOWLEDGEMENTS

For my husband Mike–the love of my life–my partner in crime–my best friend. You are my real life hero and my inspiration for every love scene! Thank you for all your love and support. I love you. Here's to making our dreams come true!

To my Dad who introduced me to books and helped teach me to read–the greatest gift a parent can give a child. I love you very much and I'll forever be grateful! I finally got it–Santa turned *with* a jerk, not *to* a jerk! Oh and as an aside, ignore the adult scenes, I don't know who wrote those. Ha ha ha!

And to my two smart, beautiful children. You make me so proud each and everyday! I love you both so much! Keep reading!

CHAPTER ONE

"I can't wait to get my toes in the sand." Nicki leaned back against her seat with a sigh.

"Oh, God, me too." Ali looked out the plane's small window watching the ground crew load the baggage into the belly of the DC-9. She had just finished her final year of business school earning her MBA and was so ready for a vacation. She wanted to do nothing but relax. She felt as though she'd had her head buried in books for the past six years, and she was ecstatic that school was finally over. Ali figured by the end of the trip, if not before, she'd know just how to put her lengthy education to use.

Nicki had also just graduated, with a masters in journalism and, thanks to her grandmother's connections, landed a sweet little reporting job on Sanibel Island. The local newspaper there was called the Beach News, and Nicki would be writing small articles of interest on local events and happenings. She knew it would be a great stepping stone to her dream job of becoming a columnist at the Boston Globe or the Boston Herald. She didn't care which; she just wanted to see her name preceding a column in her hometown newspaper.

"I'm sure you'll have your whole business plan by the end of the first week, just so you can relax and have no worries the rest of your stay." Nicki smiled at her best friend. Ali was completely organized -- an "A-type" personality, she had her priorities in order. Nicki knew Ali would one day be successful, as would she. They both had the brains and the motivation to succeed. The girls were both fortunate to come from successful families and were not strangers to a solid work ethic. Even though Nicki would be working, she was grateful her downtime would be spent with Ali on the islands. They had both worked very hard at school and couldn't wait to celebrate it being over.

It was Nicki's grandmother who had set the whole trip up for them. She was a successful real estate agent in Boston's Back Bay, and five years ago she had purchased a beautiful home on Captiva, a small barrier island in the Gulf of Mexico. A sister island to Sanibel (the larger of the two), Captiva boasted two miles of beautiful beach, laden with millions of the prettiest seashells one could hope to find. People traveled from all over the world to shell both islands and to view the spectacular sunsets on Captiva, sunsets that boasted colors straight from an artist's paint-strewn palette.

With the Gulf idly lapping the shore on one side and the stillness of the tranquil bay on the other, Captiva was a haven for true escapism. The cerulean blue water that bathed your eyes as you crossed over Blind Pass, and the occasional glimpse of dolphins lazily making their way in the shallows of the Gulf, were just two of the reasons that had people returning year after year.

Nicki had spent most of her school breaks on Captiva over the years, and some of those included Ali. They were both grateful this time to have more than just a week to spend there.

The house Nan had purchased sat directly across the street from the beach and right on the bay. At night from the backyard one might be lucky enough to hear the exhale of a manatee slumbering by, or by day be amused by the sight of a school of lady fish flying above the water, usually with a dolphin in toe.

The house usually sat empty in the summers, and Nicki's grandmother was happy to have the two women making use of it. She had bought the house as a getaway from the harsh New England winters and hoped that everyone in the family would enjoy it as well.

This would be the first time Nicki would be here without her family. Her grandmother would be taking her parents and her younger sister Jenna to Italy for the summer. Since Nicki wanted to get a jump start on her career, she chose working on Sanibel rather than the family vacation. Her grandmother's best friend just happened to own the island paper Nicki would be writing for, and Nicki was grateful for the opportunity. A foot in the door was all she needed. She hoped her writing would speak for itself, and she was certain writing for the Beach News on Sanibel was going to be fun. Not many people could boast being able to wear flip flops to work.

Ali, on the other hand, had been working all through college in her family's business and couldn't wait to have the summer off. Her parents were real estate developers just south of Boston. Ali had been working for them since high school and was ready to do something new and exciting on her own. She had her own real estate license and had even sold a few houses in the past few years. The commissions had enabled her to help pay for her education and to sock a little away. She loved the large paydays but not the headaches that came along with the job. She could have quit school and become more involved in selling real estate for the money alone, but her heart just wasn't in it. She enjoyed it solely as a hobby. The open houses she had sat had served her well as a study forum, and she was proud to now have her business degree, allowing her to move on to more exciting ventures.

She would, however, always be grateful for the experience her parents had provided and their great business sense. Ali had learned a lot through them, and she couldn't wait to do something on her own and make them proud. She had some exciting ideas and hoped this summer she could cultivate them. Meeting a hot guy on the beach wouldn't be such a bad thing, either, she thought. Although being that the islands were mostly filled with retirees and vacationing families, the odds were not in her favor.

Ali turned from the window to look at Nicki. Her best friend was gorgeous, no doubt about it -- auburn hair, blue eyes, and physically fit, she'd always attracted a lot of attention. More than one male had turned his head as the two had entered the concourse.

Nicki just six months prior had broken it off with her long-time boyfriend. He had wanted to marry her and move to Michigan to settle into his family's car sales business and Nicki, well, Nicki had not. Her ex had moved back to Michigan shortly after the breakup and just last week had married his high school sweetheart. Nicki hadn't shed a tear.

"What are you staring at?"

"I was just thinking how glad I am that I didn't have to don a light blue satin maid of honor's dress, at what would have been the worst mistake wedding in history, to that used-car salesman you called a boyfriend."

"Wow." Nicki turned to stare at the back of the seat in front of her, feigning disbelief. "It's not like it was ever a consideration." She turned back to Ali and laughed. "I had no idea you thought of him as a used-car salesman."

Ali laughed, too. "I didn't while you were dating, but whenever I picture the two of you married, I picture him on a car lot, in a plaid sport jacket, with a bullhorn, shouting, "Shop at Diamond Dave's for the deal of a lifetime."

Nicki burst out laughing. "Diamond Dave's? His name is Tom!"

"I *know*." Ali was cracking up, too. "But he looks like a Diamond Dave -- in my mind -- on that car lot."

"Well, thank God I had you to wake me up and steer me in the right direction."

"If you mean taking you to that club where you met and left with that guitar player, then proceeded to have the best sex of your life, you're welcome!"

"Yes, that's exactly what I meant, thank you." Nicki leaned back and smiled. "There's something about a guitar player's calloused fingers."

"Okay, okay." Ali laughed, covering her ears.

"Seriously, though, did you not like Tom all these years?" Nicki asked.

"Of course I liked him, but he was more like just a good friend of yours. He didn't have an exciting bone in his body, and when did you *ever* tell me how great sex was with him?"

"He was boring, I'll admit, but that's just what I needed in school. I couldn't be running off to parties and screwing off. I had deadlines at the Rag." Nicki referred to her university's newspaper. "And he was good to bounce things off of, for a male perspective."

"So basically he was just a source." Ali laughed.

Nicki chuckled, "He was more than that, and I will miss his friendship, but you're right -- after one night with the *guitar man*, I'll never think of sex the same way again. Because trust me, for four years it was the same with Tom. Although I shouldn't have to tell you, as I recall you were in a pretty stagnant relationship with John."

Ali nodded her head in agreement. She had dated this guy who had lived in her apartment building near campus. He was an aspiring day trader. In the beginning it was all paper trading, and then as his paper money grew, so did his balls. He started borrowing money from friends and family to make real trades. He assured everyone he knew what he was doing, and after a few successful trades, he'd managed to convince some people as well. But it didn't take long for him to start losing in the market, and he was unable to pay anyone back. His short-lived cocky demeanor suddenly turned to a desperate one. He was no longer the handsome, confident person Ali had first met. He became depressed and reliant on Ali to support him and pay back his debts. She quickly saw where that was headed and broke it off. Their love life had been exciting in the beginning but, like the relationship, had declined steadily. He'd ended up moving back in with his parents and sharing a room with his little brother.

After John, she'd had a few short-term relationships, some exciting, some not so, and at present she was happy to just be on her own, starting a new chapter in her life. She had her whole life ahead of her, and she was ready to jump in feet first. However, if a hot, sexy guy was in the cards for her this summer, who was she to turn him down? It had definitely been awhile.

"Now, what were you just thinking?" Nicki smirked.

"That it's been awhile and it would be nice..." Ali paused. "You know..." She grinned at her friend.

"To get laid!" Nicki finished.

Ali's face turned beet red as she quickly looked around at the surrounding seats on the plane. "Why don't you just announce it to the whole plane!"

Nicki was laughing. "Sorry, no one heard me. Besides, I agree. It *would* be nice!"

"Oh, you'll have no time -- you'll be so busy reporting how many dolphins were spotted by the lighthouse or how many baby turtles made it to the water. You'll never have time for a man," Ali teased.

"Thanks for that! I guess I'll just have to live vicariously through your lazy ass!"

Ali gave her a satisfied grin. "Yes, you will. Yes, you will." She turned to look out the window again as they took off. They'd be in southwest Florida in just under three hours. Ali closed her eyes and said her Hail Marys on the ascent.

Nicki looked out the window as well, watching the city of Boston disappear and big fluffy clouds take its place. She knew having to work that she probably *would* be living vicariously through Ali this summer.

Ali was a very strong, independent woman. At five feet, seven inches tall, Ali could have been a model for a fitness magazine. She had long brown hair and brilliant green eyes and a body sculpted from lots of running, kickboxing, and strength training. Her smooth olive skin completed the picture, giving her a healthy look even in the dead of winter, when most New Englanders were sporting their palest shade, Nicki being one of them. To Nicki, though, Ali's best attributes were her sense of humor and unconditional friendship.They had been best friends since grade school and were as close as sisters. They were close to each other's families as well. Ali had two older brothers and Nicki just one younger sister by eighteen months. They had brought their families together over the years, forming friendships between not only their parents, but Nicki's grandmother, too, who was the matriarch of Nicki's family.

A lot of Ali's strength and independence had come from her two older brothers, Jason and Matt. Jason was an architectural engineer and did most of his business alongside his parents' development company, and Matt also worked alongside the family business with his own construction company. Matt was closer in age to Ali and Nicki and had often been around during their high school years, teasing and tormenting the girls, much to Nicki's dismay. She had always felt insecure around him. He was eight years older, and he was just as gorgeous as Ali and was always with a girlfriend. Nicki had imagined herself as one of them many a time, but he had never even given her a second glance or thought of her as anyone other than Ali's best friend. He was just as funny as Ali, too. Their parents had raised all three of them to be great people, and Nicki was proud to know all of them. She hadn't seen Ali's brothers in quite a long time due to school and life in general, but Ali was always filling her in on the latest family gossip. Nicki knew Jason was a workaholic and that Matt was ever the ladies' man, currently with some blonde named Julie. Nicki didn't like her, didn't know her, either, and she couldn't help getting irritated when Ali talked about Matt, for reasons she had long since buried.

Nicki knew Ali wouldn't have any trouble meeting somebody this summer; she just had that magnetic personality. Nicki closed her eyes, smiling to herself. She just hoped whoever he was, he had a great-looking friend.

While Nicki slept through the flight, Ali took out her notebook and wrote down her business plan. She had thought about it a lot in school and knew it was something she really wanted to do. She was so excited and eager to share it with Nicki.

She'd always grown up going to flea markets and antique stores with her parents. She used to love finding the little trinkets they would let her buy: an old rhinestone brooch or jewel-encrusted compact. They made her feel so grown up. Those days always stuck in her mind, and even through college she'd stop along a main street and find a little shop that had just the right piece of furniture or picture frame. She'd buy it, take it home, and refinish it to match her own decorative style. She loved painting everything white and roughing it up with a little sandpaper to give it that worn look. It felt so homey and warm with just the right cushion or tablecloth. She'd received so many compliments from her family and friends, and it had set her mind in one direction. She was going to open her own store. She would refinish old furnishings and find little trinkets that other people would love to have in their homes, too. She would scour the antique shops and thrift shops all over New England and bring the old pieces to life.

Ali couldn't wait to get started. Her plan this summer would be to think of a name, secure a location, and of course make sure she had enough capital to get started. She was almost certain of the location. There was a great little rundown house on Main Street in her hometown, commercially zoned. It had oversized, divided light bay windows on either side of its front door that she was dying to paint white and display beautiful items in. She could just picture a comfy upholstered chair in a flowery print with a beat-up, white-painted end table holding a candlestick lamp, covered by a pastel beaded shade. The whole store was arranged in her mind. She might even get a cute little dog that would greet the customers as they came in, or a cat -- maybe a cat.

"Earth to Ali." Nicki nudged her.

"Oh, sorry, I was lost in thought."

"Obviously." Nicki smiled knowingly. "You've got it all worked out already, don't you?"

Ali laughed at how in sync they were and shared her thoughts with Nicki.

"Umm, it sounds divine. Can I work there if my gig doesn't work out?"

"As if it won't! You can write fabulous articles about me and the store so people will come from far and wide to shop there."

"Deal!" Nicki said. "It truly does sound great. It sounds like just the perfect thing for you."

"Thanks, Nick, I really feel strongly about it. I think Mom and Dad will be really happy for me, too."

"I'm sure they will, especially when you hit them up for some start-up money."

Ali laughed. "Hey, don't forget -- I've worked my ass off selling a few houses here and there and have accumulated enough for start-up. I might need a loan to sustain me if it doesn't take off right away," she conceded, "but they know I'm good for it."

"No one knows better than them. You know I was just teasing. The Rag didn't pay me much, but all that waitressing I did on the weekends will allow *me* to live comfortably this summer. Plus I'll get a small salary from the paper, which will help. Just thank God we don't have to pay room and board!"

"No kidding! Could you imagine if you had to rent a house on Captiva for the whole summer?" Ali shook her head.

"I know. I keep telling my grandmother she could probably get $20,000 a month for her house."

"Holy crap! Could she?"

"Yes!" Nicki nodded. "But then I told myself to shut up so she wouldn't rethink sending us here!"

Ali laughed. "Yeah, what were you trying to do, sabotage our fantasy lifestyle? This will be the longest we've ever stayed there. I'm going to be so spoiled, it'll be hard to leave."

"I know, I just might not!" Nicki stated.

"You couldn't stay away from Boston," Ali chided. "You'd go out of your mind without the city life."

"I know I definitely would. Maybe I'll just retire here." Nicki laughed. "Oh, look, we're coming in." Nicki pointed out the window at the palms scattered about the airport. The captain came over the speaker, announcing their approach and the current local temperature.

"It's gonna be hot!"

"It's gonna be great!" Nicki said.

"It's gonna be great," Ali agreed.

"Why the hell did we get a convertible? It's so hot!"

Nicki laughed. "Remember the island breezes at night. It'll be great."

Ali cranked up the A/C and watched the fast food chains and car washes pass by as they headed for the islands. "I'm so glad the islands don't look like this."

"I know. For the most part, they're unspoiled," Nicki agreed.

"What do mean, 'for the most part'?" Ali asked.

"Well, my grandmother's been pissed for awhile now about the developing going on, on both Sanibel and Captiva."

"Really? Like what? Fast food places?" Ali would be shocked to hear that. She hadn't been to the islands in over a year and couldn't imagine what would have been built.

"No, no, that's still not allowed," Nicki assured her. "There's been a lot of housing going up, especially on Captiva, huge homes and large buildings, completely out of place."

"Wow, you wonder where money like that comes from."

"Yeah, well, that seems to be the question at hand."

"What's the motive behind it, I wonder? And why is it being allowed? Aren't there ordinances for size and square footage?" Ali found it quite interesting, being that she grew up in the business.

"Well, apparently there are several conglomerates, some that are actually doing some good around the islands and in fact are boosting the local economy. However, there are a couple that are strictly about overbuilding and monopolizing, and the locals are afraid of chains and franchises taking over, making the islands look like any other resort area.

Apparently there is this one sleazeball agent that Nan informs me is representing one large management company in particular. He was sent there just to birddog for this company. They're buying up a lot of real estate around the islands commercially and residentially, and because of their deep pockets, this guy has managed to become one of the top ten producing real estate agents on the island, much to the dismay of the veterans out there."

"Yeah, I bet!" Ali could only imagine. "Must be nice to have deals just put in front of you like that."

"Especially when they're basically paying asking price for whatever they purchase. This realtor looks like the top dog in the MLS."

Ali loved being able to talk shop with Nicki, respecting her knowledge of real estate that she'd learned from her grandmother and Ali and her family as well. "The city must be enjoying the influx of money, though," Ali commented.

"Well, that's why Nan and her friends are pissed," Nicki told her. "Nobody is regulating any of these projects, because why bite the proverbial hand that feeds you? The taxes for one house alone they are building on Captiva could feed a small country. Nan says the city will hit them up for little things, like permitting issues, but big things like encroaching on the tide line or blocking someone's view gets overlooked."

Nicki shook her head with a chuckle. "Because Nan's an owner, we get to hear about the ugly side to the islands no one would ever want you to know."

"It sounds a little scary for the islands," Ali decided.

"No doubt. Nan hopes some of the local developers will help put a stop to it. There's a lot of people on the islands with some big bucks who don't want to see these big conglomerates from out of state trying to take over and commercializing the place."

Ali looked at her. "Do you think the locals will be able to stop it?" In Ali's experience, unfortunately, the person with the deepest pockets usually came out on top.

"Time will tell. I think with enough local backlash the city will have to start putting some restrictions in place. Wait until you see some of these new houses on Captiva."

"Ridiculous, huh? Whereabouts are they?" Ali glanced out the window and could see they were getting closer.

Nicki looked beside her at Ali. "Therein lies the punch line. One of them is directly across the street from The Three Sunrises."

Ali's jaw dropped. "Ooh, that must not have gone over well with Nan!"

"Tell me about it. Didn't I tell you about the house at Christmastime?"

"Probably," she grinned.

"Yes, well, it's an eyesore, and there's this stockade fence all around the perimeter so passersby can't see in."

"Is it permanent, you mean?"

"No, just while they build the concrete mess."

They were almost to the causeway and they both let out a sigh.

"Oh, my God! Look at the new bridge -- it's beautiful! What a difference." Ali hadn't visited since the project had been completed. "I bet it's not three bucks to cross anymore!" she laughed.

Nicki chuckled. "You're right. It's six, even for residents."

Ali's eyes were glued to the coming sight of the clear blue bay water. "With the taxes they all pay, they deserve to cross for free!"

Nicki nodded in agreement.

"Oh, I couldn't wait to see this water!" Ali looked out the window as they approached the bridge.

"It's so calming, isn't it?" Nicki felt at peace every time she crossed over onto the island.

"I cannot wait for a frozen drink by the pool!"

"I know, me, too. We'll stop at Jerry's and get all the goodies we need."

"I want to go in that little gift shop too to get some postcards and stuff."

"We will. Oh, and we have to get a new umbrella. When we were here at Christmastime it broke, and none of us replaced it." Nicki slowed the convertible. "Hi, there!" Nicki stopped to pay the toll and greeted the attendant, the hot air filling the car as soon as she put down her window. "Nan's Jeep will have the transponder," she turned to Ali, "so if you go off-island you won't have to pay coming back on." Nicki drove on, heading up the incline.

"Great," Ali said, "but I don't see myself leaving for anything. Oh!" she remembered and grinned, "except for shopping at Coconut Point." She saw movement below and yelled. "Look! Look! Dolphin at two o'clock!"

Nicki put on the brakes. "Jesus! Don't do that!" she laughed. "I almost ran that biker over." Nicki spotted the dolphins. "Oh, they are so awesome, aren't they?"

"We have to rent a boat again while we're here to see them up close." Ali remembered the first time they had done that with Nicki's Dad and sister Jenna. They'd had so much fun taking pictures of the dolphins and fishing off the back.

"We definitely will," Nicki promised."

They arrived at Jerry's and laughed at "G.W." and "Jerry," the exotic birds, taunting them as they made their way inside. They bought their groceries and beach supplies in short order and were back in the car headed for San-Cap Road and their scenic drive to Captiva.

"This will be perfect timing," Nicki declared. "By the time we bring all our stuff in, we can just get on the beach for sunset."

"Not until I've made us two frozens to walk across the street with," Ali stated.

"I thought that was just understood." Nicki glanced at her friend and smiled. "I have to call my parents when we get in, too."

"I'm not even going to bother with the cell." Ali flipped her phone open and shut it just as fast.

"No kidding -- you might as well be talking through a tin can."

"Why don't they put up a tower out this way?"

"Oh, I'm sure one of these big developers will vie for it soon enough."

"Or maybe not. Maybe they aren't the type to talk on cell phones, if you know what I mean." Ali's eyebrows rose and fell.

"Too many movies! You watch way too many movies!" Nicki laughed.

"You know, maybe the islands will flourish with the new developments. If these companies have an endless supply of moolah, maybe they'll just improve upon the islands, make them a real resort destination." Ali tried to play devil's advocate.

"Possible, but the point is the locals don't want 'resort-like.' The people that come here, come here specifically because it's *not* resort-like."

"Yeah, you're right, trying to make it something other than what it is would suck." Ali sat up in her seat as the driveway came into sight. "There's the sign! It looks great!" Ali had painted the wooden sign identifying the house as a Christmas present to Nan and Nicki's family. The words "The Three Sunrises" in black lettering were surrounded by an actual picture of three golden suns their rays rising behind the letters in shades of red, pinks, and oranges.

"It looks awesome, doesn't it?" Nicki pulled into the shelled driveway and let out a whoop. "We're here!" Nicki pulled in and stopped. "I'm just so glad we finally named it," she continued. "I kept telling Nan she couldn't have a house here and not name it!"

"I'm so glad she let us choose the name." Ali smiled. "Our favorite U2 song, such a happy song for such a happy place!"

Nicki rolled her eyes. "You're a goof!" She set the car in Park and got out of the vehicle to stretch.

Ali got out and did the same. "Oh, how excited are we? I feel like we just arrived at spring break!"

"Yeah, minus the nightlife, hot guys, and the stupidity of an eighteen-year-old."

"Well, yes, there's that, but don't you feel like we're getting away with something, getting to stay here for so long? You'll be here the whole summer, for goodness' sake."

"A little, I guess," she laughed. "But I feel like I only have this weekend to live it up before I have to report to work on Monday."

"Nick, I am not going to feel bad for you writing for a paper that gets published once a week. How hard are you going to have to work? You're on an island, for God's sake!"

"I know, I'm just kidding. I'm actually looking forward to it." Nicki found the key under the mat and unlocked the front door. "Home sweet home!"

"Ooh, it's nice and cool in here." Ali moved toward the kitchen and flipped on the lights.

"Oh, I never get sick of that view." The girls stopped to look out the back sliders overlooking the pool and to the picturesque bay beyond before going off to their rooms.

There were four bedrooms situated on either side of the house, two on each side. Each room was large and housed its own bath, and all decorated in typical island style. Ali's favorite part of the decor were the large plantation shutters that adorned all the windows. She chose the bedroom on the west side of the house with double sliders to the pool. She had stayed in this room the last time she was here and felt completely at home in it. The walls were painted a stark white with colorful local art work bringing lots of character and color to the room. The plantation shutters were stained a rich walnut and gave the room a real tropical feel. The look was completed by the large red hibiscus print on the bedspread and the palm-shaped wooden blades of the ceiling fan. Ali immediately felt herself slip into vacation mode.

Nicki took the bedroom on the opposite side of the house like she always did. It was closest to the kitchen and also had sliders to the pool. The girls loved that they could get up in the morning and be right out on the pool deck if they chose. Nan had never put up a pool screen enclosure, and it gave the house such an open feeling with unobstructed views to the vast expanse of the bay.

Nicki's room was decorated in much the same as Ali's, only her walls were painted a soft sand color and the art work was more subtle, with soft colors of the Gulf and beach. It was completely relaxing, which Nicki loved. She smiled, grateful that she didn't have to fight her sister for it, as was usually the case when they vacationed together.

After unpacking a few of their things, they met back in the kitchen to put away the few groceries they had purchased. Ali got the blender started right away and found two plastic hurricane glasses. When the mixture was a thick slushy consistency, she filled both glasses to the rim.

Nicki started to pick up her drink but stopped when Ali yelled, surprising her.

"Wait!" Ali ran to her room and came back a minute later with a paper bag.

"I should have known you would have something like that," Nicki chuckled.

Ali dropped the paper umbrellas she had brought from home into their drinks. "Of course, I can't drink these without them! You ready?"

They each grabbed their drinks and left out the front door barefoot, Nicki's eyes glued to the ground.

"You still afraid of lizards?" Ali teased.

"Only when they run across my feet. Or, God forbid, I step on one and the tail breaks off, and it's still moving!" Nicki kept looking down as they followed the path.

Ali laughed at the visual. "Ugh!"

The steps from the front door led to a well-manicured path and onto the driveway. They "ouched" their way along the shelled drive to the street and watched for any cars before they crossed.

"Okay -- and there's the hideous stockade you spoke of." Ali was looking past a beautifully manicured driveway and front entrance, which she knew led to an impressive two-story beachfront home directly across from Nan's, to just beyond it where the start of an unsightly stockade fence began.

The beach access for Nan's house happened to be between the stockade fence and the impressive beach home across from Nan's. Where there once was just a sandy path lined with cabbage palms and sea grapes, was now a tree-barren, mammoth construction site. Ali could just make out the second story being built on the massive structure.

"When you see it from the beach, you'll get the full effect," Nicki told her.

"I can't believe it," Ali remarked. "At least your grandmother's house is on the inside of the bend so she doesn't really have to look at this." As they got closer and crossed the street, they were face to face with "No Trespassing" signs on the fence.

"Okay…" Nicki looked around, "…where the hell is the path?"

Ali walked around to her left to peer around the fence. "It looks like it's right behind this fence. How can they block it like this? It's the access for, like, five houses across the street, isn't it?" Ali was now looking through the bushes at the beach house next door.

"This is bullshit," Nicki fumed. "How are we supposed to get on? The access from here is about four more houses up. What if we had all our beach stuff? No one's gonna haul all their shit that far." Nicki let out an exasperated breath.

"What about in the other direction?" Ali looked to her left, down the road.

"Same thing, it's four or five houses in that direction, too." Nicki started walking toward the impressive beach house that belonged to Nan's neighbor. "I don't think these people are here. We'll just go through their driveway." Nicki headed past the perfectly trimmed bushes and into the driveway.

"There's a gate," Ali remarked with hesitation but followed.

"We'll go around it through the bushes."

Ali laughed. "Fine by me. I just hope the snakes don't mind."

"You had to say that." Nicki stopped dead in her tracks at the gate. "Now what?" she whispered.

Ali started to giggle. "Why are you whispering? The house is, like, thirty yards away, and I thought you said no one was home."

"I'm just assuming." Nicki handed Ali her drink. "Give me a piggyback."

"What!" Ali laughed. "I'm holding the drinks!"

"Please? If a snake comes out of these bushes, I'll have a freaking heart attack!" Nicki pleaded with her. "Put the drinks on the gate post and bring me through these bushes. If you want to see the sunset, you'll do as I say." Nicki did her best to sound commanding, a smile tugging at the corners of her mouth.

"Nicki," Ali was laughing harder now, "what if *I* see a snake? I'm going to freak out and drop you!"

"Oh, shit! We just have to run through as quick as we can. Put the drinks down first, though. Ready?"

"This is ridiculous. I feel like a criminal." Ali put the drinks on the post and shuffled the ground around their feet trying to scare any critters away. "Now or never!"

"Go!" Nicki hissed.

CHAPTER TWO

He had been watching a Yankees game, half asleep, when the silent alarm went off. A full view of the driveway instantly took over the right quadrant of the fifty-inch flat screen, shrinking Fenway Park. He sat up in his chair and slowly wrapped his fingers around the Glock that lay beside him on the couch cushion.

At first he could only see an arm. He saw an object being placed on the gate post, and he used the remote control to the surveillance camera, bringing the image closer: two drink glasses. Great, he caught himself a couple of romantics trying to get on the beach for sunset. Tourists, he thought. Can't find a beach access, so they think they can just intrude on someone's property like that. He ought to go scare the shit out of them. He stayed glued to the screen as he saw the bushes come to life. Out came one and then the other: two women. Well, to each his own. They were doubled over. Were they hurt? He studied the screen. No, they were laughing. As they reached for their drinks on the gate post and walked up the drive, their images started to improve immensely.

Rafe stood up, wide awake now, leaving the gun on the cushion. Hello! If they were a couple, there was no justice in this world. The first one, leading the way, had reddish-brown hair with a killer body, tucked into a little blue dress. And behind her -- a vision in white, skirt to her ankles, tank top with her midriff exposed, bare feet, and long dark hair. She was slightly taller than the first girl and her body just as kick-ass. He watched them approach the side yard. He hit camera two, and the T.V. displayed the girls tip-toeing along the side of the house. He laughed, thinking they would soon encounter another locked gate to the pool. Rafe decided he'd do them a favor, and he hit the unlock from the remote. He hit another button and watched as camera three, now covering the bottom right of the flat screen, covered the pool area and followed their steps to the beach path. His eyes followed as they made their way toward the water and sat down on the sand.

Rafe picked up the binoculars on the sofa table and zeroed in on the two women. They weren't a couple, just friends; body language and proximity to each other told him that. He focused in on the brunette, wishing she would turn around even though the back view he had was nice, too. For the first time since arriving on the island his blood pressure was rising -- in a good way.

He had put in for some long overdue vacation time just about a month ago, with the intent of going back home to Long Island and spending some time with his family. He had been working out of Miami headquarters for the past year and hadn't seen any of them in all that time, but the bureau supervisor had asked a favor, promising an added four weeks vacation if Rafe would follow up a lead. It would mostly be downtime with just a little investigative work in between, he promised, knowing Rafe needed a break.

The favor -- live in a million-dollar beach house, on Captiva Island --courtesy of a friend of the bureau's, and gather information on one Xavier Constantine D'nafrio, who happened to be building the house right next door to Rafe's accommodations.

D'nafrio had recently come to the bureau's attention through the IRS. It seemed Xavier -- or Mr. X., as he liked to be called, and the name he christened his new fishing yacht with -- was playing a strategic game of monopoly on the small islands of Sanibel and Captiva, using his cooperation to buy up land and property faster than he could fill out a 941 form. He had purchased millions of dollars' worth of real estate in just the past year and a half and had started building monstrous properties not only on the Gulf side but the bay as well.

Since 9/11, any monetary transactions exceeding certain amounts were red-flagged throughout several federal agencies. That included the IRS. So along with D'nafrio's failure to pay certain business taxes, his numerous real estate purchases in such a short time period were questionable, sending up several red flags.

Rafe walked over to the wall of glass that looked out at the Gulf and glanced over at one of those red flags. The beach house D'nafrio was building next door on the Gulf jutted out just enough so that Rafe's view of the stretch of beach they were on was limited. At just under ten thousand square feet, the house, if it could even be called that, was an eyesore to many. Rafe had discovered at City Hall on Sanibel that several complaints had been filed on the building project due to its size and its proximity to the beach. Many neighbors feared losing their view and the general integrity of the beach itself, and many of D'nafrio's protesters, unfortunately for him, were environmentalists who believed D'nafrio was endangering the local ecosystem single-handedly.

Just before Rafe had arrived at the beach house he was staying at, it had been rigged with the best surveillance equipment the FBI could offer. Every outside angle of the house was covered by tiny cameras that were motion sensitive. All he had to do was hit the corresponding buttons on the remote and, depending upon how many buttons he hit, one or more images would appear on the flat-screen T.V., much like picture in picture, only better. Rafe could watch from the large living room T.V. or from the one on the wall in the master bedroom. So far, the two women he looked at now had been the only thing worth watching. Other than the actual building of the house next door, it had been pretty quiet over there.

Rafe wondered why D'nafrio chose Captiva. The information the SAC (special agent in charge of the investigation) had given him was that it was a somewhat small, secluded island on the Gulf, apparently home to a scattering of celebrities and extremely wealthy people who, for the most part, only occupied their homes half the year. There were only a couple of resorts, but there were many cottages and beachfront homes for rent. If Rafe had to compare, stature wise, it was more Nantucket than Martha's Vineyard. He'd spent many a summer on both those islands as a kid. Rafe had to wonder what the motivation was, buying up half the islands. Not only was D'nafrio buying up everything for sale, he was building shit much bigger than necessary, obnoxiously so. It just didn't make sense.

Talk among the locals was that D'nafrio and his major retail management company wanted to take over the islands. In the short time Rafe had been here, he'd been to three meetings at City Hall, where several residents had voiced their angst. D'nafrio's building style was a valid concern for many, and Rafe had to agree. It definitely lacked the charm of the islands. Rafe had noted the similarities with all of D'nafrio's projects that he'd seen; from homes to businesses, they all seemed to be fashioned in the same style. The roof tiles, pavers, landscape, and overall architecture all were the same, and although it wasn't unsightly, it definitely was a departure from the historic look of the islands. Rafe had learned that for years the residents had fought hard to keep the integrity of the islands safe from the mainstream. Many ordinances and restrictions were set in place, all to prevent the islands from turning into just another city or town with high-rises, malls, and franchises. It was one of the reasons why both islands were rated in the top one thousand places to see before you die. People from all over the world, year after year returned, embracing the fact that outwardly, time had not yet caught up with Sanibel and Captiva. Yes, there had been many changes throughout the years, due to obvious necessity and some damaging hurricanes, but the nostalgic feeling was still there, and the people who appreciated it most would do anything to protect it.

So Rafe had been on a few fact-finding missions as asked and at the same time was learning a whole hell of a lot about Captiva and Sanibel as well. The question of D'nafrio's business practices was still at hand, but Rafe was confident he would find something solid to go on by turning his attention to D'nafrio's realtor and right-hand man, Barry Stoddman.

He was the one overseeing all of D'nafrio's projects and brokering all his deals, and thus would hold a lot of answers to the FBI's questions. D'nafrio himself was something of an enigma, though. Rafe had only seen him once, and that was next door on the building site. Rafe had watched on the surveillance camera as D'nafrio walked the site and the shell of what had been built so far, talking briefly with a man Rafe had made to be the foreman. When D'nafrio's car had finally pulled out, Rafe had hurried to his own vehicle, following D'nafrio's car off-island for several miles. His destination had been Page Field, a small airstrip in Fort Myers, where a private plane awaited him. Rafe had dutifully called in the tail numbers and headed back to Captiva. He would find out later that a flight plan to Miami had been filed.

D'nafrio currently occupied a condo on Ocean Drive in Miami that was also under surveillance. In fact, Rafe's good friend and fellow agent, Mike Caplan, was occupying the space right next door. Mike had kidded with Rafe saying that although Rafe would be seeing some beautiful sunsets in Captiva, Mike would be seeing and enjoying the company of the many beautiful women in Miami. At the time Rafe had laughed and rolled his eyes, not doubting for a minute that that was true, but he told Mike he was actually looking forward to the sunsets. He was sick of the Miami nightlife and the emptiness that came along with it. He had welcomed the slow pace of the island and was glad to be alone these past few weeks -- until now, that is, which brought his attention back to the view at the end of the binoculars. The two women had dropped themselves on the sand right in front of his house, obviously taking in the sunset that was receding over the horizon.

Since Rafe had been here, he'd seen the sunset each and every night. He had never seen so many shades of pinks, reds, yellows, and oranges. It never ceased to amaze him that so many vibrant colors could fill up the horizon each evening. But, unlike most visitors to Captiva, he actually preferred watching the darkening sky to the sunset. Not anywhere else he'd been had he ever seen the stars so close. He was convinced he could reach right up and touch them.

He put down the binoculars and entered the state-of-the-art kitchen for a beer. There was so much stainless steel, he felt like he should put gloves on before he touched anything. He definitely wouldn't want to try to keep a kitchen like this clean. He was absolutely thankful for the weekly cleaning service that came in.

He strode back to the sliders and leaned on the frame, opening the beer. He thought about taking the stairs down to introduce himself. He hadn't realized just how much he was missing female companionship until he had laid eyes on them. If he was being honest -- sex, it was sex that he missed.

Aside from a few flirtatious conversations with the fifty-something bartender up the street, his love life was pretty stagnant. The island wasn't really conducive to dating, and it wasn't like the job was keeping him too busy like a normal assignment would. If anything, he actually felt like he was on vacation. The investigation so far had been pretty slow-going, much like the everyday pace of island life. Things didn't get done here like they did in Miami, and nowhere near like they did in his home base of New York City. "It's five o'clock somewhere" was definitely the creed around here, which was more than okay with Rafe, although he wouldn't be opposed to a little excitement.

He guessed the women must have thought the house was empty; they probably had tried the beach access first and found it barricaded. D'nafrio in all his arrogance had put a stockade fence up that ran right across it.

The house Rafe was occupying was heavily landscaped out front, and it wasn't until you actually passed through the gated drive that you could see the two-story stucco home. It was bleach white with a grand staircase leading to double French doors stained in a deep mahogany.

The large palatial windows on either side of the doors donned navy blue and white striped awnings, giving the home a nautical flair, and hurricane shutters covered the large front windows, giving the appearance of an empty house. Rafe could see why the girls would dare to come through. From the front, the house was dark and appeared empty. The beach view was not much different, although the sliders and windows on both floors were unadorned and had clear views to the Gulf. But anyone passing by would see only the bare minimum of lighting. So far Rafe had kept a rather low profile and hadn't attracted the attention of any neighbors. The house to the left of him he knew was empty until October, and he'd been informed that some houses on the bay were in fact occupied, but for the most part his stretch of beach had remained desolate.

These two women were the first people he'd seen on the beach in a week. The previous week there had been a couple walking a dog and a lone sunbather who had stayed for a few hours, but besides them, maybe just a pelican or two.

Rafe had pretty much had the beach to himself, with plenty of observation time. He had the tides pretty well down pat and had become accustomed to the dolphins showing up every day around eleven a.m., then usually again around six p.m. and sporadically in between. He had watched with fascination as loggerheads labored to the sand in the cover of night to lay their delicate eggs and watched again as their hatched babies scurried for the horizon line at dawn. He'd definitely had a lot of time on his hands, and he couldn't help but wonder if the SAC knew what he was doing by asking Rafe to come here. He kept reminding Rafe there was more to life besides the job, but Rafe had always laughed him off. Special Agent in Charge Tom Daniels had just got married and was seeing the world through the eyes of a man who was consistently getting laid.

Rafe never let anything distract him from the job, and it had definitely caught up with him, especially his last case. His burnout was evident to everyone he worked with, and he knew this assignment, albeit a soft one, was just what the SAC ordered. Rafe smiled wondering if these women were plants, Daniels' idea of a joke -- nah, he was a ball buster, but he wasn't cruel.

Rafe took a swig of his beer and continued to watch the two women. The sun had just about disappeared, and he backed up a hair as they got up to leave. He picked up the binoculars again and focused on the brunette once more. Her friend was definitely attractive, but there was something about the brunette that had his full attention. She was slightly taller, about five-seven if he had to guess, and her long hair was wavy, falling past her shoulders. He liked long hair. He also liked fit, healthy women, since he himself worked hard to keep fit. The brunette definitely appeared to be so, curves in all the right places and pretty toned from what he could see. Rafe placed her somewhere in her early twenties -- hopefully not too early.

He was thirty-three, a third of the way into his third decade. He still wasn't sure how he felt about that. He knew age was just a state of mind, though, and he was definitely feeling pretty youthful since he'd been on the island. He had nothing but time on his hands to run and work out. He was probably in better shape now than he'd ever been. He'd always kept in decent shape, but being in Miami for the past year had enabled him to be able to run outside almost daily. In New York he'd have to make sure he made time for the gym when the weather didn't cooperate, which was about nine months out of the year. And now, living on the island, he'd grown his hair out a little, and with his tan and sun-streaked hair, he could probably pass for a surfer dude, save for the lack of swell on this stretch of Gulf. He'd have to wait for a hurricane to hit before he saw a wave out here with any sky to it.

Most days his attire consisted of long board shorts, T-shirts, and flip flops. He had definitely adapted to the island lifestyle in that sense. He wasn't looking forward to Monday, though, when he'd be back in a suit and tie again. Each week he had to report to FBI headquarters in downtown Miami. He briefed his superiors and turned in the surveillance discs that would be analyzed and cataloged. He in turn received any pertinent intel about D'nafrio. He was going to try to enjoy this weekend, though, and just maybe meet himself a woman. It had been far too long, and watching these two was a clarifying reminder.

CHAPTER THREE

"I think there's someone home." Ali was staring up at the second floor. She could swear she saw a shadow through the large glass sliders. "I definitely see a light on in that room up there." Ali nodded her head to the right so Nicki could discreetly look up.

"That's probably on a timer." Nicki walked toward the home's pool nonchalantly, to get to the gate from which they'd come.

"Don't you find it odd that the pool gate was unlocked?" Ali was whispering as they approached the pool.

"No, someone has to come and clean the pool, right?" Nicki approached the gate and opened it.

"God, I feel like a thief." Ali kept looking behind her and around her to make sure they were truly alone.

Nicki laughed. "Relax, we'll be home in a sec."

"Let's run like hell through the front again. I don't want an alarm to start blowing once we hit the driveway." Ali carefully closed the gate behind her and was startled at the sound of the lock engaging.

Nicki turned around. "Oops, let's go!"

"Oh, my God! I told you!" Ali hissed.

The girls ran as fast as they could down the drive and back through the bush next to the gate. They came through the other side and to an abrupt halt as a car drove by rather quickly.

"I'll call Nan when we get in the house and see what the deal is." Nicki crossed the street to her grandmother's shelled driveway.

Ali joined her and looked back with dismay. "Now the front porch light is on!"

When the girls got back inside, Ali put the empty glasses in the dishwasher while Nicki placed a call to her grandmother.

"Hey, Nan, it's me." Nicki smiled into the phone.

"Well, hello, darlin', how's The Three Sunrises treating you girls?"

"We're loving it, of course, everything's as it should be, no problems getting in or anything -- just one little snag."

"Oh?" Nicki's grandmother sounded concerned.

"The beach access," Nicki paused, "is blocked off by your new neighbor to be."

"Are you kidding me? He can't do that!" Nan sounded furious.

"Well, there's 'No Trespassing' signs all over the fence, and the fence starts right where the path was," Nicki complained.

"Oh, I will be making some phone calls!"

Nan was definitely pissed.

"So where did you get on?" she asked.

"Well, that's the thing, we went over to the driveway and through the backyard of the house across the street." Nicki hoped Nan wouldn't care.

"Oh, Jim's place, that's okay, he's not there until October, but the gate should have been locked." Nan sounded perplexed.

"We squeezed through the bushes beside it," Nicki told her.

"Oh, for goodness' sake, I'll just place a call to Jim and ask his permission. You don't want to be sneaking around. You never know who's watching!"

"Are you sure it's empty now? Some lights came on after dark."

"Probably on a timer, but I'll call and let you know." Nan paused. "Oh, and Nicki, there'll be a surprise for you girls tomorrow."

Nicki smiled. "Really? What kind of surprise?"

"Now, if I told you..."

"I know, it wouldn't be a surprise," Nicki finished.

Nan laughed. "You'll see tomorrow. I'll call you back tonight after I've spoken with Jim."

"Thanks, Nan, I love you. Bye."

"Bye, sweetie, I love you, too."

Ali made herself comfortable on the oversized sectional that was in the living room.

"What did she say?"

Nicki joined her on the couch. "She'll call back after she calls the guy who lives there. She doesn't think he'll mind us going through his yard." Nicki was thinking as she looked at her best friend.

"What?"

"She says she has a surprise for us and we'll see it tomorrow. What do you suppose it could be?"

"How the hell should I know? What more could she do for us?" Ali stretched out her long legs and yawned. "How can I be tired at eight-thirty?"

"I know," Nicki laughed. "Me, too, but we should go party somewhere."

"You're right. I'm kind of hungry too."

"Let's go to the Crow's Nest, then -- it's close and maybe the only bar with the possibility of single men."

Ali laughed. "They do need to revamp the nightlife around here." She got up off the couch.

"Are you going to change?" Nicki asked.

"Yeah, why not, I have a cute little sun dress I could throw on."

"I'm just going to get my sexy strap sandals." Nicki winked at her and got up, too.

"Oh, you're hopeful tonight, eh? Maybe an old Wall street type with bundles of money will be there looking for a trophy wife."

"One can only hope, my friend." Nicki grinned. "How 'bout you? An old-timer who golfs all day and only needs you around for country club functions?"

"That sounds divine. My days would be free to romp with the cabana boy with the Navy SEAL bod."

"You're right -- that does sound divine!"

They both laughed and went to their respective rooms to primp. Fifteen minutes later they were in the driveway, where Nicki hit the button on the car remote to put the top down.

"The weather is perfect!"

"I know, I can absolutely get used to this," Ali agreed, looking up to the night sky. "I have never seen stars this close before. If I was on the roof, I think I could touch one!"

"It's heavenly, isn't it?" Nicki followed her gaze.

They got into the car, and Ali put U2's Best Of in the CD player. She queued up "Three Sunrises," and they pulled out of the drive, heading for the Crow's Nest. When they arrived minutes later, they easily found seats at the not yet crowded bar. The few people inside had all turned to view the newcomers, and a few lingering eyes watched as they sat down.

The lone bartender was an attractive woman somewhere in her fifties, attractive in that "been at the beach all my life" kind of way. She had dirty-blonde, sun-streaked hair and an overly tanned face. Her eyes were accentuated with a blue eyeliner that Ali could remember wearing to many a dance recital. But it was her abundant cleavage that neither Ali nor Nicki could avoid looking at as they sat down.

"Hey, there, girls, what can I getcha?" Her deep scratchy voice completed the picture.

"Hi, I'll have a Greygoose and sprite." Nicki smiled and ordered.

"And I'll have a strawberry daiquiri." Ali smiled at the woman. Behind the well-worn face and makeup were a kind smile and eyes.

"You got it. My name is Annie -- just shout when you need me."

"Thanks, Annie," the girls replied in unison.

Annie got the blender going and made Nicki's drink. "Lime, hon?"

"Sure," Nicki said.

There were two couples at the bar who appeared to be vacationers, a man alone watching the Red Sox game, and an older couple eating salads and drinking iced tea.

"Does it get much busier?" Ali asked as Annie placed their drinks in front of them.

"Oh, we have a few regulars that'll be here, and then we'll fill up for the band. They go on at ten o'clock. They usually draw a pretty good crowd."

"Oh, great!" Nicki got excited. "What kind of music?"

"It's a rock band. They do some classic stuff which I personally enjoy," she smiled, "and they cover a lot of new rock, which will probably be more your speed. They're really good," Annie offered and returned to her existing customers.

"Cool, maybe this place will get exciting," Ali hoped. "But if not," she held up her glass, "we'll make our own fun. Here's to us having an awesome start to the summer!"

"I'll drink to that!" Nicki clinked her glass with Ali's and glanced up at the T.V. The Red Sox had just scored two runs.

"Doesn't Matt have season tickets this year?" Nicki inquired casually about Ali's brother.

"Actually, Jason has them and is sharing them with Matt."

Nicki hadn't seen Ali's oldest brother Jason for a few years. "Jason's an even bigger fan than Matt, isn't he?"

"That's an understatement if ever there was one. I guarantee they're both there at that game right now." Ali looked up at the screen as well.

"Nan tells me she's been seeing a lot of Matt." Nicki stirred her drink, focusing on the ice cubes.

Ali watched her best friend and smiled to herself. She'd suspected Nicki had a little crush on Matt, even though she'd never let on to Ali. "Yeah, her kitchen is almost done, right? I can't wait to see it. I know Matt loves working there. She's always bringing the crew cannolis from Mike's Pastry. She's so nice!"

"Yes, she told me. I think she has a crush on him," Nicki chuckled.

"He loves your grandmother!" Ali laughed, too. She thought now was as good a time as any to fish around. "I'm so glad he broke it off with that EMT."

Nicki raised a brow, feeling a small jolt. "Oh, did he?" She rolled her eyes. "She was *so* not his type."

"You didn't think so?" Ali grinned. "What do you think his type is?" This ought to be telling.

Nicki was back looking at the television screen. Maybe she could spot him in the crowd. "Someone smart, who can handle his quick wit and beat him at Scrabble. That girl probably couldn't even spell Scrabble, and she wasn't even in shape. It always gets me when someone in the health field, like nurses, doctors…whatever, are not in shape. How can they do their job effectively? Do you know how many nurses I see in town smoking! I mean, are you kidding me?"

Ali suppressed her laughter. She knew Nicki was trying to steer the subject. "You always beat him at Scrabble."

Nicki looked over at Ali, realizing what she had said. "That was a long time ago, wasn't it? God, when's the last time we did that?" She knew exactly.

Ali smiled. "Thanksgiving, maybe four years ago."

"Yeah, well, I'm sure he won't have any trouble meeting someone new." Nicki was stirring her drink again, this time a little faster.

"What's wrong?" Ali asked, trying not to laugh.

Nicki looked at Ali and saw the grin trying not to creep up the sides of her mouth. "What's wrong with *you*?"

"Not a thing, I'm just sitting here having a conversation about my brother with my best friend."

"Umm," Nicki nodded. "Let's talk about something else."

"Why?" Ali prodded. "Are you mad at him or something?"

Or something, Nicki thought. More like mad for him. She'd had a crush on Ali's brother Matt since the first time she laid eyes on him. And for as long as she'd known him, he'd always had a girlfriend. It seemed every weekend growing up someone new was at Ali's house, and later when she had entered college, she'd always hear about his latest from Ali.

When Nicki was at school, she'd kind of forgotten her teenage crush and concentrated on her studies and her own love life. But there were times when the families would get together for holidays or some other occasion. It was then that Nicki would be reminded of how attracted she was to him still.

Matt had always been taller than Nicki, his over six-foot frame seeming to tower over her five-foot-six one. He'd always kept in unbelievable shape, from his hockey days in high school and college to his construction work these days. But it wasn't his unbelievably muscular body that did it for Nicki, it was his stunning green eyes. Ali had them, too, but Matt's were something else. You spotted his eyes across a room -- they actually sparkled, and he had this smile that would just melt you on the spot.

Nicki had always tried to play it cool when she was around him. She never let him see that he got to her. As far as she was concerned, he was her best friend's older brother and off limits. But oh, God! As the years passed by, she found it increasingly difficult to stick to her convictions. He was everything she tried to find in other guys: gorgeous, funny as hell, smart, strong, and sexy -- oh, so sexy…but off limits. Besides he'd never shown any inclination that he would be interested in her, so she had just put him out of her mind. Although it wasn't easy to hear Ali talk about him, and especially now, her own grandmother. Nicki had confided in Nan once about her feelings for Matt, and lately Nan seemed to always be bringing his name up. Nicki thought maybe the old woman *did* have a crush on him.

"I'm not mad at him," Nicki smiled. "I just think it's such a waste he hasn't found a good woman yet."

"Yes, I know," Ali agreed, smiling. "It's just a matter of time, though." Ali watched her carefully. "Maybe I'll try to set him up with someone."

Nicki's head snapped around. "Like who?"

"I don't know -- maybe I'll put his profile on Match.com or one of those dating sites," Ali stated.

"Yeah, let me know how that turns out!" Nicki said, dripping sarcasm. "You should concentrate on your own love life."

Ali knew she had gotten Nicki riled up and decided to give it a break. She had the whole vacation to get it out of her. "Maybe you're right." She let up for now. "How about that guy at the end of the bar watching the game?"

"Now you're talking." Nicki laughed, trying to cover the agitated state she was momentarily in. "I bet you can whip that beer belly right into shape --get him out running every morning, and nights you can cook him lots of red meat."

"We better watch it -- he could be a friend of Annie's."

They laughed, forgetting the bit of tension that had surfaced moments earlier. People were starting to filter in and the back door now stood propped open, while what looked to be the band sauntered in with various pieces of equipment.

"I hope they're decent," Ali said looking on.

"Me, too. You think people will dance?"

"Probably. Hey -- don't look now, but one of them is a hottie."

Nicki watched the guy setting up the drums. "The night just got a little interesting."

"Hey, I saw him first!" Ali teased her.

"He's so not your type." Nicki laughed, looking around the bar at the new faces arriving.

"Holy shit! ...but he is."

CHAPTER FOUR

Rafe kept his eye on the monitor as the women ran down the driveway, back through the bushes, and crossed the street. He was surprised to see them cross to the drive directly opposite him. He wondered if they were renters. He knew an old lady owned the house; he knew who owned every residence within a mile of D'nafrio's property. But he wasn't aware of any rentals for that particular house.

It wasn't long after they went inside that they were back out and getting into a red convertible. He watched as the car pulled out and drove toward upper Captiva. Probably going to the Crow's Nest, he thought. What a good idea.

He threw on a shirt, jeans, shoes, brushed his teeth, ran a hand through his hair, and was good to go. He made his way down to the three-car garage and opened the bay where his metallic gray Ducati ST3 sat waiting. He grabbed his helmet, straddled the bike, and started her up. He hit the button on his key ring that opened the gate at the end of the driveway, and hit another one to shut the bay door behind him. When the property was secure, he drove off in the same direction as the convertible.

The night air was balmy, and the moon hung over the Gulf like a spotlight. The short drive had invigorated him, and he looked forward to what he might find inside the bar. He spotted the convertible right away and parked a few spots away from it. He hung his helmet off the handle bars and made his way to the door.

Rafe had heard the band that was playing tonight a few times before, and if nothing else he'd have a beer and hear some good music. He walked into the Crow's Nest, and it was nearly to capacity. He found an open seat at the bar and ordered his usual Corona from Annie.

"Hey there, gorgeous, alone again I see." Annie couldn't help flirting with him -- he might be younger than her fifty-ahem-hem years, but damn the boy was somethin' to look at.

"You know me, Annie -- a beer and the Yankees game is all I need."

"Honey, Boston's getting the best of them tonight, so you might want to think about something else to entertain you or *someone*!" she winked at him.

Rafe flirted with Annie affectionately, but they both knew it was the friendly, harmless sort of flirting that wouldn't end up anywhere. His own mother wasn't that much older than she was.

"I just might do that tonight." Rafe looked around, and sure enough his eyes rested on the brunette from the beach. She was sitting diagonal from him on the right side of the bar. Her friend sat to her left, and was giving him the once-over.

Rafe smiled and moved his gaze back to the brunette. She had a sea-green sleeveless dress on that made her eyes pop from across the room. With her olive complexion, she was stunning, so much more so up close. She had been listening to her girlfriend talk but stopped, returning Rafe's gaze. Damn --his heart skipped and went to double time. He reached for his beer. She was unbelievably freakin' hot.

"Okay, do you see him?" Nicki turned quickly to Ali. "Over on the left?"

Ali followed Nicki's gaze at her direction, and her eyes rested on the most drop-dead handsome man she'd ever seen. He had light brown, sun-streaked hair, a killer tan, what appeared to be a very muscular upper body, and piercing deep dark eyes, set into a strong masculine face worthy of a billboard. Those eyes happened to be holding hers at just that second, and she blinked, casually bringing her attention back to Nicki. "Oh, my God, he looks like Beckham, only better, if that's possible."

"Umm," Nicki agreed while staring.

"He is dangerously good-looking, and it will suck if some drop-dead-gorgeous supermodel comes out of the ladies' room to join him." Ali sipped her drink, waiting.

"Okay, so my drummer boy doesn't look so hot any more," Nicki complained.

"He's still hot, Nick," Ali teased. "Besides, when he starts playing he'll look even better to you."

Nicki laughed. "I *am* a sucker for musicians, even though I only had just that one."

Ali laughed. "It's a total turn-on when someone can play like that, isn't it?"

"Hey, back off, sister -- you've got your GQ model over there to enjoy now."

Ali casually looked over again and caught him looking right back. She was pleased to see he was still alone. "That's the second time I caught him looking over here." She pretended to be interested in the game.

"Duh!" Nicki looked up as the band started to play. "Oh, thank God they're good." Nicki refocused her attention on the drummer.

"Yeah, they are pretty good." Ali looked around for the ladies' room. "I'm going to touch up the lip gloss."

"Uh-huh. Tell me how his ass looks when you come back." Nicki grinned.

"Shut up." Ali smiled. Her best friend knew her so well.

"Go get him, Posh!" Nicki called after her.

Ali walked through the now-crowded bar and kept him in her peripheral vision. She dared a glance and saw that his body was now turned toward the band. He wore jeans that fit him beautifully, and she could make out his muscular thighs through the denim...*and* his great ass. He had nice broad shoulders that gave way to some nicely contoured arms under the white long-sleeve shirt he wore. The sleeves were rolled up casually, and those arms looked pretty damn good as he lifted his beer.

She nearly tripped when she came up behind him and took a quick glance back at Nicki. Sure enough, she had seen her do it and was shaking her head back and forth as if to say "typical." Ali laughed and made her way to the ladies' room, resisting the urge to turn around and look at him. She had to skirt around the dance floor to get there, and once inside she went right to the sink. Her cheeks were flushed, and she took out the lip gloss from her purse to put some on. She couldn't wait to get in the sun and get some color. The guy at the bar sure had a great tan. She wouldn't mind lying beside him on the sand. She wondered how old he was. He looked about Matt's age, she thought. She fooled with her hair a bit and opened the door to go out. There were more people on the dance floor and she had to skirt around them again to make it back to the bar.

As soon as she could see through the crowd, her eyes went directly to him. He was standing up now and looked to be reaching for his wallet. Ali couldn't help notice his height and build. He was impressive, to say the least. He was as tall as both her brothers, and they were both over six feet. This guy was like a solid mass. His hair was kind of longish, too, making him even sexier to Ali than at first glance.

She moved a little quicker. If he turned around, she wanted to be there for an up-close look. She kept her eye on his back as she watched him pay Annie. Shit, was he leaving? He returned his wallet to his back pocket and, to her pleasure, he turned around.

Rafe had seen her get up, and he watched her walk to the ladies' room. Her backside was just as appealing as her front as she swayed by. He turned back to her friend and was surprised to see her watching him. He grinned as she raised her eyebrows knowingly.

"Annie," he called.

"What can I getcha, babe?"

"Do me a favor and get the two girls across the bar another round on me."

"Oh, you're breaking my heart, Rafe." Annie winked at him and got busy at the blender.

Rafe turned back around to wait for the brunette to reappear. At the same time, his phone vibrated on his hip. He checked the caller I.D.

"Yeah, boss."

"Where are you?"

"Up the street at the local bar, what's up?" He turned his eyes to the game.

"Local P.D. just got a call from someone who happened to be fishing out your way. It seems some visitors have arrived on your beach."

Rafe smirked and then swore silently as Pedroia hit one out of the park. "What kind of visitors?" Rafe was picturing a couple of loggerheads that may have come up on the sand, attracting the attention of some tourists who probably freaked out.

"The kind from Cuba who arrive on a raft."

"No shit?"

"No shit. And they made it up and onto D'nafrio's property, where apparently they were picked up in no time at all in a black Ford F-150, the kind with the bed enclosure."

"Well, that's some kind of coincidence." Rafe turned back to the bar and signaled Annie for the check. "I'm on my way back now. I'll look at the footage and give you a call. Are we sharing with local P.D.?"

"Not about the surveillance just yet. Let me know what you see, and we'll go from there. The truck has already been detained. There were nine of them, all male, plus the driver, a Mexican man. Says he was paid to pick up some passengers by a white male, maybe early twenties, over in Fort Myers early this morning. He didn't know he'd be picking up refugees until they got in the truck all soaking wet; he said he just needed the money. He didn't think he had done anything wrong, seeing that since they had made it to shore, they were allowed to stay in the country. Apparently he's savvy in laws pertaining to refugees. God bless America."

"Jesus, so what kind of shape are they in?"

"Apparently pretty good shape to have kicked all the way from Cuba on a raft."

"That's hilarious," Rafe replied, deadpan, "but not what I meant."

When the SAC stopped laughing at his own attempt at a joke, he answered. "For such a long trip, curiously, none the worse for wear."

"You know, before you met Patty, you wouldn't have made a joke like that." Or any joke for that matter, Rafe laughed as he chided Daniels.

"I'm telling you, McDonough, find yourself a good woman, and your life will change for the better."

"Yeah, well, I was going to start working on that when you called."

"Oh, really?" Daniels sounded happy. "Sorry to interrupt your night, then. I could use a cold one about now myself. Are you watching this massacre?"

"I lost interest awhile ago. I'll call you in an hour." Rafe reached for his wallet and paid for his beer and the girls' drinks. He left Annie a nice tip as usual and hung up with his superior. Oh, well, he thought -- to be continued, he hoped.

He glanced at the friend who was just now receiving the drinks from Annie. Nicki's head gave a nod Rafe's way, and she held up her glass and mouthed a "thank you." Her gaze switched from Rafe's to over his shoulder with a slight lift of her chin, and he turned his head in response. When he noticed who she was gesturing to, he turned back to her and smiled. She gave him a playful wink, and he laughed, turning his attention back to the brunette. She was walking right by him, and he just stood there staring, like a deer caught in the headlights.

Ali was walking right by him, right now, and her heart was pounding. She dared to look up, and her breath caught as her eyes met his. They were the darkest shade of brown and…penetrating was what came to mind. She was momentarily blocked by a couple getting up to leave, and she stopped in her tracks. She wanted to say something like hello, but she didn't trust her tongue to cooperate.

Rafe was staring, and he knew he should say something, but up this close her green eyes mesmerized him. He thought with regret how differently he'd like this night to turn out, but he knew he had to go.

He started toward her as her path cleared, and he had a perfect opportunity. She gave him a slight smile, eyes downcast, and then she moved away.

Damn, he blew it; timing was everything. He was kicking himself, but what could he have done tonight? He got to the door and gave a final glance toward her seat at the bar. He could see her friend chatting away and hoped she was telling her friend about the drinks. He didn't have time to find out, though, so he left. He crossed the parking lot, hopped on his motorcycle, and put his helmet back on. Revving the engine to release his frustration, he sped off toward the beach house. Please, God, don't let her be leaving tomorrow.

"Did you see that?" Ali squealed like a schoolgirl.

"Did I see that? I saw a lot more than that, my friend."

"What do you mean?" Ali's adrenaline was pumping.

"His eyes followed you all the way to the ladies' room and stayed there until you came out."

"Really?"

"Really. He got a phone call. That must be why he left so quickly," Nicki told her. "Oh, and these drinks are from him."

"What!" Ali hissed. "How did that come about? God, I was only gone for five minutes."

"Annie came over, plopped 'em in front of me, and said, 'See that gorgeous man over there? These are from him.'"

"Did you say anything?" Ali was hanging on every word.

"I indicated a thank you," Nicki assured her. "We definitely had a moment." She laughed.

"Oh," Ali said, deflated.

Nicki laughed again. "No, no, no, it was an *I know you're interested in my best friend kind of moment.*"

"What are you talking about?" Ali perked up.

"I held up my glass to say thanks, and then I saw you coming back over, so I kind of raised my eyebrows and nodded your way," Nicki demonstrated, "and he followed my gaze to look, then turned back to me and smiled, acknowledging that we both knew who the drink gesture was really for." Nicki let out a breath. "Killer smile, by the way."

"I can't believe it." Ali made a face, kicking herself. "Remind me never to go the ladies' room again." Ali was more than disappointed that he had left, but oh, so happy that he'd bought her a drink. She only wished she had been the one to thank him. "Did you see the eye contact? I couldn't stop looking at him -- he is a beautiful, beautiful man!"

"Yeah, he was blatantly staring at you, too. I thought he was going to talk to you for a second there."

"Me, too. He looked like he was going to walk right up to me, but then I kept going, like an idiot. I did manage to give him a little smile, though." Ali shrugged. "I wonder why he left."

"I don't know, but that sucks. Now only one of us is getting laid tonight." Nicki's eyes went back to the drummer.

"Nicki!" Ali followed her gaze laughing. "You better get to work, then -- he can't even see you over here. Let's go dance." Ali stood up.

"I was kidding, by the way." She smiled at Ali's doubtful look. "I'll dance with you, but don't be too obvious." Nicki stood with her, and they made their way around the bar.

"Annie, we're just going to dance -- be right back!" Nicki called out.

"Have fun, girls. I'm not going anywhere!"

The drummer was really good-looking and met Nicki's eye as soon as she appeared on the dance floor. They danced about three songs before heading back to the bar, where they grabbed their drinks and decided to move to an open table right next to the dance floor.

"I'll have a much better view from here," Nicki grinned.

They listened and danced to the music for about an hour before the lead singer announced they'd be taking a break, and Nicki just looked at Ali with disappointment and sighed. "That sucks."

"Actually..." Ali started.

"Hey, there!"

Nicki looked up at the drummer suddenly standing next to her. "Hey," she smiled, surprised.

"Can we join you?" The drummer was accompanied by the guitar player in the band.

"Sure," Nicki said, and glared at Ali.

Ali scooted her chair beside Nicki's as the guys pulled up two more to sit with them. "You guys are really good," Ali complimented them.

The guitarist was looking her up and down and not even remotely trying to be discreet. He was appealing in a scruffy, wanna-be rock star kind of way.

"What's your name?" he asked her.

"Ali, what's yours?"

He grinned at Ali like she had just asked him to sleep with her.

"John," he said.

God, he was cocky. Ali gripped her drink and sipped. She wished her hot guy would come back in. She hoped he wasn't called away by a girlfriend or worse, a wife. He didn't look like the type who would be checking her out, though, if he was attached. She was a pretty good judge of those things. For instance, this guy beside her definitely had a girlfriend, probably more than one. Ali would bet money on it.

She could hear Nicki getting to know the drummer and wished they'd get back to playing so she wouldn't have to make small talk with this guy anymore.

"What are you doing after this?" guitar man asked her.

"I'm not sure," Ali faltered. "Probably just home to bed. We just arrived today."

"Would you like some company?"

Ali's jaw dropped as he placed a hand on her knee. She laughed at the balls on him. "Are you always this blunt?"

"When I see something I want, I just go for it," he smiled.

He had to be kidding. "Well, I appreciate the offer, but I'll have to say no."

"How long are you here for?"

He stroked her knee, and Ali abruptly crossed it over her other, causing his hand to fall away. She answered. "Six weeks."

"Great, then I've got time to work on you." He flashed her a grin that probably worked on a certain, small population of women and stood up. "Back to the skins, Ace." He winked at Ali, and she smiled in spite of herself.

The drummer got up, too, and gave Nicki a "to be continued" type of look.

"Bye," Nicki said sweetly. "He's nice," she said as he walked away.

"Just nice, huh?" Ali laughed.

"Well, his hair is darker than I thought."

"Are you kidding me right now?" Ali just stared at her friend.

"He's nice, really, I just..." she hesitated. "I don't know -- I guess I could get into him."

"I'm sure he's thinking the same thing." Ali grinned.

"Sometimes you just don't click, you know?"

Ali smiled at her. Yeah, she thought she knew. "Whatever, my vacation is all planned out now. She nodded toward the guitarist. "He's going to work on me."

"Really?" Nicki laughed. "He's not bad. Are you into him?"

Ali rolled her eyes at her. "Nicki, if I don't see that guy from the bar again so I can tell him that I'll be his love slave for the next six weeks, then this part of my summer is going to royally suck."

"Wow, then we'd better keep our eyes out. From the way he was looking at you, too, he'd probably really like that idea."

"Oh, man, I really need to get back and jump in the pool!"

"I could use a swim myself," she laughed. "Just let me pay for our first round and I'll meet you on the porch."

"Take some money," Ali offered.

"You buy next time."

"Thanks, suga mama."

"You got it." Nicki waved to the drummer as she left to settle at the bar.

She caught Annie's attention. "Can I settle up?"

"You're all set, honey, you've got a friend in the band. Looks like you girls did all right tonight!" She winked at Nicki.

Nicki looked over at the drummer. Ace really was his name, and she waved again in thanks. He gave her a nod and a smile, and kept drumming away.

"Hey, Annie, did you know the other guy?"

"Rafe? Sure, he's in here a few nights a week. He'll have a beer or two, then leave. I think he lives close by, started coming in a few weeks ago."

"Really?" Nicki would have guessed he was just a vacationer. "Is he always alone?" she asked slyly.

Annie smirked, "Yes, he is. Up until tonight I thought he was coming in to see me." She winked again and got on with her customers.

"Goodnight! Thanks!" Nicki called out. She left a tip for Annie and met Ali out on the front porch.

"Okay, I got the scoop. His name is Rafe, and he comes in a couple of nights a week…alone."

Ali's eyes widened, "Rafe, huh? That's perfect -- he looks like a Rafe. I love it! So maybe he just moved here."

"Maybe, oh, and Ace paid our tab." Nicki noticed the smile play on Ali's face. "Yes, that's his real name. Don't laugh."

"Well, now, looks like you landed yourself a drummer. Are you going to become a groupie or what?" Ali teased.

"It's our first night here. I might have to audition some more bands before I go jumping into anything." Nicki played along. "Or… maybe your gorgeous man has an equally gorgeous friend."

Ali laughed. "He *was* freaking gorgeous!" She hopped in the convertible and waited for Nicki to start it. "I'm going to jump right in the pool, then get to bed. I cannot wait to get in the sun tomorrow!"

"Me, too. It's going to feel so good."

"Do you want to run in the morning?" Ali asked, hopeful.

Nicki glanced over at her. "Oh, definitely. What were you thinking, like seven a.m.? I'll only go if you're going to do, like, five miles."

"Your sarcasm hurts," Ali chuckled. She knew Nicki preferred yoga and Pilates. After taking dance most of her life, that's how she kept her lithe body. Ali, on the other hand, loved to run, lift weights, hike, bike, and just challenge her body all the time. She didn't have the patience for yoga or Pilates. Once a month she'd join Nicki, and that was enough for her.

"Plus, I was thinking more like six a.m., so I know I lost you there."

"Yeah..." Nicki agreed. She pulled into the driveway and they headed inside.

Rafe watched the convertible pull into the driveway across the street. He felt a little relief wash over him. He hadn't liked leaving her at the bar, thinking someone else might be trying to hit on her. Why the hell should it bother him? She was probably going home in a week anyway. He was already in a sour mood because he'd had to leave the bar almost as soon as he'd arrived, and the Yankees had lost to the damn Sox. That was never a good thing. But he had to stop thinking negatively -- maybe she'd just gotten to the island. He decided that was more likely, given that *he'd* been here and had only just seen *her* today. He put her out of his mind temporarily as he settled in front of the flat screen.

When he'd arrived back at the house, D'nafrio's property had been empty, but Rafe wasn't surprised when, less than a half hour later, a black SUV pulled in and parked. He called in the plate, make, and model and watched the vehicle for a little while. Rafe would find out in less than an hour who they were, and why they were there. He sat back on the couch, and because everything was digital he was able to set the surveillance tapes back and watched as the nine Cubans made it to shore.

He knew refugees had landed on the beaches of Sanibel and Captiva before this, so it wasn't that much of a surprise. The surprise and the coincidence was that they happened to arrive right on D'nafrio's stretch of beach and conveniently managed to have a ride waiting for them right out in front of his property.

Rafe watched the screen as the figures emerged from the water, letting their means of transport float back into the Gulf. He counted the nine of them and watched as the group of them ran stealthily for the mammoth structure that was D'nafrio's nearly shelled-out beach house and disappeared. Switching cameras, he rewound to the footage that would show him the front of the property. He saw the Ford pull up just moments before the nine refugees abandoned their flotation device. Rafe went back to the beach footage -- either everyone's timing was impeccable, or someone had been out there watching and waiting, giving the Ford the heads-up. Back to the front view, he watched the nine pile into the back of the covered truck and drive off. Rafe got on the phone to Daniels.

"Whadda you got?"

"Well, there wasn't any sign of a vessel in the Gulf other than what appeared to be their raft, and that appeared to have a small outboard on it."

"A Coast Guard cutter out of Fort Myers picked up an empty Zodiac with a fifty-horse engine and a portable GPS, fifteen minutes ago."

"Not exactly inner tubes and broken tree limbs." The typical mode of transportation for refugees was usually more inventive and less innovative. Rafe had seen pictures of a dozen different vessels concocted for the journeys, even floating cars.

"No, not exactly. The Coast Guard is still out there searching and will stop any boat they encounter. Meanwhile, the refugees are on route here to Miami for questioning."

"They definitely had assistance out there -- that Ford pulled up minutes after they touched the sand."

"All right, we'll see if the Coast Guard intercepted any chatter over the open channels. And let's look at the neighbors again -- someone very well could have been awaiting their arrival."

"An older couple live in the house to my left from the beach, and they're not here until October. The house beside D'nafrio's is empty and for sale. The other houses are too far away, so unless someone was in one of these empty houses, then the heads-up came from the water." Rafe didn't think someone would risk breaking into one of the beach houses just to be a lookout. It would be much easier to do the job from a boat in the water or even right from the beach. This stretch of beach was pretty private, but it wasn't unusual to see a lone fisherman down on the sand every once in awhile. "Bear with me a sec. I'm going to check something out." He used the remote to go back a few more frames before the nine refugees came ashore. He used the zoom to pull in as close as he could, and sure enough, he spotted a definite silhouette. The camera's lens didn't reach much past D'nafrio's property line, but just enough so that a form could be seen moving by the water's edge.

"I've got something here. At 21:30 there's someone by the water's edge about one hundred yards down from me. Let me get to the Ford." Rafe used the remote again, queuing up the footage of the pickup. "Here we go." Rafe found the image and noted the time. "The truck pulled up at 21:45. What time was the call placed to local?"

"Just about nine forty-five. Dan Halloran called it in -- he lives five houses east of you and was out fishing for black tips when he saw the Zodiac approach. He apparently keeps a pair of binoculars on hand at all times."

Rafe did a quick scan of the footage even though he knew Dan Halloran's image would not appear; he'd of been too far out of range. "Did he see anybody else?"

"Negative. He high-tailed it back to the house to make the call. He wasn't looking in that direction until he heard the slight drone of the inboard."

"And I'm assuming by the sight of this SUV now parked in front of his property that local P.D. notified D'nafrio?"

"They actually called his broker Barry Stoddman. He's the contact listed with the city of Sanibel for all of D'nafrio's properties."

"So you think the SUV is his doing?"

"I'll know in about twenty."

"Okay, and we need to find out who our shadow on the beach is, unless one of the refugees has anything interesting to say."

"I'll know something soon. I'm going to go sit in on this one. I'll call you back shortly. E-mail me those images."

"Will do." Rafe hung up and, using the built-in internet connection, e-mailed the night's footage to Daniels. Sitting back when he was done, he sighed, thinking how the night had started out so promising. He'd come so close to talking to the girl from the beach, but she'd kept on walking right back to her seat at the bar. He did catch that little smile, though, and he'd felt an exciting tug in his gut he hadn't felt for awhile.

The last time he'd been with a woman was in Miami six months ago. A friend's cousin who happened to be in the city for the weekend was looking to live it up while she was there. Rafe had been happy to oblige, just coming off a three-month undercover job. She was pretty and fun to hang out with that weekend, but by Sunday, he'd had enough. She had started drinking again at eleven that morning. He had been ready to detox with a five-mile run, and she had been well on her way to Margaritaville. He'd driven her back to her cousin's place and bid her farewell.

He wondered what the brunette was doing now. He wished his surveillance cameras reached across the street, specifically into whatever room she was occupying. He got aroused just thinking about watching her.

He shook his head at the perverted thoughts he was having and knew it was time for bed. He went to the bedroom to undress and placed his gun under his pillow. He slipped between the sheets and picked up the remote, bringing the flat screen to life. The picture in picture displayed all eight camera angles, and he drifted off watching the two men next door in the SUV. He was almost asleep when Daniels called back.

"Okay, the Explorer is registered to Holly Mann. She works in Barry

Stoddman's real estate office as his assistant. She has a son Timothy, and I'm e-mailing you over a DMV shot of him now. No record, but the father, Timothy senior, is up in Okeechobee Correctional for aggravated assault. The kid is twenty-one years old and hangs out with a Sean Smith, also twenty-one and no record. I'm sending his picture as well. Could be Stoddman sent them out as a precaution, to make sure there weren't any more visitors."

"Speaking of visitors, did you get any information out of them?" Rafe picked up the remote and used the T.V. as a computer monitor, accessing his e-mail and retrieving the pictures of the two men. They were DMV photos but appeared pretty clear.

"Eight of them were cleared and are being transported to our immigration offices, but one is still being questioned. He's the oldest and seemed to be in charge. When all together, the other eight seem to defer to him."

"You think you're going to get something from him?"

"Hard to say right now."

Rafe knew Daniels wasn't ready to share, so he let it go. Unless the SAC had specific facts, he didn't like to waste time speculating.

"Check in the morning, and I'll bring you up to speed."

"You got it." Rafe hung up and closed his eyes.

CHAPTER FIVE

Rafe woke with a start and reached for the gun under his pillow. His eyes swept the room and landed on the flat screen. The two "guards" appeared to still be sleeping. He relaxed, letting go of the gun, and got out of bed. It was just dawn, and he walked into the kitchen for some juice. He picked up the remote for the living room T.V. and hit the power button. The middle of the screen showed the morning news, and the surrounding edges showed the perimeters of the property in separate frames. He looked at the view from the front gate and could see the convertible parked in the drive across the street. A movement caught his eye, and he zoomed in. Holy crap! There she was. Oh, man, she had one long leg up on the bumper of the convertible, stretching -- one leg, then the other. He watched while she reached her arms up over her head and stretched from side to side. Her sports top and running shorts showed off a fit, toned body, just as he suspected. His body's response was instant.

A run suddenly sounded like a great idea. He waited to see which direction she took off in and then hurriedly returned to his bedroom to throw on shorts and sneakers. He grabbed a gray T-shirt off the back of his door, went to the bathroom to splash some water on his face and brush his teeth, then ran for the steps to the garage. He hit the button to the door, impatiently waiting for it to open, then closed it behind him from the key pad. He made his way to the gate and forewent any stretching of his own in order to catch up to her.

A glance to the right, and he could see her in the distance. He glanced to the left and was happy to see the Explorer come to life -- perfect timing. He waited until they drove past. The two young males he now had a solid I.D. on drove past without a glance in Rafe's direction.

Rafe entered out on the road and started his run at a good pace. He knew if he didn't catch up right away, at some point she'd at least have to turn around and run right by him. That probably made for a better scenario anyway. Why kill himself trying to catch up? He ran past Blind Pass and the Santiva general store. The Gulf was perfectly still at the early hour, not a ripple in sight. The beach was empty, save for a few early morning shell-seekers on the sand. He might just decide to dive in on the way back, it looked so inviting.

He kept his steady pace and enjoyed the morning air, keeping her in his sights. It was a little after six a.m. and already fairly warm. He was impressed that she was out running. They had something in common already. He could see her long brown ponytail bouncing behind her, and it didn't appear as though she was listening to any music. He normally ran with his MP3 player, but since he'd arrived on the island, he'd abandoned it, preferring to listen to the sounds around him. In the city he looked forward to blocking out the noise; now he only put the music on when he was in the workout room or out by the pool.

She was definitely running at a good clip. If he'd wanted to catch up to her, he'd have to kick it in gear. He was just waiting for the turnaround. The sun was slowly coming up over the Gulf and the temperature right along with it. He pulled his T-shirt over his head and tucked it into the back of his shorts. He was about two miles into the run when he saw her turn. Here we go. He kept his pace steady as he made his way toward her.

Ali was getting pretty hot. The sun was rising and she didn't want to get caught too far away without any water on her. She felt like she could run forever this morning, her energy level being pretty high considering the three drinks she'd consumed the night before. She couldn't stop thinking of the guy at the bar, "Rafe," and knew that it was the thought of him keeping her adrenaline pumping.

She had already gone about two miles and decided to turn back in the other direction. There was a man jogging toward her, and she started to hug the right side of the road to give him some room. Ali couldn't help but notice the muscular build on the guy -- he was shirtless, and all abs. She tried not to be too obvious, keeping her stride, all the while taking her fellow runner in. When he neared a little closer, she just about had a heart attack on the spot. She felt her heart beating double-time in her chest, and her breath got short as she tried to compose herself. "Holy mother of God!" she was screaming in her head, "it's him!" When he was practically close enough to touch, she somehow managed a breathless, "Good morning." She was rewarded by an unbelievable smile and an equally breathless, "Mornin'."

Oh, God, he was gorgeous, his body was freaking incredible. Ali was all pumped up and felt herself sprinting. She couldn't wait to get back and tell Nicki. Wait a minute, she thought, what was she doing? Was he coming or going? Would he turn around? If so, maybe she'd get a chance to speak to him and thank him for the drink. Should she slow down? No, too obvious. Shit! While she wrestled with what to do, her decision was made for her when a humongous black snake slithered out of the mangroves and onto the road in front of her.

"Ugh!" she screamed at the top of her lungs and stopped dead in her tracks, her breath coming in shallow gasps.

Rafe had turned around almost as soon as he'd passed her. He had to get close to her again -- she was something else. When he was running toward her, all he could keep his eyes on were her breasts, straining under the top she wore, and on her flat, toned stomach, but then she'd greeted him and he was again mesmerized by her extraordinary green eyes.

He noticed that she had picked up her pace, and now that he was behind her, her long legs and tight ass were the focus. His picked up his own pace just a bit, fully intending to catch up to her. He wasn't going to let her get away again without speaking to her.

He kept his eyes on her gait as he followed and was surprised when she suddenly came up short, and then he was running even faster at the sound of her screaming. He was upon her in less than a minute.

"What's wrong?" he asked, looking at her and trying to catch his breath.

Ali whipped around to see him right there beside her. Her heart was racing at the sight of the snake and now even more so at the sight of him this close to her. She couldn't speak right away, could only stare -- his eyes, the way he was looking at her was rendering her brainless at that very moment. She somehow managed to cast her eyes downward toward the snake.

Rafe followed her gaze and saw a coiled-up black racer in front of her feet. He gave a little chuckle. "It's just a black racer. He won't hurt you."

Ali knew of black racers and knew they were indeed harmless for the most part, but when the snake came out of the mangroves, she had immediately thought "cottonmouth." She wouldn't have known the difference looks-wise; she just knew a cottonmouth was bad…very bad.

"Oh, that's good news." She breathed in. "He still scared me to death, though, and he doesn't want to seem to move."

"Here, follow me," Rafe grabbed her hand and directed her out into the street, walking her around the snake. Putting the snake behind them, he guided her back onto the shoulder of the road and reluctantly released her hand, which he couldn't help notice had fit perfectly inside his own.

Ali didn't think she could be sweating any more than she was, and then he went and grabbed her hand. The current that shot through her brought on a whole new wave of perspiration. It would figure, she thought, that this was how she would meet him: dripping with sweat, hair stuck to her head, and dressed in a stupid sports bra and shorts. Her stomach was doing somersaults at a gymnast's pace, and she thought for a second she was going to throw up. She had been running pretty fast when she'd suddenly stopped, and that, combined with the snake and the sight of him -- and the sound of his oh-so-deep and sexy voice -- had her roiling. Calm down, girl, deep breaths…get it together. She wiped her brow with her forearm, and upon doing so, her eyes fell to his navel. He had the faintest line of hair below it, running down into his shorts. Oh, sweet lord. She could feel him looking at her, and she met his eyes with her own.

"Thanks."

"You're welcome." He was grinning at her and had a little glint in his eyes.

Great, he totally bagged me checking him out. "I don't like snakes."

"I'm not a big fan, either," he agreed. "Do you want to keep running?"

With you? Yes, oh, yes. Oh, yes. "Yeah, sure, I'm on my way back home anyway." Her voice wasn't quite steady, and again she caught the glint in his eye.

"Me, too." Rafe couldn't help but feel a jolt at her obvious assessment of him. They started to jog at a slow pace, Rafe on the outside.

"Do you run every morning?" she asked. Ali wasn't sure she could get her breathing on track.

"About every other day. I haven't seen you out here until today."

"I just got here yesterday." And God really loves me, she thought.

"From?" Yes! He had hoped she'd just arrived.

"Boston." Please let him be from Boston, too.

"Yeah? How long are you here for?" Work with me here, God.

"For six weeks."

Thank you. "That's great." He couldn't keep the happiness out of his answer.

Ali looked over to him. *That's great? It is?* "How 'bout you? Are you from here?" They were both running slow enough to be able to talk without losing their wind. She couldn't help feeling that there was a definite mutual attraction going on between them.

"I've been here a little over three weeks, I've been working in Miami for the past year and decided to take a break to spend a little time on the islands." It was pretty close to the truth. He didn't want to scare her away with, *I'm an FBI agent here on assignment*.

"Oh." Ali was psyched he'd be on the islands, but bummed about Miami.

They were back up by the general store.

"The water looks inviting doesn't it?" Rafe asked.

"Yes, it's so beautiful," she smiled as she pictured herself naked in there with him.

So are you, he wanted to say. "Have you been here before?"

"Yeah, a few different times, my best friend's grandmother owns the house I'm staying at, right up here." Ali gestured with her head. "What about you -- where are you staying?" Ali hoped it was nearby.

"I'm right up here, too."

They ran on ahead in silence, and Ali noticed how it wasn't uncomfortable at all. She was so enjoying his nearness to her and the sound of his steady breathing, she actually had goose bumps. Nicki wasn't going to believe this. She started to slow her pace down to a walk, and he matched her stride. She wished the house was another ten miles up the road.

"I'm right here." Ali came to a stop in front of Nan's driveway.

Rafe was walking beside her. He was a whole head taller than she, and he looked down at her face as she spoke.

Ali looked up into his fierce brown eyes. "Well, thanks for saving me from the snake." She was facing him now and feeling a bit awkward. He had the littlest bit of chest hair that glistened with sweat. She clasped her hands in front of her in case they involuntarily sprang forward and touched him. He was like a walking advertisement for Calvin Klein undies. "I think I had a poster of you in my room when

I was in high school," she wanted to say.

"Hey, my pleasure. I'm Rafe, by the way."

"I know." Ali blushed.

He cocked his head and smiled. "How could you possibly know that?"

Ali returned his smile. "My friend asked the bartender. Thank you for the drinks, by the way -- that was nice."

"You're welcome." He stared at her mouth. She was biting her lower lip, and he was finding it very distracting. He wanted to kiss her. "So Annie gave you my name?"

"Yes." Ali smiled and shifted her weight as she watched him watching her lips. Oh, God.

"She's a sweetheart. I'm in there quite a bit."

"She mentioned that."

"Oh? What else did she have to say?" Rafe was smiling, too.

"She actually spoke to my friend Nicki. I was already outside."

"I got a phone call and had to leave," he started to explain. "Otherwise..." He didn't finish because he wasn't sure what to finish with -- otherwise, I would have liked to take you home to my bed and done all the things I've dreamt of doing since I laid eyes on you on the beach.

The way he was looking at her had her nerve endings tingling, and she decided to be daring. "Otherwise?"

Rafe was taken in by her mischievous smile. Her eyes were sparkling, and her face was glowing from the run. He let his eyes drop and slowly take in her body. Her toned shoulders and arms were glistening with sweat, and the valley between her breasts had little beads dripping down into her top. Her breasts were full and perfect, her stomach flat and hard, and her shorts held some killer legs. He was envisioning those legs wrapped...

Ali cleared her throat. She could feel his eyes caressing her body, and she was getting fidgety standing there before him.

He looked up again to her face, but his smile was gone. He was looking at her hungrily, and he could see she knew what he was thinking. She was blushing again, and he was sort of glad at having caused it. He wanted her to know.

"I'm going to go in now." She thought it was probably for the better that he didn't answer. She was starting to get the shivers even though it was about eighty degrees already. His eyes had clearly answered the question that was left hanging there. "Maybe I'll see you again -- you know, running."

"Yeah, I'd like that." He felt like an ass -- she'd just given him an opportunity, he should just ask her out, but instead he just stood there while she walked toward the house. She was just about to open the door when he realized he still didn't know her name.

"Hey, green eyes!"

Ali stopped in her tracks and looked back at him. Her heart pounded again. He just called me green eyes! Get a grip, he's going to ask you out. Be calm and be cool. She just smiled.

"Yeah?"

"What's your name?" he laughed.

Oh, yeah - that would probably help, "Alison -- my friends call me Ali."

"See you around, Ali."

"Bye." *See you around? That's it?* She watched him turn to walk away, and she quickly walked to the garage door and went in. Shutting it behind her, she leaned back and sank to the ground, allowing her legs to finally give out. Holy hell, why hadn't she asked *him* out? She could only pray she would see him out running the next day. And I never even found out where he lives, she thought kicking herself, but it must be close. He said it was. Ali slowly made her way into the house and stopped in the kitchen for a bottle of water, taking it down in four gulps.

Nicki was not yet awake, so she went back to her room to shower.

She'd give Nicki all the details when she got up.

Ali checked the time. God, it was only eight a. m. It felt like so much later. She got undressed in the bathroom and didn't wait for the water to warm up. The cold water made her squeal, but she suffered through for five minutes before the water turned hot. She washed her hair and body and enjoyed the steaming water pelting her skin. She couldn't believe she had seen him out running. That had to be fate, right? she thought. She really had felt an attraction to him the night before, and now more than ever she wanted to see him again. She shaved her legs and underarms while she was in the shower and was happy to see her bikini area was still smooth, thanks to the waxing she and Nicki had put themselves through two days before.

"Why do we do this again?" she had asked Nicki.

"In hopes that we won't be the only ones to see it," Nicki had answered her, seriously causing Ali to crack up.

"Oh, and here I was thinking you signed us up to star in a porn."

"No, that's next summer," Nicki had joked.

Ali smiled, remembering their day at the salon. They'd both received pedicures too, which Ali looked down at to re-admire. She turned the water off and stepped out to dry off.

She put a new white two-piece bathing suit on, one she had bought just for the trip, and after covering her bottom half with a sarong, she headed back to the kitchen for breakfast.

Nicki was awake and eating cereal at the counter. "Hey, nice suit. How was your run?"

"Thanks -- and incredible!" Ali smiled.

"Incredible? What did you do, run ten miles?"

"No, four, and I had company toward the end." Ali's eyes sparkled with mischief.

"Really?" Nicki waited for the punch line.

"Does the name Rafe ring a bell?" Ali jumped up and down excitedly.

Nicki laughed. "Are you kidding? What the hell time was it?"

"I went out about six-thirty, ran about two miles, then turned to come back…and guess who was running toward me?"

"Rafe." Nicki nodded to go on.

"Yup, and he was shirtless and oh, so glorious, and I said "good morning,' and he said 'mornin,' and I kept going."

"You kept going?" Nicki asked incredulously, shaking her head.

"Yes," she laughed, "but listen, about a mile in on the way back, a friggin' black racer came out at me, and I had to stop in my tracks."

"Ugh, did you scream?"

"Hell, yes, I screamed!"

"And he heard you and turned around?" Nicki asked impatiently.

"It was like he just appeared. He was there right away, asking me what was wrong." She sighed. "We ended up jogging back together and walking the last few yards to the house."

"Wow, where is he staying?"

Ali grimaced. "I don't know, but he said he was nearby when we were approaching this house."

"Did he ask you out?"

"No," Ali admitted, "but he called me green eyes." She smiled.

"He did?" Nicki's eyes widened.

"As I was going in the house, he called out, 'Hey, green eyes, what's your name?'"

"Ooh, that's kind of sexy."

"Yeah, it is! There was some damn hot eye contact out there in the driveway, too."

"Really?" Nicki was excited for her. "So now what?" she asked smiling.

"We just said maybe we would see each other out running." Ali was disappointed. "I should have asked him out myself, but I was a chicken."

"Yes, you should have. Don't blow that chance again."

"I won't. I hope he's out there tomorrow."

"Or," Nicki cocked her head, "maybe back at the bar tonight."

"Right! I didn't even think of that. Damn, I should have mentioned we'd be going back there." She shook her head at her lack of skills. She hadn't done this sort of thing in a long time.

"Don't worry -- he at least knows where you live. He's definitely interested." Nicki knew that the night before. "Are you ready to soak up the sun or what?" Nicki asked.

"Oh, so ready." Ali headed to the sliders and opened them wide. She hoped Nicki was right. There had been some definite heat between them in the driveway.

"Just leave them open so we can hear the music. I'll shut off the A/C." Nicki hooked up her iPod to the sound system and joined Ali out on the pool deck. She threw her the protein bar she had left in the kitchen.

"Thanks," Ali said, catching it.

"How's the water?"

"Chilly!" Ali had a toe in. "Hey, did your grandmother ever call you back?" She walked over to a lounge chair and spread out a beach towel, then positioned the chair under the sun's rays and lay down on her back.

Nicki set up on the chair beside her. A table between them held their sun block and lip balm. "Not yet. I'm still wondering about her surprise. I haven't a clue what it could be." Her eyes were closed to the sun as she savored the heat of it on her skin.

"She's so sweet. It's probably something for us to enjoy while we're here." Ali finished applying sunscreen while Beyonce' played in the background. "There's a D.J. at the Crow's Nest tonight -- we'll have to get him to play this."

"Yeah, because we'll be the only 'single ladies' in the club!" Nicki chuckled.

Ali laughed beside her. "There were a few last night. Didn't you see them?"

"I think they were band groupies. I noticed a few wayward glances our way when Ace and -- what was the guitar player's name?"

"John."

"When they sat down with us, there were a couple of women looking over, none too happy."

"Well, they'll have to fight me for that great catch." Ali rolled her eyes.

"I think *you'll* have to fight Annie for Rafe."

Ali sat up. "I know, she seemed kind of chummy with him, huh?"

"I'm kidding. You know, she could be his mom."

"How old do you think he is?" Ali wondered. "I'd guess around Matt or Jason's age."

"Ooh, an older man, what's Jason, thirty-five?" Nicki asked lazily.

"Uh-huh." Ali thought about it. "Maybe he's Matt's age. He's definitely no older than Jay, though."

No response from Nicki. Ali knew she was zoning out in the sun, and she closed her eyes and did the same. The sun felt so good and the music was so relaxing, she found herself dozing off. It wasn't until she felt her stomach rumbling that she opened her eyes again. She never did eat that protein bar after her run, which wasn't a good thing. She had been so caught up in talking about Rafe, she'd forgotten to eat. The bar Nicki had tossed her now sat melting in its package beside her.

"Umm, what time is it?" Nicki asked groggily.

Ali stood up to peer into the house. "Kitchen clock says eleven. You hungry yet?"

"No, not yet," Nicki answered.

"I think I'm going to go across to the beach for an hour. Wanna come?"

"Nah, I want to go topless and tan my boobs -- can't do that on the beach." Nicki sat up to untie her top. She lay back down and applied a generous amount of sunscreen to her chest.

Ali laughed, "You better hope the pool guy doesn't show up today."

"Not until Friday -- already checked on the fridge. There's a schedule."

"All right, but don't burn those puppies. I don't want to hear any complaining tonight!"

Ali grabbed her towel and sarong and slipped on her flip flops. "I'm going to grab another breakfast bar. This one is all melty."

When Ali came back out, she had her towel and sunscreen in her beach bag. She bent down to the table next to Nicki for her lip balm and left a water there for her.

"Thanks, bud, have fun at the beach."

"No problem. I'm leaving through the back gate, but don't worry -- the house is locked."

"I'm not worried. I'm on vacation -- if anyone sees my boobs, they're just going to have to get over it." Nicki had positioned herself right under the sun's rays and looked thoroughly relaxed.

"If anyone sees *those suckers*, they'll have a coronary," Ali laughed.

"Funny -- are you going through the house across the street?"

"Yeah, you think it'll be okay?"

"You're fine. Don't even worry about it." Nicki waved her off.

Ali left through the side yard, eating her late breakfast as she walked across the shelled drive. She looked both ways, then crossed the road to the neighbor's gate. She scurried through the bushes flanking the side of it, and speed-walked down the paved driveway to the side of the house.

When she got to the pool gate, she prayed it would be unlocked. She pushed gently and breathed a sigh of relief as it gave beneath her hand. She walked as quickly as she could by the pool and on to the path that led to the sand. For the second time that day she was stopped dead in her tracks -- this time by a voice.

"Not a good testimonial for the security system."

Shit! Ali turned around slowly, and her eyes shot up to the back of the house. Rafe was draped over the porch railing on the second floor, a water bottle dangling in his hand. His shirt was still off, and the grin he wore made Ali blush all over once again.

"Umm, hi." Great, this was his house where she had now trespassed for the second time -- three times if you counted the going back.

"Hi, yourself." Wow, the white bathing suit top she wore was even better than her running top in the reveal department.

"I'm sorry -- I didn't think anyone was living here, and our beach access is closed, and the others are kind of a hike. Well, only if you're dragging chairs and stuff, so I thought it would be okay..." She was rambling.

He laughed. "You're welcome to cut through anytime." Rafe made his way down the porch steps, across the pool deck, and over to where she stood.

"Thanks." Ali stood rooted in the sand. She couldn't take her eyes off him, and she was suddenly aware of the heat radiating through her. She wiped a sweaty palm on her sarong.

"Where you going?" he asked with that grin that was becoming her undoing.

"Just to lie on the beach for a bit. I was lying by the pool with Nick -- she's my friend I'm staying with -- but I wanted to be on the sand, so she's home and I'm here." Please let me stop rambling. He was still grinning at her. God, his eyes were intense. She could feel the heat in her cheeks and could tell he noticed it.

"Mind if I come, too?"

Hell no. "No, of course not. Considering you didn't call the cops on me, I should be grateful."

"No need to call the cops," he laughed. If she only knew. "You look pretty harmless."

Ali shot him a daring look. "Don't be so sure."

Oh, careful how you look at me, sweetheart. "I'm going to enjoy thinking about what that could mean."

Ali just grinned. They were flirting, and she knew she was playing with fire. The air between them was electric and had her feeling weak in the knees.

They walked toward the water, and Ali took her towel from her beach bag, setting it out on the sand and sitting down. He lowered himself next to her, mere inches away.

"Don't let me stop you from lying down." He could tell she was flustered -- hell, he was, too. She was in a bikini, for Christ's sake. Although she had yet to take off the long see-through skirt covering her lower half.

"I'm fine for now." If feeling like I'm sixteen on a first date is feeling fine, she thought.

"I'm going in."

He stood back up, only seconds after he'd sat down and walked into the water. He was wearing long board shorts, and his butt looked amazing in them, hung low on his waist, his body looked hard and smooth. Ali couldn't help wondering what it would feel like to be in his arms and pressed against that chest. Was this normal after meeting someone mere hours ago? Probably not. It was full-blown lust due to lack of sex -- and being on the beach half-naked in the sun was not helping.

Why fight it, though? she thought. She was a grown woman, and this kind of chemistry didn't happen every day. She watched him as he waded in, then turned to face her. When he was deep enough, he turned, dove under, surfaced, and waved her in.

"God help me," she said under her breath, and stood up to untie her sarong. She left it on her towel, then slowly made her way toward him in the water. It was a wee bit chilly, but the heat of his eyes on her warmed at least some parts.

"It's not too bad," she lied as she came up to him. The water was up to her waist, and she was covered in goose bumps.

Rafe sank down all the way, dunking his head under and coming back up. He was thankful for the coverage of the water after watching her take that skirt off. He knew she had a fantastic body, but seeing even more of it in that barely there bikini had him staring like a teenager with raging hormones. Watching her hips move as she slo-mo'd her way in made him doubly glad he was waist deep. As it was, the thin material covering her breasts couldn't hide the two taut nipples rubbing against it. He was finding it hard not to look, and even harder not to touch.

Ali smiled and sank down under, too. "I've been wanting to do that since I got off the plane," she said, coming back up but keeping her shoulders under. The water was actually starting to feel nice.

"I'm out here every day swimming with the dolphins," he grinned. She looked beautiful with her hair slicked back off her face.

She laughed. "Oh, yeah, where are they now?"

"Just be patient and look out there." He pointed to the horizon.

They sat there, silent for a bit, letting the water lap around their shoulders, and again the silence wasn't awkward, it was rather nice. Ali felt a ripple of warmth run through her. She looked over at him and he returned her gaze.

"Look," he whispered, pointing. As if on cue, the blessed dolphins appeared. Today he had good timing. He looked at her as she followed the line of his finger.

"Oh, my God, there's two!" Ali watched the dolphins lazily make their way down the beach. "Oh, I want to be right next to them."

"They're pretty cool to watch, aren't they? I never get sick of it."

"I wouldn't, either." She looked at him. She was in big trouble here. "You must see them a lot from that porch."

"Yeah, I do." He was stunned by her eyes again. The water set their color off, and her face, reddened by the sun, enhanced them even more. "Ali, you have the most beautiful eyes I have ever seen."

Ali felt the heat rise again. "Thank you," she barely choked out. She cleared her throat, wishing she had the courage to say what she was thinking. She smiled at his compliment and had to turn from his intense gaze. "Are those lobster traps?" She noticed the scattering of buoys nearby, bobbing colorfully in the water.

"I think lobster season is over. They could be for bait fish or crabs, I guess." He grinned; he knew small talk when he heard it.

"How do the fisherman tell their traps apart? They all kind of look the same."

He smiled at her, recognizing the fact that she couldn't care less about fishing traps and that she was just trying to process his compliment. "They have registration numbers, and they mark them with their own colors or stripes or whatever."

Ali looked at one pretty one in particular. It was purplish and she couldn't see any numbers, but she thought if she had her own she would make hers pink with green polka dots, because thinking about buoys was easier than thinking about the sexual tension threatening to boil in the very water surrounding her. She suddenly felt self-conscious looking at him, or rather, of him looking into her eyes.

"You want to go get in the sun?" Shit -- he'd embarrassed her. He'd had to tell her though -- they *were* the most beautiful eyes he'd ever seen. He wanted to drown in them. He didn't want her to stop looking at him, either, because when she did, he could see something there, something he knew was reflected in his own eyes. There is a God.

"Sure." Ali stood up and started to make her way out of the water and back to her towel. Rafe was right behind her.

"I can share the towel if you don't want to sit in the sand," she offered. How subtle, Ali.

"That's okay, it doesn't bother me." He didn't trust himself in that scenario.

Ali laughed. "Won't the shells hurt?"

"Nah, I'm tough -- I can take it." Maybe the discomfort of the shells would distract from his other discomfort.

"Suit yourself." Great, he didn't want to share her towel. She was such an idiot. She lay down on her back, the warmth from the sun spreading over her and already drying her wet skin.

Rafe sat and looked over at her. Her white bikini had become quite transparent from getting wet, and before, where he could make out the tiny bumps of her nipples, he could now see their entirety. Oh, man. He felt the familiar stirring of arousal and quickly turned to lie on his stomach beside her. As if this is helping any, he thought. Talk about burying your head in the sand. What he wanted to do was roll right on top of her and let her know what she was doing to him, but considering he'd only just learned her name this morning, that probably wasn't such a good idea.

"So why *here* for six weeks?" he asked, trying to switch the gears in his one-track brain.

"Well, Nicki's grandmother has the house, and we both kind of needed a break. I just finished grad school, and Nicki's taken a summer job with the Beach News. She's going to write for the Globe or Herald someday," she told him proudly.

"Oh, yeah? And what about you? What are you going to do?"

"Well, I'm a realtor part time -- it's kind of a family business." She paused and sat up on her elbows. "But I want to open my own store."

Rafe watched her face light up as she described the business she wanted to open. She was a beautiful woman, and when she smiled, he wanted desperately to kiss her.

"It sounds great, especially the part where you travel to all the antique shops and flea markets to get your merchandise. My mom loves doing that sort of thing, too."

"She does?" Ali was surprised that he genuinely sounded interested.

"Yeah, my parents' whole house is filled with stuff my mom finds at those places."

"Really?" Ali was really interested now. "And where do your parents live?" She was loving talking to him like this. His lips looked so kissable however that she was a little distracted. He was just so damn good-looking.

Rafe was amused by the way she was looking at him. He got the idea she might be feeling a little like he did right now -- completely turned on. Man, he wanted to touch her body. She had little bits of sand stuck to her skin in various places, and he wanted to help wipe it off. "My parents are on Long Island."

Ali's eyebrows rose.

"And I'm in the city."

"Wow, you're from New York City?" Ali was impressed and disappointed at the same time.

"I've been there for fourteen years."

Ali sat all the way up and hugged her knees. "I've never been to New York City." She was staring at the muscles in his back and arms that were flexed as he rested on his elbows in the sand. He must work out…a lot.

"C'mon, never?" Rafe was surprised. "Boston's so close."

"Just never got the chance," she remarked. "So when did you move to Miami?" Just her sheer luck, of course, that someone like him would be from New York City and live in Miami. He probably had access to the most beautiful women in the world. And why was she even getting uptight? She just met him; it wasn't like they were going to have a relationship or anything. She had to learn to just enjoy the moment and stop thinking about the details.

He looked directly at her and at the sudden change in her voice. "I didn't move to Miami. I'm just working there temporarily." Rafe felt Ali's mood change and wasn't sure what happened. She seemed to get tense all of a sudden. He felt the sudden urge to wrap his arms around her, but instead he reached over and gently brushed a clump of sand off her back.

His touch sent a shock wave through her skin and had Ali snapping her head around to look at him.

"You had sand," he explained. He hoped she wasn't put off, but he couldn't help himself.

She gave him a grin instead, letting him know she definitely was not put off. "Thanks." She stood up, taking her towel, "I should probably go see what Nicki's doing." Before I throw my body on top of yours and make a fool of myself. She didn't want to leave, but she didn't know where to take it from here without looking like someone completely sex-starved. She did not want to leave him with a bad impression of her. Maybe there was a chance they could actually go on a date.

Rafe stood up too, disappointed. "Oh, you sure you can't hang out for a little while? We could go up by the pool." He prayed she would say yes. He wanted more time with her.

Ali looked up to the pool area and then back to Rafe. She *would* have the chance to get to know him better. He flashed her that devastating grin again as she was thinking it over. How could she possibly say no? "Okay -- I'm sure Nicki's doing just fine."

CHAPTER SIX

Nicki was in a state of bliss. Her body was soaking up the rays, and she was drifting in and out of a sun-induced sleep. When Ali had gone, Nicki had shut the music off so she could listen to the sounds coming off the bay. She was in pure heaven; it was so peaceful here. At some point she thought she'd heard Ali return, probably for lunch, but she didn't have the energy to get up and join her yet.

Grace had given him the key that morning before she dropped him off at Logan.

"Now, I'm counting on you to keep a close eye on those girls. I know they think they're fine by themselves, but there should be a man around to protect them."

Matt laughed, "If they ever heard you say that, Grace, they'd have a fit!" Grace was his sister's best friend's grandmother, and Matt adored her. Their families had been friends since forever, it seemed, and when Grace had called Matt two months ago to do her kitchen renovation, he was there in a heartbeat. He loved going to her townhouse in the Back Bay to check on his crew because he'd end up in a long conversation with Grace in her study. She was a smart old lady, and he respected her opinions. Grace was one of the top real estate agents in Boston, with a clientele most agents would kill for. Knowing how hard his parents worked in the real estate business, he knew the dues Grace had had to pay to get to the top. He had the utmost respect for her.

When she had asked him over coffee and cannolis one morning to fly down to Captiva to be with his sister and Nicki for a couple of weeks, he didn't hesitate. It was, however, under the stipulation that it be a surprise. Grace assumed they'd be pissed and probably say "no" to his coming if they knew ahead of time, and she was most likely right. Matt knew she wouldn't want them to think that she thought they needed protecting.

He had listened to Grace's concerns and figured, what the hell, he could spend his days at the beach and make sure the girls didn't get themselves into any trouble. Although he seriously doubted that would happen on Captiva, but he didn't argue the fact. Grace had always been overprotective of her granddaughter, and Matt knew she had a soft spot for her.

Grace talked about her all the time. Whenever Matt was at the townhouse her name always came up. He felt like he knew her better now than when she was hanging around his house all the time growing up. He knew she had recently graduated from grad school like his sister, and he thought it really great of Grace to hook her up with a summer job.

Matt knew Nicki was a smart girl -- well, woman now, but he'd always just thought of her as his little sister's friend. Ali was obviously a woman now, starting her way in the world, and naturally Nicki would be, too.

He hadn't seen Nicki in a long time. He knew from Grace that she had just broken it off with her long-time boyfriend. The guy was a tool, in Matt's opinion. Nicki was always a great-looking girl but she always seemed to be going out with some jerk growing up. Usually some hornball just trying to get in her pants.

Matt had thwarted many a relationship between his sister and some of the guys she came home with and also some of Nicki's relationships as well --unbeknownst to either of them. He and his friends had always watched out for them behind the scenes. He knew how guys could be. When they got to college, however, it was out of his hands. He did take satisfaction in knowing that both guys the girls had been with in college would never make it for the long haul, though. Ali had been too strong and independent to stay with the loser she had dated, and Nicki's guy had been so out of her league, Matt had known that wouldn't last, either. He was surprised it had lasted as long as it did.

Growing up, Matt had always shared a banter with Nicki that he'd enjoyed. She was quick and didn't let him rile her, much as he tried. He was a big brother, after all, and it was his duty to torment his sister and her friends. He looked forward to getting reacquainted with Nicki and trying to ruffle hers and Ali's feathers while he was there. He laughed, anticipating their reaction when he showed up.

He'd thanked Grace and had waved her off at curbside, then proceeded to the Jet Blue counter and checked in. He had had twenty minutes before he had to board, so he had sat by the windows and made some business calls. His last call was to his father.

"Hey!"

"What's doing, son?"

Matt knew his father had already been at the office for at least three hours.

"Just at the airport, checkin' in before I leave."

"What time is your flight?"

"Nine. Grace just dropped me off."

"That was nice of her. I told her we would have driven you."

"I know, I told her that, too, but I think she likes talking to me. She talked nonstop about Nicki the whole way over. I felt like I was getting prepped for a setup," Matt laughed.

His dad laughed, too. "Ali would get a kick out of that -- Nicki, too, for that matter."

"What's that supposed to mean?" Matt asked, feigning offense.

"I can just picture the girls laughing at the notion, that's all." His father snickered. "Just make sure you keep the wolves at bay. You've got two very attractive young ladies down there who might attract some unwanted attention."

"Yeah, yeah, never mind them. I'm hoping I attract a little unwanted attention," Matt joked.

"Oh, please," his father groaned. "Ali better not have to be babysitting you. Stay out of trouble, will you?"

"You know me," Matt grinned.

"I sure do, Romeo."

Then Matt's flight number had been called, and it was time to board the plane. He'd grabbed his carry-on and walked toward the gate. "Dad, I have to go. I left Mom the Howards' info in case they call the office. Ali's going to kill me that I'm passing them off to Mom, but Mom said she didn't mind. Besides, I can still deal with them on the phone. I just might need Mom to show the house."

"Don't worry about it -- it's a slow time of year, as you know. You should be able to relax for a couple of weeks."

"Yeah, we don't break ground on the Bridgewater development until July, so I'm not too concerned."

"We've got you both covered. Stay safe and have fun with the girls."

"Bye, Dad."

"See you, Matt."

Matt settled back in his seat and waited for takeoff. He'd never been to Captiva before, and he was looking forward to it. He'd heard so much about it from Ali, and it sounded like a great place.

He fell asleep for most of the three-hour flight and woke up to the captain declaring a balmy eighty-two degrees in Fort Myers. He was thankful for the smooth flight, and he smiled at the flight attendant giving him the once-over. She was pretty cute, and he was kind of mad he'd fallen asleep.

Matt deplaned, thankful he hadn't checked any luggage, and picked up the rental car he had arranged for. It was a shiny, new black Hummer -- loaded. He was counting on its GPS to get him to the islands, and it did, no problem. The truck was the balls and had him at the Sanibel causeway thirty minutes later. He paid the toll and started over the bridge, admiring the scenery as he drove. Glancing both left and right, he envied the people he saw fishing and windsurfing along the miles of white sand beach flanking the causeway. He would definitely have to get some fishing in while he was here.

The bay was dotted with boats and jet skis, and the beaches were combing with sunbathers and people picnicking. Wow! This looks great, he thought. Doesn't anybody work around here? It was just days before June, and he wondered if most of these people lived here or were on vacation. He was just glad to be part of the latter.

When he came to the crossroads at the end of the causeway, the GPS had him heading right on Periwinkle Way. He followed along, taking in all the businesses that lined the main thoroughfare. He took notice of all the low-lying buildings. There weren't many above one story -- must be code, he figured.

He laughed at all the real estate offices, thinking how his mother and father would shake their heads at the abundance. He could only imagine the competition. He noticed a Dairy Queen, but no other franchise-type business that he could see. He pulled into a little place called Huxters, a convenience/ liquor store, and parked. He opened his door and stepped out into the hot air. Oh, yeah, he could get used to this. He stretched by the car, then went inside the half of the store that sold the liquor. He picked up a case of Corona and some vodka for the girls. He knew that's all Ali drank and more than likely Nicki, too. He paid and put the alcohol in the truck, then went next door to get some limes and some snacks. He figured the girls had gone shopping, but he didn't want to show up empty-handed. He'd take them out to dinner and drinks later if they wanted.

Back outside, he admired the Hummer once again. He knew Ali

would flip over it. He'd toyed with the idea of buying one at home but it was pretty lousy on gas. Besides, with his line of work he really needed his pickup.

He put his purchases in the back and pulled back onto Periwinkle. There were a smattering of restaurants on either side of the road, and he made a mental note of Island Pizza -- Grace had told him how good it was and to make sure he and the girls tried it out. She also mentioned the place next door, Sweet Melissa's. Grace had suggested he take Nicki there because it was her favorite restaurant on the island. At the time he thought it odd she hadn't mentioned Ali, but now he grinned driving by the upscale establishment, thinking he knew what Nicki's grandmother was up to.

He kept following Periwinkle, then turned right on Palm Ridge, stopping for some bicyclists before continuing onto San-Cap Road. There seemed to be plenty to do; he noticed signs for kayaking and tours through nature preserves. He passed a bird sanctuary and even a seashell museum. That made him laugh. Could there be that many seashells that they warranted a museum? The school looked nice, and he wondered how many kids actually lived on the islands. What a fantastic place to grow up.

San Cap road was rather long at thirty miles an hour, and he had to remind himself to chill out and get into vacation mode -- he wasn't on Route 95 anymore. Glancing out the window, he saw plenty of people on the bike path, biking, rollerblading, and jogging, and he looked forward to running himself. He was definitely enjoying some of the scantily clad women on the bike path. "Oh, yeah, I could definitely get used to this."

When he saw the quaint Santiva general store he knew he was just about to the house. The Gulf out his left side window was breathtaking, to say the least. There were palms of all varieties lining the road, and little beach cottages in various pastel hues lining the sand. He took notice, too, of the impressive beachfront homes that were set back far off the road, their lush landscaping nearly concealing their private entrances. He smiled as he finally came up on his destination, the wooden sign his sister had made marking the entrance.

The Three Sunrises marked the way into a shell-laden driveway, which crunched loudly under the weight of the Hummer. He parked next to the red convertible the girls had obviously rented and got out. He took in his surroundings and wasn't surprised to find the landscaping at Grace's place was pretty lush, too, with all kinds of tropical flowering bushes and palms. The house was a sprawling ranch with some nice roof angles and lots of glass. By the side of the garage, he saw a white picket gate that he guessed led to the pool and dock area. He knew the house was on the bay, and he hoped he'd get a chance to do some fishing off the dock.

He took the beer and bag of groceries out of the truck and made his way to the front door. He thought about ringing the bell but decided he'd give the girls more of a surprise if he just went in. He tried the knob first and then took the key out of the front pocket of his jeans when it wouldn't turn. He let himself in, and the air inside was refreshingly cooler. The house was quiet, and he followed the large tiled floor into the kitchen. He set the beer in the refrigerator, keeping one out for himself, and put the rest of the stuff on the kitchen counter. He still didn't hear any signs of life and figured they were out by the pool.

When he approached the open sliders, he could see the backs of the lounge chairs and the silhouette of a body on one of them. Rather than going out that way, he retreated, deciding to go back out the front door and enter from the pool gate. He wanted to see the surprised look on her face. Whether it was Ali or Nicki, he knew she'd be shocked. He opened his beer, put his sunglasses back on, and headed to the foyer.

Matt shut the front door quietly behind him and crunched his way along the shelled driveway to the side gate. He was trying his best to be quiet and laughed to himself, knowing he was going to scare the shit out of whoever was lying on that lounge -- another reason he had not wanted to sneak up behind them.

He took a long pull on his beer as he went to the gate and used his other hand to work the latch. He eased it open soundlessly. He guided it back shut so it didn't slam and walked quietly along the stuccoed wall that was the back of the garage. He found himself standing on the wide expanse of pool deck and nearly dropped his beer to the concrete as he was confronted with a most unexpected sight. Holy...shit!

Nicki was lying on the lounge chair, ten feet in front of him, eyes closed to the sun, one knee up, one lean, toned leg extended, arms by her slender waist and completely, gloriously…topless. Matt was floored. He wondered for a brief second where his sister was and hoped to hell she didn't appear out of nowhere topless, too. His eyes darted quickly all around and was glad to see it was at least private back here. And then his eyes swiftly returned to Nicki.

Damn! She was smokin'. Where the hell had *that* body come from? He knew he should turn and walk away but he was rooted to the spot. He also was hot as a bastard, the temperature having just gone up about one hundred degrees.

Her long auburn hair was touching her bare shoulders, and he could see her skin was getting red, especially her two full beautiful breasts that he never remembered her having. His body was suddenly responding to what his eyes were seeing and couldn't tear themselves away. He'd better do something quick before she realized he was standing there, gawking.

Nicki stirred again and figured she better cover up -- she could feel herself burning. The only thing worse than burnt boobs would be peeling boobs. She sat up and opened her eyes. The bay was still quiet, not many boats out there at all. She reached beside her chair for her top, not finding it, and that's when she saw him.

She gasped, sitting up straighter. "Matt?" She prayed she was hallucinating as she fumbled around the side of the chair, trying to feel for her top. Where the hell was it? Was he really standing right there in front of her? How come he wasn't talking? She must have heat stroke, oh, God! Where is my top?! I'm half naked and Ali's brother is standing right here in front of me!

"Hey, Nicki," he grinned. "Need some help?"

Giving up, Nicki just grabbed her towel from beneath her to cover herself, and the bikini top fell to the ground beside her chair. "Matt! What are you doing here?" She was completely humiliated, and her stomach was in her throat.

"Is that any way to greet someone you haven't seen in a long time?" Matt teased as he approached the lounge next to hers. He thought better of a hug and a kiss and hoped that his body didn't give him away as he sat down and crossed his legs at the ankles. "I had no idea this is what went on at Grace's house. I would have been honing in on these vacations a long time ago."

Nicki looked over at him with an annoyed smirk. There he goes, right into the wise-ass remarks. She noticed he didn't even seem fazed that she had been topless. He had just seen her bare breasts, and all he could do was make a stupid joke. I guess once you've seen a hundred of them, they were no big deal. She pulled the towel around her even tighter, her anger building and her ego just a little bruised.

"I don't mean to sound rude," she said tightly, "but what *are* you doing here?" He looked pretty damn comfortable in that lounge, she thought. He looked pretty damn good, too. He was in a white T-shirt with his company logo on it, and jeans that fit him just right. His lean, muscular arms were crossed over his chest as he looked over at her. She couldn't see his eyes behind his damn sunglasses, and she was thankful. The man had eyes that made women fall for him instantly. They were green as grass, outlined with long, dark lashes any woman would kill for, and they looked right into your soul, leaving a long-lasting impression. She vividly remembered girls talking about him in high school: "Oh, Ali's brother, you know with those gorgeous 'do me' eyes!"

Those eyes she had herself got lost in so many times growing up. Yes, thank God they were covered up. There was no covering up that gorgeous smile of perfect white teeth and full lips, though, and he was laying it on her right now.

"What?" she asked, exasperated. "Aren't you going to answer me?"

"I came here to surprise you and Ali." He sounded matter-of-fact, but kept the teasing grin. "I'm staying for a couple of weeks."

"What?" She didn't believe it. Her thoughts went immediately to Nan. She wouldn't, she didn't, oh, but she clearly did. "Nan knows you're here, doesn't she?"

"Yup," he said satisfactorily. "Grace asked me to join the both of you. She thought you could use the company."

Nicki got up off her chair. She didn't know whether to be pissed at her grandmother or so utterly grateful. Her grandmother was sharp as a tack and didn't let anything get by her. Oh, man, was she ready for this?

Matt looked up at her standing in front of him. The towel she used to cover herself with didn't fully cover her long, lean legs. She just looked naked under it, and she basically was. Shit.

He took a drink from his beer while he drank her in and sat up to straddle the lounge. She was blocking the sun standing there, so he took his sunglasses off and looked at her hungrily. He wasn't expecting this at all and was overcome with desire for this girl -- woman he'd always considered to be a friend. She was freaking hot. He'd seen her coming and going through the years, but both of them had always been involved with someone. He'd never even paid attention to her in that way. What the hell happened between then and now?

"Aren't you going to ask where Ali is?" Nicki asked, losing her steam. Her voice cracked. He had to take those damn sunglasses off, and the way he was looking at her was…not what she expected. God, was he actually looking at her like *that*? She felt a little shot of confidence go through her and she stood a little straighter, loosening the grip she had on the towel.

Oh-oh. Matt got up off his chair slowly, reading her body language. He wasn't alone in this. He stood inches away from her.

Nicki had to back up a couple of inches. What was he doing? Her heart was pounding in her chest. She could actually hear it in her head.

"No."

"No, what?" She looked at him, confused, trying to avoid his eyes. It was damn hard.

"No, I'm not going to ask where Ali is."

"Well, she's at the beach," Nicki stammered.

He was grinning at her again, and the combination of that and his eyes was…damn it!

"Good," he smiled. "I'm going to go change and come back to join you." He stepped a little closer to her, and she took another step back. He made his way around the chairs and picked up her top.

"What's the matter Nick?" he asked huskily. "I don't bite." He held her bikini top in his hands, running his thumbs over the embroidered designs that covered the two triangles. "Pretty." He reached out to hand it to her, and she tried to lean in and grab it.

Nicki watched him, shocked. "Thank you...ooh!"

Matt burst out laughing as he watched Nicki fall backward into the pool, towel and all. He was still laughing as she came up to the surface. He quickly reached a hand in and grabbed the sopping towel, and threw it to the side. "I'll get you a dry one," he laughed.

Nicki was now mortified. I'm going to kill him. He deliberately got my blood pumping, getting that close to me, teasing me, only to have this happen. She swam to the edge and pressed her body against the side of the pool.

"Gee, thanks, it would have been easier to just push me!" she declared haughtily.

He laughed. "That was much more fun. Where are the towels?" They were stacked on a shelf right behind him, but he pretended not to notice.

"They're right behind you, you jerk!"

"Jerk? Is that how you talk to your guests?" He was enjoying her discomfort. Hell, he had his own discomfort going on, might as well give her some.

"Fine, *I'll* just get my top." She lifted a ways out to reach, but he was too quick. His sneaker fell down on top of the strings and stayed there. He bent down to pick it up again.

"Why are you doing this to me?" She didn't know whether to laugh or cry. He was infuriating. His muscular arms were resting on his bent knees as he squatted in front of her. She had only a brief thought before she realized what she was going to do. In an instant, she reached up, grabbed both his arms and yanked him as hard as she could. He landed with a great big splash. *She* was laughing now as she turned to reach for her top.

Matt came up for air and covered the space between them in mere seconds, grabbing her by the waist and turning her. He pulled her right into his chest and -- kissed her. By God, he couldn't help it. He pressed his lips to her surprised mouth, the mouth that just minutes ago had been pouting at him. He felt her gasp, but he didn't pull away. Instead, he used his tongue to part her lips and tried to taste her. He could feel her whole body tense and her hands pressed against his shoulders, but her reaction only spurred him on. He reached a hand behind her head to bring her even closer, while his other hand pressed against her naked back.

Oh, my GOD! Oh, my God!, What the hell is happening? Nicki was pressed up against Matt, and he was kissing her! She was in shock, and then his tongue was in her mouth. She was trying to press his shoulders away in resistance, but he had a grip on her. His shoulders were so hard and his arms felt so strong. Before she could come to a rational good reason to stop him, she found herself melting in his arms. Her body relented as she found herself returning his kiss. Her hands moved to encircle his neck, and she was aware of her legs coming up to wrap themselves around his hips. She felt him dragging their bodies through the water and over to the low end of the pool, never parting their lips. He gained his footing at last and pressed her up against the side of the pool wall. His kiss was full of passion, and there was no mistaking the message in it. Nicki was giving as good as she got and telling him with her tongue just how she saw this going down. He had no idea who he was messing with. Years of want went into her kiss, and she ran her hands right up the back of his head, gripping the short waves of hair there that were wet and dripping down his neck.

Matt didn't know what had gotten into him, but he was overcome. As soon as she relented and returned his kiss, it was on. My God, she was hot. His jeans felt heavy, and he strained against them when her legs wound around him. He put his hands on the deck of the pool on either side of her and forced himself to pull back, breaking the connection and breathing hard. Her hands stayed around his neck as he looked down at her bare breasts. Her nipples were hard, and he looked up to find her lips swollen, her mouth slightly open. Water dripped from her lashes, and her beautiful blue eyes were glazed. He bent to kiss her again, this time more slowly and deeply. He pressed himself into her, letting her know just how he was feeling.

Shit! What was he doing? He pulled away again and looked into her eyes to see what she could be thinking. What he saw there -- surprised him. There was something else besides just the heat between them, and it had him pulling back even more. Shit, shit, shit!

Nicki was looking into his eyes and could feel a slow burn creeping up her face. She was suddenly conscious of her nakedness. She released her arms from his neck and planted her feet on the bottom of the pool. She turned abruptly to face the bay, but his arms still encapsulated her on the deck. She felt him move up closer behind her.

"I'm sorry, I don't know what got into me." He leaned down and kissed her cheek, then moved to stand beside her.

Nicki looked at him incredulously, her body still humming. Was he for real? He'd just brought her from zero to a hundred in a matter of seconds -- and he was sorry?

"No need to apologize. That's what usually happens when the male guests arrive." She joked, but inside she wanted to punch his lights out. "Welcome to Captiva!" She wiped the water away that dripped from her hair and down to her face.

Matt just looked at her and laughed. He was still trying to regain some control. "Damn," he groaned. "You'd better put that top back on."

Nicki took pleasure in the fact that she'd managed to turn him on. Maybe he did see her differently now. "I've been *trying* to do just that since I saw you standing there in front of me. How long *were* you standing there, by the way?"

"Long enough," he smiled and then said, "You've really become quite a beautiful woman, Nicki."

Nicki blushed furiously and pressed her body a little closer to the wall. Could this be happening? Ali's older brother finally taking an interest? She'd been in love with him since high school, and he'd broken her heart unknowingly every time he'd start dating someone new. She'd never let on to Ali, and she did her best to put him out of her mind as she'd gotten older. It was easy to do in college because she'd been so busy working toward her degree.

When she had met Tom, he seemed like a great guy and a great way for her to bury her secret feelings for Matt. For the most part she'd gotten over him. She'd see him now and then at a family party, but she always remained aloof. She was usually with Tom, and Matt had usually been with one girlfriend or another. Small talk had been the extent of their encounters.

It had all started in high school. She would sleep over Ali's house almost every weekend, and they would stay up late. Matt would come home from a date and end up staying up to talk with them. Sometimes Ali would go to bed and Nicki would stay up with Matt alone, watching a scary movie or the late show. She used to pretend she was his girlfriend until he did something to break the spell like ruffle her hair and say, "goodnight, kid." She would even make sure to always wear her cutest baby-doll pajamas when she slept over, but the effort was lost on him. It had been pure torture back then. Sometimes when she'd come over after school, she'd see him working out in his room as she walked by to get to Ali's, and he always seemed to have his shirt off and she'd just die. She somehow managed to keep her feelings from Ali, though. Nicki figured Ali would think she was disgusting for liking her brother.

And now here he was next to her, having just kissed her like nobody's business, and she was all confused. It summoned up feelings she had thought were long buried. She felt a little differently now, though, than she did when she was younger. Now her body knew what it could take from him, where back then she hadn't had a clue. She was a full-grown woman now and not a high school girl. She had her own experiences to draw from. Back then, it would have been just Matt with all the experience and her the innocent virgin. She was sure he'd only added to his arsenal of expertise since those times, but at least she could now bring something to the table.

He was different, too, a man and not a teenager. A man who owned his own business, had responsibilities, exuded strength and confidence -- but still managed to take her breath away just by looking at her. She thought it would really be nice to get to know this Matt, the adult version.

The thought of what had just happened was so bittersweet. Nicki would have given anything for that to have happened all those years ago -- even losing her virginity to him. She had dreamt about it often enough. But the fact that this had happened today was kind of empowering. The fact that someone as gorgeous and sexy as Matt could feel that way about her made *her* feel sexy. He'd always had a gorgeous girl on his arm, and now she felt like one of them. Although, she thought with realization, I don't want to be just another one of them.

"Did you hear what I said?" he asked her quietly.

She dared to look at his face. "You didn't turn out so bad yourself."

He grinned and pushed himself up out of the pool. He held a hand out to help her out as well.

"Nice try," she smirked. "I think I'll wait 'til you go in and change."

He laughed. "Suit yourself. I'll be right back."

As she looked up, she couldn't help but notice the bulge where his jeans clung to him. She watched him walk through the back gate, water dripping off his sodden clothes and leaving a trail behind him. She hurriedly got out of the pool, found her top, tied it back on, and retreated to her lounge. He must be going to get his bag in his car, she thought. She tried to look relaxed lying there for when he reappeared. She just couldn't believe this was happening. He was actually going to be here for two weeks? How the hell was she going to suppress her feelings around Ali, never mind him? Well, at least she'd be working a lot; that would keep her mind off him. Like hell it would. How was she going to go to work now knowing that he was here or on the beach, or in a bar where women would undoubtedly be throwing themselves at him? This was going to drive her crazy! This sucked! She had to call her grandmother. What had Nan been thinking?

She got up and went to find the phone. It was on the coffee table in front of the couch, and she picked it up, dialing Nan's number. It rang three times before she answered.

"Hello, darling!"

"Nannn…" Nicki dragged out.

"Yes, dear?"

"Nan, do you know what I'm going to say?"

"I haven't the faintest."

Yeah, right. Nicki smiled at her coyness. "My surprise has arrived!"

"Oh, joy! Matt has arrived?"

"Oh, joy, he has at that, Nan -- and oh, what a surprise!" Nicki couldn't help adding a touch of sarcasm.

"Now, Nicki, don't be upset. I thought he'd be perfect to keep you girls company. He needed a vacation, too. He's been working so hard. You should see my kitchen, by the way. His crew is doing a fabulous job!"

Great, she was babbling. "Nan, I'm sure your kitchen looks great, but I know what you're up to!"

"What do you mean?"

"You're playing matchmaker!" Nicki paced back and forth in front of the open sliders and saw Matt appear back in the yard. God, he had taken his wet T-shirt off, and his wet jeans hung heavy on his hips, revealing the waistband of his boxers underneath. She watched as he put his wet sneakers in the sun to dry.

"Nicki, I don't know what you're talking about. Matt is your best friend's brother and a good friend to our family. He's your guest, and I expect you to treat him as such."

Nicki laughed and continued pacing. "Okay, Nan, you're off the hook. I'm not going to yell at you, but just so you know, this probably won't turn out like you're planning."

"All I've planned is for my granddaughter and her best friend to have a wonderful summer while I'm in Italy. Your parents and sister and I are going to miss you terribly, and I want some comfort in knowing you'll be watched out for."

"Okay, okay, I get it." Nicki rolled her eyes. "What time is your flight on Monday?"

"Eight-thirty in the morning."

"That's going to be a long one, huh?" Nicki had reverted to small talk as she kept her eyes locked on what Matt was doing. He was taking off his soaking-wet jeans right out there by the pool! She could see him looking at her and giving her that famous grin.

She turned her back to him and went into the kitchen. She noticed the bag of snacks and new bottle of vodka. He must have brought that in earlier, along with the beer he'd been drinking. Unbelievable, he'd been in the house!

"Did you give him a key?"

"Of course. Didn't he come in the front door?"

Apparently, once. "No, he came around back by the pool." She grabbed a beer out of the fridge and cut up a lime she found in the bag. She brought down a glass and mixed herself a vodka and pink lemonade.

"Oh, well, he probably didn't want to alarm you coming in the front."

"Yeah, you're probably right. It was more of a surprise out back." Wanting to change the subject, she asked, "Did you ever call the guy across the street?"

"Yes, I did -- I almost forgot! There is someone staying there. I guess he's been there a few weeks."

"Oh, God! I sent Ali back over there today to get on the beach! I hope he wasn't home."

"Well, Jim sounded kind of funny about it when I mentioned the two of you going through there."

"Really? Was he mad?"

"No, no," Nan assured her. "It was strange, though. He suggested maybe using the other access nearby so you wouldn't bother his house guest."

"Is the guy elderly or something?"

"No, I didn't get that impression. He didn't seem to want to elaborate so I just assured him you wouldn't do it again. I'm sorry I didn't call you sooner. I figured you'd wait to hear from me."

"Yeah, we were going to, but Ali just figured she'd sneak over for an hour. She's actually been gone longer than that, so I should probably go and check on her."

"Yes, please do, and tell Matthew I'm glad he made it there safely."

Nicki rolled her eyes again. "I'll be sure to. I'll call you Sunday night, Nan. Bye."

"Bye, sweetie."

Nicki laughed to herself, picturing Ali getting chewed out by some old guy across the street. She'd be mortified. Nicki picked up Matt's beer and her own drink, did a quick check in the hall mirror, sighed at her now wavy locks, and headed out the sliders. She stopped just before the opening and turned to switch the surround sound back on. Music filled the pool area once again.

Matt lay on the lounge beside Nicki's, and she set his cold beer on the table between them. He picked it up and clinked it against her glass. "Thanks -- here's to my warm welcome to Captiva. I'll never forget it." He smiled at her, taking a long sip from the bottle.

Nicki gave him a little smirk. Smart-ass. "Thanks for the vodka. I love the Citron." She took a relatively large gulp from her drink, praying the alcohol would soothe her nerves.

"You're welcome."

"Nice shorts, by the way." Turned out what she thought were boxers was actually a bathing suit. "You came prepared, huh?"

"I thought I did!" he laughed.

Nicki rolled her eyes at him. "Nan says she's glad you made it here safe."

Matt grinned. He knew it was irking her that her grandmother had arranged his coming.

"So you don't have any work for the next couple of weeks?" she asked him curiously. He had his own construction company and was usually pretty busy, according to Ali. She knew he sometimes sold real estate, too, in his parents' business, along with Ali.

"I'm a free man until July. I start a big job then. There's a few small jobs I've delegated, but nothing my crew can't handle without me."

"July is more than two weeks away," Nicki commented. "What will you do with the extra time when you leave here?"

Matt raised his eyebrows. "That depends."

Nicki looked away, swallowing a large sip of her drink. "Oh? On what?"

"How well my vacation goes here. Who knows? I might decide to stay longer. I'm sure Grace won't mind."

He was goading her, but her heart skipped a beat nonetheless. She gulped down the rest of her drink. "I'm sure she wouldn't mind."

"Would you?"

His tone was no longer teasing, and she looked over at him. No man should be allowed to be as handsome as he was. No person, for that matter. He had dark blondish-brown hair that held a little wave to it and was relatively short. His angular face was incredible: prominent cheekbones, a nose that sat just right above his full lips…and he had the tiniest dimple in the middle of his chin. But his eyes and his smile were what did it for Nicki. Those two features alone had always bowled her over, never mind his lean muscular build. The man took good care of himself, she thought as she looked him up and down, lying on the chair beside her.

His abs were ripped, and led to those two concave spots around his hip bones. She shuddered slightly, wishing she could feel him up against her again, this time skin to skin. Her skin broke out in goose bumps just thinking about it, and she had to look away. She didn't dare meet his eyes.

"Why would I mind? I'll be working all the time. I won't even know you're here."

Matt had watched her, amused as she gave him the full body scan, and felt himself stir beneath her gaze. He just nodded at her and smiled. Oh, he'd make sure she knew he was there.

"You'll probably miss Boston, though. I'm sure there's some hottie waiting for you to return, right?" She didn't know why she let that come out of her mouth. She was totally fishing, and he would know it. She toyed with the ice in her drink and looked out at the bay, embarrassed now. She saw him rise up out of the corner of her eye, and then he was in front of her. He bent down real close to take the already empty glass from her hand.

"There's nobody waiting in Boston. I wouldn't be here if there were." His tone was serious and matter-of-fact. "I'll make you another one."

He walked back in the house, leaving Nicki grinning from ear to ear. God she'd only been in Captiva less than twenty-four hours, and her life had suddenly turned upside down. She was trying to keep herself in check and not get her hopes up, but it was hard. He was throwing signals all over the place that led her to think this was going to be a fun two weeks -- and possibly more. Where the hell was Ali? On second thought, she was kind of glad she was taking her time. If she didn't show in the next half-hour, though, Nicki would go looking for her. She had probably just fallen asleep on the beach. She must be starved, though. Come to think of it, Nicki was starved, but way too nervous to eat.

Inside the kitchen, Matt mixed Nicki another drink and helped himself to another beer. His stomach growled and reminded him that he hadn't eaten since that morning. He pulled out some ingredients from the fridge, and made a couple of sandwiches for himself and Nicki. Balancing the plates on his forearm, he picked up the drinks in his hands and made his way back outside.

Nicki had risen to change the song and saw Matt with his hands full. She took the plates from him and set them down on the outdoor dining table. "You read my mind. I'm starved."

Matt followed with the drinks, once again admiring her fantastic body. Now that he'd seen what was under that bikini top, he couldn't stop staring at her chest. He wouldn't even let himself think about the bottom half. He still felt her long legs wrapped around his waist. She had a dancer's body for sure. He knew she'd been dancing since she was a little girl. He remembered Ali taking lessons with her and going to all kinds of competitions and recitals.

"Do you still dance?"

Where did that come from? They both sat down, and she pulled her chair in closer to the table. "I do, as a matter of fact. What made you ask that?" She sipped from the drink he made her. It tasted even better than the one she'd made herself.

"You have incredible legs -- strong." He figured at this point there wasn't any reason to hold back.

Nicki almost choked on her ice cube as she flashed to her legs wrapped around him and knew that's what he was thinking, too. He was blatantly flirting with her now. Was this how it was going to be? Fast moving, get right to it? He probably figured when he only had two weeks he ought to put the moves on right away. Not that he had to twist her arm. *He had her at hello.*

"Wow, I'm beginning to think you just came here to make me blush incessantly."

Matt took a bite of his sandwich, never taking his eyes off hers, and swallowed it down with his beer. "Nah, that's just working out to be a bonus." He grinned.

"What about you?" Nicki appraised him with her eyes. "You obviously still work out."

He liked that she'd noticed. "Yeah, I'm at it here and there. Work helps."

The more Nicki drank, the less inhibited she was feeling. She took a bite of her sandwich. "Umm, this is good, thank you."

"You're welcome. Hey, when *is* Ali coming back, anyway?" Not that he wanted their time interrupted, but he thought she would have made an appearance by now.

"I thought she would have been back for lunch. If she doesn't come back soon, I'll go get her." Nicki picked up her sandwich and brought it back to the table beside her lounge. "I need to lie down," she explained. The drink was getting to her, and she wanted to feel the warmth of the sun.

Matt joined her.

Nicki put her arms above her head and closed her eyes. She was definitely buzzed between the sun and the alcohol…and Matt. "I can't believe you're here. Ali's gonna freak."

Matt laughed. "I know -- I hope in a good way."

"Of course, she'll be psyched. Now she'll have someone to hang out with while I'm at work, unless she hooks up with Beckham."

"Who?" Matt asked.

"She met this guy last night, well, this morning, really. No -- she *saw* him last night and actually met him this morning, jogging. He looks like Beckham."

"Oh, jeez, I can just picture the dude now. Could I kick his ass?"

Nicki laughed. "Why is it all you Boston boys have to measure a guy by --'can I kick his ass?'"

Matt laughed with her. "It's just a guy thing, and she's my little sister!"

Nicki sat up and looked him up and down. "I'm not going to lie to you. He'd give you a run for your money."

"Is that right?" He pretended to take a knife out of his gut.

Nicki laughed. "He's definitely a hottie and built quite nice, but I'd put my money on you." She winked.

"Oh, yeah?" He gave her the eyes.

"Stop that."

"Stop what?" he asked innocently. He sipped his beer and picked up her glass, gesturing for a refill. She nodded yes, lazily. They were going down too quick. "Are you trying to get me drunk? I don't think it's even two o'clock yet."

"I wouldn't do that," he laughed. "I'm just enjoying being out here with you. When's the last time we had a real conversation?" he asked seriously.

"Oh, gee, I can't remember -- oh, wait!" She paused, pretending to think about it. "Thanksgiving, six years ago -- over a Scrabble game."

"Really?"

"You don't remember?" She wasn't surprised. "We were having a real good time, laughing and joking, and then *you* left in the middle of the game to go meet your *girlfriend*, Staacyy." She stretched the name out.

Matt laughed. "I did? I don't remember that. How rude of me." He was almost to the door. "How the hell did *you* remember that? And her name? I can't remember last week." He stepped over the threshold, one foot in, one foot out.

Nicki closed her eyes, remembering the heartbreak of that night. "Because I was so in love with you, you big jerk." Okay, probably shouldn't have let that fly. Damn that vodka and this hot sun. She prayed quickly that he was already inside, busy in the kitchen.

Matt came up short and turned to face the back of her chair. What the hell did she just say? She had to be kidding. He pretended he didn't hear her and dazedly made his way to the kitchen. Why did he feel like the wind just got knocked out of him? He'd only been here for a couple of hours, and he felt like he was on a runaway train -- one he didn't want to get off. He had never expected anything like this to happen when he got here. He didn't think Nicki had ever thought of him as anything other than a friend. Sure, he remembered a few times when they were younger that she had slept at their house, and he had stayed up late to talk to her or watch a movie, and he remembered wondering what it would be like to kiss her and whether she would like it, but she was so much younger than him -- at least, it seemed that way then. His father, not to mention hers, too, would have kicked his ass.

Had she really been that into him then? Why hadn't he taken more notice? He'd always found her attractive, but she was in high school, for God's sake, and he'd been just about out of college. He couldn't have thought about her the way he was thinking about her now. She wasn't in high school anymore, though, and if she still had feelings for him -- which he guessed maybe she might -- he was going to go for it.

He got her another drink and stopped to scroll through her iPod. He queued up U2's "Three Sunrises," then hit play. He stepped outside, moving back to the lounges.

"Someone had to be the first to play it."

"Sorry, Ali beat you to it last night!" she laughed. "It's okay, though -- I could listen to it over and over. Such a happy little song, as Ali says!" Nicki leaned back, singing along with the lyrics after accepting the drink he offered. She was feeling too good.

Man, he loved her laugh. It was kind of soft and sexy, and that was just the way she looked lying there, too. He was finding it increasingly difficult not to kiss her and touch her again.

Nicki had eaten half of her sandwich while Matt was inside in hopes of absorbing some of the alcohol. She was still feeling buzzed, but she was also enjoying herself and the fact that Matt was here. She opened an eye when she heard the splash, and found him in the center of the pool smiling at her.

"Come back in. It feels great."

"Maybe I will." She sat up and took their drinks with her. She sauntered over to the low end and stepped down into the cool water, sitting down on the first step. He swam over to her and stopped at her knees. She handed him his beer, and he was staring at her in an odd way, making Nicki feel the heat rise right to her face…again. The heated look in his eyes was there, but it was mixed with something else, something softer. Why does he still have this effect on me? Because he's a freakin' babe and you want him so badly. Her inner voice was always so blunt. "What?" she asked in regards to his stare. She kept her drink close by, like a security blanket.

"I heard you say something before, but I'm not sure if I heard you right." He realized his heart was pounding with anticipation. What was that about?

Now why did she think she could get away with that? Nothing like liquid courage. "You mean when I said Ali was supposed to come back for lunch?" She smiled at him innocently, then turned to look out at the bay. Was this really going to happen now?

"No, that's not what I'm talking about. C'mon, humor me," Matt pleaded. He wanted to hear her say it to his face. He had to know.

"Oh, I'm sure you will find it quite humorous, Matthew John Fuller."

"Oh-oh, you used my full name. Only my mother does that when I'm in trouble." He grinned at her.

"I know, I remember."

"I keep forgetting you were a permanent fixture in my house."

"*Thanks*." She smiled, not able to face him.

He reached over and turned her chin with his hand and gave her a reprimanding look, letting her know that wasn't what he meant. "Continue. What will I find humorous?"

She couldn't bear his touch, especially when it was so gentle, and the look in his eyes was…caring. She swallowed the lump making its way north in her throat and took a deep breath. She looked him dead in his brilliant eyes. "What I said before was..." Nicki turned suddenly, a noise interrupting her from behind.

CHAPTER SEVEN

Ali followed Rafe back up to the pool and sat down on one of the cushioned wrought iron-chaises. "This place is incredible, by the way. How did you come about renting it?" She looked around, admiring the large pool and spa that sat in the far corner. The water from the spa cascaded into the deep end, creating a soothing, relaxing sound.

"A friend of a friend." Rafe had to be careful here. "It's great, isn't it?"

"I could learn to adjust," she agreed.

He smiled. "Want something to drink?"

"Sure, why not. What are you drinking?"

"Corona, that good for you?" Rafe walked over to the outdoor bar set up under the overhanging porch.

Ali wrinkled her nose. "Got anything else?"

Rafe laughed. "Not a beer drinker, huh?"

"Sorry, I've tried, I really have. I just can't do it."

Rafe remembered her frozen drink from the night before. "Rum or vodka?"

Her eyes lit up. "Vodka, please, with anything."

She watched as he mixed her a drink and topped it off with -- a drink umbrella! Okay, that's a sign!

He shrugged with a grin as he brought it to her. "They were behind the bar." He indicated the umbrella.

"Thanks." She laughed and sipped from the glass. "It's good."

"You're welcome." Rafe sat down at the edge of the pool, beer in hand, legs submerged. He sat to the left of Ali so he could see and talk to her.

"So how have you been spending your time here?" Here she went with the small talk. She supposed it was better than I think you are the sexiest man I've ever seen. She'd wait at least two more drinks before that came out of her mouth.

"Just relax, mostly." Rafe knew he was in dangerous territory here; lying to a woman was no way to make friends. Not that he was exactly lying -- he was just leaving out some major details.

Ali was intrigued. There was something about him. He was a little mysterious and maybe a little dangerous, too. When he looked at her with those dark, piercing eyes she got goose bumps. "What kind of work do you do in Miami?"

"I'm doing some research and consulting." What the fuck kind of answer was that? This sucked. If he wasn't on the job, he'd just tell her.

Ali's brows shot up, "Really? What kind of research, and who do you consult with?" She gave him a teasing look, letting him know how completely vague his answer was. Now she was really intrigued.

Rafe grinned back but could only give her snippets of truth. "Mostly information gathering for different law enforcement agencies." So okay, that was partly true. As an FBI agent you do sometimes work with other agencies. He watched her closely for her reaction and was amused to see that she seemed impressed. He'd barely even given her an answer.

"Wow, like a detective? And here I was thinking I could sneak back here without getting caught." She laughed.

He laughed, too. "Something like that and -- and you can sneak back here anytime you want."

Ali smiled enjoying the compliment. "Do you have to carry a gun?" she joked.

"Yes, it's part of the job."

Whoa! Ali sat up in her seat. "Really? Have you ever had to use it?" She looked at him more closely. He kind of looked like a cop, actually, he looked more military with that body. Every time he moved, every muscle in his back and shoulders flexed. She couldn't take her eyes off him, and the thought of him with a gun was…oh, boy she was in trouble.

This conversation was not going where he'd planned. "Yes." He gave her a look to tell her he wasn't going to disclose much more.

Ali could take a hint, but now she was itching to know even more about him -- and she was even more turned on if, that was possible. The thought of him with a gun in his hands gave her goose bumps. Nicki always told her she watched too many cop shows. Maybe she was right. She should *not* be turned on by the thought of him with a gun…but she was.

"Okay, I get it, I'm intruding, but just one more thing?" she smiled.

He pretended to be put out. "What?"

"Can I see it?"

Rafe chose to use that to his advantage and gave her a look that had her blushing.

"See what?"

He was flirting with her! "Your gun!" she smirked.

"That would be a large and emphatic no!" he said, matter-of-fact.

She looked disappointed, and Rafe thought she was pretty damn cute like that. "You look like a kid who just dropped their ice cream," he laughed.

"I've just never seen one up close, let alone touched one. I think I'd be a really good shot."

He was really laughing now.

"What?" Ali loved watching him laugh. His whole face lit up and softened his chiseled features.

"What makes you think you'd be a good shot?"

Ali got off the chaise to come sit beside him, her own legs dangling in the water. "I'm pretty good at everything I do," she boasted.

Rafe raised his brows. "Is that right?"

"Yes, I'm good at most sports, and I'm pretty strong. I think I could really be good at it. You know, hit the bulls-eye or the star or whatever they hang at the end of that thing."

Rafe was pleasantly surprised at how close she had come to sit beside him; their arms were nearly touching. He really liked this girl. She was funny, and so damn sexy he was having difficulty concentrating on what she was saying. All he could think about was getting that bikini wet again.

"Maybe I'll take you to a range sometime."

She looked at him to see if he was serious. Wow, he was. "You'd let me shoot your gun? I'd love that. I'm telling you, I'll be good at it!"

The grin that crept up the sides of his mouth had Ali shutting her eyes in embarrassment. Oh, my God, could that have been any more obvious? "I didn't mean to say it the way I said it. I meant..." He was grinning from ear to ear now, teasing her. "Never mind." She looked out toward the Gulf, laughing at herself.

"You said it the right way. I just have the mind of a thirteen-year-old boy." He laughed. "I didn't mean to embarrass you. I'd take you to the range, and I don't doubt you would be good at it."

Ali turned her head back to face him, shaking her head. She could feel the heat in her cheeks. "You're pretty funny, Rafe -- what's your last name?"

"McDonough." He smiled.

"An Irish lad, huh?" Her parents would be happy. Not that his origin mattered, but it was a bonus. Why was she thinking what her parents would think, anyway? Ridiculous!

"Half." Man, even her mouth was pretty.

"I like your name, *Rafe*. It's different."

"Thank you, it was my great-grandfather's name. My mom is Italian and my dad is Irish. When I was born my dad wanted to name me Sean after his dad, but my mom didn't think I looked like a Sean, so she went with Rafe. It's short for Rafael."

"Wow, is that your full name, Rafael McDonough?" She could definitely see the whole Irish-Italian thing going on. She wondered if his siblings were blessed with the same great looks.

"It's actually just Rafe. My father didn't think Rafael would go over too well at school. He thought Rafe sounded tougher." Rafe laughed, thinking about his dad.

Ali laughed, too. "Well, they're both nice, but I like Rafe. it suits you."

"It suits me, huh?" He grinned, flirting with her.

"Yeah, you look tough, and rather mysterious." She studied his face. "But I'll figure you out."

"Oh, yeah?" he answered, amused.

"Yeah, I'll just need a little time." She looked down at the water and splashed her feet back and forth in the pool.

"I'm not going anywhere," he stated.

Ali's stomach did a little flip at that, and she turned to look at him again. "You're not? What about Miami or back to New York?"

"I'll be here awhile longer."

Ali didn't know quite what to make of that. What was awhile? She'd have to make the most of whatever it was.

"What about you? Do you think you'll get bored after awhile here? You must have things in Boston you're going to miss." He was doing a little fishing.

"No way -- I'm going to enjoy every day to the fullest. I've been in school and working for so long, I can't wait to just do nothing."

"Do you enjoy real estate?"

"My family has been in it since I was a baby. It was just something my brothers and I learned and did. I had my license right after high school."

"Wow, do you sell a lot of houses?" He was impressed she had been at it since such a young age.

She laughed. "Well, not really. I only do it part time. It helped pay for school, though, and I think it will pair nicely with my shop. People shopping for my furniture and home accessories might be in the market to buy or sell. I'll be chatting a lot of people up and hopefully gain a few clients."

"Sounds like a plan. So your parents and your brothers are in real estate, too?"

She nodded smiling, "They're all licensed, but they do so much more than just sell. Mom and dad own a development company. They design and develop new homes, and they invest in a lot of commercial properties as well. My oldest brother Jason, he's thirty-five, is an architectural engineer, so they keep him pretty busy, and my brother Matt, who's thirty-three -- I'm the youngest -- he owns his own construction company. So he's their builder. We like to keep the money in the family." She laughed.

Rafe was impressed. "They all sound pretty successful."

"They do all right, and I will, too, someday soon."

"No doubt," he said and meant it. Her family sounded very driven, and he admired that.

"And what's you last name, Ali?"

"Fuller." She smiled enjoying the exchange. "Enough about me. I want to hear about your family. Do you have any brothers or sisters?"

Rafe was enjoying the conversation with her. The more they talked, the more he liked her. She was definitely more than just a gorgeous face and body. She had a determined, confident way about her that he admired.

He nodded, taking a sip from his bottle. "I have a little brother, Jake. I say little but he's twenty-five," Rafe clarified. "But he's still my little brother -- and I have an older sister, Marly, who is married with three kids, and then my mom and dad, who are retired."

Ali couldn't help teasing him, "I'm not yet twenty-five, but I will be in August, so that makes me a bit younger than your little brother."

Rafe took another drink. "I figured as much- - and I'm the same age as your brother Matt." He waited to see what she would say.

"You say it like it's a bad thing." She smiled at him.

"When I was eighteen, you were ten."

She laughed. "It's only eight years." She grinned. "I'm legal now."

Rafe eased his way down into the pool and turned to face her. "I bet you were breaking a lot of hearts back then, too."

Too? Was she breaking hearts now? She met his eyes and watched as they slowly traveled down her body and back up again. Ali finished her drink and met his eyes as they landed back on her face. She had chills even though the sun was boring down on her back.

"I don't know about breaking any hearts, but I'm a grown woman now, so nobody can arrest you." Yup, she just said that, put it right out there.

Was that an invitation? It sure as hell sounded like one. He moved a little closer so that his chest was nearly touching her knees in the water. He wanted to pull her right down in front of him.

Keeping her eyes on him, Ali put her empty glass down on the pool deck. Between the drink, the sun, and the start of vacation, she was feeling a sense of freedom and euphoria that was all-consuming. The words "just do it " played like a ticker tape in her head. She was smiling at him as she lowered herself into the pool and had to press her body back against the wall so she didn't smash herself against him.

Rafe was pleasantly surprised by her sudden entry into the water. He guessed she answered his question. He leaned forward, and just as he was about to make contact, she dropped down below him underwater and took off for the deep end.

He groaned and turned to face her when she came up for air across the pool. She was grinning from ear to ear, her hair slicked back against her head, and she looked incredible.

"What did you think, it was going to be that easy?" she teased.

He grinned and dove under, closing the gap between them in five strokes.

"Agh!" Ali screamed as he swam at her fast. She tried to make it to the edge but felt his hand tugging her thigh, pulling her under and sending an electric current right through her body. She gasped and was suddenly choking. She'd taken a mouthful of pool water and frantically tried to come up for air.

Rafe saw her distress and grabbed her by the waist. He had her up and draped over the edge in a matter of seconds.

"Jesus, I've heard of hard to get, but drowning yourself is a little extreme," he joked while gently pounding on her back. She coughed out the water, laughing at herself.

Tears were running down her face as she tried to regain her composure. "I was just hoping for some mouth-to-mouth," she joked. God, what an idiot! I'm gagging on pool water, how romantic. She hopped onto the edge and sat, legs dangling once again as she caught her breath and just shook her head. What a way to kill the moment. "Sorry," she said, rather embarrassed.

Rafe planted his hands on either side of her legs. He couldn't help noticing her bathing suit again. He could see right through it, nipples and all. Oh, God. He gave her a minute to catch her breath, then said hungrily, "Let's try this again," He grabbed her rear end with both hands and slid her toward him down into the pool. Her arms automatically came around his neck.

This time when he touched her, her sharp intake was of air, and she pressed herself against him. One of his hands had moved around her waist, while the other hand grasped the pool's edge, holding them up.

"You shouldn't wear that bathing suit," he told her in a gruff voice.

"No?" She looked down, following his gaze, her heart pounding.

"I guess it wasn't really meant to get wet." She shrugged, looking at him. His face was inches away, and their bodies were moving against each other as they treaded water.

His muscular chest and arms were glistening with beads of water, and his longish hair was slicked back off his face. He had a strong, square jaw that she watched clench and unclench. He looked rakishly handsome.

"Are you going to kiss me or what?" she asked breathlessly, not being able to wait another second.

He didn't have to be asked twice. He pulled her even closer against him and pressed his lips to hers. She opened her mouth for him, and he moved his tongue inside to meet her own. He was even harder than he had been five minutes ago, and he ground himself against her, delivering her right into the wall of the pool. He kissed her with a need that was overpowering. He wanted her so badly and his body was on full throttle, desperate to show her.

The feel of her taut nipples pressed against his chest was too much to bear, and then he felt her leg slide up around his waist, pulling him into her hips so she could rub against the length of his erection, and he almost lost it. He groaned into her mouth and moved his free hand to her breasts, first one and then the other. He was struggling to keep their bodies afloat and wished they were in the low end.

He rubbed his thumb over the thin material of her top, stroking a nipple, and he heard her moan as he pulled his face from hers. "Can we take this out of the pool?"

Ali nodded, her stomach tight with anticipation at the searing look in his eyes. She gasped yet again as he quickly and effortlessly lifted her out of the pool and placed her on the deck. God, he was strong, and sexy and...wow! She watched as he raised himself up and out of the water. She had felt him against her under the water, but seeing him outside of it, in his shorts, was impressive to say the least -- and a little intimidating; he was a large man. She waited as he grabbed a towel off a nearby chair and spread it out on the deck's surface.

Ali moved so she was on top of it and kept her eyes locked on his face as he lowered himself down. This was turning out to be a great first day on the island, she thought.

He positioned himself between her legs, bringing his chest to hers, and his elbows rested by her head, holding him up. He leaned down to kiss her again, and she met his mouth eagerly. He was such a great kisser, and her body responded to the heat between them. She was thankful they had been in the water. She would be embarrassed if he felt how aroused she truly was. She felt completely exposed to him. The tiny bathing suit wasn't much of a barrier, and she might as well be naked.

She writhed beneath him as he ground the length of himself into her. Sweet Jesus, she was in for it. Between the hard cement deck beneath her back and his hard body on top of her, she was about to lose it.

Rafe kissed her hard, his tongue making love to her mouth. He wanted her here, right now. When he pushed himself against her, she lifted her hips right back to meet him. He caressed every inch of her bare exposed skin with his hands. Her full breasts were soft to the touch through the material of her swim suit, and hidden from him. He moved his mouth away from her lips and placed it on top of her right breast, biting with his teeth right through the material and pulling it away.

The heat from his mouth on her was unbearable. She wanted to rip her top off for him, but instead she kept her hands on his hips, helping him grind into her again and again.

He was going to explode if she didn't stop doing that. It had been six months, and she had no idea the fire she was playing with. He moved his mouth back to hers, and their kiss became out of control, like their bodies. He felt her hand start to come around between them, and he pressed his body even closer to hers. If she got hold of him, that would be the end. He grabbed her hands and pushed them up over her head. He felt like he was going to penetrate her right through their bathing suits. Damn! She felt so good. She was giving it all right back to him, and he couldn't have been more turned on -- then, of all the worst luck in the word, his fucking cell phone started to ring over by the bar. Shit! Fuck! Damn it! He knew he had to get it, but he couldn't tear himself away.

Ali heard the ringing and reluctantly opened her eyes. He was staring at her, their lips and tongues still intertwined. Her chest heaved under him and his on top of hers.

"It's okay," she said against his mouth, not really meaning it. "Get it if you have to."

He bit her lip playfully and regretfully pushed himself off her. His erection was straining to escape his bathing suit as he jogged over to get his cell.

Ali sat up and pulled her knees to her chest trying to catch her breath. Every nerve ending in her body was tingling. Her body felt like Jell-O, save for the throbbing sensation she felt between her legs. Holy hell, that was incredible, she thought. Talk about being saved by the bell -- if his phone hadn't interrupted them, they'd be naked right now. She watched him at the bar and tried to listen.

"McDonough."

"You sound out of breath. Did I interrupt something?"

"Just working out, what's up?"

"We've had a guy on Timothy Mann and Sean Smith since they left the island. Mann lives with his mother in a rundown ranch out in Estero. He and Smith have been out shooting beer bottles with 22s all afternoon behind the house. Our guy says they've been at it for three hours. You'd think they'd be tired after an all-nighter."

Rafe chuckled. "Yeah, well, they're not too useful as night watchmen. I woke up before they did." He was starting to catch his breath and he kept an eye on Ali, hoping Daniels was going to get to the good part soon.

"Well, now you know what you're dealing with. More than likely their pieces go where they go. Just a heads-up, they'll probably be back out tonight."

"Will do. Any information out of your ninth guy down there?"

"Funny you should ask," and Rafe knew the good part was coming.

"He mentioned *el paquete.*"

Rafe wasn't fluent, but he knew enough Spanish to get by. "He mentioned a package? What package?"

"Ah, the question of the hour, or the last twelve hours. We're still working on that. I don't see anything on the footage you sent, and the Zodiac's been ripped apart. If there's a package, it either didn't make it to shore or it's on the property."

"I'll check it out." Ali was watching him, and he gave her an apologetic smile. "Are you thinking D'nafrio's sudden influx of money is from drugs?" Rafe kept his voice low.

"That remains to be seen."

In other words, we don't know anything yet -- let's wait to find out.

"I don't want you seen over there. I'll send someone out to the property. If we don't come up with anything, you might have to go for a swim."

"Just let me know."

"We might get lucky, and you'll be able to skip the flippers. Hey, switching gears -- you having any fun on that island yet?"

Rafe was always amazed at the SAC's sixth sense. "Things are looking up. I've got new neighbors." Rafe watched as Ali moved onto a lounge chair by the spa. She kept watching him, too, smiling.

"Oh? Well, I'm sure I don't have to tell you how to be neighborly."

"No, sir."

"I'm waiting for more information from the Coast Guard. I'll call you back later."

Rafe disconnected the call and leaned over the bar. He had regained his composure somewhat, and he reached for another beer. "Drink?" He held up the bottle of vodka for Ali.

She smiled and got up out of the chair to come to him. She reached the bar and sat at one of the stools. "I'd love one." Her voice came out a bit hoarse -- from all the kissing, she guessed.

Rafe noticed her cheeks were still flushed and her lips a little swollen. Her green eyes were sparkling, and she looked absolutely beautiful to him. What a day he was having. He handed her the drink he'd mixed, then walked around to stand before her.

Ali couldn't help but look him up and down. His arousal wasn't as evident as before, but it was still there. She glanced back up and saw the look of desire had not left his eyes.

He liked her looking at him like that. He wanted to pick up where they left off.

"Something important?" It really wasn't any of her business, but she asked anyway.

"That was a work phone call. I apologize sincerely."

"That's okay. Work on the weekend, though?"

He was inching his way closer to her.

"Can we forget it? I don't want to talk about work. I just want to do this." He leaned in for a kiss.

Ali had no right to press him on the phone call. She'd much rather be doing this, too.

He pulled back and looked at her intently. "That was pretty damn hot back there. I'm real sorry we were interrupted."

Ali looked down at the ground, feeling her stomach tighten at the thought of what they had almost done. "Yes, it was."

He lifted her chin up with his hand. "Why are you blushing?"

She gave him a little smile. "I don't know what came over me -- you have an effect on me I wasn't expecting."

"I could say the same for you, sweetheart."

Oh, she liked that. Really liked it. Sweetheart was nice.

"Does this happen with every woman you meet for the first time? Hours later she's surrendering herself to you by the pool?"

Rafe got the hint. "Ali, you're the first woman I've touched in six months, and I don't care that I've only known you since six-thirty this morning."

She laughed and was instantly relieved.

"My philosophy is when something feels right, it is right. I couldn't be happier right now." He paused and smiled almost sheepishly. "Well, I could think of something that would make me a little happier, but who am I to rush things?"

All she heard was that he couldn't be happier right now, and oh, my God, she felt the same way. He managed to take away her trepidation in one phrase. She laughed at the smile he was giving her. "Thank you for saying that -- and I feel the same way. Everything I did, I wanted to do whole-heartedly -- and still do." Why be shy now?

Rafe pulled her stool right between his legs. "I'm glad to hear *that.*" He kissed her again, and she wrapped her arms around his neck.

Pulling back, she told him, "But I really should be getting back across the street. I told Nicki I'd be back in an hour, and that was three hours ago. She probably thinks I'm shark bait about now."

Rafe laughed, "I don't want you to leave -- ever."

Ali laughed. "Come with me and you can meet her."

He thought about it for one second. "Okay." He stepped back so she could hop down, and when she did he pulled her into his arms and kissed her.

She kissed him back, standing on the tips of her toes. His shoulders felt nice under her arms as she reached up to put her hands through the hair that hung past his ears. He groaned and pulled them apart. "Don't start something you can't finish," he ordered gruffly.

"Who said I don't intend to finish?" She pushed him away and walked over to gather her belongings. "It's just a matter of when."

Rafe watched her, desire flooding through him again. He picked up his beer. "Let's go," he said roughly.

"Is something wrong?" Ali asked sweetly, winking at him.

He glared at her and then looked down.

She followed his gaze feeling a pang in her gut. "I'm sorry about that, I truly am," she smiled, "but I have to check in."

"I'll meet you in the driveway." He gave her a look that told her they weren't finished.

"Okay." Probably a good idea that he hadn't asked her into the house, but she wondered about it just the same. She walked to the gate from which she had entered that morning and followed the path along the side of the house to the driveway. While she waited for him, she took in the surroundings. The landscaping was beautiful. There was a vibrant green lawn edged with royal palms and burgundy-red hibiscus in between them. The bougainvillea in the front by the gate was a deep purple hue and full with blooms right down to the ground. Ali heard a click and a hum and watched as the gate opened inward.

She saw Rafe coming out the side garage door, carrying his beer and her drink. He had thrown a T-shirt on and some flip flops.

"I figured you'd rather go through the gate than through the bushes."

She laughed. "I've about got it down now so I don't get any scratches, but this is okay, too."

He smirked and handed her her drink. They walked to the end of the drive and looked before crossing over.

"I wonder who's there?"

Rafe saw the Hummer as they crossed the street. "Are you expecting someone?" he asked.

"No," Ali said, perplexed.

Her mind went to the phone call from the day before. "Nicki's grandmother did say we'd be getting a surprise today, but she didn't give us any clues. Maybe she ordered us lunch from Island Pizza."

They were on the shelled driveway. "Uh-oh," Ali laughed.

"What?" Rafe looked down to see her expression.

"When I left here this morning, Nicki was lying by the pool, topless." Ali's hand covered her mouth, preventing a burst of laughter.

"Well, if it's a delivery man, then she just made his whole year." Rafe laughed, picturing the scene.

"It's been a few hours. Hopefully she's covered up by now. Let's go in the back way and see." She spoke softly.

"Okay!" Rafe agreed readily.

"Hey!" she hissed at him.

"What?" He feigned innocence. "You can go first."

"I will!" She laughed and opened the gate. It amazed her that she already felt like she'd known him forever. She felt so comfortable with him, maybe because they'd practically just had sex. She smiled at the thought.

"Oh, look, it's Posh and Becks!" Nicki exclaimed, and felt relief at not having to say what she been about to say to Matt.

Ali stood, dumbfounded, as she took in the sight of her brother Matt and Nicki in the pool together.

Rafe just looked at her with a confused smile.

"Matt!" Ali shrieked, "What the hell are you doing here?" She walked to the edge of the pool.

"Man, the welcoming I'm getting today, I gotta tell you!"

Rafe fell in beside Ali and surmised the situation. It was obviously Ali's brother. He was a big guy, about the same height as Rafe and a similar build. He was as good-looking as Ali was gorgeous; must be a good gene pool in that family. He glanced at Nicki and was greeted with a warm smile and a wink, to which he smiled back. He focused on Ali's and Matt's exchange.

"Seriously, is that your Hummer out there?" Ali was shocked he was there.

"Uh-huh," he nodded, smiling.

"And?" She waved her hand for him to continue.

"And I'm your new house guest for the next couple of weeks."

"What?" Ali whipped her head around to Nicki. Ali could tell right away she was buzzed.

"When did he get here?" Ali glared at her.

"Oh, about an hour after you left." Nicki grinned. "I was asleep, and imagine my surprise when I opened my eyes to see him standing there in front of me." She glared at Ali knowingly.

Rafe stifled a laugh. Not the delivery guy after all.

Ali tried to contain her laughter as she looked at her brother. He had a glint in his eye that spoke volumes. His proximity to Nicki in the pool was telling as well. They had been close together when she first entered the yard, and now he had put some distance between them. She looked from one to the other, and Nicki wouldn't meet her eyes. She addressed her brother.

"What about my listing?" She could tell he was feeling good, too. What the hell had gone on here?

"Is that all you can think about?" He shook his head. "Mom and dad have our backs. The place isn't going anywhere any time soon, anyway."

Ali rolled her eyes at him.

"Ali, you are being so rude right now," Matt chastised, nodding at Rafe.

Ali quickly turned to Rafe. "I'm so sorry, Rafe. This is my loving brother, Matt."

Matt swam over and reached out a hand.

Rafe promptly took it and greeted hello.

"Ha-hem," Nicki coughed.

"And this…" Ali smiled, "…is my best friend, Nicki."

Rafe waved hello and smiled.

"Nice to meet you, and thanks for the drinks last night."

"You're more than welcome, and nice to meet you, too."

"I'd offer you a drink, but I see you two have already been at it."

Ali shot Nicki a look at the obvious innuendo. Nicki gave her a wicked smile.

"I see you two have also." Ali gave it right back to her, smiling.

Matt looked over at Nicki, and Ali saw him do it. Oh, something was definitely going on over here. She could feel it in the air.

"Rafe, have a seat. Make yourself comfortable," Ali told him. "I'll be right back."

She gave Matt a parting look that said "be nice," and went into the house to use the bathroom. She checked her reflection in the hall mirror on the way back out and was surprised at how much color she had. She couldn't believe her brother was here and was so happy for Nicki. She was dying to know if something had happened between them. They were both definitely acting funny. Then it slowly dawned on Ali -- this was Nan's surprise. She laughed to herself. Well, nothing got by her! She stopped at the iPod on the way out and put it on shuffle. She could see outside Rafe was getting acquainted with Matt and Nicki.

Matt seemed like a nice guy, but Rafe knew when he was getting sized up. If he had a younger sister like Ali, he'd do the same thing -- or worse, he'd be running a background check. Matt asked him how long he was here for and what kind of work gave him that much time off. Rafe told Matt the same answer he had told Ali.

"So do you have a gun?" Nicki asked bluntly.

Ali stepped out on the pool deck. "Nicki!"

"Oh, like you didn't ask the same question!" Nicki knew her friend too well. "If you do, be careful -- she has a thing for guns."

Rafe laughed and raised a brow to Ali.

Ali blushed. "Nicki, that's not true!" she snapped.

Nicki laughed, "Okay, Miss 'I'm addicted to every cop and FBI show on T.V.'"

Ali was mortified. Nicki was drunk!

Rafe was laughing, seeing how red Ali became at Nicki's comments. How interesting for him.

"She's pretty good with a gun, too," Nicki added.

"Yeah, a screw gun," Matt scoffed.

Rafe laughed harder. "Oh, yeah?"

Ali shook her head at both Matt and Nicki as she went back to sit next to Rafe. "I'm damn good with the nail gun, too."

"Except that time you nailed your shirt sleeve to the floor," Matt reminded her.

"Matt, I was fifteen, and have honed my skills since then. Can we not talk about this anymore?" she laughed.

Rafe leaned over. "I'm having second thoughts about letting you shoot my gun."

"Just ignore them," she laughed.

"Oh, Ali, did you go through the neighbor's yard again on the way over here? Nan called, and you won't believe it -- there's a guy staying in the house. Nan's neighbor said we should use another beach access so we don't disturb him. You were gone so long I thought he might have had you arrested for trespassing or something." She was laughing.

Ali shared a conspiring look with Rafe. "Well, thanks for coming to look for me to make sure I was okay," she said sarcastically. "And, as a matter of fact, I did run into him." She grinned.

Nicki covered the laugh trying to escape. "Oh, no! Did he yell at you?"

"No, I just gave her a firm talking-to." Rafe grinned at Nicki, then quickly shot a look to Matt, realizing how that must have sounded. Matt only shook his head with a smirk. Oops.

Ali playfully hit Rafe on the knee, saw him look at Matt, and she knew he was embarrassed suddenly. She stuck her tongue out at Matt and the pretend disapproval on his face.

"Oh, my God! You're the guy?" Nicki looked to Ali. "He's the guy?" Then she couldn't stop laughing.

Ali and Rafe were laughing with her.

"Why have you been using his house to get on the beach?" Matt asked. "Isn't there a common access?"

"Well, yes, there is one right across the street, next to Rafe's, but it's blocked by a fence," Nicki informed him.

"Why?"

"They're building a house next to Rafe's, and they put a stockade up so nobody could see in, but they placed it right across the access path," Ali put in.

"There must be more close by," Matt reasoned.

"There are, but if you bring all your gear it's kind of a haul. Sneaking through Rafe's is much easier." Nicki gave him a grin.

"It's fine by me -- anytime." Rafe sat back in his chair, enjoying his beer and the company. It felt good to hang out with people. He'd been alone out here for too long. The occasional beer with a fellow agent just didn't cut it.

Matt hauled himself out of the pool, and Ali watched as Nicki followed his every move.

Rafe could see that Ali's friend was totally enamored with Matt. She couldn't take her eyes off him, and he wondered how long they'd been together.

"Nicki, are you ready for another?" Matt asked.

Nicki saw the look Ali gave her. "No, thanks, but I'll take a Dasani from the fridge, please. *What?*" she mouthed to Ali.

Ali gave her a smirk.

"Rafe, you up?" Matt took a towel and patted dry to go into the house.

"Sure, thanks." Rafe was glad he was in top shape; otherwise, he would feel pretty inferior to Matt's own build. The guy obviously took care of himself.

Matt went inside and returned minutes later with a cold beer for Rafe and waters for the girls. He gave a water to Ali and handed Rafe his beer, complete with a lime wedge, then clinked his own bottle to it. "Cheers."

"Cheers." Rafe liked Matt. He looked at Ali, who was smiling at the exchange. Her brother was all right.

Ali watched Matt go over and sit with Nicki, handing her a water as well. He seemed completely comfortable, and Nicki seemed the complete opposite. Her eyes kept darting to Ali's.

Nicki was dying! This was all too overwhelming. She was still reeling from what happened with Matt and the fact that he was here at all. She felt like her emotions were written all over her face, and she knew Ali would be the first one to recognize them. Sure enough, Ali was staring at her now, and she had that damn knowing look in that smile of hers. Nicki had to look away. She knew Ali had figured out that Matt had walked in on her topless, and she knew that Ali found it hysterical. But did she guess anything beyond that? Nicki couldn't tell. She *could* tell, however, that Ali seemed quite comfortable with Rafe. The guy was a stunner, she'd give him that, but the only guy she could focus on was sitting unnervingly close. Nicki gulped her water down. "Thanks for the water." She glanced at Ali again and was happy to see her conversing with Rafe and not eyeballing her. "He seems nice," she said softly to Matt.

"Yeah, he *seems* pretty cool. Jury's still out, though." Matt took a sip of beer. "She just met him this morning, you said?"

"Yes, but he bought us drinks last night at the bar before he left."

"What bar?" Matt inquired, turning to look at her face.

Nicki fiddled with her bottle cap. "The Crow's Nest down the street. It's at Tween Waters Inn."

"How long were you guys there?" Matt couldn't help the instant pang of jealousy that he felt.

Nicki looked at him like he had two heads. "We had drinks and listened to the band. Why the third degree?"

"Who was Rafe with?" Matt asked, looking over at the guy. He did kind of look like Beckham, only a little bigger. He hoped the guy didn't hang out with any Tom Cruise look-alikes.

Nicki had to smile. He actually sounded jealous. Her heart did a little dance in her chest. "He was alone. According to the bartender, he's in there alone all the time."

"So he left before you guys? Why?"

"He got a phone call, and then left before we even knew his name. We were only there for a couple of hours and were home by ten. We were tired, believe it or not." Nicki turned her attention to the bay. "I think I just saw a dolphin or a manatee out of the corner of my eye. Let's go see," she said to him.

Matt got up and followed. He glanced back at Ali and Rafe, who were watching them. He noticed Rafe looking at Nicki. Well, hell, I can't fault him for that -- he'd have to be dead not to notice. Matt gave him a knowing eye before he walked away.

Rafe laughed.

"What are you laughing at?"

"Your brother thinks I was checking Nicki out."

"Were you?" Ali grinned.

"Just seeing where they were going, but I'm not going to lie -- she is pretty."

"Yes, she is," Ali agreed. "She's gorgeous and has a kick-ass body, too. But the best part is she's super smart and a great friend."

"Wow, that's quite a testimonial. Something tells me she would say the same about you. I know I can attest to the first two things." He smiled appreciatively at her.

"Well, thanks," she smiled back. "I guess I'll have to show you how super-smart I am and what a good friend I can be, too."

"Oh, I already know you're smart, and the friend part? Well, you were pretty friendly earlier today." He relaxed in the lounge and straddled his legs off the sides. "C'mere." He motioned for Ali to come sit with him.

Ali glanced down at the dock, keeping an eye on Matt. She wasn't sure what he thought about this situation yet.

"Your brother seems pretty cool, Nicki, too."

Ali sat down on his chair, facing him, and he leaned over to kiss her neck. She shivered and looked into his eyes. "Do you think this is strange?"

"Think what's strange?" he asked, desire radiating through him.

"That we only just met this morning and we...you know."

"Want each other?"

Ali looked away, embarrassed. "You could put it that way." God, did she ever want him, and she was glad to know it was mutual.

"No, it's not strange, and by the way, that's how I felt last night when I saw you in the bar. It was instant." He sat up and moved closer to her. "When can we go back to my house?" he half-joked and stroked his fingers along her arm.

She laughed nervously. "I don't know. Do you think we ought to get to know each other a little better first?" She was doing her best not to jump the gun. Although, what the hell for? She practically had already. What's wrong with two people utterly attracted to each other having sex? He's into it, I'm into it, it's not like it has to mean anything, right? Or does it? Could she be okay with recreational sex?

"You think too much," he laughed.

She laughed, too. "I know, but I haven't even finished unpacking!" She laughed at his confused look. "This is happening really fast."

"Agreed, but I've decided to just roll with it." He'd never wanted a woman so badly.

"Roll with it, huh?" she smiled. How could she argue with that logic?

"There's no strings -- we're just two adults wildly attracted to one another. We can handle it."

"How do you know I won't become a basket case afterward, and decide I'm madly in love with you and start stalking you?" she joked.

"I'm not sure that would be such a bad thing. Trust me, I've been stalked by a lot worse." Rafe could name two murderous assholes right off the top of his head.

"Oh, yeah?" she asked. "You breaking hearts wherever you go, Rafe?"

"Not those kind of stalkers," he smiled. "Forget it."

She got it -- a work thing. She was again intrigued by what he did. She decided to let it go, though, for now, wanting to get back to the conversation at hand.

"I'll tell you what," she teased. "If you let me see the gun..." His brows rose, and she laughed. "…and hold it.." He smirked, as if to say *ain't gonna happen* , "…then maybe we'll finish what we started."

Rafe squinted his eyes at her. "Are you serious?"

Ali laughed a little. "Well, no, but I'm really curious."

"I'll consider it. In the meantime, I'll just try to break you down." He grabbed her by the waist and pulled her between his legs.

She adjusted herself so that she sat astride him. She felt him right away, and she leaned in to kiss him. "This is insane," she said, breathless. He was hot for her, and it was making her crazy with want. "We should probably separate before they come back up here." She made no effort to move.

Rafe peered over her shoulder. "They look like they're deep in conversation."

Ali started to look back, but Rafe stopped her with his hand. He cupped her head and brought her lips down to meet his. He adjusted his body so that it aligned perfectly with hers. He wanted her to feel how aroused she'd made him -- again. He couldn't keep his hands off her body.

Ali kept her hands splayed across his wide chest. Oh, boy, here we go again, she thought. If this didn't come to a head soon, she was going to die of frustration.

"I have to get off," she said huskily.

"Please don't -- you feel too good."

"You're making me insane. I'm going to burst!" There -- she'd said it out loud.

He laughed while kissing her. "Glad to know I'm not the only one. I told you I'd break you down."

Ali grinned. "Don't underestimate me. I have unbelievable willpower." She was totally making that up.

"Uh-huh."

"I do!" she argued and got up on shaky legs. She stared down at him, grinning, and he followed her gaze.

"That's twice in a row," he stated.

"Third time's a charm!" She laughed and dove into the pool.

Oh man, he hadn't had a case of blue balls since he couldn't remember when. She was killing him. He got up off the chair and dove in after her. The cool water helped as he swam up to the edge next to her.

"See, that's all we needed." She laughed and poked him in the side.

"If you knew what was good for you right now, you'd stop touching me and looking at me with those incredible eyes," Rafe warned her.

Ali smiled and felt a surge of adrenaline go through her.

"Will you go on a date with me tonight?"

Rafe didn't hesitate. "Yes."

Ail laughed. "Good, do you mind if it's a double date?"

He didn't hesitate again. "Yes."

She laughed again. "C'mon, we can all go to the Crow's Nest. There's a D.J. and we can dance."

"I don't dance."

"Then you can watch me dance."

"Okay." He smiled, liking that idea.

"Good, we'll eat here first, and then you will have to go so I can get ready."

"It's a date."

Her heart soared. "Okay, then."

"Okay, then." His heart rate was coming back down to normal, and he swam away to get their drinks. She took hers from him upon his return, and they hung over the side of the pool, looking down toward the dock. "I'm having a great time with you today." He drank from his bottle and stared out toward the bay. This was one of the best days he'd had in quite awhile.

Ali looked at him and smiled. "Me, too."

Rafe smiled back. "So what's up with those two?" he asked.

Ali was still feeling tingly at his nice comment. She looked down at Matt and Nicki. They did seem to be in deep discussion. They were facing each other, and both wore serious expressions. Ali would kill to be a fly on the "dock."

"Well, believe it or not, unbeknownst to my brother, Nicki has had a crush on him since high school."

"What?" Rafe laughed. "How could he not know that? And I would think the feeling would be quite mutual."

"No! It was like the picture you painted earlier, you know -- he was twenty-two, she was fourteen. He was oblivious."

"So he never knew?"

"He always had a girlfriend. He never paid any attention to us, other than to torture us." Ali shook her head, remembering. "I'm not even supposed to know, and I'm her best friend!"

"Why do you suppose she never confided in you?"

"I guess back then she probably thought I'd think it was gross. Plus, who wants to lose their best friend to their brother? But even as we got older and she had a steady boyfriend, I'd see the way she'd look at him, or how her body language would change if he was around."

"Did anyone else know?"

Ali laughed. "Apparently, because Nicki's grandmother arranged this whole thing -- him coming here. I figured it out earlier. She's definitely trying to play matchmaker. She's real close with Nicki and must have figured it out along the way. Maybe Nicki even told her."

"That's sweet. Now I'm going to be rooting for them," Rafe said, looking on. "Although it's kind of sad to think she felt that way all these years and he never knew. Who knows what could have happened?"

"I know, it kind of makes him look like an idiot, too," she laughed. "But I swear to you, it's because she was always cool as a cucumber around him. She would never let on. She's pretty tough that way."

"I can tell that about her," Rafe agreed. "So how do you explain the way Matt is acting, because I know he sure as shit is taking notice of her now." He chuckled, having a sip of his Corona.

Ail laughed. "He definitely is, and all I can figure is that the sparks started flying when he walked into this backyard and saw her lying there..."

"Topless," Rafe finished for her and grinned.

Ali smirked. "Yup!"

"That would do it."

"Plus, I can speak from experience that there's something about this place -- magical things can happen."

"I like magic." Rafe clinked his bottle to her glass and grinned.

CHAPTER EIGHT

"Did you see it?" Nicki asked

"No, you're seeing things," Matt declared.

She hit him on the arm. "Right there!" She pointed. "Are you blind?" She leaned over the dock rail and looked down.

Matt admired her from the rear. This was too much. "I'm not blind, that's for damn sure."

Nicki turned around at the tone in his voice to find him staring at her backside and not the water below.

"Funny." She was starting to feel self-conscious standing there in her bikini. She crossed her arms over her chest.

"Are you cold or something?" He was teasing her.

She was starting to get irritated. "Why are you deliberately trying to irk me?" She was not prepared for this day. So many emotions were bubbling inside of her. She didn't know if it was the amount of sun or the alcohol getting to her, but she was starting to feel weepy. Oh, don't you dare, Nicole Marie Thompson. Do not let him see you upset! He has no idea how you feel, and that's the way it should be.

Matt took in the sudden mood change. "Did I say something wrong?" he asked seriously.

There was genuine concern in his voice, and Nicki felt bad. She forced a smile. "Don't mind me. I think you got me drunk, and now I'm coming down from it."

Matt smiled, but he didn't believe her. God, her blue eyes were glistening, and he'd thought she'd been about to cry. "I was hoping you would forget that I attacked you in the pool earlier." Maybe that's why she was upset with him.

Oh, great, he was regretting it already. Nicki shook her head and stared at him. He really had no clue. "Trust me, *that* I won't forget." She continued to stare him down, her arms still crossed. She shifted from one bare foot to the other.

"I couldn't help it," he said sheepishly and gave her the eyes.

"No?" Her heart started pounding again.

"No." He took a step closer.

Nicki stood her ground, but she felt completely exposed. She'd be a lot stronger with some damn clothes on. And he was not helping with that body of his. She followed a vein up his muscular right arm. There was a matching one on the left. He was too good-looking for his own good.

"What are you thinking right now?" he asked, seeing the look in her eyes.

She smirked, keeping eye contact. "You don't want to know."

He took another step closer. "Yeah, I kinda do."

"Honestly, I'm thinking I'm on another planet, because this is the last thing I'd have expected to happen today."

"What do you mean?"

"You -- I didn't expect you and…whatever *this*…" She gestured her hand between them, "…is."

Matt nodded. "Hey, I didn't expect this either, Nicki. You think I came in that backyard expecting to see this, Nicki?" He gestured to her. "I didn't know you looked like this," he said, exasperated.

She gave a small laugh. "I haven't always. You just haven't seen me in awhile. I've grown up."

"You sure as hell have." He ran his hand through his hair. He broke eye contact with her and looked out at the bay. "Look, I apologize. I shouldn't have reacted the way I did." Shit, his hormones had taken over, and he hadn't thought about what he was doing. He thought she had been okay with it, but apparently she was having second thoughts.

Nicki reached out to touch his arm. She'd given him the wrong impression. "No, I apologize. I've made you think the wrong thing."

He turned his eyes back to hers, his skin prickling with her touch, and waited for an explanation.

"I enjoyed every second of it," she said quietly.

"You did?" His heart quickened.

"Yes -- I did kiss you back, remember?"

"Vividly," he pronounced. "So why did you get all weird on me a second ago?"

She looked down at her feet. This was turning out to be more than she bargained for, but there was no time like the present. She had waited long enough for this. "Because there was a time in my life that I would have given anything for you to kiss me the way you did today, and I thought I had put those feelings far behind me." She dared to look at him.

Matt was floored. So she had said what he thought she'd said. "What?"

"You heard me, Matt," she answered softly, looking him in the eye.

"Really?"

"Yes. really. Are you shocked?" She stood a little defensively.

"Kind of -- yes." He was astounded. "When was this?"

Nicki grinned. "Oh, let's see, freshman, sophomore, junior, and senior year of high school. Oh, and my first year of college." She refused to cry.

"Nicki..." He felt like she'd just punched him in the gut. The look on her face broke his heart. "I didn't know."

Her laugh held a tinge of irony. "I didn't want you to know." She was trying to be strong. "And stop getting all serious. I am so over you," she lied.

Matt grinned slightly, trying to read her eyes. "I really wish I had known. Why wouldn't Ali have told me?" he wondered aloud.

"I never mentioned it."

"C'mon!"

"I'm serious."

Her revelation made him feel awful, but also something deep inside was feeling pretty good. "So you got over me?" He cocked a brow.

She laughed. "Of course, I was a college woman with needs."

He smirked. "And that guy Tom filled those needs?"

"At the time."

"But obviously not good enough, or you'd still be with him."

"No, not good enough, but I didn't realize that until the guitar player." She was enjoying his pained expression.

"What guitar player?" he asked a bit gruffly.

"Just someone I met at a party. It was awhile ago."

"Oh," he said, somewhat relieved. "You don't see him anymore?"

She cleared her throat. "I actually only saw him that one time, but he left quite an impression."

"Why are we talking about him again?" Matt asked, annoyed now.

"You brought it up."

"All right, forget that, all that's in the past. You're grown up now, like you said, and I'm completely in awe. Does that count for anything?"

If he only knew. She smiled, enjoying the upper hand. "Let's just say that today…was a really good day."

"Well, there could be lots more like it," he said quietly. His eyes were taking her in again, and she loved it. He stepped closer, and she had to step back to lean against the dock railing. Her arms came down by her side, no longer defensive, and she looked up at his face.

Matt was so hungry for her. He was pumped up by what she'd admitted to, and it was spurring him on. Somewhere inside of him, he wanted her to feel that way again. He wasn't looking for love, he hadn't thought he was -- until she'd said what she'd said, and then he had felt a surge of…something…for her. She was a beautiful, smart, sexy young woman, and he'd be a fool not to want her in every way.

He leaned down to kiss her.

Nicki accepted his kiss readily. She was so happy, and her heart was filled. His lips on hers were softer this time, more controlled. He kissed her deeply, and her body was melting as she pressed herself against him. She heard him groan as he pulled her into him, his hands on the small of her back, caressing the skin there.

Shivers ran up and down the length of her body as she wrapped her arms around his neck. This was the best kiss she'd ever received. He clearly had done this before. She could only imagine the other skills he'd acquired along the way. One hand had found its way to the back of her head and was tangled in her hair. Oh, dear God, his touch was so nice. She couldn't get her body close enough to his. They were both breathing heavily.

"Nicki," he groaned.

"Umm." She kissed his neck and turned her chin up to the sky as his lips did the same to her.

"You feel so good," he breathed. "I want you."

Her stomach was in knots. How many times had she imagined him saying that to her?

"I want you, too," she told him, a little shyly. She felt so vulnerable, as if he could know what she was thinking.

"But I don't want to make love to you on a rickety old dock." He pictured having her somewhere he could lay her down and blow her away. He wanted to show her how it should be, and not what she'd had with her college guy or any one-night stand. If there was one thing he knew he was good at, it was pleasing a woman.

Make love? Nicki opened her eyes and saw the heat radiating from his. The fact that he didn't say "have sex" was all she could have hoped for from him, because even though she *wanted* to have sex with him, she knew it was going to mean so much more to her.

"I don't care where it takes place, just as long as it does." She kissed him this time with all the pent-up passion she had.

"Je-sus!" He half-laughed. "You're going to send me over the edge. Hold on." He broke the kiss and rested his chin on top of her head, holding her tight. "Let's go back up and get a drink. We have all the time in the world." Damn, the way she had just kissed him made him wonder if she wouldn't show *him* a thing or two.

All the time in the world? What did that mean? Could she allow herself to open up these feelings again? She wanted him right now. She didn't want to wait. Her body wasn't ready to back down and, from the feel of him, his clearly was not, either.

"Let's just stay here a minute." She smiled, looking down between them and holding her hips against his.

He felt her need and leaned in close to the side of her head. He whispered to her, his warm breath in her ear, telling her exactly what he wanted to do to her, and her head fell back at the promise of sheer ecstasy. He followed up by using his tongue to taste the smooth skin on her neck. She was salty and hot, and he couldn't wait to taste her everywhere, which was essentially what he'd told her.

All synapses had just been fried with his seductive words, and Nicki was having a hard time getting her brain to function. If he could make her wet just by whispering in her ear, then she could only imagine what going to bed with him would do. God, she ached for him to touch her, and he curiously hadn't, not anywhere that was throbbing for him, that is. Her breasts felt heavy, and her nipples rubbed uncomfortably against her Lycra suit. It didn't help that they were a little burned, but where her legs came together was the worst ache. She wanted to place his hand there herself.

"You got a lot of sun today."

Was he kidding? How could he switch gears that fast? She supposed she ought to come back to Mother Earth. She didn't really want to continue on the old dock, either.

"I feel it. Thank God you showed up when you did, or I would have been burnt in all the wrong places." She searched his eyes for any sign that he was still feeling this like she was.

"That would have been a shame." He laughed a little at the look on her face. She had no idea of the restraint he had. "I'm awfully glad I showed up when I did, too." He kissed her lightly.

"You got a lot of color today, too, but you always look tan." He wasn't fooling her; she knew it pained him. He tried to remain cool, but his massive erection still pressed against her. What would he do if she reached for him? As if reading her thoughts, he stepped back away from her. She smirked and crossed her legs at the ankles, leaning against the railing. She could play casual, too.

"I'm outside a lot." He couldn't believe after all that intense kissing, he still hadn't touched her. He was dying to, but he lived for the anticipation. It took all the will he had to keep from stroking her between her legs where she'd pressed against him, and not to put his mouth on her breasts. He'd especially wanted to earlier in the pool when they were bare and oh-so-perfect. He had big plans, though, and they didn't include this dock.

"It shows off your eyes. They're devastating, you know." She looked at him seriously.

"Right back at cha." He kissed her on the cheek and then on the forehead. "Let's go."

Her compliment hit him hard, especially the way she had looked at him when she said it.

She followed him back up to the pool and saw Ali and Rafe in the water, hanging out by the edge.

"Hey, you two, see any dolphins?" Ali asked, with a hint of teasing in her voice.

Matt dove into the deep end for some quick relief, while Nicki sauntered over to her lounge. "*I* did, but your dolphin spotting–challenged brother didn't." Nicki rolled her eyes.

Ali smiled. "Hey, we were thinking," she gestured to Rafe, "that we could all go out tonight."

"That sounds great," Nicki said. "To the Crow's Nest?"

"Yes, so we can dance."

"I don't dance," Matt called out from the deep end.

Rafe laughed.

"That sounds familiar." Ali smiled at him.

"Well, we do, so you guys can watch and learn," Nicki told them.

"I'm down for watching." Matt winked at her.

"That sounds familiar, too." Ali knew Rafe and her brother were going to get along perfectly.

"But we have to eat first. I haven't eaten anything but a protein bar all day, and if I don't get real food in me, I'll be passed out by six."

"I know, me, too," Nicki agreed.

Rafe and Matt shared a knowing look. Neither one of them wanted anyone passing out by six o'clock.

"I'll find something for the grill," Matt told them and lifted himself out of the pool.

"I'll fire it up," Rafe offered and lifted himself out as well.

Ali watched as the water dripped off him and his shorts hung low on his hips. She was looking forward to the night with him. She saw him grinning at her as he caught her staring. He offered her a hand to get out of the pool, and she took it. He pulled her out easily and pulled her right into him. "Careful with those eyes -- they don't hide much." He bent and whispered close to her ear.

Ali looked right at him. "After this morning, it would be impossible for me to hide what I'm feeling."

"Which is?" he prompted.

As if she would tell him. She laughed a little. "Feeling it's one thing, saying it is another."

He nodded slowly, "I get that."

He did? She wasn't sure she did. Today had been a whirlwind, a fantastic and completely unexpected whirlwind. No matter how this played out, she would not forget their time by that pool. She stood on the tips of her toes and kissed him lightly.

"What was that for?" He smiled and held his arms around her small waist.

"For today."

"That was nice," he said and meant it. "It's not over yet, though."

She looked up. "Oh, trust me, I know it's not over yet." She gave him a promising stare.

"Any chance we could skip the dancing thing and just go to my house?" he asked hoarsely.

She chuckled. "I want a first date."

"We can have as many dates as you want, but I don't know how I'm going to make it through tonight. All I can think about is touching you."

Ali was still thinking about "all the dates she wanted." Wouldn't it be nice if they actually hooked up her whole stay? She'd think about the cons to that scenario later.

"Will you do me a favor?" he asked.

Okay, yes, I'll marry you. "Sure." She smiled, laughing at herself.

"Go wrap a towel around you. I can't be out here with them," he nodded toward Nicki on the chair and Matt in the house, "and you in that bathing suit. They'll be seeing a little more of me than they bargained for."

Ali looked down at herself and laughed. "Oops, I forgot." She turned to make sure Matt was still in the house, and ran over for a towel near Nicki. She wrapped it around her as Rafe made it to the grill. He lifted the cover and hit the gas, igniting the coals, all the while keeping an eye on her as she sat down next to Nicki.

Nicki had discreetly been watching their exchange on the other side of the pool.

"Wow, you have a lot to tell me." She smiled at Ali.

Ali grinned mischievously back at her. "I could say the same."

To Ali's surprise, Nicki actually blushed and stood up, moving toward the house.

"Hmm, classic avoidance," Ali chided.

Nicki ignored her and shot her a pleading look that said she wasn't ready to talk yet.

Wow. Ali was speechless. Nicki had it bad.

"Matt!" Nicki called out.

"What?" he called back from inside.

"Put some good music on while you're in there," Nicki demanded playfully.

"Define 'good music,'" he said, coming over to stand in the door frame, "because we might have a difference of opinion there."

She laughed. "Never mind, I'll do it. You know I love the boys, but I can't hear another U2 song. I need some dance music. It'll get us pumped for tonight."

Matt rolled his eyes to Rafe. "Can't you dance to Nickleback or Three Doors Down?" he teased Nicki.

Nicki stepped by him and went to the iPod, and Matt went back into the kitchen in search of food.

"You probably won't like this," she warned him.

"I'm not expecting to," Matt answered and looked through the refrigerator. He pulled out two beers and found some chicken. "Chicken? Really? I knew I should have stopped at the supermarket."

"Your arteries will thank me," Nicki called out as she queued up Beyonce' and turned up the volume.

She went back outside singing, "Oh oh oh, -- oh oh oh."

Ali laughed at her best friend. She'd never seen her so happy, and she hoped it was because of Matt.

Rafe watched the two of them with a smile. Nicki had pulled Ali out of her chair and they started dancing on the pool deck. He downed the last of his beer and headed for the kitchen.

"Are they always like that?" Rafe asked, joining Matt.

"Honestly? I haven't seen them together like that in a very long time."

"Why's that?"

"They've both been away at school, I've been working -- life, man." Matt was hammering the chicken and sprinkling some spices he'd found.

"So what's the deal?" Matt looked at Rafe square in the eye. "Did you just get divorced or break up with your girlfriend?" Matt had to wonder why a guy like Rafe would be alone for nearly a month on an island by himself.

Jesus! "No," he half-laughed, giving Matt a look of confusion, and then getting it. Ah, the protective older brother Q & A session. This ought to be amusing.

"No girlfriend?"

"Negative."

"Ever married?"

"No."

"Where you from?"

"Currently? Miami, but home is New York City."

Shit. "Yankees fan?" Matt looked up over the salad he'd started to prepare.

"All the way." Rafe had to grin at the smirk he got to that response.

"Are you going back?"

"Eventually."

"Why have you been on the island for so long? Miami's kind of a commute, isn't it?"

Matt wasn't exactly buying the "consulting" job Rafe had described. His gut had told him there was something Rafe was leaving out, and for his sister's sake, he wanted to know just what it was.

Rafe paused and took a chance on trusting Matt. "I'm on the job."

Matt looked up again. If he was on the job and he worked with certain law enforcement agencies, then that meant he was the law. But if he were a cop, why wouldn't he have just said so? He thought he had it figured.

"So what are we talking about here -- you with the Feds?"

"Yes."

"No shit?" He knew it.

"No shit, Special Agent Rafe McDonough, FBI."

Matt whistled. "Does Ali know that?" Matt didn't think that she did, because that would have been one of the first things out of her mouth when she saw him.

"Not specifically. I told her what I told you by the pool."

"Why?"

"I'm on surveillance -- the fewer people who know, the better."

"So why are you telling me?"

"You seem like someone I could trust with the information. Getting involved while on the job isn't that smart. It could be a dangerous distraction."

"And is that what you are, *involved*, after just meeting my sister this morning?"

Ouch! He guessed he deserved that. "I like your sister, Matt." He gave him another look to let him know he meant it. "I haven't socialized with anybody on the island since I've arrived. Sure I've had a few conversations with the local bartenders," he laughed, "but other than that I do my job and relax. The threat, or danger level, if you will, has been zero on this particular assignment -- so far, and I'm fairly confident it will continue and end the same way. I wouldn't have approached Ali otherwise."

Matt nodded, believing him. He got a good vibe from Rafe, but he still had to look out for Ali. "So who's under surveillance on Captiva?"

"The property next to me and the man who owns it."

"Why?"

"That's classified, but I can tell you who owns the property. That's public information."

Rafe gave him the short version on D'nafrio and his company, leaving out his associate Stoddman.

"I can't imagine the FBI is after a guy just for building an obnoxious house." Matt continued putting their dinner together and found Rafe to be a rather interesting guy.

"If only that were illegal, then my job would be done."

"And then what?" Matt asked him.

"On to the next one."

"Back in New York?"

"Possibly."

"How long do you expect to be here?"

"I can't really say, but I've got some time coming to me, and I'm thinking of taking it here."

"Oh, yeah? How much time?"

"About four weeks' vacation time. I couldn't stay in that house, of course, but I'd probably grab a cottage up the street." Rafe could feel the inquiry coming to an end, and he admired Matt for wanting to protect his little sister.

"Well, I hope you get your man," Matt said, then added, "I'm cool with what you told me. I just wouldn't want Ali to get mixed up in anything where she could get hurt."

"I hear you loud and clear."

"Good, now have a cold beer."

Rafe accepted the beer Matt gave him. "Okay, my turn."

"Just one more question," Matt cut a lime wedge and handed it to Rafe. "I know you just met her, but do you plan to tell Ali what you just told me?"

Rafe smiled, "I do plan on it, I didn't want to..." he paused, "... scare her away with it, if you can understand that."

"I can see some women being intimidated," he laughed, "but trust me when I tell you Ali won't be." He laughed again.

"Oh, no?" Rafe didn't get the amusement Matt held in regard to the subject but okay, that was good. Ali would be okay with it.

Matt eyeballed him. "Now shoot." He laughed, realizing his choice of words.

Rafe smirked, and rolled his eyes. He could tell Matt had a good sense of humor, much like Ali. "What's with you and Nicki?"

Matt's face broke into a wide grin. "Let's just say this morning was a real eye-opener for me."

Rafe laughed. "I get that, but haven't you two ever hooked up before?"

Matt took a sip from his bottle. "Hell, no, she's always been part of the family. She's my little sister's best friend, and it never even entered my mind." Matt paused, "Okay, maybe once or twice it did when I was younger, but that was just hormones." He laughed. "She was too young."

"And now?"

"She's all grown up," Matt said satisfactorily. "I'm seeing her for the first time today. And boy, did I get an eyeful." Matt let out a whoop and picked up the plate of chicken. He was feeling pretty good.

"I heard."

"What do you mean, you heard?" Matt furrowed his brows.

"Ali happened to mention that when she left here this morning, Nicki had been sunbathing topless." Rafe grinned.

Matt started toward the door. "Hey, sometimes a man just hits the jackpot. This was my lucky day."

Rafe laughed. Yeah, I know how you feel, he thought. He was feeling pretty lucky himself, having met Ali. He glanced back at the time on the kitchen wall clock. He wondered if D'nafrio's little house-sitters would be arriving any time soon.

Ali stopped dancing when Rafe came back out. He walked over to her and took her by the hand. "Show me the dock." Ali obliged and led him down the short path.

Matt waited until Rafe and Ali were out of earshot. "Are you trying to torture me, dancing like that?" He walked by Nicki, giving her a sidelong glance. He put the chicken on the grill, set it to low, and shut the lid. He made his way over to where she stood and sat down facing her. The sun was still burning hot and bright, and he took his sunglasses off the nearby table and slipped them on.

"You look good in those," Nicki told him as she swayed to the music still playing.

"How are you feeling?" He asked her. She looked a little tired.

"Like I'm losing steam. I need some food and a shower."

"Me, too."

God, he was sexy with those glasses on. She'd thought she'd be safer without those green eyes burning into hers, but the effect was nearly as dangerous with them on as without. She knew he was looking at her intently even beneath their tinted frames.

"Can you show me where my room is?"

Nicki's stomach fluttered. Oh-oh. "Sure." She glanced over at the grill.

"It's on low," he said, standing there, "and they're pretty thick."

She knew what he was insinuating -- the chicken was going to be awhile.

"Grab your stuff." She gestured to the black bag he'd left near the garage that morning.

Matt walked over and picked it up, then followed her inside.

"You've obviously seen the living room and kitchen," she said. "That door goes to the garage." She pointed. "There's a bathroom there," pointing again. "Which side of the house do you want? There's two bedrooms on either side." She looked around suddenly, feeling uncomfortable giving a house tour in just her bikini. She casually walked into the nearby bathroom and grabbed a towel off the bar and wrapped it around her waist sarong-style.

Matt glanced at her new attire and grinned. "What side are you on?"

"That side." She pointed past the kitchen.

"Well, then, lead the way."

"What about Ali?"

"What about Ali? Her bedroom's not on this side, is it?"

"No, I mean, what's she going to think?" Nicki asked.

"She's going to be glad." Matt smiled. "She grew up with her room next to mine. I'm sure she'd be glad not to revisit that."

Nicki stalled.

"What are you afraid of?" he asked and took his sunglasses off, grinning at her.

Nicki stood up straighter putting her shoulders back. I'm not looking into those eyes, not looking! "I'm not *afraid* of anything!" She led him down the hall. "This one's mine, and you're right here." The rooms were directly across from one another.

Matt peered inside her large room, noticing the sliders to the pool. "Big." He also noticed the queen-size bed and glanced at Nicki.

She pointed to his room, indicating he should go into it. It was nearly as big, and when he stepped inside he realized it had its own bath. "This is pretty nice. Did Grace renovate this house?"

"No, actually, it had just been redone when she bought it. The guy before her bought it to flip it."

"It's great."

"Yeah, we love coming here. We always have a good time." She was thankful for the small talk, it was distracting from the huge ball of sexual tension still lingering between them.

"I'll be right back." She hurried into her room, dropped the towel, and pulled on a pair of shorts that were on a nearby chair.

Matt appeared in her door frame. "What did you do that for?" He started into the room.

Oh-oh…again. "I was chilly. I put the air back on a little while ago." She swallowed nervously.

He shut her door behind him.

"The chicken probably needs to be turned," Nicki said, suddenly nervous. Things were moving way too fast. She was still processing that he was even interested.

"They're out there; they can do it." Matt moved toward her.

He kept coming in until he was at the end of the bed. She watched him sit down on the edge.

"C'mere," he said softly.

Nicki shook her head and laughed nervously. "I don't think that's a good idea."

"Why not?" he asked. "I just want to kiss you."

Her feet were moving toward him with a mind of their own.

Man, she was sexy. The sun had dried her hair, and it fell in waves down her shoulders. Its auburn color was infused with hints of gold that the sun had lightened and combined, with her sun-kissed face, her blue eyes jumped right out at him.

He opened his knees and beckoned her to him. She moved against the edge of the bed and stood in front of him.

"This has been a crazy day," she said somberly.

"It's about to get crazier." He gave her a heated look and pulled her in by the waist to kiss her flat tummy. "You taste good, Nick, like coconut."

Nicki's skin quivered with the feel of his warm lips and hearing her name on his tongue. She placed her hands on his shoulders and lowered herself to sit on his knee.

Matt's eyes found hers, and he reached for her face with both hands and kissed her tenderly. His tongue moved around with hers in a slow, seductive dance that had him hard in a matter of seconds. He positioned her so that she was now straddling his legs and placed his hands on her hips to push against her, letting her feel his arousal.

Nicki was well aware of how Matt was feeling -- she was wet with desire for the third time that day. He was squeezing her bottom as he rubbed himself against her. Oh, God, he felt so good, and she ached for him to touch her everywhere. Her hands were in his hair and caressing his taut neck and shoulders. The hard feel of his muscles underneath his smooth skin brought goose bumps to her own skin. She couldn't stop touching him. She'd waited a lifetime to do it.

Nicki's soft hands moving over him was driving him crazy. He pulled her down on top of him and maneuvered them so that the length of their bodies now lay on the bed. He felt her press herself right into him, and he groaned with desire. He rolled her over swiftly so that he was now on top and looked down into her face as he ran a slow hand down the side of her body. He stopped at her waistband and ran a finger teasingly under the elastic.

Oh, yes, he was touching her finally. She watched him, so full of desire for him that she was going to burst. She knew he wanted her to see everything he was about to do, and she breathed his name shakily, "Matt," as his hand found its way under her shorts.

He moved to the side of her so he could have full access. "Ssh," he whispered.

"Do you have something?" Nicki asked, her subconscious thinking about protection.

Matt silently cursed himself, but he wasn't about to ruin the mood. Sure, he had something, back in his nightstand at home. He had planned on a trip to CVS later, in case he should find himself in a situation such as this during his two-week stay. He never imagined he'd be needing a rubber seven hours after takeoff, let alone with Nicki.

"Just relax," he told her. Plan B.

Nicki's hips lifted ever so slightly to accommodate his hand, while he caressed the bathing suit material that covered her. Her body was on fire from head to toe, and she dug her fingernails into his shoulders. This was way out of control, she thought. "Matt, please," she breathed. She knew he didn't have anything.

He could feel how wet she was through her bathing suit, and he almost went off at the discovery. He couldn't believe he was unprepared for this and again cursed himself. But pleasing her alone, he could do, and he was going to enjoy it immensely. He continued to caress as she squirmed beneath him. He was just about to place his hand under her suit when she rolled on top of him. She reached for his hand and pulled it out of her shorts. He looked up at her as she groaned, "Please -- stop."

"Okay, but why?" Her body sure didn't seem as if it wanted him to stop.

"Because I want us both to be able to enjoy this."

He laughed roughly. "Trust me, Nicki, I'm enjoying this." He reached back down between them and moved his hand on the outside of her shorts.

"Oh, God," she moaned. "You do not play fair." She put her face to his and kissed him hard while she ground herself down into him. He moved his hand away and reciprocated by thrusting his hips against hers. They continued moving against each other like that in a desperate, breathless rhythm until Nicki pulled away, glassy-eyed. Her eyes bored into his as she said, "To be continued." Then she reluctantly moved her body off him and ran to her bathroom, shutting and locking the door behind her.

Matt just lay there and groaned, pressing on his own discomfort and swearing at himself. He got up at the sound of Nicki's shower running and headed to his own room. To hell with the chicken; he needed a cold shower.

Nicki grabbed hold of the sink and checked her reflection. She was a complete mess. Her hair was crazy and disheveled, and her skin was all blotchy. The man hadn't been here for even one whole day, and she'd almost had sex with him. What the hell was the matter with her? She pulled back the shower curtain, turned the handle, and stepped into the ice-cold water.

CHAPTER NINE

"I like your brother," Rafe told her.

"I'm glad. You two seemed to hit it off okay." Ali was glad Matt was cool with Rafe.

"I think he's really into Nicki."

Ali met his eyes. "Did he tell you that?" she asked excitedly.

"In certain words, yes, he did." Rafe laughed.

"I knew it! I'm so happy!" She did a little dance on the dock.

"Hey." Rafe pulled her to him. "*I'm happy* that I met you this morning."

Ali's skin prickled with his arms around her. "Me, too." She looked up into his steely eyes -- ridiculously happy, which probably wouldn't fare too well for her heart.

"I'm looking forward to tonight. I wish it were right now."

Ali's stomach tightened at the thought of being with him later that night. The look he gave her let her know he wasn't talking about the dancing and drinking part. As she returned his look, she couldn't help noticing over his shoulder the great big billows of smoke coming out of the grill. "The chicken is burning."

Rafe bent down to kiss her, and Ali raised up on her toes to meet his lips. His kiss was deep and purposeful. She responded by molding her body to his.

"We better go back up," he said gruffly, pulling away.

Ali rocked back on her heels, feeling a little light-headed. She grabbed onto the railing for support.

He laughed. "Are you okay?"

"Uh-huh." She gave him a grin and took his outstretched hand, following him back to the pool.

"God, where did they go? Another second and this stuff would be cardboard." Ali took the chicken off the grill and put it on the plate Rafe held out to her.

"Will you check inside?" she asked him.

Rafe gave her a look that said that might not be such a good idea.

She laughed. "Just yell in that the chicken is done."

Rafe smiled and shook his head no. If the shoe were on the other foot, he definitely wouldn't be caring about chicken.

Ali glanced at the sliders to Nicki's room, but the shutters were drawn. "You're right," she relented. "Will you help me in the kitchen, then?"

"*That* I'll do." He followed her inside, and they were alone.

"Is that the shower?" she whispered.

"Sounds like it." He was amused by her reaction. "Are you surprised?"

"Well, God, that was quick!"

He gave her a sidelong look.

Ali realized what she'd said and laughed. "That's different!" she referred to their own whirlwind tryst by his pool.

He chuckled. "How so?"

She laughed, too. "I guess it's not."

Matt appeared as if on cue from around the corner, wearing nothing but a towel. "Did you guys get the chicken?"

"Uh, yeah!" Ali looked at him like he was daft. "Have a sudden urge to get clean?" She had her hands on her hips. "Where's Nicki?" she asked suspiciously.

Matt glanced back toward her bedroom. "Taking a shower, sounds like. She must have felt the urge to get clean, too." He winked at Ali, and she threw a dishtowel at him.

Rafe was laughing softly.

"Were you in the shower *together*?" she asked, astonished.

"Ali, what do you take me for? I just got here!" He pretended to sound hurt.

"I know how you operate," Ali told him, only half-kidding. She knew his effect on women; she'd watched it her whole life. She took some plates down from the cabinet and took some utensils from a nearby drawer.

"You make me sound like some kind of player." He gave Rafe a grin.

"Aren't you?" She made a face at him and looked at Rafe taking in the exchange. She hoped he wasn't uncomfortable. He didn't appear to be, though -- he appeared amused, actually.

"I'm too old for that now. I'm looking for an incredible woman to settle down with and have my babies."

Ali burst out laughing. "Oh, my God, if Mom and Dad or Jason ever heard you say that, they'd be hysterical!"

"What, you don't believe me?" he laughed. Funny thing was, he wasn't really joking.

"It's hard to take you serious while you're standing there in that towel." Ali filled the blender with ice and the makings for daiquiris. What if he were serious? Rafe was the same age -- was he looking for the same thing? She stole a glance at him to find him watching her. She blushed as if he could read her very thought, then looked back to Matt.

"And you didn't answer my question."

"My shower was devoid of any incredibly sexy women. I showered alone."

Ali nodded her head grinning. "Ah-ha! So you think she's incredible and sexy!"

Matt nodded back, matter-of-factly. "Uh-huh. Can you please get me a beer out of the fridge?"

Ali's mouth hung open, and Matt threw the dish towel back at her. She caught it with a wide smile, letting him know she thought that was fantastic! "Go change, for God's sake," she said, laughing and handing him a beer.

Matt turned to go back down the hall. "Nice job on the chicken, by the way!" he called out sarcastically.

Rafe shook his head, "You guys like to ride each other, huh?" He felt a little pang of envy at their closeness, surprising himself. He wanted that with her.

"He's a pest, but I'm so excited for Nicki." She finished making the frozen drinks, then put everything on a tray to bring outside. Rafe helped her by bringing the plates and utensils, and when they reached the table, Nicki came out to join them. She was fresh out of the shower and dressed in a terry cover-up.

"Sorry, I had to get all that sunscreen off me. I didn't realize Matt had gone in, too."

Ali grinned at the obvious lie. Nicki couldn't even meet her eyes. "That's okay, but you two are getting the burnt pieces," Ali joked.

Matt joined them at the table, too. "Like the rest of it is going to taste any better." He rolled his eyes. "Don't worry, Rafe, I plan on buying us all a real dinner at the bar."

Rafe laughed. "Sounds good to me…no offense." He looked at Ali and Nicki.

The girls helped themselves to the salad nonetheless. "All right, so we'll chalk this one up to too many drinks. None of us were really into cooking, it seems." Ali shot Nicki a look.

Nicki picked up her frozen drink, laughing. "So your answer is to keep drinking?"

"Why not? We're on vacation!"

"I'll drink to that!" Matt held up his beer, and they all laughed.

After politely swallowing down some burnt chicken, Rafe excused himself. "I better go across to shower and change. I'll come back in a little while?"

"How about we come over to get you when we're all ready? I'm going to head to the shower now myself." Ali got up to walk him to the gate.

"That's fine. I'll be ready when you get there."

"I'll see you later, then." She stared up at him, smiling and wishing she could just drag him back to her bedroom now.

Rafe gave her a crooked smile. "You know, waiting for you is going to be a small form of torture."

Ali laughed, "Oh, I don't take that long. I'll be ready in under an hour." She smiled, teasing him.

"That's not what I meant, funny girl!" He grabbed her by the waist and pulled her in for a kiss that showed her just what he did mean.

Ali was distinctly aware that Matt and Nicki had front-row seats to this, so she pulled back, reluctantly giving Rafe a look that had him laughing. "You'd better go." Her voice was husky.

"I'm going, I'm going. See you guys later!" he called out over Ali's shoulder.

"See you!" Matt and Nicki called back.

He bent down to kiss her again, this time on her cheek. "See you, green eyes."

"Bye, Rafe," she said softly, her heart soaring.

She watched him walk away, then started back to Matt and Nicki, meeting Nicki's eyes, her face beaming.

Nicki knew what was coming and braced herself.

Ali let out a squeal and jumped up and down, holding on to the towel that still covered her bathing suit. "Oh - my - God !" She sat back down and slumped in the chair.

Nicki laughed, and Matt shook his head, rolling his eyes.

"How friggin' HOT! is he?"

Matt slid his chair back. "That's *my* cue to leave. I'm going to change and go to the store. You guys need anything?"

Nicki looked up at him. She knew at least one thing he'd be getting at the store. She gave him a shrug. "Surprise me."

He grinned back, his face actually flushing, and said, "You know what? I am going to surprise you."

Nicki watched him walk away and couldn't help but think there was more meaning to that statement under the surface.

Ali had taken in the exchange and was about to open her mouth when Nicki started instead.

"So what the *hell* happened between you and Rafe today?"

Ali shot her a look that told her she was only off the hook for a minute.

Nicki caught it and laughed, "Well?"

"Oh, Nicki, you have no idea! I feel like I've been here for a week, and it hasn't even been a full day."

Nicki nodded, understanding full well and encouraging her to continue.

"He was on his back porch when he caught me going through the yard." She rolled her eyes, laughing. "I was mortified at first until I turned around to see it was him."

Nicki was laughing, picturing the scene.

"He came down off the porch and sat on the beach with me for a bit, and we were just talking. It was really nice -- we went in the water, too."

Nicki's brows went up. "You got wet in that thing?" She pointed to Ali's bathing suit, which could be seen above the towel.

Ali smirked, "I forgot, okay?"

"Umm-hum."

"I swear. Anyway," she smiled, "we ended up going back up to his pool, and he totally put the moves on me!"

"Damn, I knew something had gone on. You two had that post-coital glow about you when you came in."

Ali laughed. "Not quite, but almost!"

"No way!"

"Yes way." She nodded her head. "Lots of kissing, a small choking incident --" She saw the shocked look on Nicki's face and cracked up. "On pool water, I took a mouthful by mistake!" Ali shook her head, continuing, "After I recovered, things started to really get going, but then his phone rang and well, that was the end of that."

"He actually stopped to answer his phone?" Nicki was appalled.

Ali laughed. "Are you kidding? I told him to! Things were getting out of control, you know what I'm saying?" Ali swiveled the patio chair back and forth.

Nicki laughed, relieved. "Oh, all right, as long as you were okay with it. So things could have gone that far, huh?" She was thinking of her own day and glad she wasn't the only one to get carried away.

"Nicki, I could have had him right by the pool!"

"Damn, you weren't wasting any time!" she kidded.

Ali laughed. "I totally let myself go today. This place got to me, the sun got to me, and he absolutely got to me! I thought to myself, 'A guy like this, in a place like this, I'd be crazy not to enjoy myself.' You know, the life's too short, you only live once mantra that I live by."

Nicki laughed at her best friend and the humorous falsity. Ali loved to have fun, but she rarely did anything off-the-cuff or daring. She was organized and particular, and Nicki knew what she had done today had taken a lot of guts because it wasn't something she'd ever done before. And Nicki also knew that she must really be attracted to Rafe for things to have gone as far as they had.

"So what about tonight?"

"I'm going for it! No holding back, and I can't wait!"

Nicki whistled. "Don't go breaking any hearts, now."

"Ha! You know I'll be a mess by next weekend when it's over." She chuckled. "But for now I'm living for the moment. A vacation fling is just what I need."

"Nice!"

Ali stopped her swiveling and stared at Nicki. "And what's your plan for tonight?"

"Well, you're obviously going to be occupied, so I guess I'll just come home with Matt later." Nicki wouldn't look her in the eye. She heard Matt's truck start in the driveway.

Ali turned her head at the sound. "Unless of course he picks up some chick at the bar." Ali tried to contain her laughter as Nicki's face reddened in anger.

"What's the matter?" Ali coaxed.

"Allison Fuller! You know exactly what the matter is."

"I do?" Ali kept up the façade.

"You know, you two are a lot alike," she said, exasperated.

"Me and Matt?"

"Yes!"

Ali could see she was irritated and so relented. She smiled at her best friend and teased, "But you're not in love with *me*!"

Nicki's eyes got wide. "What the hell are you talking about?"

"C'mon, Nicki," Ali said, her tone now serious.

Nicki was silent for a minute. "I'm not in love with Matt." She paused, looking Ali in the eye. "I used to be -- but I buried those feelings a long time ago."

Ali could see the hurt in her eyes. "How come you never told me?"

"I knew you would think it was weird, and I didn't want it to ruin our relationship. You would have thought I was coming over just to see him."

"Weren't you?" she chuckled.

Nicki smiled. "Sometimes."

"I'm sorry," Ali said sadly.

"For what?" Nicki tilted her head.

Ali felt ashamed. "I guess I kind of knew, but I thought it was just a crush."

Nicki looked shocked.

"I didn't want to share you with him. I didn't realize it was something more."

Nicki laughed. "He was so out of my realm of possibility anyway."

"Well, I'm sorry just the same that you carried that around with you."

Nicki got up and hugged her. "It's okay."

They both had tears in their eyes and wiped them away. Ali stood up, too. "I have to get in the shower."

"And I have to go change."

"Nick?" Ali asked as they went inside. "How do you feel now? I mean there's obviously something between you."

Nicki smiled wide, tears starting to well up again. "I feel pretty happy, like I'm getting a second chance."

Ali let out a whoop. "I knew it! I'm so happy for you! Oh, and by the way, he referred to you as both beautiful and sexy," Ali told her matter-of-factly, all the while grinning.

"He did?" Nicki sniffled and smiled. She felt like they were in high school again, and was so happy to have shared her feelings with Ali.

"Now the only unfortunate part to this is you'll have to spare me a lot of the details because he is my brother, and I don't want to be grossed out."

Nicki laughed. "I won't kiss and tell."

"I love you Nicki, and I'm so glad we're here."

"I love you too, Ali -- hey, what are you going to wear?" They both walked into the house to prepare for the night.

CHAPTER TEN

Rafe entered the beach house from the garage and went right into the gym. He did a quick half-hour workout with the weights to relieve some tension, and to sweat out some of the beer he'd consumed. When he was done he went up to the shower and thought about his day as the hot water hit him.

He never would have thought after seeing Ali for the first time last night that he'd be practically having sex with her by his pool today. He'd had one-night stands before, but this was not even remotely like that. She was someone he could really be interested in, not just sexually, but in every way. There was something about her that he just connected with. And if he was going to start something with her, he was going to have to be completely honest. If not, when she saw the monitors and equipment in the house, she'd have a whole lot of questions. He felt certain he could trust her -- besides, he wasn't undercover, not really.

He shut the water off, stepped out, and wiped the steam from the bathroom mirror so he could shave. If he thought this would be another one-night deal, he wouldn't say a word to Ali, but he actually wanted to tell her. He wanted more than just one night. He wanted her for whatever time he had left here, and that scared him a little, but excited him, too.

He finished shaving and stepped inside his bedroom to dress. He decided on jeans and a long-sleeve dress shirt. Leaving it untucked, he reached for his Glock in his nightstand, checked the safety, and tucked it into his jeans at the small of his back. As he bent to put his shoes on, he thought better of it and put the Glock back in the nightstand, choosing the smaller handgun he kept next to it and strapping the gun to his ankle. If things went as he hoped they would, he didn't want Ali discovering a gun on his back. It might freak her out. On the other hand, he smiled to himself, she just might enjoy it.

He stood up and finished getting ready in the bathroom. His hair was basically dry, and he just finger-combed it back before brushing his teeth. He rolled up his shirt sleeves and put on his watch, a gift his family had given him when he'd graduated from the academy. It read six-thirty. He returned to the bedroom and picked up the remote, turning the monitors on. He checked each angle of the house and settled on the property next door. It was quiet over there. The watchmen had not yet arrived. He shut down the flat screen and left the bedroom, but not before giving it the once-over. The cleaning woman had just been in the day before and had put on a clean set of sheets, so all Rafe had had to do today was make the bed. Satisfied, he picked up his cell phone on the sofa table on his way outside to the pool bar. He took a bottle of water from the mini fridge behind it and downed it in two gulps. He reached for another and dialed his parents' house on Long Island.

"Hey, Dad," he said upon hearing him answer.

"Hey, son, how's the weather?"

"I told you it's like the movie Groundhog Day -- every day's the same. It's beautiful." Rafe laughed. It was good to hear his dad's voice.

"It's actually not bad here today, either, about seventy-five degrees," his father informed him.

"Good, how's Mom?"

"She's great, out in the garden right now, you want me to get her?"

"No, no, just tell her I said hello, and I'll talk to her later."

"I will. Hey, listen, there's a little munchkin here clamoring to talk to you."

Rafe laughed. "Okay, put her on."

"Hi, Uncle Rafe!" His four-year-old niece had the cutest little voice he'd ever heard.

"Hey, Becca!, how's my favorite niece?"

"I'm your *only* niece. Tommy and Jake are your nef-foos."

Rafe laughed. "You got me there!"

"Are you coming home soon? I miss you."

She was a little heartbreaker, no doubt about it. "I miss you, too, Becca. I'll be home as soon as I finish my job." Where once he looked forward to that, he now found himself wanting to stay. "Let me speak to pops again, honey."

"First Tommy!" she yelled into the phone.

Tommy was Rafe's oldest nephew at nine years old, who looked up to Rafe.

"Hi, uncle!"

"Hey, Tommy! How are you, bud'?"

"Uncle Rafe, did you have to shoot anyone yet?"

Rafe rolled his eyes. "No, Tommy, not yet. Put Pops on the phone for me and be good for your mom."

"Oh, all right. Bye, Uncle Rafe."

Rafe's dad came back on, laughing.

"Jesus, Dad, what does Marly tell him about me?"

"The truth, that you're a federal agent and that you bring down the bad guys."

"I don't want him thinking I'm out shooting people."

"Relax. He's nine -- that's the image he wants of you."

"Great!" Rafe said, shaking his head. He did remember being the same way as a kid, though, watching his dad go off to work in his NYPD uniform. Rafe knew he wanted to be just like him. "All right, I just called to say hello and check in. I'll call again soon."

"Careful, son."

His dad's tone made him smile. He still worried about Rafe.

"Always, Dad." He hung up the phone and finished his water.

He was happy his Dad was retired so he didn't have to worry about *him* anymore. His dad had been an NYC cop for thirty-five years and thankfully had never been hurt. It was a grueling job, and his father had done it with pride. He'd received a medal of honor during his career, and he was Rafe's hero. He was the reason Rafe had studied criminal behavior at college and had joined the Bureau right after.

While training to be an agent, it was discovered that Rafe had superior talent in marksmanship, and he'd been selected to train and be part of the bureau's SWAT division. Rafe's father had been so proud of him for that and had bragged to all his friends. It was Rafe's talent with a rifle, along with his instinct and investigative skills, that had won him the respect of his own peers.

He thought about his ten-year career with the Bureau. It had been exciting and fulfilling right up until this past year. There had definitely been a switching of gears he couldn't quite put his finger on. He was starting to feel differently about the job, not quite as fulfilled, and he knew that was part of the reason he was on this soft assignment -- to get his shit together.

He saw there was a voicemail on his phone and dialed in before shutting it closed. It was Daniels, and Rafe listened with interest. More pieces to the puzzle. Maybe this wasn't going to be a softball assignment after all.

He was looking forward to a quiet night on the beach, though. That's all he needed -- another raft to come ashore while Ali was here with him. He wanted an uninterrupted night with her. He hoped the two knuckleheads scheduled to show up next door kept to themselves, too. He was really looking forward to spending time with Ali and was surprised at himself that he wasn't just looking forward to the sex part -- and hopefully there would be a sex part -- but he wanted to hang out with her, and even Matt and Nicki, too. He had really had a good time with them this afternoon. They felt like old friends already.

He was relaxing on a barstool, his feet up on the bar, when he heard the pool gate open. Ali, Nicki, and Matt appeared, all dressed for the night out.

He tried to sound casual as he called out, "hey!" but his heart was in his throat at the sight of Ali. She wore a light blue sleeveless dress that tied around her neck and fell just above her knees. It clung to her in all the right places, accentuating her feminine curves, but what rendered him speechless was the high-heeled sandals she wore. They made her already gorgeous legs look even more incredible. Her hair hung loose and tousled around her face, which was radiant from the sun she'd received earlier in the day. He felt a burst of happiness that she was here to see him. He mentally slapped himself and swung his legs off the bar to get up and greet her properly.

"You look amazing," he told her as she approached the bar. He wasn't embarrassed that Nicki and Matt were standing right next to her.

"Thanks. You like this shirt, 'cause I wasn't sure..." Matt tried to avoid the hit Nicki was about to give him.

Ali laughed at Matt. "Thank you," she smiled, looking at Rafe, and turned to glare at her brother.

Rafe laughed at Matt and handed him a beer. The girls, he noticed, had come over with their own frozen concoctions.

Ali was rethinking this whole double-date idea. What was she thinking, having her jokester brother along? Maybe it wouldn't be so bad, but just seeing Rafe dressed like he was, much like the night before and so utterly handsome, she was definitely kicking herself a bit. Although if Matt and Nicki weren't here, she supposed things would escalate the way they had this afternoon, and she didn't want to come across as too eager. Yes, she sarcastically thought, a few more hours between them and he'd recognize her for the saint she was.

With his sleeves rolled up and his tanned forearms exposed, an expensive-looking watch on one wrist, Rafe looked like a million bucks! Not to mention the way he'd looked at her when she came in. She'd never felt so sexy in her life. She was glad she'd gone with the heels.

"This place is something. You've even got a spa back here, you lucky bastard, and look at this view." Matt took it all in. "Cool bar, too. Is that a workout room through there?" Matt looked through the sliders under the overhanging porch.

"Yeah, man, you're welcome to use it any time while you're here."

Nicki inwardly cringed at the implication Matt would eventually be leaving.

"Thanks, I might take you up on that." He glanced at Nicki and gave her a smile. "The girls keep talking about some sunset I've got to see." Matt feigned disinterest.

"You came to the right place." Rafe smiled and nodded his head toward the Gulf. "I admit I take them for granted now. I've been spoiled staying here, but I think you'll be impressed. Let's take our drinks down to the sand," he suggested. "Do you girls want something to sit on?"

"Sure," they answered in unison and smiled at each other.

Nicki had on a dress and heels as well, and Rafe was quite sure from the way she looked that Matt was appreciating her much like Rafe was admiring Ali.

Ali bent down to unstrap her heels, and Rafe's eyes fell to her backside, which was perfectly contoured under the short dress. The shoes came off, and she placed them on a barstool. Even her feet were sexy, with her painted nails and a tiny ring sparkling on her baby toe. This was going to be a long night, he thought.

He picked up two beach towels and threw one to Matt for Nicki to sit on.

Matt caught it, and he and Nicki followed Ali and Rafe down to the beach. The guys spread out the towels, and Ali sat while Nicki stayed standing next to Matt.

"I can't believe there's no one on this beach. Where are these people?" Matt gestured to the few houses that could be seen.

Rafe laughed. "It is pretty private here. Some of these people are only here half the year. It seems like such a waste, doesn't it?" It did, however, make Rafe's job easier. "It does get crowded, though, up around Tween Waters," he added. He sat down next to Ali.

"Hi, there."

"Hi, there." Ali smiled and took in the fresh, clean sent of him. She wanted to put her arms around him, but she remained still, looking out at the Gulf. The evening air was perfect, the sun's earlier heat now just a blanket of warmth. There was just a hint of a breeze, and it played with the hair around Ali's face, tickling her cheek bones. She used a hand to sweep it back, thinking how happy she was right here in this moment, and she looked at Rafe and smiled.

"Let's walk," she heard Matt say to Nicki, and was grateful as they headed off toward the setting sun. Nicki glanced back to smile at her, and Ali gave her one in return.

"Did you guys talk?" Rafe guessed from the silent exchange they shared that they had.

"Yes, she finally told me how she felt. I can't help thinking how romantic the whole story is and now, like she said, she feels like it's a second chance."

Rafe leaned over and kissed her bare shoulder softly. "And how about this story?"

He kissed her earlobe, sending shivers all over her body.

Wow. "I guess this is the first chapter, although we did get right to the juicy part. We might have to back track a little," she kidded.

"Everyone knows the juicy parts are the best." He bent to kiss her lips. "You look incredibly sexy, by the way. I can't take my eyes off you."

Ali turned her body to him, folding her legs under and beside her. "Rafe, *you* look incredibly sexy. I have to say you are *the most* handsome man I've ever seen." Ali was being completely honest, because he wasn't the type of guy who flaunted his good looks or acted overly sure about himself. If anything, it was the opposite; he seemed like he didn't care. She knew he did care because he obviously liked to work out. He had an impressive body, but if she had to guess, it had more to do with keeping healthy and staying fit for his job.

"Wow." Rafe set his beer down in the sand. "I think I'm blushing." Her words were generous, and he smiled at her.

Ali tilted her head as she studied him. "There's something fierce behind those eyes, though," she told him. "I still haven't figured it out."

Rafe felt bad holding out on her. If she only knew the things he'd seen and done. His job had definitely given him a hard edge that was sometimes hard not to show. He answered her with a kiss, and she tasted so sweet. Her tongue felt cold against his from her icy drink, and she tasted like strawberries. "Umm," he said pulling away.

"You can't keep shutting me up like that," she laughed softly.

"I think I can," he challenged.

She poked him playfully. "You're right, you can." She smiled. "So, no dancing tonight, huh?"

"Uh-uh." He drank from his beer. Sand fell off the bottom of the bottle and onto his shirt.

"Not even a slow song?" Ali moved a hand over his shirt front to brush it off, and he took it and held her wrist.

"That I can do," he relented with a grin.

"Oh, good." She smiled as he kissed the inside of her palm. "I'll look forward to that." How could this feel so…right? Was she enhancing this in her mind, or was this actually as incredible as it felt?

Rafe stood, pulling Ali up with him, and holding her back against his chest as they watched the sun start to disappear. He kissed the top of her head and took in the scent of her hair. There was a subtle flowery scent to it, and he loved it. What the hell was happening to him? He couldn't remember liking the smell of a woman's shampoo before, or feeling this vulnerable around a woman. He wanted Ali to like him, and he wanted to impress her. He'd slow dance all night with her if that's what she wanted, but he hoped she couldn't wait to get back here just as much as he did, because what he really wanted to do was rock her world. He wanted to please her to the point that she'd never want to leave his bed or his arms. Maybe it was a little insane, maybe it was this place or his lack of female companionship for six months, but whatever it was, it was strong, and he felt it, like a kick in the head.

"It's almost gone." Nicki stared at the last of the oranges and pinks on the horizon.

"That was incredible," Matt admitted. "You guys weren't kidding."

They turned and started back the short distance they'd walked, Matt holding her hand.

"Do you like Rafe?" Nicki asked him. Her hand inside his couldn't have felt more perfect.

"Yeah, I do. The more I get to talk with him, the better I like him. He's cool to hang out with."

"Ali's really into him."

"How long has she known him, six hours?" Matt laughed.

"More like twelve, but you know if there's something there, you just have to go with it." She stared straight ahead, seeing Ali and Rafe not too far away.

"Oh, yeah?" Matt dropped Nicki's hand and stopped to pick up a shell. When he stood up, he handed it to her.

Nicki took it and rubbed the little bits of sand from its smooth surface, knowing that she would have this shell for the rest of her life. The simple gesture was so endearing, she couldn't look at him for fear of revealing everything in her eyes. "It's a rose petal." She held it in her palm, giving it a closer look.

"It kind of looks like that, hence the name, I guess." He laughed softly.

He was all male, even his deep, throaty laugh, and it made her smile as he discussed the seashell with her. "They're one of my favorites. The little coquinas look like this, too, only there are so many more colors and they're smaller." She bent down and came up with a couple. She rubbed the sand off to show him. "I want to collect a whole bunch to take home."

"We should come out here tomorrow and camp out for the day," Matt suggested as they continued walking.

"That's sounds great." Nicki was again excited at the prospect of spending any time at all with him. Besides her unyielding sexual attraction for him, he made her laugh. They still shared the sarcastic banter they'd had when they were younger, and she loved it. It reminded her of back then, but it also made her realize what she had truly missed.

There was one thing that was new to her, though, and that was this gentle, sweet side he had just shown her. In all her fantasies of him when she was younger, it had never occurred to her that he would have a soft side. Although, to her discredit, most of her fantasies had been of a sexual nature; she hadn't been dreaming about him giving her seashells by the seashore.

With the small gesture, he'd managed to make her feel special. She had watched him come and go with many different girlfriends over the years, and she had always wondered where they went and what they did. She'd wanted so desperately to be one of them. And today she got to feel what it was like. She was starting to think that what was happening now was better than what could have been. What could she have offered him back then? What did she know about love, other than that it hurt tremendously? But now she stood before him as a woman who'd had relationships and who'd had lovers. She could show him how she felt and know what she was doing -- she could please him and be pleased by him without any fears or hesitations. Would she have loved for him to be the first boy to have kissed her? Yes. The first boy she had touched? Yes. But she didn't regret loving him then, and she didn't resent her heart for swelling with those long-buried feelings. If anything, she felt grateful, like she told Ali, for a second chance.

She took into consideration that Matt would definitely come to the table with more experience than she. He definitely knew his way around a woman's body. He'd made that achingly evident. She herself had only had two lovers, Tom, her ex, and the "guitar man," her one-night stand. Tom had been her boyfriend for four years, and sex with him had been dull and passionless. They really hadn't shared any chemistry. It had been more about companionship, and he had been a good friend. A one-night stand, however, shortly after the breakup had shown her that sex could be great and was great! She had completely deviated from her moral compass that night, but she didn't regret it one bit, because now she would have the courage to be with someone like Matt, someone with his experience. Today her body had come alive under his touch. Every pheromone in her body had risen to the surface. Just standing beside him now she could feel a current between them. The thought of him putting his hands on her again like he had in her bedroom made her stomach tighten and her heart race.

"Are you guys ready?" She came out of her thoughts at the sound of Ali's voice.

"Let's hit it," Matt said.

They walked back up to the pool, putting their empties on the bar top and draping the sandy towels over the back fence. Ali and Nicki wiped the sand off their feet and slipped back into their heels.

"I'll meet you guys around front in the driveway. I'm just going to lock up," Rafe told them.

"Okay," Ali answered. She thought it was a little weird again that he wouldn't ask them inside, or at least her, but she put the thought out of her head. No big deal; they were leaving, after all.

"I'll drive," he called out as he made his way up the stairs to the back porch. Ali watched as he went through the sliders. She shrugged to Matt and Nicki. "Let's go out front then, kids."

"Maybe his gun is out on the coffee table or something," Nicki whispered.

"Funny," Ali chuckled. "It's not like his gun would just be out," she said. "He just has to have it for work. I'm sure he keeps it in a safe place."

"What is it again that he does exactly?" Nicki turned to Matt, but Ali answered for him.

"He consults with different law enforcement agencies. I think he's like an expert in the criminal mind," Ali speculated. "Maybe he studies serial killers, you know, trying to figure who their next victim will be."

Ali's face was completely serious, and Nicki and Matt looked at each other and burst out laughing. Nicki was doubled over, and Matt was laughing so hard his eyes watered.

"*What* is so funny?" Ali couldn't help but laugh, too.

"You watch way too many T.V. shows." Matt laughed, trying to catch his breath.

Nicki was still laughing uncontrollably. "You make him sound like a psychic." She laughed harder at the thought.

"Well, that's what I've put together so far. He won't tell me his exact job." She sounded indignant.

"Maybe once he knows you more than eight hours, he'll open up," Matt said, and that sent him and Nicki into another fit of laughter.

"You two are quite a pair, aren't you?" She grinned as Nicki held onto Matt's shoulder, trying to catch her breath. She was failing miserably, though, because every time she looked at him, he'd make her laugh again.

"Okay, stop it Matt," Nicki warned. "I'm going to pee my pants."

He looked her up and down with a grin. "You're not wearing any."

Ali rolled her eyes at the obvious exchange. “Heh-hem. Can you two get it together before he comes out here?”

“Seriously, though,” Nicki said, wiping her eyes, “why does he have to carry a gun?”

“Why are you so concerned about the gun, Nick?” Ali asked. They were standing in the driveway when one of the garage doors started to roll up.

“I just don’t like the idea of you anywhere near one.” She half-laughed. “I know you, and you’ll try to hold the damn thing and end up shooting your eye out.”

Ali laughed, “It’s not a BB gun, Nicki.”

“You know what I mean!”

They all moved to the side so Rafe could back out.

Ali admired the shiny black Yukon Denali that rolled backward, with the roof racks and the chrome running boards. It was something right out of “Pimp My Ride”. The windows were tinted, and when Rafe came around to open her door, she whistled at the luxurious interior, with its soft leather seats, Bose sound system, navigation, -- it had all the bells and whistles, and it was spotless. “This is gorgeous,” she told him.

Matt and Nicki admired it as well. “Too bad we’re only going two miles up the road. This car is perfect for a road trip!” Nicki said.

Rafe smiled and backed out of the driveway. “It’s a great ride. I’m back and forth to Miami in it once a week -- it is really comfortable.” He did have a weakness for trucks and bikes.

“What’s in Miami?” Nicki asked.

Ali shot her a look from the front seat.

“I have meetings there once a week, for work.”

Ali turned on the sound system before Nicki added a follow-up, although she was curious herself and was dying to find out more about his job. 3 Doors Down reverberated loudly through the speakers. Hmm, she loved this band. She wondered what else he liked for music; she wondered what else he liked in general. He obviously liked his truck, and maybe she'd find out even more tonight. She had to keep reminding herself that they'd only just met this morning.

She glanced over at him. He was ridiculously good-looking, and so damn sexy. His right hand draped over the steering wheel, while his left arm rested on the window frame. With his sleeves rolled up, Ali could see the muscles in his forearm flex while he steered. Even his forearm turns me on, she smiled to herself.

Rafe felt her eyes on him, and he returned her stare. She had a dangerous effect on him that he hadn't expected. He'd had his share of short-term relationships, and because of his job, he'd never committed to anything more. He'd never wanted to, either. It had always been about the job for him. A woman in his life could make him lose focus. It would make him vulnerable, and he couldn't risk that. But something about Ali was turning all his convictions upside-down. He'd felt it right when he saw her at the end of his Bushnells on the beach. His body responded to hers like a friggin' flame to paper. It was instant. But, more than that, he found he wanted to know everything about her. He liked her brother, he liked her friend, and he really liked her. He didn't know if he was going stir-crazy on this island or what, but as soon as he'd seen her enter his driveway, he'd felt drawn.

He would tell her what he did for a living tonight. He wished the house she was staying in was about twenty miles away from him, though. He didn't like the fact that she was so close to what could potentially turn out to be a crime scene very soon.

The Ford Explorer had been parked at the construction site when they'd left Rafe's house. Rafe had taken in the young-looking dude smoking a joint behind the steering wheel, window down, and recognized him as Timothy Mann. He barely made out the passenger, but knew more than likely the both of them would be passed out in an hour's time.

He would just have to keep Ali out of harm's way. He wasn't

anticipating any problems, but in his experience, things could change on a dime. If D'nafrio was delving into the drug business, that would bring on a whole different type of investigation, involving more agencies and more involvement on Rafe's part. And, according to the message on his voicemail, things were getting interesting. Daniels had sent more manpower to the island on a fishing expedition. Apparently Operation Find *El Paquete* was in play.

He pulled into the parking lot of the Crow's Nest. Tween Waters was crowded. Rafe knew some of the cars belonged to his fellow agents, but he wouldn't be seeing them inside the bar tonight. After gearing up at the marina, three of them would be out in Red Fish Pass making their way to the Gulf side by now, and three more would be out in the channels of the bay, where D'nafrio's new 34 Express Rampage would soon be making an appearance. According to Daniels, D'nafrio was coming onto the island for a few nights and would be staying right at the marina at Tween Waters. Daniels had told Rafe he would call if anything was to go down, so Rafe knew he could relax somewhat. As it was going to turn out, once D'nafrio docked, Rafe would be the closest to him.

"It's crowded," Ali mentioned.

"Maybe because the D.J.'s really good," Nicki hoped. She couldn't wait to dance. She had so much adrenaline tonight, and she couldn't wait to release it on the dance floor.

"I hope the steak is really good," Matt put in.

Nicki nudged him playfully. "Still thinking about food."

"Yes, considering I haven't had any since this morning."

"You had *some* chicken," Ali added.

Matt grimaced, "Ali, please, look at me. Do I look like a guy who can get by on a three-inch piece of charred chicken?"

Nicki and Ali laughed.

Rafe nodded. "I have to agree with him, sorry."

"Fine, you guys eat. We'll just drink," Nicki said.

"I don't know how much more I can drink today!" Ali said, laughing.

"Oh, we'll dance it off, I've already lost my buzz from earlier," Nicki told her.

Rafe knew he would be taking it easy. Technically he was off-duty, but he still had to keep his wits about him. His phone, unfortunately, could buzz at any minute. They entered the bar and found a table close to the dance floor.

"Wow, we're lucky we got a table. Everyone seems to be at the bar," Nicki noted and sat down.

The bar was indeed packed, and tables around them were filling in fast. A waitress appeared and offered them menus while she took their drink orders. Matt and Rafe picked up the menus and looked them over briefly before placing them down again.

"Prime rib?"

"Rib eye," Rafe answered Matt.

Ali and Nicki shook their heads.

"What?" Matt asked, saying to Nicki, "You're going to share it with me."

"Maybe I'll have a bite of your vegetables," she told him. "I'll need some sustenance if I'm going to dance all night."

He gave her the crooked grin. "Yeah, that, too."

She gave him a surprised look that he would talk that way in front of Ali and Rafe, but when she stole a glance in that direction, they were close in conversation. "Are you trying to make me uncomfortable?" She grinned.

"No, just aware," he countered.

She nodded. "I'm aware."

"Yeah?" He pulled his chair a little closer and was interrupted as the waitress returned with their drink order. She set them down and took his and Rafe's dinner order, promising it wouldn't be too long.

The time actually passed quickly, as they all joked and told stories from the past. Rafe enjoyed hearing funny things about Ali, and she had him laughing at the tales she told about Matt. It sounded like they had a fantastic family, and even Nicki's grandmother sounded like an interesting lady.

In turn, Rafe shared some stories about his niece and nephews and growing up on Long Island. The girls wanted to know all about New York City, and Rafe promised them whenever he got back, he'd extend an invitation to them to come visit, and he would show them around.

Ali felt her heart drop at the thought of him going back, but she loved the idea of visiting him there. She could already see this wasn't going to be an easy fling. If her heart was doing funny things in her chest now, what would it be doing when this thing ended?

The D.J. was well under way by the time Matt and Rafe got their meals and finished eating. Nicki had shared some of Matt's meal, and Rafe had cut his steak in half for Ali. She had a few bites and had eaten half of his baked potato.

"I'm sorry," she laughed, "I guess I was hungry after all."

Rafe smiled, loving that she had just shared his food. He loved that she ate and didn't try to pretend she wasn't hungry. "Do you want something else? I'll order you whatever you want."

"No, honestly, that was perfect, thank you, A full meal would have been too much, but did you have enough?" She cringed. God, he was just being polite, and she'd eaten half his meal.

He laughed at her expression. "I had plenty -- don't worry." He took a sip from his beer and looked at her intently. He really just wanted to take her out of there and home to his bed. So far his phone had remained quiet, and he was thankful. He did wonder what D'nafrio was doing, though. Would Stoddman meet him up here and take him to the site? He took another sip and focused on Ali.

Ali gave him a smile and turned from his stare. She could tell what he was thinking, and her whole body warmed with the idea. She excused herself from the table.

"Nicki, ladies' room?"

"Yes." She excused herself, too.

Matt watched them walk away and sat back, satisfied now that he'd eaten. "Man, that's all I needed. I was starting to get a little weak there."

Rafe laughed knowing, where he was coming from. "I know, I didn't eat lunch, either, and drinking like that on an empty stomach always makes you feel sick. I feel great now, though. We'll have to grill out at my house one night this week."

"Sounds great, that place is unbelievable. Is it as nice on the inside?"

"Oh, yeah, it's all decked out. It's going to be hard to leave -- I've been spoiled."

Matt leaned forward. "I didn't know the FBI put their men up in such nice digs."

Rafe laughed. "They don't, usually. The owner happens to be a federal judge who knows D'nafrio is under investigation, and he offered to help in any way he could, so we took him up on it. Although some suspect his motives are more about losing his view of the sunset than caring if D'nafrio's guilty or innocent." Rafe laughed. "I guess it would be a crime not to see the sunset from that porch anymore."

"Is that a coincidence, him living next door?" Matt asked, incredulous.

"Believe it or not, yes. You'd be surprised at the people who own out here."

Matt didn't doubt it. "So why you? Why do you get to stay in the house?" Matt was curious.

Rafe leaned back in his chair, looking pointedly at Matt. "I was experiencing a little burnout, and I think my supervisor thought this would be an easy assignment, low stress. My last one -- not so much."

"What did it involve?"

"It's not something I really want to discuss." Rafe gave him a tired smile. During his year in Miami, Rafe had seen some despicable things. He was continually amazed how drugs could take over someone's life and make them do things only a monster would do. Four months ago he had watched as a heroin addict shot and killed his baby right in front of Rafe and most of Miami P.D. No one had seen the gun he'd concealed in his sweatshirt. Rafe had been called in because the man had threatened to take the baby away in his car, away from the mother, who was holding the sleeping baby in her arms. At best Rafe would have to shoot the tires out from his position if the guy had made good on his threat, but instead it was a worst-case scenario. The guy whipped out a handgun and aimed right for the mother but shot the baby instead. Rafe put one between his eyes before anyone on the ground could get one off. He still woke up in a cold sweat sometimes thinking about it. Then, just two months ago, Rafe had saved a little four-year-old girl from being gunned down by her mother's coked-out boyfriend, nearly getting killed himself. All he could think about as he tackled the guy was that baby and his niece Becca, and how he couldn't let that little girl die. He had sneaked up and taken the guy from behind when it was evident he was not going to get a clear shot. The guy had been moving erratically, using the little girl as a shield. When the guy had finally shoved her away, intending to shoot her right in front of her mother, Rafe had gone at him full force, knocking the weapon from his hand, and taking him bodily, clear away from the little girl, who had just stood in the street, hands over her ears while her mother screamed, tears streaming down her little face. Rafe still got nauseous at the memory.

Matt nodded. He imagined Rafe encountered some pretty nasty shit in his line of work. He wasn't about to press him. He tried to lighten the moment instead. "You could tell me, but then you'd have to kill me?"

Rafe laughed. "I think that's the CIA. I could tell you, but I'd just depress the shit out of you."

"Okay, don't do that." Matt laughed. "Ali won't let you keep anything from her, though, so be prepared. She's all about honesty and trust."

Rafe smiled. He knew what Matt was trying to say, and he didn't want to keep anything from her anyway. He wasn't about to go depressing her with his war stories, but he *had* enjoyed telling her more about himself tonight. He told her stories about his family he'd never shared with anyone. There was never a desire to. But now he found himself opening up and wanting to know just as much about her own family. In fact, after hearing about her oldest brother and her parents, he wanted to meet them, too. He drank his beer and waited for her to return from the restroom, thinking how it would be nice to have someone to be honest with and to trust.

The restroom was empty when Ali and Nicki stepped inside.

"Can you believe we've only been here since last night?" Ali asked.

"It's insane," Nicki agreed. "who would have thought we'd be having this much fun so soon?"

"I think I'm in love," Ali half-joked.

"I think you're in lust," Nicki returned.

"That too," Ali agreed, laughing softly.

"Do you think you'll go back to his house tonight?"

"Are you kidding? I'm counting the minutes!"

Nicki laughed. "Wow, okay then! Be careful," she added.

"Always." Ali looked at her in the mirror.

"You know what I mean." Nicki looked back, meeting her eyes.

"I know." Ali did know, but she knew she wouldn't be able to stop her feelings; she never could. If she got hurt, she got hurt, but she wasn't not going to sleep with Rafe because of being afraid of that. She was definitely throwing caution and her feelings to the wind, but right now, she was okay with that.

"What about you and Matt?"

"What about us?" Nicki laughed, somewhat embarrassed by the subject in front of Ali.

"Okay, pretend he's not my brother. I can take it," Ali promised.

Nicki thought about it. "All right, but you can't get weirded out."

Ali primped in the mirror. "I won't!" she lied, but she knew Nicki needed to vent.

Nicki proceeded to tell Ali in detail about her day with Matt, up until she'd gone into the shower and ending with the seashell he had picked up on the beach and given her.

Ali's mouth hung open just a little, and she tried to process what Nicki had told her as a best friend. "Okay, I know I asked for that, but from now on, I just want to hear things like the seashell part."

Nicki smirked. "I knew you couldn't handle it."

"Seriously, Nick, I'm over-the-top happy for you both, and I wouldn't expect Matt to be any other way with you. Look at you, you're gorgeous! If I were a guy, I'd want to do you, too!"

"You're an ass, but thank you!"

The door opened, and they could hear one of their favorite songs playing by Estelle.

"Ooh, let's get out there!" Nicki pulled Ali out of the ladies' room.

The guys watched with amusement as the two women walked right by them straight to the dance floor, stopping only to toss their small purses on their chairs.

Rafe noticed he and Matt were not the only men with their eyes on them.

Man, she can move, Matt thought to himself, watching Nicki

dance with appreciation.

Rafe couldn't take his eyes off Ali. Her body was going to be his undoing, that and those high heels.

Matt glanced at Rafe and saw the way he was looking at his sister. He knew she was a grown woman and was obviously beautiful, but he couldn't help being the big brother. Old habits died hard. "She's a good girl."

Rafe turned at Matt's words and looked him in the eye. "I know that, and you have no worries with me, man."

Matt nodded, looking back at Nicki. He'd made his point. He wouldn't say any more to Rafe about it; anything that happened was between him and Ali. He'd probably be pretty pissed if Nicki had an older brother who kept playing the part around him. He really liked Rafe, too, and hoped he hadn't made him uncomfortable.

"Hey, Rafe." He turned sideways to look at him. "Don't mind me, man, it's just in the hard wiring, you know? I have to remember she's an adult. I know she's really into you, so go for it, man."

Rafe nearly spit out his beer at Matt's last words and looked at him in disbelief.

Matt laughed. "Forget I said that last part. You know what I'm saying."

Rafe kept laughing as they both turned back toward the dance floor. Not that he felt he needed Matt's blessing, but it was nice to have nonetheless.

Ali and Nicki danced the next four or five songs, until Ali suggested going back for a drink. "Okay, it's really hot out there," she laughed, sitting back down and using a napkin to fan herself.

"This guy is so good, he's playing all our stuff." Nicki still moved to the music while sitting in her seat.

Matt leaned over and moved the hair that fell across her eye. Her skin prickled at his touch.

"You look great out there," he said softly so that only she could hear.

"Thank you. You should come out there with us."

"I think I like watching better." He grinned.

Nicki was melting under his gaze.

A slow song finally came on, and Ali leaned back in her chair, settling next to Rafe. "Did you get this?" She picked up a glass of water that was in front of her and sipped from it.

"I figured you'd want some."

"Thank you, I do. I'm done drinking -- I think I just sweat all the alcohol right out of my system out there." She laughed. "Sorry, that's not very appealing, is it?"

"Everything about you is appealing, even your sweat." In fact, seeing her like that only made him picture her sweaty between his sheets.

Ali was self-conscious now. She probably looked a mess.

"C'mon." He pushed back his chair and took her hand, leading her to the dance floor.

He took her in his arms and pulled her close.

"I'm all wet and sticky." She was embarrassed as she wrapped her arms around his cool, dry neck. He was probably regretting he took her out here.

"I like you wet and sticky," he whispered in her ear.

Or maybe not! She pressed herself a little closer and felt the muscles in his neck twinge. In her heels, she was almost eye to eye with him. Almost. "I need to wear these shoes all the time with you," she told him. "Now I can look right into those mysterious brown eyes of yours." They swayed against each other as the slow beat played on, their bodies aligned perfectly.

"I'd like you to keep them on all night," he said gruffly. He pulled her in even closer so there was no mistaking what he meant.

"You're a pretty good dancer," Ali whispered in his ear. Her whole body was taut with anticipation against him. He really was a good dancer, and his body felt nice and solid against hers.

"I want to leave," he whispered back.

Ali shuddered. "Okay."

Yes -- that was the answer he was hoping for. Rafe took her hand and led her back to the table.

Ali took the lead and said, "We're going to head out, maybe go for a swim. I'm dying in here."

Matt looked over at Nicki. "You ready to leave?"

Nicki wasn't; she was having too good a time talking with Matt. "We can just walk back," she offered. "It's not that far."

"We'll see you guys later then," Matt told them. "We're fine with walking."

Rafe was relieved. "You sure?"

"Absolutely, you guys go ahead," Matt assured them.

Rafe threw some money on the table, which Matt tried to hand back, but he turned away, ignoring him and calling out, "See you later."

Ali followed him out, and when they got to the truck, he opened her door, helping her in, then got behind the wheel to drive the short distance back to his house.

Ali's heart was pounding as she thought about what was going to happen when they returned to his house, and neither one of them spoke on the short drive back. The truck's windows were open, and she just enjoyed the soft sounds coming from the beach and the Gulf beyond. She knew she would implant this very moment into her memory. It was a perfect, nearly summer night, and she hoped it was only going to get better.

They pulled past the gate, and he parked the car inside the garage. Ali got out and couldn't help but see the big silver motorcycle parked beside her. "Is that yours?" she asked, impressed.

He came around to meet her. "Yes, it's a Ducati ST-3. Do you like it?"

"It's gorgeous! Can I sit on it?"

He looked at her and grinned wickedly. "Not unless you want to spend the rest of the night right here." She looked at him like he was crazy, but the thought of her straddling his bike, in that dress and those high heels, had him leading her out of the garage and up into the house…fast.

Ali took in her surroundings as Rafe led her into the main part of the house. Everything was a soft white. The only pictures on the wall were of the local landscape. Most were in black and white, and the contrast was stunning.

"I wonder who took these shots?" she said out loud. They had come up a set of terra cotta tiled stairs that emptied out into a grand room with vaulted ceilings and which opened up into the kitchen. The kitchen was state of the art, all stainless and natural stone, and the whole back of the house was glass, overlooking the Gulf.

Rafe heard her intake of breath. "Pretty nice, huh?"

"It's breathtaking." She walked forward to the sliders. There was a grand covered porch that took up the whole length of the house just beyond, with big comfortable furniture spread all around it.

"Do you want something to drink?" Rafe asked. "We could go outside to the bar."

"Actually, I'd just love an ice water." She was starting to shiver. The sweat had dried on her body, and the air conditioning was giving her goose bumps -- that, and knowing what was to come.

Rafe poured her a glass from the refrigerator and filled it with ice. He brought it over to her and noticed her shivering. "Do you want to sit outside? It's warmer out there." He rubbed his hand over the bumps on her arm.

She smiled at the contact and nodded, following him out through the sliders. He led her to a large, oversized cushioned couch and she sat down, putting her drink on the glass coffee table. Rafe sat down beside her, and she tried not to let on how nervous she actually felt. "Got any music out here?" she asked. Music would definitely make her feel less anxious.

"Yeah, sure I do. It won't be anything the D.J. played, though." He grinned at her as he got up and went back inside. He found the remote and turned the CD player on. The outdoor speakers came to life, and the Foo Fighters' Best of You was playing.

"Loud enough?" he asked as he came back on the porch.

"Perfect," she answered. She loved the Foo Fighters. So far they shared the same taste in music -- okay, so maybe he wasn't into the dance music, but most guys weren't. She took a sip of her water and waited for him to sit down again, but instead of sitting, he went over to the porch railing and leaned his back against it, resting his hands casually on the rail.

Ali fidgeted with her dress hem and felt him watching her. She looked up expectantly to meet his eyes. "It's warm," she noted. This was brutal; they both knew what they were there for.

"Uh-huh," he nodded.

"The moon looks pretty." Ali was starting to feel pretty ridiculous sitting there. She was doing all the talking.

Rafe was trying to exhibit control and take it slow. He wanted nothing more than to take her in his arms, but he wanted to be a gentleman, although his primal instincts were having trouble cooperating.

Oh, this was silly, they weren't teenagers! Ali got up with a sudden burst of courage and walked over to Rafe. She couldn't take it anymore. She was jumping out of her skin. She bravely stood just inches from his face and softly told him just that: "I'm jumping out of my skin." Then she pressed her hands to his shirt front and put her lips to his.

His response was immediate. He placed his hands on either side of her face and took over the kiss with a moan of sheer pleasure. He explored her mouth with his tongue and tasted her sweet, soft lips. God, he loved that she'd come over to him like that.

Ali's body filled with heat as she moved her hands over his chest and arms, lingering over every muscle, admiring him with her touch.

His own hands moved across her bare shoulders and taut back, feeling her shiver beneath him. He kissed her slower then, and deeper, making love to her mouth, envisioning what he would do to her body.

Ali adjusted herself so that she could press herself against him. She was rewarded with the swell of his arousal, and she groaned with her own pleasure.

With his arms still around her back, Ali was standing against him one minute, then being lifted and laid back on the cushioned sofa the next. She looked up at him, taking a deep breath in. Oh, God, he was strong, he'd just lifted her like she weighed nothing, and now he was staring at her like that, with such heat in his eyes -- she pulled him down to her.

With her hair splayed around her, and the heat she returned to him in her eyes, Rafe was burning hot for her. She pulled him down to kiss her, and he grabbed her arms and brought them up over her head, holding them there. He kissed her more intently this time, his desire overcoming any slow measures he had planned to take to seduce her. She wanted it just as bad, and he was going to give it to her. His hands traveled down the underside of her arms to find her breasts, rising and falling with each deep breath she took. He caressed them through the thin material of her dress and watched as her back rose up to the feel of his touch. He was ready to rip the dress right off her. As their kissing and heavy petting kept time with the fast beat of the music, Rafe had never been more turned on.

Ali sat up and started to untie her halter. She had to feel his hands on her bare skin now, but Rafe put a hand on hers to stop her.

"I want to take you inside," he said, his voice deep and gravelly, and Ali's stomach flipped at the sound of it, knowing he was in the same amplified state she was.

She followed his lead as he made his way into the house. He led her through the large living room, past the long couch, and on into the spacious master bedroom. Once inside, the moon was their only light, coming in through the large glass windows that overlooked the beach, and she glanced at the shadow it cast on the oversized bed in the middle of the room. The bed was neatly made, and the room was impressively clean. She took a deep breath, trying to calm her nerves as she looked around.

Rafe was facing her and watched as she took the room in. "Hey." He held his hand out to her, and she closed the gap, taking it. "You're thinking too much again."

She smiled. "I know, I just can't help thinking what you might be thinking of me, being here like this -- so soon, and how I was this afternoon by the pool. I just don't want you to think..."

He pulled her in against him, arms around her waist. "I think you're great, that's what I think. I've been waiting for this all day." He kissed her then, wanting to show her that what he told her was true.

She kissed him back and started to unbutton his shirt. "I've been waiting for it, too. I couldn't wait for your hands to be touching me again," she answered him in barely a whisper, as she separated all the buttons successfully and pushed the shirt away from his shoulders. Her hands moved all over him, memorizing every muscle beneath her fingers, outlining his frame, starting with his wide shoulders, down over and across his pecs, over his perfectly sculpted six-pack, and resting briefly at his navel and the thin vertical line of hair that led down into his waistband. She felt him flinch and looked up to see the searing heat in his eyes. His body was so hard and such a turn-on. She was in awe. He was perfect.

She moved her hands again, slowly, traveling up from his trim waist on to the wider expanse of his muscular back. She could do this for hours, she thought. The contrast of his soft skin over his hard muscles was scintillating, but there were other hard parts she wanted to touch and explore too.

The feel of her hands, so soft and gentle on him, was mind-numbing. How could her touch be so erotic? Instead of picking her up and throwing her on the bed, he went slow, reaching around to untie her dress. Using both hands, he slowly pulled it down over two of the loveliest breasts he'd ever seen, not too big and definitely not small. He stared at them in full appreciation before he found his mouth on first one and then the other. She was incredible, and he felt and heard her moan at his mouth on her. He used his hands as he molded each breast and sucked on one nipple while giving full attention to the other with his thumb and finger. Her hands were grasping his hair and head in pleasure, and he smiled at her as he pulled away. This was going to be such a great night.

He stepped back and slowly peeled the rest of the dress down and off her. She stood before him in just her underwear and those high-heeled sandals. As he made his way back up, he caressed her long, smooth legs, stopping to rest his hands at the sides of the white lace thong she wore. His erection was straining against his jeans uncomfortably, but he wanted to savor every inch of her before anything else. Hands still at her hips, he gently lowered her back onto the bed, heels still on, and eased her head back onto a pillow. He lowered himself so that one leg fell between her own and pressed against her heat, and he kissed her deeply, squeezing and kneading her breasts.

Ali's body was in another stratosphere, and she could do nothing to stop it. Rafe's touch was exquisite, and she only wanted more and more. Her hands found his waistband, and she ran them along inside, touching the skin of his lower back. When they came around to the front, he lifted himself slightly, giving her access to his button and zipper. Once there, she worked fast to free him but had some trouble doing so.

Rafe rolled off her quickly and sat up to finish undressing. He bent down to unstrap his ankle holster and slipped it under the bed. Before he could come back down on top of her, Ali was sitting up on her elbows, staring at him, wide-eyed.

"Was that what I think it was?"

Rafe was on top of her in a flash, pinning her arms down. "Ssh, no talking."

He was naked on top of her now, and her hips rose up to meet his. He had her damn arms pinned, and she struggled to free them. She wanted so badly to touch him and see him.

"Let me..." she started, as he kissed her hard, and he did as he was told, releasing her arms, letting her put her soft hands over the hardest erection he could ever remember having. He had tried to prevent her from reaching for him, just for this reason -- he was about to explode with her touch. He pulled away abruptly.

"Hey, no fair!" she whispered, out of breath.

"I want these off," he whispered back, and sat up to use both hands. He slipped his fingers under the thin material, feeling her soft skin, and slowly pulled the lace down and over her.

His eyes went wide at the sight of pure male fantasy as the material came away. What he saw there made him groan out loud in pleasure. "Oh, my God." She was shaven in a such a way that hid very little of her sex from him. She was all smooth skin, and he couldn't wait to touch and taste.

Ali felt the heat rise in her face as she watched his reaction. "Nicki convinced me to do it."

"Remind me to thank her later," he breathed. He finished pulling her underwear off, getting it around the heels of her shoes and dropping them to the floor. He was between her ankles now and looking at her body splayed on his bed. Holy God! She was all his right now, and he was going to make this last all night.

Because he had the surround sound on, the music still played throughout every room, the beat having slowed somewhat as the Foo Fighters sang about a little bit of "resolve." He smiled happily as he bent down and gently pushed her legs apart, then traveled the lines of her legs with his hands, stopping at the shaven mound between them.

He put a hand to the smooth skin and swelled even more at the wetness he felt. She squirmed beneath him, pressing into his hand, and he touched and probed her some more, enjoying her reaction. He moved around her wet, warm opening expertly and played with the pink swollen nub he could so plainly see. He watched her all the while as he stroked her, her head lolled back, her eyes closed, and her breasts rising and falling. He had to struggle to keep control as he touched her, especially when he felt her whole body go taut, and she cried out as she came, spilling right into his hand.

"Rafe," she pleaded breathlessly, "please!" Oh, my God!

He smiled and did it again and again, torturing them both as his hand and fingers brought her repeatedly to orgasm, her body quivering under him, his own body threatening to detonate.

"Rafe, I mean it, I need you inside me now!" Ali's arms beckoned him forward and Rafe reached across into his nightstand for protection.

Ali watched his every move, and she couldn't help but see the dark outline of a gun in his nightstand drawer. Her eyes found his as he rolled the condom on. She was *so* turned on. She had felt a little jolt of fear at the sight of the gun, but it only served to make her more excited for him.

Rafe knew she had seen the Glock he kept nearby while he slept, and he watched her eyes for her reaction. God help him, she was turned on by it. He laughed as he got on top of her and spread her legs apart with his own. He looked her in the eyes before the fullness of him found her wet entrance. She was tight as he pushed his way gently inside her warm, wet opening, fighting to stay in control with the feel of her wrapping around him. He had all he could do not to just thrust his way in.

But Ali didn't want self-control, and she knew he was trying to be gentle. She had seen the size of him, and she wasn't afraid. She wanted him -- all of him. She moved her hips up, enveloping him, showing him just how much she wanted it, her rhythm matching that of the music in the background.

Rafe had been holding himself up, and upon her invitation he lowered himself to her, his forearms at the sides of her head, and he matched her rhythm, thrusting himself hard into her like she wanted. She met him thrust for thrust, her legs coming up to encircle his back, high heels digging into his ass and pushing him deeper inside of her. He almost lost it when he felt the hard heels of the shoes touch his skin. The music pounded in the background, and their pace was fast and furious, neither of them letting up. She was taking all of him and he of her. His mouth was on her breast, and he cupped her rear, bringing them as close as their bodies would possibly allow.

She moaned with ecstasy. Their bodies were so slick with sweat, they were actually slippery against each other. She unwound her legs from his hips and set her heeled feet on the bed, her knees up and spread, his legs between hers. He kept pushing into her, and she gained the leverage she wanted by pushing her heels into the bed, their bodies connecting together in a force of energy and heat. She had never, ever, been so turned on in her life. She ran her hands all over him. The muscles in his arms and back were flexed as he held himself from crushing her, and she stroked them and kneaded them, giving him relief as he worked hard at pleasing her. Physically he was a god, and the feel of him was bringing her to the end very fast.

Rafe couldn't believe how wet she was. He could feel it all over him, and he knew he wasn't going to last much longer. He gripped her hands in his and plowed himself into her a final time, grunting as he came forcefully inside of her.

"Oh, my God, Rafe!"

"Ali, you're incredible," he breathed and kissed her, his body crushed to hers. He didn't want to move. He throbbed inside her as he felt her clench around him. He was pretty sure his fate had just been sealed, and a feeling of warmth rushed over him.

Ali held onto him for dear life, trying to catch her breath and wrapping her legs back around him so he wouldn't leave her body. She felt an overwhelming urge to cry, and she kissed him back so that he couldn't see that. Why the hell was she crying? That was undoubtedly the best sex of her life, and rather than laugh with glee or shout with happiness, tears sprang from her eyes. She was most definitely happy, so she had to guess they were happy tears, but he was going to think she was a weirdo. She'd just have to keep kissing his beautiful mouth until the feeling passed. Only she had a feeling -- *what* she was feeling wasn't going to pass.

Rafe kissed Ali back for a long while. He finally pulled away and felt her legs come down to rest beside his. He lifted himself off her, not trusting himself to look at her, and walked to the bathroom on rubbery legs to clean himself off before returning to the bed. The rubbery legs were no surprise after the workout they'd just given each other, but the feel of his heart lodged in his throat was a definite surprise. Oh, man, this was crazy.

Ali had watched his big, strong body walk away, and she settled into the pillow with a sigh, quickly drying her wet eyes. Her body felt as if she'd just run a marathon. She felt a dull throbbing between her legs and smiled. It had been even better than she'd imagined it would be. She kicked off her heels and arched her feet, stretching, while she pulled back the covers and slid beneath them, welcoming the feel of the cold sheets on her still overheated skin.

Rafe returned, slipping in beside her, and Ali rolled to her side pressing herself against him, her hands rested on his warm chest, as he wrapped his arms around her, loving the feel of her bare skin.

"Wow," she said.

He laughed out loud. "Yeah, wow!"

"That was...pretty damn good," she added.

"Babe, that was friggin' beyond pretty damn good."

"Yeah, it was," she agreed, laughing, too. "Who knew?"

"Oh, I was pretty sure it would be like that as soon as I saw you."

"Oh, yeah," she laughed, "you determined that in fifteen minutes at the bar?"

"No, I determined that before the bar, in about five minutes, after I saw you sneak through the yard and onto the beach." He realized what he said and cringed inwardly.

"What do you mean, before the bar? You saw us come though the yard?" Ali sat up on her elbow.

Rafe clasped his hands behind his head and nodded.

"How? Were you at the window or something?"

Rafe stared at her and thought about it. They had just been as intimate as two people can get, and keeping anything from her seemed ridiculous at this point. As soon as he'd got up out of the bed, it had struck him like a freight train -- he already cared about this girl. He had loved spending all that time with her today, and now this. He had never felt this way about sex with any other woman. This was on a whole new level, and he damn well knew it and it scared the shit out of him.

"Well?" She poked him.

Rafe leaned over to his nightstand and picked up the remote. He pressed a button, and the fifty-inch flat screen on the wall in front of them came to life with six different images.

Ali sat up quickly, staring at the images before her. Each one held a different view of Rafe's house, and it was real time -- she could see the palm trees swaying in the driveway. One picture was of the front entrance.

She turned slowly to look at him, and Rafe braced himself.

"I knew it!" She squinted her eyes, "You're a spy!" This was why he hadn't invited her in earlier.

God, he loved this girl. Whoa, did he just think that to himself? Okay, he did. It's just an expression, right?

Most women would have freaked to find out they were on a surveillance video, but it didn't even faze Ali. That's what he thought was great, he loved *that about her,* not loved her, *loved her.* Oh, shit.

Rafe laughed, or was that a choke? and pulled her on top of him. "You knew it, huh?"

"I've been putting the pieces together." She held up her fingers. "First, you're built like a commando, which, by the way, *I looove* ."

He laughed at the sexy expression she gave him. "That makes me a spy?"

"Ssh, I'm not done. Second, you carry a gun, which, by the way, *totally turns me on.*" She whispered the last part, knowing it was so bad to say that.

He laughed again. "Anybody can carry a gun."

She ignored him. "Third, you won't come out and say what it is exactly that you do, and spies are evasive, right? And you are so evasive!" She grinned as he continued to laugh. "And four, now four is just an instinctive opinion on my part, but it's your eyes. They are so intense, like a predator, and I mean that in a good way, not like you're scary or anything, just like you've seen some things, not so good things." He still looked amused, thank God, so she went on. "I mean, I really love your eyes." She noticed the flash of surprise on his face. She couldn't shut up all of a sudden. "I mean, your eyes are..."

Rafe leaned down and kissed her mouth.

Ali pulled away. "I told you, you can't keep shutting me up like that." Although it worked every time. She'd gladly kiss him instead of talk, but she wanted to know. "Am I right?" She sat up again and pulled the sheet against her chest.

"What happened to your shoes?" he asked, smiling.

"I kicked them off when you got up. Don't change the subject."

He sighed. "No, I'm not a spy like you're imagining." Rafe sat up, his back against the headboard.

"But I'm close?"

"FBI." He watched for her reaction.

Ali's eyes widened, and she studied his face. This brought a whole new dimension to him that she couldn't help but be turned on by. "Wow," was all she could think of to say.

"Disappointed that I'm not an international spy?" he teased.

"Disappointed, no, thoroughly impressed, yes. I think that's really cool."

Rafe found it amusing that she was impressed. "You're impressed, huh?" He tried to pull her to him.

"Wait." She put a hand on his chest. "Tell me about it. I mean, can you tell me about it? Do you have a badge?"

He laughed. "It's an I.D. It's over on the bureau next to my wallet."

Ali tore back the covers and hopped off the bed, making it to the bureau in two strides. She reached on top of the chest and picked up the leather case. It felt strange to be holding something so personal of his, and she looked at him before she opened it. He gave her a nod, and she flipped it open and recited, "Special Agent Rafe McDonough."

"No one has ever addressed me completely naked before." Rafe was eyeing every blessed inch of her. "Come back here."

Ali put the I.D. down and walked to the edge of the bed, standing before the nightstand. The drawer was open slightly, and he knew what she was thinking. "Ali, I want you to close that drawer all the way and come here."

"Ohh," she groaned. "Just a peek?"

"No."

She turned at the serious tone in his voice, and she was afraid she'd crossed the line. "I'm sorry," she said, closing the drawer and getting back under the covers he held up for her.

"I promise, another time, okay?" he placated her. She needed to understand his gun was not a toy.

Ali nodded, feeling pretty stupid and like a naughty child.

"Hey." He lifted her chin. "I'm not upset. I just want you to remember that it's a weapon, a dangerous weapon."

"You're right. I'm just curious, that's all."

"You know what, I'll show you tomorrow, and you can finish asking me all the questions you want." He smiled.

"Promise?" Her face lit up.

"Within reason on the questions," he laughed, "but right now, I don't want to talk anymore."

She moved closer and then covered his body with her own. "No more talking, huh?" she kissed his neck.

"None." He showed her what he wanted to do instead.

CHAPTER ELEVEN

Nicki and Matt had left the bar shortly after Ali and Rafe left, and headed across the street to the beach. They walked the one and a half miles back to the house on the sand, quiet for most of the way, just enjoying the warm night air and their own thoughts. They left the beach through an access just a few houses away from Rafe's' and walked on the side of the road until they were almost across from Nan's. In fact, they were just approaching the construction site next to Rafe's when they heard someone whistle. They had just walked by a parked truck and were about to cross the street.

Nicki whispered to Matt, "That just scared the hell out of me. I didn't think there was anyone in there, did you?"

Matt looked back and was trying to get a clear view of the driver. "No," his voice tight, "I didn't think there was anyone in there, either." But now Matt could see that there were two guys, and they were slumped down in the front seats. His back went up, and he moved Nicki in front of him, getting ready to cross.

The passenger yelled out, "Hey, gorgeous, why don't you say goodnight to your boyfriend and come say *hello* to us."

This guy had to be fucking kidding. "Nicki, go across. I'll be right over." Adrenaline suddenly surged through Matt's veins.

"Matt, please don't go over there. Let's just both cross, okay?" Nicki pleaded with Matt. She knew he wouldn't hesitate to pull both guys out of the truck and beat the hell out of them. She knew he was no stranger to fighting, at least not when he'd been younger.

Matt looked at Nicki, his arm still around her protectively, and turned back to the truck. "Hey, assholes, get the fuck out of the truck and come say hello to the boyfriend." Matt waited, his stance defensive, staring them down, but didn't get a reaction. After a couple of minutes, he shook his head and took Nicki's hand to cross the street, directing them past the front door and down toward the driveway, where they could no longer be seen by the two jerks in the truck.

"Thank you for not approaching them. They were probably drunk," Nicki guessed.

"They're lucky they didn't get out of the truck."

Nicki laughed. "Or what, you would have got all Boston on them?"

"Damn right."

They both laughed at the silliness of it, and Matt reached over to tickle her. "You are gorgeous, though. I can't argue with them there."

Nicki smirked. "Coming from you, it's much nicer, *boyfriend*." She teased him, laughing and was glad he hadn't let the jerks spoil their night.

He gave her his famous crooked smile and a raised brow. Okay, so maybe he liked the sound of that as much as she did. Nicki looked away so he wouldn't see too much.

They finally approached the front door to Nans', hidden by the lush landscape, and Matt took her key to let them in. The cold air assaulted them first thing, and Nicki immediately went to the thermostat.

"Want the windows open instead?"

"Sure." Matt put the key on the counter and watched her open the sliders.

Nicki turned back to face him and found him watching her. She knew what he was thinking by the look in his eyes, and she found herself suddenly nervous. This was going to be a lot more difficult for her than it was for him. Being with him -- making love with him -- was going to overwhelm her heart and her mind, and she was frightened to hell he was going to see that.

"Do you want to go out by the pool?" she asked.

"No," he answered matter-of-factly.

Oh-oh, he wasn't going to waste any time. Time she needed to gain courage.

He leaned against the kitchen counter, just looking at her. She was incredibly beautiful in her dress. It fell over her body just right, revealing the feminine curves he'd been longing to touch all night.

"Do you want to sit down?" Nicki moved toward the sofa and away from his seductive gaze, but before she could sit, he was suddenly in front of her, taking her hand and kissing the inside of her palm, sending tremors up and down her arm. She looked into his eyes, and he let go of her hand, bringing his lips to hers, kissing her like he had just that afternoon. He was showing her mouth just what he wanted to do to her body, and Nicki swooned, becoming light-headed at his expert kissing. She held on to his strong back and traced her hands around the hard muscles in his shoulders.

"This is what I want," he breathed into her ear, and she realized happily she didn't need any courage, just him. She took his hand with a smile and led him down the hall to her bedroom, stopping just before the bed.

Matt pulled her in at the waist, then slowly and deliberately lowered the zipper at the back of her dress. He pulled it down gently, using his hands to help the thin material fall away from her.

Nicki's heart leaped as she stepped around the dress and stood before him in her bra and panties. She reached her arms up around his neck and stood on her tiptoes to kiss him. Her body tingled with anticipation as her hands fumbled with the buttons of his shirt, and she felt him smile under her lips. She was nervous and he knew it. When she got the last of them undone, she slipped the shirt from his shoulders and pulled back to look at him, and under his watchful eye, she traced the sexy line of coarse hair that led down beneath his waistband. God, if she didn't think that was the sexiest thing ever, especially on him and his washboard stomach. Her hands stroked him there some more, until he was straining against her, and then she deftly unbuttoned, then unzipped his jeans, helping him out of those, too.

He wore tight boxer briefs that molded to the large shape of his arousal, and that had Nicki instantly pressing herself against it. Matt groaned at the contact and lifted her up in one effortless swoop, and her legs instantly wrapped around his waist. He kissed her hard as he walked her right through the open doorway, across the hall, and into his own bedroom.

Nicki was reeling; she was putty in his arms as he laid her back on his bed and molded his perfectly hard body to hers. He looked at her with such desire in his green eyes as he ground himself against her, and she knew he could probably feel her own arousal through the thin cotton panties she wore. They kissed with such need and desperation for one another, grinding and pressing into each other as if they couldn't get close enough, then Matt reached around her back and unclasped her bra, removing it skillfully with one hand. He took turns on both breasts, kissing them and filling his mouth with them until she cried out in pleasure. She reached down with a desperate urgency to the waistband of his shorts, pushing them down, using her bare foot to help guide them all the way off, and then receiving a wide smile from him at her method. When he was completely free of them, she took him greedily in her hands and was more than surprised, meeting his desire-filled eyes she gave him her own wide grin. Oh, boy. She kissed him again and moved her hands around to his hard round ass, pressing him down more firmly against her, her hips moving under him more urgently.

Nicki was driving Matt wild, and he had to get inside of her. Her hands were like smooth silk touching the length of his hard cock, and now with her gyrating under him, he felt like he was going to burst in a hurry. He got off her quickly while he got protection and put it on. He watched her watching him, waiting there, lying there -- beautiful. He admired her long, lithe body for the hundredth time, her chest rising and falling under his gaze, and he put his hand possessively on the small piece of material that covered her. When he felt the dampness of it, he groaned in pleasure. This is what he wanted, what he'd wanted to do all day, to make her so hot and wet she'd be crying for him. Now he wasn't sure if he could control himself because she was making him so hot, *he* was ready to cry. He dared to move the thin, damp material aside with his fingers, and- oh my god! He moaned in awe at the bare, smooth skin he found underneath. Oh, man, she's killing me here. There was only a tiny patch of hair meant to tease, that led to the glorious place his fingers sought readily, and he really, really had to fight for control now because what he desperately wanted was to bring his mouth right down to that smoothness and taste and lick and...damn. Instead, he touched and rubbed and teased and watched as her body writhed appreciatively under his touch.

His arousal pulsed against her as her hand reached down to stroke him and hold him, but he couldn't get enough of touching her and pleasing her. She was loving it, and he was loving her loving it.

"Oh, God, oh, God!" Nicki moaned loudly. Her head was spinning in ecstasy. She came hard and forcefully, again and again under his touch. Just when she was coming out of one orgasm, he started stroking her again, his finger expertly moving at just the right speed and just the right pressure. She cried out in undulated pleasure, "Matt!"

Matt couldn't believe how wet she was. He could do this all night, but he was about to explode in her hand. Every time she came, she gripped him harder and stroked him faster. He got rid of her underwear in one quick motion and that was it -- he was on top of her and thrusting himself deep inside. She was so wet and warm and felt so unbelievably good as she stretched around him, his whole body trembled in response. He heard her moan against him, and he wrapped her in his arms, keeping her body pressed to his own as he pushed deep inside her, meeting her hips as she rose and fell beneath him, their pace steady and determined, until she gripped his back and started pushing him even deeper and he lost all sense of control. In one swift move, he lifted her up and had her on top of him as he thrust into her hard and fast from beneath her. He watched as her head fell back and he reached for her breasts bouncing back and forth in front of him. She was moving right along with him, keeping the pace, He held her hips while she rode him and fought the overwhelming need of his release. He could see she was on the edge of her own release, and he quickly rolled her on her back again, coming down on top of her, pressing his lips to hers, kissing her hard and inhaling her cries as he exploded deep inside her, feeling her whole body shake and squeeze and tighten around him. Holy mother of God! That was fucking unbelievable!

He was breathing heavily, and he tried to roll off her gently so he wasn't crushing her, but she caught him with strong arms, pulling him back and hugging him to her chest tightly. When he lifted his head to look down into her eyes, they were closed, and he was taken aback by the tears he saw glistening on the lashes just underneath them. His heart sank in fear as he kissed them away, tasting the salt.

"Hey," he whispered, "look at me." Now his heart was pounding in his chest for other reasons.

Nicki turned her head into the pillow, trying to wipe her eyes. Then she hesitantly looked up at Matt, and the look of concern he gave her brought more tears to the surface. She didn't dare speak. She was so overcome with love for him, her heart was going to burst.

"Are you okay?"

She nodded, not trusting her voice.

"Did I hurt you?" he asked fearfully.

She shook her head no and pulled him back down to her so she could wrap her arms around him. She just wanted to hold him and savor it -- know that it was real. It was everything she had ever dreamed and so much more. She didn't want to let him go.

Matt wrapped his own arms around her and held her close, knowing that something huge had just happened between them but that he wasn't willing to explore it just yet. He shifted them so that she was tucked right up against him, his weight off her and her head cradled against his chest. He slowly stroked her hair, inhaling the sweet scent of her, and he could feel her body start to relax against him. She was so soft and warm, and he pulled her in even closer, his big arms around her small frame. And that was how he fell asleep, overwhelmed with feelings and hiding them in a warm embrace.

CHAPTER TWELVE

Ali stretched her body against the warm sheets and sneaked a peek over her shoulder, only to see an empty spot. The sliders were open to the morning air, and she could hear the sound of the Gulf just beyond. She smiled serenely as a warm breeze flowed through the room, washing over her, and she smiled to herself, thinking of the night before. Rafe had taken her above and beyond anything she could ever have fantasized -- more than once. After the hours of mind-blowing sex, they had gone for a late night swim in the pool to cool off. They had kissed for what seemed like hours, naked in the water, and had finally come back to his bedroom, where she had fallen asleep peacefully tucked into his warm side.

She sat up, taking in her surroundings in the light of day. The room was large and warmly decorated in shades of browns and blues, beachy and masculine at the same time. It actually suited Rafe, even though it wasn't really his. Her eyes came to rest on the flat screen, which was off, but she couldn't erase the images it had shown the night before. She wondered why the homeowner would need all that security in a place like Captiva, then realized it was probably there for Rafe. But why would he need all the cameras? That would be one of her questions. She couldn't believe he was an FBI agent.

How friggin' cool was that? Wait until she told Nicki -- she wouldn't believe it. She couldn't wait to ask Rafe more about it. She glanced over at his night stand and felt a surge of excitement knowing his gun was in there. She wondered if he'd let her hold it. Probably not. Her thoughts were interrupted by the sound of clanging dishes.

She got up and padded into the bathroom. Oh, God! She'd fallen asleep with wet hair, and it now lay around her head in a wavy, tangled mess. That's pretty, she thought and splashed some cold water on her face. She found some mouthwash on the counter and helped herself, then used her fingers as a comb, trying to at the very least not to look like she'd been electrocuted. Back in the bedroom, she found Rafe's shirt on the floor and put it on. She inhaled his scent as she worked the buttons and rolled up the sleeves, knowing it had just become her favorite pajamas -- he so wasn't getting it back.

She walked out of the room barefoot and smiled as she saw him in the kitchen.

"Good morning," he said, seeing her approach. His stomach did a little dance as he saw her wearing nothing but his shirt, her hair mussed and her face fresh and clean. She was beautiful.

"Hi," Ali said, taking a seat in the living room on the comfortable white sofa.

"Hungry?"

"Yes, actually." She smiled, feeling a bit shy. He was looking at her and smiling, and she wasn't sure if she should go to him. She didn't want to seem clingy or anything.

"Good. I made everything since I didn't know what you like for breakfast."

She laughed and stood up walking toward the kitchen. "Everything?" He was setting more food down on the glass kitchen table, already full with dishes of food. There were pancakes, eggs, bagels, cereal, fruit, and three different kinds of juice.

"The coffee just finished brewing."

"You're crazy. There's enough here to feed a family of five! But thank you!" she added. He made her breakfast!

"Help yourself, I'll pour the coffee. Cream? Sugar?"

She made a face of apology. "I'm sorry, I don't drink it."

"No? Good for you. I have to have it." He came over to the table and sat down.

Ali sat, too, making a plate with one of everything. "What time did you get up to make all this?" she laughed.

"Not that long ago." He had actually got up around six, watching and waiting to see when the Explorer would leave next door.

Ali looked him over. He had on a T-shirt and jeans and no shoes, just his bare feet. He looked incredibly sexy. She made a plate for him and handed it across the table.

"My shirt looks good on you," he said and took the food from her. She looked sexy as hell, and he thought about skipping breakfast.

Ali returned the look he was giving her and grinned. "I've already decided to keep it."

"It's all yours."

Ali knew breakfast was about to be over before it had even begun, and as much as she wouldn't mind that, she wanted answers, too, so she quickly derailed him. "So tell me all about it."

Rafe grinned, knowing what she had just done, and figured he'd better keep his end of the bargain. "I work for the Criminal Investigative Division of the FBI. I've been with the Miami field office for about a year."

"That is so cool." She rested her chin in her hand, elbow on the table.

Rafe chuckled. "You sound like my nephew."

"Well, it is! I've never met an FBI agent," Ali told him, smiling. "So why Miami? What about New York?" she asked seriously.

"Miami is just a temporary transfer."

"Did you put in for it?" Maybe he was trying to get away from something, or more specifically someone, in New York.

"I was asked to come."

"Oh." She thought she understood. She studied him, sitting back in his seat relaxed, his knees apart and his arms behind his head. He was one cool character.

"Are you special ops?"

He laughed out loud. "Nicki was right -- you're really into cop shows, aren't you? What's your favorite, The Shield?" he teased.

Ali made a face. "I do like that show, but you're changing the subject."

"They needed my input on a particular investigation, a type of case I had worked before with success. An agent I had worked with in the past suggested coming to Miami to help them out. The timing was right, so I went."

"So how did you find yourself here?" She thought that was less invasive than, *Have you ever shot someone?* which was what she really wanted to ask.

"I'm kind of on a working vacation." He smiled at her confusion. "I'm trying to get over a bad case of burnout and doing a little investigative work at the same time."

"How do you expect to get over burnout if you're still working? Whose idea was that?"

She sounded indignant on his behalf, and he laughed softly. "Trust me, compared to what I've been doing for the past year, this is nothing. I'm barely working, more like watching and asking a couple of questions here and there. And when this one is over, I'll get a real vacation to myself."

Ali wondered about that briefly. "So what or who could you possibly be investigating on Captiva?" She watched him, watching her, thinking about it. "I understand if you can't tell me."

Rafe looked at her across the table, wearing just his shirt, the buttons fastened just short of her cleavage. "Are you wearing anything under that shirt?"

Ali took a sip and swallowed her juice, feeling the heat wash over her body. "No." It came out rather gravelly, and she cleared her throat.

He sighed, knowing his desire was plain to see in his eyes by the way she shifted in her seat. He wanted her again, but not just her body. Last night had been somewhat of an earth-shattering event for him, and he was still coming to terms with it. He had woken up beside her and watched her sleep, naked under his sheets. His first instinct hadn't been to wake her and tell her he had to get to work or that he had a pressing appointment, no, his first instinct had been to kiss her cheek and go make her breakfast. He wanted to keep her there all day and into the night and all the next day and on and on. At first his feelings had scared him a little, but then while cooking, he realized happily that this is what people do -- they start committed relationships when they care about someone, and he did care about Ali. So what if he'd just met her? He lived by what he'd told her: if it feels right, it is right. It was true in his job and in his life. And he lived by the opposite, too -- if his gut didn't like it, it was wrong, and this was definitely not wrong. He knew he could trust her; he wanted to trust her.

"Do you recognize the name Xavier D'nafrio?"

Ali shook her head. "Should I? He sounds like a mob boss."

He grinned. "No, He's the guy building the house next door, so I didn't know if you'd heard his name around Nicki or her grandmother."

"Oh! So that's why you have all the cameras outside. Nicki never mentioned his name, but I bet her grandmother knows it. Nicki mentioned that there were a bunch of neighbors protesting the construction. Is that what you're investigating?" She couldn't imagine what the crime would be there.

"No," he laughed. "Let's just say a little matter with the IRS has brought him to our attention, and I'm just here to see if things are on the up and up."

"And if things are not on the up and up, you'll take him out?"

Take him out? He smirked, seeing the teasing look in her eye. "You're pretty funny, you know that?"

Ali shrugged. "Why do need to carry a gun?"

"It's required as an agent."

"So can I see it?"

Rafe studied her, reminded of their age difference. She looked even younger than twenty-five with her fresh, clean face and her mussed-up hair. "Are you sure you're old enough to be here?" he smiled, teasing her.

"That's not funny." She looked at him seriously. "Does it bother you that I'm a little younger than you?"

"No, it actually doesn't. You just look pretty cute right now, and it reminded me that there *is* an age difference."

"Eight years, so what? Twenty years from now, you'll be proud to have a younger woman on your arm."

Rafe raised his eyebrows. "Twenty years from now, huh?" He liked the sound of that.

Ali felt her face turn beet red as she realized what she'd said. "You know, if you're still into dating younger women." Nice cover -- he won't see through that. Shit! Next she'd be telling him where she sees them retiring. Captiva's as good a spot as any.

"I hope I'm not still dating twenty years from now. I want to be with my hot, younger wife, maybe lying on a beach somewhere." Rafe smiled at her, knowing they were dancing around a topic that usually took place much further into a relationship.

Oh. Huh? Was he talking about...? She couldn't think of anything witty to respond with, because she was actually picturing that beach twenty years from now, with *her* beside him, so she got back on subject. "You must have been in some dangerous situations before." The realization that Rafe's job was more than just a glamorized image in her mind hit her with full force as she pictured him having to shoot someone, or worse, getting shot. "Is this guy D'nafrio dangerous?"

"We treat every situation as dangerous, but we also have the best-trained agents on the job who take every precaution to be safe, but no, so far this guy has remained on the sidelines and hasn't posed a threat."

"Are you one of those 'best trained agents'?"

"Yes, SWAT certified."

That sounded impressive. "That's when you shoot with a rifle?"

He nodded.

"So I shouldn't worry about you?"

"No." He smiled at her.

His confidence was comforting, and she believed he probably was indeed the best at what he did, but she would worry anyway. How could she not? She finally finds someone that she could see being with twenty years from now, and he's part of a SWAT team for the FBI? Perfect, no fears there. Could she handle it every time he walked out the door to work, wondering if he would even come home in one piece? She looked at him carefully. He exuded pure strength, and he had a confident and calm demeanor about him. He didn't seem like the type of guy who would be careless or who took unnecessary risks. "I believe you. I bet you are really good at what you do."

Rafe smiled at her compliment and was happy to see that she didn't seem afraid of his job. He knew a lot of women who wouldn't even want to get involved. Did she want to? That was all he could think about right now. How could he hold on to this girl and do his job at the same time?

Rafe pushed his plate back and stood up. "I've decided I want my shirt back."

Ali stood up and started toward him. "You'll have to shoot me for it." She winked and sauntered past him back to the bedroom.

He laughed incredulously and was right on her heels.

Nicki awoke around seven to a sliver of light coming through Matt's window. She quietly got up, leaving Matt gloriously spread out over the bed. What a great ass, she thought as she covered him with the sheet. She was walking on air as she remembered their night, smiling to herself at the condition of the room and the torn condom packages all over the floor. She was surprised to feel so refreshed after having had barely any sleep at all. Her body was sore, but pleasantly so, and she smiled happily as she shut his door softly behind her and entered her own room to start her day.

She used the bathroom to clean up a bit and dressed for her workout in shorts and a tank. Grabbing her yoga mat, she headed out to the pool deck and proceeded to do her stretches.

Matt was up an hour later, and that was how he found her, in the lotus position, facing the bay. "If I did that, I'd roll right over into the pool."

She laughed and turned with a big smile at the sound of his voice. "It's relaxing. You should try it."

"It looks painful." He smiled back at her.

Nicki unfolded her legs and stood up. She reached her arms up over her head, stretched, and yawned.

"Sleep well?" he asked, coming to her and taking her in his arms.

He was dressed just in a pair of shorts, and Nicki once again admired his strong, muscular body. She wrapped her arms around his neck and kissed him softly.

"Last night was..." She didn't get to finish.

"Friggin' unbelievable," he finished for her.

"Yes, that!" she laughed. Among other things, she thought... heartbreaking...soul-shattering.

He looked at her closely, about to mention the tears, but thought maybe he'd keep it light for now. Besides, he still wanted to sort out his own strong feelings. "I'm starved. Want to go out to breakfast?"

Nicki smiled. "I'd love to."

They walked back inside, and Matt picked up a T-shirt he had left on the counter, along with the convertible keys from the key rack in the kitchen. "It's incredible outside. Let's put the top down -- I'll drive."

Nicki slipped on some flip flops and took a hoodie she had hanging by the door. They walked out to the car, and Nicki glanced across the street. "Ali didn't make it home last night."

Matt laughed. "I figured as much."

Nicki grinned, happy for her best friend. She got in the car beside Matt, and they pulled out, heading toward Sanibel. "Oh, it's heavenly out today."

"I'm going to enjoy this weather every day that I'm here, that's for sure."

Nicki's heart lurched at the thought of him going back, and she started up the small talk to keep from thinking about it. She talked about starting her job the next day and how excited she was, but it also reminded her that it would be time apart from him. She asked him about his work as well and listened to him intently on the fifteen-minute drive.

When they arrived at the café, they took a table outside. "What will you do while you're here?" she asked, sitting down.

"You're looking at it, kid -- breakfast, beach, run, drink, eat, sleep, start again."

She laughed. "Sounds like the makings of a good vacation."

"Although," he said, looking at her," I'm starting to realize the real reason I was asked to come here." He grinned at her.

"And what reason would that be?" Nicki asked with a smirk, thinking she knew where he was headed.

"I think your grandmother is trying to get us together." He saw the pink rise to her cheeks and smiled.

Nicki shook her head. "My grandmother thinks she's got it all figured out."

Matt smiled, "Does she?"

Nicki looked at him seriously. "I guess she can be pretty perceptive."

Matt reached across the table and took her hand, holding it in his, watching her blush again.

"Well, I for one don't want to disappoint her. Do you?"

Nicki shook her head no, cautiously, just looking at him. What was he saying?

"I mean, if she thinks we should be together, maybe we should try it."

He was still grinning. Was he kidding with her? "After last night," she spoke somewhat quietly, "I would say mission accomplished, wouldn't you?"

"I think she was hoping for something more than that."

Nicki was taken aback by his serious demeanor. He *wasn't* kidding with her, and her hand started to feel sweaty under his. "Well, maybe she is." Nicki dropped her head to the menu in front of her, trying to sound nonchalant. Her grandmother had always known how she felt about Matt. She had been the only one Nicki had confided in and the only shoulder she'd cried upon.

"And what about you?" Matt pressed her.

Nicki kept staring at the menu, trying to register what he was asking and also trying to take in the fact that *he* seemed as if he wanted more than that. Her heart was in her throat. "I..."

She was avoiding his eyes purposefully, and he knew his words were coming as a surprise. He knew he had shocked her, but the way he was feeling about her was unlike anything he had ever felt, and if he had any kind of chance with her, he was going to take it.

He didn't let her finish once again. "I was thinking, maybe while I'm here, I could get you to fall in love with me again."

Nicki jerked her head up at his soft-spoken words. Her stomach flipped repeatedly, and she stared at him as if he had just spoken in a language she couldn't understand -- except she absolutely did understand, and she was beaming inside. That wouldn't be hard to do at all -- in fact, just kiss me right now, and I'll tell you your job is done, I'm in love with you again. And even though those words were on the tip of her tongue, she had the good sense not to make it so easy. She deserved a little fun after years of self-torment, right?

"That might take a lot of time and effort, and repeat performances." She grinned slyly, feigning complete composure. "Are you up for that?" If only it were acceptable to dance on the breakfast table.

He let go of her hand and reached under the table to bring her chair closer to his, the heat in his eyes wiping the grin off her face. "Are you challenging me?"

"Maybe," she answered quietly. His eyes were too much, but she couldn't look away. "But how will you be able to focus on the challenge? There are beautiful women all over the island who'll take one look into these eyes of yours and throw themselves at you." She was only half-joking, but the thought of losing him to another woman shot pangs of jealousy right to her gut.

Matt saw the uncertainty flash behind her eyes, and he reached in to kiss her, seductively, trying to convey that nobody could stand a chance against her. "Sweetheart, after yesterday, and last night..." He didn't finish, but kissed her again.

"Yes?" She waited when he pulled away.

"Let's just say I've never had trouble focusing. When I see something I want, I work hard and I get it."

Nicki got the chills with the thought that he would actually pursue her. "Well, then, who am I to stop you?" She smiled. Thank you, Lord… thank you, fate…thank you, mother earth…thank you, universe!

"You couldn't if you tried," he said matter-of-factly and picked up his menu. He knew he was already a goner.

Nicki was out-of-her-mind happy, and she picked up her own menu, trying to just smile normally and not like a woman prepared to dance all over the breakfast tables. She pretended to read the menu, but her mind was all over the place, and she couldn't read a thing. She could only picture the time she would be spending with him while he was here, trying to get her to *fall in love with him again*. Ha! Thank you, Nan!

"Oh, and by the way," he said, not looking up from his menu, "repeat performances are a given."

Nicki laughed soft and deep. "Now you've got me wanting to skip breakfast."

"Let's go." He started to push his chair back.

"No! Wait, sit, sit," she laughed. "I need sustenance."

"You sure, because I can wait 'til lunch." Hell, he would skip eating altogether to have her in his bed again.

She hit him playfully in the chest, still sitting close, "I plan on skipping lunch." She laughed as Matt flagged down the waitress, eager to order breakfast.

CHAPTER THIRTEEN

"I suppose I should go across the street and make an appearance," Ali said as she lay against Rafe.

"No offense, but I have a feeling no one is missing you over there."

Ali laughed. "You're probably right, but I should go home to shower and change."

Although her body wasn't making any move to do so. "It's already ten."

"My shower works just fine."

Ali laughed. "But I don't have any clothes."

"And that's a problem why?"

She slapped his chest lightly.

Rafe grabbed her hand and rolled her on top of him. "Come with me. I'll get you nice and clean." He scooped her up and brought her to the large walk-in shower in his bathroom.

Ali stood back while Rafe started the water and waited for it to warm up. The water was tepid at first, but as he held her in his arms, the heat gradually fell upon them, steaming up the clear glass doors.

Ali's hands traveled lazily all over Rafe's wet body, enjoying the feel of his hard skin beneath her. His own hands lathered her skin with the body wash he kept on the shower shelf. She inhaled the masculine scent and smiled at the thought of smelling like him all day. She tilted her head up to kiss him, and as the water rained down between their bodies, she couldn't ever remember feeling so intimate with someone. Her heart was full as she kissed him. What was happening to her? She'd had the greatest sex of her life with this man, not just once, but again and again, and now she was standing in the shower with him and feeling...what? Like she didn't want it to ever end? Like she'd found her soul mate? She squeezed her eyes shut tighter as she kissed him, their moisture mixing in with the water.

Ali was kissing him so tenderly and with such feeling, that it hit Rafe right in the gut. He closed his arms around her tight and savored her lips and tongue. She felt so good against him, her lithe body fitting perfectly against his, and he wondered how something like this could happen so quickly. No woman had ever evoked the kind of feelings from him that Ali was capable of. God, he had to be careful. He couldn't let his feelings cloud his mind. He was here to do a job, and he couldn't let her be a distraction. He gently washed her exquisite body, then pulled away to rinse the soap from her. When he finished he reluctantly shut the water off, stepping out first and producing an extra-large towel to wrap her in.

"Umm, thank you, I feel sufficiently clean." She smiled and kissed him on the cheek.

He smiled back and inwardly cursed. This was not going to be easy. He watched as she put his shirt on again and slipped her dress on underneath, wearing it like a skirt. She picked up her sandals and walked to the bedroom door frame. "I'm going to go across and change. Do you want to come?"

More than anything he did. "I've got a little work to do first. Can I see you later?"

"Sure." Ali ran her fingers through her wet hair like a comb and tried not to let her disappointment show. Why should she feel bad? He wasn't going to spend every minute of the day with her, and he did ask to see her later. Jeez, she had it bad.

"I might come down to the beach later. Maybe I'll see you then." She attempted to sound nonchalant, as if she'd be doing her own thing anyway.

Rafe noticed the slight change in her demeanor and knew that it was his fault. He should go with her, damn it, but he was holding back

-- for both their own good, he told himself.

"That sounds good. I just have some things to prepare for Miami tomorrow."

"Oh, I didn't realize you were going there tomorrow."

"I'll be gone 'til the afternoon, then I have a few things to do on the islands."

"Oh." Ali knew she was acting petulant all of a sudden, and she couldn't help it. Get a grip, she yelled at herself. You had an incredible night -- be gracious! She smiled and walked over to kiss him. "I hope I see you later. I had an unforgettable time," she said, meaning it.

"Me too." It came out as a whisper as he bent to kiss her longingly. She sounded cavalier all of a sudden, and he knew he should say something to make it right.

They pulled apart and he reluctantly walked her to the front door. "Ali, I..." Rafe was at a loss for words. There was so much he wanted to say, but what would she think?

She looked at him questioningly. Just say it, just say it, she pleaded with her eyes. Let me know I didn't just make a huge mistake. What did he want to say? She knew he must be feeling something, too, maybe not like she was, but something. But he only gave her a crooked smile, so she waved, hiding her disappointment again. Rather than continuing to stand there looking like she was waiting for him to say something, she hurried down his front steps and across the driveway to Nan's, berating herself for being such a glutton.

Rafe shut his door, leaning against it, running a hand through his hair. He felt like a piece of shit. The best night of his life, and he let her walk away without telling her. She *should* be pissed at him.

He went to find his phone, and he checked his e-mails while sitting on the living room couch. Glad to see there was nothing of importance, he brought the monitors up and used the remote to go back to the images captured the night before. He watched as the SUV pulled onto D'nafrio's property and parked, and saw his own truck drive by shortly after. He could see that the passenger had kept himself occupied with a magazine. Rafe could just make out the nude image on the front cover. God, these two were idiots, he thought.

He hit the fast-forward and stopped when a movement beyond the SUV caught his eye. He sat up as he recognized the images of Matt and Nicki enter the frame. Shit, they must have used the access just before his when they left the bar, not wanting to come through his yard. He watched as Matt turned toward the truck, his lips moving and not looking too happy. Rafe could only guess what had happened. He saw Matt's arm go protectively around Nicki's waist as they crossed the street.

Shitheads, he thought with some unease. Matt would have kicked their asses, but considering they were probably carrying, he was grateful Matt had not approached them.

Rafe continued to check the footage, this time from the beach angle, and saw his fellow agents out "fishing" the shoreline in their center console. The boat was a 25-foot Boston Whaler, and Rafe noticed the absence of the dive flag off the stern, but he knew his good friend Mike, the avid diver, would be down under searching the area where the refugees had come ashore. He wondered if he found anything and kept watching. He watched as two other agents repeatedly cast off the bow, and he saw one actually reel something in. Rafe smiled, knowing whoever it was, he was probably enjoying that particular assignment. It was awhile before Rafe saw him come up, and Rafe recognized the shocking blond hair that was Mike's. Even wet, one couldn't miss it.

The boat floated in the Gulf with its side hull facing the camera, so Rafe was able to see Mike emerge in full dive gear, climbing the short ladder at the stern into the boat, and he wasn't empty-handed. Rafe could see he was holding something, although it was dark in color and Rafe couldn't quite make it out. He zoomed in as much as he could, pausing the frame, and could only make out the square shape. It was about the size of a box that maybe a basketball would come in. Once inside the Whaler, in short order the other two agents reeled in and they took off toward North Captiva. Mike had been fast and discreet.

So the refugee had been telling the truth about a package. Rafe got on the phone, bringing the real-time images back to the scene. Rafe put in a call to the SAC. "It's McDonough. I just watched the footage in the Gulf. What did they find?"

"MDMA, a special mix, we haven't seen before, and about 4 kilos of it. The DEA lab has it as a 3-2-2 mix, MDMA, meth, and hydrocodone."

"Jesus, Ecstasy? What the hell were Cuban refugees doing with 4 kilos of 'x'? How many pills is that?" Rafe knew the "feel-good drug" was prevalent in Miami, especially in the club scene. Most people who took it touted its endurance effect and being able to party all day and night while experiencing a feeling of euphoria. Rafe also knew it wasn't uncommon for the pills to be enhanced with other drugs like methamphetamines and common prescription drugs such as hydrocodone, or "Vicodin," as it was more commonly called.

"A bit over 14,000, and apparently they were promised five grand to deliver it."

"I suppose we don't know by whom yet." That would be too easy.

"All we've got so far is that the refugees were approached by a woman who offered them five thousand dollars in cash to take the package. She told them she would provide the boat, and the coordinates to leave the box. When they made it to land, they would be picked up and driven off the island to a motel in Fort Myers, where they would have a room waiting for them with five Gs inside. All they had to do was get the key at the front desk. The person on duty would be expecting them."

"Okay, first, how is it that the box was where they left it, and not riding the tides back to Cuba?" Rafe was standing now at the wall of glass that looked out at the Gulf. It had to have been weighted down somehow.

"They were instructed to place the box inside a crab trap that would be marked by a purple buoy. The box was airtight and plastic, in a waterproofed shell."

Holy shit, of course, the very same buoys Ali had been inquiring about yesterday, when all he could think about was...shit. "So someone placed a trap out there just for this package." He tried to recall from the footage when they could have placed the package in the trap, and he tried to think of anything he may have seen in the last three weeks on the surveillance footage. Nothing came to mind.

"I know what you're thinking, and you didn't miss anything. I've gone over the footage myself. The trap must have been put in place weeks ago, before you even arrived. We're running the registrations on all the surrounding traps. Mike took them down last night. And if you look again at the footage of them getting out of the Zodiac, you'll see one guy swim around from the back. We all thought they'd cut the motor and he was just guiding them in, but that's most likely when they placed the package."

Rafe pictured the footage. One man had been at the back, and it had appeared as if he'd been hanging on to the vessel, perhaps kicking his way in with it. Son of a bitch.

"And what about the motel and the money? Any leads there?"

"We've questioned the staff, and there was a room booked but unoccupied. Whoever left the money was either waiting to see if everything went as arranged and when the refugees didn't show, took the money back, or they never left any money in the first place, knowing the refugees would never make it there. The motel has one security camera at the front desk, and that's being looked at. We're going over all the bookings for the past couple of days and questioning the employees. Apparently, one woman got called out on an emergency during her shift that night, something to do with her kid. She's the only one we haven't spoken to yet. Her name is Misty Spencer.

"And what about the woman who approached the Cuban?"

"We've got a pretty good description, and know that she approached the Cuban man at the tobacco plant he works at back in April -- this has been in the works. We're checking the airlines for flights in and out of Cuba for that month. Once we sift through it, we'll see if there's any connections to D'nafrio. Until then we just watch and wait."

"I think it's time to make contact with Stoddman. I'll make an appointment for tomorrow after the meeting."

"That's fine, but tell him you can't go beyond the three-million-dollar range -- you aren't up for a raise for another six months."

"C'mon, Daniels, if I'm going to buy on Captiva, it's gotta be on the beach. Three million is going to be tough; I was thinking along the lines of six to seven mil." Rafe laughed as they joked about the absurdity of the notion.

Daniels laughed with him. "That ought to get Stoddman salivating."

"No doubt, maybe Ms. Mann will be in the office, too. Call me if you get anything else."

When Rafe got off the phone, he sat back on the sofa to think. It made sense to him that Holly Mann would be the woman in Cuba and that perhaps her son or the friend had hired the driver of the Ford, so who was the shadow on the beach, and was D'nafrio indeed orchestrating this whole deal? He'd make one more phone call and hopefully have some answers tomorrow.

He dialed Information and got patched through to East End Realty. It was just about eleven-thirty on Sunday, and Rafe wondered as the phone kept ringing if they worked on Sundays. He left a message when the machine came on, telling him their hours were from noon to five. He left his real name since there wasn't any reason to lie. He wasn't really intending on buying anything, so his identity was safe. "I'm interested in looking at some beachfront property in Captiva tomorrow. Please call me back if this is convenient." He left the number to his beach house and his cell. He was sure he'd get a call back. He didn't see anyone turning away the prospect of making a commission on a beach house in Captiva.

He felt good about the case and had a feeling it was all going to come to a head soon. He was at that familiar midway point, where things started to fall into place. When the case was over he would get his real vacation time, and he knew he was definitely going to spend it on Captiva. There was no way he could leave here now. His stomach knotted up with the thought of when he would have to leave Ali. He knew after his three to four weeks he'd have to go back to New York, but he didn't want to think that far ahead just yet. He'd have to make the most of his time here with her, starting today. He had to go apologize for his lousy goodbye this morning and to tell her how much last night had meant to him. He got off the couch and went to change into his bathing suit and a T-shirt. He put his phone in his pocket and went out the door. The rest of the day was his, and he was going to spend every minute of it with Ali.

Ali returned to a quiet house. She noticed the convertible was not in the driveway and figured either Nicki or Matt took it to get the paper. When she got inside and walked into the living room, she noticed Nicki's yoga mat on the pool deck and thought maybe she was in the shower and Matt had taken the car.

She wandered down the hall and poked her head in Nicki's room. The room was empty, and her bed was made. Ali went across the hall to Matt's room. His room was also empty, but his bed was unmade. Ali couldn't use that as conclusive evidence, but she smiled, thinking she knew what had gone on, and now they were out together. The realization put a smile on her face. She wished she were spending more time with Rafe right now. She tried not to let it bother her that he hadn't come with her.

Oh, well, she thought, I'll just beach it by myself and hope to see him later. She went to her room and took off Rafe's shirt, changing into her bathing suit. She slipped on a pair of shorts, put her hair into a ponytail, then picked his shirt up again, inhaling the fresh soapy scent of him. She had it pressed to her face when she heard the doorbell chime, startling her. She dropped the shirt on her bed and headed down the hall to the door. A great big smile spread across her face when she saw Rafe on the other side dressed for the beach.

"Hi."

"Hi." Rafe took her in. She looked pretty cute with her hair pulled back off her face.

"Done with work stuff?"

"Yeah, I did it as fast as I could."

"I'm glad you're done. Come in -- Nicki and Matt aren't here." She couldn't believe he was here, just when she was doubting their incredible night.

"Yeah, I noticed the convertible was gone."

"They must have gone for a ride. I was just getting ready for the beach. Want to help?"

Rafe followed her into the kitchen. "Sure, but first I want to apologize."

Ali stopped, heart thumping, and turned to face him. "Apologize? For what?" She took in his expression; he looked pretty serious.

"For letting you leave this morning the way I did."

Ali's heart soared. "What do you mean?" She knew just what he meant, but was dying to hear what he would say.

Rafe took a deep breath. "I wish I had told you that I wanted to come back here with you, because I did, more than anything. I really did have work to do, but I should have asked you to stay until I finished, and then I would have come here with you."

"Rafe, I completely understand about your work. Don't even think twice about it -- there is absolutely no need to apologize." But she was glad he did just the same.

He still wasn't saying quite what he wanted to say. "I'm not apologizing for work."

He noted her look of confusion. Why was this so hard to do? "I'm apologizing for not telling you how I felt." He cleared his throat. "How I *feel*," he corrected himself.

Oh, boy. Ali leaned against the counter, not taking her eyes from him.

"Last night, and this morning..." He watched her smile. "It was something else, I mean, really something else, and I just wanted you to know I didn't think it was anything less." Shit, this was not coming out the way he wanted. "I guess I'm trying to ask you to keep seeing me while we're both here. I would really like that -- I really like you and would like to spend a lot more time with you."

"I would like that very much. I really like you, too, Rafe, and while we're being honest," Ali took a deep breath herself, "I have never had a night like last night, it was pretty..." She wanted to say special, momentous, earth-shattering, or absolutely life-changing but wanted him to actually stay and not run out of the house scared. "Well, I'll never forget it." She settled on safe and hoped she conveyed her feelings. By the intense look in his eyes, she just may have. Oh, God, she was falling hard.

Rafe wondered what she really wanted to say. She definitely had just held back on him, but then again, there was so much more he could have said, too. He took the few steps toward her that separated them. "I'm really happy you feel that way. I won't forget last night, either." He bent to kiss her and pulled her up against him as he did.

Ali's heart was beating so fast, she was still reveling in his words. She was so glad it wasn't just going to be a one-night stand. She was sure something had happened between them on a much deeper level, and he had just confirmed it for her. Maybe there was something there -- only time would tell.

"What can I do to help?" he asked, pulling away, feeling better now that he'd told her somewhat of how he felt.

Ali smiled. "I'm just going to make sandwiches and pack a cooler.

I'll leave a note for them." She turned to the refrigerator and rifled through it for ingredients, a smile plastered to her face.

"Cooler in the garage?" Rafe headed to the door off the kitchen.

"It should be," Ali called out. "I'll take a couple of chairs and an umbrella too. There's a new one leaning against the wall out there."

"I've got chairs, no sense in dragging yours over," he called back. Rafe found the cooler and umbrella and noticed all the fishing gear along the back wall. "Maybe Matt and I can put some of those rods to use," he said, coming back in with the cooler and umbrella.

"He'd love to have someone to go fishing with," Ali told him. She made sandwiches for everybody and placed them in the cooler with some ice.

"No vodka and lemonade today?" he teased.

Ali rolled her eyes. "No. As a matter of fact, I'd love to go for a run tonight just before sunset. You interested?"

"Absolutely -- I'll race you!" he challenged.

"You're on, sucker!" she laughed, thinking of how she'd dismantle him at the start line.

"What's so funny?" he grinned.

"The vision of you trying to catch up to me."

"You're awfully sure of yourself." Rafe shook his head. "You know, I held the best time at Quantico."

"Are you trying to get me to stay here and skip the beach?" she asked him, desire in her voice and eyes.

He laughed. "You're nuts, but if that's what turns you on, I'll tell you all about my training at Quantico -- whatever you want."

She knew he was kidding, but she looked him up and down seductively, pretending to think about it. "You know what, as tempting as that is, I'm looking forward to spending time with you on the beach today."

He went to her and kissed her. "Later, then." He picked up the full cooler easily and waited in the hall for her.

Ali's heart skipped just thinking about "later." "I have to get my bag and leave them a note." She scribbled a quick note, letting Matt and Nicki know where they'd be and that she had packed them a lunch. She stuck it on the fridge with a magnet, got her bag and umbrella, and followed Rafe out, shutting the door behind her.

CHAPTER FOURTEEN

After they had finished breakfast, Nicki and Matt had gone in and out of all the little shops in the small plaza, just poking around and looking at the souvenirs. He had held her hand while they walked around, and Nicki was in seventh heaven. Even after the night they'd shared, she still couldn't believe she was here with him, window shopping, of all things.

"Let's get out of here and get on the beach," he suggested.

"Umm, that sounds great," Nicki told him. "Maybe Ali and Rafe will join us."

"They're probably already out there," Matt said, walking to the car. "They just had to roll over this morning, and they were on the sand," he exaggerated.

"I know." Nicki laughed. "Can you imagine having a house on the beach?"

"Oh, I can imagine." He laughed as he opened the car door for her, then got in on his own side. Truth was, he had already found a piece of land on the beach for a second home, only it was on Cape Cod, not Captiva. He wondered if Nicki liked the Cape.

Nicki put the radio on as Matt left the parking lot, and they drove most of the way back in silence. Nicki thought about their breakfast conversation and couldn't stop smiling. She stole a glance at him and was once again struck at how handsome he was. She wondered what their kids would look like and then blushed furiously as he turned to catch her staring.

"What was that look?" he asked, grinning.

"Just can't take my eyes off you," she teased, and he gave her the grin she loved. God, if he only knew what she'd been thinking, he'd probably be on the next plane. They pulled into the driveway and she noticed the time. "It's noon already? How can that be?" They had lingered over breakfast, and she had enjoyed listening to him tell her all about his business. She had asked him a gazillion questions about it and had laughed when he told her she was going to make a great reporter. She hadn't thought they were in the shops all that long, but time obviously had flown.

"Who's thinking about time? It's endless here," he remarked as they got out of the car and walked up the path to the front of the house.

Nicki only wished that were true. She unlocked the front door, and he followed her in.

"Ali?" she called out and didn't receive an answer.

Matt walked into the kitchen and saw the note on the fridge. "They're at the beach."

Nicki turned to see him reading the note.

"She made us lunch." He grinned at Nicki and put the note on the counter. He slowly walked toward her, and she started backing up down the hall toward her bedroom. She was laughing at his knowing look.

"I believe you said you were going to skip lunch."

"She probably went to a lot of trouble." Nicki was almost to her doorway.

Matt grabbed her before she could get away. "I'm not hungry for lunch at all."

"Me, either." She grinned, giddy with anticipation.

"So are you up for a repeat performance?" he asked, kissing her neck, his voice thick with desire.

She nodded yes as he guided her away from her room and into his own. He shut the door behind him, locked it, then went to the windows, where he tightened the shutters, closing out most of the light.

He turned to Nicki. "Lie down."

Nicki raised her eyebrows. "Is that an order?"

"It is," he answered, and she watched as he lifted the T-shirt he wore off his perfect body. She lay back on the bed obediently, impatient for his touch.

Matt straddled her hips and lifted her tank top off, then reached around her back to unhook her bra. He was enjoying the look of surprise on her face as he discarded the bra and adjusted his body so he could peel first her shorts off, then her underwear. In the filtered light of the room, he studied her.

Nicki watched his hot gaze travel over her body, up and down, and she felt desire wash over her.

"I'm going to make you feel so good," he said.

Nicki's body tensed in anticipation. Oh, God, what was he going to do? Last night he had driven her to the edge and back, and she'd felt completely vulnerable. She watched as his head bent down to her breasts, and she placed her hands through his hair, massaging his head and neck. He kissed her breasts until they were red and swollen with pleasure, then his hands took over as he inched his lips down her belly and she quivered at their soft touch. She was aware of the weight of him between her legs as he moved his way down. He paused to look up at her as his hands found their way to her hips, and he rubbed his thumbs over the bones that protruded there. Nicki let herself relax when she looked into his eyes.

What she saw there made her reach a hand to his cheek, and she held it there, not wanting him to stop looking at her like that. There was more than desire in his eyes, and if she let herself believe what it was, she just might cry. She returned his look and saw the glimmer that took over in his eyes as he broke the gaze, only to place his open mouth between her legs, his tongue finding and tasting the wetness that covered her. Holy God! She lifted herself eagerly to him in response, gripping his head as he made love to her expertly with his mouth and tongue. She whimpered in complete and utter ecstasy, which only spurred him on.

Matt tasted the sweet juices flowing from her and was rewarded with her cries. He placed his hands under her firm little ass and pulled her as close as he could, burying his face in her. He loved how her body reacted to him, and he didn't want to stop pleasing her. He pulled his mouth away to kiss the silky skin of her inner thighs.

"Matt," Nicki whispered, "I want you."

"I want you, too, sweetheart, but I'm not done yet."

Nicki moaned at that. She didn't know how much more she could take. Her body felt like a limp noodle.

Matt brought a hand up to caress her smooth mound and parted the little strip of hair that covered it. His finger found the little nub at the center and he slowly rubbed it back and forth, feeling it swell beneath his touch until Nicki cried out again.

Nicki gripped his shoulders and dug in. "You have to stop," she breathed.

Matt's response was to grin and to rub her again, only this time a little faster. He smiled in satisfaction as her whole body bucked beneath him.

Nicki reached down and put a death grip on his wrist. "You are in so much trouble," she told him, sitting up and breathing hard. She pushed him forcefully down on his back and pulled his shorts off roughly, surprising him. She reached over to his nightstand, found what she was looking for, and, instead of one, pulled out the whole box. "And by the way, we are going to use every one of these."

Matt's brows shot up and he almost laughed, but he saw the determined look on her face and wisely kept his mouth shut and his eyes wide open. He watched as she tore one package open with her teeth and rolled it down the hard length of him. He groaned at what she was about to do, and he grabbed her hips, holding on, as he watched her lower herself onto him.

Nicki was fraught with desire for him. He had just turned her body to Jell-O, and she was going to try to return the favor. He started to move underneath her, and she stopped him by moving his hands off her hips. She took them and clasped them with her own, placing them above his head as she lowered her chest to his. "Let me," she told him.

Matt gladly let her take control and was pleasantly surprised at her aggressiveness. However, she moved herself over him in such a way, slowly and methodically, contracting herself around him, using muscles that...holy shit! He found himself coming fast and furious. "Jeez-uss! What the hell was *that*?" he panted, exasperated. He wasn't even inside her five minutes.

She smiled satisfactorily. "*That* was years of dancing and muscle control. It's all in the hips, you know." She kissed his forehead and slid off him. "I'm going to get ready for the beach."

He watched her walk out of his room, bare-assed, and tried to figure out what the hell she had just done to him. He managed to get into the shower and shave, and met Nicki in the kitchen a short while later.

"Look at that, it's only twelve forty-five," Nicki declared, smiling at Matt in a teasing way.

"Yeah, well, we'd still be in there if you didn't take me out with that kamikaze move." He pretended to be upset.

Nicki kissed him on the lips. "You get what you give, darlin'." She was on cloud nine and enjoying their banter.

"Did you like what I gave?" He watched the pink rise to her cheeks and grinned, his eyes searching hers.

Just the thought of what he'd done had her hot all over again. "You can't lay those eyes on me like that, it's just not fair," she complained. "And oh, my God, yes," she whispered.

"*What*?" he asked, holding a hand to his ear.

"You heard me." She laughed softly.

"No, no, I didn't, could you repeat that?" he teased her.

"I think my response was evidence of how much I liked it," she told him, heading out the front door.

Matt followed, smiling, remembering her response. "Are you in love with me yet? Because that was some of my best work."

Yes. Nicki didn't dare turn around to answer him. She just kept walking. "I told you it was going to take a lot of time and effort, but that was a definite start in the right direction." She laughed as he grabbed her ass playfully crossing the street.

"I've got a lot of staying power. I'm in this to win."

She gave him a sidelong look and a crooked smile.

"That move wasn't fair. You can't judge me on that," he sighed. He'd get her back for that one. He couldn't wait.

They went through Rafe's gate, down through the pool gate, and over to the sand.

They could see Ali and Rafe set up a few feet ahead.

"Don't worry, you'll have plenty of chances to redeem yourself." She smiled, tickling him, and in one motion he scooped her up and ran full throttle to the water, with her screaming all the way.

Ali and Rafe turned at Nicki's screams and laughed as Matt buzzed by, carrying her.

"Oh, that's just cruel." Ali laughed, watching them. Suddenly Rafe's body was blocking her view. "What are you doing?" She gripped the sides of her chair.

"I think we need to cool off, too." He picked her up easily out of her chair and threw her over his shoulder.

She pounded his backside. "Rafe!" she screamed, laughing. "It's gonna be cold!"

Rafe ran into the water and deposited her next to Matt and Nicki. She came up from under and jumped on him, knocking him down and submerging him with her body. "Gotcha!"

They were all laughing and splashing around, enjoying the water and each other.

"Oh! It's chilly in here." Ali shivered, rubbing her goose bumps.

"Ali, the water is eighty degrees, for God's sake." Matt splashed her.

"I've been baking in the sun," she laughed. "It feels cold to me."

Rafe pulled her back against his chest and wrapped his arms around her. "Better?"

"Yes, thank you." She stuck her tongue out at Matt. "Where were you two this morning?"

"Breakfast," Nicki answered, her eyes meeting Ali's as she tried not to giggle.

"Where were *you* this morning is the question." Matt said. "Mom called, and I didn't know what to tell her."

Rafe laughed in Ali's hair, catching the look Matt shot him.

"What?" Ali asked, horrified.

"Don't listen to him!" Nicki laughed and splashed Matt. He pretended he was going to dunk her under.

"Oh, that so wasn't funny." She may be an adult, but she still didn't want her mother thinking she hadn't come home last night.

They all hung out in the water for awhile, talking and having a good time, then headed up to the sand, where they sat in the chairs Rafe had brought down.

"Oh, this is going to feel good," Nicki said lazily as she removed her wet T-shirt and shorts to reveal her bikini underneath. She plopped down on a beach chair, positioned it under the sun's rays and lay back, her body instantly warming under the hot sun.

"Matt, what do you think about some fishing this week?" Rafe asked him.

"Oh, man, that would be great. Are you interested in getting a boat?"

"Sure, we can go right up the street to Jensens. I'm in Miami for part of the day tomorrow and then I have some appointments on the island, but how's Tuesday?"

"I'm free!" he smiled.

"You guys can use whatever Nan has in the garage. That's what it's there for," Nicki told them.

"Are there any surf casters in there?" Matt asked.

"You're asking the wrong person," Nicki said. "They all look the same to me."

Matt laughed. "Rafe, let's go check and see. If there are, we'll bring 'em down and fish right now."

"What about bait?" Ali asked.

"I saw a tackle box -- there's got to be some lures in there," Rafe said.

"We'll be right back, ladies." Matt headed off the sand, and Rafe followed, calling back.

"Hey, Nicki."

When she looked up at him, he yelled, "Thank you!" then he winked at Ali and kept walking.

Nicki turned to Ali with a sly grin. "Why is he thanking me?"

Ali shook her head, laughing. "He's thanking you for the porn star makeover you talked me into getting."

"Ooo-kay!" Nicki sang. "Spill it!" She got up and moved under the umbrella where Ali sat.

Ali looked at Nicki. "You…have…no…idea," and then her eyes widened and she said quickly, "and if you do, I'm happy for you, but keep it to yourself."

Nicki winked. "Fair enough, and didn't I tell you that trip to the salon wouldn't go unnoticed?"

Ali rolled her eyes, laughing, "Yeah, it was a big hit." She proceeded to tell Nicki every detail about her fabulous night and her equally exquisite morning.

Nicki whistled. "He sounds way too hot to handle!"

Ali laughed. "I'm telling you, it's even hotter than you think."

Nicki tilted her head. "Elaborate, please."

"He's an FBI agent," Ali whispered excitedly.

"Shut up!" Nicki's mouth hung open. "I thought he was some kind of research consultant or something like that."

Ali shook her head no. "And he's part of a special SWAT team."

"You are totally making this up!" Nicki laughed and thought if Ali were to describe her fantasy man, then Rafe was it.

"I swear to you, he told me last night. He didn't want to scare me away telling me right off."

"My God, Ali, it's your fantasy come to life -- that's kind of weird," Nicki said seriously, scrunching up her face.

"I know!" Ali shook her head. "I still can't believe it. I think I'm in real trouble here Nick."

Nicki knew just where she was coming from. "Ali, I know just how you feel."

"Oh?" Ali smiled, but Nicki wanted to hear more about Rafe.

"So did he tell you anything about his job?" she asked with interest.

Ali hesitated. "Just that he's here investigating someone."

"Really?" Nicki looked back toward the beach house. "Someone on the island?" There was a note of disbelief in her voice.

Ali could see Nicki kicking into reporter mode. "Please don't ask me any more. I probably shouldn't even know what I know," Ali pleaded.

"You're killing me right now, you know that, right?" Nicki sighed. "This will be all I think about."

Ali gave her a wry grin. "Something tells me it won't be all you're thinking about." She hoped she could change the subject.

Nicki gave her a smirk. "All right, I understand." Then she smiled. "You're right -- lucky for you, I do have other things to occupy my mind."

"So things went well last night?" Ali asked.

"Your brother is..." Nicki searched for the appropriate words.

"Oh, please, Nicki." Ali cringed.

"No, listen," she laughed. "He's caring and thoughtful and...incredible! I can say that, right?" She laughed, seeing Ali's face contort. "I just didn't expect to see a serious side to him. He's very intelligent and knows so much about business."

"He's been around it and in it for so long," Ali put in. She couldn't believe Matt and Nicki were actually starting something -- it was great.

"I know, but I never saw that side of him. I only knew him as the wise-ass who teased us relentlessly."

"You always gave it back to him, though," Ali laughed. "He liked that."

"Well, he was always so sure of himself, and all those girls he went out with, it used to drive me crazy!" Nicki huffed.

"It did?"

"Yes! I wanted to be them!"

"Oh, Nicki," Ali said sympathetically.

"You know what I've come to realize?"

Ali's brow lifted.

"If something had happened between us back then, it probably wouldn't be happening now, and I'm thankful to have the opportunity as an adult, if you know what I'm saying." She grinned.

Ali laughed. "I know what you're saying, and you're right. What the hell did we know back then? And for that matter, what the hell did he know back then?"

"I'm quite sure that he knew plenty back then. Only now, he's a master at his craft." Nicki grinned.

"I'm going to pretend you are talking about his carpentry experience and end this conversation." Ali said, smiling at her best friend. She loved picturing them as a couple and hoped it turned out that way.

"Okay, okay," Nicki relented. "What's for lunch?"

The guys returned shortly, poles and tackle box in hand, and Matt sneaked up behind Nicki's chair, stealing the sandwich she was holding. "I thought you were going to skip lunch," he teased.

Nicki tilted her head back to see him. "I worked up an appetite." She smiled. "Did you find everything you needed?"

"Yeah, we're just going to do some casting. If you want, I'll fix you up a rod." He took a big bite of her sandwich and handed it back to her.

Nicki gave him a smirk at his choice of words, and he laughed when he realized what he'd said.

"Your bad." He smiled.

Nicki took in the sight of him with his shirt off and his already tanned torso; he looked like he'd been on the island for a week instead of a day. She couldn't see his eyes behind his sunglasses, but she knew he was looking at her in much the same way. "Go fish," she told him with a crooked smile.

Matt bent down and kissed her right on the lips, and laughed at the shocked look on her face. He walked toward the water with his pole, knowing she was probably bright red and checking to see if Ali had seen him kiss her, which he made sure she had.

Ali had indeed seen Matt kiss Nicki, and now Nicki wouldn't meet her eyes. Ali thought it was great, and she just laughed as she looked up at Rafe. "Hungry?"

"Not yet. I'm going to cast for awhile. Do you mind?" He put a hand on her shoulder and rubbed it gently, sending a current right through her.

She smiled up at him and his touch. "Of course not. I'm going to soak up some more sun." Ali was happy Rafe was going to spend some time with Matt. She really wanted Matt to like him. If she had Matt's stamp of approval, chances were the rest of her family would approve, too. Of course she *was* getting ahead of herself, but she couldn't help feeling optimistic. She watched as he took two beers from the cooler and walked to the shoreline, where he handed one to Matt.

"That man has some intense eyes." Nicki commented.

"Oh, yes, he does," Ali agreed, looking after him. Both he and Matt made quite a pair standing at the shoreline fishing together.

"Your brother damn near melts me when he looks at me with those eyes of *his*," Nicki sighed.

"Yes, I've noticed how he's been looking at you. I have to say he seems..." Ali thought about it. She'd never seen Matt look at any woman that way, actually. Wow, could he actually feel the same way that Nicki did?

"He seems what?" Nicki sat up at full attention, watching Ali's face. If anyone knew Matt, it was his own sister, and Nicki was dying to know what Ali thought.

"I don't know, pretty into you, I guess, for lack of a better way to put it."

"I'll take that." Nicki laughed and then asked seriously, "Do you really think so?"

Ali smiled at the question. She could see that Nicki was still unsure about Matt's feelings for her. Maybe he hadn't quite let on the extent of them yet, but Ali knew he would; it was just a matter of time. She felt a little envious at their budding relationship. They had the advantage of being friends and knowing each other for many years. Ali wished she knew Rafe as well, so she wouldn't have that tenuous feeling she got when she thought about the end of his time on the island, which would no doubt be soon. She knew she was setting herself up for major heartbreak, but she wasn't going to pass up the chance to be with him while he was here. It felt too good, in every manner.

Ali had a feeling Rafe thought so, too. She could tell he had wanted to say more to her in the kitchen, but he'd held back. She could only imagine what he would have said. If it was anything like what she wanted to say, she understood his hesitation. It was crazy to think in such a short amount of time two people could know for sure how they felt about each other, wasn't it? But the truth was, she did know exactly how she felt, and she prayed Rafe felt the same way. As if he knew she was thinking about him, he turned around and winked at her, spreading a smile across her face.

"Yeah, I really think so, Nick." She smiled at Nicki and lay back in her chair. Maybe she and Nicki would get exactly what they wanted this summer.

Nicki sat back, too, her face to the sun, praying Ali was right. Could Matt really settle down? And would he choose her to do it with? Or would he break her heart…again? He had seemed so sincere at breakfast, and she had taken it all in, wanting to believe he could love her. The way in which he had pleasured her just that morning surely was an indication of his feelings. She had seen the look in his eyes, and it had floored her. How could she have doubts after he'd looked at her that way? It just felt too good to be true, that's why. Was it just because they were here in Captiva? And what would happen when he returned to Boston? She didn't even want to think about it.

"So what's up for tonight?" she asked, trying to think in the present.

"I don't know. We should all go out again, maybe go out to eat. Let's ask them."

"I can almost guarantee they'll want to." Nicki laughed. "Remember, Matt's been inside our refrigerator."

"You're right." Ali laughed, too, getting up. "Maybe we can take a ride to the lighthouse after we eat. I love that beach -- it has the best shells."

"That's sounds great. We should eat at Sweet Melissa's," Nicki said, getting up, too. It was her favorite restaurant on Sanibel. "Then we can scope out my new workplace on the way to the lighthouse."

"That sounds good. The food is incredible there. I want to see where the Beach News is, too. What time do you start tomorrow?"

"I have to be in at nine. That's not so bad," Nicki said as they approached Matt and Rafe.

"What's not so bad?" Matt asked without turning around.

"Poor Nicki having to go to work at nine tomorrow." Ali made a sad face at Nicki, who dutifully stuck her tongue out in return.

"I've got that beat," Rafe told them. "I have to be in Miami at nine."

"Ooh," the three groaned collectively.

"We'll be thinking of you working stiffs, won't we, Al?" Matt reeled in his rod and picked up his beer.

"Of course we will. We won't do anything fun without you guys -- we promise." She winked at Rafe.

"Sure we will. We're going parasailing." Matt turned to Ali, who gave him a skeptical look.

"What? You don't think I'd do it?"

"*You* would, but I have zero interest in that," Ali told him.

"Why not?" Rafe asked, laughing a little, "Don't you want to see all the sharks swimming out there?"

"Sharks?" Matt asked.

Then Nicki laughed. "That was good, Rafe. You just rendered them pool side all day tomorrow. Now we won't have to be jealous."

"That was the plan." He laughed at the look still on Matt's face. "You can see everything from up there. My friend Mike has done it, and he says if people only knew what they were swimming with, they'd never step foot in the water again."

"Thanks for that." Matt sounded discouraged, "I'm just going to stay in and hide under the covers tomorrow."

They all laughed as they headed back to the chairs.

"Do you girls want to go out to dinner? Rafe and I feel like some seafood."

"We were just going to ask you both the same thing. We were thinking Sweet Melissa's, and afterward maybe we could take a drive to the lighthouse." Nicki settled back in her chair and Matt took one, bringing it up beside her.

"Sounds good to me." Matt looked to Ali and Rafe, who nodded their approval.

"What about our race?" Rafe asked Ali.

"Let's go now," she offered. "I'll run across and change and meet you in the driveway."

He smiled. "You got it."

"Want me to take the poles back?" Ali asked the guys.

"I'll bring them over with me," Matt answered, waving her off.

Ali walked with Rafe back up to the pool area and left him to go change into some running clothes while she did the same. By the time she'd tied her sneakers, he was already waiting in the driveway.

"It's hot," she said, coming to meet him.

"You sure you have the energy?" he teased.

"I run even faster in the heat," she lied with a grin. They started off in a jog to warm up.

"We'll stop at the Crazy Flamingo and start on that side street," he said, teasing her.

"It's Lazy," she laughed.

"What is?"

"The restaurant. Lazy Flamingo."

"Right." He grinned. "You ready to get your nice little ass handed to you?"

"Them's fightin' words." She grinned.

They got to their starting point, and she bent down to stretch her legs. Rafe did the same and waited for her signal. He smiled as she put a hand on his shoulder for balance while she stretched her quads one at a time. When she leaned in, he thought she was going to kiss him, but instead she whispered in his ear.

"Tonight, after dinner and the beach, I was thinking you and I could go back to your spa and I could..." She explained in erotic detail what she could do to him, her breath hot in his ear and her lips just touching his skin, sending a jolt from his brain to his cock, and then she removed her hand from his shoulder, placed one foot in front of the other, and yelled, "Go!"

Rafe's eyes were wide, watching her run, but his own legs wouldn't cooperate, due to the fact that a different part of his anatomy was now in command. Her words had taken him by surprise and sent a signal right down south. He had to walk over to the side of the road and sit down as he watched her running at full throttle away from him. He shook his head in disbelief at his good luck. She was awesome, and he hoped she wasn't kidding.

Ali jogged back moments later with a satisfied grin on her face. "Watch out for fire ants down there." She nodded her head at his resting spot while trying to contain her laughter, well aware of what she had done to him.

Rafe stood up, standing very close, his full height looming over her. "That was just plain dirty cheating," he said in his low, deep voice.

She laughed. "Did I shock you?"

He looked down between them so she'd follow his gaze. "What do you think?"

She grinned. "You're right -- that wasn't fair. I take it back. Let's start over. Competition brings out the worst in me." She was feeling immensely embarrassed now at her bold declaration.

"Oh, no, you don't," he growled. "You are definitely not taking *that* back!"

"No?" she teased.

"Hell, no!"

Ali looked at him with her bright eyes, smiling and laughing nervously. "That all just kind of slipped out. I'm sorry if I was a bit *forward*, for lack of a stronger word." She laughed again. "I don't...that's not... I was just..." she put her face in her hands. "Oh, God! Never mind."

Rafe laughed, watching her face turn bright red as she tried to backtrack. She was obviously embarrassed. But he knew the kind of person she was. He knew she wasn't the type to whisper intimate words like that to a man -- unless it was someone she was already intimate with, and he certainly fit the bill for that. He also knew what she thought he thought…and he definitely did not want her to think that!

Oh, no! The more Ali replayed the words in her head, the worse they sounded! He must think she's a total slut! Sleeps with him on the first date and in so many words offers him oral sex on the next. Her parents would be so proud! What the hell was wrong with her? It was him, damn it -- he just made her think about sex! She couldn't look at him or touch him without thinking about it. Now she just couldn't look at him! And he was laughing at her! She started to turn away and then felt herself being picked up and thrown over his shoulder. She didn't so much as yelp in surprise. She just hung over his back, head upside-down, and said in defeat, "I've completely humiliated myself. I wouldn't blame you if dumped me in the Gulf and washed out my filthy mouth with salt water." Her arms hung limply down the back of his legs, and her lips were mere inches from his nicely rounded rear end. Even now she was thinking about sex. His own hands were awfully close to her own butt as he held her in place. Why was he holding her like this?

"Rafe? Say something." At least he had stopped laughing.

"I know you were just playing around, Ali. A certain part of me that doesn't have a brain didn't realize that." He laughed. "But don't worry -- I won't hold your filthy mouth against you. In fact, as soon as I put you back down, I'm going to kiss it."

Oh, God! "You do think I have a filthy mouth! Is that why I'm like this? Are you going to spank me?" She grinned in her upside-down state. She knew he was teasing her, and she was glad he didn't hold it against her. She was tempted to squeeze his butt, or bite it.

"You're like this because you couldn't look at me, and you needed to see how silly it was for you to be embarrassed. You had a good strategy, it worked, score one for you." He laughed, then spanked her behind. "Are you ready to come down?"

"I actually kind of like it here. Do that again." She couldn't resist a little squeeze.

He laughed and used his arms to guide her back down, holding her close so that she had to slowly slide against him. When she was on her feet, he bent down to kiss her. It lasted a good solid minute before he finally pulled back. "Just so you know -- you know for the future, I liked what you said, and I wish you weren't embarrassed by it. You could say anything to me, and it wouldn't change my mind about you."

The future, huh? She gave him a sheepish grin. "Really?"

"Yes, really." He smoothed the loose pieces of hair around her face.

"Good, because I really do want to please you," she said more seriously, "I want to do to you what you did to me." Couldn't she just quit while she was ahead?

Rafe moaned. "When I said you could say anything to me, I didn't mean in the middle of the street so that I had to walk home with a full-blown hard-on." He grinned at her.

"I'm not going to apologize this time." She grinned back, looking down at him, "I loved what you just said to me."

"I meant it." Rafe kissed her again. "Now let's head back so we can get this night going."

"What's the big rush?" she teased.

Rafe gave her a crooked smile and adjusted himself.

Ali laughed happily as they crossed the street to the beach. They jogged the rest of the way back on the sand until they reached Matt and Nicki again.

"That didn't take long," Nicki commented.

"She cheats," Rafe said matter-of-factly.

Ali smiled, pleased with herself. "I'll let you have a rematch."

"Oh, don't worry, I'll get my revenge," he warned, and leaned down to kiss her.

After a few more hours on the beach of sunning and swimming, the girls went ahead to shower and change for the evening, while Matt helped Rafe bring up the beach equipment.

"Did you tell her?"

Rafe grinned. "Yeah, I did."

Matt laughed. "How did that go?"

"She was great about it, full of questions." He laughed.

"Yeah, just be careful. She probably thinks fate has somehow interrupted her life." Matt laughed softly, but was trying to tell him that Ali could easily get hurt.

"Maybe it has." Rafe looked him in the eye, taking two chairs from him. Not just her life, either.

Matt gave him an appraising glance, understanding. Maybe it had for him and Nicki, too.

"All right. man, I'm headed across. Come over when you're ready. I'll drive."

"See you in twenty." Rafe watched him walk out the pool gate and went inside himself to shower and change. He dressed casually, in shorts and a short-sleeved shirt, leaving his piece in the nightstand. Before leaving he picked up the remote and turned the flat screen on, happy to see that from all angles, it was quiet. He expected the Explorer to pull in any minute if they were going to make it a nightly ritual, and he wondered briefly how deep their involvement was -- if any -- in the case. He wouldn't think about it until tomorrow, though. He wanted another night with Ali. He looked forward to officially putting in his vacation time at the office tomorrow so he could tell Ali how much longer he would be here. He wanted more than anything to spend his vacation time with her. He would call for availability on the drive to Miami and see about a cottage at Tween Waters.

The couples all piled into Matt's Hummer and drove into Sanibel. After feasting on various seafood and pastas at Sweet Melissa's, they made the short drive to the East End.

Nicki had pointed out the offices of the Beach News to them and seemed excited about starting her new job. Rafe had already known where Nicki would be working. He'd driven by East End Realty, which abutted the Beach News, quite a few times, and tomorrow he would actually enter Barry Stoddman's office as a buyer.

Once they parked and got on the beach, Rafe had taken Ali's hand and led her on a walk toward the setting sun, while Matt and Nicki headed off in the opposite direction toward the lighthouse pier to see if the fish were biting.

"Dinner was great," Ali said as she walked along the sand beside Rafe, seashells crunching under their flip flops.

"Excellent," he agreed, smiling down at her. He took her hand and held it as they walked. He was thankful the beach wasn't too crowded, just a few shell seekers and some dog walkers. They both laughed as a golden retriever ran by them at full speed, soaking wet, chasing seagulls along the shoreline, his owner clearly miffed that he wasn't heeding her call.

Ali was thrilled to be walking on the beach with Rafe, her hand warm and secure in his.

"Have you ever seen so many seashells?" she asked.

"I have not, and I keep meaning to scoop some up to take back to my niece. She'll love them. I have to do that before I leave."

Ali's heart sank. "So do you think your job will end here soon?"

"I'll know more tomorrow, but I think things are coming together now. It might not be too much longer."

"And then what?" She felt a wave of sadness wash over her.

"I have some time off coming to me and I was thinking of putting in for it."

"Oh, what will you do?" The thought of him leaving really sucked. What was wrong with her for falling so hard so fast? It wasn't going to be easy to hide her feelings when he did leave.

"I was thinking I'd like to spend it on Captiva. It would be nice to relax on the island and not have to investigate bad guys."

"Really?" Ali's stomach flipped. "That would be kind of nice. We could still get to hang out." She tried to sound casual as she looked up at him, then, suddenly feeling presumptuous, said. "If you wanted to."

"That's what I was hoping, actually." He was looking at her and knew they were both still feeling their way around each other. He stopped her from going any further by placing his hand over her arm, and she turned to face him. He could see the questions in her eyes.

"I was thinking of staying on here before I met you." He watched as she nodded, thinking she understood, but she clearly didn't. "I was just going to stay a week or more and go back to New York..." She turned her eyes away from him, looking toward the water, and he gently cupped her chin, directing her eyes back to his. "But now, I don't want to leave at all. I'm going to take my whole time off here..." Her eyes were glistening, and he felt the thud in his heart, "...because I want to spend it with you -- if *you* want to."

Ali let out the breath she hadn't realized she'd been holding and blinked away the moisture that had started to pool beneath her lids. She was so happy she could have him for a few more weeks, maybe longer, depending on his job. She didn't know how their time together would turn out in the end, but in the meantime, she was going to enjoy every second with him. "I'm so glad to hear you say that. I definitely want to." She smiled up at him.

Her green eyes danced with the now setting sun behind them, and Rafe pulled her close against him. "Ali, I want to be with you." Only he didn't mean it just sexually. He just couldn't leave her now -- it wasn't even an option for him. He was hooked, but it was too soon to tell her that.

"I want you, too," she whispered and wrapped her arms around him. She stood on her toes to kiss him seductively, for that's what she took his words to mean, and she was surprised at his return kiss. Instead of the hungry, passionate kiss she had expected, he kissed her slow and gentle, his strong hands coming up to hold her face. She was instant mush, and the swelling of feelings he brought forth threatened to surface.

He pulled away, and his dark eyes were piercing her own. "I don't know what you're doing to me," he said gruffly.

Ali swooned, and she looked down so he couldn't see her eyes. "Right back atcha," she said softly.

"Maybe we should head back. I have to get up early." Rafe's heart was doing funny things in his chest. "Besides, there was some mention of some activity by the spa, and I don't want to miss that."

She laughed, hitting him playfully on the arm, grateful that he'd broken the serious moment.

He bent his head to kiss her earlobe and her neck, his tongue sending chills up and down her body. Ali knew he was teasing, but she was more than ready to please him, and she grinned mischievously, taking the hand he offered once again. They headed back with a quicker pace in their steps.

"They've been gone awhile," Nicki mentioned as she and Matt sat on a large piece of driftwood jutting out of the sand. They had walked the pier, watching a few fishermen reel some in, then had walked a ways down the beach to sit.

Matt rifled through the sand, coming up with shell after shell for Nicki. "I'm sure they're fine. She's in good hands."

Nicki looked up at Matt. "I'm glad you like him."

"I do, I think he's a great guy."

"She told me what he does today," Nicki said conspiringly.

Matt grinned. "Oh, yeah? What's that?"

Nicki looked around. "He's an FBI agent." She waited for Matt's reaction.

"I know." He laughed slightly.

"You know?" she asked, surprised.

"He told me last night."

"Wow, so what do you think about that?"

Matt shrugged. "It's definitely interesting, and pretty funny that she would meet her dream date the first night on the island." He laughed. "Does it impress you?" He couldn't help wondering.

Nicki smiled. "Sure, but not in the way your male ego is thinking."

He laughed. "No?"

"No," she assured him. "I'm much more into the rock star type," she teased.

"Oh, really?" He poked her stomach. "I play guitar."

Nicki laughed. "Ha-ha."

"I do, honest."

Nicki laughed with a skeptical grin. "Ali has *never* told me that, and I've never seen or heard you play in all the years I've known you."

"Jason and I used to play when we were younger and I kept at it. I took lessons all through school. I was a big hit at college parties." He grinned back.

Nicki smirked. "Oh, I bet you were! Why didn't Ali ever tell me this?"

"She hasn't heard me play since she was little, I kind of keep it to myself, Jason's the only one who's heard me play recently. My parents haven't even heard me play."

"Why?" Nicki feared it might be because he wasn't that good, but she didn't care.

"It's just a private thing for me, I guess, unless I'm drunk and at a college party." He laughed.

She rolled her eyes. "I don't even want to know." She did not want to picture him in college, then she'd have to picture the women around him. "Well, I was just kidding about the rock star thing anyway. I'll take a guy in a tool belt over a rock star, all those muscles and swinging a hammer…umm." She smiled. "Besides, who wants to compete with all those groupies."

Matt laughed at her. Funny thing was, he was actually pretty damn good on the guitar, but his brother Jason was one of the only people who knew it. He'd always wanted to pursue a career in music, but the family business had sort of taken over his life. He wasn't complaining; he made a great living, but he loved to play his guitar any chance he got. He wished he had brought one with him. "Let's go home now so I can build you something." He got up off the driftwood and pulled her with him.

Nicki laughed. "I didn't realize you brought your tool belt."

"I'll find one in the garage," he promised. "Look, here they come." He nodded toward Ali and Rafe walking toward them.

Nicki and Matt closed the distance, and they all went back to the car for the ride back to Captiva, stopping only for a mother raccoon and her babies on SanCap road along the way. When they reached the driveway twenty minutes later, Ali informed them she'd be across the street with Rafe.

"I'll leave the porch light on for you." Matt winked at Rafe.

Ali blushed, but grinned at her brother. "Don't bother." She laughed at his feigned shocked expression. "Goodnight, Nick." She smiled at her best friend, giving her a knowing look.

"Yoga by the pool at sun-up?" Nicki teased

"No." Ali shook her head emphatically."

"Just thought I'd ask."

"Go for a run at seven?" Ali countered.

"No." Nicki shook her head, just as emphatic.

"Just thought I'd ask."

Rafe bid goodnight to them, and he and Ali crossed the street to his driveway. He saw the SUV in his peripheral vision as he made his way to the front door. He didn't see any movement, only the parked vehicle. Once inside the house, he flipped the lights on and went to the kitchen to get them both a water.

Ali excused herself before taking it from him and went into his bedroom to use the bathroom. On her way out she made a quick stop to his nightstand. She found what she needed and saw the gun that lay inside, causing her to draw a breath. She shut the drawer quickly and quietly and returned to the living room, where she went over to the couch to sit.

"Tonight was nice." She made herself comfortable and took the water he offered.

"It was," he agreed, sitting down beside her. He put an arm around her shoulders, and she pressed herself into his side. She put a hand on his chest, feeling the hard contours beneath his T-shirt. "You work out a lot, don't you?"

"There's a gym downstairs that's better than the one I pay for at home." He laughed. "I've had a lot of time to make use of it."

"It shows." Ali moved her hand along his arms, traveling over his biceps and down his forearms. He was muscular, but not in an obnoxious way; he was lean, like she preferred. "You have an incredible body," she told him, her voice filled with desire.

His own hand moved along her arm. "*You* have an incredible body, and I like it best when it's underneath me."

Ali laughed softly, excited by his words and his touch. "Show me the gym."

"Now?" Rafe was thinking of another room in the house, but okay.

"Why not?"

Because I was going to take you to my bedroom and… He let his thought drift as she stood to take his hand, leading him down the stairs to the gym.

Ali entered the room. Two whole walls were mirrored floor to ceiling with every type of fitness equipment available, filling the center. The room took up the whole bottom footprint of the house. "God, is this guy a body builder in his free time?"

Rafe laughed. "He just might be."

"Treadmill, elliptical, spinning bike -- Jeez, can I get a membership?"

"Use it anytime," he said seriously.

"This is fantastic." Ali admired all the strength-training equipment and noticed the sliders on the back wall that led to the pool. She went over to them, found the lock, lifted it up, and moved aside the heavy glass door.

Rafe's blood pumped as he watched her. She turned to him and beckoned him outside with her index finger. He followed the sway of her hips as she led him purposefully over to the hot tub. There were two lounge chairs set up beside it, and she gently nudged him down into one. He didn't take his eyes off her for a second as she stood at the end of the lounge and slowly began to peel away the simple sundress she wore. Underneath it she wore a matching white lace bra and panties, and he was rock solid in an instant looking at her.

Her smooth, tanned skin stood out against the white lace and his eyes traveled up and down as he admired her fit body. She looked both strong and soft at once. He watched as she kicked off her flip flops and came up to straddle his extended legs, her warmth radiating on top of his thighs. Her breasts were inches from his face, with the top half spilling nicely from her bra.

"I'm sorry I cheated today," she said, bending to kiss his neck.

Rafe leaned back and put his hands on her hips. He shifted her body so she could feel his reaction to her, and she replied by rubbing herself against him. *Oh, yeah.*

"But I'm going to make it up to you."

Rafe kept his eyes locked on her, not saying a word, rigid with anticipation.

Ali wanted to please him in the worst way. She wanted him to see and feel how much she desired him and how much he turned her on. With light fingers she lifted his T-shirt off up over his head and let it fall to the ground. Her hands seductively ran over his chest and the smattering of light brown hair that covered him, and she continued caressing him with both hands and lips, well aware of his swelling arousal underneath her own.

As she moved her hands down to his waistband, she scooched her body down so she could put her lips on the sexy line of hair that disappeared down into them. She followed the line with her lips, kissing until she reached material, then she carefully lifted herself off him and came around to the end of the chair again, kneeling down on the hard cement deck. She used both hands to guide his shorts down over his rather large erection, and met his eyes, seeing the heat shining out of them, the look on his face a mix of pleasure and pain.

Rafe just watched her, not believing what she was getting ready to do. She was really something else. The desire in her eyes shone bright in the darkness, and the way she was looking at him was melting him right there on the spot. He was so hard for her, and waiting for her touch was agony. He couldn't remember ever wanting someone as much.

Ali placed her hands on his big, strong thighs and felt their muscles twitch beneath her touch. She bent down and kissed his legs, then slid her hands to his center, where she gently took hold of him. She looked up at the sound of his low moan and smiled. This was what she wanted, to be in charge and make him crazy. She kept eye contact as she cupped him with one hand and lowered her mouth down over his long, hard, fully erect shaft.

Oh Fuck! Rafe's whole body tensed as her lips neared him and then opened to take him into her warm wet mouth. Just the feel of her breath on him was enough to make him explode. He moved his hands through her hair as she slowly and methodically moved her mouth over the length of him. He was going to need every bit of self-control for this. He wanted to enjoy every minute. Who was he kidding? -- Every second.

Her lips were wet and soft, and her tongue teased him relentlessly. He moved in and out of her mouth, keeping her rhythm. Oh, man, it felt unbelievable. Her silky hair was wrapped around his fingers, and he pulled and pressed gently, guiding her head.

Ali knew he was nearing the edge, and she increased her momentum, wanting his release. She gripped his thighs and moved her mouth faster and faster, but just when she thought she had him, he let out a groan and leaned forward to lift her up and off the cement where she knelt.

"Hey! I wasn't finished," she demanded in a husky tone.

Rafe could have gone off easily, but he wanted in. "We need to go up."

Ali grinned at the sound of his voice. He had clearly been about to shatter, and she was glad she'd brought him there. "No, we don't." She reached into her bra and produced the condom she had taken from his nightstand.

Rafe groaned again, happy that he wouldn't have to wait another minute. "Give me that thing," he said, and took it from her. She was looking at him as she slid out of her panties and bra. He could barely concentrate, watching her as he rolled the damn thing on.

Ali watched him sheath himself and lowered herself to the ground, sitting up on her elbows in invitation.

Rafe came down on top of her quickly and put his hands under her head to cradle it as he lowered her back. He entered her fast and hard, kissing her swollen mouth. Their pace was aerobic, and Rafe couldn't plunge himself in deep enough. "Ali... Ali," he cried out. The feeling was so intense he wasn't going to last.

Ali cried out with him as they came together explosively, her body convulsing under his, his body pulsating on top of hers. She was throbbing around him. He was still so deep inside her, and she was pretty certain most of the skin on her back was missing, but she didn't care.

Rafe breathed heavily on top of her, not wanting to leave her warm insides, but he worried that the cement may have done to her what it had done to him. He slowly withdrew, kissing her soft lips, and pulled her to a sitting position. He gingerly placed his hands on her back. "Are you hurt?" He winced, fearing she might be bleeding.

"I won't hold it against you. It was self-inflicted." She reached out to softly touch his scraped knees.

"Yeah, you definitely asked for that." He grinned.

"You didn't have to stop me, you know."

"Oh, believe me, babe, I did." He pulled her onto his lap and kissed her. "That was so worth losing the race."

She laughed softly. "So you enjoyed it?"

"I'd like to return the favor." He cupped her breasts, and she felt his arousal again.

"Are you kidding me right now?" She laughed incredulously.

Rafe wasn't kidding, and even he was surprised at his quick recovery. The image of her going down on him was sealed in his mind, and that was all he could think about.

"I guess I underestimated you when I went in your nightstand." She laughed.

"Never underestimate me, babe."

She loved his term of affection. "I guess I won't. Stay right here."

He watched as she got up and walked away up the stairs and into the house. He wished she could just live here with him and be naked all the time. He got up and rid himself of the spent condom he wore and thought fleetingly how he'd like to take her without one.

He went behind the bar and powered up the jets to the hot spa. He got some bottled water and brought it back over with him, setting it down on the ledge. Lowering himself down, he felt the water sting his knees and the back of his hands and arms. It was a pain he could smile about.

When she reappeared, he watched her come back down the stairs and thought how fortunate he was to have met her. She had definitely turned his world upside-down in a matter of days. "Go real slow," he warned. "I thought I just saw a snake slither by."

Ali stopped in her tracks, and Rafe just took her in. Her long wavy hair touched her bare shoulders, and her beautiful breasts were pale against her browned skin. He studied her long, lean legs and rested on the smooth mound where they met. "I was thinking what a shame it was that you couldn't be naked all the time."

Ali saw the look in his eyes and figured out quickly that there wasn't a snake, but she enjoyed him looking at her anyway. "I can be," she teased him, moving forward and getting into the hot bubbling water, "but I think the FBI would frown upon you having your own personal sex slave."

He laughed. "Some might think I'm a hero."

Ali's scraped back was on fire, but she wasn't complaining. She had checked it out in his bathroom mirror and was happy to see it wasn't as bad as it felt. Just a little red, nothing some aloe wouldn't fix.

"You're *my* hero," she teased.

"Oh, yeah? What did I do?" He pulled her between his legs.

"You sent me up for another one of these." She held up the condom package.

"Let's not waste it, then."

They aroused each other under the steaming, hot frothy water until their desire once again became unbearable. It was then that Rafe led Ali out of the spa, took the cushions off the lounges, and placed them on the ground. He laid her down gently, making sure she was comfortable.

The moon was low in the warm night sky and sprinkled with millions of brilliant stars that Ali could almost reach up and touch. She stared at them, eyes wide as Rafe hovered over her, entering her ever so slowly this time. She thanked each and every one of those stars as he continued to move into her in a slow, gentle rhythm, bringing her to a state of euphoria she wasn't aware existed. She knew, lying under this star-filled night, that she was gone, she was head-over-heels in love with him.

When they lay spent next to each other, Rafe took her hand, and Ali basked in the warmth and comfort of his body beside hers. The only sound came from the swaying palms that separated the pool area from the beach, their fronds colliding gently in the night's breeze. They each took a deep breath. "This is so peaceful," she said softly.

"When I'm done with this job, Ali, I really want to spend some quality time with you."

Rafe's voice was thick with emotion, and Ali didn't dare look at him.

"This isn't quality?" she joked quietly, loving that he'd said it. She kept looking to the stars. If she didn't joke with him, she was afraid she wouldn't be able to suppress what her heart was truly feeling.

"I'm serious. I want to get to know everything about you," he told her.

"You do?" She dared to turn and face him, their naked bodies intertwined.

"Yeah, I do. I really love spending time with you."

"I love spending time with you, too." She kissed him softly. Okay, so they had each said the "L" word, maybe not the way she wanted to say it, but it was good enough to make her heart pound with joy.

"I'm glad you're here...with me." Damn it, this was as close as he could come to revealing his feelings. She'd think he was a nut case if he told her what he was really feeling.

He wasn't even sure what he was feeling was even real. Two days? Ridiculous. Who falls in love in two days? Maybe he was confusing a perpetual hard on with being in love, but somehow he didn't think so.

"I can't think of any place I'd rather be than right here, right now," Ali told him at the risk of revealing herself.

"Will you sleep over again?"

She could hear the unsure tone in his voice and see the hopeful look in his eyes. How could he possibly think she would say anything else but yes? She placed her hand on his cheek. "I would really like that." She was beaming now and was happy to see he clearly was, too.

"Great!" he said enthusiastically, getting up. "I'm hungry -- do you want a snack?"

"I like snacks." She smiled and watched as he went up the porch stairs, disappearing into the kitchen.

Ali stood up lazily, and sauntered over to the beach path illuminated by the bright moon. Her hands rested on the wooden gate as she stared out at the still Gulf. Far offshore she could see a light from a boat and wondered briefly where it might be going. How romantic it would be to be headed somewhere with Rafe out on a boat, just the two of them. She laughed to herself, thinking just about anything with Rafe would be romantic.

The moonlight and the stars were so bright that most of the beach was lit up. Ali had never felt so sensual and alive as she stood there, looking out without a stitch of clothing on. Her whole body felt sated, and she looked forward to crawling into bed with Rafe later and having him close. The memory of it from the night before was cloudy because it had been so sporadic. If either of them had seemed even remotely awake, the other was touching them in such a way that sleep was no longer an option. She had had more sex last night than she had had in the past year. She laughed again, thinking about it. When Rafe had asked her if she would sleep over tonight, she knew he meant for more than just sex, and that's what had set her heart pounding. The thought of them lying in bed just holding each other was a happy one.

She turned with a smile sensing his presence behind her. "What did you get…" She didn't finish her question, for standing off to the side of Rafe's property was a young man who just stood, leering at her.

Her eyes took in the tall, skinny man with blond disheveled hair hanging in his face, his creepy eyes staring, his mouth hanging open. Then her eyes followed the movement of his hand, which moved deliberately over the crotch of his shorts, sending her own arms and hands to instinctively cover herself as best she could while backing away and screaming Rafe's name as loud as she could. It only seemed to encourage the weirdo, and he seemed to move a little closer. She didn't dare take her eyes off him, but she wanted desperately to find a towel to wrap around herself. She heard the pounding on the porch steps as Rafe ran down them at full speed toward her.

He had only been in the house five minutes, putting shorts on and checking the monitors on his way into the kitchen. When he'd zoomed in on the SUV, he swore to himself and wondered where the passenger had disappeared to. Rafe's eyes scanned each angle, and then he saw him, son of a bitch, taking a piss right on the beach in front of D'nafrio's foundation walls. Rafe also saw Ali standing there naked at the beach-path gate, and if she was there, then…shit! He ran through the slider opening and took the stairs two at a time just as he heard her scream his name. He scaled the last few steps and made it across the pool deck, hurdling the fence, and started after the little bastard as he took off away from the building site, up the beach. Rafe was right on his heels and could have tackled him easily, but thought it through. He didn't want the driver to come looking for his friend, thereby endangering Ali, even though he hoped she was safely in the house by now, and he didn't want to engage in fucking up either one of these assholes, blowing his cover and possibly any leads on the case. His frustration was palpable. He slowed his pace, breathing heavily, letting the jerk think he couldn't keep up. He watched as the prick cut through one of the beachfront properties up ahead, then Rafe turned to jog back to see how Ali was. He swore to himself because he hadn't protected her better. They never should have been out there so exposed. He had to get his head in the game.

He hurried back to the pool deck and up the stairs inside.

Ali was under the covers in his bed, sitting against the headboard. "Did you catch him?"

"I let him go," Rafe went to the edge of the bed and sat. "Are you okay?"

Ali nodded to show she was.

"Did he say anything to you?" Rafe was still fuming, and seeing Ali in this vulnerable state made him want to go outside and pull them both out of the truck.

"No, he was just standing there."

"He was taking a leak. When you moved to the gate, you caught his eye."

"How did you...?" Understanding, she nodded. "The monitors -- you saw him before I did."

"As soon as I saw him, I came running." He reached out and took her hand.

"God, where did he come from?"

"There's two of them. They're watching the property next door." Rafe felt guilty for not telling her before. He honestly thought he wouldn't have to.

"Why?"

Rafe exhaled. "They work for D'nafrio, the owner. They're making sure there's no trespassing." Rafe didn't want to get into the real reason, although he was starting to think if he didn't he could be putting her in danger.

"He seemed kind of young," Ali commented.

"Yeah, they're just twenty-one."

"Jeez, I was just starting to feel good about being naked, too."

Rafe laughed softly at her serious tone. "I think we should keep you naked *inside* from now on."

"Imagine if he had been there any earlier?" she asked, horrified.

That reminded Rafe that he'd better delete the images camera four had captured before Smith had showed up.

Ali's eyes widened in comprehension. "Oh, Rafe, what about..?"

"I'll delete it tomorrow."

"That's all I need, to be naked in an FBI file somewhere."

Rafe laughed, "You would give new meaning to the FBI's most wanted list."

Ali hit him playfully on the arm and rolled her eyes. "Seriously, Rafe!"

"No worries, love." He kissed her forehead. "I'm sorry -- I hope that didn't spoil the night for you."

Did he just call her 'love'? "Can I ask you a question?"

"Of course."

"Why did you let him go?"

The sound in her voice nearly crushed him. "I didn't want to, Ali, I had to." And he wouldn't let something like that happen again.

"Because you would blow your cover?"

He smiled half-heartedly, "Yeah, but know that with all my heart I wanted to beat the living shit out of him."

Ali smiled. "Thanks, that means a lot, and I understand." She shrugged. "So he got an eyeful. Worse things have happened."

Rafe shook his head, smiling at her.

"What?"

"Nothing."

"What?" she prodded.

"You're an incredible woman." She had handled the situation quite well, and he had to admire her for it. He started to calm down and slowly started to peel back the covers.

"Hey!" Ali held tight to them. "I thought you were getting snacks."

"Later." He whipped back the covers and laughed at her squeals.

CHAPTER FIFTEEN

"Where the hell you been, man?" Timothy Mann asked his friend.

"Holy shit, man, I just got chased down the beach by this big fucking dude."

"What the fuck for?"

"His girl was outside at the pool next door -- fucking naked, man, what a piece of ass! I couldn't help but look, but she saw me and started screaming, then he came running."

"Right next door?" Tim looked in the direction of the home next door, but the heavy landscape prevented him from seeing the house.

"Yeah, dude, I fucking gunned it up the beach, and he gave up." Sean was still breathing hard, his smoker's lungs preventing him from breathing normally.

"He doesn't know you came from this truck?" Tim knew they'd be fucked if they screwed this job up.

"No, man, I was back there taking a leak, not even close to the house," Sean lied.

"Good, we can't fuck this up. That asshole banging my old lady is paying us good."

"Nah, he doesn't know where I came from." Sean sank down in the passenger seat and shut his eyes. "I'm going to dream of that naked ass tonight man. You know, she reminded me of that babe from last night."

"Now that was a piece of ass." Tim closed his own eyes and let his high take over.

CHAPTER SIXTEEN

Nicki woke up and looked at the bedside clock. She was in her own bed -- alone. It was seven o' clock. She didn't have to be to her new job until nine, and she got up to stretch. She was dressed in Matt's T-shirt, and she smiled, thinking of the night before.

They had actually just gone for a late-night swim and talked for hours under the stars. The night was perfect. When he had walked her to her bedroom door, she was expecting him to follow her in, but instead he kissed her mouth softly, and with a wink and a smile he said goodnight and had retreated to his own room.

Nicki didn't know whether to feel disappointed or touched that he could just go to bed without having sex with her. She'd slept like a baby, though, and was glad to be so refreshed for her first day of work. She would have liked to have slept in Matt's arms though, and she felt a twinge of remorse that that hadn't happened. She opened her sliders and went out to the pool deck. She unrolled her yoga mat and started her stretches. After a half-hour she rose to go back to her room to get ready for her day. She figured Matt was still asleep and kind of wished he weren't. She was curious as to how he felt today. They had shared a lot the previous night, and she hoped he didn't regret it.

Back in her room, she undressed and put on the short silk robe she'd packed. Sitting on the edge of her bed, she picked up the phone and dialed her mom's cell. Nan and her family would be at the airport already, but their flight didn't leave until eight-thirty, so she could still catch them. She had totally forgotten to call last night. Her mom picked up on the second ring.

"Hello, honey!"

"Hi, Mom." Nicki smiled at the sound of her mom's voice.

"I thought we'd hear from you last night."

"I'm sorry, I forgot." Nicki had been so engrossed in conversation with Matt that the night had just passed by so quickly.

"Well, we don't have much time. Is everything going well? What time do you have to be to work? Oh, Nan tells me Matthew is there. How's that working out?"

Nicki waited until she was sure her mom was finished. "Everything's great. I leave soon, gotta be there at nine, and yes, Matt's here and it's fine."

"Okay, great. Dad and, Nan too, I'm sure, have e-mailed you our itinerary, so check it out and write down the number to the hotel. I don't know if we'll have cell service. Gosh we wish you were with us. Do you want to speak to Dad?"

"Sure, Mom, put him on -- and don't worry, I'll check my e-mail. Have a great flight and call when you get there, okay?"

"Will do. I love you, Nicki."

"You, too, Mom." Nicki waited.

"Hey, kiddo!"

"Hey, Dad! Are you excited?"

"You know me. I'll be happy when we are on the ground."

Nicki laughed. Her dad hated to fly. "So what kind of meds will you be on for the long flight?"

"Mom wouldn't hear of it, so I'll have to rely on the drink service."

"You'll be fine. Take a long nap!"

"That's the intention -- hey, your sister wants to say something quickly. Love you, sweetheart. We'll call when we get there."

"Bye, Dad! Tell Nan I'll talk to her soon, too." Nicki waited again for her sister's voice.

"Nan filled me and Paige in. So is he as hot as I remember?"

Nicki rolled her eyes. Great, between her sister and her cousin, word would spread fast. "I have no idea of what you speak."

"Bullshit," Jenna whispered into the phone. "Does he know you've got it bad for him?"

Oh, I believe he has an idea. "Again, I don't know what you're talking about, or who you're referring to. I have to get off the phone and finish getting ready for work."

"Nick, *please*, give me something," Jenna begged.

Nicki laughed, enjoying teasing her sister. "Okay, okay, he's amazing and just as hot as he ever was."

"Oh, I knew it! How come Nan knew all about your feelings for him, and I didn't until she had to tell me?" her little sister complained.

"Nan is just a freak and knows things before anyone else does. She knew before I even knew. It's disturbing, and she had no right to tell you anything. I don't even know what I'm feeling." That wasn't completely true.

"Oh, come on, she's just excited. She promised to tell me more on the plane. I should be all filled in by the time we get there," Jenna boasted.

"Hey, there's nothing to tell!" Nicki half-shouted. "When there is, I'll do the talking." Jeez, was nothing sacred?

"What about sex?"

"Jenna -- where are you standing right now?"

"Relax, they're all in Dunkie's getting coffee. The only one who can *maybe* hear me is a hot pilot standing nearby -- man I hope he's ours. So?"

Nicki rolled her eyes again. "What *about* sex? Are you looking for advice?" Nicki teased.

"I'm looking for details."

Matt's hands framed Nicki's doorway above his head. The sound of her voice had brought him out of his room, where he'd been dressing. "Amazing? Hot?" Who was she talking to? And did it really matter? She had just called him amazing and hot. He grinned as he watched her lying there on her bed, her back to him. She wore a short silk robe that rode up on her thighs, giving him a nice view, and a hard-on.

Nicki laughed out loud. "You can't handle the details, baby sister. Now go get on your plane and don't talk about my love life with our grandmother!"

Love life? Is that how she saw it? He shifted from one leg to the other, waiting to hear more. He kept an interested eye on her hand, which was playing with the hem of her short robe.

"So are you in love with him?" Jenna pried for more.

Nicki sighed. Why deny it? It would feel so good to say it out loud. "Jenna, I am truly, madly, deeply in lo..." Nicki fell back on the bed, about to finish her confession, when the sight of Matt lingering in her doorway had her jumping three feet off the bed. "Jenna, I have to go!" She nearly shouted into the phone.

Matt smiled at the sight. Her robe was slightly parted, and he could see the outline of her breasts and the skin of her stomach. His gaze stayed there until she felt his stare and pulled the robe snug around her.

"How long have you been standing there?" Oh, God, what had he heard her say? His gaze was hot and was giving her goose bumps all over.

"Long enough."

He was dressed and looking damn good with his tanned skin and his eyes even greener because of it.

"I was just saying goodbye to my family. They're leaving for Italy."

"I heard." He grinned.

Nicki fixed her robe so that it covered her properly, and she blushed furiously, not because of modesty -- he'd seen all there was to see -- but out of fear that he'd heard what she'd been about to reveal to Jenna.

"I have to get in the shower and get ready for work." She stood perfectly still.

"I know, I just wanted to tell you to come have breakfast with me when you're done." He smiled at her, wishing she wasn't so embarrassed, or he'd go to her and take her in his arms. He would have loved to hear her finish that sentence, but he didn't have to. He just had to process it himself.

"Oh, okay, thanks, I will..." Relief washed over her. If he had heard anything, he wasn't going to call her on it. He was a gentleman. Maybe it wasn't something he *wanted* to hear, she thought, maybe he had just been kidding when he said he would get her to fall in love with him again, but that didn't mean she should expect him to fall in love with her. Why should she expect that from someone like Matt, who was just here on vacation, right?

Matt watched the gamut of emotions play over Nicki's face, and his gut wrenched at what he saw in her eyes. He wanted to reach out, but he let her walk away to the shower instead. He could see the doubt that had played over her eyes, and it killed him. It had taken all of his restraint the night before to leave her with just a kiss, but he wanted her to know she meant more to him than just someone he wanted to take to bed. He'd learned so much more about her last night, and he told her things about himself he'd never told anyone. He was gone, and he would do whatever it took to be with her and to love her. His heart pounded, thinking that she had just been about to tell her sister that she loved him -- deeply, madly, and truly. Man, if that were true he could die right now, happy, but he wanted to hear her say it to *him,* and he wanted to tell her just the same thing. And now she was in the shower thinking he didn't feel that way. Shit.

Nicki took a quick shower, cursing herself the whole time. She should learn to keep her feelings to herself! Why had she decided to tell Jenna that? Because she'd been so happy, realizing it was the absolute truth, and she wished she could shout it from the rooftops, but a lot of good that would do. Matt's expression had said it all. He had actually looked uncomfortable and scared at the end there. She would have to suck this up big time.

She got dressed and did her hair quickly, with Matt at the forefront of her thoughts. This wasn't going to be easy. She couldn't even be around him without her body responding. She was actually in a state of discomfort, needing some relief. She should have gone to him last night. Now it sucked -- she would have to work all day, sexually frustrated for a man who didn't love her. Hell, she knew that going in, right? She was a big girl; she handled it once and she could do it again, although this time her body was involved and she didn't know how well *it* would cooperate.

She found him at the counter, reading an island guide. "Going to do some sightseeing today?" She sat on the stool next to him.

Matt inhaled the clean scent of her and leaned over to kiss her lips. "Ummm, you taste good. Good morning."

"Good morning." Nicki looked away, not wanting him to read what she was sure was in her eyes. "Thanks for the fruit and bagel."

"I would have made eggs and bacon, but there's none in the fridge." He smirked.

"Sorry, I'll pick some up on the way home from work, if you want." God, if that didn't sound domestic.

He laughed. "I'll be out and about today. I'll get some stuff. Are you excited about today?"

She let out a breath. "Yeah, I am. I'm not sure what to expect, but I think it'll be fun."

"Good, I hope you love it."

"Thanks." Nicki ate some fruit and half her bagel while he flipped through the guide.

How could he just ignore the obvious tension in the room?

"Anything that interest you in there?"

"Yup."

"Like?"

He gave her the once-over and she turned, heat rushing to her cheeks. Damn it!

"Kayaking."

She smiled. "Don't tip -- there's gators out there."

Matt stood up and flexed. "They're no match for these guns. You've never seen *me* do the death roll."

Nicki shook her head and rolled her eyes, getting off the stool. "You're right. I should be worried about the gators," she said drolly. Okay, he was just going to ignore what he heard from her phone conversation to avoid the awkwardness, so she would just play along as well. "What else are you going to do today?"

"Why, are you going to miss me?" He pulled her in close, putting his arms around her waist. He kissed her lips and let his hands slide down to her bottom and squeezed.

Nicki's body automatically contoured itself to him. "I just might." Oh, brother, would she miss him. She just wanted to turn right back down the hall and stay in bed with him all day.

"You look too good in this dress. I hope there are no men in the office." He wasn't kidding, either. The thought of anyone looking at her made him jealous.

Nicki laughed. "I think Nan said it was all old women." Could he possibly be jealous? Man, what was she supposed to think about him? It was all so confusing.

"Maybe I'll just sit outside in the parking lot all day until you're done."

"I'd like that, only because it will keep you from encountering any bikini-clad females who might turn your head." Might as well be honest.

"You're the only one who can turn my head." How could she not know that? Maybe because he needed to tell her and get that look of uncertainty out of her eyes that kept kicking him in the gut. What was he so afraid of?

"Really?" She cursed at herself for the pathetic way that came out.

Matt kissed her again, taking her head in his hands, then pulled back, still holding her face. "Nicki, in two days you've managed to do to me what no woman has ever done to me. I have no desire to look at anyone else. All I can think about is you -- looking at you, being with you, touching you." His hands traveled back down and slowly lifted the back of her dress, revealing the thong she wore.

Nicki's throat constricted at his words, and moisture gathered behind her eyes. She pressed herself to him, feeling his erection. Her arms went around his neck. "I have to go to work," she whispered into the side of his neck, inhaling him and swallowing back her emotions. She gasped at the feel of his hand between her legs. She was wet, of course -- all he had to do was look at her.

"Umm, you feel good, too." He was moving his fingers under the thin cotton material.

"Matt, I have to go." She took a sharp intake of breath. "I can't go into work in this condition."

"That's why I'm going to relieve a little tension so you can start your day out right."

He spun her around so her back was to his chest, his hands never leaving her wet opening. "I thought about you all night," he whispered hoarsely.

"Oh, God," she moaned in pleasure. How did he know this was exactly what her body craved? She rubbed her backside against him, his arousal straining and pressing against her under his shorts. He kissed the nape of her neck while one hand moved across her breasts, squeezing and pulling on her nipples. He took his other hand away, and she heard the sound as he placed his fingers in his mouth, sucking her juices from them. Then they were back on her, and in her, wet from his mouth and tongue. She could barely stand as he pressed them in and out repeatedly, finally resting a calloused finger on her clit and rubbing ever so gently, applying a little pressure until she ached, then more pressure, and even more and rubbing faster and faster in a circular motion until she screamed,

"Oh - oh - God!...Matt!" She nearly collapsed, bending at the waist as he held on to her, his arms around her, steadying her.

Matt pulled her in against him and whispered in her ear. "Oh, yeah -- that's what you needed." It was what he had needed, too. He wanted nothing more than to please her.

"That was...how am I going to go to work now?" Nicki asked, breathless, and leaned her bottom against a stool.

"Wait right here." Matt headed for the kitchen, and Nicki heard the sink running but didn't turn around. As if she could even move.

He came back with a damp towel and bent down in front of her, lifting her dress. Nicki blanched as the hot towel touched her inner thigh, and she watched, not embarrassed, as Matt wiped away the wetness that had trickled onto her skin. Oh, he was good. He cleaned her up in all the right spots and gently pulled her panties up and pulled her dress back over her legs.

"There, like it never happened." His satisfied smile had her blushing from ear to ear. Every nerve ending in her body still crackled with electricity, and she didn't trust herself to stand. They both held each other's gaze, and she felt every urge to tell him what she was feeling -- but she was so afraid, she couldn't stand the heartbreak if he didn't feel the same, and how could he possibly after only two days? She kept her mouth shut and swallowed the lump in her throat.

"You'd better get going." He watched her eyes; they were filled with heat, and something more. Something he found himself wanting to see there. He wondered if she could see it in his own eyes.

"Matt," she said, her voice coming out in a soft whisper

"What is it, gorgeous?" He loved that he'd pleased her and made her come. She was so damn sexy, and he couldn't keep his hands away. He hoped the day went by fast. He leaned in, placing his hands on either side of her, pinning her to the counter.

Nicki was at a loss. "I..."

Matt's heart pounded. Say it, baby, say it.

Nicki saw the expectant look in his eyes. What did he want her to say? "Thank you."

He laughed softly. All right, he'd have to be satisfied with the look in her eyes for now. After all, he hadn't quite worked up the courage yet, either. He kissed her forehead and pulled her off the stool. "My pleasure -- have a great first day."

Nicki looked down at the towel he still gripped in his hand. "I will now." She was smiling as she headed out the door. Oh, sweet Jesus, make this day fly by.

CHAPTER SEVENTEEN

When Ali woke up, the first thing she noticed was the quiet. The second was the crinkle of paper she heard as she rolled over to see the time. Reaching underneath her, she pulled the paper out and held it up. Even his handwriting was nice. She smiled as she read.

Sweet, beautiful woman in my bed, I didn't want to wake you, I did, however, stare at your exceptional naked backside for some time before I got in the shower. Trust me when I say I'd rather be in bed with you right now than driving. Help yourself to food, to the gym, the shower, whatever you want. I'll be back early this afternoon, and I wondered if you would spend some time with me today? I have a little investigating to do, and it would help if I had a beautiful woman by my side to pose as my fiancée. Don't panic -- this isn't some crazy attempt at a proposal. I can be much more romantic than a note by the pillow. Anyway, will you do it? And no, you won't get to carry a gun! I'll call you from the road on my way back. --Rafe

Ali lay there with her mouth hanging open. Would she do it? Hell, yes she'd do it and enjoy every second of it. She laughed about the gun. Funny that he would know already that it briefly crossed her mind, envisioning herself in the stance, saying, "Hold it right there!" She took a deep breath and read the note again, stopping at the part where he said he could be more romantic than leaving a note by the pillow. Was that an indication that he planned to be? Her heart raced at the thought, and a hundred images flashed before her eyes, from the proposal, to the wedding to the honeymoon, to the babies. Talk about panic -- if he knew what she was thinking because of that one statement, he'd keep driving and never come back. But he was the one who wrote it, and she couldn't help but read into it. Whatever -- she would look forward to this afternoon. Even if it was pretend, it would be fun.

She folded the note and got out of his bed. It was eight o'clock according to the clock on his nightstand, and her eyes lingered on the drawer, curious as hell. She slowly drew it open, only to find it devoid of the gun. Of course it wasn't there. Rafe was responsible and professional, and she was an idiot. She laughed as she left the room to meander through the kitchen. She fixed herself a bowl of cheerios with a banana and ate at the large glass table overlooking the Gulf. It was another stellar day, and she wanted to run. Putting her bowl and spoon in the dishwasher, she cleaned up Rafe's dishes as well and wiped down the countertop. It felt nice being here amongst his things. She was wearing one of his T-shirts and decided to keep this shirt as well. She was tempted to use the gym, but she didn't want to miss the morning air. A run would feel great.

Ali went back to the bedroom and quickly made the bed, then slipped her shorts on from the night before and gathered her shirt, bra, and flip flops from the floor. She grabbed Rafe's note from the nightstand and made her way to the front door, where she was faced with another note giving her the key code to lock the door behind her. She prayed she didn't set the damn alarm off as she punched in the numbers, but she was successful, and she breathed a sigh of relief as she jogged down the stairs and across the driveway. The gate was open, so she was spared the scratches from the bougainvillea flanking it. When she got to the front door of Nan's house, she realized she didn't have her key. Shit! She tried the knob, and it was indeed locked. Nicki's car was already gone, and she hoped Matt was awake. She rang the bell and waited.

"Who is it?" She heard his gruff voice on the other side of the door.

"Matt, it's me. Let me in -- I don't have a key.

"Me who?"

Ali smirked. "Me your sister, now open the door."

"I do have a sister, but she's in here tucked safely in her own bed."

Ali rolled her eyes. "Well, this is her wicked twin who *didn't* come home last night, and she's going to kick your ass if you don't open the door!"

Ali heard the click of the lock and the door opened, revealing Matt on the other side, grinning like an idiot. She hadn't woken him -- he was clean-shaven and dressed.

"Good morning, sis." He winked at her.

Ali backhanded him in the arm. "Good morning. Why are you up so early?"

"Seeing my woman off to work."

Ali laughed. "Your woman, huh? Does she know that?" Ali arched a brow.

"Not yet, but she will."

"Seriously, what's up with you guys?" Ali took a seat on the couch, hugging a pillow to her chest.

Matt leaned against the back of the couch and turned so he could face her. "How does it appear to you?" He wasn't asking sarcastically.

"It *appears* like you're really into her. I can't say that I'm surprised, though -- she's awesome." Ali waited for his response, watching his face.

"Yeah, she is, and yeah, I am." He smiled.

Ali smiled, too, at what she saw in his eyes. "Do you love her?" She really didn't need to ask. His eyes told her the answer.

Matt gave his sister a slight smile. He wasn't ready to share his feelings quite yet. If and when that came out of his mouth, it would be to Nicki first.

Ali got up off the couch. "You don't have to answer that, but I'm happy for you, and I'm especially happy for Nicki."

"Why especially for her?"

"Because she's waited a long time for this."

"I know." He looked down at the floor, feeling foolish.

"She told you?" Ali was a little surprised.

"Yeah, but I honestly had no clue! I wished I had."

He sounded remorseful, and Ali felt bad for him.

"What would you have done?"

"I don't know, I guess the timing wasn't right anyway, but I still feel bad, like I let her down."

Ali loved her brother and his obvious feelings for Nicki.

"And the timing now?"

"For me, it's perfect. I can't say for her -- that was a long time ago that she felt that way."

"Some old feelings are hard to forget."

"That's what I'm working on." He smiled.

"I have a feeling you'll be successful." Ali gave him a smile. He was a great- looking guy with a tough, hard exterior, but he had a heart of gold, and she was glad he was going to give it to her best friend.

"I'm going to go for a run before it gets too hot. Interested?"

"I ran at about six, believe it or not. I couldn't sleep."

"Why not?" she teased.

Because Nicki wasn't in my bed. "Who knows?" Matt shrugged. "Rafe drove by me and beeped. Gone to Miami, huh?"

"Yeah, he'll be back this afternoon." Ali contemplated telling her brother his profession.

"He told me what he does, Al."

Ali's eyes widened. "He did? When?"

"At the bar the other night."

"So what do you think?"

"I think Dad is going to flip out, that's what I think." He laughed, just picturing his father's face.

Ali cringed. "I know, promise me you won't say anything."

"I'm not going to say a word. I don't have to ask what *you* think about his job," Matt gave her a smirk, "but how do you feel about the guy?"

"Oh, Matt, I know it's been only a couple of days, but I've got it bad."

He smiled gently. "Just be careful, Al. You said it yourself -- it's only been a couple of days."

"I know, I know," She looked at him, concerned. "You like him, right?"

"Yeah, I like him a lot. I think he's a stand-up guy, but I'm sure there's a lot more to know."

"It's just the craziest thing, I feel so..." Ali searched for the right words.

"All right, you know what?" Matt sighed, stopping her. "Let's just see what happens with everybody and enjoy the ride. We're just here to have fun, right?"

Ali laughed at his obvious discomfort with the intimate conversation. "I'm going to change." She left him and went to put on her running clothes and sneakers. She put her hair up, brushed her teeth, and went back to the living room to stretch.

Matt was on the phone. "Fax it to this number." She heard him rattle off her parents' office fax number. "We'll look it over and present it tonight." He gave Ali a look from the kitchen.

"Offer?" she mouthed.

He nodded. "They're coming in a little light, but I'll see what I can do. Thanks, Bob." Matt hit "end."

"Bob Santos? How much?" Ali crossed her fingers.

"Two seventy-five," Matt told her.

"A little light? They're 175 off," Ali huffed.

"His clients are saying they'll need to put at least that much back in."

"That's laughable. All that house needs is a new kitchen and baths and some paint. Everything else is sound. People suck." Ali stretched while thinking. "I'll call them today. They're going to be pissed."

"Santos says they're cash, thirty days, no contingencies."

"Have you ever met him?" Ali asked about the realtor.

"A couple of times. He lives in that neighborhood I built off Maple."

"Figures." The neighborhood consisted of million-dollar homes and over.

Matt chuckled. "What's that got to do with the deal?"

"I don't know. I just already don't like the guy, and I'm insulted on behalf of my clients."

"Ali, just drive him up and be psyched you've got an offer -- on paper. Let's start the process."

"You're right. I'll run and think about what I'm going to say to the Howards. They just want to retire, and I've got to get them everything I can."

"You will, and I'll help."

"Thanks, I'll see you in awhile."

"You taking a key? I'm going to head down to Tarpon Bay and see about kayaking."

"Oh, fun -- be careful, and yes, I have a key." Ali left the house and started a slow jog. This time she headed right out of the driveway toward the center of town. She would try to make it all the way there and to the tip of the island, then back.

Thinking about the Howards, she would suggest they counter at $440,000. The house was worth it-- the comps were there, and the work was mainly cosmetic. She didn't want to lose these buyers, but she wasn't about to give her clients' money away. She picked up her pace and let her mind think about the upcoming afternoon.

CHAPTER EIGHTEEN

Rafe had left the house reluctantly, not only because of the beautiful naked woman in his bed, but because of the two shitheads still parked next door. His only comfort was the fact that they usually pulled off around sun-up, so Rafe had made sure he gave them a wake-up call. He had made quite a racket sounding the alarm on his car, and it had worked because moments later he had heard their truck start and watched as they drove by his gate. He had followed them as far as Huxters on Sanibel, where they stopped, probably for Yoo-hoos and donuts. Rafe had kept going, knowing a tail would pick them up at the crossroads.

The dress shoes he'd put on with his suit now sounded their way along the marbled hallway in the building that housed the Department of Justice in downtown Miami. FBI offices were held on the fourth floor of the posh building, and he headed to the boardroom three doors down from the elevator where the weekly meeting took place.

Rafe entered the room and took an empty chair. Seated around the table were a few fellow agents and some DEA representatives as well.

"Good morning, Agent McDonough. We are just waiting for Agent Simmons." Daniels gave him a friendly smile.

Rafe nodded in greeting and pulled forward a yellow legal pad and pen from the center of the table. A secretary poured coffee and water around the table, and Rafe gladly took a cup of the steaming liquid. Agent Simmons made his way in and took a seat, also helping himself to a cup.

"Okay, people, let's get right to it." SAC Daniels stood at the head of the conference table, and all eyes were on him.

Rafe waited to hear what Daniels would have to say. Right after he'd listened to his voicemail and heard Holly Mann's voice telling him Stoddman was available at two o'clock for a meeting, he had called Daniels on the drive in to tell him, and to tell him about the incident with Ali and Sean Smith. He hoped that Daniels would leave that out of the meeting but knew it wasn't likely. Rafe had the SIM cards from the surveillance cameras and had made sure to delete the parts with Ali and him by the pool. Unfortunately, he'd had to make the tough decision of leaving the footage of Smith leering at her on there and the chase that ensued. Ali's face had been well concealed from the cameras, but there was no mistaking her naked body standing in the moonlight by the beach-path's gate. Rafe had to rely on Daniels' discretion as to whether it would be brought up in the meeting.

"We know now that it was Timothy Mann's friend Sean Smith who approached the driver of the Ford. The driver I.D.'d him last night by his DMV picture. We also know that it was Holly Mann in Cuba at that tobacco plant. She has also been identified by our refugee. We've got her on a flight to Havana out of Miami on April 10th. From there she took a bus to Pinar Del Rio, where she made contact. It turns out D'nafrio owns a piece of this tobacco plant. The majority shareholder of this plant is his long time friend and business associate, Jay Scintillo.

Several heads nodded in recognition of the notorious Miami night-club owner. He was a business man from Cuba but had been living in Miami for the past ten years. The FBI had a separate investigation going on inside one of his gentleman's clubs.

"Turns out Scintillo also owns beachfront property on Captiva." Daniels waited a beat. "Looks like he and D'nafrio will be neighbors."

Rafe nodded along with several others at the table. Things were starting to make sense.

"So there's our connection. Now we just need proof D'nafrio himself was involved in the smuggling of the drugs." Daniels hit a button, and a large screen behind him came to life with head shots. "We know Holly Mann works at East End realty, and Timothy Mann and Sean

Smith are now guarding D'nafrio's property. Special Agent McDonough will be on Barry Stoddman this afternoon and report back with me this evening."

Rafe nodded.

Daniels pointed to another female on the screen. Rafe noticed the resemblance to Holly Mann.

"This is our motel desk clerk, Misty Spencer, who, according to her boss, had to leave suddenly on Friday night due to an emergency with her kid. She's been an employee there since April first, doesn't really have a kid, and is Holly Mann's younger sister. We're guessing she got the call to get the hell out of there when it was clear nobody would be arriving for the money."

"Where is she now?" a DEA agent asked.

"Holed up in a trailer park not far from Holly Mann's home. We've got someone on her. It would be easy to bring anyone of these people in now for questioning." Daniels gestured to the screen. "But we don't want to risk losing D'nafrio. We want him first and foremost; let these people hand him to us. If he is behind all this, he'll send someone for the drugs sooner or later and they'll have to deliver them to D'nafrio."

"Is it possible he knows the drugs have already been confiscated?" Simmons asked.

"It's possible, but unlikely. It's clear now the two goons were put at D'nafrio's place to guard the drop sight -- but McDonough can tell you they're not very bright." Daniels nodded to Rafe.

"Why not just send the two goons in for the package? What's D'nafrio waiting for?" Simmons asked again.

"My bet is they were just told to watch out for anyone coming and going on the property. It's unlikely those two know about the package." Daniels surmised.

Rafe spoke up. "Cheech and Chong couldn't be trusted to get the mail, never mind retrieve a package with over 100 grand worth of ecstasy in it." A few chuckled at the reference. "D'nafrio's waiting to see if any of these refugees talk before he makes a move."

"He's probably right," Daniels added. "That's why we've sent out a statement to the press that tells of the release of the nine refugees and the help they'll be receiving from our government to start their new lives in the U.S. It's also why we aren't going anywhere near these suspects," he gestured again toward the screen, "with any capacity of the law. We are taking a big risk today putting McDonough on Stoddman, but if we can get audio on him, it'll get us D'nafrio on a silver platter."

"What's the plan there?" another of the DEA agents inquired.

"I'm meeting him this afternoon to look at property. I'll put audio surveillance in his office, in his car, and hopefully his cell," Rafe answered the man.

Daniels nodded. "It's the fastest way, and it won't be complicated. In the meantime, our refugee will be in protective custody, continuing to be questioned. Scintillo is obviously a major component to this case, and we're finding out all we can as I speak."

Daniels handed out assignments to the various agents around the table and dismissed everyone, asking Rafe to hang back.

When the room was clear, he spoke. "I have to turn that surveillance in, you know."

"I know, and I appreciate you not mentioning the incident at the table."

"What you do on your own time is your business, you know that. Just remember next time to stay the hell away from the camera. You can't be playing editor with the evidence if there's a possibility something important could be on that footage."

Rafe was duly reprimanded. "I hear you, and it was an error I won't make again." Shit if he didn't feel like an ass.

Daniels laughed, "I'll try to keep the audience to a minimum. It's not like you're going to marry the girl." He smiled, looking at Rafe, and just as quickly frowned as he saw Rafe's face. "Oh, shit, McDonough, what'd you go and do, find the girl of your dreams and get her mixed up in this shit?"

Rafe swore. "Not intentionally."

"Jesus." Daniels sat in the closest chair. "Do you want to tell me about it?"

Rafe grinned. "No, but I want that time off when this is over."

"To be with her?"

"Yes."

Daniels sighed. "Well, what do you know. It's finally happened to you -- how does it feel?"

"Off the record?" Rafe smiled.

"Of course, you think anyone else cares?" Daniels laughed. "Although Caplan's going to be pretty disappointed."

Rafe smirked, knowing Daniels was right. "It feels great -- more than great."

"Well, I'm happy for you pal. Just keep her off surveillance. Trust me, none of us would mind seeing a show, but you don't want everyone on the case envisioning her naked when she walks down the aisle."

Rafe definitely wouldn't want that. "That's hysterical, Daniels. There you go with the jokes again."

"Who's joking? I've seen that look before. Hell, I had that look -- still do, see?" Daniels was grinning from ear to ear, and Rafe threw his pen at him.

Daniels caught it deftly between his fingers. "Hey, seriously, get the surveillance equipment you need for today and see Mary about the paperwork for your time off. Let's get this case closed so you can live life the way it's supposed to be."

Rafe shook his head, smiling, and left the room. He suddenly couldn't wait to get back to the island where hopefully Ali waited to be his pretend fiancée.

CHAPTER NINETEEN

Nicki had been introduced to the four other women in the office. She would be filling in for a woman named Mary who went north for the summers. An intern from one of the local universities usually filled her place, but because Nan had made a phone call, Nicki would be taking the spot, and the other women were more than happy to help Grace Thompson's granddaughter out.

Nicki's first day was mostly getting acquainted with her co-workers and the paper itself. She would be covering local happenings, which meant she wouldn't be spending much time in the office at all. Her first assignment would start tomorrow, when she was to interview and photograph a new real estate agent for Beach Realty Company. Then she was off to the Sanibel School to interview and photograph the science teacher, who was just finishing her first year at the school, then over to the new rec. center to take photos of the swim team who were happy to now have a place to practice and have meets. Finally, she would stop over at C.R.O.W. (Clinic For The Rehabilitation Of Wildlife), where a new intern was busy rehabilitating a screech owl.

Nicki smiled at the simplicity of the island life as she sat at her new desk to get familiar with the paper. She was really going to enjoy this job. It was a few hours later, after familiarizing herself with the inner workings, that she set out to get some lunch.

"Excuse me! Hello there!"

Nicki looked up as she made her way to the convertible to see a short, balding man exuberantly heading her way.

"Hi, there! I'm your neighbor. I wanted to introduce myself."

Nicki took stock of the man before her. He was about fortyish, she guessed, and overly dressed in a pale pink suit jacket and tie from another decade on this rather hot day. Her neighbor? Next to Nan's house? He didn't look familiar. "Hi..." She waited.

"Here, I'm your neighbor here -- right next door at East End Realty. Barry Stoddman."

She should have guessed. He held out a meaty hand to her, which she took reluctantly. Sweaty, just as she'd guessed. He was a definite throwback to the eighties Miami Vice style -- minus the vice.

"Oh, nice to meet you, I'm Nicki Thompson. I just started at the paper."

"I know, I heard all about you from the girls inside."

Nicki smiled. The "girls" inside were all around her grandmother's age.

"They've been looking forward to your arrival."

"Yes, I'm glad to be on board for the summer."

"Now as I understand it, you are staying at your grandmother's house in Captiva, The Three Sunrises?"

Nicki cringed anticipating the pitch. She casually looked down at her watch. "Yes, that's right."

"That's a beautiful, beautiful home. Great spot she's got there. I actually represent the owner across the street. We do a lot here on the islands. If there's anything I can ever do for you or your grandmother, please don't hesitate to call."

Nicki accepted the business card he offered with feigned interest. Of course he represented monster-house guy. "Well, thanks, I appreciate that. I'm sure I'll be seeing you around."

"Sure thing. Maybe we can share a lunch one day soon."

Ugh, he actually winked at her. Nicki let the invitation go without responding, as she forced a smile. She started her car and waved goodbye as she pulled off. Her first shark, and she hadn't even entered the water yet. Wait until she told Nan.

After her run and a shower, Ali spent the rest of the morning in downtown Captiva exploring the little shops and stopping for an early lunch at R.C. Otters. She just loved the little street it was on. The magazine-worthy, cottage-style homes that lined it led right to the pristine beach.

She stopped in at the general store and picked up some groceries for the house. Her plan was to go home, call the Howards, and relax by the pool writing her postcards until Rafe called.

Ali returned to Nan's Jeep, which she was having fun driving, and put her few bags down in the back. She loved the Jeep. It was probably about twenty years old, but it had started right up for Ali. She wasn't crazy about the stick shift, but wasn't about to complain. She was grateful to have a car at all and grateful for older brothers who had taught her to drive a stick. With the top down and the breeze blowing around her, she thought it was the perfect island vehicle.

When she arrived back at the house, she put the few groceries away and went to her room to phone the Howards. There wasn't any sign of Matt yet, and she didn't expect to see Nicki for hours. She got Mr. Howard on the phone and explained to him about the offer and what she thought their counter should be and why. After briefly speaking with Mrs. Howard, they agreed with Ali and gave her the go-ahead to verbally counter the offer.

"Right now they're just fishing, so don't let this first offer scare you," she told them. "I'll flush them out. Just sit tight."

Ali called the buyer's agent, Bob Santos, when she hung up with the Howards. "Hi, Mr. Santos, this is Allison Fuller."

"Hello, there, Allison. Please call me Bob."

"Okay, sure, Bob. Listen, I've got a counter for you. My client sure does appreciate you bringing a buyer. However, they did feel the offer was way off. They are willing to take ten thousand off the asking price, and they did ask me to reiterate that the roof is only a year old and the plumbing, heating, and electric have all been updated within the past two years." Ali took a deep breath. "All the windows have been replaced as well. My clients actually put a lot of time and money into the house before putting it on the market. They realize the kitchen and baths need updating, but basically the house is sound and well cared for." Ali finished her spiel.

"Yes, yes, it's a fine house, and my buyers did take all of those factors into consideration, but what they want to do is put an addition on and flip the house, so they obviously want to keep there overhead down and their equity up."

Ali's jaw dropped. Oh, sure, my clients will pay for their built-in pool, too. "Well, Bob, with all due respect, that has nothing whatsoever to do with the sellers. Your buyers are coming in well below comp value, and quite frankly it's a little nervy." Ali found herself using one of her mother's favorite expressions for lack of a better one.

She heard him chuckle, and she found herself gripping the phone tighter.

"Now they are cash, no contingencies as I told -- your brother, is it?"

"Yes, Matt is my brother. I understand your clients' position, and you have our counter. I hope we can come to a reasonable and *fair* place." Ali was ending the conversation before she said something unprofessional.

"I'll pass it along, Ms. Fuller, and get back to you."

"Thank you so much." Ali hung up. Ugh! What an arrogant jerk! Did he actually laugh at her? She may be rather green as a real estate agent, but she'd been around the business long enough to know a crap offer. She wasn't going to get her hopes up on this one.

She heard the front door open, and she left her room to see who came in.

"Oh, good, it's you." She followed Matt to the kitchen and waited while he downed a bottle of water.

"Did you go kayaking?"

He nodded. "It was fantastic. We'll all have to go soon -- you'd love it, and it's an awesome workout."

"Cool. Hey, listen, I just got off the phone with Bob Santos and gave him the counter -- 440, by the way."

Matt nodded, smiling. "What did he say?"

Ali relayed the conversation, and Matt laughed.

"Doesn't that make you mad?"

"He's just trying to feel you out. They'll come up," he assured her.

"They'd better." Ali took the postcards she had purchased with Nicki their first day from her pocketbook. "I'll be out by the pool. I want to relax and forget about that jerk."

Matt laughed. "Yeah, I'll be out there soon. I've got to check my messages and make some calls first."

Matt went to his room and picked up his cell, which he'd purposely left behind. It had been great to have a few hours without it. The workout and the surrounding nature had done him good. It had given him an opportunity to really think about his relationship with Nicki and where he wanted it to go.

He sat on the edge of the bed and opened the phone, shaking his head at the eleven missed calls. Five were from Rick Tosca, one of his crew. He immediately got a bad feeling as he dialed him back.

It only rang once before Matt heard, "Matt, thank God. It's Sean, man, he's in the emergency room."

Matt stood up at the fear in Rick's voice. "Tell me what happened."

"He fell off the roof on Kelly Drive."

"Holy shit!" Matt ran a hand across his head. He pictured the steep slate roof on the 150-year-old home his crew was rehabbing. "How bad is it? What the fuck happened? Wasn't he tethered?"

"He was, but the tiles were slick from the rain the night before, and when he slipped, the damn rope split like it was kite string."

Oh, God, it was supposed to be just a simple patch job. "Is Terri with him?" Matt's heart went out to Sean's wife, who was pregnant with their first child.

"She's with him. He was hurtin', Matt." Rick sounded worried.

"So is there word yet?"

"No, but he's definitely got a broken leg -- he fell right to the ground from thirty feet. I think one of his arms is fucked, too."

"Did he hit his head?" Matt prayed not.

"Yes, but he was talking when they put him in the ambulance, answering their questions."

"Shit, I've got to get up there." Matt had to be there for Sean; not only was he his right-hand man, but a great friend.

"He's at Mass General."

"All right, I'm coming home. Call my cell as soon as you hear anything else."

Matt hung up the phone with a heavy sigh. Fuck! He prayed he would be okay. He dialed information and got connected to Mass General. "Emergency, please." He waited impatiently until he was connected. "I was wondering if you could tell me anything about Sean Thayer. He was brought in sometime in the last couple of hours, I think. Yes, I'll hold."

It had to have happened this morning, if the tiles were still slick from the night before. He'd forgotten to ask Rick the time.

"He's still in surgery, sir," a nurse informed him.

"Okay, thank you." Matt hung up and got his bag out of the closet. He threw his stuff in it and headed to the kitchen. He saw Ali out by the pool and went to tell her.

"Ali, I have to leave."

Ali turned around in her chair. "Okay, where you going?" Ali stood up at the look on Matt's face. "What's wrong?" Her stomach flipped over, thinking the worst.

"Sean fell off the fucking roof on Kelly Road."

Ali was familiar with the renovation job Matt's crew was working on -- Matt had given her a tour of the old home when they'd first started. "Oh, my God, Matt, how bad is it?" She pictured the steep roof line.

"I don't know, he's in surgery, but I have to get back there. Terri's pregnant."

"Oh, Matt, I'm so sorry. I hope he'll be okay. Did you book a flight already?"

"No, I'm just going to go to the airport and get on the first one out."

Ali's face fell. "What do you want me to tell Nicki?"

Matt felt horrible leaving without saying goodbye, but he had to get back ASAP. If Sean wasn't okay, he needed to be there for his family. "Please explain why I left and tell her I'll call her tonight."

"Of course. Is there anything I can do?"

"Call Mom and Dad. They may have already heard, but let them know I'm on my way."

"I will." Ali walked over and gave her brother a hug. "I'll pray."

"Do that." Matt grabbed his bag and keys and left the house through the front door. He thought briefly that he should have left Nicki a note, but he knew Ali would explain.

Ali came into the house for the cordless phone and took it outside with her. She dialed her dad's cell.

"Hey, Dad." He had picked up on the first ring.

"Hi, honey! How are you?" Her dad sounded enthusiastic and obviously had not yet heard the news.

"I'm calling because Matt's on his way to the airport."

"Oh?"

Ali filled her dad in, and in turn he told her to call Matt's cell and let him know he'd pick him up at Logan.

"Have him call me from the airport when he gets a flight."

"I will. I'm going to call him now."

Ali did just that and told Matt how sorry she was again. Man, what a horrible thing to happen. She couldn't help feeling bad for Nicki as well. Ali's eyes found the clock inside, and she wondered when she'd hear from Rafe.

She sat back in her chair and silently prayed for Sean. The ringing of the house phone startled her, and she nearly dropped it trying to answer it

"Hello?"

"Hey."

It was Rafe. Her heart leaped. "Hey, yourself." It was so good to hear his voice.

"What's wrong?" Rafe could hear in her voice that something was off.

Ali explained what had happened. "It's awful, and I feel so bad -- I just pray he's all right. His wife is pregnant with their first child."

"Wow, so Matt left already?"

"Yes, he was really upset."

"I'm sorry for him. I hope everything will be okay, too." Rafe felt kind of silly now asking Ali to accompany him. He was nearly back to the island and had just about an hour before he met Stoddman.

"Are you on your way back?" Ali asked, hopeful.

"Yes, I'm just about over the causeway." He hesitated, "I understand if you're not up for today."

Ali smiled, "Unfortunately, there is nothing I can do but pray, but I'd still like to help you out if the offer still stands."

Rafe smiled wide. "It definitely does. I was hoping you'd still want to."

"Be your fiancée? Of course, I've already booked the church. I was thinking the Chapel by the Sea one year from now -- is that good for you?" Ali smiled as she teased him.

"You bet, but do we have to wait that long?" Rafe laughed, but the prospect of it really happening didn't scare him one bit.

Ali laughed, too, knowing they were kidding around, but envisioning it as a real possibility thrilled her. Get a grip, girl! "We could probably get it done by the end of the summer. Is that soon enough?" Just joking about it excited her.

"Sounds good to me." He consciously left any humor out of his voice.

He actually sounded serious. Ali cleared her throat and laughed nervously. "So how should I dress for this?"

"Just casual. I like when you wear dresses, if it matters." God, he wanted her again just hearing her voice.

Ali grinned. "It matters." More than you know.

Rafe was smiling, too, like an idiot. Why was he so excited about this? He had to remember the task at hand. He had picked up the audio surveillance bugs that he would attach to the interior of Stoddman's office, car, and hopefully his cell before leaving headquarters and signed the paperwork for his vacation time. He needed this case to be over and had to get his head in the game, but he couldn't wait to have Ali on his arm posing as his fiancée. "I'm just about to the house. Do you want me to come get you?"

"Sure, I'll be ready when you get here." Ali hung up with Rafe and quickly went inside to slip on a sundress and sandals. She let her hair down loose around her shoulders and put a little lip gloss and mascara on. She went to the kitchen to leave Nicki a note, leaving out the part about Matt leaving and asking her to call her cell instead in case she was home before Ali.

Ali was gathering her phone and purse when she heard the knock at the front door. She took a deep breath, trying to calm her suddenly nervous stomach, and went to the door. She gasped silently as she opened it and saw Rafe standing there in a dark suit and sunglasses. He was an FBI agent, all right, right off the set of a movie, and all she could do was stare. The expensive suit looked as though it were tailor-made to fit his tall, muscular frame handsomely. His tinted sunglasses only enhanced his gorgeous face, and with his deep tan and sun-streaked hair, he made quite an impressive sight in her doorway. "Wow."

Rafe smiled, taking off his glasses. "Wow?"

"Yeah." Ali nodded appreciatively, looking him up and down. "Wow."

He laughed. "You like the suit?"

"I love the suit." Ali let him in and stood close by, unable to stop staring. "You should be a model."

He laughed loudly at that. "Now you're embarrassing me. C'mere."

Ali didn't have to go far to be in his arms. She rubbed her hands over the smooth material of his suit jacket. "Aren't you hot?"

"I had the A/C on in the car," he answered huskily as her hands caressed him. His own hands smoothed over the naked skin of her back and shoulders, and he felt her shudder against him. "I was going to go home and change into shorts real quick before we go. Want to come?"

Ali smiled up at him. "Uh-huh."

Rafe looked at her with hooded eyes. "It shouldn't take too long today. We're just going to look at a few houses."

"Okay." She didn't care how long it took as long as she was with him.

She locked the front door and followed Rafe across the street and into his house. The house was cool, and she got goose bumps as she followed him into his bedroom.

"I'm just going to change," he told her, watching as she sat on the bed.

"Can I stay?" she asked, smiling.

Rafe let out a small groan. "You're going to see more than I intended you to see right now."

Ali grinned. "I was hoping so."

"You're also going to make it difficult to be on time. If it weren't so important, I'd cancel right now."

"I don't want you to cancel. I've been looking forward to being your sidekick all day."

Rafe laughed as he took off his shoes and suit jacket, revealing his shoulder holster with his Glock safely harnessed inside it. He hung the jacket up on the hanger he'd left on the doorknob. "You're my fiancée, not my sidekick. The fewer words you speak, the better."

"Oh, the submissive little woman, I get it," she teased, and her heart thudded at the sight of the gun strapped to his side. "Don't I get a say in where I want to live?" She got up off the bed and went to him.

"Of course." He smiled, knowing full well why she had stood and come over to him.

"I know it's ridiculous, but you have no idea how badly you're turning me on right now." Ali's whole body hummed with excitement being near him.

Rafe laughed softly and reached for her. "You're crazy, but I have an absolute idea because I feel that way every time I look at you."

Ali reached up to kiss him, putting her arms around his neck, careful not to let them go to his side where she really wanted to touch.

Rafe kissed her back, returning the heat she was giving him, and reached for her hands, unclasping them from his neck. He slid them down his sides and let her right hand rest on the harness and slide over the bulk of the gun. He felt the intake of her breath and kissed her harder. Her hand came away just as quickly as he'd put it there, as if she'd touched fire. He pulled away and looked into her green eyes. "Is that what you wanted?"

She nodded, looking closer at it. "It's scary."

"You should always think so." Rafe stepped back and removed the holster, placing it atop the bureau. He unbuttoned his white dress shirt, and Ali's hands were immediately on his bare chest. "I should have come home to change first before I came for you." He was smiling down at her.

"And deprive me? No way. I'll go back on the bed and just watch. I'm sorry." She grinned.

"*I'm sorry* that we don't have any time before we have to meet him, because I want you naked right now, and that's going to be all I think about. Maybe this wasn't such a good idea." He was seriously thinking he'd made a mistake in asking her to come along.

Ali saw the worry on his face. "I can behave. I promise, I'll keep my mouth shut and be the best pretend fiancée there ever was."

Rafe laughed as he put a more casual dress shirt on and some casual shorts. He tried not to notice the heated look in Ali's eyes as she watched, especially when he'd slipped his shorts over his obvious erection. He shook his head and tucked his now unharnessed gun into the back of his shorts. His loose-fitting shirt hid its form, but there was no hiding the fact from Ali that it was there. She was making him squirm under her gaze, and he had to get them the hell out of his bedroom.

"Let's go," he barely got out.

Ali followed Rafe back outside and smiled as he opened the passenger-side door of the Yukon for her. She was so excited she couldn't stand it. She was actually going to be in the presence of a supposed criminal and the hottest FBI agent on the face of the earth, and she got to pretend to be his fiancée. She had to calm down and play it cool -- she didn't want Rafe to worry she couldn't handle herself.

"So fill me in. What do I need to know?"

Rafe shook his head, laughing, as he started the truck and pulled out of the drive. They had to drive to the East End, so they had about twenty minutes in the car. He told her he just wanted to get a feel for Stoddman, and that they were really just going to look at property and nothing else. He did not tell her he'd be discreetly bugging the guy's office, car, and phone. "Really, all you have to do is pretend you love me with all your heart and want to spend the rest of your life with me." He smiled as he drove.

Ail swallowed the sudden frog in her throat. "Okay, I can do that." Easily.

Rafe looked over at Ali, who sat staring intently out the windshield. He'd managed to render her silent. "What are you thinking? Is it going to be difficult?"

Ali turned her head just slightly, not wanting to look at him dead-on. "Hardly."

Hardly? Good, because it wasn't going to be difficult for him at all.

When they arrived at East End Realty twenty minutes later, Rafe came around to Ali's side to help her out of the truck. When she was on her two feet, he bent down to kiss her gently, and she responded in kind. "Ready?"

She nodded and felt him take her hand as they walked up the two steps to the entrance. Ali glanced quickly around the parking lot but didn't see Nicki's car, thank goodness. She forgot to consider they might run into Nicki.

They were greeted by a middle-aged blonde woman who reminded Ali of Annie the bartender, only a little rougher around the edges.

"Hi, may I help you?"

She definitely possessed the same smoker's voice as Annie at the bar, maybe worse.

"Hi, Rafe McDonough and Allison Fuller to see Mr. Stoddman," Rafe announced.

At the sound of his name, Barry Stoddman came out of his office to greet his potential new clients. Ali's first inclination was to laugh, but she held it together, plastering a big smile on her face as she felt Rafe squeeze her hand. The short little man was dressed in a suit jacket and dress pants, both in colors Ali would have loved to see in her Crayola box as a child. His tie was a blend of the two, with pink flamingos adorning it.

"Hello there! Welcome, this is my assistant Holly. Can she get either of you a drink while we talk?"

"No, thank you," Rafe answered politely. "Hon?"

Ali smiled sweetly. "No, thank you."

"Well, then, let's get acquainted in my office. Follow me."

Perfect. Rafe guided Ali ahead of him and smiled at Holly Mann, who had her eyes fixed on him. They took seats facing Stoddman's desk and still kept their hands intertwined.

"So, Holly said you wanted to look at beachfront property. Did you have any particular homes in mind?" Barry sized the couple up. They were stunning together, to say the least, a perfect match in the looks department. She was as hot as they come, and he looked like a movie star he couldn't place the name of readily. They were dressed casually, and he had taken notice of the Yukon when they drove up. They could just be a couple of looky-loos, Barry thought. They looked rather young to afford a beach house in Captiva, but one never knew on the islands.

Rafe sat in his chair, relaxed as could be, and discreetly took in the office. It was pretty bland in the decor department, the most color coming from the man who sat behind the desk. The walls held a couple of department store–type pictures of island landscapes, and the desk and chairs were straight out of IKEA. Rafe took stock of the desk's belongings, noting the phone, a stack of files, a glass paperweight with a teal-colored dolphin poised inside of it, and a gold-framed picture.

"We do have a couple in mind." Rafe gave him the addresses, one of which was Scintillo's beach house. He watched with hidden amusement as Stoddman's face went from casual to bright eyed -- dollar signs dancing in his pupils. Rafe could see him mentally calculating the commission on either of the houses he mentioned.

"Those are fine properties. I have a few others that might interest you as well. For not much more, you could have both bay and beach access."

Ali wanted to throw up at the obvious push but her smile stayed right where it was as she asked him some benign questions about the islands.

Rafe was proud of Ali, keeping him talking, which Stoddman couldn't stop doing now that he thought he had a big fish on his hook. Rafe almost felt bad for the guy. He let go of Ali's hand as he reached for the framed picture. He picked it up and stared. It was Stoddman on the back of D'nafrio's Rampage holding up a huge tarpon.

"Wow, is this recent?"

Stoddman grinned like a kid. "No, last year, actually. About this time, though, caught that sucker up in the Pass. Hell of a day, one hundred and twenty pounds. What a fight -- still have the scars to show for it." He held up his hands and Rafe smiled, putting the frame back on the desk.

"That looks like a hell of a boat. Wouldn't mind having one of those in the backyard."

Rafe smiled over at Ali, taking her hand again.

"Let's concentrate on the house first, babe."

"You're right." He winked at her, giving her a loving smile.

Stoddman watched the exchange and thought enviously about the relationship these two seemed to have. "Well, why don't we head out and see what appeals to you. We'll start with the two you mentioned, and then I'll show you what I had in mind. Luckily each home is unoccupied, and we can get right in."

Rafe knew Scintillo's house was empty because it was just yards away from the house he was staying in, and it was Stoddman's own listing. Rafe wanted to get in there and see the vantage point from the beach. He knew it had been the lookout point awaiting the refugees, and he wanted to get Stoddman out there. He could later compare his form in the light of day on the monitors, to the image captured the night the refugees arrived.

The second home Rafe chose was on the bay side, in town, a block from the Gulf. He chose it for no other reason than it, too, was one of Stoddman's listings and Rafe knew it would keep the realtor interested. Coincidentally it was also situated just doors away from a piece of land owned by one of D'nafrio's holding companies, that as yet had not been developed.

"You're welcome to jump in with me or follow, whichever you're more comfortable doing."

"We'll ride with you. That way you can fill us in on everything we need to know about the islands," Ali told him, smiling at Rafe. He looked at her appraisingly. She was making a good little sidekick after all.

Ali kept Stoddman talking by asking all the pertinent questions one would ask when buying a home. She was a pro and seemed to know the right balance of stroking the guy's ego and keeping him on his toes, having to answer her sometimes pointed questions about homeowner's insurance and taxes. He seemed impressed, and, thanks to Ali, Rafe knew he looked upon them as serious buyers.

They had headed back toward Captiva, Stoddman not knowing that they had only just come from there. Rafe found it humorous that Stoddman had yet to ask where he and Ali were staying or where they were from. His mind was obviously focused on a big fat commission check.

When they pulled into the driveway two doors down from Rafe's, Ali did the obligatory intake of breath at the sight of the massive beach home. It was impressive, to say the least, but not her style. Stoddman had handed the listing sheet to her when they got out of the car, and her eyes immediately went to the listing price - $6.5 million, a four-bedroom, four-bath home on the beach. There better be solid gold bricks holding up this mother, she thought to herself. She glanced at Rafe and smiled, her eyes teasing, telling him this could be the one.

Rafe wanted to take her in his arms and kiss her. She would make a hell of an actress.

"This house was built in 2000. It has all the amenities, and a finished lower level. Wait until you see the view. Just the backyard alone will thrill you. It has a saltwater pool with a ten-seat Jacuzzi spa."

"Did you say a saltwater pool?" Ali grimaced.

Barry stopped to look at the young woman and at the tone of her voice, he felt his stomach drop. "Yes, but it can easily be converted."

Rafe shook his head when Stoddman turned to work the lock box, giving Ali a big smile. She was enjoying making Stoddman sweat, and Rafe was enjoying her.

"It's just that the saltwater really bothers my eyes," Ali complained dutifully like a good little rich girl, and followed Stoddman into the house.

"Well, like I said, it can easily be converted. I can get an estimate for you by tomorrow, if this house interests you." Great, a prima donna, Barry thought.

I bet you'll have it by tonight. Ali smiled. "Thank you, that's above and beyond."

"Nonsense, comes with the service." Barry smiled at the couple. He hoped she didn't make things difficult.

It ought to come with the service, at...she tried to remember...a six-percent commission, that was if he didn't shave any off and he got both sides of the deal -- and of course if this were real and she and Rafe were actually to buy the house. That's the commission Nicki had told her Nan had paid when she bought her house. Six percent of 6.5 million. Ha! She worked in the *wrong* zip code.

She and Rafe continued to hold hands as they toured the house. Just the simple act of doing so felt so natural to Ali. His hand was large and solid around her much smaller one, and they fit together perfectly. Every so often he would absentmindedly rub his thumb over the back of her hand, and it was nothing, really, but to her it felt like everything.

The house really wasn't anything exceptional other than the views of the Gulf, but Ali oohed and ahhed just the same. When they made it down to the pool, Ali had to admit the surroundings *were* beautiful, and it reminded her of the backyard of the house Rafe was staying in. She caught his eye, and she knew he was remembering the previous night as well.

"Do you mind if I take a look at the house from the beach?" Rafe asked.

"Of course not. Follow me -- there's a well-manicured path over here."

"I'll stay here. I want to look on the inside again," Ali told them.

"Go right ahead. I saw you eyeing that little room off the master. It would make a great nursery." Barry winked at Rafe, and Rafe had to contain his laughter at the brief horrified look on Ali's face.

"That's right, honey, I noticed that, too." Rafe grinned at her.

"I was thinking more of a walk-in closet -- but okay, now you've got me thinking." She played along and gave Rafe a mischievous smile.

Ali went back inside and into the kitchen. She could see Rafe and Mr. Stoddman making their way to the water's edge. She wondered if Rafe was getting the information he needed. She ran a hand over the granite counters. Stoddman thought that the counters would be a huge selling point for her, and in fact they would be the first thing she ripped out- *if* she were to buy the six and a half million dollar home. She was so sick of granite and everyone using at as a selling point still today. Sure, natural stone was nice, but it had become so overdone. If it were her own kitchen she would use wood, a nice thick piece of cherry, stained just the right hue with a waterfall or Dupont edge. Maybe she'd have an island done in stone to add some contrast, but something consistent, not the potpourri of colors she was tired of seeing in the granite.

She checked out the appliances as well. They were all stainless, but old, not like the streamlined look of Rafe's kitchen. She wouldn't have a stainless refrigerator, either, she thought as she opened the side-by-side Sub Zero. She'd have her fridge paneled to match the cabinets. She loved that look. She looked again through the glass and could see Rafe and the realtor looking at the back of the house. Ali wondered how she would feel to really be house shopping with Rafe, and what kind of house they would look for, and where would they look? Could she see herself living in New York? She didn't think there even were houses in the city. Could she live in an apartment? She didn't even know if Rafe lived in an apartment, or where he lived when he was in Miami. There was a lot she didn't know, she realized, and watched as he and Stoddman made their way back to the house.

When they got inside, Rafe gave her a big smile, not for the benefit of Stoddman, but a genuine smile, and Ali's heart warmed at the sight of it. He came to her side and put his arm around her.

"Ready for the next one? I'm just not feeling it here, are you?"

"I'm not, and that room would be too small for a nursery, I think. What if we had twins?"

Rafe kissed the top of her head and pulled her in closer. "You're right -- we might need something with more bedrooms, big enough for five kids."

Ali choked back her laughter.

"Already planning that big family, eh?" Stoddman asked, smiling.

"The bigger the better." Rafe squeezed Ali's backside, and she had to bite her tongue to stop from laughing.

Rafe could cross two things off his list and was starting to relax. He was having fun teasing Ali. Stoddman was anxious and seeing dollar signs, making it easy for Rafe to do his job.

They made their way back outside and over to the car.

"I'm sorry. Do you mind if I run back in and use the bathroom?" Ali asked. She actually had to go.

Barry was only too happy to let her back in. He could get Rafe alone and feel him out, maybe get a better idea of how serious they were. He walked Ali back over to the house and fumbled with the lock box on the garage door rather than the front entrance. "You can go in this way. There's a bathroom to your right down the hall."

"Thank you." Ali slipped inside and found the room. When she was done, she quickly looked around. They had skipped the finished basement on the tour and now she knew why. As she stepped toward the sliders that led to the pool, she could smell the mildew all around her. Looking down, there was definite water damage to the carpet and to the bottom of the sheet rock on either side of the glass doors. She shook her head, thinking of the asking price, especially since the finished basement wasn't technically part of the living space, but she would think as the realtor Mr. Stoddman would disclose the problem or handle fixing it himself.

She continued on, opening a door she guessed led to the garage. She stepped inside and was surprised to see how full of stuff it was. One wall was lined with lots of wood slatted boxes that Ali deduced to be crab or lobster traps, given that beside them was a shelf full of colorful buoys like she had seen on the beach with Rafe. On the back wall hung all kinds of diving gear -- masks, flippers, wetsuits, and tanks. The owner was obviously a fisherman of some sort. She carefully shut the door behind her and made her way back outside, pulling the exterior door closed and making sure it locked behind her. Rafe and Stoddman were leaning against Stoddman's Beemer, talking amiably.

"All set?" Rafe asked, smiling. "I'm anxious to see this next house on the bay. Barry says it's a nicer home, although it's not on the beach."

Ali smiled, getting into the back seat. "That's okay. The bay is pretty, too." She watched as Rafe got into the front seat and wondered briefly about it. He had sat with her in the back on the way here.

"I was telling Barry we'll be getting married at the end of the summer and how we'd like to have something purchased by that time."

"It would be nice to have one less thing to worry about," Ali agreed from the back seat. Talking with Rafe like this was feeling way too natural, and she had to remind herself she was driving around looking at multimillion-dollar houses in the back of a BMW. Reality check, please! They passed the downtown area and pulled onto a little sandy side street, and then onto a shelled drive where at the end stood a tall narrow house overlooking the bay.

"It's tall, isn't it?" Ali commented, getting out of the car. It was interesting architecture for sure; she was curious about the inside.

"Can we start around back? I'd like to see the view," Rafe asked and took Ali's hand as Stoddman led them through a side gate.

The view was magnificent. They watched as several boats meandered by. They could see the sign declaring a No Wake Zone. "That's good -- nobody can go buzzing by, disturbing the peace and quiet," Rafe commented.

"Yes, it's very peaceful back here," Stoddman agreed. "This home was built in 1985, destroyed in Charlie, and rebuilt in 2005. It was built to all the new codes and has state-of-the-art hurricane protection."

"That must have cost a small fortune." Ali looked quickly at Rafe apologetically. She had to remember *they* were supposed to have a small fortune if they were out shopping in this price range.

"Worth every penny, I bet. Hon, think of how much safer you'd feel living in a house like this, protected from the elements."

"You're right, I would. Let's go see the inside. The outside is absolutely stunning -- I have a feeling the rest will be too."

Barry eagerly took them inside, again giving them the tour. This was on at 5.9 million, and he could see they were really liking it. "Again, it's not on the beach, but from the top decks you can see the Gulf, and you've got direct access here on the bay. You can get that boat you're dreaming of and head off fishing." Barry gave Rafe's back a manly slap and winked at Ali.

Ugh! She could practically see him salivating and decided to feed the fire. "I really love this, Rafe. I can see us entertaining here, having our family and friends visiting. It's really something special, don't you think?"

Rafe nodded. "I love its location. We could walk to town for dinner and drinks or walk to the beach for the sunset. It is pretty perfect." He smiled at Ali, and she returned it with her own.

Barry could see they were falling in love with the house, picturing themselves in it already. His heart raced thinking about it. Yes, he had these two lovebirds; he just had to get them on paper.

"I know there's been some other offers, but we can go back to my office after we look at the other homes I'd like to show you and look at the history."

Ali refrained from rolling her eyes. Here was where Ali, as the woman, was supposed to get anxious and emotional, worried that somebody else would swoop in and buy it. She decided to give it to him. "Oh, Rafe, do you think we should put in an offer tonight? I'd hate to lose it."

Rafe took a deep breath, watching Ali's performance. He had to give it to her, and would for sure when he got her back to his place. Even as his pretend fiancée she turned him on -- maybe it was the real thought of it. He turned to Stoddman. "How long has it been on the market?"

Oh, good question, Rafe, can't wait to hear this guys bullshit answer. Ali looked at Stoddman, too, with feigned concern.

Barry cleared his throat. "I've had the listing for two months."

And there you go. That wasn't the question. Ali didn't do the obvious, which was to call him to the carpet. Instead, she looked at Rafe. "Oh, wow, only two months. This won't last."

Rafe had everything he could do not to laugh at her and shake his head. "Yeah, we have a lot of thinking to do. You know what, Barry, I don't think we need to see anything else, but we'd like to sleep on this tonight and maybe tomorrow night, too. Would you mind taking us back to the office now?"

"Sure thing, sure thing. Let me just go up and lock those sliders to the roof top deck. I'll meet you all by the car."

"Great, thanks, Barry." Ali started toward the stairway down.

"Oh, Barry," Rafe approached him. "Would you mind if I used your phone? We didn't take ours today, and I'd like to put a quick call in to my accountant. I know he'll be a big help in our decision."

"Absolutely." Barry couldn't give Rafe his phone fast enough.

"Thanks, Barry, see you outside." Rafe was dialing as he followed Ali down the stairs. The phone rang on the other end.

"Daniels."

"Hey, boss, what's my cap again?"

Daniels shook his head. "You're calling me from his phone, aren't you?"

"Yes, is 5.9 million in the budget?"

"Why, did you find a small country you want to buy? I could probably get it approved."

"Great, I'd like to make the purchase by the end of the summer." Stoddman was coming out the door.

"Yankees are up by two, bottom of the fifth."

"That's what I like to hear, we'll talk more about this tomorrow." Rafe hung up and dropped the phone by accident. The battery fell off the back, and he apologized as Barry came over to the car. Apologizing and placing it back on, he handed it to Barry.

"Don't worry about it. That happens at least once a day to me."

Rafe laughed. "I know, me, too. It always amazes me how easily they fall apart."

Ali got into the back seat and again watched as Rafe took the front seat. He had essentially made the realtor his friend, calling him Barry now, and sitting next to him, relating with him on life's little annoyances. He was good, and Ali wondered again if Rafe had garnered from Barry what he needed. She listened as Rafe got Barry talking about himself and his life on the island. He seemed like a harmless guy other than being a smarmy realtor, and Ali wondered if he was indeed a criminal.

They made it back to the office and promised to call within a couple days' time with their decision on an offer. They thanked Barry profusely and couldn't help but see the hopeful look on his face as they left him.

"I'd feel bad for him if he wasn't so full of shit." Ali perused the parking lot once again for Nicki's car, but it was still not there. It was after three, and Ali figured she'd see her at the house in a couple of hours. She didn't look forward to it, and her mind went to Matt. He would hopefully be arriving in Boston soon.

"Why, because he's subtly trying to pressure us into buying a five-million-dollar house?" Rafe laughed.

"There *are* other offers, you know. We should make our move tonight. God, did he think we wouldn't look at the bottom of the listing sheet? It's been on the market for over a year." She shook her head. "Did you like how he made it sound as if it had only been on for two months?"

"Yeah, I caught that." Rafe smiled over to her. "You're all riled up, huh?"

"People like him give realtors a bad name. He's like the used car salesman everyone pictures in their mind."

Rafe laughed again. "His choice in clothing didn't help, either."

Ali burst out laughing. "I almost lost it when he first came out of his office. If you didn't squeeze my hand, I may have."

"You were great the whole time. I was impressed. I kept thinking what a good little sidekick you really are."

Ali grinned. "Would I make a good agent?"

He laughed heartily at that.

"What?" She pretended to be offended.

"I'm laughing because I'm picturing you as one of Charlie's Angels."

"The original, or the remake?"

"Does it matter?"

"I guess not. I should be offended either way."

He smiled. "I'm not being sexist. It's just that you *are so sexy,* and the idea of you running around with a gun in a bikini makes me think of that."

"No, Rafe, that's not sexist at all." Ali rolled her eyes at him, but wasn't really offended since he thought she was sexy. Besides, she hadn't any designs on becoming an FBI agent -- she just enjoyed the idea of it.

"I wouldn't want to have to worry about my fiancée out there in the field, anyway. It would be too stressful." He gave her a slight grin.

"No, you'd rather have me at home pregnant, right?"

"Not until after we're married -- and married for a couple of years. I'd want you to myself for awhile before sharing you with our five kids."

"Five? Really? I say three tops. One of each sounds even better, but I know that doesn't always pan out." Ali was enjoying the teasing, and she wondered if he really did want that many kids. She was playing along, but her answers were honest ones.

Rafe looked over at her. He knew they were kidding around, but it felt kind of nice to think it could be a real conversation. "Whatever you want. If two or three makes you happy, then that's what makes me happy. I'm just going to enjoy the gettin' it done part."

Ali laughed, meeting his eyes. God, he almost looked serious. She turned to look out the window. "I had fun today, anyway. Thanks for trusting me to help you out."

Rafe reached for her hand and settled it on his thigh while they took the Gulf road back to the beach house. "Like I said, you did great. You were the perfect distraction."

"Can I ask what I was trying to distract him from?" She looked at him again, and loved him holding her hand like that. It had been such an intimate gesture, and it felt comfortable, like they'd been together for a long time.

Rafe thought about her question. “I made it possible for headquarters to now be privy to Stoddman’s conversations.”

Ali nodded. “Is that what you were doing when you put the battery back on his phone?”

“And here I was worried you’d think I was a klutz.”

“If I didn’t know who you really were, I would have. I was pretty impressed how you made him think you had so much in common. Are you sure you don’t have any light pink sports coats or lime green pants in your closet?”

Rafe laughed. “Thanks, and maybe just a few pink ones.”

“The difference is, *you* could pull it off. You’d look great in any color.” Ali smiled at him, meaning it. He truly was the most handsome man she’d ever laid eyes on. It got her thinking again of babies. What would theirs look like?

“Thank you, but I should be saying that to you.”

“I thought you liked me best naked?” she boldly teased him.

He gave her a hungry look. “Just picturing that is enough to make me drive off the road.” He pretended to swerve onto the shoulder and got a shriek out of Ali.

“Hey!” she laughed. “I didn’t mean to distract you. Tell me what’s going to happen now with Stoddman.”

He smirked at the change of subject. “Hopefully now we’ll gain some knowledge as to what’s next, and when I can put an end to this case and move on.”

“When it’s over, can you tell me what it was all about?”

“Sure, if you’re interested.”

Ali gave him a look that read “duh.”

Rafe laughed. It would be nice to share his work with her. He knew she really was interested, and he knew after the previous night’s incident he should probably explain some of what was going on. The refugee story would be all over the news today, so that wasn’t an issue.

He just had to be careful of revealing too much about D'nafrio's involvement until that was evident itself.

"Do you want to come back to the house for a late lunch?"

Ali smiled. "Sure, that would be great. You must be starving -- we went right out when you got back. Have you eaten anything since this morning?" Ali remembered his cereal bowl in the sink.

"Just a cup of coffee at the meeting. I am pretty hungry. Do you want to pick something up? Or I could cook us some burgers on the grill," he offered.

"That sounds good." Ali just wanted to get back to the house with him. He still held her hand, and she turned her body so that she faced him.

"I put in for my vacation time today, officially." They were almost to Captiva and Rafe was enjoying the drive with her. The weather was ridiculously beautiful once again, and he looked forward to a drink with Ali by the pool.

Ali's heart soared. "That's great. So will you have to leave the house right away?"

"Not until the case is officially over, but I've made a call to Tween Waters. They have some cottages available."

"Oh, great, those look so nice to stay in. I would stay there in a heartbeat if we didn't have Nan's house." She would also ask him to stay with *her* in a heartbeat if it wasn't Nan's house.

"Yeah, it should be nice." Rafe was envisioning her there with him, but didn't want to be presumptuous.

Minutes later they pulled into the garage and headed inside the house. Rafe turned on the T.V. in the living room and the property's surveillance covered the screen.

"Do you have to watch that all the time?" Ali loved watching him in "FBI guy" mode. It was such a turn-on.

"Pretty much. The days are pretty dead -- the construction going on is generally the only activity I'll see. Once in awhile someone of interest shows up on site, but my only job so far has been to make sure the footage gets to H.Q. That'll change soon."

"How so?"

"Well, the situation is starting to heat up. Some things have happened in the past few days that are bringing us closer to a finale."

Ali's brows arched as she went over to the couch and sat. "I know you can't tell me a lot, but I'm dying to know." She looked at one corner of the flat screen and watched as two men hauled lumber up a makeshift ramp into the shelled-out structure. They must be putting up the second floor, she thought. The other camera angles that surrounded the beach house were pretty dead, as Rafe described -- some palm trees swaying in the breeze and images of the vast, empty beach. Every once in awhile a car would drive by on the monitor that covered the front of Rafe's property, and it would catch her eye. She noticed that she could see the bottom of Nan's driveway, and she looked up at Rafe who was watching her.

"It wasn't a coincidence that you were out running Saturday morning, was it?"

Shit. "No." He walked over to the chair across from her and sat. He couldn't tell if she was mad, but she appeared to be thinking about something.

"So you purposely went out to meet up with me?"

He nodded yes, and she smiled, thank God. "But I didn't know what I would say or do, I just wanted to see you again. I'll forever be grateful to that black racer."

Ali laughed softly. "Me, too, then, I guess." There was one for the grandkids. Seriously, what was wrong with her?

"I wanted to come down to the beach the night you and Nicki sneaked back there, but I didn't have the courage."

"I knew someone was watching. I felt it."

"I couldn't take my eyes off you."

"Why not Nicki?" Ali was curious.

"I don't know. She's obviously beautiful, but I was drawn to you. I am drawn to you."

Oh. Ali sucked at her lower lip. What could she say to that?

"I'm sorry about all this." Rafe gestured to the flat screen. "I don't want you to feel like your privacy has been compromised. I did take advantage of the situation by tailing after you Saturday morning."

"I would have been sorry if you hadn't. My hope was that I would see you again at the bar. Although I must admit Saturday I was foolish enough to think fate had somehow intervened and had you out running at the same time as me." She laughed at herself.

Rafe looked at her face, and she seemed a little embarrassed. "You weren't foolish. You were just a day off. Fate arrived Friday night, putting *you* on the beach right outside this house."

Ali's heart was pounding. He was totally serious. "Wow." She blinked as she stared at him. She wanted to ask if he really felt that way but had the feeling he'd just so plainly told her that. Now what?

"Yeah, wow." Rafe held her gaze. He knew she was surprised at his admission, and he hoped it hadn't sounded ridiculous, but he actually believed what he'd told her. "I'm going to start the grill."

Just like that? And leave me sitting here to ponder the rest of my life with you, because you're saying fate put us together, and who screws with fate? No one. Which means that we're going to be together right? And have those babies we pretended about earlier. Oh, my God.

As if he were hearing her silent conversation with him, he smiled and said, "Let's just start with the hamburgers."

Ali laughed, grateful for the break in the all too overwhelming moment. She added her own humor. "That sounds good, because I was just about to start a mental list of baby names." She gave him a teasing smile.

Rafe got up off the chair and held out a hand to help her off the couch. Pulling her into him, he kissed her softly. "Thanks for today."

"Any time." Ali kissed him back and then followed him to the kitchen to help him prepare the burgers to bring outside. She grabbed a couple of plates and some napkins, and they went outside to the pool bar, and she sat while Rafe tended to the grill.

"I'm hoping I'll hear from Matt soon. I hope things are going well. I'm not looking forward to telling Nicki, though. She is going to be so bummed out."

"Yeah, the timing definitely sucks for them, but I'm sure she'll understand."

"Oh, of course she will. She'll want to fly there to be with him, except her new job will prevent that."

"That's tough, but maybe things will be okay and Matt can come back soon."

"I hope so." Ali looked out at the Gulf and watched a lone pelican bounce in the tide.

Rafe sat down next to her on a barstool and looked at her.

"What?" She smiled, seeing he had something on his mind.

"You know how I got the phone call in the bar the other night?"

Oh-oh. "Yes." Please don't let this be bad, she thought.

Rafe could see she was thinking it had something to do with them, and he reached for her hand, bringing it to his lips and kissed it. "This has to do with work."

Ali relaxed and listened. "Go on."

Rafe told her about the refugees arriving on the beach, his suspicions that Stoddman had been the one to announce their arrival to the driver, and he told her about the package. He let her draw her own conclusions as to what was in it, but he explained that that was the reason for the two idiots next door and that he wanted her to be wary of them. He also explained why he had wanted Stoddman on the beach today, to compare the footage in the daytime to what he had from that night.

"So the FBI has this package, and the bad guys don't know it yet?"

"We don't think so. We think they were waiting to see that all nine refugees were released without incident and that none of them talked."

"That was quite a risk, wasn't it? What made them think none of them would talk?"

"Well, we aren't dealing with the smartest bunch, I think it was more along the lines of they didn't think we would ask. This isn't the first time refugees have arrived on these beaches, and so far they've just been people looking for a new life in the U.S. If these nine hadn't landed on D'nafrio's stretch of beach -- a man already heavily being investigated by the government -- it's possible certain questions *wouldn't* have been asked. But of course nobody knows he's being investigated, so whoever's running the show thought nothing of directing them here."

"Wow, so where did they leave the package, in the house being built?"

Rafe smiled, "Remember those pretty buoys you were asking about in the water the other day?"

Ali was nodding enthusiastically as it registered, and Rafe got off the stool to flip their burgers.

"Yes, yes!"

Rafe looked at her funny and laughed, "Well, anyway, one of them marked the trap that held the waterproofed package. It was placed weeks ago, before I arrived, meant to blend in with the others."

"So you have no footage of anyone placing it." Ali said it as a matter of fact, and Rafe looked at her with amusement as she nodded her head, as if she were trying to piece the puzzle together.

"Exactly, but I have my suspicions of who may have."

"I'll be right back." Ali ran up the porch steps, into the house, down the steps to the garage, and opened the passenger side door to Rafe's truck. She took the first folded-up listing sheet from the dash where she'd left it, then made her way through the workout room to get to the pool area faster.

Rafe saw Ali appear at the lower-level sliders and waited as she lifted the lock and slid them open. "Where did you go?"

Ali was reading as she made her way back to the stool at the bar. Rafe was taking the burgers off and setting them on buns. He handed her a plate and went around to the mini fridge for ketchup and pickles.

"He's had the first listing for two months as well. That would give him plenty of time to set up shop and get the buoys out there. I can look up who owns the house. It's public record, maybe the owner is involved." Ali's adrenaline was pumping, thinking she was figuring things out, and maybe being able to help Rafe.

"A man named Scintillo owns the house, a business partner of D'nafrio's. That's why Stoddman has the listing." Rafe told her.

"Well, that answers that. So you already know there's a connection. You just need proof of Stoddman's involvement, right?"

"Yeah." He grinned at her enthusiasm. "Proof is always good for a conviction."

Ali smirked. "What if I told you I know where you can find some?"

Rafe came around to her side of the bar and stood in front of her. She was adorable playing junior detective. "I'd kiss you on the lips and ask you to marry me."

She knew he was teasing, but she couldn't help smiling at the thought.

"You might regret you said that," she told him. "When I went back in to go to the bathroom, I took a tour of the lower level. That basement was all mold, by the way. They totally had some major flooding."

Rafe sat down next to her and shook his head with a smile, taking a bite of his burger. She kept amazing him. She hadn't touched her own burger yet; he could see she was all excited about something. Rafe had been busy bugging Stoddman's car while Ali had gone back inside. He had pretended to admire the BMW, caressing the soft leather seats and the burl dash. All the while she had been snooping. He chuckled on a mouthful.

"Go on." He took another bite. He would eat hers, too, if she didn't. He was famished.

Ali knew he was laughing at her attempts to help him, but she ignored him and went on. "So then I went into the garage, and what do you think I saw?"

"A car?" he teased her.

Ali rolled her eyes. "Crab traps, and purple buoys, like the one out there," she pointed to the Gulf. "I saw paint cans and dive gear, too." Ali sat up straight, pleased with herself, as she waited for Rafe's reaction.

Rafe swallowed his burger down, it suddenly tasting like a lump of sand instead of the soft juicy meat of a moment ago. Why hadn't he asked to go down to the lower level? He had been so concerned about getting a shot of Stoddman on the beach and concerned about getting the audio surveillance in place, it hadn't even crossed his mind. He slipped big time, and Ali may have just saved his ass. He washed the lump down with his water and stood up.

"Tell me again exactly what you saw, and where exactly you saw it."

Ali wiped the proud look off her face, seeing Rafe the "FBI guy" appear, and she told it to him again, this time a little nervous she would forget an important detail.

"I have to make a phone call. Will you excuse me?" Rafe pushed his stool back and started to walk away, but came right back to her.

He took her by surprise as he bent down and kissed her on the lips. Ali hoped that meant she'd done well. He had become real serious real fast. She thought about calling out after him, "Hey, what about the asking me to marry you part?" but decided he probably wasn't in a joking mood.

Rafe dialed Daniels from his bedroom. He had the flat screen on, and he watched the construction site next door. It was business as usual; the same pickup trucks were parked there, and Rafe could see men working inside and out. He could also see that Nicki had just pulled in the driveway across the street and he knew Ali would want to know. When Daniels didn't answer, he hung up to go inform Ali that Nicki was home. He was glad to see she'd eaten half her burger.

"Is everything okay?" she asked.

"It will be, thanks to you. I'm just waiting for a call now, but I wanted to tell you I just saw Nicki pull in."

"Oh, I'd better get over there, then." Ali made a face, indicating she wasn't looking forward to it.

"It'll be okay. I'll come over when I'm done here?" Rafe asked with a slight smile. He didn't want her to go, but he had to talk to Daniels.

"I'd like that." Ali smiled back. "Thanks again for today. I had fun."

"I did, too." Rafe took her in his arms. "You made a great partner."

Ali smiled. "You want to take me to the firing range now, don't you?" she teased.

"That's not the kind of partner I had in mind." He grinned. "But I suppose I owe you now."

Ali wondered what he did have in mind. "Yeah, you do, and I intend to collect."

Rafe laughed. "Get out of here before I don't let you leave."

Ali laughed, too. "It's kind of difficult with your arms around me -- not that I'm complaining."

"It's just hard to let go." He bent to kiss her and they stayed, lips and tongues intertwined for awhile, before Ali pulled away.

"No fair," she said softly.

Rafe pressed her to him and groaned.

"That's definitely not fair," she laughed. "Come over as soon as you can, okay?"

"Uh-huh." Rafe reluctantly let her go and walked her out and down the driveway. "I'll see you in a bit."

Ali said goodbye and ran across the street, her heart filled.

CHAPTER TWENTY

Nicki decided to stop into Periwinkle Place before she went home. The shops looked so inviting this morning when she'd driven past. She'd done a little window shopping and found some great jewelry in Pandora's Box, hers and Ali's favorite store on the island. It was now nearing four-thirty, and she was starting to get hungry already. She wondered what they'd all do tonight. Smiling, she got back in the convertible and took the drive back home to Captiva. She glanced at the school and was looking forward to going there tomorrow for her interview with the science teacher. Her eyes back on the road, she had to slow the car suddenly as she saw a turtle lazily crossing to the other side. It made it to the oncoming lane, and Nicki laughed as she looked in her rearview mirror. A driver had had to stop to get out and move it to the shoulder of the road. That turtle was lucky he wasn't crossing the expressway in Boston, she thought.

When she finally pulled into the driveway, the first thing she noticed was the absence of Matt's Hummer. Only Nan's old Jeep sat parked off to the side. She wondered where he went. She went in through the pool gate instead of the front door, figuring she'd find Ali back there, but no one was out back. She tried the sliders and found them unlocked and went inside. "Hello?" she called out, but didn't get a response. In the kitchen she found Ali's note to call her, so she went to her room to change and do just that. Maybe Ali and Matt were together.

Nicki heard the front door open and shut moments later. Ali found her in her room.

"Hey."

Nicki looked up from the edge of the bed where she sat, about to call Ali.

"Hey," she smiled, "I was just about to call you. Are you with Matt?" Nicki took notice of her best friend's forlorn look, and her heart sank. "What's wrong?"

"Nicki, Matt had to leave."

Nicki didn't understand. "Leave?"

"He had to go back to Boston. His foreman fell off a roof and got taken away in an ambulance."

"Oh, my God!" Nicki stood up. "Is he okay? Sean?" Nicki had heard Ali and Matt mention him on several occasions. Matt had just mentioned him the night before, saying what a good friend he was.

"When he left, Matt didn't know Sean's condition. He's at Mass General."

"Oh, no, I hope he'll be okay. Isn't his wife expecting their first baby?"

"Yes." Ali cringed. "I feel so bad."

"Me, too." Nicki felt bad all around. Just when things were going so well, she couldn't help but think a little selfishly. She was crestfallen that Matt had had to leave. She didn't even get to say goodbye.

"Did he...say anything before he left?"

"Of course, Nick." Ali reached a hand out to her best friend. "He said he would call you tonight. I could tell he felt real bad about leaving."

"Well, he should be with his friend, of course," Nicki said, meaning it. "I hope he calls us with good news."

"Me, too." Ali could see how badly Nicki was feeling, and her heart went out to her. "Want to have a drink by the pool?"

"Sure." Nicki followed Ali to the kitchen and thought about Matt. She wondered if he was in Boston yet.

"How was your first day?" Ali tried to get her mind off Matt as she mixed them each a drink.

"It was good, got to know everyone, got the rundown on the paper and how it all works. Not much different from the college paper, actually." She half-laughed, then continued, "Drove around the island a bit, getting my bearings for tomorrow. I've got some interviews to do that should be interesting."

"That's sounds fun." Ali knew Nicki would only be thinking about Matt tomorrow, and she hoped he would call soon. They took their drinks outside and sat looking out at the bay.

"This sucks." All Nicki wanted to do was cry. Of all the worst luck!

"Want me to put an umbrella in it?" Ali knew Nicki hadn't mean the drink, but she hoped she could put a smile on her face.

Nicki gave her a sad smile and a little laugh, but it led to a burst of tears.

"Oh, Nicki." Ali got off her chair to hug her. "He didn't want to leave."

"I know, I know, I feel like a jerk. Matt's a great friend going back to be with him. I'm just being selfish. Things were going so well, and now I'm just afraid the spell will be broken, you know? He'll be back home and reality will settle in -- you know, maybe wondering what he was doing here with me. Maybe this was all just a fantasy."

"No, Nicki, it's real. I know Matt. I don't think anything's ever been so real to him."

Nicki sniffled. "I wish I could have gone with him."

"When he calls Nick, tell him how you feel, okay?"

"Maybe." Nicki sipped her drink, swallowing the lump in her throat.

CHAPTER TWENTY-ONE

"Holly, I'm going to be in the office on an important call, so please, no interruptions." Barry watched as Holly continued to file her nails.

"How did it go with those two?"

She said *those two* with a touch of condemnation that Barry interpreted right away as jealousy.

"I'll probably have them on paper by tomorrow," he answered her with confidence. He knew by looking at Rafe that that man would give his fiancée anything she wanted, and she wanted that house. Barry would take that commission and maybe trade the Beemer in for a Mercedes. Xavier drove a Benz, and it was sweet.

Holly looked the realtor up and down. She'd been sleeping with him for a few months now, and he'd finally started paying her rent. As soon as she'd started getting creative with him in the sack, she had him hooked. He wasn't as disgusting as the last guy, but she was finding it harder and harder to look at him in his stupid Easter egg–colored clothes. She looked forward to when Tim Senior got out of prison. He was the only man who did it for her, but in the meantime, she had to make ends meet. Although, now that Timmy Junior was on D'nafrio's payroll, things were starting to get a little easier. Even her sister had made a little extra cash, and *she* didn't even have to sleep with anybody.

With Barry now paying her rent, Holly could start socking away money for Tim Senior's release. They would move up to North Carolina, to the mountains. Each day when Barry was out of the office, Holly would look online at the land for sale. She and Tim Senior could buy an acre real cheap and put one of those nice double-wides on it for when Timmy Junior came to visit. She just had to make sure neither she nor Timmy Junior and his friend Sean fucked things up.

"Glad to hear it." She focused on Barry and gave him one of her best smiles leaning forward on her desk, giving him a great view of the cleavage that spilled from her low-cut blouse. She *was* glad to hear it -- the more money he made, the better for her.

"*You* can interrupt me in about twenty minutes." Barry gave her a wink and went into his office, shutting the door behind him.

He took his suit jacket off, taking care to hang it up in the closet behind him, rather than on the back of his chair. The last time he had done that, it had got wrinkled to shit from Holly grasping it while he fucked her in the chair. He sat down and picked up the phone. D'nafrio was in Miami, and Barry knew to call the condo on his secure line instead of his cell.

"Where were you today?"

Barry blanched at the lack of greeting he received. "I was out showing property. I think I've got a buyer."

"One of my properties?"

Barry cleared his throat. "They actually like our newest listing, on the bay in Captiva."

"Did you show them the Gulf front?"

"Yes, it wasn't what they were looking for." Barry knew he was supposed to push certain properties, including the Gulf-front home of D'nafrio's business partner and he waited for the lecture.

"That's fine. Scintillo's thinking of giving it to his daughter anyway. She's getting married in the fall."

Barry let out a sigh of relief. He'd rather forgo the commission on that property than deal with the pressure of having to sell it.

"Are we still on for tomorrow night?" Barry was anxious to retrieve the package. They had waited long enough, and Barry thought it was now safe to go after it. He knew the authorities had been combing the Gulf that first night and all the next day like they always did when refugees arrived on the beach, but by now the activity would have died down and just the Coast Guard would be out there -- way out there. No one was going to bother a lone diver close to shore. The plan was to dive for the package, rather than motor out to pull the trap up and risk being seen in a boat.

"Yeah, we're on. I want *you* to go, though. Don't send one of those young idiots."

Shit. Barry didn't like to dive at night; he'd been planning to have Holly's son do it. "No, I won't. I'll be diving myself, no worries."

"It needs to be in your possession tomorrow night. Then you need to bring it to the site the next morning."

"Are you still expecting a shipment to the site Wednesday morning?"

"Yes, I'm just waiting for the final word from the city on what time the barge can come through. Once the beams are off-loaded, Joe will be taking inventory. When he discovers the shit on the pallets isn't what he ordered, he'll call you. That's your cue to call in the truck I'll have waiting over the bridge, to come and get it. I want those pallets and the package on that truck and brought to the warehouse in Estero. The pallets will have five-gallon buckets of mortar on them instead of the plaster Joe needs. Inside some of those buckets on each pallet is more precious cargo, so get them on the truck as quick as you can. I want that shit sorted and bagged by Thursday and in the clubs this weekend. This is going to make you extremely rich, Barry, so don't fuck it up."

"Yes, sir, I mean, I won't, sir." Barry was sweating just thinking about it. "The buckets will have the same content as the package?"

"Yes, I negotiated a fair deal with Jay. If we can get rid of it all in a month, there will be more where that came from." D'nafrio had no intention of telling Stoddman what else would be in those buckets. Stoddman was getting his cut based on the amount of Ecstasy that would be sold and nothing more. The larger profits from the Cocaine would be lining D'nafrio's pockets.

The coke was coming right out of Miami. Scintillo would supply him directly. They both recognized the danger in having the Cubans bring the Ecstasy over. It had been an ingenious idea the first time, but the risk was far too great. The tobacco plant Scintillo owned was working out as a great front for the manufacturing of the drugs, but now Scintillo had found someone to ship the Ecstasy straight to him in Miami. With the drugs coming out of Miami, and not via Cuban refugees, D'nafrio could now pay less for them and be able to expand his product line with the coke, along with lessening his risk.

"Where would you like me to keep the package until Wednesday?"

"Strapped to your body. Don't let it out of your sight."

"Okay, I get it. No worries, Xavier."

"Don't fuck up, Barry."

Barry heard the click of the phone and hung up himself. He wiped the sweat from his brow. He was about to be a very rich man, and he rocked back in his chair, thinking of his new Benz. "Holly!"

CHAPTER TWENTY-TWO

Daniels called Rafe back thirty minutes later. "Nice work today, in the nick of time, too. I've got a nice clear signal from the office. We've already got information. Stoddman's going for the package tomorrow night."

"So are we going to take him then?"

"No, there's more. I'm sending Mike back out to replace the package so Stoddman has something to retrieve."

"What's going on?"

Daniels told of the conversation between Stoddman and D'nafrio to Rafe.

"Man, this'll be over in a couple of days." Rafe was excited, and adrenaline rushed through his veins. "With the sound of the size of this shipment, he's looking at twenty-five plus."

"If all goes as planned, yes. I'm waiting for some more information on the particulars of the delivery, so sit tight. Tomorrow night, we'll have men out there, but be in place. Stoddman will be diving for it, just like Mike did, so as not to be seen. The package will look just like we found it -- only the contents will have changed. We are not expecting Stoddman to open it."

"What will be in it?"

"Candy."

Rafe laughed, "Candy?"

"Yes, made to look just like the pills." Daniels chuckled. "I actually have some extras in a bowl on my desk right now. They're pretty good."

Rafe laughed, "Yeah, well, if you start making love to your desk, you'll know they weren't extras."

Daniels laughed.

"Hey, why do you suppose they even bothered with the refugees bringing in the package if they've got this big shipment coming in by barge? Seems like a calculated risk for a relatively small amount."

"Yeah, well, we are looking into that particular reasoning now. I'll let you know."

Rafe took a deep breath, "Listen ,Tom, I fucked up today."

Daniels listened while Rafe explained what happened with Ali.

"Rafe, you did your job today, and because of it we now have information we can use to bust D'nafrio. Stoddman didn't show you that garage for a reason, and I'm sure he didn't expect your girlfriend to go in there. It was actually a great idea bringing her with you, and now because of your great idea, we've got some concrete evidence. Do you get what I'm saying here, Rafe?"

Rafe understood loud and clear. Daniels wasn't going to look at it as an error on Rafe's part; instead, he saw it as a bonus that Rafe took the initiative to bring Ali along. Because of what she saw in the garage they would have substantial evidence to help bring down D'nafrio and whoever else was involved.

If Rafe had gone in the garage, he supposed Stoddman would have passed the items off as the owners' -- after all, it wasn't as if any of the items in the garage were illegal. To any real buyer, those items would appear right at home in that garage. Many people on the islands had crab and lobster traps on their property and were divers as well. "Thanks for that, but you and I both know that it was a rookie mistake."

"What I know is, I sent one of my best agents to that island to assist on a case, not work it to the bone like he's done all through his career with everything else. This was supposed to be a soft one, so you could relax a bit and get your head on straight. Your job today was to plant the surveillance, and you did that and it was a success. We now have solid information.

Do not beat yourself up over this. When this is over, you'll have your time off and you'll set your mind right, to where it should be at this stage of your life. Not on filthy murdering drug dealers and baby killers, but on life with real people who you can hang out with and call your friends, people you can love, *someone* you can love and let love you."

Rafe was momentarily speechless. "Jesus Daniels if I didn't know any better, I'd say that candy on your desk has kicked in. You're some kind of life guru now?" Rafe was teasing him, but he was so appreciative of Daniels knowing he needed a break. They had been friends and colleagues for many years, and Rafe had always looked up to him. "All kidding aside, thanks, Tom."

Daniels only wished the best for Rafe and hoped this girl worked out for him. "Hey, if things go south with this girl, I'd like to get her in the academy. We could use someone like her." He kidded Rafe and waited for the rebuke.

Rafe laughed. "Not a chance, on both parts of that sentence."

"Wow, I like that optimism. I'll be rooting for you. Hey, I'm getting a call. I'll call you back when I have more information."

Rafe said goodbye and pressed "end." He wanted to give Ali some time with Nicki, so he decided to hang around and wait for Daniels to call back. He hit the remote and brought up the day's footage from the beach. When he got to the frame he was looking for, he e-mailed it to Daniels. By Rafe's eye, Stoddman had been the lookout on the beach that night, and H.Q. would have one of their techies confirm it. He definitely had the same build as the shadowy figure caught on camera just a few nights ago.

He switched back to real time and shrunk the image, bringing up the local news. He didn't have to wait long for the anchor person to mention the refugees. It was a relatively short story, and Rafe was glad the news van had shot pictures from a stretch of beach on Sanibel, and not the actual location, as per the FBI's request. D'nafrio had been contacted as well through the proper channels that his privacy would be respected. There had been no mention of D'nafrio or his property.

When the phone rang again, Rafe muted the T.V., looked at the caller ID and answered. It wasn't Daniels.

"Hello, Barry." Rafe smirked, thinking how the guy couldn't even wait two hours, never mind two days.

"Hi, there, Rafe! I just wanted to follow up real quickly. The home your fiancée and yourself are interested in? Well, I just had an offer come in, and I thought you should know."

"Wow, what a coincidence." Rafe couldn't wait to tell Ali this. "Is it strong?"

"Well, now, I can't really divulge that information, but if you were to come in close to asking, I think you'd have a fair chance." Barry couldn't believe his luck, he had to make one of these deals work.

"I'll have to speak to Ali, but I honestly don't see us making a move tonight." Rafe could almost hear Stoddman's heart beating.

"That's okay, the offer is contingent to financing, and that may very well fall apart. I just wanted to relay the information."

"Thanks, Barry. We'll get back to you when we've made a decision."

Rafe hung up and shook his head. The phone rang again, and this time it was Daniels.

"What, you're going to leave the guy hanging like that? I thought that was very considerate of him to call. So Ali, huh?"

"What do you do, sit around eavesdropping all day? And yes, her name is Ali -- Allison. If you want to loan me 5.9 mil., I won't leave him hanging."

"Sorry, I'm only worth that much on paper. I won't be liquid for another thousand years."

Rafe laughed. "What did you find out?"

"I'm going to conference you in on an emergency meeting. I've got Agents Simmons, Lambert, Gogin, and Bealls on the wire and your good friend Agent Caplan on the phone as well."

"Shoot." Rafe sat forward on the couch and listened.

"First off, we've got a barge out of Miami scheduled to make its way into the bay Wednesday morning. It'll be carrying the steel support beams for D'nafrio's second floor, along with half a dozen pallets loaded with five-gallon buckets of plaster. His foreman will be off-loading and taking inventory. He's going to find that those pallets contain five-gallon buckets of mortar that he doesn't need. They are supposed to be filled with plaster, and he'll call the error in to Stoddman to take care of it. Some of those buckets on those pallets are filled with the drugs, and they're marked. Stoddman's job is to call in the truck that'll be waiting just over the causeway, and to make sure that the pallets and the package he's already retrieved get on the truck and over to D'nafrio's warehouse in Estero. McDonough and Caplan, that's where you two come in -- as soon as Stoddman places the call for the truck, you two are headed off-island to the warehouse to await its arrival. We have a feeling D'nafrio will make an appearance and we'll take him down there along with Stoddman. If he doesn't show, we have enough evidence to find him and bring him in."

"How the hell did he get clearance for this barge, and where are they going to offload?" Special Agent Mike Caplan was currently staring out at the shallow channel and bay beyond from his balcony room at 'Tween Waters.

Rafe thought he had a pretty good idea. Shit.

"The barge will dock in the waters right across from D'nafrio's building site. There's a cleared lot right there, and he's already got clearance from the town. There'll be detail cops handling traffic on the road while the beams are being craned over to the site. Everyone will be in position, although we are not expecting anything to go down on the island. We'll have men in the bay and in the sky. We watch and wait, then get to the warehouse."

Daniels was referring to the lot right next to Nicki's grandmother's house. Rafe would have to get the girls out of there.

"There's a small matter of some neighbors in the house next door." Rafe was up and pacing now.

"If I'm not mistaken, McDonough, you've become familiar with them. Buy 'em lunch, send them to a movie, whatever, just get them out of there for a couple of hours. You'll need to be on that roof."

"Yes, sir." Rafe was grateful Daniels hadn't said more. But he was aware of a soft chuckle in the background he recognized as Mike's.

"Agent Caplan, you'll be on the ground over there, so make sure you stay out of McDonough's cross-hairs."

Rafe laughed. Daniels hadn't missed the chuckle either and knew Mike would be busting Rafe's balls about Ali as soon as this call was finished.

"What about local P.D.? Are they informed?" Agent Simmons asked.

"Once the barge is within one hundred yards from the causeway, it'll be escorted by two P.D. tugs ensuring its safety to Captiva. They'll be there mainly to pull the barge out if she runs aground, but also to ensure there's no foul play. The captains of the vessels are aware of the cargo aboard the barge. They'll be armed but know their jobs are only to escort.

On the ground, like I said, local will be on detail for traffic and anything else that might come up."

"Like protesters?" Rafe wouldn't be surprised if they caught wind of the delivery.

"Unfortunately, yes. We'll let local deal with that if there are any incidents."

"What kind of protesters?" Mike asked.

"The LAOB," Rafe spoke. "Locals Against Over-Building. They've been pretty vocal at the town meetings, and at the local realtor meetings."

"Why the realtor meetings?" Gogin asked.

"Some of the agents are actually part of the group. D'nafrio and his parent company are trying to control the market by buying up as much real estate as they can. The LAOB want to put a stop to it and they're also trying to get rid of a few city officials at the same time. They're convinced some of them are taking bribes to push through D'nafrio's permits."

"With all the money he's bringing to the island, who's going to turn him down?" Mike asked rhetorically.

"Well, add it to the list. Hopefully he'll be toast by Wednesday afternoon." Daniels was concluding the meeting. "Caplan, call in as soon as you've dropped the package. I'm assuming it arrived in one piece."

"Yes, sir, sitting right beside me."

"Who's taking you out?"

"Agent Reynolds." Mike answered.

"Good. Rafe send that footage as soon as they are clear."

"Will do." They discussed the teams and manpower a few minutes more and concluded the call. Mike was calling himself seconds later.

"So the neighbor, huh? Is she hot?"

Rafe laughed. "You are so predictable. Yes, and oh, yes!"

"Nice, when do I get to meet her?"

"Never. I've got to go." Rafe hung up on his friend, anxious to get to Ali.

"I think I heard the door. I'll get it." Nicki got up to go in, composing herself along the way.

"It's probably Rafe," Ali called out. She was excited to see him, even though only just an hour had passed.

Rafe waited at the door and smiled at Nicki on the other side. She didn't look like her usual chipper self.

"Hey, everything okay?" He hoped Matt hadn't called with bad news.

Nicki let Rafe in. "Yeah, you heard the news?"

"I did. That sucks -- I'm sorry. Is there anything new?"

"We haven't heard from Matt yet."

"I'm sure he'll get back here as soon as he finds out his friend will be all right."

"I hope so." Nicki gave him a grateful smile. "I'm going to make a drink and make some calls in my room. I haven't heard from my parents or grandmother yet."

"They're all went to Italy, right?" Rafe asked.

"Yes, this morning, so they should be landing about now if they haven't already. Did you guys eat?"

"Yes, we had a late lunch at my house. How was your first day at the paper?" Rafe leaned against the counter while Nicki made herself a drink and a snack.

"It was good. The usual -- you know, get introduced to everybody, see how things work, but I've got actual interviews and writing to do tomorrow. It should be fun."

"That's great." Rafe started to head to the pool deck, where he could see Ali sitting down having a drink.

"Hey, I'm sorry, I forgot my manners," Nicki called after him. "Would you like a beer?"

"Sure." Rafe waited while she took a Corona from the fridge and cut a lime for him.

"Thanks, Nicki." Rafe hesitated, not sure he should intrude.

"What? I can tell you want to say something." She smiled at him.

Rafe smiled, too. "I was just going to say that I know it must have killed Matt to leave."

Nicki felt the lump in her throat again. "Thanks, Rafe."

He turned and went to join Ali outside. She greeted him with a warm smile that went straight to the heart.

"Hey, again, how are things here?"

"Kind of grim. I wish we'd hear from Matt so we knew what was going on. He should have been in Boston hours ago. I'm going to call my dad if you don't mind and see if he's heard anything."

"Of course not, call. I'll take a walk down to the dock."

"I'll just be a minute." Ali took her cell from the nearby table and dialed her dad, who answered right away.

"Hi, Dad, have you heard from Matt?"

"Yes, honey, I'm at Logan now. He should be landing any minute. I guess he had to take a connector and had a little layover in Atlanta."

"Oh, that stinks. Has he been in touch with anyone at the hospital?"

"Not yet, but I've heard from Rick, and Sean is still in surgery. I'll take Matt there straight from the airport."

"Okay, call us when you hear anything." Ali hung up. Matt must be on edge, having had to take a connector. At least he'd be at the hospital soon.

Ali got up and brought her drink down to the dock to meet Rafe. He took her hand and helped her settle in beside him. She sat, her legs dangling off the dock next to his.

"Still no word. Matt is just getting to Boston now. He couldn't get a direct flight out."

"That sucks. At least he's there now. Did you tell Nicki?"

"Not yet. I know she wanted to call her family. How did your call go?" Ali was interested to see if what she had seen was going to help in any way.

"My boss wants you to join the academy and become an agent." Rafe grinned at her.

"Ha ha," she laughed. "Seriously, is the stuff in that garage related?"

"We think most definitely. I wasn't focused enough to go in there, Ali, and I'm grateful to you that you did, even if finding that evidence was unintentional."

"You sound disappointed in yourself. How come?"

"I should have asked to see the lower level. I knew the house had been used as a watch point, but I was too concerned with the who and not the what."

"That's crazy. You were busy doing your spy thing!"

Rafe laughed. "Yeah, that's what Daniels said -- he's my boss and my friend. He's the one who sent me here."

"For the semi-vacation?"

"Yes. It was a tough year in Miami; he thought I needed a break."

"You know, I'm a good listener, almost as good as being a pretend fiancée." Ali smiled at him.

"I don't doubt it." Rafe took a sip of his beer. He didn't want to dampen the mood with his war stories.

"I want to know about you, Rafe. I was thinking in that house today that I don't even know where you live." He looked at her. "I mean, do you live in an apartment or a condo or a brownstone or a tent?"

He laughed. "In Miami, just a small condo near the beach. It's nice. In New York -- an apartment in the city. Two bedrooms -- I use one as an office -- small living room, beat-up leather sofa, small kitchen, but nice view. You should see it at night."

"I want to." Ali looked at him. Was it obvious to him how she felt?

"I want you to, too." He held her gaze for a long moment before he spoke. "I saw two babies get hurt this year, one shot dead before my eyes, and one almost. She stood in the middle of the street with her hands over her ears, rocking back and forth and screaming for her mama. The first one was not even a year old and the second was around four, same as my niece."

Ali stared at him, wide-eyed. How horrifying that must have been to witness. No wonder he was "burnt out." God, she could only imagine what he'd done about it. "Did you have to shoot someone?"

"Yes."

"Did they die?"

"Yes."

"Was it the person who killed the baby?" Tears formed in Ali's eyes for that poor infant and for the pain she saw in Rafe's eyes. He worked in a world she knew nothing about.

"Yes, I shot him between the eyes from a rooftop. But I had no way of saving that baby."

"Oh, Rafe." Ali put her arm around his waist, her arm coming in contact with the solid shape at the back of his shirt. She lifted her arm a little higher and rested her hand on his side, her head on his strong arm. "I'm sorry."

"Me, too. When I thought it might happen to that second little girl, I left my position and tackled the guy full on. I couldn't take the chance of shooting him and have his gun go off, killing her."

"You saved her, Rafe."

"Yes, but I don't know how she'll ever get over the trauma she went through."

"Children are resilient. You've given her a chance." Ali felt the deep exhale from Rafe. She could tell he'd been holding it all in and was touched he'd opened up to her. "Thank you."

Rafe laughed in disbelief. "For ruining your night?"

Ali shook her head against him. "For trusting me with your feelings.

"Oh, that." He smiled and kissed the top of her head. "You make it easy. I should thank you."

"You have a hard job. Do you ever think about quitting?"

"No, it's in my blood. I guess what happened in Miami just made me realize how short life is, and maybe there's more than just the job."

"Like?"

Rafe smiled, looking out at the bay. Like what Daniels had with Patty or what his parents had, and his sister -- family, kids, a normal life.

Ali looked up when he didn't respond to see him looking out at the water. "I know what you mean," she answered for him.

"So I don't have to embarrass myself by saying it?"

"Why would you be embarrassed? It's normal to want more out of life than just your career. No matter how good you are at it, everyone wants...." to be loved, but she couldn't say that. "...more," she finished.

Rafe turned to look at her and smiled. "And how about you? Are you looking for more than what you have now?"

Now Ali was embarrassed, and she avoided his eyes. "Sure I am. I'm no different from any other woman who's head over heels in love, looking at million-dollar beach houses with the man she's going to marry." She dared to look at him then, to let him see she was teasing.

Rafe knew she was kidding, but for a second he let himself believe she wasn't. Head over heels? Marry? His heart beat a little faster at the thought, thoughts he had never even considered until he'd met her.

"Whoa, relax, you know I'm teasing you, right?" Ali half-laughed, seeing the look on his face, thinking she'd gone too far. "I mean I don't even know your favorite... anything." God, he was just looking at her all serious, probably thinking how he could politely get up and leave. Way to go, Ali.

"Green, pizza, baseball, Yankees, the city at night, my motorcycle..."

Oh...wow. Now it was Ali's turn to stare.

"Favorite color, food, sport, team, favorite view, my ride -- you know?" Rafe grinned.

As if he had to clarify. She nodded in response.

He laughed. Good, he'd managed to fluster her. Now she knew how it felt.

Ali tried to comprehend the underlying meaning of this conversation while her heart pounded in her ears. “Green huh?”

“Yeah, that’s new. I never had a favorite color before until I saw those eyes of yours.”

Oh, God. Her heart was melting. “What kind of pizza?”

“Big, flat, round, New York style.” He smiled even more as he felt her scoot a little closer to him.

“The Yankees could be a problem.” She looked out at the water, grinning, liking where this was going.

“There’s nothing wrong with a good healthy rivalry. Besides, I could bring you over to the dark side.”

Ali laughed, putting her head back on his shoulder. “Over the dead bodies of both my brothers.”

Rafe laughed, too. “Not gonna happen, huh?”

“Uh-uh.” He felt so good and solid under her.

“What is going to happen, you think?” Well, hell, he just put it out there, can’t get it back in. He felt her still against him. “Don’t answer that, okay? Stupid thing to ask.”

It wasn’t stupid. Ali wondered all the time what was going to happen, and she thought all the time about what she wanted to happen, and apparently it had crossed his mind, too, which made her unbelievably happy.

“Are you in danger a lot?” She stayed leaning against him, and obliged him by not answering the question -- not yet, anyway.

Okay, switching gears. He could understand. He had probably just scared her with that one.

“It’s always a possibility.” He wasn’t going to lie to her.

“Do you really love your job?”

“Yes.” And he did -- good and bad, he loved it.

“Why?”

“Because I get to get bad people off the street and away from good people...like you.”

Ali smiled a little. "Is your job here going to end soon?" God, she hoped so.

"As a matter of fact, sooner than later. I wanted to talk to you about that, and Nicki, too."

"Nicki?"

"I have to ask you both to leave here for a night or two." Rafe looked at her and waited for her reaction.

Ali's eyes widened. "What for?"

Rafe explained about the barge delivery on the lot next door, and followed Ali's gaze toward the property. "It's just a precaution. We are not expecting anything to go down here, but I'm going to need to be on the roof, and my friend Mike will be here, too, just in case."

Ali couldn't believe it, a real drug bust. Rafe's job was definitely real and dangerous, not the glamorized vision she had in her head. "Where would we go and when?"

"We can talk about it with Nicki."

"Okay." Ali's heart was pumping. "Should we be scared?"

"No."

God, he was so cool about it. He was a different man when he was in work mode. Ali found it sexy as hell.

"Should I be worried about you?" she asked quietly.

Rafe lifted her chin and stared into her eyes. "Absolutely not."

She believed him.

Rafe put his lips to hers and kissed her softly. "Let's go find Nicki. We need to talk."

Ali let him help her up and led him back up the dock and into the house. She found Nicki at the counter in the kitchen and told her Matt had just arrived in Boston and was going straight to the hospital with Ali's dad.

"They'll call when they get news," Ali assured her.

"Thanks, Al. What are you two up to?" Nicki smiled as Rafe took a seat at the counter next to her.

"Rafe needs to ask a favor of us." Ali looked at him as he explained to Nicki as much as he could.

"So, Tween Waters, huh?"

"Yes, Tomorrow night and Wednesday night to be safe, that's it. It's all paid for. You'll have to share a bed, but it will have everything else you need."

"I'm fine with it," Nicki told him, "but only if you promise to give me an exclusive when it's over."

Rafe smiled. "I promise."

Nicki brightened. "Really?" She imagined walking into the Beach News with a story straight from the FBI. "So nobody on the island knows what's going on?" She was already thinking like a reporter worried about someone else scooping the story.

Rafe grinned. "Only those who need to know."

"Gotcha." She wondered who was involved but she trusted Rafe to tell her. God, she wished Matt were here.

Ali reached for a pan and filled it with water to boil. "Pasta?" she asked Rafe. She had only eaten half the burger he'd made her, and she was hungry for dinner already.

"Sure, that sounds great." Rafe would have to get back to his place soon, though, and get Cap's footage over to Daniels.

"It'll be kind of fun," Ali said, getting out the pasta. "I'll be dying to know what's happening down this way, though."

Rafe smirked. "I know you will, but you'll have to sit tight and wait for me to come get you."

Nicki got up off the stool. "I'm going to try my parents and Nan again." She looked at Rafe. "Don't worry, I won't say a word." She didn't think Nan would appreciate knowing there was a drug bust about to go down practically on her property.

Rafe nodded.

Nicki went down the hall and went into her room. Shit, this sucked. Would Matt come back? She turned around and went through the doorway and into his room. All his things were gone. She opened drawers and looked in the bathroom -- nothing. She closed the bathroom door and saw the T-shirt that hung on the back of it. Nicki pulled it off the hook and put it to her face. His masculine scent was all over it, and she wanted to cry. What shit luck, she thought. She immediately felt bad for his friend. "C'mon, buddy, I don't even know you, but I'm pulling for ya. You need to be there for your kid, and I need Matt back." She went back to her room and lay down on the bed, keeping the T-shirt against her face.

"Nick," Ali said softly from the doorway a few minutes later. She recognized the shirt Nicki held to her face and felt her pain.

Shit. Nicki heard the caring tone of Ali's voice. I will not cry, I will not cry.

"Pasta's ready if you're still hungry."

"I'll be out in a minute." She knew her voice betrayed her, but it was Ali and Nicki knew that she got it.

"Take your time."

Ali returned to Rafe. "I wish this night would go by fast."

Rafe had just been thinking the opposite, and he looked up at her from where he sat.

"Only because I want to hear from Matt." Ali had noticed the look that had come across Rafe's eyes.

"I won't see you tomorrow night or Wednesday."

"I know," Ali said quietly. "And what about after that? Is it really going to be over?"

"Yes, if everything goes according to plan."

"And then what?" She wished she hadn't asked, it was reminiscent of Rafe's question on the dock, only she sounded needy and pathetic asking it. The way he was smiling at her, though, made her feel a whole lot better.

"Then I'm on vacation, for real."

Ali's face lit up. "That's just fantastic."

"What's fantastic?" Nicki joined Rafe at the small dinette off the kitchen.

"When Rafe's done working, he'll be on vacation."

Nicki looked at him. The guy was stupid good-looking. "What's your plan?" He'd better not be going anywhere -- one aching heart was enough around here.

Rafe chuckled at Nicki's protective tone. She'd slipped right into Matt's role. "I'm going to stick around here for awhile."

"What's awhile?" she asked pointedly.

"About four weeks." Rafe caught Ali's smiling eyes.

"Now we just need good news from Matt," Ali said, placing plates of pasta in front of them.

Ali and Rafe ate while Nicki pushed hers around on the plate. She wasn't even hungry, but she didn't want to be alone. She practically jumped out of her seat when her cell phone rang and couldn't help be disappointed to see it was her parents and not Matt. She excused herself to take the call.

Rafe helped Ali clean up.

"The cottage at Tween Waters, is that going to be yours?" Ali asked as she washed their dishes.

"That's the plan." Rafe looked for a towel to help dry.

"You could stay here, you know," Ali offered cautiously. She was sure now neither Nan nor Nicki would mind.

Rafe took the dish towel she offered and took her in his arms. "That's a nice invitation," he kissed her lips, "but wouldn't that be a little awkward when your brother comes back?"

"I guess it would," she agreed. "I don't know when he'll be back, though."

"If I had to guess," Rafe motioned his head toward the hall, "it'll be as soon as he can."

Ali smiled, "I hope so. She's a little hurt, I think."

"I'm sure she understands."

"Yeah, she does, but I know her. She would have liked to have said goodbye. He wanted to get right to the airport, though, and not miss any flights heading out."

"He'll make it up to her." Rafe could tell Matt really cared for Nicki, and he wasn't the kind of guy who would hurt her intentionally.

"I should probably go see if she's okay."

Rafe led Ali out of the kitchen and over to the couch where they sat. "You should probably do that, but I just wanted to thank you first, for dinner. It was great."

"You're welcome. I'm glad you stayed -- I know you probably have work to do."

"Yeah, a little." Rafe glanced at the wall clock and figured Mike was out in the Gulf about now. He still had a bit of time with Ali. "Thanks again for today."

"My pleasure, anytime. In fact, I'm going to go online tonight and see what the prerequisites are for joining the FBI."

Rafe took her by the shoulders and pulled her toward him. "Please don't."

His face was inches from hers, and Ali saw the heat in his eyes and felt it radiate over her own body. "Why not?" she asked softly.

He kissed her with such passion, Ali found herself molding to him in response.

Rafe pulled his lips away briefly but pulled her down on top of him, his desire for her evident as she rested between his legs. "Because we wouldn't be able to do this."

"Well, then, forget I said it," Ali whispered, kissing him back. Oh, he felt good. She moved against him and was rewarded with a groan of desire.

"Unfortunately, I have to go."

"I know, but this feels too good. Give me a minute." Ali shut her eyes and lay on his chest, hearing and feeling his heart beat beneath her. She was going to worry about him something awful. "I'm going to think about you in that suit this morning, Mr. FBI."

"The suit does it for you, huh?" He laughed softly, rubbing her back.

"Actually..." she touched his chest, "what's underneath the suit does it for me."

Rafe grinned up at her. "I told you that you can't play with my gun."

"I wasn't talking about your gun, smart ass."

"Smart ass?" Rafe picked her up and set her across his lap. "Who you calling a smart ass?" He squeezed hers as she squealed and squirmed on his lap.

She laughed. "You know what I like?"

"I'm starting to." He kissed her neck.

"I like how you pick me up like I don't weigh a thing. It's very sexy."

"You don't weigh a thing." He kissed the other side of her neck.

"Liar." She laughed and tilted her head so he could nuzzle her some more.

"You know what I like?" he asked, moving his hands up and down her thighs.

"I'm starting to," she mimicked.

He smiled. "I like the way you look when I touch you."

Ali blushed at that and fell silent.

"I should go."

"I want you to stay." She had her arms around his neck, and she kissed him softly and sweetly, trying to convey with a kiss everything she was afraid to say. When they finally pulled apart, she could see the message had been received.

"Ali." Rafe swallowed and tried to form a coherent thought. "It's been a long day for everyone. I have to go get my head on straight."

Ali tilted her head. "Is it not on straight?"

"Since I've been around you? No, it's definitely not straight."

"Is that a bad thing?"

"When I'm working -- yes."

Ali put her hands on either side of his face, feeling the shadows that were two days' worth of growth. "This makes you look kind of mean."

"You kept me up late, and I left early this morning." There'd been no time to shave.

"It's a sexy mean. I like it."

He laughed. "You're too much." But if she liked it, what the hell?

"Will I see you tomorrow?"

"Only to take you up to the cottage and get you settled in."

"I'm going to worry a little." She was actually very worried. This was real and not some T.V. show where the good guys always come out on top.

He kissed her gently and lifted her up to stand in front of him. He placed his hands on her legs. "I'm going to do my job and come back to be with you, and I want you to celebrate with me that it's over. I also want to start my vacation waking up next to you."

Ali's heart quickened. "That sounds really nice."

"Good," he said, getting up. "And tell Nicki she has nothing to worry about."

Ali smiled. "How do you know?"

Rafe smiled back. "I've seen the way he looks at her -- I can relate."

With a kiss to the forehead, he left her standing there, smiling.

CHAPTER TWENTY-THREE

"Thanks for picking me up, Dad. Can you believe this?"

"It's awful. Let's just be glad he's going to be all right."

Matt had called the hospital as soon as he'd landed and found out from Rick that Sean was out of surgery. He was indeed going to be all right. He had a broken left leg, a broken right arm, and two ruptured discs in his back, but his head was uninjured, and besides some intense pain, he would make a full recovery.

"He'll have quite a story to tell his first-born."

"I feel so bad for Terri. She must have been sick while he was in surgery."

"Well, Mom's there now and says she's doing much better. She says she'll be gone when we get there though."

Matt's dad had been making his own phone calls while Matt had talked to Rick. He was thankful his mother had gone to the hospital to represent the family.

"Has Terri talked to him yet?"

"Yes, he's still a little groggy, but she said he was in relatively good spirits."

Happy to be alive, no doubt, Matt thought. They made it to the hospital a little after eight, and thankfully Matt was able to see Sean for a few minutes. He embraced Terri outside Sean's room when he got up there and expressed his sympathies, offering to furnish whatever she needed. She cried as she hugged him, then sent him into the room.

Matt entered the room to see his good friend's limbs suspended in mid-air. From the cast on his elevated arm to the cast on his elevated leg, he was something out of a spoof movie.

"Jesus, Thayer, there's more plaster on you than the walls of that house you fell off."

"What the hell are you doing here, man?" Sean asked in a low groan.

"I heard you were dead. I came back for your beautiful pregnant wife."

"Fuu..."

"Ssh, don't try to talk. I know you're in pain. So you foiled my plans, but it's okay. She still wants to run away with me -- the doctor told her about your dick."

"Fuu..."

"Ssh," Matt said again and could see his friend trying not to laugh. "You might have a full recovery one day, but she just can't take that chance."

"You can *suck* my dick," Sean forced out.

"Does that have a cast on it, too?" Matt joked.

"No, I already checked." Terri had walked into the room. "Thank God that was spared."

Matt gave her a grin.

"Thanks for coming, Matt."

"Where else would I be?" Matt enclosed his hand over Sean's and gave it a squeeze. "You sure scared the shit out of me, buddy."

Sean coughed then grimaced in pain. "Can you believe this, man? It's not like me -- I just lost it up there."

Matt could hear the wounded pride in his friend's voice. "Sean, it could have happened to me or anybody. The pitch on that roof is crazy steep. We're all lucky you're alive."

"Oh, by the way, Matt," Terri gave him a stern look, "he'll never be on a slate roof again, got that?"

"Yes, ma'am." Matt winked at Sean.

"Babe, get me some more water, will you?" Sean asked.

"Yeah, I get the hint."

Matt laughed. "I'll be out of here in a minute, Ter."

Sean waited until the door closed behind his wife. "You didn't have to come back here. I'm fine."

"Yeah, you look great." Matt smirked.

"What are you going to do?"

Matt knew he was referring to the rest of the jobs that the company had on the board.

"No worries -- me and the guys can finish what's on the board. It's not much."

"I'm sorry I fucked up your vacation."

"Hey, it's not like I went there and met some beautiful girl I might want to spend the rest of my life with."

Sean gave Matt a roll of the eyes. "You've only been gone three days. What the hell?"

Matt laughed. "I'll tell you some other time. Get some rest."

"Tell Terri to send in some more drugs."

"Will do. I'll check in on you tomorrow."

After they left the hospital, Matt's dad got on the highway to drive them back to their family home. His mother was already there, having left before them.

"Mom says you're welcome to stay with us tonight."

"I'm just going to go home, Dad. I've got some calls to make and figure out my day tomorrow."

"Don't let this ruin your vacation. I can run your jobs for you. There's only a couple on the board, right?"

"Thanks, Dad, but I'll stay the week and make sure things get done. You've got enough to do. Besides, I've got to make sure Sean will be okay."

"He's going to hurt like hell for a while."

"Ugh," Matt groaned. "That must have scared the absolute hell out of him."

"I'd say so."

Twenty minutes later they pulled up in front of Matt's house. It was a three-bedroom bungalow he'd purchased a year ago. He'd been fixing it up in his spare time and was nearly finished. "I'll call you tomorrow."

"Goodnight, son."

Matt let himself inside and went right up to his bedroom. He threw his bag on the floor and took out his cell phone. He realized he didn't even have Nicki's phone number or the phone number to Three Sunrises, and he swore. He only had Ali's, and he hoped she answered; it was almost ten.

She did, on the third ring. Matt filled her in on Sean. "Is Nicki nearby?"

"She went to bed pretty early, but I told her I'd wake her when you called."

"How did she seem?"

"Bummed."

"Bring her the phone, okay?"

Ali smiled at the tone in Matt's voice. She could tell he was worried about Nicki. "Hold on."

Ali padded out of her room and down the hall. She knocked softly on Nicki's door.

"Nicki?"

"Come in," came her muffled voice.

Ali opened the door. Nicki lay in bed, her bedside light on, and a pile of crumbled tissues beside her on the covers.

"Are you okay?" Ali mouthed. "It's Matt."

Nicki nodded and held out her hand for the phone.

"Goodnight." Ali left, closing the door behind her.

Nicki took a deep breath. "Hello?"

"Hey."

Her stomach tightened at the sound of his voice.

"How's your friend?"

"He's going to be fine. He's out of work for a long while, but he's alive."

"Thank God." She took slow deep breaths. Relax, relax.

"Nicki, I'm sorry I didn't wait to say goodbye. I wasn't sure how serious his injuries would be and I felt a responsibility to get there as soon as I could."

Don't cry, don't cry. Breathe. "Don't be silly. I understand completely."

"Your voice sounds funny."

That's because I'm a big crybaby who managed to fall in love with you *again* in three days time, and then you left. "I was asleep."

"Do you want me to let you go?"

"No, no, I'm awake now." That was the last thing she wanted.

"Good, because I really want to talk to you." Matt was so glad to be finally talking to her and wished he were there beside her.

"About what?" She tensed.

He laughed. "I don't know, about anything."

She laughed, too, so glad he had called finally. "Okay."

"How was your first day?"

Nicki told him about the office and the people she met and about her interviews the next day.

"That sounds like it'll be fun for you, and at least you're not holed up in some office. You'll get to see the islands a bit."

"Yeah, I think it'll be a pretty fun job, actually."

"Did Rafe come by tonight?"

Nicki sat up, "Actually, he was here for dinner and asked a favor of Ali and me."

"What kind of favor?"

Nicki told Matt what Rafe had asked of them, and he didn't sound too happy.

"Is he saying it would be dangerous if you stayed at the house?"

"He didn't come out and say that -- he just said he would feel better if we weren't here. I don't even know exactly what the hell is going on, but he promised me an exclusive when it was over."

"Just make sure you both stay the hell away until he tells you to come home." Shit, the timing of all this couldn't suck worse.

"We will." Nicki couldn't even think about any of that. "So is that it for your vacation?"

She felt weepy again as she asked.

"Hell no, I've got some things to do here that Sean would have been doing this week, but then I'll be free again. I hope to be back this weekend, if that's okay?"

Nicki squeezed her eyes shut. "You have a job to finish here as well, so yeah, it's okay."

Matt laughed low into the phone. "I plan to wrap that one up real soon too."

"Oh yeah, how are you going to do that?"

"I've got a lot of tricks up my sleeve."

Nicki laughed softly. "Yeah, I've experienced a few."

Matt smiled, picturing her in bed. "Did they work?"

"I'm not prepared to comment at this time."

"Why's that?"

Because it's only been three days and I'm not just going to hand you over my heart.

"So would you like my cell phone number?"

"Are you changing the subject?"

"Uh-huh."

Matt chuckled. "All right, I'll let you off the hook, and yes, I want your digits."

Nicki smirked and gave him her number.

"I'm glad I was able to talk with you tonight."

"Me, too." Now she would be able to sleep.

They were both silent for a moment.

Matt pictured her in bed, and his body ached for her. "I just want to tell you before we say goodnight," he paused, "I had an incredible weekend, and I won't forget it, no matter what happens."

No matter what happens! What the hell did that mean? "Neither will I. It was a surprise, to say the least."

"For me, too." The best surprise he had ever had. "Well, stay safe and listen to Rafe, okay?"

"We will. Goodnight, Matt."

"Bye, Nicki."

Nicki pressed "end" on Ali's phone and sank down to her pillow. What did he mean, no matter what happens? Like, if he doesn't come back? Nicki pounded her pillow. Why was she automatically thinking the worst? He had a legitimate reason to leave, and he had real responsibilities to stay there for. She had to stop thinking negatively. If anything else this weekend, she had lived out a fantasy from her youth, and it was everything and more she'd ever dreamt of. The problem was the more part. There would be no forgetting him now; he'd been inside her, and she wasn't about to let that feeling go. If he didn't come back to Captiva, then she was going to Boston. Her feelings now were too strong to suffocate, and she was old enough now to convey them, no matter the consequences.

CHAPTER TWENTY-FOUR

Rafe woke up early to watch Shithead One and Shithead Two rise with the sun. He was surprised, turning on the monitors, to see them already awake. The driver was gesticulating behind the windshield, and his passenger was laughing at whatever he was saying and doing.

Rafe surveyed all the other angles on his flat screen and stopped as Ali appeared on camera one, stretching, her leg extended on the Three Sunrises sign. His eyes shifted back to the SUV. Shit, they were watching her. His first instinct was to run over there and lay a beating on them, but he couldn't -- he still had to maintain cover. Just the same, he hopped out of bed to throw on shorts and sneakers. He kept his eye on both pictures as he brushed his teeth and watched as Ali moved out of the camera's view and he saw the SUV slowly pull out of the drive. Son of a bitch! They'll probably drive right alongside her.

Rafe went to the front, down the stairs, and through the front gate as quick as he could. He could see Ali a ways ahead, and sure enough, the SUV was slowly tailing behind her.

Turn around, sweetheart, turn around.

He started a slow jog, keeping her in his sights. Two pickups drove by with their heads turned as they passed her. Rafe recognized both trucks from D'nafrio's job site. Jesus, she shouldn't be out this early -- the sun was only just starting to rise. He saw her stop and turn to face the truck. What was she doing? He slowed and watched as she said something, then gave them the finger. Thankfully, she turned back toward him and started running again. He could see that her pace had quickened.

The SUV's brake lights shone, and Rafe picked up his pace, closing the gap between him and Ali.

He saw the look of relief on her face as she approached him. "Hi," she said, breathing heavy and clearly upset.

"Hi, yourself. What the hell are you doing out here this early?" He could see she was trying to pretend she wasn't shaken by what had just happened.

Ali was taken aback by Rafe's obvious anger. "I thought I'd go for a run, like always." She studied the look in his eyes and realized he wasn't angry at her, but had obviously seen the encounter she'd just had. "I'm sorry." She didn't know why she was apologizing, but she didn't want him to be angry.

Rafe felt like an ass and took her against his bare chest. "I'm sorry -- I just saw them tail after you and wanted to prevent exactly what just happened. What did they say?"

Ali hugged him, feeling safe now in his arms. "It doesn't matter. It was gross. Seeing that creep again wasn't pleasant, either, but I knew I could make it back to your house even if I had to cross over onto the beach. I wasn't worried." She had feared that one of them might get out and chase her, though.

Rafe stroked her hair, blood boiling inside him. When he got his hands on those two little pricks…

"I'm glad you were heading back for me, but they still could have chased you. Ali, I need you to lie low until this is over, okay?"

Ali nodded against him. He had come running outside to help her. Tears formed behind her eyes, and she tried to swallow them back.

Rafe could feel her heart pounding and the sudden wetness against his chest. He pulled her back to look at her. "Are you okay?"

"Yeah." She laughed, embarrassed. "I'm just glad you came out."

"Of course I came out." He wiped the moisture away from under her eyes. "How about we run some of this adrenaline off?"

She smiled, "Sounds good."

They ran together stride for stride for a couple of miles, then turned to head back home. Ali noticed that Rafe was acting a little differently on the way back.

"You're quiet."

"I don't mean to be." He smiled. "Just thinking about the next couple of nights."

"What time do you want us to leave today?"

"You can wait until Nicki gets out of work, and then I'll follow you two up there."

"Okay." Ali slowed as they approached the driveway.

"Thanks for the run."

"Anytime," Rafe reached for her hand, squeezed, and let it go. "I'll see you later on?"

Ali nodded and smiled. She could definitely tell he was distracted, and she was determined not to take it personally. She knew he had a job to do. Still, her heart thudded as she watched his shirtless body walk away from her.

Rafe went right to the gym and worked off the rest of the anger he felt toward the two scumbags who had shaken Ali up like that. He didn't want to ever see her afraid like that again. If he ever got his hands on either one of them, it wasn't going to be pretty. He hated leaving her upset like that, but he wanted this job done, and he needed to be focused.

He showered and got ready for his day. He'd be coordinating with all the other agents and going over their positions for the following morning. Tonight he would be on full alert, waiting to see if Stoddman or someone else would retrieve the package Mike had planted. Rafe had watched Mike make the drop the night before on the surveillance monitors. His well-trained eyes had spotted Mike; clad in his black wet suit, breaking the surface of the water, and then swimming up beach where he was picked up in the fishing boat the FBI was using as a cover. Rafe had e-mailed the footage to Daniels as planned and had contacted Mike to confirm a successful drop.

Now Rafe opened the closet and walked to the back of it, where he kept the small arsenal he would need for the next day. He checked his rifle, ammunition, and gear, then walked out, heading for the kitchen and some breakfast. It was going to be a long day.

Ali came out of her room showered and dressed for the day, just as Nicki entered the kitchen.

"Want to have breakfast with me before you leave for work?"

"Sure." Nicki helped Ali fix bagels, fruit, and juice in the kitchen, and they both went outside to sit in the morning sun.

"What do you have planned today?" Nicki asked.

"Nothing. I was going to beach it, but I'm kind of anxious about tonight and tomorrow and don't think I could sit still for very long."

"I know -- I feel like something major is going to happen. I wish I knew more," Nicki complained. "Is Rafe going to have to..." Nicki paused. "...shoot anybody?"

"He says they"re not going to let anything happen on the island, so no I don't imagine so." Ali didn't want to think about it.

"You're not worried?"

"I'm a little worried," Ali admitted, finishing her juice.

"You really like him, don't you?" Nicki smiled.

"I feel foolish about how much I like him."

"Why?" Nicki laughed.

"Because, like you said, three days! How does anyone know anything about a person in three days?"

Nicki just stared at her, as if to say "look who you're talking to."

Ali laughed. "But you and Matt are different. You've actually known each other for, like, thirteen years."

"I thought you believed in love at first sight," Nicki half-joked.

"I believe in lust at first sight," Ali replied seriously, "but I've never had love at first sight, and I'm afraid to call it that for fear of sounding like a complete idiot, I guess."

"You wouldn't sound like that to me." And then she did say, "Look who you're talking to." Nicki picked at her fruit. "How do you think he feels?"

Ali swallowed a bite of bagel. "I think he really likes me, too. But my God, these past three days have been all about sex, so it's hard to say. When he talks to me, I do believe he's being honest and sincere, and he has shared some personal information. I guess the biggest thing of all was confiding in me about who he is and what he does, right?"

"That was pretty big. I don't think he would have told you if he didn't care or wasn't very interested."

"Right. So I'm just going to hope things move forward. He is going to take his vacation time here. Four weeks is a long time."

"Do you think it's because of you?"

Ali smirked. "Well, he was going to just take a couple of weeks, anyway -- before me -- then go home to New York, but now he's going to stay the extra time here, yes, to be with me. He says he wants to get to know me better."

"Well, he's obviously feeling the same way you are if he's going to skip going home to his family." Nicki smiled. "If nothing else, you'll have amazing sex while he's here."

Ali laughed. "True, at least for a few weeks." But then what? She'd be that much more into him, and he'd be leaving. She couldn't even bear to think about it.

"He is pretty damn good-looking, by the way."

"You should have seen him yesterday in his suit." Ali closed her eyes just thinking about it.

"Good stuff, huh?" Nicki grinned.

"Holy crap, yes!"

"Well, give me rugged good looks and a tool belt," Nicki winked, "and apparently I'm done."

"How did the conversation go last night?"

"It was okay."

"Just okay?"

"Well, he said he would be back by the weekend."

"That's great!"

"But then later on in the conversation he said that no matter what happens, he had a good time this weekend."

"No matter what happens?" Ali narrowed her brows.

"That's what I said -- to myself, of course."

"I think he meant with your relationship," Ali surmised.

"You don't think it meant he might not be back?"

"I can't imagine him not coming back, Nick."

"Well, I can't obsess over it. I've got work to keep me busy, and apparently we're going to be on an episode of COPS, so 'no matter what happens,'" she said sarcastically, "I guess we'll see."

Ali chuckled. "I'm betting on something good happening between you."

"I hope you're right." Nicki sat back and stretched. "Hey, you want to come with me today?"

"Really? Won't your boss mind?"

"Not at all, you'll be my photographer."

"That might be fun. It'll keep my mind occupied, too."

"There you go! Let's get out of here then."

Ali picked up their dishes, and she followed Nicki in the house. As they left through the front door moments later, she was singing, "Bad boys, bad boys, whatcha gonna do, whatcha gonna do when they come for you..."

"You're an ass." Nicki shook her head, laughing, walking to the car.

Ali took pictures for Nicki all day and enjoyed meeting everyone she interviewed.

"That teacher was really nice," Ali commented.

"I know, what a cool school to go to. Imagine having your locker outside?"

"What was the matter with our parents not moving someplace warm?" Ali asked, really wondering.

"Who knows?" Nicki shrugged. "The girls on the swim team were nice, too."

"That one on the end was trouble."

"Why?" Nicki asked laughing.

"Because every time I tried to take the group picture, she scowled at me."

"You want me to crop her out?" Nicki joked.

"Definitely." Ali laughed.

They were both laughing and having fun together, forgetting temporarily anything that might have been bothering them. They got back in the convertible and headed back to the offices of The Beach News.

"I just have to run in and get tomorrow's assignments."

"I'll be out here," Ali leaned against the headrest, her eyes closed to the sun. Not a minute had past when her daydream was interrupted.

"Excuse me, Ms. Fuller, is that you?"

Shit. Ali recognized Barry Stoddman's voice instantly. She hadn't even considered the possibility of running into him. She'd make a lousy agent after all. Opening her eyes, she looked up and let a smile adorn her face. "Hi, Mr. Stoddman."

"Barry, please. Are you here with Rafe?"

"No, no, I'm with a friend today." Ali was sweating. She hoped she didn't say anything wrong, and she prayed Nicki stayed inside until he was gone.

"Nicki is your friend? This is her car, right?" Barry was confused. How did Ali and Nicki know each other?

Ali kept her smile plastered on. "You know Nicki?" Oh, no.

"Sure, we met just yesterday."

Ali heard somewhere once that when telling a lie, sticking to as much of the truth as you could was the best bet. "Rafe and I are staying with Nicki at her grandmother's house."

That's funny, Barry hadn't even thought to ask them where they were staying yesterday. "Well, no wonder you're in love with the Captiva house -- you've experienced how lovely it is up there."

"Exactly." Ali figured it best to let him do most of the talking.

"I hope you weren't disappointed to find out about the offer on the house, but like I told Rafe, things could fall apart, and if your offer is a strong one, we just might have a chance."

Ali tried not to let it show that she had not heard this information. Barry must have called Rafe last night. "Well, we are still taking advice from our accountant and mulling it over. I wouldn't want to lose it, but I'm a big believer in 'if it was meant to be, it will happen.' I expect we'll know something soon." Shut up now, Ali.

"Sure, besides, I've got plenty of others we can still take a look at."

"Great." Ali smiled and caught sight of Nicki coming toward them.

"How long are you all here for again?"

Ali swallowed, hoping she was giving the right answers. "Just a few weeks."

"Great, that gives us plenty of time to find just what you're looking for if this house on the bay doesn't work out. I've got just the one in mind, too, perfect for the large family you both want to have."

Nicki stood behind Stoddman, slack-jawed, and Ali had to give her a look that said, "play along." "That sounds just fine, Barry. I'll have Rafe give you a call."

Nicki came around and smiled as Barry greeted her. "Hi, there, how are you today, Barry?"

"Just great, Nicki. How is the new job treating you?"

"Just wonderful, thanks."

"I didn't realize Ali was a guest of yours, what a coincidence. She and Rafe looked at some beauties yesterday. You must be spoiling them up there in Captiva." He winked at Ali, who smiled at Nicki.

"I'm doing my best." Nicki smiled at Ali but gave her the eyes that said "what the hell"?

"Well, you two have a nice evening and remember, Nicki, anytime for lunch!"

"Oh, thank you, Barry, I'll keep that in mind." Nicki got in the car and pulled out of the parking lot. She waited until they were on the main road before turning to Ali. "What the hell was that?"

Ali laughed nervously. "I kind of met him yesterday under the pretense of being Rafe's fiancée, and we went looking at five-million-dollar beach homes in Captiva."

"Which part should I ask about first?" Nicki asked incredulously.

Ali explained what Rafe had asked her to do, and why.

"This keeps getting better and better. So you mean to tell me, that little sleaze is involved in this drug business going down tomorrow?"

"Oh, God, Nicki, I should not have told you. You promise to keep it between us?"

Nicki rolled her eyes. "As if you have to ask. This is unbelievable. Wait 'til Nan hears this."

Ali shot her a look.

"I mean, when it's over and safe to talk about. Are you hungry?"

"Yes, want to go to the Cow?"

"Umm, sounds good, then it's off to the safe house," Nicki kidded.

"Ha-ha, and it's safe cottage, remember? I'm psyched, I've always wanted to stay in one of those."

"Me, too, actually."

"Maybe we can drink by the pool tonight," Ali suggested.

"I'm up for that. Not too many, though -- I still have to get up for work."

"Sure, we'll take it easy and then maybe take in the sunset."

"Sounds romantic. I'm in." Nicki winked at her.

Ali laughed. "Hey, take what you can get."

"It won't be the same when you lay your green eyes on me, as pretty as they are," Nicki teased.

"That's because when I look at you, I'm not trying to get you naked."

"That's true." Nicki cracked up. "And remember, you said that, not me!"

They had a nice meal and light-hearted conversation at the Cow, and it was fun, just the two of them sharing some time together. They had had a great day, and Nicki was grateful to have her mind off Matt for awhile.

Ali ordered a large sandwich to take back to Rafe. It was still relatively early, and maybe she could get it to him before he ate. When it was ready, they paid the bill and headed back to Nan's.

"Trying to win him with food?"

Ali laughed. "I feel bad. Since we've had dinner together the past three nights, I feel like I broke the trend. Now at least he'll know I was thinking of him."

"So thoughtful."

"Oh, be quiet." Ali turned up the volume, and they sang along with the radio the rest of the way home.

Ali smiled to see Rafe waiting in the driveway when they pulled up, but the smile quickly disappeared when she saw the look on his face.

"Hi," she said when Nicki had parked and she could get out. He was leaning on the Jeep, looking heartbreakingly gorgeous as usual. The man should be modeling jeans for a living.

"Where were you?" He crossed his arms in front of him, and he looked angry.

Nicki gave them a look and disappeared into the house.

"We stopped for some dinner." Why was he mad? Maybe Stoddman called him and she'd screwed up by talking with him.

"It's six o'clock. I thought you'd be home well before this."

Ali was starting to get a bit irritated. "I worked with Nicki all day, we left the Beach News and went to get something to eat. I wasn't aware we had to be back at a certain time." Her tone was equal to his own.

"You were at the Beach News offices?" Rafe swore to himself, he hadn't thought she'd go to work with Nicki. "Did you see Stoddman?"

Ali felt guilty all of a sudden. "Actually yes, he was surprised to see me with Nicki. I told him we were staying with her here." She grimaced at Rafe's obvious displeasure upon hearing that news. "I hope I didn't say the wrong thing but I was waiting for Nicki in the car and he approached me. He told me about the offer on the house and then asked how I knew Nicki." Ali looked at Rafe apologetically. "I'm sorry if I screwed things up." Shit!

Rafe shook his head telling her no. "I thought we agreed when Nicki got out of work, we'd leave." Rafe ran a hand through his hair in frustration. This was all his fault.

Ali looked down at the driveway and moved some crushed shells beneath her sandal. Her stomach was tight, and the dinner she had just eaten sat like lead in her belly. "I'm sorry. I didn't think an hour would make a difference."

"I tried calling your cell." Rafe had in fact started to panic when he couldn't get in touch with her. He was worried sick something or someone had happened to Ali. He could see she wasn't too happy with him right now for questioning her, but he had wanted her long gone to the cottage by now, before the two shitheads came back on duty. He didn't want the two thugs across the street driving by and seeing them together out here. Not only didn't he want the two thugs to know where Ali or Nicki lived, Rafe also couldn't have Stoddman finding out he was staying next to D'nafrio's house and not with Nicki; like Ali had told him. Barry might start getting curious and it could jeopardize the retrieval of the package, and then they'd have a problem. He just wanted her safe at the cottage and out of harm's way.

"I left my cell here." She had actually forgotten it. She had left it charging on her nightstand after getting it back from Nicki that morning. It had never occurred to her that Rafe would try to call her. Ali looked up at him now, and he was looking at her intently, but his eyes didn't hold any anger as she had first thought; there was something else there. The irritation she had been feeling left her instantly. "You were worried about me."

"Yeah, I was." It came out sounding harsh. He was still tense, but the tension quickly evaporated at the sight of a smile playing at the corners of her mouth. He came off the Jeep and came up in front of her. "I was real worried."

Ali melted at his softer tone. Oh, wow. Now there were butterflies swarming around the dinner in her belly. "I'm really sorry. My phone was charging, and I actually forgot it. I didn't think you would try and call me."

"Why not?" What if he just wanted to say hello? Did she not want that kind of thing with him?

Ali shrugged. "I honestly don't know -- this is all new. Yesterday you had a reason to call, you know -- about work and helping you out."

"You're right. I called you because I wanted your help, and today I tried calling because I was worried and wanted to get you to safety, but there are other reasons I would call you." God, he sounded needy and possessive all of a sudden.

He was standing so close that Ali had to crane her neck to look up to him. "Oh, okay."

She'd make damn sure she didn't forget her phone again. If she had thought for one second he might call her just to say hello, her phone would have been glued to her hand all day.

"Oh, okay?" Rafe wondered if she even had a clue about how he felt about her. If she didn't, it was his fault. Why, after just a matter of days, would she think it was anything more than casual between them? How could he tell her that in just one weekend with her, he was reevaluating his whole future, a future that he now envisioned with her in it?

Ali looked up at Rafe. "I mean, okay, I'm glad you would want to call for other reasons."

Rafe took a deep breath. Now was not the time to lay his feelings on the line. It was still way too soon. He took a step back and leaned against the Jeep again, watching her. He was still surprised himself how worried he had been about her; the thought of anything happening to her had made him weak. He couldn't afford to be weak in his job, and he was really upset with himself for letting this happen. Getting involved with Ali while on the job, no matter that it was supposed to be a softball assignment, had put her in danger and him in a weakened position. Because he had feelings for her, he couldn't focus entirely. He had fucked up yesterday, and he couldn't let that happen again.

Ali could see Rafe was struggling with something, and she couldn't help but feel responsible. Maybe he was regretting this whole whirlwind thing they had going. She wondered if she was complicating things for him at work. He sure didn't look too happy that she'd spoken to Stoddman. She walked to Nicki's car and took the takeout bag off the front seat. "Here," she said holding it out to him, "I picked you up a sandwich from the Cow -- that's where we were."

If Rafe hadn't felt bad already, he now felt worse. She picked him up a sandwich? Who did that? He stared at her and the slightly sad smile that he knew he had put on her face. He was an A-class jerk. "Thanks, that was a really nice thing to do." He took the bag from her and felt the twist in his gut.

"I just figured since we've been..." Ali stopped herself. What? Like he was going to think like she did, and think they had started some dinner tradition because they had eaten together the past few nights? She was starting to get why he was acting the way he was. She was totally trying to accelerate this "relationship," and she needed to back off. "I just figured you might not have time to cook for yourself because you'd be getting us settled and working tonight, no big deal. I'll go in and pack quickly. Did you want to come in?" She turned and started toward the front door.

Rafe guessed what she'd been about to say, and yes, he was hoping he would have dinner again with her, every night for the rest of his life. He watched her walking away and started after her. "I can't -- I have to run across to the house for something. I'll be waiting for you to pull out and I'll follow you in the Yukon." God, he felt horrible.

Ali couldn't help but be disappointed, but she understood. "Okay, we won't be long." She entered the house and found Nicki packed and ready in the living room.

"What was *that* about?" She stood with her hand on her hip in defense mode for Ali.

Ali smiled. "It was nothing. He was just worried -- he expected us a little sooner. I'm going to pack quick and meet you outside. He's going to follow us up there." Ali didn't really want to talk about what *that* might have been. She had been over the top to find out he had been worried about her -- not that she wanted to worry him, but it meant he cared. But then he became rather distant and had her questioning his feelings. Maybe she had read too much into the worrying part, but she had seen the look in his eyes, and in her estimation, the eyes never lied. Nevertheless, her stomach was in turmoil.

"Ohh-kay." Nicki knew not to press. "Do I have to roll down the hurricane shutters or anything? Is this place going to get riddled with bullets?"

Ali laughed in spite of her now dour mood. "Now who watches too many T.V. shows?"

"I'm just sayin'." Nicki raised her brows and started toward the door.

Ali was outside five minutes later with her bag, and she threw it in the back of the convertible, seeing Rafe's truck idling at the end of his driveway. She got in and Nicki pulled out, making the short drive to 'Tween Waters.

Rafe pulled into a spot beside them and got out. "I'm going to check in and get the key. I'll be right back." Ali was determined not to let him see she was upset. He had a job to do, and she didn't want him to have to think about anything but that. When it was over they could sort out whatever it was they needed to sort out.

"This feels so…clandestine," Nicki remarked as she sat waiting behind the wheel.

"I think it'll be fun." If nothing else, she and Nicki could make a good time of it.

"Of course you do." Nicki looked at her best friend. "Leave it to you to meet an FBI agent who looks like a frigging movie star and three days later have us in the witness protection program." Nicki turned to face the windshield as if she were talking to herself, "I just wanted to come here and start my new job, enjoy life on the islands. Now, between you and your brother, my heart is in pieces and I'm living out an episode of CSI: Miami."

Nicki's exaggerated montage brought forth instant laughter from Ali, and she found herself unable to stop. She was laughing so hard she was doubled over in the front seat.

Nicki shook her head, laughing herself. "Here comes your G-man. Get it together."

Ali wiped her eyes as she sat up and tried to compose herself. Just seeing him approach sent a current right through her.

Rafe could see something had occurred between them as he made his way to the convertible. He looked them over, curious, as he took their bags from the back seat. "I'll take you to the cottage."

Ali looked at Nicki, and they both got out to follow him. They exchanged a look, realizing Rafe was all business now.

The cottage was one that looked right over to the Gulf, complete with a screened-in porch perfect for watching the sunset.

"This is great," Ali said, admiring the quaint structure. Rafe unlocked the door and led the way inside.

"I love the porch," Nicki said, poking her head out there.

"It's got everything you need, and I had it stocked with food earlier so you should be all set while you're here. And if you go to the bar or restaurant, just charge it to the room."

"How 'bout the spa?" Nicki joked.

"Anything you guys want. I know this is inconvenient."

Okay, he was still all business. "We're not going to the spa." Ali hit Nicki's arm. "We appreciate you doing this."

Rafe nodded. "You'll be back at the house in a couple of days."

Oh, really? Me, too? Ali wondered.

He handed her a piece of paper "That's my cell and the house phone, in case you need to reach me."

Ali held his gaze, trying to read his thoughts. "Thanks."

Nicki felt the already small room get a little smaller and excused herself to check out the bedroom.

Ali sat down in a chair at the small dinette in the kitchen. "This is just a precaution. Everything's going to be fine -- you're going to be fine." She said it as a statement, but wanting reassurance. No matter what he was feeling toward her now, she cared for him, and she would worry.

Rafe went over and squatted down in front of her chair, resting his arms on his thighs. "I'm going to be just fine, and I'll be back here in a couple of days to take you back to the house."

Yeah, you mentioned that already, I get it. "So this is no big deal for you right?"

"It's my job, Ali." He looked her in the eye, then shook his head slowly back and forth.

"What?"

"I just wasn't prepared for," he hesitated, "this."

"This?" Ali's heart started to sink. She was such a glutton.

Rafe exhaled in frustration and looked out the window beyond Ali. The beach was starting to thin out for the day, and the resort staff were stacking the wooden lounges offered to the guests. "For meeting you and being with you like I have these past few days -- it's crazy." That didn't come out quite the way he meant. He saw her physically withdraw in front of him.

"I didn't exactly expect it, either, and I know we got off to a quick start..." And Ali was feeling pretty foolish at the moment. This is what happens when you fall into bed with a guy you just met, you idiot. She knew going in, that this was a potential outcome, yet heart be damned, she dove in head-first. "Maybe it's just this place. I got swept up in it, I guess. It's not like I've ever done something like this before." If that didn't sound cliché. God, why was she defending herself?

She was a grown woman. If she wanted to have a weekend fling with an unbelievably sexy man, she had every right! Guys did it all the time. It wasn't her fault if he somehow developed feelings for her and it was affecting his focus. She thought about that for a second. He had feelings for her, and now he regretted getting involved because he didn't want to have feelings for her? Why? On the dock he had alluded to the fact that maybe that was something he was looking for in his life, and Ali had foolishly imagined herself being the recipient of those feelings. Why did shit have to be so complicated? Why couldn't she separate great sex from falling in love?

Rafe heard her defensive tone, and he felt awful. How could he make her understand without just coming out and saying it? Because he knew he was too afraid to do that, tell her that he cared, that he really cared. He was sure she was thinking he was an absolute jerk right about now, and he wasn't doing anything to dispel her opinion. "Ali, I don't think you are understanding what I'm trying to say, and I don't blame you." He stood up and paced the small area.

Ali watched him, hurt evident in her eyes. If she could grab Nicki and run out of there right now, she would, but she knew he would stop her. Instead, she stood and opened the door that led to the screened porch.

Shit. Rafe watched her go and followed her out there.

"Is it really necessary that we're here?"

His stomach roiled hearing the hurt in her voice. "It would make me feel better knowing you weren't in the house at the time of the delivery, so yes."

"Because it's your job to keep people out of harm's way, right?"

Rafe was feeling worse by the second. "Of course," he said quietly. "I would feel terrible if something happened to you or Nicki because I didn't make an effort to keep you safe."

Ali nodded. "Well, like I said before, we appreciate your doing this, so we'll just wait to hear from you then? Or should we just consider it safe to leave on Thursday?"

Her tone was cold, and he didn't do anything to change it. He wasn't about to tell this woman after four days how he really felt about her. She'd think he was crazy. He wasn't kidding when he told her he hadn't expected "this" to happen. As soon as he'd laid eyes on her he had been drawn, and then actually meeting her and talking with her, he had become lost in those sea-green eyes. He'd been blown away. But when she let him kiss her and touch her and be with her in the most intimate of ways, that's when he fell -- and fell hard. He heard about it happening to people, but he didn't believe it. He'd been with plenty of women, and he had had lots of great sex, but nothing like it was with Ali. She was different. When he was with her, he felt connected. He wanted to know everything about her, he wanted to protect her, and he especially wanted to love her. And how do you not scare someone away by telling them that after only four days? He knew their attraction was mutual -- she'd told him and showed him in a multitude of ways, but did she feel the intense feelings he did? He couldn't take the chance of blowing what they did have by scaring her off. He could be patient, he hoped, and tell her when the time was right. And now was obviously not that time, when he'd just managed to hurt her with his lack of courage.

"I'll come for you Thursday if you don't mind waiting."

"No, I guess not. I'm on vacation, remember? No plans, no worries, no ties." She gave him a smile that did not quite reach her eyes.

Okay, he deserved that. He didn't like it, but he deserved it. But the "no ties" thing? That was bullshit. She was his, and he had better make her realize it before he left this cottage. He closed the gap between them and pulled her to him roughly, emotions getting the best of him. Her arms immediately pressed against his chest in resistance, and the wounded look in her eyes crushed him. He couldn't bear it, and he put his lips to hers and kissed her, not with the intensity in which he'd grabbed her, but with the gentleness he wanted to convey to her.

He kissed her with the feelings that were overtaking his heart and soul, but which he didn't have the courage to say. He was rewarded by the fact that she didn't pull away, but her body remained tense.

Ali didn't know whether to cry at the earth-shattering kiss or slug him in the gut. What the hell? Talk about confused -- she was officially dumbfounded. The kiss said everything she wanted to actually hear, but his words were, well...the opposite.

Rafe pulled his lips away reluctantly, but his arms still held her close, and he looked down into her eyes. "On Thursday, when I come back, I'd really like another chance to talk to you. Would that be all right?" He'd get his shit together and just lay it out there, maybe not the extent of it, but enough to let her know he was serious. He realized by not saying anything, he could blow it with her, too.

Ali nodded, her hands still pressed against him. She could feel the beat of his heart, and her own was keeping the same time. Was that a goodbye kiss -- "I'll dump you properly on Thursday"? Or something she shouldn't let herself hope for? "I'll be here." She attempted a brave smile. She didn't want him to go away thinking she hadn't had a great time with him. She had to learn to be more like a guy and be nonchalant. She needed to adopt the "we had great sex, let's end it on a good note" type of attitude.

"Stay safe. I wouldn't want to see anything happen to that handsome face of yours." It came out sounding cavalier and a bit sexist, and she supposed she wanted it to, but she was kicking herself on the inside for letting herself be so vulnerable.

So she was incapable of just a sexual relationship with him. She'd fallen in love with him in a matter of days. The first day, if she was being honest. She did believe in love at first sight. There, she said it, and because she was a dreamer, she let herself be open for the hurt that now resided in her chest.

His response was to drop his arms and touch her face, giving her a smile that appeared to her to be filled with regret. Just great. She watched him leave the cottage, and when the door shut behind him, she sank down onto the small wicker sofa, put her head in her hands, and sobbed like a baby.

Nicki's arms were around her in a matter of minutes. "Oh, Ali, what happened?"

"I think I just got the blow-off." She looked up at Nicki. "What's the matter with me? I should have known better!"

"I am not going to let you beat yourself up!" Nicki got mad and stood up. "Are we on a beautiful island?"

Ali looked at her like she had three heads. "Yes," she sniffled.

"Did you meet an incredibly handsome guy and have mind-blowing sex?"

This brought more tears, but she nodded. "Yes."

"Will you ever forget it?"

"Are you trying to make me feel better or worse here?" Ali whined.

"Listen." Nicki stood her ground. "You did nothing wrong. You had a great time. If nothing happens from here -- which I have my own opinions about -- you know this cottage is pretty small -- then be glad it happened in the first four days and not the last. We have the whole summer ahead of us!"

Ali sniffled again. "What do mean, you have your own opinions, about what?"

"Ali, I couldn't see Rafe's face when he was talking to you, but it was pretty obvious to me from inside that bedroom that he has a whole lot more he wants to say to you, and that he was finding it, for some reason or another, difficult to do. And if I had to guess, he's scared."

"Scared? Of what?"

"Of his feelings." Nicki could relate. After all, she was scared shitless to tell Matt how she felt, scared of her heart breaking in a million pieces. It was one thing to get over a teenage crush, but she wasn't convinced her adult heart could handle it.

"You think that's what this was all about?" It would explain that heart-wrenching kiss. Could she actually let herself believe he felt like she did and was too afraid to tell her?

"Yes, I do. Ali, I've seen you two together. It's like you've been together for years -- you fit. I'm envious. It's surprising, yes, at the short amount of time, but then again, why does time have to enter into it? If there's something there, you both owe it to yourselves to explore it. I know you're not afraid to, but he might be, so cut him some slack, and see what he has to say on Thursday, okay?"

Ali stared at Nicki. "Wow, I can't believe I just let him walk out of here like that. What if I screwed things up, letting him think I didn't care?" Ali stood up and looked out at the Gulf, feeling that sick feeling in her stomach again.

"Don't do that to yourself. Just have faith and talk to him on Thursday." Nicki gave her a hug. "We could both use a drink. Let's put on our best bikinis and go get a frozen at the pool bar. Maybe there'll be some old geezers to give us a boost."

Ali laughed, wiping her eyes. "I didn't bring my best bikini."

Nicki rolled her eyes. "Like it really matters."

CHAPTER TWENTY-FIVE

Rafe had pulled out of the parking lot, his tires kicking up shells and sand, swearing out loud in his truck. That could not have gone worse. He may have just lost the best thing that ever happened to him, all because he was afraid to speak his mind. And when in all his life had he ever been afraid to do that? He couldn't dwell on it; he had to get his head back in the game. If he wanted to keep Ali safe and end this so he could try to redeem himself, then he had to focus.

The damn SUV was parked for its nightly stint outside D'nafrio's, and he had to resist the urge to jump out and beat the crap out of both assholes who had bothered Ali. Instead, he parked his own vehicle in the safety of the garage and went upstairs into the house to make his phone calls. They were all expecting Stoddman to retrieve the package tonight, and Rafe wanted to make sure nothing had changed. His first call was to his friend Mike Caplan and fellow agent, who was staked out at Tween Waters, on the bay.

"What's up, McD?"

"Where you at?"

"Sitting at the pool bar with a club soda and a twist of lime." Mike pretended to be happy about it.

"Yeah, well, the beer will come later. Listen, I've got my neighbors in cottage 101, keep an eye out, will you?"

"Sure, man. Going above and beyond the call of duty, wouldn't you say?" Although Mike would do the same thing if involved a woman he liked.

"Yeah, well, I didn't want to send them to a movie."

Mike grinned, "Hey, you said neighbors plural; what's her friend like?"

Before Rafe could answer, he heard a low drawn-out whistle come from Mike.

"What's that?"

"The view by the pool just got a lot nicer." Mike kept his eyes on the women that had just arrived.

Rafe rolled his eyes. Mike, ever the ladies' man. He'd probably have whoever she was eating out of the palm of his hand in a matter of minutes. "Behave, you have a job to do shortly."

"Yaaa, I'm not really listening to you right now. I gotta go." Mike ended the call and smiled at the two Sports Illustrated swimsuit models who just sat down at the bar.

Rafe shook his head, staring at the phone. He tossed it onto the coffee table. What the hell, the guy was totally driven by his cock. He went into the kitchen for a bottle of water, opened it, and took a long drink. He looked out at the Gulf and wished to hell things had gone better with Ali. It just hadn't been the right time for him to tell her how he felt. Who was he kidding? He was terrified of telling her how he felt, and he'd left there knowing she wasn't happy with him. He took another drink from the bottle and thought about what she might be doing. Then a resounding gong went off inside his head. Son of bitch! He ran for the phone on the coffee table and pressed redial.

"You're killing me here, man. What is it now?" Mike paused. "Excuse me, ladies. I'll be just a sec." He got a brief smile from them while they ordered their drinks. Holy shit, they were hot!

Rafe was suddenly fuming. "Who are you talking to?"

"This really isn't a good time." Mike turned in his stool to get a better look. "I know you're hearing me, man." Mike grinned at the ladies, rolling his eyes as he gestured to his phone. They really weren't paying any attention to him, so far just a couple of polite smiles, but

Rafe didn't need to know that.

"Listen you, prick, if one of those girls has the most incredible green eyes you've ever looked into, and the other one has blue just as deadly, back…the…fuck…off now!" Rafe could just imagine the things Mike may have already said to them. Unfortunately, the guy oozed charm, and he was great-looking, not a good combination for two women who weren't exactly happy with the men in their lives at the moment.

"Whoa, easy there. You forgot to mention the kick-ass bodies, too." Mike winked at Ali and Nicki as they turned his way, finally.

"I mean it, Mike."

Light dawned. "Don't tell me." Disappointment rolled off Mike's tongue. "These are your neighbors."

"Yes, and they're both spoken for."

"Wow, aren't you being a little greedy there, buddy?"

"I'll explain another time."

"Thank you, Agent Killjoy. The highlight of my stay here, and you ruin it with one phone call."

"Glad to do it. Now, be nothing more than polite, then get the hell back to work."

"Yes, sir -- oh, and Rafe? Which one is yours?" Mike was smiling flirtatiously at the women. "No, wait, don't tell me. I already know."

"How's that?" Rafe's heart was beating double time.

"Because at the mere mention of your name, those green eyes you were telling me about? Are now staring me down."

Rafe swore. "Shit, Cap, your discretion must be a real asset to the FBI." Rafe slammed the phone shut and swore again.

Ali continued to stare at the good-looking blond guy two stools over. "You're a friend of Rafe's?"

Mike scooted over to the stool nearest them. "One of his best friends. Agent Mike Caplan." He peered around Ali to greet Nicki. "Hi, there."

Nicki couldn't help grinning. "Hi." She wondered where the FBI were recruiting their men these days. "I'm Nicki."

"And you must be Ali." Mike gave them his megawatt smile. "Rafe told me you were his neighbors."

"We're staying right across the street from him at my grandmother's house," Nicki told him.

Mike nodded. The lucky bastard.

"So you're an agent, too?" Ali asked keeping her voice down.

Oh, boy, no wonder Rafe had got so hot under the collar. "I sure am, and I'm here to make sure you two lovely ladies stay out of trouble." He winked at them, his blue eyes smiling.

Ali laughed. "No, you're not!"

"You're right. I'm here for other reasons, but if either of you need anything, I'll be close by."

"Thanks," they said together, laughing.

Mike paid the bartender for his club soda and for Ali and Nicki's drinks as well.

"You didn't have to do that. Thank you."

Ali smiled at him, and once again Mike thought, lucky bastard. "My pleasure, ladies," and to Ali, "Rafe's a lucky guy."

Nicki leaned back in her seat. "You ought to mention that to him," she said, smiling.

Ouch! Mike laughed. He would definitely mention that and find out what it meant, too.

"And what about you?" He gave Nicki the eyes.

She laughed. What a flirt!

Ali swiveled around to respond, "My brother's the lucky guy." She laughed when Mike shook his head in defeat.

"Goodnight, ladies. It was nice to meet you. Painful, too, but nice."

The girls laughed. "Goodnight, Mike. Nice to meet you too."

"He was cute." Nicki was still laughing. "See, don't you feel better?"

"I do, and he was, and did you happen to catch any of that phone call?" If Ali had a smidgen of hope before, it was now amplified.

"I did." Nicki grinned. "But I won't say I told you so."

Rafe did not want to think about Ali at the bar. He hit the remote and brought up the surveillance. The flat screen came alive, and all angles covered the screen. His eyes went to the SUV. They were still awake, and Rafe wondered if tonight they would stay that way. Did they even know Stoddman would be diving for the package? That there was a package? D'nafrio made it clear he wanted Stoddman and only Stoddman going for it, so there was a chance they had no clue.

Rafe knew there were agents surrounding the beach and out on the Gulf at a safe distance as he sat there. If he had to guess, Stoddman was up the street at Scintillo's beach house right now, suiting up for the dive. Rafe would be alerted to Stoddman's every move by Agent Gogin until he had him in his own sights. He would document his actions, then follow by car to wherever Stoddman was taking the package. Mike would be covering the bay where D'nafrio's Rampage still sat in the marina, knowing it was a distinct possibility Stoddman would bring the package there. If he did that, and D'nafrio were aboard, the FBI would have a slam dunk, but it wouldn't be quite the same bust as it would be if they waited just one more day for the mother lode, which they were going to do. Besides, Mike had seen D'nafrio board a fifty-foot Prestige in the marina just this morning, and there had been no word of his return as of yet. Mike had taken advantage of D'nafrio's absence to install listening devices aboard the Rampage for when he returned.

Rafe left the monitors and picked up his binoculars from the sofa table. The sun had long disappeared, and he switched to infrared as he focused on the buoy. He spotted the Whaler out deep, about three hundred yards from the shore due east. All was quiet on the Gulf, so Rafe dialed Daniels.

"You in for a long night?" Daniels skipped the hellos.

"I'm thinking he'll get this over with right away. Doesn't strike me as the type who likes to dive at night -- alone. He's the type who would have gone out this afternoon if he thought he could walk up the beach in a wet suit and with a big package under his arm unnoticed."

"Maybe you're right. He did sound a little nervous about the retrieval when he spoke to D'nafrio. He probably had designs on sending one of the little punks out there."

"He still might. I've got my eye on them."

"Mike's relieved Reynolds. Still no sign of Mr. X., but guess who the Prestige belongs to?"

"Scintillo." Rafe wasn't surprised, and he was glad to know Mike was back on duty and not at the bar. Not that he'd have to worry about him with Ali since Mike now knew the deal, but he didn't want to have to explain to Matt if Mike decided to hit on Nicki.

"You got it. I wouldn't be shocked if they took a cruise around your way."

"Simmons and Bealls are on the Whaler. Do they know about the Prestige?"

"They were on the bay when D'nafrio boarded."

"Good, maybe Scintillo will board the Rampage for a nightcap and a little conversation when they return, make it a two for one."

"Can we be that lucky?" Daniels asked with a chuckle.

"Hell, it doesn't matter. D'nafrio will give him up in a heartbeat trying to plea out."

"You got that right. I hope they're whooping it up out there -- you know the difference a day can make." Daniels huffed.

All too well. If Rafe could start this day over, he would in a second. He looked over at the handheld, which crackled with sound. "Gotta go, boys are calling."

"Keep me posted."

Daniels hung up, and Rafe picked up the handheld and said, "McD." His fellow agents said it took too long for "McDonough" to come out over the radio, so it was significantly shortened. "What do you have?" Rafe picked up his binoculars and focused on the water right beyond the glass. Rafe's house was in complete darkness, and with the moon shining so bright, he almost didn't need the infrared.

Simmons came over as clear as if he were in the room. "Prestige, two hundred yards off our stern."

Rafe swung around and looked past the Whaler at the yacht steadily making its way along the Gulf toward upper Captiva, where he knew it would turn at Red Fish pass and head back to the marina. Or maybe they would stop to check on Stoddman. That would be nice; Rafe could get out the Nikon with the long range lens and get off some shots. He moved his sights back to the buoy, then to the yacht again. "Gogin."

"Right here."

Gogin was covering the beach house. "Anything?"

"Nada."

"Cap you having fun yet?" Rafe grinned picturing Mike looking out at the bay from his hotel room, his feet up on something.

"Do I have time to go back to the bar?" Mike asked trying to rile him.

"Cap, take a nap. We'll call you when they get close," Rafe answered just a little peeved.

Rafe could here Mike cackling. Rafe shook his head. Mike loved to bust Rafe's balls. He watched the Prestige get closer and finally pass by without slowing. Interesting.

"Cap, you've got about a half hour before your boys are back."

"That's all the time I need." Mike chuckled again.

And on it goes. Rafe ignored him and put down his binoculars, making his way to the kitchen. He opened the fridge and reached for the sandwich Ali had bought him. Sitting at the table, he unwrapped the wax paper to find a large Italian sub, everything, no hots. God, he loved her.

He'd never even mentioned that this was one of his favorite sandwiches, but yet that's what she picked out for him. He tried to imagine what hers would be -- turkey and cheese, lettuce, tomato, maybe a little mayo, maybe a few pickles, and probably on a wrap, no, a pocket. He took a big bite and chewed. What the hell was he doing? Was he seriously sitting here thinking about what her favorite sandwich was? He was losing it, no doubt about it. Daniels did the right thing sending him away. He just had to keep his head straight for the rest of tonight and tomorrow. He took another big bite and wrapped the sandwich back up for later.

"McD, subject has arrived. Black Beemer just pulled in."

Good, he wanted to get this moving. "Copy that."

Barry pulled into the driveway at Scintillo's beach house and killed the engine. He wanted to do this as quickly as possible. The thought of diving in that water with sharks and God knows what else was terrifying, but he kept thinking about his cut of the profits.

He used the key to the basement door and stepped inside, locking it behind him. He gratefully used the restroom first, thinking about the wet suit he'd be encased in for the next thirty minutes or so. When he opened the door to the garage area, he put the overhead light on, illuminating the whole room. There weren't any windows, so he stripped down to his briefs. He found a wetsuit that looked like it would fit and tugged it on. He knew D'nafrio expected him to put the tank on and enter the water right from here, swimming underwater unseen for the less than hundred-yard distance to the marker, but Barry didn't want to be in that water any longer than he had to. He would walk on the sand, toward the buoy, getting as close as he could, then go in with just a mask, underwater flash light, snorkel, and flippers. He was already nervous about trying to juggle the package and the light as he made his way to the surface. What if a shark swam by? He really wished he could have gotten one of those lunkheads to do this -- they were just sitting out there in that truck, fucking off. Some watchmen; they hadn't even noticed when he'd slowed by them. He looked around on the shelves and grabbed the rest of the gear he needed, then headed for the basement sliders.

"We're on."

Gogin's voice cut through the silence of Rafe's dark surroundings, and he went to the sliders, binoculars to his eyes.

"He's moving toward you, McD, hugging the dunes."

Rafe adjusted his aim and spotted the dark figure. He could make out the flippers Stoddman carried in one hand, a smaller object held in the other; flashlight possibly? A mask was already atop his head, snorkel attached, dangling by Stoddman's face, which was stark white in the moonlight against all that black. Rafe chuckled. Apparently Stoddman had never received any SEAL training. When he reached D'nafrio's monster house, he started walking toward the water. He stopped just at the shoreline, bent down to put the flippers on, adjusted his mask and air tube, then entered the Gulf.

"Diver in, boys." Rafe double-checked the monitors behind him. The boys were dozing.

"There goes the incredible Mr. Limpet," Gogin joked.

Rafe laughed. Stoddman had looked pretty damn funny waddling down the beach.

"The incredible Mr. Who?" Mike watched as the Prestige docked.

"Never mind, Romeo. Your friends back yet?" Rafe asked.

"Just arrived." Mike answered.

Rafe kept his eyes on the water and saw the Whaler puttering close by. "Keep that engine off, guys. Don't want to scare the fish."

"What, are we new at this?" Simmons came over.

"You? No, you're a friggin' dinosaur. Bealls is a newbie, though, and he's in the driver's seat."

"Fuck you, McD. I may be a dinosaur, but I've never been sent on a head vacation."

Ouch. He deserved that.

Mike came over. "What's that, Simmons? You were breaking up. You say you never get any head when you go on vacation? That's a damn shame. You need me to have a talk with the missus?"

Rafe chuckled, appreciating the defense.

"Caplan, when I get back there I'm going to kick your ass."

"At shuffleboard maybe, but that's about it."

"Guys, anyone keeping an eye out for Mr. Limpet? He's been in the water five minutes." Gogin, the voice of responsibility.

"I still got his air tube in sight. He's just about to the buoy." Rafe checked the monitors. They were still quiet. There was no movement from the SUV.

"Is anyone going to tell me who Mr. Limpet is?" Mike was thankful for his earpiece as he shot a few candids of D'nafrio stepping off Scintillo's yacht. Gotcha! Now he just needed Scintillo to appear.

"Ask the dinosaur," Gogin told him.

Rafe shook his head at the conversation. "Okay, he's down."

"What's your bet?" Mike asked. Mike could hold his breath for two and a half minutes, and defied anyone to beat his time.

"I don't think you have to worry about him breaking your record, Cap. Oh, look, he's already up for air." Rafe watched as Stoddman treaded water, catching his breath, then he was back down again. "Deeper than he thought. Should have strapped on the tank."

"You boys prepared for a rescue at sea?" Mike switched out the camera for his scope. He watched D'nafrio climb aboard his Rampage alone.

"Hell, no, I'm not getting in with the sharks," Bealls put in.

"Snakes, too." Mike smiled.

Rafe waited for what seemed like several minutes, but in actuality was just about one, and then he saw him. "He's up!" Rafe adjusted his lenses. Stoddman was swimming, or rather kicking, back to shore on his back, hands full. "He's got it." Rafe again checked the monitors. The boys were fast asleep. He turned back to the beach and waited for Stoddman to reach the sand. Stoddman emerged, package in hand, and kicked off the flippers. Pushing the mask off his face, he appeared to be checking out the waterproofed box.

"You don't think he'll open the damn thing, do you?" Gogin asked.

"No, he's just checking it out -- there he goes." Stoddman had picked up the flippers and was awkwardly jogging up the beach, arms loaded.

"Gogin, keep him in your sights. Let me know when he pulls off. I'll be in the Yukon. I'll have my ear piece in."

"Caplan, get your shuffleboard shoes on, I'm coming home." Simmons told Bealls to start the engine as soon as Stoddman disappeared into the beach house.

"Mike, be ready in case he's coming your way." Rafe wondered if Stoddman wouldn't pay D'nafrio a little visit at the marina.

"I'm good to go, buddy." Mike kept his eye on the Rampage. D'nafrio was inside the cabin, smoking a cigar. Waiting for Stoddman? He doubted it. D'nafrio wouldn't be stupid enough to have the drugs brought right to him.

Barry finally made it to the sand, his heart beating wildly. He was sure something had bumped him down there. The box had been easy to lift out, but not easy to swim back with along with his light. He checked out the densely wrapped package, and it looked okay to him. It was wrapped in a sealed tight plastic cover and another waterproof shell under that. It should fit just right into one of the five-gallon buckets. Barry started jogging, wanting to get back to the safety of the beach house as soon as possible. He didn't want to be mistaken for a refugee. That was all he needed.

He made it up the beach in minutes even with the heavy wetsuit and his arms full, and let himself back inside through the sliders, being careful to lock them behind him. Once in the garage, he set the package down, stripped out of the suit, hung it back with the others, and put his own dry clothes back on. He returned the mask and flippers to a shelf that was laden with pool supplies, and reached for the large bucket of pool shock that he saw. He pulled it off the shelf, estimating by its weight to be about half way full, then carried it with him to the bathroom in the basement. It took him some effort to get the top off, but when he did, he had been right in his estimation, and he dumped the half-filled bucket into the toilet. He held his breath at the strong chemical smell, then used a nearby towel to dry the container out. This would be perfect, he thought, to store the package tonight. If he got pulled over, no one would question a bucket of chlorine for his pool. Besides, it was a good disguise, seeing as how tomorrow the other drugs would be in similar buckets.

Coming back into the garage, he picked up the package, gave it a shake, and, hearing the tell-tale rattle, placed it inside the bucket. He had to poke a little hole in the outer plastic to let some air out and squeeze the box all the way in, and only then was he able to screw the cover back on. He breathed a sigh of relief, happy to have retrieved the box without incident, and he left the garage, shutting the door behind him. He locked up the basement and brought the bucket to his trunk. He looked at his watch. He still had time to get over the causeway, grab a late night dinner, and get over to Holly's. He hoped she'd let him spend the night.

CHAPTER TWENTY-SIX

"Coming your way." Gogin informed. "Trunk is loaded, looks to be concealed inside a large bucket."

Rafe started the Yukon. He saw the headlights approach and, with his own lights off, slowly rolled forward down the drive. When Stoddman was well ahead, Rafe pulled out, lights on, and followed at a discreet distance. He hoped Stoddman went right home.

His cell rang, and he saw it was Daniels.

"Our boy just made a phone call to the boss, confirming he made the pickup and ensuring the delivery was still on for tomorrow. They're expecting this barge bright and early, so be ready."

"I'll be ready." There were no cars between his and Stoddman's, and Rafe slowed to put even more distance between them.

"What do you make of D'nafrio still at the marina?"

"I think he wants to be close by when that barge comes in. Maybe he'll make an appearance."

"And if he does?"

"Nothing. We take him at the warehouse only."

"And you're certain he'll go there?" Rafe took a left on Periwinkle and now had two cars between his and the Beemer.

"As certain as the sky is blue. He'll be dying to know if Scintillo screwed him or not."

Rafe approached the four-way stop minutes later, but Barry didn't go left. "Looks like we're making a pit stop." Rafe knew Barry would head to the office, so he let a few cars pass him before he continued on.

"Have you thought about what you're going to do after your vacation time is up?" Daniels asked, curious.

"I've been thinking a little about it, yeah." Rafe drove past East End Realty and pulled off to the nearest side street. It was an unpaved dead end that looked over the bay. He turned around, cutting his lights, and slowly crept back up the street. Cutting the engine, he turned to see that he had a good view of Stoddman's office and the Beemer in front of it. Barry was at the trunk and taking the large bucket from it. "He's bringing it in the office."

"Makes sense. Why drive all the way home with it?" Daniels continued on his fishing expedition. "I'd love to have you stay working out of the Miami field office, but I know you're dying to get back to New York."

Rafe watched Barry unlock the office and disappear inside with the bucket. "Actually, I was wondering about Boston." There was silence on the other end, and Rafe thought he might have lost Daniels. "You there?"

"Boston, huh? That's not quite the speed of Miami or New York that you're used to."

"I know, but I've been thinking about changing speeds."

"Change is good."

Rafe could hear the smile on Daniels lips. "He's back out, locking up." Rafe watched him get back in the car and pull out. "And there he goes." Rafe followed him to the four-way and watched as he proceeded over the causeway, a tail following him. "My job is done for tonight. I'm heading back."

"Does your family know what you're thinking?"

Rafe exhaled. "I don't even know what I'm thinking, but I know what I want."

Daniels gave a soft laugh. "Then go for it, my friend. I'll do what I can on my end."

Rafe hung up and grinned. He would go for it, as soon as tomorrow was over. He touched his ear piece and spoke to Mike. "Marina still jumpin'?"

"Nope, lights out, must have an early bell. Still following Mr. Limpdick?"

Rafe laughed. "Mr. Limpet. And no, he brought it to the office and headed over the causeway. There's a car on him, so I'm off. Don Knotts is Mr. Limpet. Didn't you ever see that movie? He turns into a fish?"

"No, man, but I've seen every Andy Griffith. I'll have to check that one out. Stoddman kind of resembles Don Knotts, doesn't he?"

"Yeah, with about forty pounds on him." Rafe paused, "Anything else happening over there?"

Mike chuckled. "Wouldn't you like to know."

Yeah, he would. He was dying to know what she was doing this very minute. "Just check on the cottage for me at some point, will you?"

"Now, you know it'll be my pleasure." Mike left his balcony and stepped inside the room for a cold beer. D'nafrio had locked up the cabin, so Mike didn't expect him to go anywhere until morning.

"Yeah I do know, but lucky for you I trust you."

"Now, why did you have to go and say that? That's just the kind of guilt trip that will make me behave."

"That's the idea." Rafe hung up and made the drive back to Captiva in fifteen minutes. He pulled into the garage and went right back upstairs to turn on the monitors and…shit! The passenger side was empty. Sean Smith was no longer sitting in the truck.

"This was such a good idea," Ali leaned against the heated jets of the hot tub, her upper back getting the brunt of the force.

"Wasn't it? And extra nice having it all to ourselves. It's pretty dead out here at night, huh?"

"Once this outdoor bar closes, forget it. Everyone must be in the

Crow's Nest. Plus, it is a Tuesday night."

"True." Nicki leaned her head back, looking up at the moon. It was huge and brilliant in the pitch-black sky and made her long for Matt.

"It was fun working with you today. I hope the pictures come out good."

"Oh, I'm sure they will. You can come with me anytime -- it's a pretty relaxed atmosphere at the paper. I'm so glad. It would suck if it was like a nine to five thing, all day stuck in an office."

"I know. It seems like it would be pretty laid-back everywhere on the islands. That's why people live and work here, right?"

"Could you live here?" Nicki lifted her head to ask Ali.

"My first instinct is to say, most definitely, but if I had to think about it, I'd miss too much back home." Ali shifted positions so the jets aimed at her lower back. "Umm."

"Yeah, me, too. I'm so glad Nan has a house here, though!"

"Me, too!" Ali smiled. "I'm just glad she adopted me as another granddaughter."

"Nan loves you so much. She loves your whole family," Nicki added.

"She's going to be really happy about you and Matt. Did you talk to them last night?"

"Yes, they arrived safely and are staying at a villa in Tuscany. Can you imagine? I'm a little jealous," Nicki admitted, "but Nan promises to take me back sometime."

"I bet it's heavenly." Ali had always dreamed of going to Italy.

"Oh, you know you'll be invited." Nicki laughed.

Ali smiled. "I'm in. Did you mention anything about Matt?"

"No, I kept it pretty general. What could I say?" Nicki pretended to be talking to her grandmother. "Matt arrived, and in less than an hour we were making out, and then most of the weekend we had earth-shattering sex, until he left for an emergency Monday, leaving me to wring my hands with worry if he'll ever come back." She laughed.

"I'm not sure that she's ready for that. I know I wasn't."

Ali looked at her. "Earth-shattering, huh?"

Nicki grinned. "I'm sorry. That slipped out, but oh, yes!"

"Well, I'm happy for you, but you could have told her the G-rated version."

"Until I'm sure of what's happening, I'm going to keep it right here." Nicki touched her heart, and Ali knew just how she was feeling, except Ali *was* sure of at least one man. Her brother would come back for Nicki.

"This weekend will be interesting," Nicki said, looking up to the stars again.

"If we have to, we can make our own fun." Ali hoped they wouldn't have to.

"Yes, we can. That's why we came here in the first place, right?"

"Right! That band is back Friday night. Let's just plan to come here." She wouldn't sit inside pining for Rafe if he blew her off. She'd get right back out there. What a horrible thought. "Ace will probably be looking to hook up with you," she teased.

"Your brother has ruined me for anyone else." Nicki said it with an exasperated sigh.

Ali laughed. "He'll be here, Nick. He said he would."

Nicki tried not to get her hopes up. "What about Rafe?"

Ali stood up, getting out of the hot tub. "I guess that depends on how things go Thursday. He said he wants to talk more then."

"Why can't guys just spit it out? We wear our hearts on our sleeves, and we have to pull it out of them."

"Says the girl who wore her heart *under* her sleeve for the past dozen years."

"Touché, but seriously, why is it so hard for some guys to say how they feel?"

"Fear of rejection, I guess." Ali patted herself dry, and wrapped the towel around her.

"Well, we're all afraid of that." Nicki definitely feared not seeing Matt again. She followed Ali out of the spa and grabbed a nearby towel to dry off. "Damn, it's chilly when you get out."

They started the short walk back to the cottage, anxious to get inside and warm up.

"Hey, look at this guy," Nicki said softly. "He looks wasted."

Ali looked over, and her stomach lurched immediately to her throat. It was the jerk from the beach who had seen her naked, and then had bothered her on her run just this morning. What was he doing here? She and Nicki were dressed only in their bathing suits and towels, and were mere steps from him. "Get to the door," Ali whispered, her voice frantic. "Go, go!" she hissed and practically shoved Nicki forward.

"Okay, jeez." Nicki looked at Ali as she fumbled for the key. It wasn't like her to be so freaked out.

"Hey, ladies."

Ali kept her back to him, but he was close enough to see her face.

Nicki rolled her eyes and tried to work the lock. Just great, a friggin' drunk was going to harass them. "Goodnight!" she called back.

"Hey, what do you mean goodnight? I just got here, babe. How about I come in for a drink?"

Neither she nor Nicki would look at him.

"Or we could go for a swim. You all look like you're ready for a swim."

Ali no longer thought he was drunk, but possibly high on something instead. He talked like he was a stoner, not slurry, just lazy. But stoners generally weren't aggressive. Maybe he was on something else. She really didn't care to find out.

"No, thanks," Ali moved Nicki aside and tried the credit card type key herself. Where was the green light, damn it?

"I have a friend and we could all go down to the beach, smoke a little, fuck a lot." He laughed at his own crudeness.

"That's it!" Nicki yelled, and Ali turned to face him with her. "Get the hell away from us, or we'll call the police!"

He zoomed right in on Ali now that he could see all of her face. "Hey, I remember you," he said real slow. "Why don't you take that towel off? I've already seen the goods, remember?" He laughed.

Nicki looked at Ali and saw she was now shaking. What the hell? "Did you hear what I said, you little prick?"

"Hey, I remember you, too. Where's your boyfriend tonight?"

Ali looked at Nicki this time, then turned her attention back to the lock. She sure wished Rafe's friend would make an appearance. She saw the green light. Yes! The door clicked and she turned the handle, pulling Nicki inside. They heard him say, "See you real soon!"

"Go home, loser!" Nicki yelled before Ali slammed the door. She went right to the phone and called the front desk. After explaining what happened, they promised to send security to check it out right away.

Nicki pulled the curtain back on the door and peeked out. "What a creep. He must have been in that SUV the other night when Matt and I walked back to Nan's from here." She turned to Ali. "You've obviously seen him before, too."

Ali nodded. "You and Matt saw him?"

"We didn't see him -- we heard him and his friend. They made some rude comments when we walked by and Matt called them out, but they stayed in the truck, obviously afraid," Nicki added, thinking how Matt would have pounded them. "They were sitting outside the monster house."

"They're guarding it. The one who was just here saw me naked in Rafe's backyard." Ali grimaced as Nicki's jaw dropped.

"What? How? They're guarding it for what? Were you skinny dipping?"

Ali cleared her throat. "No, we were...we had just finished... Rafe went inside to get us something to eat. I was just standing by the gate to the beach, looking at the water. When I turned he was just standing there on the beach, staring at me."

"Ugh! My God! What did you do?" Nicki peered out through the curtain again and saw security roll by in a golf cart. Okay, so not exactly intimidating, but maybe the creep would get the hint not to come back.

"I screamed for Rafe, who came running and chased him down the beach."

Nicki turned back to face Ali, not quite getting it. "Well, the guy still appeared to have all his teeth, so what the hell did Rafe do about it?" From the way Matt had reacted to just their words, she knew if one of them had been looking at her naked, he wouldn't be back for a second chance.

Ali went on the defense for Rafe. "He couldn't do what he wanted to do because they're not supposed to know who he is. He purposefully didn't catch him."

Nicki shook her head. "Oh." She was a little confused. "Why are they guarding that house?"

"Supposedly so nobody trespasses." She hesitated. "They harassed me this morning, too, when I went for a run."

Nicki's face was wrought with anger. "What did they do?"

"Did nothing -- *said* gross things. I gave them the finger and told them to go to hell, and when I turned to run back, Rafe was running toward me, thank God."

"Ali, I think you should call Rafe. I don't have a good feeling about those two jerks, especially them being so close to Nan's house. Did they see you come out of there?"

"I don't know. I didn't see them until I had already started running."

"Well, I think you should let Rafe know." Nicki double-checked the lock and peered out one last time. Neither the golf cart nor the jerk were in sight.

"It's over now. I'm not going to tell him tonight -- he's working, and this nonsense would just be a distraction." Ali headed into the bedroom, Nicki on her heels.

"I think he'd want to know, but it's your decision." Nicki dressed and got into bed while Ali went into the bathroom. "I should have let Matt kick their asses," she said, loud enough for Ali to hear.

"He wanted to, huh?" Ali came out and joined Nicki in the bed.

"I begged him not to go over to the truck, so he just told them to get out and come to him."

Ali grinned, picturing her brother. "He would have laid a beating on them."

"No kidding. Remember that high school party we were at junior year, and Matt showed up because he was friends with that girl's older brother?"

Ali laughed. "Yes, and he and his friends beat the hell out of those jerks who showed up from Quincy?"

"Yes!" Nicki pulled the covers around her. "God, I remember thinking how great he was that night. He even looked good throwing punches."

"I just remember how he threw us in the car right before the cops came." Ali laughed.

"Oh, I remember that, too." She smiled, thinking back, "I got to sit right beside him, between him and that kid John, while Matt drove. I was in absolute heaven!"

"Oh, my God! Meanwhile, I was stuck between two huge guys he played hockey with who stunk like the keg they'd been drinking from."

Nicki laughed. "They were pretty gross!"

Ali sighed. "If we only knew then what we know now."

"The things I know now, after this past weekend, would have made me the class slut back in high school, so no thanks! I'm glad we were oblivious."

Ali giggled. "I guess you're right."

"Goodnight, Al. Forget tonight, and dream of something good, okay?"

"I'll try." She smiled. "Goodnight, and you do the same."

Nicki's eyes focused on the ceiling fan spinning lazily above her head. No phone call, no messages. Not a good sign.

Tim was startled awake as Sean opened the door and climbed in the truck. "Where the hell you been, man?"

"The fuckin' lady wouldn't serve me, said the kitchen was closed, but guess who I ran into when I was leaving?"

Tim lit a joint and inhaled. "Who?" He passed it to Sean. They'd already blown through their stash of coke for the night.

Sean took a hit. "That fine piece of ass from the other night and this morning, and she was with that other fine piece of ass. You know, the one with the boyfriend who walked by here?"

"Did he give you any shit?" Tim ran a hand over the gun in his lap. "I should have put a cap in his ass that night, then fucked the shit out of his girlfriend while he watched."

Sean laughed, passing the joint back. "No, man, he wasn't there. They were alone, going into one of those cottages overlooking the beach. Dude, they were in their bathing suits with just towels covering them. I had a boner the whole time."

"What did you say?"

"I told them I had a friend and we could all go down to the beach and get high and fuck, but they weren't into it."

They laughed out loud and high-fived each other. "Yeah, dude! I could've gone for that! You just have to work on your delivery." Tim took another hit and passed it over.

"They called security on me." Sean laughed. "This little dude in a golf cart drove up alongside me and was like, 'Excuse me? What is your room number?'

So I go, 'Fuck off, rent a cop, I'm in room go fuck yourself.'"

Tim was really laughing now, the pot kicking in. "What did he say?"

"Nothing. After he closed his gaping hole, he drove off. Of course, he might have been a little scared when I lifted my shirt and showed him my piece."

Tim sobered instantly. "You did what? Are you fucking stupid? What if he calls the cops?" Tim looked through the windshield out to the empty road.

"Relax, dude, I cut over to the beach when he left and walked back that way. He doesn't know where I came from."

Tim breathed a little easier and took another hit, "Still, man, don't be waving that shit around."

Sean leaned back against the seat, settling in. "Maybe we can both go back there tomorrow, huh? I'll work on my delivery."

Tim was back to laughing. "Yeah, I wouldn't mind working on my delivery, too." They finished the joint and fell asleep, smiling with their own lewd thoughts.

CHAPTER TWENTY-SEVEN

Rafe scanned all the monitors and saw nothing. Where was the son of a bitch? Rafe went to the sliders and scanned the beach with his binoculars. Nothing. Hey, wait a minute. Rafe went back to the monitors and picked up the remote. He rewound the footage and watched. The monitor read 2150, thirty minutes ago. Rafe watched as Sean Smith exited the vehicle and headed north on foot until he was out of camera range. Where the hell was he going? To the beach house? Rafe got on the handheld to Gogin. "It's McD. You still covering the beach?"

"Yes, sir, just me and the turtles out here now."

"So you didn't see a white male, tall, skinny, early twenties, out there?"

"Nope, I've got oval shell, probably greenish brown, female, by the looks of what she's doing, and maybe a hundred. I don't know -- how old do turtles get to?"

Rafe rolled his eyes, about to comment on Gogin having been out there too long, when he heard Mike come over the radio, chuckling. "Lost one huh?"

"I was a little busy, but yeah, passenger's gone. I've got him walking your way street side, half an hour ago."

"I'll check it out. I need to stretch my legs anyway." Mike had been sitting on his balcony for far too long himself. D'nafrio was definitely in for the night.

"Thanks, man." Rafe went back to real time on the monitors and watched. Tim Mann appeared to be asleep, so Rafe went into his bedroom and put the flat screen on in there, changed, and got ready for bed. He put his Glock under the pillow and his cell phone on the night stand. He thought about calling Ali, but then decided against it. She was probably still angry, and he wasn't about to spill his guts tonight. He still had to focus and get through tomorrow. He propped up his pillows against the headboard and kept his eye on the truck. Gogin sounded over the handheld.

"White male, tall, skinny, early twenties, headed your way Rafe," Gogin's voice sounded in his ear. "Beach side. He cut through near Scintillo's house, but didn't pay it any attention. Looked like he came right off the street, kind of like he was in a hurry."

Rafe watched him appear at the bottom of the screen. "Thanks, call in your relief, will you? You're sounding a little punchy." Rafe could see Smith cut through from the beach behind the site. Then he reappeared at the top of the screen and entered the passenger side of the truck. Where had he gone? Rafe's cell phone rang, and for a brief moment he thought it might be Ali. Caller ID said otherwise.

"Why aren't you on the radio?" Rafe picked up, asking Mike.

"I didn't think you'd want anyone else to hear this."

Rafe sat up. "Hear what?"

"I just left the front desk. I went in because I saw the security guard waving his arms around to the woman on duty. It seems your boy wanted some food from the restaurant but got shot down because the kitchen was closed. The restaurant manager called up front to complain when the kid called him a fucking tool. Then apparently upon his stroll back toward the road he encountered two women, whom he proceeded to harass." Mike paused. "They called security, and the guard went out on his dune buggy to follow the guy."

Rafe swallowed, knowing exactly which two women. "And?"

"And then your boy let some profanity fly and flashed the guy his piece."

Oh, shit. "And security high-tailed it out of there. They don't get paid enough to deal with that kind of shit."

"More or less, he came back and called local, but nobody's been up here yet." Mike hesitated. "You know where he was, right?"

"Yeah, I know. Thanks for calling me on the cell." Rafe ran a hand through his hair. He wanted so bad to go out to that truck, he could taste it.

"Don't do anything stupid, brother. This will be over tomorrow."

Rafe knew Mike read his mind, because Mike would be thinking the very same way if it were his girlfriend. His girlfriend. Shit! She would have been better off in bed right next to him and Nicki in her own bed at home. The bastard had been carrying -- he could have threatened them. "Did security ask them any questions, like what he did or said to them?"

"I asked the same thing. Apparently the guard is new. He didn't even knock on their door. I think he was hoping for local to do it. When the girls called they just said they had come back from the hot tub, and that there was this guy who was propositioning them, and seemed to be high on drugs."

"Jesus." Rafe pictured Ali walking back in just her bikini. Smith would have surely remembered her. Maybe by some miracle she was fully clothed, her and Nicki. Doubtful at 88 degrees.

"I'm standing out front now. It's dark -- they're probably asleep. Do you want me to knock?"

"No, but I want you to stay there. Is Reynolds covering for you tonight?"

"He's there now. Hey, there's a nice beach chair here that looks pretty cozy, but you will be paying for the massage I'm going to need at some point tomorrow."

"I know, I know, and thank you, I'd do the same for you."

"Yes, but you're so loyal, you wouldn't be dreaming about yourself in there between them."

Rafe laughed. "You've met Nicki? She's with Ali's brother, and he could kick your ass six ways to Sunday, not to mention you're already aware of what I'm capable of."

Mike laughed at that. "Oh, yeah, I met Nicki…and nobody can kick my ass. You got lucky that one night. I was drunk."

"Sleep tight." Rafe smirked and hung up, feeling slightly better that Mike was outside and both assholes were accounted for. And Mike was right -- nobody could kick his ass, but Rafe liked keeping him on his toes. If anything, Matt would want to kick *his* ass for getting Nicki mixed up in this shit.

CHAPTER TWENTY-EIGHT

Matt had had the day from hell as he'd gone from one job to the next, trying to tie up loose ends. He had ended up on the slate roof himself, tethered to the chimney. He took his time and patched the areas Sean didn't get to, and it was dusk by the time he'd finished. It was a relief to have it done. The pitch on that roof had been steep as hell, and Matt was amazed Sean was even alive after falling from it.

He'd had a quick bite to eat with his parents at his mother's insistence, and then he'd gone right to the hospital to see Sean and Terri. He knew Sean would feel better knowing the roof was done, and he left him in good spirits, promising to be back the next day.

On his way back home, he stopped at the office to check off the job board and line up his work for the next day. By the time he got home, it was ten o'clock. After a quick shower, he lay down in bed and put the game on. He fell asleep minutes later, watching the Yankees get the best of the Sox.

It was a couple of hours later that Matt woke up abruptly, in a cold sweat. He'd had a nightmare about Nicki. She had been standing on her grandmother's dock and fell off into the dark water. Matt had tried to pull her to safety with a rope, but it broke in two and she went under. He had jumped in to save her, but both of his legs had been in casts, and he sank to the bottom.

Matt sat up and took a big gulp of water from the bottle on his nightstand and looked at his phone plugged into its charger. Jesus, he hadn't called Nicki. He was going to just watch the game a minute, then call to say goodnight. He must have drifted off. What the hell time was it, anyway? He opened his cell. It read one a.m. Shit. He knew she had to get up for work, but he decided to take the chance that she'd pick up.

Nicki awoke, thinking the bedside alarm clock was going off. She hit the button groggily, but the noise kept on coming. It took her a minute or two to realize it was her cell phone ringing, and she reached an arm over to the night stand to find it. She didn't recognize the number, but she recognized the area code, and hope filled her. "Hello," she whispered, turning away from Ali so she wouldn't wake her.

"Hey, sleepy head."

Nicki's heart soared at the sound of Matt's voice, and she was instantly awake.

"Hey." She gently got out of bed and left the room, leaving Ali soundly asleep.

"I'm sorry I'm calling so late. I fell asleep, believe it or not, watching the game."

"I'm glad you called." She opened the door to the porch and went to sit on the wicker sofa. The moon was shining bright over the Gulf, illuminating parts of the beach and casting a small shadow on the deck of the small porch.

"I'm glad you answered."

Nicki wrapped an arm around her bent knees and smiled. "You must have had a busy day."

Matt lay back in bed and told her about it, and how Sean was feeling better. He did make sure to leave out the nightmare.

"That's great about Sean, and I'm glad you made it off the roof safely." Nicki was glad she hadn't known he was up there.

"Of course I did. You don't send a boy to do a man's job."

Nicki could hear the infamous grin through the phone. "Oh, brother, I hope you didn't tell that to Sean." She laughed.

"Oh, of course I did. He can't get up, remember? His wife gave me a good whack, though."

"I'll bet she did." Nicki laughed softly as she watched a couple walk arm and arm across to the beach, going for a moonlit stroll, no doubt.

"How are things there?" Matt asked.

Nicki filled him in on her day with Ali at work, but left out the creep at the end of the night. No need to get him upset.

"What's it like right now?"

His voice was low and deep, and she wished with all her heart she were lying beside him. "It's about eighty degrees out, and the moon is so bright over the water, it's really pretty. I'm sitting on a little enclosed porch."

"Sounds nice. What are you wearing?"

"Matt!" She laughed, her body warming instantly.

"I'm serious. Tell me."

Nicki looked down and smiled. His T-shirt came to about mid-thigh, and she could still smell him on it. "It's nothing exciting, really."

"Let me be the judge of that."

The desire in his voice came burning through the phone, sending shivers all over. "You really want to know?"

"I'm waiting."

"I'm wearing your T-shirt. You left it hanging behind the bathroom door." Talk about wearing your heart on your sleeve.

Matt shut his eyes and smiled. Now that made him feel good on *so* many levels. "Picturing that is going to make it hard for me to fall back to sleep, pardon the pun." God, he missed her.

She laughed, but was feeling miserable. "I wish that had never happened to Sean." She paused. "You know," she faltered, "obviously, but..."

Matt's eyes were open again. "I know, Nick, me, too. I really wish I were there with you."

Oh, God, that's what she wanted to hear, and naturally she couldn't hear it without tears springing to her eyes.

"Nicki, you still there?"

Nicki sniffled away from the phone. "I'm here."

Matt's heart wrenched. Was she crying? "Is everything okay?"

The caring in his voice was not helping her very much. "Yes," she whispered, "it is now."

"I didn't think this would be so hard." He heard his own voice, thick with emotion. It killed him to think he had somehow brought tears to her eyes.

Ha, *she* knew it would be hard -- been here, done this, but what did he think was hard? "What do you mean?" Just come straight out and ask, right?

Matt took a deep breath. "Being away from you, Nicki. It's hard. This weekend was incredible. I want more."

More what? Sex? Yeah, so did she, but she wanted oh, so much more than that. "Me, too." Way to bare all. If it ended up that all he wanted was sex, well, she would take that and be happy.

Matt didn't want to bare his feelings in a long-distance phone call. He wanted Nicki in his arms when he told her that he loved her, even if it meant hearing the tinge of doubt in her voice now. "I'm going to let you go back to sleep. I know you have to get up early, and I really want to fall asleep and dream about you in my T-shirt."

Yup, all about the sex. Oh, well, what did she expect, a declaration of never-ending love, after just one weekend? She needed to get a grip. "Unfortunately, my dreams will be G-rated, given that I'll be sleeping beside your sister."

Matt laughed. "I'm just glad you guys are safe."

If he knew what had happened tonight, he might not think so. "We're fine. I guess I'll talk to you soon?"

"Very soon. Goodnight, Nicki."

"Goodnight, Matt." And I love you -- still.

Mike had heard the one-sided conversation from where he sat uncomfortably in the beach chair, and the little crying jag that followed after the call had ended. He had been tempted to offer some comforting arms, but he knew better. Instead he just cursed the schmuck who had made that beautiful woman cry.

CHAPTER TWENTY-NINE

Rafe had slept, but not soundly. He'd kept waking to check the monitors, making sure both men were accounted for. It was only after he remembered Mike sitting guard outside the cottage that he finally fell asleep, but it wasn't long before six-fifteen rolled around and he was up for the day, watching them pull off. He took solace that in a few short hours they'd be arrested and held for questioning.

He got out of bed and called Mike.

"Let me get this straight -- not only do you ask me to sleep outside in a beach chair all night, but then you wake me up at the ass crack of dawn?" Mike yawned and stood up to stretch.

Rafe grinned. "I know Ali's going to come out to run..."

Mike interrupted. "That's pushin' it, buddy. I'm not running anywhere except to the coffee shop."

Rafe laughed. "No, no, I'm not asking you to run with her, but if you could maybe mention that I asked you to stay last night -- you know, because I couldn't be there myself -- I'd appreciate it."

Mike shook his head. The boy had it bad. He looked up at the sound of the door opening and smiled large at the sight of Ali in her running outfit. "You definitely missed out, buddy." Ali was smiling at him, albeit a bit confused. "Tell her yourself." Mike took a step toward Ali and handed her his cell, gesturing for her to take it.

What the...no! he didn't want to... "Hello?"

"Hello?" Ali spoke but kept her eyes on Rafe's friend. What was this all about?

Damn. "Good morning, Ali." Rafe was fully awake now.

"Hi, Rafe, what's up?" Ali looked Mike over. He sat down in the lone beach chair outside the door. His long muscular legs were outstretched, and his arms were crossed over his wide chest. Why was he here? And why was she now on his phone?

What's up? Okay, that was a little cold, but it was nearly six thirty in the morning and she was probably surprised to see Mike outside her door this early. "I just wanted to let you know that I'm aware of what happened last night, and that's why Mike spent the night outside keeping watch. I would have done it myself, but I had to keep an eye on things here."

Ali looked at Mike again. He had slept out here all night? Because Rafe had asked him to? Rafe was aware of what happened, and he didn't call? But she hadn't called him, either, if she wanted to be fair. "That really wasn't necessary, Rafe. This couldn't have been very comfortable," she said, turning and speaking to Mike directly.

"It was fine, nothing a nice massage won't work out." He winked at her, and Ali couldn't help but laugh. She heard Rafe clear his throat.

"I'm sorry." God, he really didn't want to do this now.

He's sorry. "Sorry?" Ali's stomached fluttered.

"I should have called to see if you were all right." He'd been too afraid he would hear fear in her voice, and he wouldn't have been able to stop himself from going down to that truck and making that little bastard pay for putting that fear into her.

Ali turned slightly away from the direction of Mike's gaze. "It's okay -- it was no big deal."

No big deal to be harassed for the third time in two days by the same asshole. Some called it stalking, but maybe that was just him, and here he was, an agent with the FBI and had done nothing yet to stop the guy. Ali must be real impressed. "Ali, it was a big deal, and after today, it will never happen again." Not if he had anything to do with it.

Ali held the phone tight, not knowing how she should respond. He certainly sounded as if he cared, but was it because of who he was or how he actually felt about her? "Did they leave?"

"Yeah, ba -- Ali. They pulled off about twenty minutes ago. You're good to go running. I wish I could join you."

He had almost called her babe, and the disappointment she now felt that he hadn't, sucked. If she could only rewind yesterday, she would -- she would just tell him how she felt. Maybe not the L- word, but she'd make it more clear that she was really into him, and damn the consequences. He had said he wanted to spend his vacation with her and get to know her better, but then he'd become a little distant, and it had thrown her. She really didn't know him as well as she wanted to. Maybe that's just how he was when he was in work mode. Maybe she should stop being so damn paranoid. "Why did you just do that?"

Rafe got up and went to the sliders. He wished he'd woken up next to her. "Do what?" Just the sound of her voice made him a happier man.

Ali's voice held a hint of teasing. She wasn't going to start her day or his by being glum. "You were about to call me 'babe,' and you changed your mind."

Rafe grinned and breathed a sigh of relief. She wasn't mad. "I was afraid you wouldn't like it, that maybe you were still a little upset with me."

"I liked it the other day when you said it, and I would have liked it just now, too." She could see Mike grinning at her out of the corner of her eye. She shook her head at him. He was trouble, but she liked him a lot. Anyone who could sleep on a beach chair all night for his friend was a good guy.

"Oh." Rafe found himself pacing around the room. "Well, now it seems too obvious if I just call you that, but I really want to, and I'm glad you want me to." He was babbling like a fool.

Ali laughed. "I'll let you off the hook, but next time don't hold back, okay?" About anything, she wanted to add.

He smiled. "Funny you should say that. I was planning on not holding back the next time I saw you."

"Wow, I'm impressed, at…" she looked at her watch, "…six-thirty in the morning, you're thinking about sex." This got a full- blown gape and a chuckle out of Mike. She winked at him this time, and he was shaking his head.

Rafe grinned again. She was something. If she only knew that when he wasn't having sex with her, he was definitely thinking about having sex with her. He'd tell her that later, too. Then he remembered Mike. "Hey, is that ... is Mike still standing there, listening?"

Ali laughed. "Don't worry -- he looks like he's seen and done it all before. I don't think I've shocked him."

Ali laughed as Mike said with a wide smile, "You got that right, baby."

It was time for Mike to go. "Ali, as much as I can't stop thinking about sex with you, I meant not holding back when we talk tomorrow."

That got her adrenaline pumping. "Well, I'm all for that, Rafe. I look forward to it." She couldn't wait to hear what he had to say.

"Would you mind putting Mike back on? I have to coordinate with him about today."

"Sure." She paused. "And Rafe?"

"Yeah, babe?" He laughed a little, and finally stopped pacing. He was glad Mike had passed him the phone. He suddenly felt one hundred times better.

Ali laughed, too. "That works, and I just wanted to tell you to be careful today."

"Always. Have a good run." He hesitated, not wanting to sound demanding. "Do you think you can kind of stick around up in that direction today, for me?"

God, for him? Double yes. "I planned on going into town and maybe hitting the beach right out front."

"Good. I know Nicki will be well away from there today, right?" The last thing he wanted was to have Matt think he wasn't watching out for her as well. They had become friends in a short time, and he could only imagine how badly he wanted to get back to her.

"She'll be on Sanibel until at least five. Is that okay?"

"I'll get word to one of you if it isn't."

"I know you'll be busy, but is there any way you can let me know when it's over and you're safe?" Ali would worry all day.

It was odd, having someone other than his family say something like that to him, and it felt kind of nice. "I'll call you, okay? I just don't know when."

"Thanks." Ali knew she was smiling ear to ear because of the way Mike was mocking her with a smile of his own. He already felt like an old friend. "Hey, by the way, where did you find this joker?" Mike made a face, pretending to be hurt.

Rafe laughed. "Believe it or not, just this past year in Miami. He was hard not to like and hang out with. He really is a funny bastard when he's not trying to get laid."

Ali cracked up laughing, which made Mike say, "Hey! What did he say about me? It's probably true, but you shouldn't have to hear it."

"Goodbye, Rafe," Ali said, smiling. She was so glad she had spoken with him.

"I'll talk to you later." Rafe couldn't stop smiling himself.

Ali handed the phone to Mike again and waited until he was through.

"He says I should stick to you and Nicki like glue all day."

Ali laughed. "That's definitely not what he said -- he's met my brother."

"Yeah, yeah, I've already heard about your bad-ass brother." Mike feigned a face of annoyance. "It's always the way, well, not always." He grinned. "But it's not fair. I could have just as easily been your neighbor."

Ali was really laughing now. "You're a big flirt, you know that, right?"

Mike smiled. "A big flirt who has to go get some coffee and brush his teeth, maybe not in that order."

"C'mon, I'll walk you to the breakfast hall." Ali started out, and Mike hesitated. She looked at him.

"She gonna be all right?" He bent his head toward the cottage.

Ali tilted her head. "Why wouldn't she be?"

Mike told Ali the late night conversation he'd overheard on the porch, and in turn Ali gave him a brief history of Nicki and Matt as they walked, ending with Matt's arrival and departure this past weekend.

"Wow, so the guy's probably hurtin' as much as she is."

"Yeah."

"And here I was ready to knock some sense into him."

"It was nice of you to care, though." Ali thought he must have a big heart under that big sense of humor.

"My motives were strictly sexual." He tried to look serious.

Ali teased him. "I don't blame you. She's hot, isn't she?"

The look on Mike's face was priceless, and Ali was laughing, hard.

"You realize the image you just planted in my head, right?" He looked at her, incredulous. "You do, dontcha? Does Rafe know how fresh you are?"

Ali raised her brows. "What do you think?"

Holy shit, Rafe was a lucky bastard. "Holy shit, he's a lucky bastard!"

Ali left him at the restaurant and ran away, laughing, toward the street. She even thought Matt would like Mike, as long as she left out the flirting with Nicki part.

After an intense workout in the gym, Rafe took a shower and geared up for the day. A small handgun was strapped at his ankle, and he placed his Glock and his HTR(heavy tactical rifle) in the large duffle that held his Kevlar vest, along with extra ammo. He didn't anticipate having to use the rifle, but he would be in ready position just the same. The workmen had already arrived next door and were milling around, having their first cups of coffee. It was just a matter of time before the fun began. He put his earpiece on and checked in with Mike. "Heading across now."

"Be there in ten. Waiting for Reynolds to stop primping and get over here."

"Fuck you, Cap," came Reynolds' retort.

Rafe laughed. They were all on the same signal and would be able to communicate throughout the day, making it easy to know what was happening from all angles.

Rafe left the house, and crossed the street, his own cup of coffee safely ensconced in one hand and his other holding the duffle with all his gear. He used the key Ali had given him and went inside. He unlocked the sliders to the pool, then brought his things to Ali's room where he could get situated. He opened the duffle and pulled out the Glock, tucking it into the back of his jeans, then put the Kevlar vest over his T-shirt. He called Daniels from his cell, cutting off sound to his earpiece and waited when the SAC answered and asked Rafe to hold.

"Okay, I just got word, the crane has just made it to the four-way on a flat bed," he came on, informing Rafe.

"What about the barge?" Rafe took the duffle and headed out the sliders. He looked up to the roof and tried to gauge his best way up. It was a ground-level home, and the roof appeared to be the flattest over the garage, so he walked in that direction and put his gear down on the outdoor dining table.

"We're expecting it to be closing in on the lighthouse in about an hour. What's the situation there?"

"Just the normal construction crew right now. When I get up on the roof I'll be able to see who else pulls in." Rafe went over to the sliders that led to the living room, then went inside to the garage, where he found a small eight-foot ladder. Holding it under one arm, he brought it back outside and leaned it against the back of the garage.

"The lot's covered from all angles. Agent Murphy is in the bay directly across from you, Simmons and Gogin are Gulf-side, Reynolds is on D'nafrio at the marina, and Mike's coming to you. No one moves unless I give the order. This is still going to go down at the warehouse -- we just want to make sure this delivery goes smoothly. Once everything has been off-loaded and brought across the street, then you and Agent Caplan will proceed to the warehouse. That'll give you plenty of time to get into position and wait for Stoddman and the truck. D'nafrio shouldn't be far behind."

Rafe acknowledged the plan and hung up with Daniels. He'd done his fair share of waiting around before, and today apparently was going to be another one of those days. He hauled the duffle up onto the roof and chose the best area to settle in.

The spot he picked was well concealed from the street and the bay due to the large palm fronds that dipped low toward the roof, providing a nice canopy to hide under and get a little protection from the sun at the same time. He was wearing jeans to protect his legs from the asphalt shingles and was thankful Nicki's grandmother hadn't gone with a metal roof, or worse, clay tiles. That wouldn't have been comfortable. He set up his rifle on a tripod, and adjusted the scope using Murphy's flat boat as his target. He touched the small button to his wireless earpiece and was back on comm.

"Hey, Murph, leave some of those fish in the bay, will ya?"

"You wouldn't believe this shit. I take a day off to go fishing, and I get nothing. Today they're practically jumping in the boat."

"I think they call that Murphy's Law." Rafe chuckled at his own bad joke.

"McD, if I had a nickel for every time I heard that, I'd be..."

"Yeah, yeah, if my grandmother had a set of balls, she'd be my grandfather," Mike interjected as he pulled into the driveway in his bureau car. "Face it, Murph, you got the luck of the Irish."

"Hey, at least I didn't crash and burn at the bar last night."

"Ooh, he's got you there," Rafe laughed.

Mike shot Rafe a look up on the roof as he got out of the car and came around to the pool gate by the garage. His look told Rafe to be careful, or Mike might just let slip why he indeed crashed and burned at the bar.

"I admit I was off my game last night, but I guarantee tonight I will be in that hot tub with a hot female, smokin' a cee-gar and drinking a frosty."

Now it was Rafe's turn to shoot Mike a warning look.

Mike grinned, knowing what Rafe was thinking, and he laughed. "I was thinking of that cute little waitress from breakfast. Did anyone see her? The blonde, had an accent, Dutch or something."

"Way out of your league, man," Simmons chimed in. "Besides, she looked about eighteen."

"She's twenty-three -- I asked her." Mike defended himself, while taking Rafe's ladder away with a grin. He leaned it horizontally along the bottom of the garage wall, then went down to the dock to get a view of his surroundings.

"You asked the woman her age?" Where Simmons came from, that just wasn't done. Of course, he was part of a generation where men still opened doors for a lady.

"I asked her if she were old enough to be handling that many sausages at one time."

A rise of laughter came forth from all positions.

"You did not, you asshole, and if you did, you really are an asshole." Murphy was still laughing.

Rafe just shook his head. He knew Mike had a reputation around the guys, but Rafe himself had never seen Mike be anything more than "charming" with women, always a flirt, but never rude.

Mike walked back into the pool area, grinning. He liked making the guys laugh. There was nothing worse than sitting surveillance where nobody talked or joked. It was God-awful boring. Sure, on some cases silence was imperative, but on a case like this, he liked to break it up. He walked over to where the trees and fence surrounding the pool area aligned with the adjacent lot. He could see the lot was pretty clear from the bay side, but when he'd driven by, he noticed the street side had some brush the crane would have to maneuver through. Driven over once, the brush would be flattened right out.

"Is that the only ladder we've got?" Mike was looking up at Rafe, speaking one to one.

"No, I saw a twelve-footer in the garage, too. Go in through the sliders -- the door is right off the kitchen."

Mike did so, but opened a bay door to bring the ladder out and around the side of the house. He set it up on the far side of the house away from Rafe, but with a clear view of the vacant lot and the open fence at D'nafrio's job site. To anyone nearby, he would look like a man cleaning his gutters.

Rafe and Mike exchanged glances as simultaneously they heard, then saw the crane being driven up San Cap Road on a flat bed. "Crane's here," Mike reported.

CHAPTER THIRTY

"I don't want any problems today, Barry."

"No sir, everything is running on time so far. Joe just called, said the crane is just arriving."

"I want you there watching every last pallet come off that barge, and I want you to watch Joe inventory it all. When he makes a stink about the order being wrong, get on the phone to that truck right away. The driver will be waiting for your call just over the bridge."

Barry was sweating listening to D'nafrio on the drive to Captiva, even with the A/C on. Today was a big day, and he had to do everything right. He just hoped it wouldn't take more than a couple of hours. He had a showing late this afternoon for one of his own listings, and had a chance to make forty grand. He didn't know when he'd see his cut from the Ecstasy shipment, so forty grand after D'nafrio took his cut was going to be sweet.

"Call me when the barge is there." D'nafrio didn't tell Stoddman he was only up the street at the marina. He didn't want that idiot trying to do something stupid like coming to find him.

D'nafrio hung up before Barry could say, "Will do." Barry hung up the phone and took a deep breath. Between his cut of the Ecstasy money, possibly selling a house today, and getting that young couple from Monday to buy, he'd could be sitting pretty real soon.

"How was your run?" Nicki asked as she sat having a bowl of cereal at the small dinette.

"Just what I needed." Ali had just come in and sat down

across from Nicki.

"I wasn't sure if you'd go after last night."

"I'm not letting that bother me. Besides, it turns out we had our own personal bodyguard last night." Ali grinned at her.

"What are you talking about?" Nicki got up and brought her bowl to the sink. "Who?"

"Apparently Rafe called his friend Mike -- you know, from the bar? He kept watch outside all night. He slept on the beach chair out there."

"Oh, my God, what? That couldn't have been very comfortable." Nicki scrunched her face.

"Did you speak to him?"

"Yes, he was standing out there talking to Rafe on the phone when I came out."

"Wow, that wasn't really necessary, was it?"

"That's what I said, but Rafe was worried, I guess, so he asked Mike to do it."

"Nice friend. I don't know if I'd sleep in a beach chair for you all night." She laughed. "Did he have a blanket at least?"

"Sure you would." Ali smiled. "I don't think so -- he had a T-shirt and shorts on."

"Man, that's crazy. I would have thrown one out there had I known. I was up at about one."

"Yes, I know." Ali looked at her.

"Oh, did I wake you? I'm sorry, I thought I was quiet."

"No, you didn't wake me. Mike heard you on the porch."

"Oh." Nicki scrunched her face again. "What did he say about that?"

"He was nice, concerned, actually, but I gave him the condensed version of the Nicki and Matt story."

Nicki laughed. "Great, one more person to know what a glutton I am."

"You're not a glutton any more than I am." Ali grinned.

"That's reassuring." Nicki laughed.

"I know, we're both screwed." She said it matter-of-factly and got up to head to the shower.

"It's still early. Do you want me to wait while you get ready? You can come to work with me again today."

Ali smiled. "No, that's okay. I think I'm going to hit the beach for a bit, do some reading."

"You sure?" Nicki raised her brows up and down. "Today I interview the cast of The Fabulous Fifties at the School House Theater. Think of how fun the pictures will be."

Ali laughed. "Sounds fun, but I think I'll just hang out." She wanted to stay in Captiva. Knowing Rafe was nearby made her worry less -- this way, if she heard any sounds like sirens or... anything alarming, she'd be here. To do what, she didn't know, but it would make her feel better.

"Okay, I get it." Nicki knew just why she was hanging around, and she didn't blame her. "But hey, if you find any junonias on the beach, call me and I'll get you on the front page!"

"It's a deal! See you later." Ali chuckled, heading into the bedroom and on into the bathroom for a quick shower.

Nicki left the cottage a few minutes later and had to slow down as she approached her grandmother's house. The construction site across from Nan's was busier than she'd ever seen it. The whole front sections of the stockade fence had been removed, and a man was driving back and forth across the road bringing large pallets of something to the job site. Apparently they were under way. She wondered what Rafe was doing.

There was a local cop who was letting a few cars go at a time as the man on the little machine either loaded up on her left side or unloaded on her right. She was glad she'd given herself some extra time this morning -- this totally would have made her late. As she approached the empty lot, she was once again stopped in traffic, and she could now see where the pallets were coming from. There was a huge crane on the lot next to Nan's, and it was hauling things off a rather large barge in the bay. Nicki instinctively grabbed her camera from her bag and got off a few shots. Aside from the drug angle, she might be able to work up a little side article on the building that was going on on the islands and the lengths certain people were willing to go -- or were *allowed* to go, was more like it. She'd run it by the editor.

It was her turn finally to go, and she took a few more shots of the off-loading on the job site before she rolled forward. The cop gave her a wary glance, having seen her taking pictures, but she just smiled and said "good morning." She went as slow as she could by Nan's and saw an unfamiliar black sedan at the back of the driveway. She was dying to know what was going on, but supposed she'd hear soon enough. Maybe something big would go down on the island. It was kind of exciting. She called Ali, hoping she was out of the shower already.

Ali heard her cell ring and spit the toothpaste out of her mouth into the sink, and ran for the night stand. "Hello?"

"Just me. Hey, there's all kinds of activity down by Nan's."

"What? Already?" Ali sat on the bed. "Do you see Rafe?"

"No, not that kind of activity, but the construction site is busy. There's more crew than ever, and there's a big huge crane on the lot next to Nan's, and the barge Rafe told us about is in the bay."

"What are they doing?" Ali wondered if Rafe was inside Nan's.

"They're hauling supplies, I guess, back and forth." Nicki drove by the Sanibel school and had to slow for some cars turning in.

"I'm dying to know what's happening there."

"I know, me, too, but stay up that way, will you? I don't want to have to worry about you today. In fact, after the beach you should hang out by the pool or go to the spa. Rafe said it was okay."

"Maybe I will, but I'd pay for it myself." The idea of a getting a massage or a facial actually sounded kind of nice.

"Well, whatever, just stay at the resort today like Rafe wanted."

"I will, don't worry."

Nicki ended the call and arrived at work ten minutes early despite the hold-up, and went in to start her day. She sat at her desk and stared at her computer screen. She didn't know how she was going to concentrate today between thinking about Matt and wondering what the hell was happening at Nan's. It was going to be long day.

Ali put on her bathing suit and slathered herself with sunblock, then packed her beach bag with a book, sunscreen, her cell phone, and the room key. She left the cottage and walked across the street to the beach. It was another beautiful day, and the staff were busy setting up the beach chairs and cabanas for the guests. Ali helped herself to a chair and moved it a little closer to the shoreline, feeling bad when she scared off some sandpipers who skittered away. She had to laugh, though, at the brazenness of the large blue heron that stayed close by. She took a picture of him with her cell and emailed it straight to her mom.

She couldn't help but wonder and worry what was happening just a short distance down the road and wondered what Rafe's job would entail today. Would he actually have to shoot someone, or just make an arrest? Wouldn't something like that cause a huge commotion on the island, or would people not even know what was happening? She picked up her book and tried to read, but after reading the same paragraph four times, she gave up and closed her eyes. The sun was getting hotter as the morning progressed, and Ali reclined her chair back to soak it in. She didn't last but a couple of hours, and by then she had had enough sun.

She was feeling restless and wished she had gone to work with Nicki after all. Maybe she should call her and meet up with her. It would keep her mind off Rafe. She wondered what it would be like if she were his girlfriend. Would she be sick with worry that he was going to get hurt every time he went out on a job? The excitement she had felt when she first found out he was with the FBI, today had turned into fear and anxiety. The "what ifs" that were flying freely through her mind and the realization that the bad guys carried guns, too, was unsettling to say the least.

She had to get off the beach. She couldn't relax knowing Rafe was potentially involved in something serious down the street. She collected her things and walked back across to the cottage. She inserted the card key and swore as the light shone red. "Not again," she muttered. She tried it three more times and finally got the green light. Breathing a sigh of relief, she entered the cottage. She decided to go into town to shop and threw a sundress on over her bathing suit. She could shop, come back for lunch, and maybe take an afternoon nap before Nicki came home, then maybe they could go to the pool together.

As she shut the door behind her, she suddenly realized she was without a vehicle. It wasn't that far into town, but she didn't feel like walking in the heat, so she went to the front office to see about a bike. Fifteen minutes later, she was putting her bag in her basket and pedaling toward town. It felt great riding, and she took her time, meandering in and out of the side streets along the way, admiring the beautiful beach houses that lined them. It was fun reading some of the names of the houses -- some had obvious names, and some she enjoyed wondering about. But out of all the names she saw, she still liked The Three Sunrises the best, even though "The Three Sunsets" would have made more sense in Captiva.

She got to town and secured her rented bicycle in one of the racks provided outside the shopping area. She climbed a set of stairs that led to a handful of shops and browsed in each eclectic one. One of the stores carried some very cool surf wear, and Ali found a fantastic dress that fit her to a tee. She also picked up a couple of fun "life is good" beach bags, a pink one for herself and a yellow one for Nicki. She admired some unique artwork from various local artists and then retreated back down the stairs to her bike. She'd only been shopping for an hour and she was already hungry, so she decided to head back.

Moments later she was pulling over to a side street when she heard her cell phone ring from within her bag. She dug for it, saw Nicki's number, and flipped it open on the fourth ring.

"Hey, there!"

"Where are you?" Nicki asked.

"In Captiva, on a bike, making my way back to the cottage."

"Oh, good, you rented a bike. After I hung up with you earlier, I realized you were stuck there anyway."

"Yeah, it's okay, I'm loving it. Some of these houses are crazy beautiful."

"I know," Nicki agreed. "Next time I'll come with you. There are bikes in Nan's garage."

"Definitely. I want to go farther up, but I'll wait to do that with you because now I'm starved and just want to get back to eat."

"So you're just going to be at the cottage then, right?"

"Yeah, I'll eat and maybe take a nap. When are you done for the day?"

"I'm not sure. I just found out I might have to sit in on a city meeting at seven if this one woman in the office can't do it. So if I'm way late, it's because of that."

"That stinks. What are you going to do until the meeting starts?"

"Maybe hit Periwinkle Place again, get something to eat."

"Okay." Ali was disappointed but figured it might be better for Nicki not to be up this way after all. "I was regretting that I didn't go with you. The day is kind of dragging by."

Nicki felt bad. "Shut the shades and take a long nap after you eat. When you wake up, a few more hours will have passed, and maybe everything will be over."

"I hope so. Call me later -- I'm heading back."

"Okay, see you."

Ali hung up and continued on. Maybe she would try to get a massage before she took a nap. That would take her mind off things.

When she made it back to the cottage, she leaned the bike near the door and got inside after her fourth attempt with the key. She'd have to remember to get a new one at the front desk.

She went over to the counter in the kitchen and looked through the various pamphlets the resort left in the room. She found the glossy card advertising the spa and called the number at the bottom. They had an opening at three for a full-body massage, and she booked it. She didn't mind splurging. She fixed herself lunch and ate it on the screened-in porch so she could watch all the people on the beach and hoped to see some dolphins out playing in the Gulf. The resort was pretty crowded, and Ali wondered how Rafe managed to snag a cottage with such a great view. She wondered if all he had to do was show his badge.

She cleaned up after lunch, and with only a half-hour to kill before she had to be at the spa, she returned the bicycle and walked around the resort. The clay tennis courts were hidden beneath a canopy of palms and various tropical plants, and Ali watched as a couple rallied back and forth. She continued walking along a wood-slatted path until she came out to the sandy lot that led to the bay. The resort contained its own marina, and she admired many of the boats docked among it. There were plenty of boats motoring along the bay itself, and she thought it looked like a lot of fun. She started away from the marina and in the direction of the spa. She still had ten minutes to spare. Having the uncanny feeling someone was staring at her, she looked up to see a man sitting on his balcony. He had sunglasses on, similar to the kind Rafe wore, and binoculars around his neck. He smiled when she looked up. Ali smiled politely, but quickly looked away and made her way to the spa.

She was immediately relaxed once inside the calm atmosphere. The cool, soft colors and the sound of running water from the wall fountains put her right in the mood to be pampered.

An hour later she made her way back to the cottage on rubber legs. She had been rubbed, pushed, and pressed by a pair of expert hands, and she was ready to lie down and go to sleep for awhile. She cursed herself for forgetting to get a new key as she patiently tried and retried to get into the cottage. Eventually she made it inside, shut all the blinds, and crawled between the cool sheets. Her body still had the oils all over it from the massage, but she didn't care. She'd shower again when she wokc up. Once her head hit the pillow, she was out in a matter if minutes.

CHAPTER-THIRTY-ONE

The barge had made it in, and the crane was working at a steady pace to off-load the supplies. The steel beams had come off first, which had been a harrowing ordeal, and now they were onto the pallets. Rafe kept his position, snapping pictures, and Mike his as they watched the continuous movement from next door to across the street. Rafe was grateful for the palms that gave him some shelter from the sun, but for the most part his ass was still pretty much baking up on the roof.

"Can you guess what buckets are marked from here?" Mike asked Rafe, sounding as if he himself knew.

"Are we playing 'find the narcotics'?"

"I've got it figured out," Mike bragged.

Rafe used the zoom on the camera and snapped away. "There's one, third down from the bottom."

"Wow, you're good. I had that one, too." Mike said admiringly. "What gave it away?"

"The color of the lid is off from the others. There's another one, second from the top on the next pallet over. The majority of the covers are bright blue. Those other few look faded."

Mike looked at Rafe from where he perched at the top of the ladder as they both wondered whether the majority of the buckets held drugs or mortar.

"All right, new game. How many..."

"Heads up, fellas," Reynolds interrupted. "The Rampage has left the marina. He's bayside and heading your way."

Rafe had expected that. D'nafrio would want to see for himself that the barge had indeed made it. "Was he still by himself?"

"Affirmative, gassed up and went." Reynolds cleared his throat. "Hey, now that D'nafrio's gone, you guys don't need me for anything, do you? One of those babes Mike was talking to last night at the bar just strolled by. I think I'll head over to the pool."

In a tone that could best be described as ferocious, Rafe commanded, "Stay right where you are, Reynolds. We don't know if D'nafrio will come back that way."

"Man, McD, forget the coffee this morning? I thought we pretty much did know he wasn't coming back."

Mike chuckled. "Just stay put for now, Reynolds." Mike shot a look over to Rafe and shook his head, laughing while he pulled some grape leaves out of the gutters.

Rafe smirked. So Ali was out walking around, maybe now at the pool. Not that he would have worried about Reynolds, but the thought of anyone else approaching her made him crazy. He wished this day would end.

"Mr. X, nine o'clock," Mike announced.

They all watched as the Rampage fishing yacht slowed and seemed to linger in the bay.

"Murph, can you see anything?"

"Just him at the helm, smokin' a stogie."

"Oh, I'm going to enjoy taking him down." Mike came down off the ladder and brought it more toward the front of the house. "Last pallet coming off. Stoddman's in the driveway, talking with the foreman," he reported to everyone.

Rafe kept his sights on D'nafrio. The man had balls of steel, like the beams that would hold up the second floor to his mega-mansion. The Rampage appeared to be slowly heading off, and Rafe gave the heads-up to the agents covering the bridge. The barge, too, was moving with the help of the tugs that had been idling nearby. Rafe watched for the second time that day as they maneuvered by the dock attached to Nicki's grandmother's property. He was glad that hadn't been an issue. There were only a half dozen homes in this part of the bay that had docks, and from attending the few town meetings that he had, he knew they were grandfathered in. If the barge had somehow taken it out, Rafe doubted another could have been built in its place.

"Stoddman and the foreman seem to be having a little disagreement." Mike kept watching. "Stoddman's on the phone," Mike informed Rafe. He got off his ladder and made his way back over to the garage, where he put Rafe's ladder back in place. "C'mon down, big guy, time to fly."

Rafe grabbed his gear and handed it down to Mike, then made his own way off the roof. They went through the sliders and through the front doors, locking up as they went. They would take Rafe's truck, and Rafe waited back in the driveway while he sent Mike over to get it, keeping out of Stoddman's sight. Mike pulled the Yukon in seconds later, and Rafe hopped in. His phone rang as he sat down, and he saw that it was Daniels.

"Stoddman called for the truck. It's headed over the bridge now. One male driver, 22-foot white box truck. Where are you two?"

"Just pulling out."

"Okay, I'm going to meet you at the warehouse. There's a plant nursery two buildings down. Park there and make your way over. There's a back door -- enter there. It's wide open inside, no windows. Your only coverage will be a small bathroom in the back and an office-type room up front. We'll secure the perimeter, and you two will take your positions. D'nafrio is pulling into Sanibel Harbor Resort as we speak. That's where his car is. We've got men on him."

"He's going to get a jump on us," Rafe said, matter-of-fact.

"I don't think he'll get in the car until he gets the call from Stoddman that the truck is loaded and heading back."

"And if he does?"

"Then we maintain outside positions and make sure D'nafrio's inside when Stoddman and that truck show up. Then we go in when the first pallet hits the cement floor of D'nafrio's warehouse."

"Roger that." Daniels had a few more things to say, and then Rafe hung up. He relayed the parts of the conversation Mike didn't hear, and Mike picked up speed. He wanted to be inside that warehouse waiting. He did not want a free for all between the FBI and the DEA. He wanted this bust.

"There's our truck." They both checked out the driver as he drove by them in the opposite direction. He appeared to be young, and he was indeed alone, which made one less problem. Several minutes later they were finally driving the Yukon over the bridge.

When they reached 41, Mike disabled his earpiece and looked over at Rafe. "Okay, we've got a little drive time, so tell me about Ali and Nicki."

Rafe looked over and smirked. "Not now." He took off the sunglasses he'd been wearing and cleaned their lenses with the bottom of his T-shirt.

Mike ignored Rafe, "You were right about those eyes by the way. You should have seen them this morning, green as grass looking up at me. It was stunning."

Rafe let out an exasperated breath and put his sunglasses back on. "Seriously, I don't want to talk about her right now. I want to focus and get this over with."

Mike nodded. "I get it, I get it. So tell me about Nicki. Is she really in love with Ali's brother, because if there's even a chance she's not, you gotta hook me up, man."

Rafe looked over again at Mike and lowered his glasses, giving him a menacing eye.

"What? Ali and I talked this morning before her run. She's awesome, by the way. I like her for you."

"Gee, thanks, and yes, Nicki's off-limits. She and Matt are a done deal." What else had Ali said to Mike?

"What about you?" Mike laughed. "Are you a done deal?"

Rafe didn't answer but looked out the window, trying not to give away his feelings.

Mike looked over at Rafe. "Oh, shit, brother, you *are* done for, aren't you?"

Rafe still didn't answer, but he couldn't help the slight smile that started to spread. "Turn left at the next light."

Mike nodded and took the turn. "Lucky bastard." Their topic of conversation ceased as Mike turned into the industrial-looking area. There were warehouses and Quonset hut–type buildings lining the street, housing businesses of all kinds. They saw the nursery ahead on the left and pulled into it, driving all the way to the back where they wouldn't be noticed. They parked beside stacks of stored clay pots and rows of small flowering shrubs.

Before they left the truck, they each donned their Kevlar vests and put their earpieces back on. Their weapons in place and extra ammo in their pockets, they each put on lightweight jackets concealing their vests and the small arsenal each of their bodies held. They exited the vehicle and discreetly made their way to the backside of D'nafrio's building. The parking lots were abutting without any obstacles, and they were at the back door in under a minute.

Rafe tried the knob, and it was locked. He used the small kit in his jacket pocket to pick the lock, and they cautiously stepped inside. The inside of the warehouse was wide open and devoid of any partitioning walls. It was also completely empty, with not a soul around. There was one small room in the far right corner of the structure, and diagonal from that what appeared to be a small bathroom in the back left corner. Other than that, the place looked like it had never been used. There were two large bay doors facing the front of the building which would allow for the height and width of any box-sized truck to enter seamlessly, and a standard entry door to the right of those.

"I'll take the front," Mike said as he walked that way. He looked around as he went, his eyes focusing up to the steel rafters that made up the ceiling. "Looks brand-new."

Rafe headed toward the back and slipped inside the rather small bathroom. "It is -- it was put here six months ago. It's prefabricated. Anything of interest in there?"

Mike took the room in, gun in hand, it was about 12x12 and housed a metal desk and one matching chair. The walls were painted an industrial gray, not one thing hanging on them, and the floor was carpeted in much the same color. "Not even a sticky note." Mike opened the one drawer in the desk. "I take that back -- there's a note here that says, 'Dear FBI, please go easy on me. I'm new to this business and pretty stupid when it comes to drug trafficking. Maybe I shouldn't have named my boat Mr. X, huh? I'm much better at tax evasion and various forms of racketeering. Please keep this in mind while you have your knee in my back, and you're handcuffing me'."

Rafe laughed. "Was it signed?"

"Shit." Mike laughed and heard a few of his fellow agents who were surrounding the place laugh as well. He knew he forgot something.

"I guess we'll have to get him the hard way." They waited with the patience that only years of experience on the job had trained them to do. It was forty minutes later that they heard the SAC say, "Truck's rolling into the parking lot, Stoddman's Beemer right behind."

"We're in position," Rafe responded, and held himself still behind the bathroom door. It was open enough so that he could peer through the crack.

"Bay door closest to you, Cap." Daniels came over. Mike crouched beside the metal desk, giving him the best view into the warehouse.

They both heard the diesel engine outside the bay door and then the sound of the lock being disengaged on the front entry. Rafe peered through the crack and watched as Stoddman opened the door and came inside. He went over to a switch on the wall beside the door and hit a button. A loud noise reverberated through the empty warehouse as the motor on the bay door closest to Mike came to life and the door slowly rose up to lie beneath the rafters. Stoddman stood back as the box truck drove inside, cutting off Rafe's view of the office and Mike's view of the bathroom. He relayed that information over the wireless.

"Sit tight," was the response.

Rafe breathed a sigh of relief as Stoddman signaled the truck to pull farther in, parallel to the overhead door. Now Rafe had a clear view of the office and the driver as he cut the engine and stepped out of the truck. Stoddman walked back to the wall switch again, engaging the door and also flipping the switch to illuminate the overhead lights.

From where Mike crouched he could see the driver come around to the back of the truck. He was about mid-twenties, slight build, and brown-skinned. Mike watched as the driver unlocked, then rolled the truck's overhead door up. He got a clear look at the inside, seeing the pallets that had just come off the barge that the foreman wouldn't accept, along with a pallet jack tucked firmly under the closest one. The driver jumped up into the truck, his shirt rising at the movement, revealing a hand gun pressed against his back.

"Driver armed," he reported in a trained whisper. "Truck fully loaded."

"Copy that." Rafe's own gun was at the ready.

The driver engaged the lift gate and maneuvered the first pallet onto it. He pressed a button on the back wall of the truck and rode the lift gate down. "Donde lo quieres?"

Barry looked at the young driver blankly for a minute. It was clear he wanted to know where to put the pallet, but Barry's Spanish was limited to few words, never mind sentences. Barry pointed to the back wall gesturing with his hand. It seemed to do the trick, because the driver steered the jack that way.

Barry was sweating. The vast space was cool, but he hadn't been able to regulate his body temperature since he had left the job site. He hoped Xavier would show up soon. As soon as he took inventory,

Barry wanted to be out of there and right into a barroom.

His nerves were definitely shot from all the stress. He just wanted to get the fuck out of here. He wanted to make that showing. If he sold the house this afternoon, he might start getting some proper respect from the other realtors, instead of just being known as D'nafrio's bitch. He still had some work to do at his desk to prepare for the showing, and now he'd have to take another shower again. He looked at his watch, chances of him making it weren't looking so good.

Rafe could see that the realtor was a nervous wreck. The way he paced and kept looking at his watch, Rafe knew he was in way over his head. So far he had shown no signs of a weapon, and Rafe was doubtful he was armed. D'nafrio would be, though, if only to protect the amount of drugs Rafe and Mike suspected were on those pallets.

"Stand by -- subject on approach."

Moments later, they heard three beeps from a car horn outside. Stoddman ran to the wall switch and hit the button. The bay door cranked to life again, letting in the bright light of day and D'nafrio's black Mercedes sedan. When the sleek car was completely inside, Stoddman hit the wall button again, and the bay door rolled down, shutting out the last of the natural light.

Barry stood at the front bumper of the Mercedes, nervous as a cat, waiting for Xavier to get out of the car. He seemed to be taking his sweet time. Barry watched as Xavier slowly removed his sunglasses, then reached into the glove box. Sweat rolled down Barry's back, and he wondered if D'nafrio had been reaching for a gun. He himself was unarmed, but he knew the truck driver was carrying; Xavier had insisted upon it. Xavier wanted the driver prepared in case anyone had tried to stop the truck. Barry had stressed about it the whole three miles over the causeway. Before the new construction of the bridge to the islands, trucks were sometimes pulled over because of their size and weight, and Barry had said many a prayer as they'd crossed over.

Rafe watched as the driver's door opened, and Xavier Constantine

D'nafrio stepped out. He was dressed in a tailored, pin-striped charcoal suit more suitable for a boardroom in the city than an empty warehouse in a dirt-water town, closing in on ninety degrees. The leather driving gloves topped off the look. He oozed money as he stood looking over the warehouse, but Rafe knew nearly every dime the guy had ever made was born from ill-gotten gains. Rafe was going to enjoy taking him down and watching his face as his buckets full of club drugs were seized right in front of him.

"Give us the go, and we're in." Daniels was in Rafe's ear. The warehouse was surrounded with FBI and DEA agents just waiting on Rafe or Mike's word, but they both held them off for now.

D'nafrio approached Stoddman but did not shake his hand or give him a manly slap on the back that might be indicative of their partnership or friendship. Instead, in one quick move, he pulled out a gun and fired it at the truck driver point-blank in the chest. The sound was like a cannon going off in the vast empty warehouse. Stoddman's subsequent scream echoing after it.

"Stand down, stand down," Rafe hissed, his heart beating wildly. "Truck driver down." If they stormed the place now D'nafrio just might shoot Stoddman too.

Holy shit! He could hear Mike breathing in the earpiece and knew he was just as shocked.

The driver had moved in front of the pallet jack when D'nafrio got out of the car, having just off-loaded the last shrink-wrapped load. He didn't see it coming and went down fast and hard, face up on the rusted jack, his body splayed over the two parallel pieces of metal.

Mike had moved quickly and made his way to the office door, adrenaline pumping through his veins, and positioned himself against the back of it, gun drawn. He could just make out the back of D'nafrio's balding head.

Barry thought he was going to vomit on the spot. He looked up at Xavier in total horror. "You shot him." It was an obvious statement, and Barry thought he might be in shock.

"Yeah, I shot him. Now get him off that jack and into the back of that truck." D'nafrio slipped his gun into his waistband and removed the gloves he'd been wearing. There was no way he could risk having that driver talk about anything he'd seen or done today or find his way back to this warehouse. Better to just eliminate the potential problem. From now on he'd get Barry to transport the drugs, the less people involved the better. He glanced at the dead body. All those hours practicing on the range up on his ranch in Ocala had paid off. It was a nice, clean death shot.

Barry looked at the young man, whose blood was fast becoming a puddle underneath him. "Move him by myself?"

The look Xavier gave him was enough to get him moving, albeit slowly. How the hell was he going to lift this dead weight? He'd have the man's blood all over him.

"Drag him onto the lift gate, raise it up, and roll him into the truck."

Barry again looked at Xavier. He had given the order much the same as someone would say, "Get in the car, turn the key, and start the engine." Matter-of-fact, no emotion. What the hell was happening? This was not what he'd signed on for. He knew D'nafrio was a crook, but a killer? Had he done this before?

"Move a little faster, Barry. I've got a seven o'clock."

Barry lifted the young truck driver from under the arms and started to drag him backward toward the truck, his body bumping over the metal arms of the jack and jarring it sideways with a noisy scrape as Barry pulled him along. Oh, dear God, life as he knew it was flashing before his eyes.

Didn't bargain on this, I'll bet, Rafe thought as he watched the stout realtor dragging the dead man and waited for the right moment to announce their presence. They had to take D'nafrio by surprise now that he was armed.

Barry watched as D'nafrio approached all the pallets. Would he shoot him, too? "I put the package in a bucket like these and added it to one of the pallets. I'm not sure which one it's on now but it should be easy to find since it's a little smaller than the others." He hadn't paid attention once the pallets went on the truck. He'd been too nervous and had just wanted to get off the island without incident. "It's probably right there in the back." Barry was babbling, and he didn't recognize his own voice. He was actually trying to talk while his arms were wrapped around a dead man, dragging him backwards. He was definitely going to vomit.

D'nafrio walked to the back wall where the pallets were lined up. He removed a pocket knife from his pants and cut the shrink wrap on the pallet closest to him. Rafe could see that the pallet he was cutting into did indeed have the smaller bucket Stoddman had added.

D'nafrio put the knife back, and went for one of the buckets with a faded lid, not the bucket that contained the package of fake Ecstasy that Stoddman had retrieved. With some effort D'nafrio removed the faded lid off and reached inside. He pulled out one bag after another of white powder setting them aside on the pallet beside him.

Holy shit! The bucket was filled with Cocaine and if Rafe had to guess so were all the others. A might sight more profitable than the "x".

"Bingo," Rafe announced and moved forward, while Mike did the same.

Xavier reached for the next bucket and began working the lid. He lifted more packages of cocaine from that one as well and held one in each hand while staring at the rest inside. Scintillo had hooked him up big-time, scoring some of the best Colombian cocaine he'd seen in awhile. Xavier himself hadn't dabbled in the drug business for nearly a decade, but his friend Jay was turning quite a profit these days and was willing to share the wealth. Xavier was going to be *the* supplier on the west coast of Florida.

It had started with just the Ecstasy. He couldn't complain about the profit margins on that, especially since Scintillo had started his own meth lab and cut out the middle man, but when he'd found out what a kilo of coke was going for these days, D'nafrio wanted in on that, too. Five buckets out of every twenty-seven on a pallet held a dozen kilos each, sixty kilos all together. Yes, indeed, this was going put him on the map as a key player in the drug business and make him an even wealthier man.

He placed the bags back in the bucket and started to open the next one. The buckets containing the drugs all had a faded lid on them, as if they had been sitting on a shelf for too long, to distinguish them from the others. Xavier opened the next bucket and reached in again, excitement running through him momentarily, but then the hairs on the back of his neck suddenly rose, and he found himself reaching for his gun.

"Freeze, D'nafrio. FBI."

Xavier did, then slowly turned his head around to face the agent who was looming over him. Tall, with a build meant to intimidate, he looked more like someone who played a cop in the movies. D'nafrio would have snorted in annoyance had it not been for the menacing eyes the guy was glaring at him with. He silently cursed. He'd have to let pretty boy arrest him, but his lawyers would make sure none of the charges would stick. He paid them monumental amounts to make sure he would never be behind bars -- not for long anyway. He was going to miss his seven o'clock, though, and that pissed him off.

Barry dropped the dead man's arms just as he had been about to get him on the lift gate, as he, too, became aware of his own eyes staring down the barrel of a gun. A gun that looked like it would blow a hole right through him and then some. His guy identified himself as FBI, too, but his build and spiky haircut suggested something more along the lines of a military commando. Barry's world collapsed around him as, in what seemed like in slow motion, the bay doors rolled open and the warehouse started filling up with men and women all wearing protective vests and pointing guns.

It was surreal, really. He thought about his last real estate commission, at $64,000. It was incredible -- the money had been infectious, and when he realized he could make twice that even easier with D'nafrio's new enterprise, greed had taken over. He hadn't thought twice about it. So what if he was helping to put drugs on the street? Nothing but lowlifes and junkies were buying, and who cared what happened to them?

He was aware of cuffs being placed on his wrists, and someone was saying something about rights. He was trying to focus on the words, but the warehouse seemed to get smaller and smaller and very dark. Then everything disappeared as Barry passed out.

"You're under arrest for the murder of --" Rafe looked over to Mike, who was squatting beside Stoddman's body, and the dead body of the truck driver. He saw Mike check his pockets, then shake his head to Rafe. " -- for one John Doe," Rafe continued, "and possession of illegal narcotics." Rafe could now see that there was enough coke in those buckets to put D'nafrio away for a long ass time.

He relieved D'nafrio of his weapon and his pocket knife, holstering his own weapon while he cuffed him. He reached into one of the empty buckets himself and pulled out a kilo of coke. He held it up and reached for another. There had to be a dozen bags in just one bucket. Rafe could see at least three buckets on the pallet in front of him that had a faded lid. Rafe looked at D'nafrio and whistled in awe, "Steppin' up in the world, huh?" The coke would obviously bring in much more money than the "x". If Rafe had to estimate, there was probably close to a million dollars' worth of coke here, assuming each pallet contained the same amount of drugs.

D'nafrio knew enough to ignore him, and Rafe led him over to Daniels, who had pulled his vehicle right into the warehouse. Daniels relieved Rafe of D'nafrio and read him his rights before depositing him in the back seat.

The DEA were all over the shipment, slicing through shrink wrap and opening buckets, faded lid or not. Rafe couldn't imagine if all those drugs had made it to the street. He felt a jolt of pride that he had helped to prevent it.

He looked around the warehouse. There were law enforcement agents everywhere, photographing the scene, chalking the body, or gathering evidence, and Rafe chuckled at one particular agent trying to roust one stupid-ass real estate salesman.

"Wow, Mike," Rafe said, walking over to him, "I knew you were capable of making the ladies faint, but perps, too?"

"I'll say he is." Rafe and Mike both turned at the voice of a young female DEA agent passing by, giving Mike an admiring glance.

Rafe and Mike looked at each other, eyebrows raised, then Mike looked right back at the agent, following her with his eyes. "Damn! They're recruiting 'em hot these days!" He turned back to Stoddman.

Rafe smirked at him. "Wake him up, will you? I want to get the hell out of here."

Mike hefted him up under the arms and dragged him into the office he had been hiding in. He sat Stoddman in the metal chair and gently slapped his face. "C'mon, asshole, wake up." Mike grinned at Rafe. "This guy's up shit creek without a paddle, huh?"

"He definitely took up with the wrong crowd," Rafe joked.

Barry opened his eyes to the commando agent who had pointed a gun at him and to -- Rafe McDonough? What was his client doing here? "Rafe?"

"Hi, Barry." Rafe smiled and crossed his arms, leaning against the door jamb. "Special Agent Rafe McDonough with the FBI. Nice to see you again. This here is Special Agent Mike Caplan."

"Hi, there sleepy." Mike smiled. "Can we get you some water or anything?"

Rafe was an FBI agent? Not a client? He must have known about the drugs all along. Barry dropped his head and fought the tears that were threatening. How had he screwed up so badly?

D'nafrio had always taken care of him. Barry looked up to him, trusted him, and when D'nafrio wanted to go into the drug business, Barry didn't necessarily agree with it, but he knew if anyone could do it successfully it would be Xavier, so Barry went along. He could still be sitting in the real estate office now, working on leads if he had only minded his business and had not tried to play in the same league as D'nafrio.

He couldn't go to jail -- he would die in jail. He tried to compose himself and absorb what was happening. He tried to see into the warehouse for D'nafrio, but all he could see was that dead body and people hovering over it. The nausea started again. "I didn't know what was in those buckets," he tried to defend himself. He certainly hadn't known about the cocaine.

"No? Well, then, the judge will probably go a little easier on you." Rafe used his most sincere voice. "Don't you think, Agent Caplan?"

Barry looked at him gratefully. Rafe was being kind to him. Maybe he could get off with just a slap on the wrist. He'd deny everything, and maybe Rafe would still be interested in working with him.

Barry felt a little twinge of relief until he saw the look of amusement come across Rafe's face.

"They are going a little easier on drug trafficking these days." Mike lied nodding his head. "It's just the accessory to murder charge that might do you in."

"I didn't murder anyone!" Barry whined. This was all wrong, all wrong! "It was Xavier!"

"Oh, we're well aware of how it went down. By the way, would you like to use the restroom to wash that blood off your hands and shirt?" Rafe indicated with a nod of his head toward Barry.

Barry looked down at his cuffed hands and his Hawaiian shirt, both covered with blood, and he started to cry. Then his cry turned into a full-blown wail.

"That's it, get it all out now, Barry." Mike sat on the edge of the desk and spoke above the noise. "Where you're going, if you cry, you die." Mike chuckled at his own joke.

That brought more tears.

"Oh, c'mon Stoddman," Rafe laughed, "he's just pulling your leg. You don't die for crying -- you might get the crap kicked out of you, but nobody's going to kill you for crying."

"C'mon, Cap, let's leave him to the professionals." Rafe started to leave the room but stopped. "Hey, Barry, I meant to congratulate you the other day when you were showing me property. That was a hell of a sale you made last week on that beach house. I've been watching you -- you were starting to creep up on some of those realtors out there. It's a real shame, this whole mess." Rafe gestured with his hand toward the warehouse. "That must have been one hell of a commission." Rafe left the room, followed by Mike, leaving Barry to contemplate, his wails becoming louder.

Rafe and Mike spent the next two hours at the scene talking with the SAC. They watched as the DEA team sorted through the pallets finding, as Rafe guessed, nearly a million dollars' worth of cocaine among them and as the coroner finally loaded the young tuck driver's body into the back of his vehicle.

"Wow, if he didn't murder that dude, he might have only been looking at twenty to thirty years instead of life." Mike said sarcastically and shook his head after finding out the amount of cocaine that was confiscated.

"He didn't even put up a fight," Rafe commented.

"I think he's cocky enough to believe his team of expensive lawyers will get him out of this." Daniels smirked.

"I don't care who his lawyers are, he's fucked." Mike half-laughed.

"I'll say one thing for the guy, he's got the kill shot down." Rafe had been surprised that not only had D'nafrio pulled the gun, but managed to kill the guy with one bullet.

"He's got a range up at that ranch of his in Ocala. He's got about ten acres up there," Daniels informed them.

"Any word from Simmons and Gogin?" Mike asked.

"Yeah, they shut the job site down right after we came in here. Joe Trainor, his foreman, has been detained and will be brought into headquarters for questioning. The other crew members have all been questioned and let go."

"Reynolds and a few other men are over at Scintillo's beach house cataloging the evidence. Stoddman's office has been taken over, too -- our guys are in there now gathering up his files. Holly Mann has been taken in as well." Daniels phone started to ring, and he walked away to answer it. He came back moments later and slapped the two men on the back. "Good work, you two. I'll expect reports by the end of the day. Fax 'em to me -- I don't care, just get 'em in. Rafe, email whatever footage you've got and leave everything for the techs to come in and dismantle. I'll expect you out of there by Friday. Where you going to go?"

"Cottage up the street." Rafe grinned, looking forward to it.

"Have a nice vacation, and I'll keep you informed of the details."

"Thank you, sir." Rafe would be interested to see how the arraignment went for both D'nafrio and Stoddman. He gave D'nafrio a final glance in the back of Daniels' car. He just sat there, stoic.

He and Mike walked outside the bay doors into the bright hot sun, and they both removed their lightweight jackets.

Mike caught the eye of the DEA agent who had flirted with him. He lowered his glasses to look at her and said to Rafe, "Hey, partner, didn't you say you were having some car trouble?"

Rafe followed Mike's gaze and rolled his eyes.

"I think I'd better try to find a ride back onto the islands."

"What if she's going to Miami?" Rafe grinned.

"Dude, I don't care what coast I get laid on, just as long..."

"Yeah, yeah," Rafe interrupted and chided him, "just don't call me from South Beach when she discovers you're an asshole."

"That hurts." Mike kept his eye on the hot blonde, who had not broken eye contact with him. "How much you want to bet I'll be poolside at Tweenies with her by eight o'clock?"

Rafe started walking back toward the nursery and his truck. "Your confidence is never waning, I'll give you that."

"Meet us for a drink later!" Mike called after him. "We'll celebrate!"

"Maybe," Rafe yelled back. He made it to the Yukon and got in. He took a deep breath, finally calm from the adrenaline surge that had stayed with him most of the day. It was always a good bust if he didn't have to shoot anybody, although he hadn't expected D'nafrio to shoot anyone but he did.

Rafe started the Yukon and pulled out. It was six-thirty. He couldn't believe it. It had been a long day, and he finally let himself think about Ali. He needed to call her and let her know it was over and he was coming back -- to her. He dialed the resort and asked to be connected to the cottage. It rang several times before prompting him to leave a message, which he did. He let her know it was safe for her and Nicki to go back to the house, but that he hoped she would stay to wait for him. He called her cell, too, just in case she was out by the pool or at the beach but she didn't answer that, either. Shit. He didn't know Nicki's cell, so he dialed information and tried the Beach News. Someone answered after three rings and informed him Nicki was at a town meeting. Rafe put his phone down and wondered where Ali was.

CHAPTER THIRTY-TWO

Ali woke from a sound sleep just as the phone rang for the last time. She looked over at the bedside clock. It was six-thirty? How could that be? That massage must have really done her in. She saw the red message button blinking on the cottage phone, so she picked up the receiver and pressed it. Her stomach fluttered at the sound of Rafe's voice. Oh, thank God -- he was safe and on his way to her! She wouldn't have to wait until the following day to see him. She jumped out of bed and found her cell to call Nicki.

Nicki answered right away. "Hey, there!"

Good ol' caller I.D. "Hi, are you at that meeting?"

"Yes, it doesn't start until seven, but I'm at town hall. Why?"

"Rafe called. It's safe to go back to Nan's. I guess everything is all right."

"That's a relief. Are you going to go back?"

"I think I'll wait," Ali answered sheepishly.

Nicki laughed. "I would, too, if I were you. Call me later -- I'll probably be back to the house by eight-thirty."

"Okay, I'll let you know what happens. Bye." Ali hit "end" and went to the bathroom to take a shower. She was nervous as hell and excited at the same time. He wanted to talk, and she couldn't wait to hear what he had to say. While she rinsed her hair, she thought she heard a noise from the next room, so she finished in a hurry. She had wanted to be dressed and waiting for him, but maybe this would work out just as well, she smiled to herself.

"What are you doing? We're supposed to be at the site, like, right now! I thought we were coming back here late night." Tim looked around. The area was pretty quiet, but someone could walk by any minute and wonder what they were doing.

"I don't want to wait until tonight. I been thinking about this all day." Sean rubbed his crotch to prove his point.

"Well, fucking be quick. If Barry drives by and sees we're not out there, we'll lose the job, and I need that cash."

"Don't you want to come in for some?" Sean smiled lasciviously.

"Someone's gotta keep watch in case one of those boyfriends show up, or both." Tim lifted the hem of his T-shirt, revealing the handgun tucked in his waistband.

Sean grinned and approached the door to the cottage. He looked around. There were a couple of people crossing over to the beach, but no one too close by. He tried the knob, but it was locked.

"How the fuck you gonna get in, Einstein?" Tim sat in the beach chair right outside the door.

"Hell, I'm just going to knock." He grinned wickedly.

Ali stopped the shower and dried herself quickly. She went into the bedroom and grabbed some underwear and a sundress from her over-night bag. She got dressed and managed to put her hair back into a ponytail before she heard the knock at the door. Her heart beat double time as she padded out in bare feet to open it. Rafe was probably having the same trouble with his key. She took a deep breath and opened the door, then froze on the spot, her breath holding.

At the door was not Rafe, but the slimebag who had harassed her. Ali's eyes quickly scanned him as her brain tried to register his presence. Up close in the light he was even more repulsive. His greasy blond hair hung to his shoulders, and his face was drawn and pale, against the black

T-shirt he wore, emphasizing sharp cheek bones and a long pointy nose. His eyes were just as spaced-out as they'd been the night before. Ali's inner alarm kicked in, and she automatically slammed the door. Only he stopped it with his foot, keeping it from closing all the way.

"Whoa, aren't you going to invite me in?" He pushed the door open wide with strength she never would have guessed he had, forcing her to take a few steps back.

"Hey!" she screamed. "Get the hell out of here! Who the hell do you think you are?"

He slammed the door shut behind him and started for her. "C'mon, baby, you know you want some -- you let me get a good look the other night."

Ali was sick. He couldn't be more than twenty-one, and was skinny as a rail. She was pretty sure she could take him, but his strength had surprised her when he shoved the door open. She just had to wait for the right moment, and then everything her brothers had taught her she was going to unleash on this motherfucker.

She instinctively backed up into the kitchen. She hadn't really explored much in the cottage and found herself in front of the most logical drawer to hold the utensils. She just hoped she was right. "Get the fuck out now. I'm calling the police."

"You're not being very nice to me." He pretended to lunge for her, then laughed when she backed up quickly.

Ali's blood was pumping furiously, her initial fright turning into unabashed anger.

"You have ten seconds to turn around and walk out that door."

"Or what?" He laughed, coming closer.

"Or a federal agent is going to come inside and kill you!"

He laughed hard. "That's a good one. FBI, huh? Yeah, 'cause they're just all over the island." He laughed again.

Ali laughed herself. "You have no idea, you little prick. It's your call, scumbag."

"I think I'll take my chances."

He was only inches away now, and Ali was going to have to defend herself. Where was Rafe, for the love of God?

Rafe passed Nicki's grandmother's house and his own beach headquarters, noting the relative quiet of both properties. Just as it should be. It wasn't until he was a little farther up that he realized the SUV had not been parked at the construction site. Did those two little twerps know what had happened today? He didn't see how they could. Holly Mann had been arrested -- would she have used her one phone call to call her son? Or had they somehow found out and were now on the run?

He pulled into the Tween Waters parking lot and got out of the truck. His heart was beating hard. God, he hoped she was inside the cottage waiting for him. If she wasn't, he'd look for her by the pool, or maybe she'd be at the beach, waiting for sunset.

Rafe was on approach when he spotted Timothy Mann sitting in the beach chair outside the cottage door. What the fuck? Rafe immediately turned toward the street, making it appear as if he were going to cross over to the beach. The kid hadn't spotted him, and Rafe cut back over quickly to the front of the cottage, coming around from the screened porch, surprising the hell out of Mann.

"What the fuck are you doing out here?" Rafe growled at him.

The kids eyes darted to the door nervously, and Rafe realized in a heartbeat what was happening. Oh, Jesus. Turning away from Mann, he tried the knob, and it was locked. "Ali!" he yelled. "I'm here!"

Ali almost cried in relief at the sound of Rafe's voice. She had been struggling for nearly ten minutes with this doped-out pervert. She'd managed to knee him in the balls and give him a good punch to his ugly face when he had doubled over, but when he realized he was bleeding, he forgot about his balls and straightened up. "You broke my nose, you fucking bitch!"

He spit the blood that was dripping down his face and went for her. She tried to punch him again, but he grabbed her wrist and pulled her against him hard, grabbing her other wrist, too, as she tried to swing at him.

"Not so tough anymore." He swung her around so that her back was to him, and she had to kick backward, only managing to catch his shins. She squirmed and wiggled with all her strength. She would not let him win. What was taking Rafe so long? It had to be his damn key -- she had to try to get to the door to open it.

"He probably already fucked her," Tim said, confident, his hand resting at his shirt hem.

Rafe shot him a look to kill and let out a loud angry grunt as he kicked the door to the cottage right off its hinges, ignoring Mann.

With the noise of the door crashing open, the sleazeball jumped back, and Ali turned around. She had never been so happy to see someone in her entire life. She wanted to cry in relief at the sight of Rafe standing there, looking so fierce and ready to protect her.

"Rafe!" she screamed as she looked over his shoulder.

Rafe had just been about to tackle the dickhead who'd had his body wrapped around Ali's when he registered her scream. Shit! He had taken his eyes off the shithead outside, who had tried to intimidate Rafe with his hand at his waistband. Rafe turned, and out of the corner of his eye he saw the gleam of metal.

He heard the shot go off as he slammed Timothy Mann into the wall, yanking his arm back, and hearing the bones snap as he broke it. The gun fell, and Rafe instinctively kicked it away, watching it slide under the sofa.

Time seemed to stand still for Rafe as a mix of screaming and yelling filled the room. He took in Smith yelling and holding his bloodied nose, he took in Mann on the floor screaming and trying to hold his now-broken arm, and then he turned his eyes in the direction of Ali's scream. The only scream that was making his gut turn inside out. One minute she had been standing up, relief written all over her face at his presence, and the next minute she lay slumped on the tile floor.

Smith now stood frozen, staring at her with a look of horror, blood dripping down his chin.

"What the fuck, man?" he yelled to his friend, his eyes going wide in fear as Rafe moved fast, grabbing him hard and easily throwing him out of the way so that he fell into the dinette set, sending both him and the two chairs there flying.

"Fuck you, man!" Tim yelled back at him trying to get up. "This was all your idea. Now my fucking arm is broken!"

Rafe blinked as he looked at Ali's blood, and the reality of the situation took hold. These little punks had just hurt her -- she'd been shot, for God's sake. "Baby, look at me." He crouched down beside her. There was blood all over the tile, and Rafe tried to see where she'd been shot. She had on a sleeveless dress, and he followed the blood trail up to the wound in her left shoulder. Her eyes were still closed, and he had to fight the tears that were stinging his own. He could see and hear that she was still breathing, even though it was labored.

"Ali, honey, can you hear me?"

Ali couldn't believe the pain that was resonating in her arm. She felt as if someone was resting a red-hot fireplace poker right on her skin. "It hurts," she managed to respond.

"I know, darlin', I know. Just keep breathing for me -- every thing's going to be okay." Rafe was aware of Smith and Mann hurriedly making their way out of the cottage and of the sound of tires peeling out of the parking lot, but he didn't care. He knew they'd never make it off the island. He flipped open his cell and dialed 911, then he called Mike. Mike had started to say something before Rafe started to talk, and he interrupted him, asking if he were on the island and relieved when Mike said he was just coming over the bridge. Rafe spoke quickly, keeping his eye on Ali and his bare hand on her wound, trying to stop the flow of blood.

"Listen carefully, a white Ford Explorer, license plate X1O UVF, is heading toward you. Take Gulf Drive. Stop them. Two white males, one armed, possibly another weapon in the vehicle. One of them assaulted Ali at the cottage. The other one shot her," Rafe took a deep breath. He wasn't about to say in front of Ali how worried he was about the amount of blood she was losing.

Mike's demeanor did a 180. "I got it bud, no worries." Mike could hear the strain in his friend's voice. He was sick for him, and for Ali. He hung up with Rafe, and instructed his new friend to drive a little faster.

"An ambulance is on its way baby." He didn't like how damn far they were from the hospital, though. "I'm going to look more closely at your shoulder, sweetheart. Just try to be still, okay?" He pulled his hand away and looked, but there was so much blood.

Rafe grabbed a clean dishtowel and tried to wipe away some of the blood. Ali seemed to be sliding down, and he was afraid she'd pass out. He picked her up off the floor and brought her to the sofa, trying to keep her upright. By the look of her arm, the bullet had just grazed her, but it had taken enough skin with it to make it appear much worse. Rafe confirmed this by looking back into the kitchen. Sure enough, there was a hole in the cabinet door right behind where Ali had been standing. The bullet had grazed her and lodged right into the wood. He sighed with monumental relief and applied pressure to her wound, causing her to cry out. His gut wrenched.

"Listen, Ali, you're going to be just fine. The bullet just grazed you -- it's not in you, okay? Can you hear me?" She was definitely on the verge of passing out.

Ali opened her eyes, and tears streamed down her cheeks. It nearly broke his heart. Her hair was back in a ponytail and was damp. She looked like she had just come out of the shower. She was all fresh and clean, minus the blood that now ran down her arm and onto her cotton dress. She looked so young and precious to him. He wrapped his arms around her, being careful of her shoulder, her blood now soaking him, and he wanted to cry. How could he have let this happen? He should have never gotten involved with her; he'd put her in danger. "I'm so sorry…I'm so sorry," he choked out.

The blood wasn't stopping, and he needed something better than the damn towel. "I'll be right back." He leaned her back against the couch so she wouldn't fall over and hurried to the counter to search for something. He spotted some kind of elongated hair elastic and used a knife to cut it in half, then went back to Ali and tied it around her upper shoulder, causing her to cry out again. "Damn it, where is that ambulance?" He had no sooner said it when he heard the telltale sirens pulling into the parking lot along with a cruiser.

"Ali?"

She was staring at him, her eyes glassy, and she whispered, "I should have looked out the window, but I thought it was you. I just wanted to see you. I was so glad you were okay and coming back to me tonight."

Oh, God. His heart was shattering -- she'd been worried about him. "It's not your fault," he assured her. He hadn't even considered how long Smith may have been in the cottage. A feeling of dread washed over him. "Ali, did he hurt you?" He waited for her to answer, his heart in his throat.

"No way, I kneed him in the balls," she said breathlessly.

Rafe shut his eyes and laughed, his grief mixing in. "Good girl."

"I punched him hard, too." Her eyes were closing again. "He said I broke his nose."

Oh, God, he loved her. "That's my girl." He picked her up again, and she cried out. "Oh God, I'm sorry babe, I'm just going to bring you outside." He carried her out just as the EMTs came to the door.

"Where will you take her?" Rafe asked.

"Healthpark, sir."

"I'll be right behind you."

"Rafe," Ali whispered against his shirt.

"What is it, Ali?" he asked, his lips against her soft damp hair.

"Please, don't leave me."

She was killing him. "Darlin', I have to tell the police what happened here, and then I gotta get those guys. I'll be right behind you, okay?"

"Be quick." She looked up at him and she was clear - eyed for an instant, her eyes so green and revealing so much with just one look that he faltered before he spoke.

"I ...will, I promise." He kissed her lightly on the lips.

"And call Nicki," she said as he placed her on the gurney. "But tell her not to tell."

"Not to tell?" He didn't understand.

"Not to tell," she said again, then passed out.

"Go! Get her out of here!" Rafe slammed the back doors of the ambulance shut and got on his cell. He could see the officer waiting for him as he opened his phone to call Mike. Rafe had identified himself when he had called 911, and he flashed his I.D. now. The officer just moved past him and on into the cottage to seal it off. A small crowd had been lingering, and hotel security was finally ushering them away. Mike picked up right away.

"We're just about to Gulf. Simmons and Gogin are on Periwinkle, and we've got local all over the four-way stop just before the causeway. They're not getting off."

Rafe took a breath, the anger he felt threatening to consume him. He glanced briefly at the cop and waved. He'd give a statement later. He jumped in the Yukon and peeled out of the parking lot. Another cruiser was pulling in and he paid it no mind as he sped off toward Gulf Drive. "I want you to hold them there, you hearing me?" Rafe knew without a doubt they'd be on Gulf Drive.

"Loud and clear, Rafe, loud and clear." Mike knew this wasn't going to be pretty.

They drove through the four-way and down to Gulf Drive. Mike finally explained why they would be a little late getting to the resort, and he grinned happily when his new friend smiled back at him and drew her gun.

"Man, I can't believe you shot her!" Sean said with a thick nasal voice, his nose in immense pain.

"Shut up and drive me to the hospital. My fucking arm is broken!" Timothy was screaming at Sean.

"Do you think she's dead?"

"She's not fucking dead!" He had no idea if she was or not, and he didn't want to think about it or how fucked he was now.

"Do you think he called the cops?"

"Of course, you asshole, that's why you have to drive a little fucking faster off the island! And you're getting your fucking blood all over the steering wheel!" Timothy yelled, disgusted.

"At least nobody knows what we're driving, and they'll expect us to be on the main road." Sean tried to reason.

"Watch out for that car!" Timothy screamed. "What the fuck are they doing?"

"He's wasted! He's driving in our lane!" Sean swerved the SUV.

"Go around! Go around!"

"I can't! There's another car coming! Oh, shit!"

Sean slammed on the brakes.

"What are they doing?" Timothy asked, confusion and pain in his voice. The force of their stop had thrown him into the dash, igniting a fresh wave of pain to his arm.

"They're coming over! Holy shit, they're cops!" he yelled, seeing their guns drawn.

Timothy swore, remembering his own gun back on that cottage floor. He reached for the glove compartment, where he knew Sean had put his.

Mike and his newfound partner jumped out of the sedan and approached the SUV, guns pointed at the vehicle. Mike was on the driver's side, and his new DEA friend had the passenger side. Lucky for them, both the windows were down. Mike stopped the passenger with a stern warning before he could get the glove box open. His pretty DEA agent had the passenger out of the car and up against the hood of her own in record time. Mike couldn't help but be turned on.

"You, too, dickhead, out. FBI."

Sean nearly shit his pants. FBI? Oh, man, they were going to jail. He got out of the Explorer and walked over to the black sedan at gunpoint, his nose still bleeding from that little bitch. It was definitely broken, but at least he had the feeling back in his balls. He knew enough to keep his mouth shut as he met Timothy's eyes across the hood, but moments later after they had been searched and cuffed, a defeated "oh, fuck" left his lips as he saw the boyfriend pull up, a police light flashing from behind the windshield of his truck. "Oh, fuck." Timothy followed Sean's gaze and repeated his sentiment.

Rafe got out of the car and strode over, the fury evident on his face. "Did you call it in?"

Mike nodded almost apologetically, but the last thing he wanted was for Rafe to have any length of time with these assholes. Mike was already sweating that local wasn't here yet. The look in Rafe's eyes was pure murder. His shirt was covered in blood; Mike presumed to be Ali's.

"Thanks for stopping them." Rafe looked from one low life to the other.

"Hey, our pleasure. Agent Taylor and I were glad to take the scenic route."

Rafe nodded to the DEA agent from the warehouse.

"If you don't mind, I'd like to search the vehicle," she said to Rafe.

Rafe walked over to where she held Timothy Mann, the piece of shit who shot Ali. He was actually whimpering. "Go for it," he said to Agent Taylor while glaring at Mann but he didn't touch him.

Mike kept his eye on Rafe. It was clear that Rafe had already broken the kid's arm, probably trying to disarm him, but Mike couldn't be sure he wouldn't break the other one as well, or worse.

"There's nothing in the truck. What does the FBI want with us, anyway?" Mann complained.

Rafe grabbed the bad arm that hung lamely by Mann's side and gave it a good tug. He was rewarded with a loud scream.

Mike winced.

"She's DEA, asshole. You'd better hope you've only got a map of the islands in that glove box." Rafe kept pressure on the kids broken arm.

Tim swore, thinking not of Sean's gun in the glove box, but his stash of weed and bag of blow under the driver's seat. He knew if he said another word he'd be in agony again.

Mike grinned at his own detainee. "Why do I know she's going to find something?"

Rafe heard, then saw the local P.D. car pull up in front of them. They had attracted a little bit of a crowd over on the bike path, and one of the officers got out to move them along.

Rafe still glared at Mann. He had intended on hurting the little fuck some more, but now that local was here, he just wanted to get to the hospital.

"Mike, can you fill these guys in and let them know these boys are also part of a federal investigation?"

The look on Smith and Mann's faces would have been amusing at any other time, if Rafe wasn't so anxious to get to Ali. He peeled away in the Yukon and kept his flashing light on the dash, making it over the causeway in record time. He pulled out his phone and realized he still hadn't notified Nicki.

Shit! He still didn't have her cell number. He called the Beach News again, doubting anyone would answer; it was already eight o'clock. And nobody did. He dialed Mike and explained. "Can you swing by her house and let her know what happened? Oh and tell her not to tell anyone just yet; Ali's request not mine."

"No problem, we're just finishing up here."

Rafe hung up. Thank God for Mike. He followed the signs to Healthpark and hoped to God Ali wouldn't hate him for this. He swung into the parking lot and ran through the doors of the E.R. He flashed his I.D. at the nurse stationed behind the reception desk and inquired about Ali. "A woman was just brought in here with a gunshot wound. Can you tell me the status?" He waited impatiently while she flipped through some charts.

"Sir, they did bring a woman in a short time ago, but I haven't any information yet. We don't even have a name."

Oh, God, she either hadn't come to or they knocked her out. He told the nurse her name, and she promised to go check on her.

Rafe waited anxiously by the desk for the nurse to return.

Mary Lou couldn't help noticing the obvious distress on the handsome FBI agent's face as she returned. She wondered if he had been the one to shoot her. "Sir, they are stitching her up now, and she'll be brought to a room shortly after. You can wait in recovery if you like." She noted the instant relief that spread across his face, and when he smiled, she realized 'handsome' didn't quite fit, but drop-dead gorgeous was more accurate. She also came to realize that he couldn't have been the one to have shot her. His smile told an altogether different story. He thanked her and headed to the bank of elevators. Lucky girl, Mary Lou thought, and went back to work.

Rafe was on the recovery floor and paced until he heard the ding of the elevator doors. Twice other patients were taken off, but still no sign of Ali. Then finally the doors opened again, and Ali was being wheeled out on a gurney being pushed by a male nurse. Ali was upright, and her eyes were closed.

Rafe approached and flashed his I.D. again. "Where are you taking her?"

"201. Is there a problem?" The nurse wondered if he were wheeling some kind of criminal around. If so, she was the hottest criminal he'd ever seen.

"No, no problem, I just need to ask her some questions." Rafe knew because he wasn't family, his I.D. would be the only reason he could get in to see Ali.

"All right, but you'll have to check in at the front desk. She's sedated right now anyway. She should come around soon, though."

Rafe hadn't stood there to let him finish he was already at the front desk. He got his permission and headed back to 201, where the nurse had taken Ali. As he entered, the nurse was leaving, and Rafe thanked him. He went over to Ali in the darkened room and pulled a chair up next to her bed.

Now that he was sitting down and staring at Ali, the weight of the day hit him hard. She was so beautiful lying there, and he'd never felt worse in his life. This was all his fault. He shouldn't have gotten involved with her. He should have caught that bastard that night on the beach when he had the chance. They wouldn't be here now. He leaned forward, resting his elbows on the mattress, and took hold of her hand. He held it between his own, bringing it to his forehead as he wished again this hadn't happened to her. He felt her stir, and then her free hand was on his face, and he joyfully took that one too. Oh, thank you God. He felt his love for her wash over him and his throat grew tight.

"Hi beautiful."

"Hi," she answered, her voice raspy.

"Are you in pain?"

"No, I feel heavenly." She smiled.

Rafe smiled, too, happy the painkiller they gave her was working.

"Ali, I'm sorry about this."

"Don't be silly, I'm going to be fine. That's what the doctor said."

Rafe grinned at the sound of her voice. She was definitely feeling no pain.

"Why are you smiling like that?" She grinned herself.

"I'm just so happy you're okay." He still held her hands in his, and he kissed them.

"You called me 'babe'."

"What?" he smiled. Jesus, his eyes were clouding over.

"And you called me 'sweetheart' and 'darlin'' and 'honey,' I think."

Rafe laughed, "Yeah, I guess I did."

"I liked it."

"Yeah?" His heart did a little dance in his chest.

She nodded and pulled his hands toward her. Rafe came closer so that he was leaning right by her face.

"Thank you," she whispered.

Rafe's heart was now pounding, and he wanted to take her in his arms so badly, but he didn't want to hurt her. "For what?" For calling her babe, sweetheart, darlin', and honey? He'd do that for the rest of their lives if she let him.

"For saving me from that jerk."

"You were doing pretty good on your own before I got there. You definitely broke his nose." He spoke softly, since his lips were inches from hers.

"I didn't know the other one was out there." Her eyes were getting heavy again.

"Yeah, but they're behind bars now. I made sure of it before I got here." He was whispering, and he could see her drifting.

"My hero."

"Ali?" He could see he was losing her to the painkiller.

"Goodnight, Rafe...I love you." Ali closed her eyes, and she dreamt of lying next to Rafe at the beach house. They were in love, and they were naked in each other's arms. She hoped she didn't wake up for a little while.

It was spoken so softly, but Rafe pulled back as if she had just shouted it. Her eyes were closed, and he watched her sleep. Wow! Had he just heard that, or was he dreaming? He knew she was all drugged up, but still, he couldn't help but be ecstatic at what she had just whispered. He sat back in his chair, still holding on to one of her hands. He pressed it to his lips and whispered right against it, "I love you, too, Ali." And he did, and it felt great to say it out loud, even if she couldn't hear him. She would soon enough.

CHAPTER THIRTY-THREE

Nicki drove home from the meeting and couldn't wait to fix herself a drink. It had been a rather long day, and sitting with a bunch of complaining locals had sucked the mojo right out of her. Who lived on an island and complained? She had just encountered the select few. One guy complained about his neighbor's boat in the yard, and another about a boat trailer in *his* neighbor's yard. Nicki wanted to laugh. In Massachusetts, lots of people had boats in their yards. Not only did they have the right to do so, but the damn things actually sat there nine to ten months before they even dreamed of touching the water. The people being attacked tonight lived on this island year round, surrounded by the Gulf and bay, and used their boats all the time. Not to mention with the real estate taxes they all paid, they should be able to put their boats anywhere on their property they damn well pleased.

Nicki had heard about these meetings from Nan. Nan's theory was the people complaining had a little too much time on their hands in their golden years. People really needed to lighten up. The islands were considered paradise to most people, for goodness' sake. What was there to complain about?

Yet still another resident complained about people going too fast along the bike path, and there was also a complaint about the noise coming from a local restaurant. Nicki couldn't wait to get out of there. If those were the worst of those people's problems, they should feel lucky. She'd love to turn in an article saying what she really thought about their complaints, but she knew she could only stick to what was said at the meeting. Oh, well, she thought, someday she'd be expressing her own opinions.

She pulled into Nan's driveway and was glad to see the house was still standing. The black sedan was still at the back of the driveway, and she wondered about it. She needed a hot shower, and she hoped there wasn't anybody still there.

Once inside she was relieved to find she was alone, and she made herself a drink. She wondered how Ali was doing with Rafe up at the cottage as she sat down on the couch for a minute to relax. No sooner had she sat when the doorbell rang. She walked over to the door, wondering who she'd find on the other side, and opened it to see Rafe's FBI friend Mike and a cute little blonde standing there.

"Hi," she greeted them and was sure she looked surprised to see them, but then she realized they must be there for the car. Although there was something in the way Mike was looking at her and even the blonde whom she'd never met held an almost apologetic look. Nicki's heart immediately sank. "What happened?"

Mike gave her a little smile. Man, she was something to look at. "Rafe asked me to come by. He couldn't get in touch with you. Ali's at the hospital."

"Oh, my God! Oh, my God! Why? What happened? Is she all right?" Nicki was frantic and was imagining the worst. Had she come back here today and gotten mixed up in something?

"Calm down, she's going to be all right." Mike hesitated, not wanting to tell her the news. "She was shot."

Nicki stumbled, drink in hand, and nearly fell backward, but Mike and the blonde reached out to steady her. "Shot!" she yelled, and looked at them both like they had three heads. How was that possible? Oh, God, did she do it herself by accident with Rafe's gun? Nicki had been afraid of something like that. She felt the blonde's hand on her arm, leading her to one of the kitchen stools. She took Nicki's drink from her hand and set it down. But Nicki couldn't sit; she hopped off the stool and grabbed her keys. "What hospital? How did she get shot?" She was headed out the door.

Mike reached her and took the keys from her hand. "We'll drive you. You've been drinking, and you're upset."

"I just walked in. I've had two sips. How did she get shot?" Nicki waited for them to follow her outside, and she shut the door. She saw Mike give the blonde a look as he locked it for her. When they were in the car, another black sedan, Mike told her what happened while they drove.

"Oh, my God." Nicki shook her head in disbelief. "I have to get there -- I have to call her family."

"Ah, apparently when she asked Rafe to call you, she told him to tell you 'not to tell.'"

"Don't tell." Nicki shook her head. They'd been saying that to each other since they were kids. If either of them did anything remotely embarrassing or out of character, "don't tell" meant keep it in the vault. How could she not tell Ali's mother and father about this? They'd never forgive her. "This is unbelievable," she said, more to herself.

Mike made the introductions, and Nicki could only nod to the blonde. She got the feeling Mike had just met her himself. "Is Rafe with her at least?" Nicki couldn't help but be a little angry with him. How could he have let this happen?

"He is." Mike knew enough to keep his mouth shut. She sounded pissed now. He gave a look of regret to Agent Taylor. Their poolside drinks were going to be put off yet again. Rafe was really going to owe him one.

Mike got them to the hospital in thirty minutes, pulling up to the entrance and helping Nicki out of the car. He offered to wait, but Nicki thanked them both and waved them off.

"Rafe can take me back. I really do appreciate you both taking the time to drive me here. I probably was too upset to drive." Nicki smiled.

Mike gave her a wink. "No problem. Give her my best."

Nicki chuckled. He was still flirting -- the blonde was in for it. She entered the hospital and made her way to the elevators. When she got off on the second floor, she immediately saw Rafe in the hall. He was on the phone, and he abruptly hung up at the sight of her.

Rafe could see Nicki wasn't too happy.

"Where is she?" she demanded. She knew she sounded angry, but actually, the sight of his bloodshot eyes, as if he'd been crying, disarmed her and she felt sorry for him.

"201." Rafe pointed to the room and turned to the nurse at reception. "She's with me." The nurse rolled her eyes, knowing damn well the woman wasn't family, either.

Nicki entered the room with Rafe right behind her and cried out at the sight of Ali in the bed, all bandaged up. "God, Rafe how did this happen?"

While Rafe explained, Nicki held her best friend's hand. Nicki actually found herself feeling grateful to Rafe that he had arrived at the cottage when he did. If any more time had passed, something even worse could have happened to Ali. "She's pretty tough, but I hate to think of what would have happened if you hadn't shown up."

"I couldn't feel worse," he admitted quietly.

Nicki looked up at the sound of his broken voice. "You really care about her, don't you?"

The look he gave her in return spoke volumes.

Nicki smiled. "She'll be happy to know it. I do assume you'll be letting her know?"

Rafe laughed at her stern tone. Ali was lucky to have a friend who looked out for her. He knew what that was like. "As soon as I can get her out of here. Hospitals aren't the most romantic place on earth."

Nicki smiled again and looked at Ali's sleeping form. "Jesus, what the hell did they give her, a horse tranquilizer? Look at the stupid smile on her face." Nicki laughed. "Oh, and you're going to have to drive me back to the house, too, so you'll have to wait until you spill your guts, okay?"

He grinned. "Okay."

They talked while Ali slept, and Nicki took the opportunity to ask Rafe about what had gone on at her grandmother's house and with Xavier D'nafrio. He gave her lots of great information, and she hoped the paper would let her write about it. They laughed about Rafe's friend Mike, too.

"He's quite an operator."

"That's one word for him," Rafe laughed, "but I wouldn't have anybody else at my back. He's a great friend."

"I can see that, and that's nice. I wouldn't know what I'd do without my girl here." Nicki started to get teary-eyed. She just couldn't believe this had happened.

"You're stuck with me," Ali whispered.

Rafe and Nicki looked over at the sound of Ali's voice.

"Oh, Al, how are you?" Nicki stood up.

"I'm good," Ali whispered. "My shoulder aches a little, but they told me I'll be just fine." Ali glared at Nicki and asked, "Did you?"

"No." Nicki smirked. "I didn't tell anyone, but you know I'm going to have to."

"Nick, my mom and dad will have a heart attack and be on the next plane down here. Please don't!" Ali's pleading was raspy.

Nicki knew they would indeed do just that. "I have to tell Matt, then. Someone should know."

Ali thought about it. "You have to make him swear he won't say anything to them. Tell him you'll never sleep with him again if he does."

Nicki shot a look at Rafe, her face reddening. He was grinning at the exchange.

"Uh, I'll handle it, don't worry." Nicki glared back at her.

Ali smiled and looked up to Rafe, standing at the foot of the bed, "Do you think I'll have a cool scar from the bullet?"

Rafe looked at Nicki, and they both rolled their eyes.

CHAPTER THIRTY-FOUR

Matt had been trying to reach Nicki for the last hour. He tried Ali's cell as well. He knew they were up at the cottage, but even that phone went unanswered. It was ten o'clock, and he wondered if everything was all right. He hadn't liked the idea of them having to leave Nan's house in the first place, but he felt he could trust Rafe. Besides being a federal agent, he was a pretty stand-up guy, and Ali liked him a lot. Matt assumed he'd keep the girls safe.

He turned the Sox game on and kept trying them both intermittently. He was frustrated as all hell. He went over to his computer and went online to check flights. He hadn't planned to return until Friday, but maybe he could get a flight out tomorrow instead. He had one more job Sean was supposed to finish up, but maybe he could have Rick take over.

He studied the screen mindlessly, and his phone finally rang around eleven. It was the number he'd been dialing all night. "Nicki?"

"Yeah, it's me." She was so happy to hear his voice. "I see I missed a few calls from you. I'm sorry, I didn't have my phone."

"Where are you guys?" Matt felt relief wash over him at the sound of her voice.

"We're back at the house now." Nicki watched as Rafe carefully carried Ali into her room. The first thing Nicki had done when they came in was go for her phone. Besides a long-winded message from her boss at the paper in regards to today's arrest of one of the island's most notorious contributors and one of its realtors, the rest of the messages had been from Matt asking her to call. She was amazed that the paper had already heard about D'nafrio, and she was excited to tell them what she knew.

"Is everything all right?" Matt detected something in her voice, and he was instantly on edge.

Nicki took a deep breath. "There was a little incident at the cottage." How was she going to make this sound less horrible?

"What incident?" His voice was tight.

Nicki could here the gruff tone and knew this wasn't going to go over well.

"She's okay now, but Ali was shot in the shoulder tonight." Nicki held her breath and waited.

Matt took a deep breath and spoke slowly. "Did you just say she was shot?" He must have heard wrong. "Please tell me that's not what you said."

"I'm sorry, Matt, that's what I said. Trust me when I tell you she's okay. The bullet grazed her shoulder, and she had to have stitches and some staples, but she's actually here now back at the house with Rafe and me."

"What the FUCK happened there?" he couldn't believe what he was hearing.

Nicki cringed at his angry tone and felt awful having to tell him. "Do you remember those jerks parked across the street from the other night? You know, the guys who gave us a hard time?"

Matt felt the anger boiling in his veins. "Yes."

"They went to the cottage. One of them had harassed us there the night before, and I guess he decided to take his friend back there tonight. I was at work and Rafe was -- well, thankfully on his way back to her from a drug bust." She paused. "One of them went in and tried to attack her."

Oh, sweet Jesus, his little sister. He should have taken care of those bastards when he had the chance. "Go on." He was beyond angry.

"Rafe got there just in time. He barged in, but the other one was still outside, and he followed Rafe in with a gun. When Rafe knocked the gun out of his hand, he broke the guy's arm, but the gun went off and the bullet hit Ali before lodging into a cabinet."

"Holy shit, she could have been killed!" Matt's stomach turned, thinking of his parents knowing this. "And you were at work?" He hadn't even considered that Nicki could have walked into that.

"Yes, I had to go to a meeting at town hall, so I wasn't back here until eight-ish and found out myself."

Matt was suddenly grateful for town meetings. "Who told you?"

"One of Rafe's friends and fellow agents. Rafe couldn't get in touch with me, so he sent him by, and he took me to the hospital."

Matt felt a brief twinge of jealousy. "That was good. Is he still with you guys?"

"No, no, he and his date or whoever she was dropped me off at the hospital, and then I came back with Rafe and Ali." Nicki felt so bad for him. "Matt, please don't worry about her. She's really going to be fine. She was shaken up, but she did manage to kick the kid's ass a little."

"Really?" Matt laughed, relief sweeping over him.

"She broke his nose, and he'll probably be peeing blood for a while." Nicki smiled.

"That's my baby sister." He laughed, filled with emotion. He was proud of her, but he knew she must have been scared shitless. "What happened to the guys?"

"They were arrested. I guess they had drugs in their car, too, so they'll go away for awhile."

"Man, I wish I'd taken care of them that night."

"Then I'd be talking to you through a glass partition."

Matt laughed. "Probably." Matt took a deep breath and sighed, sitting back in his desk chair. "I'll be there as soon as I can. Tell her that, will you?"

"You're coming back, then?" Nicki dared to hope.

"Of course I am. I was planning for the weekend, but just before you called I was trying to find flights for tomorrow." And it wasn't looking all that good. "Did you think I wouldn't come back?"

"I wasn't sure. I know you've got responsibilities there."

Matt could hear the uncertainty in her voice, and he ached for her. "Yeah well, I've got responsibilities there, too."

Nicki knew he would want to be here for Ali. "She wants to make sure you don't tell your parents. She doesn't want them to fly down. She's afraid they'll try to get her to come home."

Matt sighed. "I'll decide when I get there if I tell them or not."

"Okay, I guess that's fair."

"Nicki?"

"Yeah?"

"I wasn't talking about Ali when I said I've got responsibilities there."

Nicki leaned against the kitchen wall and put her head back. "Oh." She wanted to cry. She was already so grateful Ali was going to be okay, and now she just wanted to put her arms around Matt and feel his body beside hers.

"Is Ali right there, by the way?"

"No, Rafe brought her to her room. She's still a little out of it from the painkillers. She's actually excited about the prospect of a scar." Nicki laughed softly.

God, he missed Nicki. "*She would* be excited about that." He shook his head. "Well, tell her I'll be there soon." Matt smiled. "I'm glad you're both safe."

They ended the call, and Matt got right on the phone to his older brother Jason.

"It's the bottom of the ninth, bases loaded. This better be good."

Matt could actually hear the crowd in the background. "Don't even tell me you're at the game." The Red Sox were playing the Rays in Tampa. His brother was a die-hard fan, and they shared season tickets to Fenway, but Matt was surprised Jason was in Florida.

"Hell, yes, I'm here, was here last night, too."

Matt could hear the crack of a bat. "Jesus, where are your seats?"

"Right behind home plate, baby. Ohhhh! She's outta here! Woo!"

Matt held the phone away and watched on T.V. as Big Poppy brought all his teammates home, adding three more to the board. "Nice one," he agreed a little less enthusiastically.

"So what's up, little brother?"

"It's Ali."

"What about her?"

Matt heard the instant concern. "She's okay, but she was shot in the shoulder tonight." Man, now he knew how Nicki must have felt delivering the news to him. There was no easy way to say it.

"Matt, please tell me you just said someone was *doing* a shot off her shoulder tonight, because the other way is incomprehensible to me." Jason was standing now.

"I know, I know, but it's true." Matt gave him the short version, starting with Rafe and ending with Nicki's phone call.

"Holy shit, I'm leaving now. I'm two and a half hours away."

"All right, but listen -- you can't tell Mom and Dad yet."

"They don't know? Why the hell not?" Jason was outraged.

"She's just afraid they'll want her to come back home, and she really doesn't want to do that."

Jason smirked. "Because of this FBI guy?" He couldn't wait to meet him.

"Yes, basically."

"What's he like?" He let the skepticism drip from his question.

"He's actually pretty cool. He's around our age, maybe somewhere between; tall, built, and not as good-looking as me, but I guess I can see the attraction."

"You sound like you want to date him. Is she sleeping with this guy?"

Matt cringed. "God, I guess. I haven't asked, but I think it's safe to assume."

"I'll be there as quick as I can." Jason had already left his seat.

Jay didn't sound happy. "Just be cool about it. I like him. If I didn't, I would have told him to take a hike."

Yeah, he'd make his own decision about that. "When are you coming back down? I heard about Sean, by the way. That sucks." Holy fuck, his sister got shot!

"Yeah, it does suck," Matt agreed. "I've got a few loose ends to tie up. I was trying to fly out tomorrow, but there aren't any good times that work for me. If you're going to be with Ali, then I won't worry about not getting there until Friday."

"I'll let you know when I arrive."

"See you." Matt hung up the phone and felt relieved Jason would be with Ali in just a matter of hours. Although he should probably warn Nicki. It would be about two to two-thirty a.m. by the time he got there. He called her cell.

"Hey, me again."

"Hi." Nicki's mood brightened considerably. She had just been brooding in her room.

Nicki sounded happy to hear from him, which was good. "Listen, my brother Jason is on his way there."

"Really? When will he get here?"

"In about three hours."

"Oh, God, Ali's going to kill me. I told her I was only going to tell you."

"I had to tell him, Nicki, and it just so happened he was at the game in Tampa. He wants to see for himself that she's all right." He paused. "And he wants to meet Rafe."

"Oh-oh," she laughed. So this was what it was like to have older brothers. "I get it. All right, I'll let him in, and he can sleep in your room." She felt kind of funny calling it that.

Matt grinned. "Why don't you put him in the room next to Ali's?" He didn't want Jason in the bed he'd made love to Nicki in.

"Oh, yeah, I guess that would be better, but Rafe is, you know

-- in there with her."

"She's a big girl. Jason can handle it."

"Okay." Nicki sighed, not sure if she believed him.

"Are you still trying for tomorrow?"

"Well, it's not looking too good. It looks like Friday is going to work out better. I feel better knowing Jay is coming, though. I'll definitely be there by the weekend."

Now it was the weekend? She let out a sigh. "Okay." She wasn't going to whine and complain; she had no right.

Matt could hear the disappointment in her voice and he felt bad, but he planned to make it up to her. He said goodnight again, and when he hung up he turned back to the computer and booked his flight for first thing Friday morning.

When he woke up on Thursday, Matt hit the ground running. He went into the office, paid some bills, went to the bank, deposited some checks, and made it over to the Back Bay, where he went to check on Nicki's grandmother's kitchen. He was happy with the work his guys had done and knew Grace would be, too. His next stop was to the Howards. He was going to get their house sold before he left. It would be a great surprise for Ali.

Forty minutes later he pulled into their driveway. He knocked on the door to their well-kept Colonial. Mrs. Howard answered the door, and Matt introduced himself. She invited him in, and Mr. Howard joined them in the living room.

After briefly explaining why Ali couldn't be there and thanking them for their sympathy and understanding, he got down to business. "I've heard back from Mr. Santos. His client received your counter and are coming back at 350,000, which is good news."

Mr. Howard sat forward, confused, "But we're still 90,000 apart."

"I understand," Matt nodded, "but they came up 75,000, so they're serious, and I think I can get this done for you both." He had their attention. "Now, we could keep going back and forth, but my suggestion is to split the difference. I think 395,000 is a strong number. It's close to 90% of your asking price and, I think, worthy of consideration. I honestly think the buyers will go for it. You could be fishing in the Bahamas next week." He winked at Mrs. Howard as he smiled at her husband.

Matt could see them thinking about it. Yes! Just get them to consider it.

Mr. Howard stood up to shake Matt's hand and told him they'd be in touch later that day. Matt left and had one more stop to make before he went home to pack.

CHAPTER THIRTY-FOUR

Nicki woke up with a start. She wanted to be up before Ali to explain why her older brother was crashed on the couch. She had let him in quietly around three a.m., and he insisted on heading straight for the sofa. He sent Nicki back to bed and told her they could all talk in the morning. He apologized that she had had to let him in, and he didn't want to keep her up any later. So Nicki had gone right back to bed, grateful she didn't have to stay up and make small talk. She still had to get up for work.

It was funny -- she remembered Jason differently than how he had looked when she opened the door. His features were darker than Matt's. Jason had real dark brown hair as opposed to Matt's golden brown, and Jason had deep blue eyes that were definitely engaging, but not quite as lethal as Matt's heart-stopping green ones. He was dressed in khaki shorts, a Red Sox T-shirt, and sneakers. He was built pretty much the same as Matt, maybe not quite as muscular, but he appeared lean and fit. He had a reserved demeanor about him too, although she supposed that was because it was nearly three a.m.

Nicki also did not want Rafe to appear in the living room before her either. That might not go over too well with Jason. It was only seven, and Nicki threw on her workout clothes, hoping to sneak some yoga in before the inevitable meet and greet began.

She opened her bedroom sliders and rolled out her mat on the pool deck. She faced the bay and stretched languidly out on the mat. She would spend the day writing her little pieces for Friday's run, and work on the extra piece she would try to submit on D'nafrio. She was so excited thinking about seeing her name appear in print. She'd have to send a paper to her family in Italy -- Nan would get a kick out of it especially.

The morning sunlight washing over the room woke Jason. He adjusted his eyes and sat up, the previous night coming back to him clearly. He looked around, but the house was dead quiet. Ali must still be sleeping, he thought.

He saw movement out of the corner of his eye and turned to look outside. He watched with an admiring eye as Nicki stretched by the pool. Man, she turned into quite a beautiful woman. He hadn't seen her in quite some time. He turned away quickly as he heard Ali gasp behind him.

"Jason?"

He got up and went to his little sister. Her hair was mussed from sleep, and she wore an oversized man's white T-shirt and a pair of shorts as her pajamas, the T-shirt not completely covering the large white bandages on her arm. Hugging her gently and kissing her forehead, he asked, "What the hell happened to you?"

"What are you doing here?" she asked, ignoring him.

"You first."

Ali shot a glance outside to Nicki and noticed Jason do the same. "I'll go first, but forget about her." She gestured with her good arm to Nicki. "She's in love with Matt."

"Figures." He pretended to be upset about it, but he was happy for Matt and definitely envious. "Now spill it."

"I got shot."

"Matt told me that last night, but I didn't quite believe it until now." He lifted up her shirt sleeve to peek at the bandages.

"Did you tell anyone?"

"Nooo," he drew it out, "I can see you're fine, and I won't say anything because *you're* going to."

"When I'm ready," she challenged.

"Don't wait too long. They deserve to know."

"Why? They'll just worry," Ali argued.

"That's their job." Jason gave her that older brother look that said stop arguing, and she did.

"Well, how long can you stay?" Ali was thrilled that he had come.

"I have to be back in Tampa by Saturday. I'm leaving Sunday. I'll wait until Matt gets here, though, so you'll be in good hands."

"I'm already in good hands," she said with a coy look.

"Yeah, so I heard, but I think I'd like to be the judge of that."

"Ssh!" Ali hissed.

"Jesus, Ali, he's in your room?"

"Jason, for God's sake -- I'm a grown woman."

"You're my kid sister."

"You were just checking out my best friend, who happens to be my same age," she countered.

Jason stole another glance at Nicki and smiled. "Okay, you got me there."

Ali rolled her eyes. "C'mon, I'll make you breakfast."

"Whoa, you go sit. I'll make breakfast."

Ali laughed. "Oh, yeah, I'm injured. I'll have scrambled eggs, toast, orange juice, and a Vicodin, please." She grinned. "They're on the counter."

"Breakfast of champions!" he teased. "Coming right up."

"Hey, I'm in serious pain here."

"Yes, I can tell. Why's your guy so sleepy?" he asked suspiciously.

Ali looked at her oldest brother, then at her shoulder, and said sarcastically, "We were at it all night."

Jason's jaw dropped. "Don't say things like that to me!"

Ali laughed. "Get used to it!"

"Ugh! I'm telling Mom and Dad!" They were both laughing, enjoying each other's company.

Rafe woke up in Ali's bed to the sound of laughter and the smell of breakfast. Both things were welcoming. He recognized Ali's laughter but not the deep tones that obviously belonged to a man -- and it wasn't Matt.

He got up and slipped his jeans over the boxers he'd slept in, and he *had* actually just slept beside Ali, all night. She had lain on her good side, her back molded comfortably to his front and the surge of emotion that had overtaken him had been overwhelming. He never wanted to let her go. Seeing her bleeding the way she had in the cottage had leveled him. If he wasn't certain of his feelings for her before that, he was now. She had whispered his name a few times in her sleep, and he had held his breath, desperate to hear again the words she had whispered in her hospital bed. She had made him the happiest man in the world last night, and she didn't even know it. He hoped to hear her say it again, minus the painkillers. He laughed to himself as he splashed some cold water on his face in the bathroom. She would be mortified when he told her she had talked in her sleep. He found a new toothbrush in the vanity drawer and used it. He'd have to have a little fun teasing her about that.

He went back to the bed in search of his T-shirt, then remembered Ali was wearing it. He had slipped it over her because it would be loose and comfortable over the bandages while she slept. He'd wanted to do so much more as he'd lowered the blood-stained sundress from her body, but she was rather out of it, and he had held back even as she'd reached for him. He told her he would protect her all night and he had -- and it had felt amazing.

He left the bedroom and walked down the hall toward the sounds and smells. There was definitely a man in the kitchen, and he was cooking. He saw Ali sitting on the couch, and she was watching Nicki through the sliders, who appeared to be doing yoga. Rafe came up behind Ali and ruffled her already messed hair.

Ali turned her head at the feel of Rafe's hand. "Good morning."

she gave him a big smile that radiated through her eyes.

"Morning," he smiled back. Those eyes got him every time and he felt that all too familiar tug in his gut.

Ali took in the sight of him, knowing he could read the desire flashing in her eyes. He wore just his jeans, and with that ripped upper body and that line of hair leading to places she wanted to go, he was too damn sexy.

Rafe saw the fire in her eyes, and he held it with his own, his body beginning to stir. As much as he had enjoyed holding her all night, it had been real hard not to touch her intimately, real hard. He cleared his throat and shot a look into the kitchen and then back at her.

Ali laughed at the predatory look Rafe gave her and got goose bumps. She felt so deprived of his body. They hadn't been together, naked, in two nights. Two nights too long. Last night had been like a dream as she'd slept against his large, warm body. She had felt so safe and so…loved. When she awoke this morning, it was with a new determined attitude about him. She wanted him in her bed like that for the rest of her life, and she would do anything to make it happen.

Jason was aware of Rafe's presence in the other room. He continued to cook as Ali spoke to the guy, giving Jason a chance to sneak a look. The guy was shirtless, tanned, and cut, with muscles Jason wasn't sure he himself possessed. Oh, give me a break, buddy -- his movie star profile sealed the deal. Jason was already passing judgment until he saw the looks exchanged between them. Okay, so *maybe* there was something there. He'd have to feel this guy out.

"Hey, good morning!" he called out, breaking their spell.

Rafe turned and was surprised at the resemblance to Ali. This was obviously her older brother. They had the same dark complexion, only his eyes were blue. Rafe walked toward him and held out a hand. "Good morning. Rafe McDonough."

Jason took his hand and was surprised at the genuine smile and look in the guy's eyes. "Jay Fuller, Ali's brother." They did that manly grip handshake, and Jason handed him Ali's breakfast plate. "For the patient. I'm making more -- you interested?"

"Sure, that would be great. It smells great," Rafe told him as he picked up a fork and napkin, bringing it all over to Ali. "Do you want to eat on the couch or outside?" he asked her.

She smiled. "Outside would be nice." She was grateful Jason was being friendly.

Rafe opened the sliders and brought the plate to the table, greeting Nicki. "How you doing today, Gumby?"

Nicki chuckled. "I think I've rid myself of yesterday's stress." Nicki rolled up her mat and told Rafe about the call from her boss and how the paper was handling it.

"Well, I hope my information was helpful. Call me today if you need anything else."

"Thanks a lot, Rafe." Nicki was truly grateful. It would be a huge deal to get the scoop on that story.

"No problem." He nodded toward the inside. "It seems you girls have yourself a chef. I'd go put my order in if I were you."

Nicki went inside and winked at Ali. Rafe was sure a sight with his shirt off, and she teased Ali, bouncing her eyebrows up and down. God, she wished the weekend would get here faster. She had her own hottie she'd like to ogle.

Rafe came back in to help Ali outside and she was grinning. She knew Nicki was a sucker for that jeans and no shirt combo.

"Hey, I hear you're cooking to order in here."

Jason laughed and came over to hug Nicki. "Sorry about last night. It's great to see you again."

"You, too, now that I'm actually awake. That was nice of you to haul ass and get here," she laughed.

"Well, it's not every day Ali gets shot. I wouldn't have missed this for the world."

Nicki laughed at his sarcasm.

"So what's this guy like? Do you like him?"

"Right to the punch, eh?" she grinned. "He's great. I do like him, and I believe..." she turned to make sure she couldn't be overheard, "...it's love."

"I kind of figured. I saw the way she looked at him, but how do you think he feels. Is it serious?"

"Judging from last night at the hospital, I honestly do think it's serious -- that *he's* serious," she corrected.

"And Matt likes him," Jason commented.

"Yes, he does."

Jason noted the sudden change in Nicki's voice. "So what, everyone who comes to this island falls in love in a matter of days?" he teased her.

Nicki's eyes widened. "What?"

Jason poured juice and finished putting the breakfast he prepared on plates. "Don't try to hide it. Ali already told me."

Nicki felt the heat rise to her cheeks. "I'm not that cavalier," she joked. "My plight was years in the making."

Jason just stared at her with surprise. "No kidding?"

"Unfortunately not." Nicki shrugged and picked up two of the plates to take outside.

Jason took the rest and followed her to the patio. "So are you telling me my little brother is a moron?" Jason winked at Ali.

Nicki laughed, "No! *I'm* just really good at keeping secrets." She met Ali's eyes.

"Ah." Jason decided to let that go for now. He'd have to get more details from Ali.

They all ate their breakfast outside in the warmth of the morning sun, and Jason demanded a detailed rundown of the previous night.

He also asked Rafe all about his career with the FBI and general background information about himself. He had to admit he liked what he heard. Rafe seemed like an intelligent, caring person. The way he referred to his parents and siblings was heartfelt. Jason could tell he had a loving relationship with his niece and nephews, too.

"So you're here for another month?"

"Pretty much," Rafe told him.

"Nice, where are you going to stay if you have to vacate the beach house?"

Rafe laughed knowing what Jason was wondering, he was having that sense of déja vu. "I'll be at Tween Waters up the street, in a different cottage now, I guess."

Ali laughed. "If they let you back in."

"Right," he agreed, "I might be doing some renovations in order to stay."

"We'll just get Matt to do the remodel," Ali joked.

"When's he coming back?" Rafe asked. It would be good to hang out again, maybe do that fishing trip they'd talked about.

Ali's eyes were on Nicki.

Nicki pushed her chair back. "First he said tomorrow, then Friday, and last we spoke he said by the weekend so I don't know if that means Friday, Saturday, or Sunday. I guess we'll know when he gets here." Nicki knew she sounded frustrated, and she tried to be gracious, "Thanks for the breakfast, Jason. I have to get ready for work -- see you guys later."

They all watched her disappear behind her bedroom sliders, and they all shared a look.

"I guess I shouldn't have asked that question." Rafe made a regretful face.

"She's just missing him, and he's probably having a hard time trying to get all the work he needs to get done in just a few days." Ali felt bad for Nicki and just wanted to see her happy again. "He better get here soon, though."

Jason laughed. "He'll be here tomorrow for sure. I know *I* wouldn't wait another day."

Rafe grinned at him, understanding, and Ali kicked him playfully under the table.

"What? Can you blame me?" Jason laughed.

"What's the plan for today? Do you want to see the islands?" Ali asked, shaking her head.

"You can't go anywhere like that! You need to rest." Jason looked at her like she was insane.

"It's a glorified scrape! I'm fine," she insisted.

"You have twenty-five stitches and staples in your shoulder. A whole chunk of you was ripped off. I don't think you'd make a very good tour guide today." Jason looked to Rafe for support, who was nodding in agreement.

"If I'm uncomfortable, you can bring me back here. Rafe, do you want to come?" Ali asked, hopeful. She wasn't about to admit to any pain -- she was just happy to be sitting there.

"I'd love to, but I have to get my stuff out of the beach house and work on getting a new room at the resort." He also owed Daniels his report, which he never did last night, and he supposed he'd find a message at Tween Waters from the local P.D. about giving them a statement.

"You know, you're welcome to stay here," Ali offered again.

Rafe smiled. "That's a generous offer, but I already paid for my stay up there. Who knows, maybe they've already replaced the door and the cabinet." He was only joking; he would take anything they gave him at this point.

"They probably have," Jason put in. "I'm sure it doesn't bode well for the resort for the other guests to see a crime scene out their windows."

"Yeah, you're probably right about that." Rafe laughed, picking up their plates. "I'll give you a call later this afternoon, Ali. I'm going to head across the street."

Ali stood up to follow him. She knew today was the day they were supposed to talk. She was anxious to do so, too. Although, she held a little trepidation at the thought of what he would say. Going out with Jason for a ride, she'd be able to put their talk off for a couple of hours. She couldn't bear it if it turned out to have a negative outcome.

Rafe placed the dishes in the sink and turned to face Ali. "How are you feeling?"

"Much better. The Vicodin is in full effect."

He grinned. "I kind of like you all drugged up."

"Oh, yeah?" She laughed. "Why's that?"

"You say some interesting things under the influence."

Ali paused at that revelation. "Oh? Like?" Oh-oh.

"You don't remember?"

"No I don't. Are you going to tell me?" Maybe she should be embarrassed. Something told her she should.

"Nah, I won't tell you... it was nice though." He grinned.

Oh, shoot, she was racking her brain. What did she say? She remembered how blissfully good it felt to be held by him all last night. Maybe she said something to that effect.

Rafe kissed her beautiful mouth. "I still want to talk with you today, okay? Even if it's not until tonight. It really can't wait."

God, he was so serious. She couldn't decide whether that was good or bad. "Rafe....I..."

He stopped her with another long, lingering kiss. "We'll talk later."

Why did he always stop her from talking like that? His kisses certainly didn't feel like the kisses of someone who wanted to end things, so maybe she should stop being so damn paranoid. "Okay," was all she managed in response. Her knees were feeling a tad weak. She walked him to the door and shut it closed when he left, and then she went to find Jason. He was still on the patio, at the table.

"So what do you think?" she asked right off the bat. His opinion was important to her.

Jason swiveled in his chair. "I was skeptical at first. You know I don't like to feel inferior first thing in the morning," he joked.

Ali laughed. "He is a god, but you're pretty cute -- you shouldn't feel that way.

"Gee, thanks." He rolled his eyes. "Anyway, after talking to him, I can see he's pretty smart and not a meathead."

"Jason, when have I ever been attracted to meatheads?"

"I'm just saying," Jason conceded. "I think he's all right."

Ali was so happy about that. "Do you think Mom and Dad would approve?"

He rolled his cyes again. "Mom will fall in love with him on the spot, and Dad will be skeptical like I was until he talks to him."

"Well, that's why I don't want to tell them about yesterday, until they can meet him face to face. Otherwise, they'll never want to meet him, thinking it was somehow his fault."

"I gotcha. I'm not going to say a word."

"Thank you."

"Tell me about Nicki and Matt. This didn't just happen this past weekend did it?" Jason had lowered his voice, knowing Nicki was still inside.

"Well, for him it did, but apparently for her, it started a long time ago."

"Apparently? *You* didn't know?"

"No, she never said a word. I felt bad when she admitted it. That would really suck to love someone and not have it returned."

"But he had no clue, right?"

"None. If he had, who knows, but she was a little young for him in high school, you know?"

"Yeah, that probably wouldn't have worked." Jason laughed.

"But now," she laughed softly, too, "Matt obviously sees her as a grown woman."

"How do you think he feels?" Jason was fascinated that the two of them were together. It was a rather touching story, he had to admit.

Ali smiled. "I think he wants to marry her and have tons of kids with her."

"No shit?"

"No shit!"

"Wow, that's great, huh?"

Ali filled him in on how Nicki's grandmother had kind of put things in motion.

"That was pretty astute of her."

"I guess she's known all along."

"Do Mom and Dad know?"

"No, I haven't said anything, and I don't think Matt has either."

"Well, I'm happy for him." Jason truly was.

"Yes, me, too."

"And for you." He smiled at her.

"For me?"

"You seem really happy."

"I am Jason -- over the moon."

He grinned. "All right, I've heard enough. Point me to the shower, and then let's go exploring."

Ali set him up in the guest bath and went to find Nicki. She was in her bedroom, putting her earrings in.

"What's on the agenda for today?" Ali asked.

"Just writing in the office, getting ready for tomorrow's paper!"

Ali was happy Nicki seemed to be in better spirits, excited even.

"It'll just be a couple of paragraphs, but it's a start," she explained.

"It's a great start. We'll have to celebrate tomorrow night!"

"Yeah, sure." Nicki nodded.

Ali noticed the sudden swing in her mood. “Hey,” she touched Nicki’s arm, “I know my brother, and he won’t disappoint you.”

Nicki smiled. “I guess I know that, but why can’t he just tell me exactly when he’s coming? I’m dying here!” she complained.

Ali laughed. “So punish him when he gets here for making you crazy!”

“Oh, I plan on it!”

CHAPTER THIRTY-FIVE

Rafe entered the beach house and opened the sliders to the back deck. He sat down and stared out at the Gulf. He was going to really miss this spot. The time he spent here with Ali especially. He was going to tell her that he loved her tonight, and he prayed that his honesty wouldn't scare her away.

He got up to pack. He wanted to do what he needed to get done and settle in at the resort so he could plan a perfect evening for them. He had a few ideas and hoped she would be feeling up for it.

"Don't you love the Jeep?" Ali asked Jason.

"Yes, but are you sure you're comfortable?"

"I'm fine, Jay, I'll let you know -- honest."

"Okay, but every time I go over a bump, I cringe for you."

"Don't worry. Where do you want to go first?"

"I don't care. How about we start at one end and end up at the other?"

"Good. Head to Sanibel, and we'll start at the lighthouse. We can have lunch at Grandma Dot's. It's in the marina -- wait until you see some of the boats."

"Do they serve cold beer at Grandma's?"

"Yes, not to worry," she assured him.

They made it to the lighthouse, and Ali took him down to the fishing pier. There were a handful of men angling, and she and Jason stayed awhile in the hot sun watching, even though the fish didn't seem to be cooperating. They moved down to the sand after awhile and shelled on the beach for a time until they both became quite hungry for lunch.

After some cold drinks and some food consumed at the marina, they got back in the Jeep and took Gulf Drive back toward Captiva.

"How's the shoulder?" Jason could tell Ali was a little uncomfortable.

"It's starting to hurt a bit. I need another pill."

"Don't get hooked," he half-joked.

"No worries there. I don't think I'd be able to work out feeling all loopy."

Jason knew how important that was to her. "I didn't even think. You won't be able to run for awhile. That sucks."

"Don't remind me." She wasn't happy about it, and she'd have to figure out a workout for her legs that didn't involve any impact. "I guess I'll be doing a lot of lunges."

"I think you can afford to take a break for awhile."

"How nice of you." She smiled. "You've been working out, too. I can tell."

"I have to offset all the drinking I do at the games," he laughed.

"Yeah, don't get one of those beer bellies. The chicks don't dig that."

"I know, I know."

"So are you seeing anyone?" Ali asked with a smile.

"Not anymore, and it wasn't anything serious anyway. I'm too deep into a project at work right now to concentrate on my sex life." He looked over at Ali. "I mean, my love life."

"Right," she giggled.

They pulled into the drive finally, and Ali gratefully got out of the Jeep. She wondered if Rafe was still at the beach house.

"I'm going to take a ride up into town; look around some, maybe grab a beer." Jason told her.

"Okay, have fun. I'm going to lie down for awhile. I'll leave the door unlocked for you."

Jason stared at her, incredulous.

"Okay, okay, let me unlock the door, then you can have my key." Ali made her way to the door, unlocked it, and came back over to the Jeep to toss Jason her key.

"Lock the door behind you!" he commanded as he pulled back out.

"Yes, sir!" Ali saluted with her good arm. "Have fun!"

"I intend to."

Ali went back inside and took a painkiller. She went to her bedroom and picked up the paperback she had started on the beach. She lay down to read it, but after a few pages felt her eyes getting heavy. She was aware of the book falling from her hand and onto the floor before she drifted off completely.

Rafe made it up to the resort in good time, after faxing a report to Daniels; a day late, speaking on the phone with the local P.D., and transferring all his gear and belongings into the truck. He parked and went right to the front office to speak to the management. After a lengthy discussion that involved writing a healthy check, he was able to check into a new cottage. This one was much like the other, only nestled back by the pool area. It still had the screened porch, and although it didn't look over at the Gulf, it was cozy and somewhat private. He had also arranged for them to transfer his belongings from the old cottage to the new one. They were really Ali's and Nicki's belongings, but the staff were also going to unload the refrigerator and cabinets and bring everything over to him.

He walked over to cottage 101 before he started to unload his truck to see that they had indeed already fixed the door. Someone would be vacationing in there by tonight, no doubt. Rafe went back to the Yukon and began to unload. The only thing he had left to do was jog back to the beach house for the Ducati. He'd ship it back north in a few weeks, and until then he hoped to get Ali out riding with him. He had a feeling she would love it.

It was nearly four-thirty by the time he got back to the cottage, and he thought he'd better call her. He didn't want to wait any longer than necessary. It was five rings before she answered.

"Hey, did I wake you?"

"I'm glad you did." Ali sat up, favoring her shoulder. "That pill knocked me out."

Rafe could hear the grogginess in her voice. "Sober up, kid, I'm coming to get you in one hour."

"One hour?" Ali swung her legs off the bed, looking at the bedside clock. "What's the plan?" she asked, feeling a surge of excitement.

"You'll see."

"What should I wear?"

"Wear a dress." He loved her body in a dress. "And pack a bag."

"Okay," she smiled. "I'll be ready." "Pack a bag" sounded promising.

"See you soon." Rafe hung up, his excitement outweighing his nervousness.

Ali hung up the phone. He wanted her to wear a dress. He obviously had something in mind, and if he were giving her the brush-off, he probably wouldn't have asked her to wear a dress for the occasion, let alone pack a bag. She was feeling positive. She knew without a doubt that she was in love with him. She didn't care whether it had happened in days or hours, it was just so, and she wasn't going to pass up the opportunity to tell him.

Whatever he was going to tell her tonight, she would face it and try to be strong if it didn't have the outcome she wanted, but she would not let the night end without sharing her own feelings. Life was too damn short. She'd tell him there were no strings attached -- she just wanted him to know how he made her feel and that their time together would forever be special to her. If he had to go back to work in New York City after his four weeks were up, then she would understand. She hadn't any hold on him, but she would make sure he knew that he would forever be in her heart. She could only dare to hope that they could have any kind of future together.

Ali made her way to the shower. She wasn't going to be able to stand under the shower head without soaking her bandages, so she lifted the shower nozzle off its cradle and proceeded to wash and rinse herself that way. It wasn't easy, but she managed to wash her body and to shave without cutting herself.

After drying off, she picked out the white tank-style sun dress she had bought in Captiva and a pair of white wedge-heeled sandals to wear. Drying her long hair proved to be rather difficult, making her good arm almost as sore as her bad one, so in the end she let what was still damp air dry. She finger-combed it through and left it loose and somewhat tousled around her shoulders.

Ali's attempts to pull out all the stops were marred by the stupid bandages covering her left arm and shoulder, but she wanted to try to look her best for Rafe. After a little makeup and some lightly scented body lotion, she headed to the living room to wait nervously.

The sound of the front door opening had her turning before she sat down, and she saw Nicki stride through.

"Wow, look at you!" Nicki whistled. "What's the occasion?"

"The big talk." Ali raised her brows.

"Ooh, what do you think, proposal?"

"Ha-ha," Ali scoffed. "I don't know what he's going to say, but I've decided I'm going to be honest. Why not, you know?"

Nicki nodded. "Definitely! You've been through kind of a big ordeal with him -- I think it would be appropriate."

"Me, too. I've decided life is too short."

"That's for sure. You're a living example of that. You never know what tomorrow's going to bring."

"No kidding." Ali laughed, looking at her bandages. "Can I really be taken seriously looking like this?"

"Trust me, he won't be looking at your bandages."

Ali smiled, "I hope not. This wasn't easy to pull off."

"You did good, kid." Nicki gave her the once-over again. "Where did you get that dress, by the way?"

"When I was shopping the other day. You like?"

"Gots to get me one." Nicki sat at the kitchen stool. "Hey, where's Jason?"

"He went into town for a beer. You should go find him," Ali suggested.

"Maybe I will. I don't want to just sit around."

"Waiting?" Ali smiled.

"Yeah." She gave Ali a half-smile. "Plus, I'm off tomorrow, so I can have more than one and enjoy it."

"I'll give you his cell. If you don't see him anywhere, just call him."

"Great. I'm just going to change. If you're not here when I come out, good luck and have a great time. You deserve it, and I know it's going to be all good!" She winked at Ali and disappeared down the hall, a spring in her step. She had done it -- she had written the piece on D'nafrio and submitted it. Her boss had given her a doubtful look but told Nicki she'd see what she could do.

Why did Nicki wink at her? Did she know something? Ali went over to the counter and left her Jason's number. She checked her voicemail while she was at the notepad, realizing that in all the chaos she hadn't checked it since the day before yesterday.

The first one was from her mother, saying hello and telling her to call; the second one was from her father, saying hello and telling her to call; and the third one was from Mrs. Howard, thanking her for sending Matt by and that they were seriously considering his advice.

What advice? She felt bad that she hadn't even been thinking about the Howards since her ordeal, and she would definitely have to put a call in to Bob Santos to see if his buyers responded to the counter. Probably not, if she hadn't heard from him. She was pretty sure they had just been fishing, anyway. She started to dial Matt when the doorbell chimed. She hit "end," forgetting about the call, and went to the door excitedly.

Rafe rang the bell and waited nervously. He suddenly felt like he was on a first date. The door opened and he stood, riveted. He was momentarily speechless as he took Ali in with his eyes. Her long hair hung loosely around her face and shoulders -- it was messy in a really sexy way, and a total turn-on. Rafe's eyes traveled down the rest of her body, and he felt his own respond to the white dress that clung to her beautiful curves and showed off her deep brown tan. It was when his eyes made it back up to her face that his heart skipped a beat. Her brilliant green eyes shone up at him, and he could see all that he wanted to see right in them, all he'd been hoping for.

"Ali, you look incredible."

She smiled, her own heart pounding. "Thank you." She opened the door to let him in. "I found something to wear to match the bandages."

He laughed, but he could tell she was self-conscious about them, and he hadn't even noticed them. He couldn't keep his eyes off her face.

Ali was flattered immensely at the way he was looking at her, and she was taken aback herself. Rafe was so utterly good-looking that she couldn't believe he was standing in front of her. His hair was slicked back and slightly damp, just touching the collar of his crisp white shirt, and his skin was golden from the sun, making his eyes even darker than ever as they looked into her own. He was wearing khaki cargo shorts that accentuated his narrow hips and strong thighs, and she wondered if he were carrying his gun at his waistband.

The heat between them was volcanic, and it took a lot of restraint for Rafe not to just lead her back to her bedroom. He cleared his throat. "Are you all set?"

Ali finally broke his gaze. "Yes, I just have to get my bag." She picked the small backpack up off the floor and headed out the door with Rafe in tow. When she saw the motorcycle in the driveway, her eyes lit up, and she turned to him, smiling.

"I had to get it out of the garage, so I figured I'd take it. I hope you don't mind. It's a short ride."

"I don't mind at all -- I've been dying to have a ride." Ali stared at the motorcycle admiringly. "I just hope I can hold on!"

Rafe grinned. "Just put your good arm around my waist and lean into me."

That sounded fine by her. She smiled up at him, and he was smiling back. She knew what they were both thinking, and she felt herself blushing. Two days too long!

Rafe picked up his helmet and placed it on her head, then took her bag and placed it in the compartment under the seat.

"I bet this looks attractive," she said with sarcasm.

"You look sexy as hell." And she did. He got on the bike and turned to help Ali settle behind him.

"Good thing it's a short drive. This dress isn't exactly conducive to motorcycle riding."

He laughed. It was working for him; her bare legs surrounding his were almost too much to handle. He'd be driving a little faster back to the resort.

Ali did as she was instructed and leaned into Rafe's back, her good arm around his waist, her bad arm dangling by his side. He felt so good and...male. She breathed the fresh soapy scent of him in, and her legs inadvertently squeezed against his.

"Are you kidding me right now?" he groaned, turning to look at her.

"What?" Ali's cheek rested on his shoulder blade, and she moved her eyes up to meet his.

"Your…umm...legs." God, he wasn't going to make it up the street -- it had been two days. He looked at the smooth skin that enveloped him and to where the dress rode up to accommodate her position.

"You're the one who told me to wear a dress," she said innocently, but her own eyes held the same amount of desire as his.

"Just hold on." He turned back with a groan.

"Yes, sir!" Ali smiled against him, loving that she had got him all stirred up. He pulled out of the driveway, and she squealed with delight as the tires hit the pavement. She had never been on a motorcycle before, and it was exhilarating. "Faster!" she yelled.

Rafe laughed. He knew she would love it. "The speed limit's thirty. I can't go much faster," he told her, his head turned her way so she could hear him. He would love to take her out on the open roads in upstate New York. He would show her how beautiful it was in the fall. "Another time, I promise."

Ali loved the whole five-minute ride and definitely wanted to do that again. They pulled into Tween Waters, and Rafe parked them outside a little cottage set back on its own and surrounded by tropical plants. He helped her off the bike and took the helmet off her head for her. "This one is cute, too," she said, looking it over. The cottage was painted an ocean blue and looked so pretty surrounded by the lush landscaping. Ali's heart started to pound again at the thought of going inside.

"Are you hungry?" Rafe asked, "I know it's kind of early, but we could have a couple of drinks, eat, and then go over for the sunset."

"That sounds great. I am hungry -- Jason and I had lunch a long time ago." She took his outstretched hand and walked beside him on the sandy path to the resort's restaurant.

"So what happened with the other cottage?" She couldn't see it from where they walked.

"Like it never happened."

"Really? That was fast! So why didn't they just let you keep it?"

Rafe wouldn't have brought her back there if they had offered it for free. "I could have kept it, but I thought you'd be more comfortable in a different one." He looked down at her and smiled.

He was thinking of her comfort? "But you're the one staying here, not me."

Rafe kept walking, "That's one of the things I'd like to talk to you about."

Oh! Ali looked up at him, but he stared straight ahead, grinning, pulling her along toward the restaurant. Ali was beaming, suddenly realizing that their talk *was* going to be "all good" as Nicki predicted.

Once inside they were seated at a small white-clothed, candle-lit table in the back. Soft mood music played in the background, and waiters and waitresses poured water and wine in goblets and glasses on the elegant tables around the room. Ali immediately felt self-conscious of her bandages as she felt the stares upon her. Rafe came around and held her chair as she sat, then whispered in her ear, "White gauze and surgical tape have never looked so good." He was trying to make her feel at ease, and she smiled up at him gratefully.

Ali was self-conscious for another reason as well -- she felt like she was on a first date, which, if she thought about it, she was. She and Rafe had pretty much skipped the formalities when they'd first met.

Rafe could see Ali was a little tense, and he was feeling much the same, wondering if this had been such a good idea after all. He felt like a hormonal teenager.

The waiter took their drink order, and Ali sipped on the ice cold water he had poured and left for them. She was thankful it was on the table, because for the first time in her life she was at a loss for words.

Then Rafe started to laugh, and she put her water glass down.

"What?" She was laughing now, too. She loved how his face lit up.

"This." He motioned with his hand at their surroundings. "My attempts to wine and dine you."

"Is that what you're trying to do?" She grinned.

"Yes," he admitted and grinned right back.

Ali scooted her chair a little closer to his. "I'm flattered, but it's totally unnecessary."

"You are? It is?" He reached over and swept a lock of hair away from her eye.

She laughed softly, loving the intimate gesture. "The motorcycle ride was enough for me."

"Wow, if I had known it would be that easy…"

"I thought *that* had already been established," she teased.

Rafe brought his own chair closer to hers. "Well, I wasn't talking about *that*, but I plan to later."

Ali shivered at the thought of later and the look Rafe held in his eye. "Well, then, what are you talking about?"

All *she* could think about was putting her hands all over him. This was going to be a long dinner. They were momentarily interrupted as the waiter placed their drinks in front of them.

"Would you like to hear the specials?" he asked.

"I think we'll wait a few minutes, if you don't mind." Rafe couldn't think about food at all right now. He looked to Ali to make sure it was okay, and she nodded in agreement.

"Sure thing, I'll come back." The waiter disappeared.

Rafe took a deep breath. Did he really want to profess his feelings in this restaurant with a bunch of people in the room? Not really. "Tell me more about your family."

Her family? What the heck just happened? That was definitely *not* what he had been about to say! He had switched gears in an instant

-- he had been all serious and then had obviously re-thought what he was going to say. Okay, if he wanted to keep it light she could do that, but by the end of this night he would at least know how *she* felt. If she didn't chicken out like he just did.

"Well, you've met Jason. He's a die-hard Red Sox fan. That's the first thing that comes to anyone's mind when they hear his name."

"Yeah, I noticed the T-shirt, but I won't hold it against him." Rafe smiled, relieved that he steered the conversation in a different direction. He wanted the timing to be right.

"I'm sure you two could have some spirited conversations." She laughed.

"You look a lot alike."

"You think so? Everyone always says I look like Matt because of our eyes."

"You do look like him, too, but you and Jason have a few of the same facial expressions. It's funny."

Ali smiled at the compliment. "What about your family? I'd like to hear more about them." They were sitting real close now, and Ali was enjoying herself. Talking to him was fun and interesting, and it felt comfortable.

"My older sister is married with three kids. I think I told you that. And my younger brother Jake is just out of NYU."

"Are you a good uncle?"

He laughed. "When I'm around, I try to be. The boys are kind of impressed with the whole FBI thing."

Ali gave him a sexy look. "I know what that's like."

He laughed, enjoying the compliment and the look that went with it.

"My brother is making the family proud, heading to law school in the fall, and my parents are…" He paused, thinking about them and how they would love her, "…great. They're retired and still actually love each other after forty years of marriage."

"That's really nice. My parents are pretty cool, too. They've been married for thirty-five years and are also still in love. It's a nice thing to see and aspire to. I think they did a good job with the three of us."

The waiter was back, and they placed their dinner order, then remembered their drinks as they continued to talk about their families. Ali laughed at the stories about his niece and nephews, and she could see that he adored them.

"I want to hear more about your business plans." Rafe listened to her talk and loved how enthusiastic she got when she spoke about the store she planned to open.

"I'd love to get a few of the local artists from here to put things in my shop, too."

"I'm sure they would. Who wouldn't want to have a chance to sell their art, right?"

"That's what I'm hoping." Ali blushed. "I'm sorry, I hope I'm not boring you."

"You could never bore me. I asked because I'm interested."

Could he get any better? "And what will you do after your vacation? Will there be another case to work on right away, or do you have to sit around and wait for one?"

He laughed. "No, unfortunately there's no shortage of crime in this country, so I'll be assigned right away."

"And you'll be in New York City?" God, it was like pouring salt over her own wounds. Why was she asking him these torturous questions? She didn't want to think about him going back to New York.

"Possibly." Rafe was watching her, and he could see a slight change in her mood. "It could be Boston, for all I know."

"Really?"

Her face lit up at his words, as he had hoped. "It could be." He paused. "Or I could make sure it was."

Ali just stared at Rafe. What was he saying? Her heart rate increased. "You could?"

"Agents transfer all the time."

"Wouldn't you miss New York?"

"Boston's a pretty great city." He smiled at her.

"It's not as big as New York City, though, and it doesn't have as many things to do." Okay, why was she down playing Boston? She clearly had an opportunity here, and she better run with it.

"But we do have fantastic food, and shopping and the Public Gardens. I know they're not nearly as big as Central Park, but you can still take a horse and carriage ride around the city, and we have a great theater district. There's Newbury and Boylston streets for great shopping and the Aquarium..." The Aquarium? Like he cared, but she didn't want to leave anything out. "Oh, and once you've had pizza from the North End you'll never want to go back."

He was grinning at her. "Are you finished?"

"Well, I could think of plenty more attractions, like the Sox, the Celtics, the Bruins and Pats, but when you look at me like that, I get distracted."

"I'd only go to Boston for one reason, Ali."

The Waiter interrupted again to place their meals on the table, saving Ali from having to absorb that statement fully.

"Can I get you anything else?" he asked.

Rafe ordered them two more drinks, and they started on their meals when the waiter left.

"This is probably the best steak I've ever had." Ali cut off a piece and put it on Rafe's plate. "Try it." She was still basking in his declaration that he'd only come to Boston for one reason -- and she knew it wasn't for the Sox.

Rafe watched her cut her steak carefully. "How's the shoulder? Are you in any pain? I could cut that for you," he offered.

Ali smiled. "Thank you, but it's okay. Go ahead -- try it."

He did, and he shook his head. "Mine's better." He offered Ali a taste of his.

"No, thanks," she declined. "I haven't seen that much blood since --yesterday."

His head went back, and he laughed loudly. "Suit yourself, but I bet Matt would appreciate it."

"No doubt." She laughed, too. "He'll have to bring Nicki here, although she wouldn't be able to sit at the same table with that."

"She doesn't do red meat, huh?"

"Uh-uh. She'd be appalled to see me eating it." Ali took another bite of her steak.

"Your secret's safe with me." He winked.

"Thanks." She smiled.

They finished eating and enjoyed the rest of their drinks, then Rafe paid the bill the waiter had left for them. "We're just in time. Let's go across the street," he suggested.

Ali made a quick stop in the ladies' room, primped a little, and joined Rafe at the exit.

"How's the arm?" He was so worried that she was uncomfortable and not telling him.

"It's good, no throbbing yet. I brought a pill if I need one."

"Hopefully, you won't, although I do enjoy the things you say after you've had one," he teased.

Ali looked up at him as they stepped outside, "You better tell me what I said, I'm feeling a little self-conscious about it."

"You shouldn't."

Ali could only imagine what had come out of her mouth. It was probably something sexual, which would make sense, since sex with him was on her mind most of the time. He took her hand, and they walked across the street and onto the beach. The sun was setting right on cue.

"It's gorgeous. You have good timing," she proclaimed.

"You're gorgeous," he told her, stopping her on the sand.

"You just feel bad for me and my injured appendage."

Rafe shook his head in amusement and led her over to one of the empty cabanas. He sat and gently pulled her onto his lap, his hands finding their way through her hair as he pulled her head to his. Rafe kissed her gently, opening her mouth with his tongue and tasting her.

Ali put her good arm around Rafe's neck and felt the rush of heat as his tongue met hers. She was so hot for him, and she didn't know how long she could stand it before they could be naked. Their kiss went on and on, and she was pleased when she felt his arousal beneath her bottom. She felt such a sense of empowerment that she could do that to him.

He pulled away. "I've been wanting to do that all day," he said huskily.

"Umm, I've been wanting you to do that all day."

He laughed and adjusted her on his lap so that she could know the full extent of his wanting.

Ali acknowledged him by squirming just so. "Sunsets are kind of overrated, don't you think?"

He laughed, knowing what she wanted. He wanted it too, but not just yet. "Not this one."

"Why not?" She started kissing him again and caressing his strong jaw line with her hand.

Rafe pulled back just a little to look her in the eyes. "Because this is the sunset where I tell you that…" he smiled slightly, "…that I'm in love with you."

Ali pulled back so far that Rafe had to catch her before she fell off his lap. The look on her face made him smile, and then he watched as sudden tears flooded her eyes.

Oh, shit. That wasn't the reaction he was expecting.

She was shaking her head, and she dropped her forehead to his shoulder. Her good arm still ensconced around his neck. "Rafe," she whispered, trying not to outright sob.

"Yeah?" He still held onto her, and she hadn't tried to remove herself, so that had to be a good sign.

"That's what I was going to tell *you* tonight."

He pushed her back to see her face, his heart filled with her words. "You were?"

She nodded. "I know it's crazy -- it's been what, five or six days? But I can't help it. I'm crazy in love with you. I don't care what anyone thinks or says. The moment I saw you, I was gone." She smiled and waited for his reaction, her heart beating wildly.

Rafe kissed away her tears and then put his lips on her mouth again. If he ever felt happier, he couldn't remember. Hearing her say it right to his face and not while she drifted off into a drug-induced sleep was beautiful. "Ali, I don't care how short a time it's been, either. I feel the same way. I think about you every minute of the day, and I want to be with you. You're incredible and -- I love you."

Ali was numb. "Rafe?" she asked sweetly.

"Yeah, babe." He gave her a crooked smile.

"Can you take me back to the cottage now?"

He stood up with her still in his arms. He didn't need to be asked twice.

Ali was laughing hard. "You can't carry me all the way back!"

"Yes, I can," he answered gruffly.

"People are going to know what we're going back there to do." She was giggling.

"Yeah, and pretty soon they might be hearing it, too!"

She kept laughing as she bounced in his arms all the way back across the street. "Okay, but no Foo Fighters this time, not until my shoulder gets better."

He laughed and stopped to kiss her mouth, recalling their marathon session that first night. "They have a few slow songs."

He brought her right to the cottage door and set her down on the step while he grabbed her bag from the motorcycle. Then he went back to open the door.

The key card worked on the first try, and Ali smiled, grateful for small favors. They both went inside, and Rafe shut the door behind them, dropping her bag and the key on a nearby table. He pulled her against him with his back against the door and cupped her rear, bringing her in close.

"You know I can't even listen to that music now without getting all, well, you know." Ali was kissing his neck and moving her good arm and hand all over him.

Rafe reached one hand greedily under her dress and put it right on her wet heat. "Yeah, I know."

That was all it took, Ali lifted her leg around his hip and pressed herself hard, into him. Their kissing was fast and furious as they ground into each other, desperate for the contact. Rafe half-lifted her right into the bedroom and gently laid her back on the bed. He stood, looking down at her, and took his shirt off. He had never wanted any woman more in his life. He placed his hands on her shins and ran them up her smooth silky skin, not stopping until he reached the hem of her dress. Then he lifted it slowly, painstakingly so, torturing them both but wanting to prolong the anticipation. He gazed down at the pretty white panties and felt himself throbbing to get inside her, but he was going to try to savor this, and he fought himself for control. He bent down over her, hands astride her legs, and kissed her right through the thin cotton that covered her.

Ali's body jerked up in response. The heat from his breath on her was maddening. She gripped his hair in her hands, and any pain in her shoulder was forgotten.

Rafe continued to kiss her just like that. She was wet for him already, and he could taste her sweetness and smell her. He continued to suck on the material and then pulled it away with his teeth. The taste of her was driving him wild. His hands rubbed the tops of her thighs as she writhed sensually beneath him, then he moved to push her dress up even further to reveal her naked breasts. He held them and fondled their fullness, bringing her warm pink nipples to hardened peaks between his fingers. He heard her cry out and was aware of the soft groans coming from his own mouth.

The pressure he felt through his shorts threatened to release, and he had to concentrate really hard. With his arms outstretched, hands still fondling her breasts, he used his teeth again and pulled her panties to the side, they rested against his cheek while his lips and tongue found the wet, hot flesh he craved. She whimpered at his touch, and he brought his hands back down, caressing the sides of her body and stopping at her hips so he could pull the material completely out of his way. He brought the panties down and over her legs, leaving her with nothing but her dress up around her neck, which he sat up to carefully lift off her. He threw it to the floor and bent back down to kiss her slick, wet opening. His tongue went right to her clit, and he sucked and laved her with his tongue until she arched her hips right up into his face, pressing her smooth mound hard against him and he felt her explosive release all over his skin.

"Oh, yeah, baby, that's it." He wanted more -- she was so great.

"Oh, my God, Rafe." Ali's chest was heaving. Holy God!

He couldn't get enough, and so he took his fingers and spread her swollen lips apart. His tongue found the same spot again, and he sucked and licked and touched. This time when she came, he drank her in, and he could feel her reaching for him and trying to get to his shorts. He came up, laughing huskily. "I'm not done yet."

"Please," she groaned, "I need to feel you." Ali was desperate for him; what he was doing to her felt like an assault on all of her nerve endings. She was so wet and open for him that she throbbed where his mouth had been, ached for him to fill that opening and bury himself deep inside her.

Rafe wasn't about to argue, so he got up and stepped out of his shorts quickly. He brought himself down beside her, and she rolled onto her good side and grasped him. Her hand was like soft silk on his hard cock, and he moved deliberately inside her grip, torturing himself. "Oh, God, Ali, your touch is heaven."

"Rafe, please," she begged softly, "I need you inside me, deep, deep inside me."

He saw the need in her eyes, the fullness in her lips from his kisses, and the sheen of sweat on her skin. He knew she was more than ready, and still he prolonged it. "I told you, I'm not done. You don't know how badly I want to keep pleasing you and watching you come. It's exquisite, Ali. Let me enjoy this a little more, and then I promise to bury myself so deep inside you and fill you up with everything I have."

His words were whispered so softly in her ear, with the heat of his breath on her skin and his hands slowly caressing her breasts as he spoke, Ali could only throw her head back in submission, waiting for the next soul-shattering attack on her senses.

He helped to roll her to her back again, taking care to keep her shoulder stable, and then his hand traveled ever so slowly to the sweet spot he craved. Her hands gripped the spread underneath her in anticipation, and he grinned down at her, loving that he could make her come so forcefully -- she held nothing back. He bent his head to her breast and moved his middle finger slowly around her clit in a lazy circle while he sucked on a taut nipple. His cock pressed against her side, and he felt her reach for it with one hand. He watched her as her head sank into the pillow and her heavy eyes shut. She was stroking him as he stroked her, her pace quickening and matching that of his finger swirling on her swollen bud. He increased the pressure and speed until her hips rose up, and he felt and saw everything tighten. Her muscles clenched and she gripped him tighter, emitting a soft moan of pleasure from him while her body spasmed and she cried out again, her bottom sinking back on the bed, her legs splayed in utter surrender.

Ali lay there with her eyes still closed, her chest rising and falling with each labored breath, and her mind and body somewhere in another dimension. What he had just done to her had left her reeling. She was almost embarrassed and afraid to show him the vulnerable look he would clearly see in her eyes. He had stripped her bare. She had just given everything up under his touch, and it was overwhelming. She had never experienced anything like it. "You're like magic," she whispered, her eyes still closed.

"Open your eyes, Ali, and see what you do to me." Rafe looked into her eyes and saw the hesitancy there. He brought her hand to his cock again and used it to help him roll the condom over his length, her eyes never leaving his. He positioned his body above her and leaned his head down to kiss her lips. "You're beautiful, Ali, everything about you -- your taste, your smell, your touch. I love you."

Oh, God! "I love you too, Rafe." Tears stung her eyes as he entered her, slowly and deliberately.

She rose her hips up to meet him and found herself moving with a desperation that resonated from deep in her heart. She wanted to feel him touch her soul. She wanted their bodies to become one, and knowing he loved her intensified all her feelings. As she wrapped her legs around him and used her hands on his hips to push him deeper inside, she knew he could feel it too.

Her eyes watched as his gorgeous body moved over hers, the muscles in his arms straining as he held himself up, his tight abs flexing as he moved his hips to thrust in and out of her. She was more than turned on -- she was filled with an all-consuming passion and lust for him, and she reached up with her good arm to cradle his neck and bring his head down to hers so she could kiss him with all of that passion and lust. When he kissed her back she could feel the love flow through them both. Tears came careening from her lids and onto her cheeks, their salt finding its way between their kisses. She moved her bad arm up and around him so that both her arms could hold him tight against her as they moved together, the weight of him not crushing her, but bringing him closer to her heart.

Rafe kissed her, matching her intensity, his emotions threatening to spill forth like Ali's. He could taste the salt of her tears and knew without a doubt why they were there. He felt it, too, the raw, deep need to be as deep inside her and as close to her as he could. The fact that they had professed their love for each other had amplified their sex. He never imagined it could get any better than what they had shared just days and nights ago, but it was better, so much better. He knew without a doubt that she was his now, and he was letting her know it with each glorious thrust inside of her. It was a primitive feeling that over took him, especially when he'd seen the passion and want in her devastating green eyes.

He was really pounding into her now, and she against him, and he knew the end was near. He could feel her muscles contracting around him, squeezing his cock and bringing forth the start of a mind-blowing orgasm. He kept pressing into the tightness, feeling the spasms rack him again and again, every muscle in his body taut with the onslaught of his explosive release, made even more so with the breaking dam of Ali's own release. It surrounded him, dripping between them, sealing them together.

He lay on top of her, kissing her, their bodies still joined, her breasts pressed against his chest, her arms and legs wrapped around him. He came up on his elbows to relieve her but not wanting to break their connection. He kissed her eye lids and the remnants of her tears; he kissed her cheeks, her nose, her mouth, and her chin. "That was incredible. Promise me you'll stay naked in my bed forever."

She laughed, feeling sexy and feminine underneath him. "I promise, as long as you promise to do all those same things again."

He nibbled on her earlobe. "Deal." He reluctantly slipped out of her warmth and moved to lay beside her on his back, her hand resting on his chest and caressing him.

"That really was unbelievably great." She stared up at the ceiling, smiling.

"You're unbelievably great." He bent to kiss her.

"My shoulder doesn't even hurt," she realized. "I didn't need the Vicodin -- I just needed you."

He laughed. "Well, you can throw those away. I'm prepared to give you an overdose."

"Yes, and then I won't be able to say things I won't remember later on."

"Like telling me that you love me?" He grinned wickedly.

Ali's eyes got wide, and she laughed. "Is that what I said?"

"Yup. In the hospital, you said, 'goodnight, Rafe, I love you,' and made me the happiest guy on the planet until I remembered you were on drugs." He laughed. "And then I could only pray I'd hear it again, you know, without them."

"Well, sometimes the truth comes out while you're under the influence." She smiled at him. "Now you know that either way I meant it." Ali sucked on her bottom lip; the words still new and hard to say. "I love you, Rafe." Her chest tightened at the words.

Rafe sat up on his side, looking down at her, about to tell her, but his eyes got wide instead at the blood he saw seeping through her bandage. "Shit, Ali, you're bleeding. I was too rough." He felt horrible as he sat up to tend to her, but she just lay there, still, looking up at him expectantly, and he cursed himself. She had just told him she loved him again, and he was talking about her shoulder. She didn't seem to be in pain, so he forgot it for the moment.

"Ali." He placed a hand on her smooth, flat stomach, feeling her flinch at his touch. He moved his hand along her soft skin. "I want to apologize for the night I left you in that cottage. I kicked myself all that night and all the next day. I should have told you then that I was in love with you, but I was scared. I was scared you'd think I was crazy." He saw tears forming again, and he moved his hand to her face and smiled slightly. “I saw doubt in your eyes and hurt, and I let it stay there because I was afraid, and I’m sorry.”

“I was scared, too, Rafe, but after last night I made up my mind that I didn’t care -- I was going to let you know. Life’s too short, and I feel lucky to be alive, thanks to you.”

He kissed her again and whispered against her lips, “I love you Ali...I love you.”

CHAPTER THIRTY-SIX

Nicki parked the convertible in the sandy lot adjacent to the general store and walked across the street to the outdoor bar, where a man played an old summer song on guitar under a palm-thatched hut. She spotted Jason right away, kicking back with a Corona and talking with a waitress who was being plenty attentive. Nicki grinned as she approached. The Fuller children were all blessed with the good looks and charm, that was for sure.

She sneaked right up on him when the waitress walked away to tend to her customers. "Do you always drink alone?"

"Only until a gorgeous girl walks up and joins me." He smiled, happy to see her.

Nicki pretended to look around. "Well, you're shit out of luck. I'll have to do."

"You're pretty funny." Jason stood while she sat beside him. He cursed his little brother for the second time that day.

A waiter appeared, and Nicki ordered a fruity vodka concoction.

"So how was work today? Ali told me about the newspaper job. That sounds like fun."

"Yeah, it is so far. I typed mostly today and turned in my copies. Tomorrow's my big debut." She smiled, raising her brows, and took a sip of the water the waiter had just left.

"Well, here's to Lois Lane." Jason clinked his beer bottle to her glass.

She laughed. "Well we'll see about that, but it's exciting anyway, and now I'm off until Monday."

"So we're getting drunk, right?"

"That was my plan. I don't know what the hell you were thinking."

He laughed. She was a little wise ass; no wonder Matt liked her. "Hey, I'm already ahead by one."

"I'll catch up -- no worries!" As if on cue, the waiter appeared with her drink, and she took a long sip as if to prove it.

"Are you hungry?"

"I could nibble on something, but if I'm going to get drunk, real food can't enter into the equation."

"Oh, I see." Jason picked up a menu. "There's a method to your madness."

She nodded, laughing.

"Nachos?"

"Too fattening."

"Wings?"

"Too messy."

"Oh, look, here's a nice vegetable platter with fat-free dip." Jason feigned interest.

Nicki cocked her head. "I recognize sarcasm when I hear it." She smirked and acquiesced. "All right, I'll eat a few nachos. That's what you're supposed to eat when you're getting drunk, right?"

"Now you're talking." Jason signaled the waiter, and Jason placed their order. They both sat back and listened to the man cover Buffet on his guitar. He had a pretty good voice, too.

"This is nice, huh? I could get used to this." Nicki relaxed and sipped her drink. It was delicious and going down fast.

"I could, too. I've never been here before."

"Oh, you'll have to come back when you have more time. My grandmother's house is always open to your whole family."

"Wow, that's a generous offer. I might take you up on that someday."

"Please do. I'm not kidding." Nicki drank from her glass. "This is sooo strong, by the way. I'm already buzzed."

"You're a lightweight," he teased. "How are you going to keep up with Matt?"

"I can hold my own!" she challenged.

"I don't believe you for a second, but okay."

She laughed. "All right, so tell me, why is a great-looking guy like you still single?"

He gave her a wide smile. "You think I'm great-looking? Wait 'til I tell Matt -- that'll really burn him!"

"Stop, will you, I'm serious." Nicki did think Jason was really handsome. No one could compare to Matt in her eyes, though. He was a sex god of mythical proportions, and she got excited just picturing him. She wondered if he was wearing a tool belt right this very minute somewhere on a job site. God, she was buzzed.

"I don't even want to know what you were just thinking about." Jason might be single, but he recognized the look on Nicki's face and knew it wasn't directed at him. Damn that Matt!

Nicki laughed and acutely blushed.

"I'm single because I'm a workaholic."

"That's just sad. Don't you at least go out with your friends?"

"Sure, to games, but most of my friends are married."

"I could set you up with so many women it's not even funny." Nicki could think of two friends right away.

"I do all right on my own, thank you." He feigned indignation.

"Yeah, I'm not talking about Red Sox groupies you pick up at the Cask & Flagon. I'm talking about someone you can have a relationship with."

He grinned. "There's nothing wrong with those girls. They're fun and vivacious."

"Translation -- they'll have sex with you, and they have big boobs."

He cracked up. "And that's bad because?"

Nicki liked him -- he was cute, and they got along well. "That can't last."

"Well, when I want something to last, I'll make a go of it."

"So you're not looking?" Nicki persisted.

"When you're looking for it, you don't find it. It has to smack you in the face, surprise you."

"Ooh, that's deep," she teased, "but I do believe you're correct."

"So is that what happened with you and Matt?" Jason gave her a small smile, hoping he wasn't prying.

Nicki smirked. "Is this on or off the record?"

"Off, Lois."

"He definitely surprised me." She laughed at the memory of him standing before her on the pool deck.

"It sounds like there's a story behind that."

The waiter set their nachos before them, and they ordered another round of drinks. They picked at the food, and Nicki was feeling good. She was happy to finally have someone to talk to about Matt. Ali got too freaked out, but Jason was a guy, and she knew he'd be able to handle it.

She grinned mischievously. "I hope you can handle this better than your sister."

"Ali's not cool with you and Matt?" Jason hadn't got that impression.

"No, no, she is." Nicki laughed. "Just not the parts that, you know..."

Jason grinned, nodding. "I'll try to be a good listener."

Nicki rolled her eyes. "Thanks, I figured you would. Guys don't care -- sex is sex."

Jason laughed. "Well, there are some things off limits, but you're mostly right. Tell the story, will you?"

Nicki laughed at his impatience. "All right, all right." She told him how Matt had arrived that first day at the house.

Jason's mouth hung open, and then he leaned back and laughed his ass off. "Are you telling me he came into the backyard, and you were lying there topless? C'mon!"

Nicki laughed. "I'm not kidding! It was mortifying!"

"Not for him!" Jason cracked up.

Nicki smiled shyly. "Well, no, he seemed to not mind so much."

"*That*, Nicki, I can say without a doubt, is the understatement of the year." Jason took a swig of his beer, shaking his head, and cursed his brother for the third time. "But there's more, right?"

She smiled. "Have you got five hours?"

"I got all night, sweetheart." He clinked her glass again. "Go on."

Nicki told him everything, from the first time she saw Matt working out in his bedroom to the late nights watching Letterman and to the agony of seeing him go out on dates. She told him how she'd put him out of her mind and ended up in a mediocre relationship at school, and even how Dan had gone on to marry only six months after their breakup.

"So you had put him out of your mind and were moving on," he said it as a matter of fact.

"Yes, I mean I was young. Everyone has a first love, whether it's reciprocated or not, right? I had to get over it."

"And then he showed up here. What did you do?"

"Well, after realizing I wasn't hallucinating, I cursed my grandmother!"

Jason smiled, encouraging her to go on.

"She set the whole thing up! " She filled him in on how her grandmother had always known.

"Wow, she's like Yoda."

Nicki couldn't stop laughing. "Exactly!"

"So now what?"

"I don't know. I'm just waiting for his fine ass to return." Nicki looked down at her drink and stirred the remnants.

The waiter returned with new ones just in time. Jason said, "Let's call him."

"What?" Nicki was slightly drunk now, and she wasn't sure that was such a good idea.

"Let's call him and ask him when he's getting his fine ass back here." It was that moment that the waitress Jason had been talking to earlier chose to reappear. She paused only briefly, looked from Jason to Nicki, and moved on. They in turn looked at each other and cracked up. "So much for that." He laughed. "I think my ass is much better by the way."

"Just ask you, huh?" Nicki grinned. "I'm going to the ladies' room. You can do whatever you want."

"Anything you want me to say?"

She rolled her eyes. "What, are we in high school?"

"I'm just saying, I'm his brother, and I can convey things to him in a way that maybe you can't."

"Trust me, I've conveyed quite a bit to him in a short amount of time."

Jason's jaw dropped again as Nicki walked away. He was chuckling and feeling pretty good as he dialed Matt's number to curse him over the phone.

Matt answered the phone and smirked, hearing the buzz in his brother's voice. "Where are you? And no, I can't give you a ride home."

"I'm not legless yet, but I am sitting in a nice little outdoor bar up in Captiva, getting my drink on with your girl."

Matt's heart beat a little faster, and he felt a stab of jealousy. "Oh, yeah?"

"Don't worry -- all she's talking about is you, you little prick."

"That's a nice endearment, Jay. Is that jealousy I hear in your tone?" Matt was now smiling from ear to ear.

"Maybe a little," Jason admitted, "but we've become friends in the last two hours over nachos and drinks, so you're safe."

"Well, that's good to hear. Is she right there?"

"No, she went to the restroom. I told her I was going to call you to ask when you're getting your fine ass back here -- her words, not mine."

"Glad to hear that." And he was. "I'm coming tomorrow, but don't tell her that."

"Why the hell not?"

"I want to surprise her."

"Aren't you afraid you'll piss her off? She seems a little unsure about where she stands with you. By the way, where does she stand with you, because after what I just heard…well..." Jason decided to let Matt answer before he said anything further.

"What did you just hear?" Matt's curiosity was definitely piqued.

"Answer me first."

"If you can control your Corona-speak, I'll tell you."

"I'm not going to say anything to her." Jason watched as Nicki returned. He mouthed to her that it was Matt and held a finger to his lips conspiringly. He rolled his eyes when she actually blushed. Jeez. "Did I tell you you're a little prick by the way?"

"Yeah, you mentioned that, and -- I'm in love with her."

Jason whistled and stared across at Nicki. "Okay, I can understand that."

Nicki listened and wondered why Jason sounded so disappointed.

"I don't know how she's going to react to that, but I suppose it's best if you tell her yourself."

"She's sitting back down now, right?" Matt rolled his eyes. He was going to strangle Jason when he saw him.

"That's affirmative, baby brother. I should go."

"Tell her I'll call her tomorrow."

"Okay, as long as you realize that's just cruel."

Matt ground his teeth, "Jay," he warned, "goodbye." He was dying to know what Nicki had told Jason. He was dying to get back there.

"Don't tell me he's not coming tomorrow." She'd heard enough of the conversation, and she wanted to cry, but she was too pissed. She took a long sip of her drink.

Jason couldn't stand to see her so upset, especially when he knew the truth. Screw it.

"I don't like to see that unhappy look on your face. We were having such a good time."

"*You* had to go and call him," she complained. "My ignorance was bliss."

He laughed. "You're right, it's my fault, but I can make it up to you even if Matt might hate me."

"How?" she asked suspiciously.

"By telling you that he's definitely coming back tomorrow."

She squealed with happiness, drawing a few looks from the crowd. "Really? Really?"

"God." He smirked. "The news isn't that great."

"Oh, yes it is!" She slammed her palm down on the table. "And he didn't want you to tell me that?"

"He wants to surprise you."

Nicki put her hand over her heart, "Oh, how nice. And you're such a good friend telling me, thank you." She grinned. "A lousy brother, though," she teased.

He laughed. "Can you blame me?"

She caught his innuendo and smiled, "Oh, Jason, you'll make some woman very happy someday."

"I'm enjoying making a lot of women happy now."

"Oh, God!" she groaned. "Hey, I love this song. This guy's pretty good."

"He's all right." Jason glanced over at the guitar player.

"Matt told me you guys play," Nicki said as she enjoyed her drink and the music.

"He told you that?" Jason grinned. Now he knew Matt was in love if he told Nicki about his playing. And when she heard him, she'd be blown away.

"Why are you grinning?" Nicki squinted her eyes at him.

Jason pondered over the perfect opportunity before him. "What did he say about it?"

Nicki tilted her head a little, hesitant. "Just that he's been playing since he was in high school and that you have, too. Why, is he not very good or something?" Nicki would feel bad for him if that were the case. He talked as if he loved it.

Jason had to bite back his laughter at Nicki's little nose all scrunched up on her face, worried that Matt might not be good on the guitar. How sweet. This was too good.

"He always wished he could play like me but..." he paused for effect, "...he's really not that good."

"Oh, no." Nicki instantly felt sorry for him. "Does he think he is?"

"Yeah, I'm afraid he does. I let him play with me but never in a crowd. I wouldn't want anyone to heckle him, you know?"

"You're a good brother after all." She smiled and giggled a little. "I know it's not funny, but is he that bad?"

Jason let out a little bit of the real laugher he was holding back. "It's pretty bad."

Nicki made a face of sympathy. So he wasn't good. So what? He excelled in far more important areas. "Well, he could keep learning, right? As long as he enjoys it, that's all that counts."

Jason took a gulp of beer to stop from laughing. "Yeah, maybe in time." Truth was, the kid could be on stage today with any current band, singing and playing the shit out of the guitar. He figured Nicki would hear him for herself someday soon, so he couldn't resist the harmless joke.

"I'm officially toast. Want to go back to the house?" Nicki leaned back in her chair.

"Sure," he agreed. "Leave your car -- I'll drive."

"Okay, I can walk up and get it in the morning."

Jason paid the bill, shooing Nicki's money away. "It was my pleasure. This was a blast."

"I had fun, too, but I'll pay tomorrow night."

"What's tomorrow night?"

"We're all going out to celebrate my name in the paper!" she sang.

"Sounds great. Where we going?" They walked across to the parking lot, and hc opened the passenger door for her.

"Just to the resort up the street. They have a cool bar with a really good rock cover band. They play every Friday night."

"Really?" Jason got in the driver's side, his wheels turning.

CHAPTER THIRTY-SEVEN

Matt made it to the airport in the nick of time. Traffic had been a bitch on 93, and he had just enough time to grab a cup of coffee before they called his flight number to board.

He went over the Howards' paperwork on the flight. He knew he could get them to sign a deal. They had called him yesterday afternoon and gave him the go-ahead to negotiate. He was now looking at a signed accepted offer to present to Ali. She'd be psyched. The Howards had followed his advice and split the difference. The buyers made out great, and the Howards could still retire comfortably.

By the time he collected his bag and rented a car, it was two-thirty. He stopped for a quick bite to eat on his way to the islands and was driving over the causeway an hour later.

He took a left at the four-way and headed to the Beach News offices. Nicki would probably still be at work, and he thought he would try to surprise her there. If she was out doing her thing, he would just head to the house.

When he pulled into the parking lot a few minutes later, he was surprised by all the activity around the building. Inside the Beach News, a small older woman informed him that Nicki was off today -- which he would have known if he'd talked to her the night before, he thought. He had tried to call, and it had gone right to voicemail. He hoped Jay wasn't right, that she was pissed at him for not telling her when he was coming. He wondered how long the two of them had stayed out.

"What's going on next door?" he asked the woman, curious at all the suits going in and out of the office outside next to them.

The little old lady leaned forward and whispered, "It's the FBI. They've been here since yesterday, confiscating all the records that belonged to the realtor there. Barry Stoddman, have you heard of him?"

Matt shook his head. "No, can't say that I have. Thanks, though, I'll try Nicki at home." He left the newspaper and glanced over at the realtor's office. This obviously had something to do with Rafe's case.

Before he got back in the car he picked up the folded-over paper that was the Beach News for the week and paged through it. There she was on page two, and he smiled. There was a small picture and a paragraph about her, welcoming her to the staff. At the bottom it gave the pages of the two interviews she'd done and credited her with an article on the front page. The front page? He turned back to the front and saw the small headline in the right-hand corner. "Local Investor Turned Drug Smuggler/Murderer," by Nicole Thompson. Wow.

Saving the best for last, Matt opened to the interviews first and read a nice little piece about the science teacher who just completed her first year at the Sanibel school, her accomplishments in the field, and the strides she hoped to make with the science program there. Her second piece was about the new show at the Island Playhouse. She had interviewed a couple of cast members, informing everyone of their upcoming performances and their experience and accreditations. It was short and to the point and well written. Matt was proud of her, and it was cool to see her name in print. He flipped back to the front page, wondering how she possibly managed that her first week on the job, and then he read it.

Most of us know Captiva as a small barrier island in the Gulf of Mexico, known for its breath-taking sunsets and its abundant shell-filled beaches, but to one local businessman Captiva was merely a conduit for drugs, dangerous drugs to be sold on the streets, drugs that impair and even sometimes kill the person who takes them. These kind of drugs were smuggled onto Captiva Island Wednesday afternoon.

Nearly a million dollars' worth of cocaine was confiscated Wednesday by the FBI after audio surveillance revealed that the drugs would be coming in on a delivery barge Wednesday morning to a construction site out on Captiva. The drugs were concealed in ordinary five-gallon construction buckets of what appeared to be plaster -- plaster that was to cover the walls of a luxurious home being built on the beach in Captiva , owned by one Xavier Constantine D'nafrio. Known to many on the islands as a recent local investor and contributor, Mr. D'nafrio is also the owner and CEO of a major retail management company. A company that finds specific locals to open up large chain stores and franchises.

D'nafrio made his mark nearly two years ago when he started purchasing failed businesses and properties among the islands. Talk among the locals is that D'nafrio planned to place a variety of popular retail stores into many of those recently purchased properties. However, it was his latest endeavor on Captiva that garnered many protests and an outcry from area residents, due to an imposing structure on the Gulf that he plans to call home. According to sources from the LAOB (Locals Against Over Building), the structure does not adhere to the coastal construction line, as all new construction must, and neither does it adhere to the "points of light," building code, to ensure unobstructed Gulf views from neighboring homes. The LAOB's most important concern thus far is the effect the structure will have on the environment, specifically, the habitats of the nesting sea turtles. Still months away from completion, the site did, however, lend itself to being an ideal spot for drug trafficking.

According to Special Agent Rafe McDonough, the construction site has been under surveillance for a number of weeks. Just one week ago, nine Cuban refugees came ashore to the beach front that abuts Xavier D'nafrio's property, bringing with them four kilograms of the "club drug" Ecstasy. According to sources at the DEA, that equates to approximately 14,000 pills, an estimated $150,000.00 street value.

Allegedly, one refugee in particular was offered five thousand dollars to transport the drugs from a meth lab in Cuba that operates as a tobacco plant in which Xavier D'nafrio has a financial interest. The majority owner, Jay Scintillo a Cuban businessman and owner of several downtown

Miami nightclubs, couldn't be reached for comment and is actively being sought by the FBI. Eight of the nine refugees were released after questioning, and the one man still remains in the custody of Immigration and Customs Enforcement until it is known if he will be called to testify.

Continued on page 5

Matt flipped to page five.

The cocaine smuggled onto Captiva Wednesday was confiscated at an Estero warehouse owned by D'nafrio. It had been delivered there by truck from D'nafrio's construction site in Captiva. Special Agent Rafe McDonough was on the scene, along with Special Agent Mike Caplan, when the delivery arrived. It was then that the two agents were witness to the murder of Juan Travez, 23, of Miami, the driver of the delivery truck, who was shot and killed in cold blood by Xavier D'nafrio. Mr. D'nafrio is facing lifetime imprisonment and at press time was out on a million-dollar bond. Upon his arrest, all of Mr. D'nafrio's assets were quickly seized by the government, including the 10,000-square-foot beach front home in Captiva. Along with his impending murder charge, Mr. D'nafrio is facing tax evasion charges by the IRS in regards to his retail management company.

And as an added mar on an otherwise sleepy community, realtor Barry Stoddman, known on the islands as D'nafrio's right-hand man and business confidant, has been arrested on drug smuggling and distribution charges. He faces a minimum of ten years imprisonment. Also in FBI custody are Stoddman's secretary, Holly Mann, believed to have participated in the voyage of the refugees, and her sister Misty Spencer, believed to have knowledge of Wednesday's activities. The FBI have appropriated the offices of East End Realty for the investigation. Local officials were not available for comment due to the tarpon running.

Matt laughed, thinking she's awesome.

In related news, Timothy Mann, Holly Mann's son, and friend Sean Smith were also detained, then arrested Wednesday night for breaking and entering, assault and battery and illegal possession of drugs. Mann's husband and father to Timothy resides at the Okeechobee Correctional

Institution and could not be reached for comment.

Beautiful. Matt took a couple of extras, got back in the car, and headed up toward the house. He was so proud of Nicki -- he couldn't believe she was on the front page. He called Ali's phone on his way. He knew she was okay but reading the list of charges and knowing they had happened to her made him sick to his stomach.

"Do you realize it's almost four o'clock in the afternoon?" Ali asked as she lay, spent, beside Rafe.

"Um-hum."

"We're still in bed."

"Uh-hum." He pulled her right up against him.

"What are you trying to do to me?" She laughed lazily.

"Remember I told you I wished you could be naked in my bed all the time? I'm making my wish come true." He moved his fingers softly over her breasts.

"Well, we've already had breakfast *and* lunch in bed, so I think we should make an effort to get up for dinner. What do you think?"

"Nope." He nuzzled her neck and started kissing her collarbone, moving his lips steadily downward.

She laughed. "Aren't you sick of me yet?"

Rafe popped his head up and said seriously. "I cannot get enough of you."

Ali warmed at his tone and reached for him.

The sound of her phone ringing made her pause. "I should get that."

"Do you have to?"

She nodded apologetically. "I haven't answered all day."

"I'll get it for you, but try to be quick." Rafe got off the bed and walked to the table where Ali's phone sat ringing. He brought it over and handed it to her. Ali took it and watched him walk out of the room naked. His body was so damn incredible, and she couldn't get enough of him, either.

She opened the phone and recognized the number. "Hi, Matt," she answered happy to hear from her brother. "Where are you?"

"Hey! I'm on the island. Are you at the house?"

"Oh, good, but no, I'm at Rafe's cottage. Nicki and Jason should be there, though."

"I don't want Nicki to know I'm here yet. Can I come to you?"

Ali looked down at herself. "Yes, of course. How far away are you?"

"Twenty minutes. How's the shoulder, kid?"

"It's okay." Ali gave him the cottage number and said she would see him in a few.

"Rafe!" she called when she had hung up.

He appeared gloriously in the door frame. Her gaze sauntered over him.

"Matt's on his way. He'll be here in twenty minutes."

Rafe frowned. "But I had big plans for us."

Ali grinned. "I can see that, but he's coming now, so would you help me in the shower?"

Rafe gave an enthusiastic nod and led her into the bathroom. He ran the water and waited for it to warm.

"You know, I can get a lot done in twenty minutes," she told him, taking the length of him in her hand.

He pressed into it and groaned. "Or less."

She laughed and sat down on the generous edge of the tub. "C'mere," she said seductively.

Rafe obliged and watched as Ali took him fully in her mouth. Oh, man, did he love her. He ran his hands through her hair as she held him and sucked him, looking up at him as she did it. Oh, yeah. And when he was just about to his boiling point, he pulled back and led her into the warm shower. He turned her body so that her bandages didn't get too wet and so that her back was to his front, then he kissed her neck possessively. He put one hand on her stomach and one on her back and bent her at the waist with purpose. He heard her small gasp, and grinned as he placed her good arm up against the back wall so that she could rest her hand there.

Ali cried out as Rafe entered her from behind. The feeling was shocking, but yet so familiar after their hours of lovemaking. She closed her eyes, taking him in. It was so intense as he moved in and out of her slowly, his hands holding her at her hips, the warm water spilling around them, and then she opened her eyes back up, and turned around to look at him. They stared at each other, realizing this was happening without a condom.

He hadn't even given it a thought as he'd entered her. "You feel so good, Ali," he groaned. She felt so good around him, he didn't want to leave her.

Somewhere between the night before and that afternoon they had discussed safe sex and past partners. They had both had a recent clean bill of health, but Ali wasn't on the pill and feeling him inside her now, she so wished that she were because, oh, God, he felt so good in there.

She knew they were playing with fire and that all it took was a drop, but she moved against him anyway and let him give it to her good right under the pelting spray of water. He held her tight, making sure she didn't slip, and she turned to watch him. He was watching her, too, as he slammed into her again and again. She felt him start to contract inside her, and she carefully slipped off the length of him and turned to hold him in her hand, forgetting about her bandages, just taking him in her hand and coaxing him to come all over her skin with a satisfied grunt. She tilted her head to kiss him and hugged him tight with her good arm. She loved him so much.

Rafe's knees were weak as he kissed her. She had felt so good, even though he hadn't been smart. "That was dumb, and my fault."

"You didn't hear me objecting, did you?" Ali felt even closer to him than before.

"I didn't really give you a chance." He had just wanted to feel as close to her as possible, and it was great.

"I'm not worried about it, are you?" She could think of worse things to happen than having his baby.

Rafe looked at her. No, he wasn't worried about it; in fact, there was a selfish part of him that would be extremely happy if she got pregnant. But he just shook his head no and lifted her chin to kiss her. "I love you, green eyes."

"I love you, too."

They stood, holding each other under the spray, and he started to wash her.

"Your hair feels so good in my hands. It's like silk." He shampooed her, and she slumped against him.

"That feels soo good. I could fall asleep right against you," she moaned.

"Except that you told your brother to come here," he reminded her playfully.

"I know, I know," she whined.

"It's okay, it's great that he's back." He rinsed her hair and washed both of their bodies before shutting the water off. "I'm going to have to re-bandage you."

She smiled. "Okay."

They stepped out, and he carefully unwrapped the wet bandages from Ali's shoulder and arm. They needed to be changed anyway, since some bleeding had occurred while they probably weren't being too careful in bed. "Am I hurting you?"

"Quite the contrary." She smiled loving, that he was caring for her.

He smiled and got the last of them off, depositing them in the trash and cringing at the large area of stitches and staples that held her skin together. He patted it dry with a clean towel and couldn't help but feel remorse.

Ali saw the look on Rafe's face and smoothed the wet hair back from his forehead. "It wasn't your fault. If you didn't break his arm, he may have shot me right in the chest."

He couldn't even think about that. He would have been a broken man if he had lost her. He kissed her lips softly. "Don't remind me," he said quietly, and found the clean bandages on the counter that she had taken from her bag, along with her toothbrush. He placed a large square adhesive bandage over the wound, then wound the clean cotton around her upper shoulder and arm expertly. "Too tight?"

"Just right," she grinned. "You're hired."

He bent to kiss her and was aware they still stood there naked and dripping.

"I don't know how long I'll make it out tonight," she warned as he dried the rest of her body off.

"Just say the word, and we're back here in a flash." He smiled. When he moved the towel between her legs, they heard the knock at the door.

Ali pouted. "I was hoping you could have finished before he arrived." She looked down as his hands came away.

"Don't worry -- when we get back here tonight, I'll start something you'll never want me to finish."

"Promise?" She grinned.

He groaned, throwing the towel around himself, and he left the room.

Ali leaned against the wall. How was she going to handle this at the end of his four weeks?

Rafe threw on a pair of board shorts and went to open the door. "Hey man, come in. Glad to have you back."

Matt shook Rafe's outstretched hand, taking in the wet hair and half-dressed man before him. "I hope I'm not interrupting." Matt grinned.

Rafe actually felt himself blush and turned away quickly. "Not at all. Have a seat on the porch -- I'll get us a beer. Ali will be out in a minute."

"How's her arm?" Matt called out.

"Good. She doesn't complain about the pain, even though it's got-ta hurt like hell," he told Matt, bringing him a beer and joining him on the porch.

"Nicki told me what happened, but I'd like to hear it from you."

Rafe told him his account of the story and all about nabbing D'nafrio, too.

"So that's why the Feds are all over that real estate office?"

Rafe nodded, taking a sip of the cold beer.

"I read Nicki's piece in the Beach News. Did you help her out?"

"I gave her all the info I could. Ali and I were so happy to see she got on the front page."

"I know, I can't believe it. Looks like she couldn't have done it without you, so thank you."

"My pleasure. I just did it to get my name in the paper."

Matt laughed. "You can send it to your mom."

"Don't think I won't." Rafe laughed, too.

"I spoke to Nicki this morning about it, and apparently local officials were leaning on the paper not to print anything about it since D'nafrio is such a big contributor to the islands. Nicki said the paper basically told them to screw, freedom of the press and all that."

"Typical small-town politics." Matt shook his head.

Ali stepped onto the porch, freshly bandaged and dressed, and smiled seeing her brother relaxed and talking with Rafe. He jumped up when he saw her.

"Oh, Al, c'mere, bud." Matt took her in his arms and embraced her gently. He pulled back to check out her bandage, then embraced her again silently.

Rafe smiled as he watched the two of them and as tears welled up in Ali's eyes. He was touched at their close relationship, and because this was all new, a little jealous, too.

"Don't make me cry, you jerk! You are so lucky you came back here!" she scolded him.

He laughed, pinching her cheek playfully. "Oh, yeah, why's that?" He sat back down next to Rafe and winked at him.

Rafe knew Matt loved riling Ali, and he laughed.

Ali shot him a pretend look of reprimand. "Don't encourage him, Rafe. That's all I need." It made her happy that the two of them got along so well.

"I'm not saying a word." He grinned and drank his beer.

"Nicki is why! For God's sake, you took long enough getting back here! She's been walking around not even knowing how you feel about her. Meanwhile, there are a ton of guys ready to take your place!"

Matt's facial expression changed dramatically, from good to bad. "Like who?"

"I knew that would wipe the smirk off your face. *Like* Rafe's friend Mike -- he's FBI, by the way," she added for effect. "There's this drummer she met when we first got here, and even Jason, for God's sake!"

Oh, shit. Rafe looked at Matt and caught the look of betrayal that flashed across his eyes. He had to straighten this out quick. "First of all, I wasn't here when Mike hit on *both* of them, *and* he was informed that very night that both women are unavailable." He pulled Ali onto his lap but not before he gave her a playful slap on the rear. "And he has quickly moved on. He's probably at the pool right now with his new friend." Rafe looked Matt in the eye. "I would never have let that happen, man. I consider you a friend."

Matt nodded believing him. “Thanks.” But he was still mad, and he turned to Ali. “Jason? What the fu...?”

Ali held up a hand. “Don’t get the wrong idea,” she yelled out before he could finish his question. “I’m just saying, he obviously couldn’t help but notice her, and he is a red-blooded male, so I just think you were playing with fire being away like that. She shrugged her disapproval.

“Hey!” Matt said defensively, “I had to go, and I would have thought I could trust my own sister and brother to have my back!” Jesus, should he be worried?

“We do,” Ali said, backing off, seeing that she had upset him. “I’m just giving you shit on behalf of my best friend. She’s been moping around for the past few days, and don’t tell her I told you so.”

“Wow, and here I was all concerned for you and even brought you a surprise,” he huffed. “Forget it now.” He took a drink and grinned at Rafe, who was trying not to laugh.

Ali hit Rafe in the shoulder. “Ouch!” He laughed. “You did just torment the guy. Give him a break -- he’s here now right?”

Ali ignored him, smiling. “What’s the surprise?”

“She was really moping?”

“C’mon, Matt, please? I’m sorry, okay?”

“This is a nice little place you got, Rafe, huh?” he asked, his turn to torment Ali.

“Yeah, it’s pretty cozy,” Rafe agreed with a grin. “Want another beer?”

“Sure, if you’re getting up.”

Ali looked from one to the other. She smiled that they were both teasing her, and she stood up so Rafe could get up for the beer. She sat right back down when he left. “Okay, I’m really sorry -- I didn’t mean to mislead you about the guys. Rafe’s friend was harmless, and I told Jason right off the bat that you and Nicki were together.”

Matt squinted his eyes at her. “How sorry? Because that wasn’t very nice. You scared me a little," he admitted.

"Real sorry," she said seriously. "C'mon, tell me."

He laughed, giving in. "We've got a done deal, little sister." He placed the envelope he'd been carrying in his back pocket on her lap.

"What?" Ali didn't know what he was talking about, and she opened the envelope. She unfolded a real estate contract and moved her gaze to the bottom where she saw the Howards' signatures, along with another set that were the buyers. She looked back up to the top at the price, then to Matt with astonishment. "How the hell did you get them to agree to this?" She was ecstatic.

"You know me," he kicked back. "I can talk a penguin into an ice cream cone."

Ali scrunched her face and laughed. "What?"

"I don't know -- it just came out." He shrugged and laughed, too.

Ali rolled her eyes at him, still laughing, "This is amazing! Thank you! Now we all have something to celebrate tonight!" She stood up, still looking at the sales contract.

"Oh, we're celebrating tonight?" Matt asked

"Yes, if you checked in once in awhile, you would know. We're celebrating Nicki's debut in the paper. Have you seen it, by the way?"

"I did -- I stopped at the paper before I came here. It's fantastic, isn't it?"

Ali could see the pride in her brother's eyes and she smiled, happy for him and Nicki. She couldn't wait until Nicki saw him here. "It's awesome. We read it this afternoon." They were naked in bed and eating lunch, too, but he didn't need to know that. "So we'll celebrate *that,* me being alive," she laughed, "Rafe's bust, and the start of his nice long vacation, Jason being here, *you* coming back here, and now this!" she held up the contract.

"I thought that would make you happy." Matt smiled, finishing his beer.

"Did you tell Mom and Dad?"

"About the contract? Of course. They were psyched."

"I'm going to call Nicki and Jason. I still haven't congratulated her yet."

"Do me a favor and tell Jason to come up here, and you can go see Nicki, congratulate her in person."

"You trying to get rid of me?" she asked, suspicious.

Rafe came back to the porch, handing Matt another beer and Ali a water. "Sorry I took so long, I was on the phone."

Ali took the bottle and thanked him, looking to see if the call had been important, but he just smiled.

"What's going on?" he asked, taking his seat back.

Ali told him about the contract.

"That's great news!" He was genuinely pleased for her. "That'll help with your plans, huh?"

"It'll help so much," Ali nodded. Her plans. Her plans of owning her own business in the small town she grew up in, a dream that had been born in college, one she could finally bring to fruition, except now there was Rafe. And he was a dream she never imagined. He had bowled her over and encircled her life in a matter of days. He was a dream she didn't want to give up. How would he affect her other dreams and goals? Could she give them up to be with him, to follow him wherever his job took him? She felt him watching her, as if reading her thoughts, and she looked away quickly as Matt spoke.

"I was telling Ali she should go see Nicki and send Jason down to have a couple of beers with us. We can hang out while the girls get ready."

Rafe looked to Ali to see if that was okay with her. He didn't want her to go, but if she did, he had no problem hanging out with her brothers.

"It's okay," she told him, "you can all do some of that male bonding stuff. I have to put something different on anyway." She was dressed in shorts and a tank and wanted to wear something special for tonight.

Rafe got up and kissed her. "Do you want me to drive you?"

Ali shook her head. "I can manage."

"Take the Yukon then. The keys are by the door there on the table."

"Not the motorcycle?"

He smirked. "Not until you learn how to ride one."

Ali walked back in the cottage saying, loud enough for him to hear, "Great, you can teach me how right after you teach me how to shoot."

Matt shook his head. "You realize what you're getting yourself into, right?"

Rafe laughed softly. "Yeah, I do."

Matt could see it written all over Rafe's face that he really cared for Ali, and he was truly happy about it. He liked Rafe a lot, and he hoped things worked out with them.

Ali had gathered her things and was walking out the door.

"Hey, walking wounded, don't crash the Denali -- that's a sweet ride," Matt called out.

"Ha-ha." Ali was out front, heading to the truck.

"She's going to have your seat pulled right up to the windshield, and all your mirrors will be out of whack. I made the mistake once of letting her borrow my truck to pick up some furniture."

"I can hear you! You're like five feet from me on a screened-in porch!" Ali called out from where the truck was parked. "And for Rafe, I'll put it all back where it goes." She smiled at Rafe, stuck her tongue out at Matt, and left them chuckling on the porch.

Ali pulled into the driveway at Nan's moments later and went around to the backyard. She found Nicki by the pool sunning herself and saw Jason fishing down off the dock.

"Well, you two certainly look like you're relaxing."

"Hey!" Nicki sat up, smiling. "How was last night?"

Ali came to sit beside her, surprised and glad she seemed to be in a good mood, considering she was miserable without Matt. It must be because of the paper, she thought. "Magical -- and congratulations! You're big-time now!"

Nicki laughed. "Thank you! And magical? Wow, meaning he had some good tricks in the bedroom or...?" She was teasing.

"Oh, shut up." Ali laughed. "Meaning we bared all, and it's out there now."

"Really? That's great." Nicki lowered the sunglasses she had on. "You mean the actual L-word?"

Ali nodded yes. "I'm bursting, Nicki. I've never been happier in my whole life." Ali grinned, embarrassed at the tears that kept springing up.

"Oh, I'm so happy for you, Al." Nicki stood up and gave her a big careful hug.

"Thank you," she sniffed, and smiled as Jason came walking back up. "Catch anything?" she asked, trying to contain her emotions.

"Nah, but I saw a manatee, and that was pretty cool. How's the shoulder?" He'd clearly interrupted some girl talk.

"It's okay, hurts a little but nothing I can't put up with. I think that's the same manatee I saw the other day. I bet it hangs around these docks a lot, looking for food. They are cool, huh?" Ali held Jason's eyes and gave him a heads up with a conspiring look. "Rafe was wondering if you wanted to go hang out with him and have a couple of beers while we get ready."

Jason gave his own conspiring look to Nicki and said, "Sure, I'm showered already. I'll head right up there."

Nicki winked at Jason. "Oh, Ali, we can be quick. Let's just go with him."

"No!" Ali nearly shouted. "Let's take our time and look nice for tonight." She knew Nicki would want to look her best if she were going to see Matt. She watched Nicki's face and furrowed her brows as she looked back at Jason. They both found something funny, apparently. "Am I missing something?"

"I know he's here, Al." Nicki laughed.

"You do?" Ali was confused. "Did he call you?"

"No, Jason told me last night that he'd be here today."

"Oh, you are in deep shit," Ali told him.

"He'll get over it." Jason laughed. "Why torture the poor girl?"

"Thank you, Jason, for caring," Nicki teased.

Ali smiled at the two of them and the obvious camaraderie they had struck up.

"Okay, but she's supposed to be surprised," Ali warned.

"Trust me." Jason laughed again. "She will be."

"What's that mean?" both girls asked in unison.

"Just go get ready. I'll see you both up there." After getting the simple directions from Ali, Jason left the house with a big grin on his face.

When Jason pulled into the parking lot minutes later. He parked and walked past the different cottages, trying to find number 10. Ali had said back by the pool area, so he headed that way. He found Rafe and Matt sitting on the porch of a little blue cottage set back on its own. Jason laughed, seeing them out there. Had they been in rocking chairs, he would have given them some shit.

"Hey, big brother, nice to see you!" Matt called through the screen.

"Hey, yourself. When did you get on the island?"

"A little before five, I guess. What were you doing at the house?"

Jason entered the cottage and stepped into the porch area. He shook Rafe's hand and accepted a hug from his brother. "I was actually doing a little fishing off the dock. No bites, though." He sat down in the chair Rafe offered him and said yes to the beer offered as well.

Matt called to Rafe, who was heading to the fridge, "Now that you're on vacation, let's get that boat this week and do some fishing in the gulf." To Jason he asked, "Can you stay a few more days?"

"No way -- I'm out of here tomorrow. My flight leaves out of Tampa on Sunday morning."

"That sucks," Matt replied.

"Well, I can't fuck off for as long as you. I've got work to do." Jason smiled, antagonizing his brother. He gratefully accepted the beer Rafe handed him. "Thanks, man."

"You work too hard. You've got to hire someone to help," Matt told him.

"I'm seriously thinking about it." Jason was seriously considering it.

"Good, then we can get to some games together." Matt looked at Rafe, grinning, and Jason followed.

Rafe rolled his eyes. "You'll never turn me. I'm a Yankee through and through."

"This is good, though -- a little rivalry in the family will be fun," Matt joked.

Rafe couldn't help feeling flattered with the comment. He could only hope to be part of Ali's family someday.

The three of them sat on the porch for another hour talking about sports, Rafe's job, and his family, and then finally what his intentions were with Ali. He had wondered how long it would take them to get around to that. He felt a bit like one of the many suspects he'd interrogated over the years. He was definitely in the hot seat, but he could respect Ali's brothers for caring like they did, and he wouldn't have had it any other way. The looks on their faces as they awaited his response was almost comical. He imagined their dad would be proud.

He smiled at them and just decided to throw it out there.

"Guys, I am unequivocally 100 -percent head-over-heels in love with your sister." He watched as Matt nodded, smiling, clearly pleased, but Jason held his look a bit longer.

"What about the distance?" Jason leaned forward, his beer hanging casually between his fingers.

Rafe had thought a lot about the distance and had already been making some calls. He hadn't discussed anything with Ali on the subject, though, and wasn't quite ready to do it with her brothers. "Can I just say I'm working on it?" he asked.

"That's good enough for me." Jason reached over and shook Rafe's hand. "You're a good guy. I like you."

Rafe chuckled at the compliment. "You two aren't so bad, either."

Matt cracked up looking at them. "Are you guys serious right now? I think I need a tissue."

Jason shot him a stern look, much the same as he had given Rafe. "And what about you, asshole? What are *your* intentions with Nicki?"

Matt got serious. "What's it to you, *asshole*?"

"I like her a lot and want to make sure you realize what you have there."

Rafe took a drink from his beer feeling a little uncomfortable on Matt's behalf. He knew how Matt felt about Nicki and that his intentions were nothing but good.

Matt's defenses were up. "Don't *you* worry about *my* intentions. I know damn well what I have there."

"Relax, I just want to make sure you don't fuck it up. I'm here to help." Jason grinned.

Matt laughed with disbelief, "Oh, really, what the hell are you gonna do?"

"We'll talk about it later. Right now I'm starved. You guys hungry?"

Rafe stood. "I'll call the restaurant and get us a table."

"I'll call Ali and tell them to get their butts up here," Jason said, pulling out his phone while Matt still glowered at him. He just laughed at him and shook his head.

"I'll just sit here and drink my beer." Matt put his feet up on the sill of the porch and watched the guests come and go from the pool. He thought about Nicki. It had only been a couple of days, and yet both Ali and Jason had given him shit about his feelings toward her. Did he have that much of a bad rap? Did Nicki doubt him, too, thinking their weekend together had been nothing more than great sex? He knew he could have been more forthcoming in the feelings department, but damn, it had all come as a surprise and in the blink of an eye. Who could blame him for wanting to sort it out and be sure? He had been pretty sure about his feelings when he left, but now he was damn sure and he intended to let her know. He just hoped he hadn't screwed things up.

Ali came down the hall to Nicki's bedroom to tell her Jason had called, but came up short in the doorway as her eyes fell upon her. "I told you that would look incredible on you." Her best friend looked beautiful.

"Are you sure? I feel like I'm spilling out of the top here." Nicki gestured to her boobs.

"They look fantastic, and he'll drop dead when he sees you in it." Ali had loaned Nicki her new white dress, and it looked stunning on her. Nicki was a bit more endowed, so the sex appeal factor was sky high. "I'm jealous," Ali admitted.

"Rafe's going to recognize the dress, don't you think?" Nicki asked, embarrassed.

"Considering I didn't have it on for very long, I doubt it." Ali laughed, "Besides, I've been saving this one for a special occasion and hopefully he won't be looking at you!"

Nicki laughed, too. "I didn't mean it that way! He won't be able to keep his eyes off you. He can't, even when you're swallowed up in his T-shirt." She smiled.

Ali loved wearing his T-shirt for pajamas and the way he looked at her in it -- well, she hoped for a similar response tonight. She had on a pale yellow spaghetti-strap dress that fell just above the knee. Its silky fabric hung loose but revealed her curves as she walked, making her feel both sexy and feminine. She wasn't as self-conscious of the bandages anymore, either. Instead, she chose to look at them as a reminder of how lucky she was, lucky to be alive and lucky to have met Rafe.

"I'm so nervous. I don't know why," Nicki said, putting some last minute things in her purse.

"He's dying to see you," Ali assured her. "And Jason just called. He said to get up there; they're at the restaurant."

"Oh, God, my stomach is in knots, like it's a first date."

Ali laughed. "That was me last night, and look how it turned out." She smiled.

"I won't be able to eat," Nicki warned as they left her bedroom.

"Just relax, it's Matt. He'll have you laughing in no time, and you'll forget the knots."

"Okay, okay." Nicki followed Ali out of the house. She locked up and they both got in the convertible for the short drive to Tween Waters.

Ali started laughing as they entered the parking lot and got out of the car.

"What?" Nicki laughed nervously, nearly twisting her ankle as the heel of her sandal sank into the shelled lot. "God!"

"Be careful!" Ali warned, still laughing. "I'm just thinking how Matt is going to react when the drummer starts hitting on you tonight."

"Oh, I hope that doesn't happen," Nicki worried, wiping the dust off her shoe. "I think when he sees me with Matt, he'll get the picture."

"For his sake I hope so." Ali could only picture what Matt would do.

"That didn't make me feel any less nervous, by the way. Thanks."

"I'm sorry -- it just came to my mind when we pulled in and I saw the band's name on the sign. I'm sure it'll be fine." She'd keep her fingers crossed, anyway.

Nicki's heart was beating double time as they entered the restaurant through the resort's small gift shop. They stopped at the hostess stand, and Ali gave her Rafe's name. The hostess was expecting them, and she led them through a set of wide French doors and into a semi-private dining area.

There were only three other parties seated in the room, along with Rafe and Matt, who sat talking in the far corner at a large round table. They appeared relaxed and confident, sitting back with their drinks and holding a conversation. Nicki wondered briefly where Jason was, but she couldn't keep her eyes off Matt. He was laughing at something Rafe said, looking as handsome as ever. Her heart beat wildly at the sight of him.

Ali kept her eyes on Rafe as she entered the room and smiled self-consciously when he looked up and noticed her. She was suddenly aware of each step she took and how her body moved toward him. The way his eyes washed over every inch of her had her catching her breath and making the distance to the table seem endless. She could feel the heat in her cheeks and neck as she approached, and she gripped her purse a little tighter. He looked impossibly handsome, with his tanned face freshly shaven, and his intense dark eyes even darker against the deep navy color of his shirt. His shirt sleeves were rolled up, casually revealing the impressive watch that encircled his wrist. He looked perfectly elegant, right off the cover of GQ, and Ali felt so lucky to have found him as he got up from his seat to take her hand. She was surprised when he excused them both to Matt and Nicki and led her right back out of the room and through the doors to the outside porch.

Matt couldn't have been more grateful to have Rafe and Ali leave the room. He was dumbstruck when he saw Nicki walk in. He had never seen a more desirable woman, and he was aware of the other men in the room taking notice right away -- their women companions as well. Maybe they were looking at Ali, too, but all *he* could see was Nicki.

His body responded right away as she walked gracefully toward him. Her hair was loose and fell in waves around her face and shoulders, creating an auburn halo as the late afternoon sun filtered into the room. She looked like an angel in white as she came to him, sun-kissed to a golden brown, arms and oh-so-long legs toned from her daily yoga, and, God help him, cleavage he could dive right into. Her body was meant to be noticed in that dress, and he was at full attention. Their gazes locked and didn't break until Ali and Rafe left the room and Matt stood up to greet her.

Nicki took sight of him as he stood, and her heart threatened to beat right out of her chest. If he wasn't the most gorgeous man she'd ever seen, then she didn't know who was. She tore her eyes away from his to look at all of him. The white long-sleeve shirt he wore accentuated his broad shoulders and fell over his muscular chest perfectly, and with his sleeves pushed up she got a glimpse of the golden hair that barely covered his arms. Her eyes continued down to the faded jeans that fit him -- oh, boy, she looked back into his eyes and saw the hunger there -- that fit him so well.

"Hi," they said at the same time, and Matt laughed softly as she smiled. He couldn't take his eyes off her. He knew she was aware of the effect she was having on him, and he wanted to pull her in and let her feel it, too.

"Jason told me you were here," she confessed.

"I figured he would." He wanted to kiss her, but he held back. He didn't want to presume she was just going to fall right back in his arms, although there was no mistaking the heat he saw in her eyes when she had given him the once-over. She was even more beautiful than she was four days ago, if that were possible, and his heart was in his throat.

"How have..."

"Is Sean..."

They laughed again, both feeling awkward.

"Maybe if we sit down, I can stop looking at you in that dress and actually hold a conversation." He laughed trying to ease the moment.

Nicki smiled and laughed, too. God, she was actually blushing! She felt like her boobs were set out on a platter, and she wished to God she had rethought this dress. The air between them was electric and making it hard for Nicki not to wrap her arms around him and kiss him desperately. Instead, she sat perfectly still in the seat he offered beside his own. He turned his chair to face her, and his knees touched hers where they crossed, making the small hairs on her arms stand on end.

"All right, you go first." He smiled. Her lips held the lightest amount of gloss and he watched as she licked them before she spoke. He leaned forward, one elbow on the table, his other hand resting on his thigh, but wanting it to be on the smooth skin of her own. Her bare legs were crossed, the hem of the already short dress riding up slightly and making it hard for him to focus.

"I just wondered how your friend was doing." She was making small talk, being polite, but she wanted him desperately to kiss her. She ached for it. God she had missed him. It had only been days, but it felt like months.

"He should be leaving the hospital tomorrow. He'll have a good six to eight weeks in the plaster but should be back to new after that." He tried to hold her eyes to his. He wanted her to see what he was thinking and feeling. "Thanks for asking."

Nicki's body was humming with those eyes on her. They were like a friggin' aphrodisiac. She looked at the table cloth instead.

"Hey, congratulations. I read your stuff in the Beach News -- front page huh? That's quite an accomplishment your first week. It was really great. I was impressed."

She dared to look at him then and smiled, happy that he had taken the time to read the paper. "Thank you, it was exciting to see my name in there today." She paused. "I'm glad you came back. You can help me celebrate."

"I plan to," he answered her, in a tone that suggested more than drinks and laughter.

Nicki cleared her throat, and forced her eyes back to the tablecloth. She'd never been so physically aware of herself than right now sitting at this table, so close to the one man whom she'd loved for half of her life.

Matt pulled his chair closer. He couldn't stay away another minute. He picked up her hands from her lap, grazing the front of her dress where they had sat clasped, and he held them in his own. She was forced to turn her body toward his. He stared at the tops of her breasts, lifting and pressing against the bodice of the dress each time she took a breath. He looked at her face and took in his own deep breath. "Why can't you look me in the eyes for more than ten seconds?" He feared the worst, that he had put too much distance between them and she had rethought her feelings.

Nicki half-laughed. "Because I feel naked when I look in your eyes." Might as well be honest.

He laughed huskily with relief. "Good, because that's how I'm envisioning you."

Oh, sweet lord, she was in trouble -- again. She looked into them now and found the desire she was so afraid of, but also a hint of amusement, and she saw the crooked smile he gave her, the one he knew was her undoing.

Matt leaned in and kissed her, kissed her beautiful sultry mouth, kissed the gloss right off it, slowly and softly at first, until he parted her lips with his tongue and tasted her hungrily.

Nicki's hands pulled from his so she could touch him. She rested them on his strong thighs, feeling the hardness through his jeans. His own hands gripped the sides of her chair, pulling it in that much closer, sending vivid images through her mind of them naked in bed. She had to remind herself that they were in a restaurant, and it took everything she had to pull away. He was smiling at her rather triumphantly, and she couldn't help but return the grin.

Man, her hands on him made him crazy. He couldn't wait to touch her all over. It was going to be a long night.

Nicki laughed, starting to relax a little. "You don't have to look so satisfied," she said, turning toward the table, wary of hands -- his and hers.

"Not even close, Nicki, not even close." He signaled for the waiter and ordered her a Grey Goose and Sprite.

She raised a brow. "Good memory."

"It's all up here," he tapped his head, "everything you like." He kissed her again, this time on the side of her neck, inhaling the scent of her. "I missed you."

He whispered it to her, and she could hear the emotion behind the words. Her stomach tightened as she looked into his eyes, and her heart was bursting at what she thought she saw there. "I missed you, too." Her own whisper left him smiling.

His hand rested like a hot coal on her upper thigh, and she kept her own hand comfortably placed on his. She melted with the contact and blushed as the memory of what he had done to her the morning he left the islands played in her mind. She wished Ali and Rafe would hurry back in and force her to think about something else…and give Matt something else to rest his dangerous eyes on.

Ali followed Rafe willingly, thinking this was something Matt had worked out with Rafe in order to be alone with Nicki for a few minutes. When they reached the gift shop, Rafe took her by the hand and led her outside to the porch, taking her almost all the way to the end, where no one sat or stood. She turned to face him, and he backed her against the railing, his dark eyes predatory and fierce. She looked up into them, trying to gauge his look.

"Ali..."

His voice was low and gruff, and his stance was close and brooding. She found herself trying to take a step back, but he pulled her against him instead, and she found herself melting into his hard body. He wasn't angry, but he was determined about something.

"What is it?" she asked against his chest, her one good arm circled around his back, feeling the cords of muscle there.

"You walked into that room and took my breath away." He bent to kiss her, and she was thankful for the porch railing to steady her.

Rafe pulled away and looked into her eyes. "You're so beautiful, Ali, and when I look at those bandages on your arm, I think about what could have happened and how..." He took a deep breath, and his heart expanded as she looked at him expectantly. "How much worse it could have been. It overwhelms me."

Ali stared up at him. He was so intense, so serious, and she could see the emotion in his eyes. She moved her hand up to his cheek, and he kissed the inside of her palm. "Rafe, nothing worse did happen, thank God." She laughed ironically. "Do you know how frightened I was when I saw him come in with that gun? I never thought he was going to shoot *me* -- I thought he was going to shoot *you*. I was terrified," Ali moved her hand down to his chest and placed it over his beating heart, staring up into eyes that bored into her own.

"I was going to tell you I loved you last night no matter what you had planned to say to me. I woke up yesterday morning determined to tell you, because yes, it could have been worse, much worse than this," she pointed to her shoulder, "and when something like that happens to you, you realize how short and precious life is. I was so freaked out over the weekend when I was coming to terms with how I felt for you, I was actually berating myself for feeling so strongly in such a short amount of time, can you imagine? I was trying to talk myself out of love, convince myself it was just lust, which yes, it was definitely that, too, but why was I doing that? Because we're not supposed to believe it's possible to fall in love at first sight? Well, what if I had died -- people would have heard the story from Nicki and said, 'Oh, how sad, she had fallen in love with that impossibly handsome man, and she never got a chance to tell him.' But I think it's sadder if I walk on this glorious earth next to you, alive as can be, and *don't* tell you because it's 'too soon', even if it hadn't been reciprocated, which would have sucked, by the way." She smiled when he laughed softly. "At least I put it out there in the universe. I could tell my grandkids how 'yes, I did fall in love at first sight once upon a time, and at first kiss, and at first...' -- well, maybe I'll leave that part out, but you understand what I'm saying, right?" She took a deep breath.

Rafe took her face gently between his hands and kissed her with all the emotion rioting inside of him. She'd taken the words right out of his mouth. He had felt all of those things, too, and when he saw a glimpse of what life would be like without her in it, he knew he had to tell her how he was feeling. He pulled back to look at her, at her lips so full and sensuous, her eyes hooded and glazed, and his body ached for her. "*Our* grandchildren."

Ali was dizzy from his kiss. "What?" Ali leaned against the railing behind her for support. What did he just say?

Rafe smiled down at her, knowing he had just shocked the hell out of her, but he had never felt so connected to someone and so overcome with emotion than when he was with her. She made him laugh and made him crazy with lust. He couldn't get enough of her, and when they came together so explosively, it rocked him to his core. The sex with her was beyond words, and the way her beautiful body molded to his, was as if God had made her just for him.

She brought out the primitive male in him; he wanted to protect her with his life. She stroked his ego -- she was so impressed that he was FBI, and she made him smile with just one look in her extraordinary eyes. She made him happy just being in her presence, and just thinking of her warmed him from the inside out. When he looked at her, he saw his future.

He wanted to take her home and meet his family, show her New York for the first time, and experience it all with her. He wanted to go to Boston and meet her parents and her friends and gain their respect. He wanted to marry her and make babies with her, and have those babies grow up and give them grandchildren. He'd seen enough ugliness and brutality in the last decade, and he wanted to change that. He wanted to see more of the good parts of life with someone he loved by his side.

"You look awfully serious right now, Rafe," Ali said softly. His strong hands cupped her face again, and it made her want to melt.

"I've never been more serious in all my, life Ali." The look he saw in her eyes was all he needed to make his decision.

"Oh, God, Rafe I'm so in love with you. When you look at me like that and hold me like this, I want to cry. I feel so happy it's ridiculous," she choked out, embarrassed by the tears that threatened to fall. Why was she such a crybaby around him?

"Hey." He lifted her chin. "I'm the happiest man in the world right now, and yes, it's crazy, and yes, it's fast, but it's the real deal, Ali."

"It is, isn't it?" she laughed, smiling up at him. She reached her arms up around his neck, grimacing as she lifted her injured shoulder, and kissed him, her own emotions jam-packed into it.

"Careful," he said, lowering her arms as he pulled her against him in an embrace. He rested his chin on her head and stared out at the Gulf, feeling her heart beat against him. The sun was getting ready to set on the horizon. "I want us to be together, Ali." He felt her intake of breath. "I want to go back to Boston with you."

He felt her answer before he heard it. Her arms wrapped around him tighter, and her head nodded into his chest. He could feel her own chest heaving against him and felt the dampness from her face through his shirt. He pulled her back to see the tears steadily streaming down her flushed cheeks. If it were possible, her eyes gleamed even greener. "Is that a good cry or a bad cry?" He laughed because he already knew and was rewarded with a huge smile.

"Are you serious?" She started to laugh -- she was overwhelmed and shocked.

"I told you, I've never been more serious in my life. Would you like it if I moved there?" he asked, looking right into her eyes this time.

"Yes," she barely whispered. "Yes!" she said much louder, drawing some attention.

He picked her up at the waist and kissed her. It was a slow, sweet, and tender kiss that only brought more tears to Ali's eyes. When he set her back down, she was weak in the knees. "Wow, I never expected this, but I hoped for it."

"I've been thinking about it since the night you were shot. I don't want to lose you, Ali. When I think of my life, and my future, you're in it. I picture us having a life together, having beautiful babies together, and I picture being on this very beach twenty years from now vacationing with my 'young' beautiful wife. You know the morning you joked about that? I could picture it then. You knocked me off my feet, Ali."

"Rafe?" Ali was floored listening to him. Was he actually saying he wanted to get married? And have babies? Oh, my God!

"I know, I'm getting ahead of myself, but I don't care." He saw the surprise on her face, but he also saw the love and hope in her eyes. "I'm not going to rush you. We'll take it one step at a time, but I want you, Ali. I want you in my life as my friend, as my lover, and someday soon as my wife."

"Rafe," Ali said, barely breathing. Hadn't she just imagined all this the day she had pretended to be his fiancée? "I..." she swallowed the lump in her throat and pressed her face against his chest, feeling his arms go around her. "I want all that, too. I want it so much. I'm never going to forget this," she promised, "all of this, Rafe -- this bar, that black racer." She laughed. "The beach house, last night, and right this minute. I'll never forget any of it."

"I won't either, Ali. This has been without a doubt the best week of my life." He laughed against her head. "Minus the criminals and the shootings, we can tell *our* grandkids together someday, okay?"

Oh! She nodded as the tears poured. He was laughing at her, and as she looked around, she noticed they had drawn a little crowd, who, to her mortification, started to clap. She looked up at Rafe, and he was grinning from ear to ear. She put her hand over her mouth and buried her face in his shirt. He smiled to the people and walked Ali a little farther down the porch. They clearly thought he had proposed and, in a manner of speaking, Ali realized, he had.

"Are you okay?"

"I'm a lot of things right now, but okay doesn't describe it." She took a deep breath. "I'm worried about you and all you'll be giving up. How can you move to Boston? What about your job and your family?" Would they live together?

Rafe kissed the top of her head, reading her thoughts. "Ali, don't worry about anything, okay? Let's have a blast tonight and celebrate -- everything. We'll talk about the logistics tomorrow. I've got it all worked out."

He did?

"Do you trust me?" He pulled her back to look at her.

"Yes," she smiled, "with my life."

"Then let's go back inside and have some fun." He took her hand, and some of the same people who had overheard them still stood outside, waiting for the sun to set. They clapped again as Ali and Rafe stepped inside, and Ali and Rafe laughed, not disillusioning them.

CHAPTER THIRTY-EIGHT

"I can only imagine what my face looks like right now. Do you mind if I clean up a bit?" Ali wiped at her eyes.

"You look amazing, but you're going in there anyway, so I'll get us a couple of drinks."

Rafe smiled at her as he left to go to the bar, and she sought cover in the ladies' room, where she immediately went into a stall and pressed herself against the door. Holy shit! She took several deep breaths and came back out to face the mirror. Her eyes were puffy, her cheeks were red, and her lips were swollen from kissing. Great, no one will have a clue what I've been doing. She splashed some cold water on her face and tried to register all that Rafe had just said to her.

She looked at herself in the mirror again, wiping the water away with a paper towel, and thought about him coming to Boston. Her life had changed dramatically in a week's time, and she knew beyond a doubt that it was fate. She couldn't wait to introduce him to her parents -- she couldn't wait to get him back to Boston. Her brothers would be so happy for them. They really liked him, she knew, and she hoped his family would like her. She couldn't wait to meet them, especially his niece and two nephews. It would be interesting to see him interact with children. Children. Ali couldn't believe he said he wanted babies with her. Her heart had filled with the sheer joy at that thought. Just the thought of someday being his wife filled her with enough happiness for a lifetime.

She dried the rest of the water from her face and left the ladies' room. She strode over to where Rafe waited with their drinks and lifted her face to kiss him.

"Get a good look at this face now, because this is what it'll look like on our wedding day." Whoa, that sounded weird. "So if you want to rethink any of what you said, I understand completely." She took the drink he handed her and drank down half of it like a shot. She felt like a live wire. Had she just said "wedding day"? Now she felt presumptuous.

"You're crazy," he laughed. As they walked back into the dining room, he bent down to whisper in her ear, "I hope you look just like this on our wedding day. Your eyes are greener than ever, and your lips are pure sex."

Ali felt the rush go right through her. "Whoa, that's better than what I saw in there." She grinned. What a sweet talker, *and* he said "wedding day" too. She had some more of her drink.

He laughed and couldn't wait to take her to his bed.

Ali could see Matt and Nicki head to head in conversation. "Where's Jay, by the way?"

Rafe laughed again. "He wanted to sit in the bar and eat. He didn't want to be a fifth wheel."

"That's crazy! He wouldn't have been!" Ali felt badly.

"Don't worry -- there were a couple of women in there that he struck up a conversation with."

Ali smiled, nodding. "Good, maybe he'll get lucky tonight."

Rafe looked at her with a cocked brow, grinning. "What about me?"

She leaned up to whisper to him, "Oh, that's a guarantee, babe."

Babe? He liked that, too.

Nicki was on her second drink and far more relaxed then when she had first entered the room. Matt was making her laugh now instead of trying to seduce her with his eyes, Nicki figured it was as much torture for him as it was for her, but she didn't doubt that it would start up again as the night wore on. For now, they were back to teasing and talking. She smiled when she saw Ali and Rafe reappear.

And okay, Ali had definitely had a good cry fest somewhere along the way, Nicki noticed immediately, but she was also grinning from ear to ear. Nicki sought her eyes, but Ali just smiled. Nicki would have to wait until they were alone.

"Hey, you made it back. We thought we lost you for the night. Where's Jason?" Nicki had figured they had all purposefully left her and Matt alone.

"He's actually going to eat at the bar -- he found some friends." Rafe grinned, holding out a chair for Ali, then sitting himself.

"More like fans, I'll bet." Nicki laughed and noticed the disgruntled look on Matt's face as he moved his hand over her thigh. "What? Your brother's pretty cute, and he's a very nice guy."

Matt harrumphed. "He's okay."

Ali laughed. "You're cute, too, Matt when you're jealous."

Nicki looked at him. "Are you jealous?"

Her eyes teased him, and he gave her a smirk. "Let's just say I didn't like being away."

"I didn't find it all that enjoyable myself," she said matter-of-factly and loud enough so that Rafe and Ali could hear. The drinks had loosened her tongue, and she felt comfortable talking in front of Ali and Rafe. They were well aware of how she felt.

"We can vouch for that." Ali and Rafe both nodded at Matt.

"Really? You missed me, huh?" He was teasing her now, and he squeezed her thigh. He leaned in close to her ear and whispered, "It was the longest four days of my life."

Nicki blushed and looked away, but knew by his tone that he wasn't teasing her now. She was in dangerous territory where her heart was concerned. Their sexual attraction was intense, but her feelings went so much deeper than that, and she could only hope that his did, too. She felt his hand again, coaxing her to look at him, which she did.

"Okay, that's good," Ali interjected. "We still have to eat dinner."

Matt rolled his eyes at his sister, and they all picked up their menus. Who the hell could think about food?

As if reading Matt's mind, and knowing everyone at the table was pretty much thinking the same thing, Rafe suggested, "Why don't we just get some apps., then hit the bar?"

At a collective yes, they all laughed, and by the time they made it to the bar, the band was already setting up.

CHAPTER THIRTY-NINE

Ali and Nicki exchanged glances as they noticed Ace the drummer and the guitar player who had tried to pick them up their first night on the island.

"This will be interesting." Nicki spoke from the corner of her mouth.

They made their way to a six-top on the edge of the dance floor, garnering a few glances as they sat. The table faced directly at the stage where the band was warming up, and Jason stood talking with them.

"Figures Jay's over there already, trying to play their instruments." Matt laughed.

"Does he still play?" Ali asked. She hadn't heard either of her brothers play since high school. She remembered Matt taking lessons, but she'd only heard him practice a handful of times, and she thought Jason had lost interest as well.

"Yeah, once in awhile," Matt told her, then gave the waitress who came over everybody's drink order.

"These guys are pretty good. You're going to like them," Nicki told him.

"You've heard them before?" Matt asked.

She glanced at Ali. "Yeah, the first night we got on the island, we came in for a drink -- that's the night Ali kind of met Rafe. I thought I told you that."

Ali and Rafe exchanged a smile.

"What kind of music do they play?" Matt glanced at the drummer, then back to Nicki.

"They're pretty good," Rafe said to Matt. "I've actually heard them a couple of times. They cover Foo Fighters, Creed, Nickleback, and some classic stuff."

"No U2, though," Ali put in.

"Good. There aren't many bands who can cover the boys, and sometimes it's painful to hear." Matt did like playing the music from the bands Rafe mentioned, though. "I'm surprised you girls like them -- they must play Justin Timberlake and Beyonce', too."

"Ha-ha." Ali smirked, laughing. "I love those bands, and Nicki does, too. She's got a thing for guys who rock." She smiled at the heated look Rafe gave her. He definitely knew which band was her favorite.

Nicki kicked Ali under the table. "Thanks, that's helping," she said sarcastically. She had seen Matt's wary look to the drummer.

Matt shot Ali a look that said "haven't you tormented me enough today?"

Ali shrugged. "She's got a thing for construction workers, too." Ali laughed at Nicki's face. Obviously her attempts to rectify her previous statement hadn't gone over that well.

Nicki just stared at Ali, her mouth ajar, "How many painkillers did you take before we left the house?" she asked seriously.

Rafe couldn't contain his laughter.

Ali laughed, too, hitting him on the arm, "None, I swear."

Matt laughed. "It's okay, Nicki, I can appreciate fantasies."

"Oh, God!" Nicki rested her head in her hands, embarrassed.

"Myself, I have one about a hot newspaper reporter who does yoga by my pool in just her bikini."

Nicki lifted her head, smiling. "And where are you ever going to find one of those?"

Matt grabbed her chair and pulled it to him in a swift motion, causing her to squeal.

"Right here," he said through clenched teeth, and kissed her hard.

Rafe laughed at them and at Ali's look of shock. "What? Does that make you uncomfortable?"

She turned to face him. "I'm still getting used to it," she laughed.

"Well, come a little closer. If you're kissing me, you won't have to look."

Ali scooted her chair right up against his, facing him so that her knees came between his straddled legs. She placed her hands on his thighs and lifted her head to kiss him.

"Umm, you taste good," he said softly.

Chills ran through her; kissing him was dangerous in a public setting. She pulled back and took a sip of her drink. "I'm having fun."

"I'm glad. You deserve to. I'm having fun, too." Rafe turned to Matt. "It's too bad you couldn't convince Jason to stay longer."

"I know, maybe I can get him to come back next weekend."

Nicki's stomach tightened. Now she knew Matt would be here at least until next weekend, but what about after that? He hadn't said how long he was planning on staying. He had originally planned to stay for two weeks. Would he still? She watched him as he talked to Rafe. He leaned forward to talk, his shirt pulling across his back where she could make out the outline of his muscular form, and with his shirt sleeve pushed back and his arm bent on the table, she could see the swell of his biceps through the material. His hair looked nice, too, flecked with gold from the sun and working outside, and when he turned to look at her, his eyes were exceptionally green against his tanned face.

"Hey," he said softly, turning to her. "What are you thinking about right now?"

"I'm wondering how long you're here for."

Matt could see the uncertainty in her eyes and knew he had caused it by leaving the way he had. He wouldn't make that mistake again. "I can stay for a couple of weeks, if that's okay with you." He glanced over to Ali and Rafe to see that they were now in their own conversation, and out of the corner of his eye he saw Jason heading back to the bar to sit with a woman there.

Nicki's heart leapt at the thought of two weeks with him, but she couldn't help but wonder what would happen after that. She had committed to a whole summer on the islands working, and now the prospect of being without him made her sad and worried. The past four days had been torture without him. She didn't know if she could handle a couple of months. The band started to play, and she had to speak up to be heard. "Of course it's okay. I think that's great." She looked at the band playing and away from Matt.

Matt followed her gaze but then guided her face back to his with his fingers. "So what's bothering you?"

Nicki couldn't avoid his eyes, and the jolt they sent went right through her, hovering between her legs. She couldn't even look at him without thinking of him touching her there. But she was going to be honest. Ali was right -- life was too short. "I'm scared about what happens after the two weeks, because these past four days really sucked for me. I'm sorry," she said, seeing the look on his face. "I know you had to leave, it was the right thing to do, but selfishly I wished you'd stayed. I was afraid when you were home that the intensity of the weekend would wear off for you and your life would just go on. I know what took place, happened because we were here, and it's hot and it's sexy and it's just paradise, and those kinds of things happen in places like this, but I figured with you being back in Boston and back to reality that you might think it had all been just...I don't know, just a great weekend and nothing more."

Matt watched as she spoke. She was so sincere, and she wore her heart right out there for him to see, and it nearly broke his own. How did he get so lucky? She had been under his nose for years and years, and now he finally saw her. She had astounded him last weekend, and slammed his world upside-down, yet she thought that he thought it had just been a "great weekend," a fling in paradise.

"Nicki." He leaned in close as the music played loudly. He was inches from her lips, his forehead resting on hers. He could see the deep breaths she took, as her cleavage rose and fell, and okay, yes, that was a distraction, but he wanted to set things right. "I'm sorry I left the way I did. I should have come to find you to say goodbye, to tell you I would be back as soon as I could because I didn't want to leave in the first place. Last weekend was unbelievable, but make no mistake, it didn't happen because of the weather, or the palm trees -- it happened because we couldn't stop it from happening. When I saw you that first day, out there by the pool, I became a walking hard-on." He laughed as her shoulders shook from laughing. "I'm not kidding -- it was instant, I had to have you, but then after the most incredible sex of my life, yes," he nodded as she shot him a skeptical look, "the…most…incredible…sex of my life, Nicki, then getting to know you all over again, talking all night and laughing all night -- forget it! I was toast!" She laughed softly at him, and he kissed her gently.

"These next two weeks are going to be like heaven. I want to do everything with you, share everything with you, do everything *to* you," he added huskily, "and after the two weeks are over? Well, that's something I intend to talk to you about, okay? But not right now -- later, when we're alone and it's quiet. Are you okay with that?" He pulled back to take a drink of his beer. The way she looked at him and the way she looked in that dress, he would rather it be much sooner than later.

Nicki was reeling from his words, but she could only nod for fear her answer would come out in a sob. She took a sip of her drink and reached over to kiss him with the pent-up passion she was feeling. Her hands feathered over his hard chest and then came up around his neck possessively. Her kiss was hungry and filled with her desire for him. She wanted him to know how much she had missed him.

"Whoa," he said softly, pulling back, "are you prepared for everyone in this room to see you naked? Because I'm about to clear this table with my arm and take you right on top of it. I would like nothing more than to peel that damn dress off you."

Nicki smiled wickedly at his hoarse, desire-filled tone. "You like the dress?" She teased and stroked his thighs, scratching the denim with her nails.

Matt practically choked, "Are you trying to torture me? I've got a raging hard-on for you right now."

"I know." She let the back of her knuckles brush up against the large bulge straining against his jeans.

"Hoo, Nicki, please." He half-laughed and looked around. God, was there a corner he could take her to?

"Hey, you two, check out Jason at the bar!" Ali shouted above the music.

Nicki gave Matt a "to be continued" seductive look, and her eyes went to the bar.

Matt groaned out loud in frustration and reluctantly turned that way himself. His brother was talking to a leggy blonde who seemed rather enamored by him. "Go, Jay!"

Rafe laughed. "That wasn't the girl he was talking to earlier. I wonder where she came from?"

"I think she's with that little blonde girl in the corner with -- hey, that's your friend Mike!" Ali smiled and waved as he spotted her.

Matt, Nicki, and Rafe turned to see Mike and his date coming toward them. Rafe stood up and clasped hands with his good friend.

"Hey, how's your second day of vacation treating you?" Mike grinned at Rafe and came around to give Ali a gentle hug and a kiss. Rafe smirked, and Ali laughed.

Mike introduced his date, leaving out that she was a DEA agent, but Ali had heard from Nicki that she was, and that she had been there at the arrest of Timothy Mann and Sean Smith. It was strange putting names to them. She didn't really think of them as people at all.

Ali shook Agent Samantha Taylor's hand and thanked her for all her help, telling her it was nice to meet her.

"Sit down," Rafe offered, and introduced Mike and "Sam," as Mike called her, to Matt and Nicki.

"*This* girl, I know." Mike winked at Nicki and said to Matt, who had stood to shake Mike's hand, "you're a lucky guy." Mike held his arm around Sam, letting her know that he felt pretty lucky, too. She was pretty damn sexy, especially when she was arresting someone. In fact, Mike had made her cuff him just last night. He smiled down at her remembering.

Matt stood, and shook the guy's hand. He was as tall as Matt, with spiky white blond hair, tanned, and had definitely logged a few thousand hours at the gym. Matt knew he was FBI, and he also knew he was a player just by looking at him. The guy oozed charm and was clearly a relentless flirt. All the girls at the table were either blushing or giggling at whatever he said to them. Jesus, he *had* been playing with fire being away. He decided to give him the benefit of the doubt, though, sincc he was Rafe's friend, and he seemed genuinely friendly to Matt.

"Thanks, man, I know that I am." Matt gave Nicki's hand a little squeeze, and he sat back down.

Mike and Sam sat down, too, beside Ali. Sam was next to Nicki.

"So when are you heading back to Miami?" Rafe asked Mike.

"I'm staying the weekend, buddy. This place is great. Sam and her friend are staying the night, too." Mike gave Rafe the wagging brows.

Ali shook her head, catching it. "You're bad," she told Mike. "Is that your friend, Sam, at the bar?" Ali asked, leaning around Mike.

"Yes," Sam answered with a nod. "We don't know who she's talking to, though. I guess I'll find out later."

Matt grinned at that and winked at Nicki, who knew what he was thinking, that that leggy blonde would most likely be eating breakfast with them by the pool tomorrow. He picked up his beer and listened to the music. The band was really good. Nicki, bless her heart, was paying attention to the band, too, and not Rafe's charismatic friend, her hand resting comfortably in his. Why was he so jealous?

Ali laughed. "That's actually my other brother, so you don't have to worry."

"Oh, good." Sam laughed, pleased.

"No shit." Mike glanced over. "The whole family come down to see our injured girl here?"

Ali smiled, enjoying his affection. "Just my brothers."

"Nice brothers," Mike commented and held his beer up to Matt in a cheers. He could tell *that* brother was a little tense. Mike looked to Rafe, but Rafe just shook his head at him.

What? Like if the roles had been reversed, either one of them wouldn't have tried with Ali and Nicki? Damn right they would have.

"So what do you say, Sam, moonlight stroll on the beach?" Mike knew when it was time to go.

"Who knew you had a romantic side?" Ali teased.

He leaned down close to Ali. "Have you seen those cabanas out there? The tops roll right down over the chairs." He gave her a wink and took Sam's hand.

Ali rolled her eyes. "Watch out for splinters," she laughed.

Rafe stood up and shook Mike's hand again. "Thanks for everything Wednesday night -- you were a big help. I owe you."

"You know I've got your back anytime, every time." Mike slapped Rafe's shoulder and turned to the tense brother, Matt. "Nice to meet you, man, your sister's a class act."

Matt shook Mike's hand, feeling bad that he should have been more friendly. "You, too, Mike. Thank you for what you did, and thank you for helping Nicki out that night."

"No problem, Sam and I were glad to do it. Maybe we'll see you all again before the weekend's through." His subtle hint that it was a joint effort the other night was noted.

"Sound's good." Matt said goodbye to Sam, and the couple walked away, stopping at the bar to say something to Sam's friend and meet Jason. They left a minute later, and Jason came walking over with the blonde.

"Hey, guys, this is Katie. I guess you know her friends." Jason helped her into a seat but didn't sit himself, just stood behind her chair.

The introductions were made, and Rafe told Jason a little bit about Mike and how they had all just met Sam.

"Are you a federal agent, too?" Nicki asked Katie.

She laughed, "No, I'm a dancer."

"Oh," Ali and Nicki said together, and Matt shot Jason a look, a smile playing at the corners of his lips.

Rafe knew enough to keep a straight face and his mouth shut.

Jason just shook his head at Matt and excused himself, walking over to the band.

"Nicki's a dancer, too," Ali said, winning herself another kick under the table.

"I'm not a stripper." Katie laughed, sensing what they were all clearly thinking. "I'm a principal dancer with the Miami City Ballet."

"Oh!" Nicki and Ali said together again with much more emphasis.

Matt shot Rafe a look -- that works, too.

"That's amazing!" Nicki said. "And I'm not a stripper, either." She laughed in apology and at the wishful look Matt shot her.

Katie smiled and went on to answer questions about the ballet for Nicki and Ali.

"The band is pretty good, huh?" Matt commented to Rafe.

"Real good tonight," Rafe agreed. "Hey, sorry about Mike -- he can come off a little aggressive sometimes."

Matt laughed and joked, "I'm just glad I came back when I did. He even had me blushing at the end."

Rafe laughed. "He's a real charmer, but he's a funny bastard."

"Yeah, and I can tell he's harmless, and I know you had my back while I was gone."

Rafe nodded. "Absolutely." He stole a glance at Ali. She was beautiful sitting there, alive, having fun. She was going to be his wife someday. His chest filled, and he looked at his watch.

Jason came back and sat down next to him, Katie on his other side.

The band was in between songs, and Matt couldn't help noticed how the drummer kept looking over at the table specifically at Nicki. The guitar player was looking, too, for that matter -- at Ali. Matt looked from Ali to Nicki and then back to Rafe, who seemed to have picked up on it as well, because he was now intently looking at the guitar player.

"Just how long were you girls here listening to the band last Friday night?" Matt asked out of curiosity.

Ali looked at Nicki. "A couple of hours, why?" She looked at Rafe, who was smirking.

"Because you two have a fan club," Rafe answered dryly.

Jason laughed, overhearing. "Those guys are cool -- I met them. I told them you all came in to hear them play."

"Well, do they see Rafe and me sitting here?" Matt asked, his back up.

"Relax, they're harmless," Jason assured him.

"They are nice -- we met them," Nicki admitted.

"You met them?" Matt was definitely jealous.

"They bought us a drink on their break and sat down to talk," Nicki told him with a smile as she watched his expression.

Ali looked at Rafe to judge his reaction.

If Rafe had known that night what had gone on, then he would have been insanely jealous, but he sat back now, relaxed and happy, a content man with no worries. However, it *would* be polite if the guy stopped looking Ali's way.

Ali was laughing at Matt's reaction and how Nicki seemed to be enjoying it.

Matt looked at Nicki and grinned. He'd put an end to any confusion right now. He gripped Nicki's chair on either side.

Nicki laughed at the predatory look in Matt's eyes and knew he was coming in for a kiss. She was ready for him and accepted it with fervor. She didn't want there to be any confusion, either.

Ali was still laughing and looked over at the drummer, who had caught the display and gave an "oh, well" shrug in defeat. "Okay I think he gets it!" she laughed to Matt and Nicki, who still hadn't separated.

Rafe nudged her and gestured for her to sit on his lap. The band started up again, and he shared a smile with Ali as she made herself comfortable. The band played "Everlong" by the Foo Fighters, and Ali groaned.

"I told you, I can't hear this music without thinking about our first night together."

Rafe teased and nuzzled her neck. "They're the only CDs I brought to the cottage."

She laughed. "That's fine with me -- at least I'll get a good workout now that I can't run for awhile."

"Oh, you'll get a good workout, all right." His hands shifted her rear strategically.

Ali felt him. "Jason's friend seems nice."

Rafe paid no attention. "You smell nice, and you feel nice."

"You feel nice, too." She moved just enough to tease him.

"I want to touch you so badly."

"You are touching me," she teased.

His hands moved slowly under the hem of her dress, under the cover of the table. "I want to touch you under here." He caressed her bare thighs.

She leaned down to his ear. "So go ahead." Heat soared through her body, and she could feel the wetness dampen her panties. He groaned as she took his hand, discreetly, placing it on her, letting him feel it for himself.

Rafe tried to keep his hand there, his arousal painful in his pants, but she moved his hand away, smiling.

"I'm going to the ladies' room."

"You can't get up now!" He laughed.

"Just pull your chair in under the table when I get up." She grinned.

"You're brutal." But Rafe did just that and took a long pull on his beer. Was it time to go yet? Thank God they were steps away from the cottage.

Ali stood up and straightened her dress. "Nick, Katie, ladies' room?" Jason gave her a thankful look for including Katie, and she smiled at him.

When the girls were gone, Jason winked at Rafe and turned to Matt. "All right, little brother, I'm about to give you an awesome gift."

Matt cocked his head. "Oh, yeah? Your season tickets?"

Jason laughed. "Better."

Matt took a drink and looked at Rafe, who shrugged. "What kind of gift and why?"

"You'll see, and it's because I think you're great, and I want Nicki to know it too."

Matt looked at Rafe again, a little embarrassed, "What, are you drunk?" He laughed. "What the hell are you talking about?" Jason seemed pretty pleased with himself, and Matt was just confused.

Jason looked over at the band, who were just finishing their song, and caught the singer's eye, giving him the heads-up.

Matt followed Jason's gaze and then looked at Rafe. "Oh, shit."

"Okay, ladies and gentlemen, we have a special guest in the house tonight representing Boston..."

There were a few cheers and hollers as Rafe looked around. He saw Ali, Nicki, and Katie emerge from the restroom, making their way back to the table.

"What's going on?" Nicki asked, returning and sitting down.

The band had stopped playing and were making some kind of announcement.

"Let's give it up for Matt Fuller, everybody!"

Huh? Nicki looked at Matt with surprise.

The crowd clapped as Matt shot Jason a look. "You are so lucky I've been drinking, or I'd beat the living shit out of you right now!"

Jason grinned. "Yeah, yeah, just get your ass up there!" he said sternly.

Rafe was watching the exchange and looked at Ali, who seemed just as confused.

Nicki was glaring at Jason. How could he do this? He was deliberately setting Matt up as a joke. She couldn't let him go up there, but he was already rising and walking away.

"Matt!" she called out, and he turned and gave her that crooked smile and a wink. Oh, no. "Jason!" she hissed across the table. "This isn't funny!"

"I think it's fucking hysterical!" he answered her, laughing at the horrified look on her face.

God, she had thought he was so nice! Why would he want to embarrass Matt this way? She turned to face Ali for help and grabbed her drink. She couldn't bear it if Matt saw any judgment on her face. Oh, God, she prayed it wasn't too awful.

Ali and Rafe looked at Nicki's face and then at each other. What was happening?

"Jay, what the hell is Matt doing up there?" Ali asked him. "He hasn't played since he was fourteen!"

Jason sat with a smile and stared at Matt, just waiting and ignoring both Ali and Nicki, who were glaring at him.

Rafe was a little uncomfortable for Matt's sake and gave him a half-hearted smile in encouragement when Matt looked over at the table. He didn't know what was about to happen, but he prayed it wasn't going to be awful. He looked over at Jason, wondering if he was the guy he thought he was. He was somewhat relieved when Jason leaned over and said, "It's all good."

"Thanks, guys." They all heard Matt come over the mike. "I won't bore you for too long -- I'm just going to play a song for my lady over there." And he gestured to Nicki, who had been forced to turn at the sound of his voice filling the room. Everyone cheered as their eyes fell upon Nicki, and her face turned beet red.

"Our Father, who art in heaven." Nicki prayed silently for the electricity to shut off. She watched as Matt slung a guitar over his body and said a few words to the band. She shot one last desperate look to Jason, but he just winked at her, and she looked at the floor in despair. Her stomach was in knots, worse even than when she had left the house earlier, and she was sick for Matt -- but then the room quieted, and he started playing the guitar…and her head almost snapped off her neck.

It was just him at first, for the first few chords, and she recognized the introduction, and then her eyes grew wide as the band came to life, joining him -- and he started to sing! Oh, my God!

"Hello, my friend, we meet again,
It's been awhile, where should we begin?
Feels like forever
Within my heart are memories of perfect love, that you gave to me
Oh, I remember

When you are with me, I'm free
I'm careless, I believe
Above all the others, we'll fly
This brings tears to my eyes
My sacrifice"

Nicki's eyes immediately brimmed with tears, and she sat on the edge of her seat. Holy shit! He was singing Creed to her, and he sounded just like the lead singer! Matt was phenomenal on the guitar, *and* he could sing! He was playing the bridge with the band, and she swiveled around to Ali, whose jaw was practically on the ground. Tears ran down Nicki's face now as she quickly looked to Rafe, who, judging by his own look, obviously hadn't known, either, and then she swiveled the other way and turned on Jason, who was looking at her with a huge satisfied smile. Then he winked.

"There's your rock star, Nicki."

Nicki quickly turned back to Matt. She gripped the sides of her chair and took in every word he sang from his lips, his beautiful eyes looking right at her and giving her that crooked grin.

"We've seen our share of ups and downs
Oh, how quickly life can turn around, in an instant
It feels so good to reunite
Within yourself and within your mind
Let's find peace there

'Cause when you are with me, I'm free
I'm careless, I believe
Above all the others, we'll fly
This brings tears to my eyes
My sacrifice"

Nicki watched him play, his hands and fingers moving effortlessly over the guitar like it was part of him. He looked like he belonged up there, like it was his band. She laughed in awe of him, wiping her tears, and never taking her eyes off him. He was grinning at her as he played, knowing she was surprised. She saw him look at Jason, too, and shake his head with a laugh. He started singing again, low and gritty, and just like a rock star.

"I just want to say hello again,"

Then louder.

"I just want to say hello again,"

And the drummer did his thing. And then Matt was singing again, just him and his guitar, looking right into her eyes, the band hanging back. *"'Cause when you are with me, I'm free. I'm careless, I believe, above all the others, we'll fly. This brings tears to my eyes, my sacrifice."*

The band kicked in to bring the song to an end, and the place went nuts. Ali was standing up cheering, screaming, and clapping, along with Rafe and Jason, who were whistling and hollering, and Nicki just sat there with her hand over her mouth, more tears running down her cheeks.

Rafe was blown away. Matt could be in his own band selling CDs -- he was awesome. He looked down at Ali, who was cheering for him, shaking her head in awe.

Jason was so proud of him. He looked at the expressions on everyone's faces and knew they thought he was great, too. He hoped Matt was taking it all in.

Matt was on a definite high. He felt incredible; his body was pumping with adrenaline. All this week whenever he had heard that song it had made him think of Nicki. It was perfect, and he knew he had blown her away playing it for her. He laughed, looking at her. She couldn't stop crying, and he wanted to go to her, but if he had the chance to impress her a little more, he was going to take it. He turned to the band, who were all encouraging him to do another song. Hell, yeah!

Matt came back on the mike. "Hey, they're going to let me be a rock star for a couple more minutes, so..."

The crowd screamed their applause, and Matt went into Nickleback's

"Rockstar," getting some appreciative laughs from the crowd, especially Ali, Rafe, and Jason. Nicki still sat there, looking straight at him, a smile playing at her lips. She was definitely into it and moving to the music, but he knew that look in her eye, and he flashed her his best rock-star grin and watched as she shook her head at him real slow. This was *so* going to be a good night.

Ali moved on the other side of Rafe to stand beside Jason and Katie. "Uh, how long has this been going on?"

"Like you said, since he was fourteen." Jason laughed. "He's a bad ass, isn't he?"

"Uh, yeah!" Ali agreed, nodding her head emphatically. "I guess I'm just wondering why I didn't know about it?"

"He keeps it to himself. Don't take it personal," Jason tried to assure her.

"Do Mom and Dad know?"

"No, he's a little self-conscious about it. He only plays in front of me. He used to play at college parties when he was drunk and he had some balls," Jason laughed, "but now he just plays at home by himself."

"Do *you* play like that, too?" Ali couldn't believe this.

He laughed. "Shit, no, mediocre at best."

"Why don't I believe you?" Ali rolled her eyes.

"Trust me, or I'd be up there, too." Jason smiled at Katie.

Ali looked at Rafe. "I had no idea."

"He's awesome, Ali. He should be on stage every weekend."

"I know!" She laughed happily and continued to watch and listen. She looked at Nicki, sitting down, facing Matt, riveted to her chair, and then started laughing even more, pointing to her.

"What?" Rafe asked.

"I can only imagine what's going through her head."

"I got her good, didn't I?" Jason was cracking up. "I told her yesterday while we were out drinking that Matt couldn't play for shit but that *he* thought he was great. Did you see the look on her face when they called him up there? I thought she was going to kill me. She was petrified for him. Oh, my God, that was priceless!" Jason was laughing so hard, trying to catch his breath.

"Oh! You are so mean!" Ali, Rafe, and Katie were laughing, too.

They watched as Matt ended the song, and everyone clapped and cheered. He thanked the crowd and the band as he handed them back the guitar.

"Thanks, guys, that was fucking awesome!" Matt shook their hands.

"Hey, any time, man. We're here every Friday night."

Matt laughed. "I might take you up on that -- that's addictive!" Matt thanked them again and turned to step off the stage. As his foot hit the floor, he looked up to see Nicki standing. She was coming toward him, and he was aware of people shushing, and the room getting quieter. What the hell? He looked to their table to see Ali, Rafe, Jason, and even Jason's date or whoever she was watching Nicki come at him, and holy shit if she wasn't coming at him!

Ali nudged Rafe and Jason, and they followed Ali's gaze to the dance floor where Nicki walked, all long legs and sexy dress, toward Matt coming off the stage. All eyes were on her -- in fact, the room had settled down to a dull roar. There were even a few whistles from the crowd, cheering on whatever was about to happen.

Nicki saw him take that guitar off, and she stood right up, wiping her eyes and straightening her dress. She made the short walk across the dance floor and came to a stop right in front of him. Reaching up with both hands, she grabbed his face, then kissed the living hell out of him.

Matt pulled her right into him and laughed against her mouth as the room erupted and cheered loudly, but her determined heated kiss soon had him replicating her passion.

Nicki didn't pull away until she was sure he got the message. "I want you to take me home right now."

Damn! Matt saw the look on her face and picked her right up off her feet. More cheers ensued, and he was laughing as she was kissing his face all over. He reached in his pocket, digging around as he walked toward their group. He pulled out some cash, threw it on the table in front of Jason and Rafe, gave them all a wide grin, and called out, "Oh, man! See you later!"

The room exploded in hoots and hollers as Matt carried Nicki right out the front door.

Ali, Rafe, and Jason couldn't stop laughing. Katie was cheering just as much as the crowd, and she said loudly, "God, that was just like the end of An Officer and a Gentleman!", which had them all bursting into another bout of laughter.

Ali remembered the scene well. Way to go, Nicki -- way to go!

CHAPTER FORTY

Matt couldn't stop laughing as he fumbled for his keys. Nicki was kissing him relentlessly, and her hands were all over him.

"I'm not going to get us there if you keep doing that."

"I don't care if you lay me down in this sandy parking lot. I want you so badly."

"Wow, what got into you?" Matt teased her.

"You know damn well what got into me, and what I *want* in me right now!" she said against his ear.

Whoa!

Nicki felt an urgency she couldn't describe or control, and she reluctantly let him put her down and into the passenger side of his car. Her hands went right to his thighs when he got in and started it.

Matt cursed the speed limit, feeling as if they were going at a snail's pace the whole three-minute drive. When he finally pulled into the driveway, he slammed it into "park" and hopped out to open Nicki's door. He pulled her right up against him as she stood up. He closed the door, pushed her right back against the car, and grinded himself into her. "I've been waiting for this all week," he said gruffly.

Nicki kissed him with a desperate need. She moved a leg up around him, her heeled sandal digging into the rear of his jeans, her dress riding up to her hips. She couldn't get close enough.

Matt lifted her other leg so that they both hugged his hips and he could carry her to the front door. Her dress was now bunched at the waist, and he held her bare ass in his hands. Oh, man. "Where's your key, Nicki?" She was busy separating the buttons on his shirt and kissing his neck. God, her lips felt so good on his skin. The key, focus on the key.

"It's in my purse." She kissed his lips. "Back on the table." She kissed his neck. "In the bar." Back to his lips.

"What?" He nearly whimpered.

"There's a spare under the mat."

Oh, thank Christ. Matt squatted down, holding on to her, and found it while she laughed.

"I got it!" he said triumphantly and stood back up.

He managed to get the key in and open the door, locking it behind them. He carried her right past the kitchen, down the hall, and right into her bedroom, where he tore off the bedspread and laid her down on the soft cool sheets. The reflection of the moonlight off her bedroom sliders provided them with just enough light.

Nicki lay on the bed and watched as Matt took off his shirt, revealing his muscled chest. He came toward her with both hands and slid her dress up and over her head. She lay there in just her thong underwear, and she looked at him as he stared down at her.

"Oh, Nicki," he whispered in awe.

She sat up and reached for his waistband. It took some doing, but she got the zipper down and reached in to set free his impressive erection. He started to lean her back again, but she put her hands on his hips to stop him. She scooted off the bed instead and guided him over to the edge to sit.

Matt watched in awe as she knelt on the floor before him, her beautiful full naked breasts touching his knees. She placed her hands on his thighs and kissed the tip of him softly. Oh, sweet mother of God. His jeans were still on, and she grasped the bottom of his cock, keeping him free of his shorts. His fists clenched the sheet on either side of him. "Nicki." It came out like a warning.

She smiled up at him as she opened her mouth all the way to take him in. Jesus! The sight of her doing that was all he could stand, but selfishly he wanted to enjoy it. He put a hand to the back of her head, guiding her. Her warm mouth and tongue moved over him at an erotically slow pace. Every muscle in his body tensed and twitched. He moved his hands off her head and gripped the sheet again, leaning back slightly on his elbows, letting her suck the length of him. Her pace increased, and he watched her head move faster, her hair moving around the insides of his thighs. Oh, shit! He pulled back out of her mouth and had her up and on her back in an instant. Reaching into the pocket of his jeans, he grabbed the condom he'd placed there, shucked the jeans, shorts and shoes, and rolled it on. He hovered over her, taut and ready, and watched as she slipped out of her panties. He was rewarded with that nearly hairless mound that he'd been dreaming about the past few nights.

Nicki just watched him as she took her undies off. The want in his eyes filled her to her core, and she moaned with pleasure as his hand went right to her, feeling her heat.

"Jesus," he breathed. She was so wet.

"That's what you do to me," she whispered.

Matt brought his body down on top of hers, and he entered her with sheer primal need. Nicki cried out as he filled her, and he repeated the movement over and over. He couldn't get deep enough or close enough. He moved a hand to the back of her leg and propped it up on his shoulder. He was fucking her so hard and so deep that she cried out his name, urging him on. Their bodies were slamming together, slick with sweat, and Matt knew he was going to come any second.

Nicki pushed back as hard as Matt pushed in. They were fucking each others brains out. She couldn't get enough -- he had turned her on so damn much up on that stage, and she wasn't going to let him forget it. She adjusted her other leg and let it rest over his other shoulder, allowing him to sink even deeper inside of her. Oh, God! It was so intense she cried out. How could something feel so good? She felt the sensation inside her building, felt him, too, tensing inside of her, and she contracted around him, gripping his arms with her hands, her nails digging into his biceps, and oh, God, they pushed so hard against each other, and then she felt him burst and shatter into her very core.

Matt grabbed the headboard with one hand and grunted loudly as his body rioted with the most intense orgasm he could remember having. He reached for Nicki's hand and interlocked their fingers, squeezing tight as shockwave after shockwave ripped through him.

"Matt, oh God, Matt!" Nicki brought her legs down, letting them fall to the mattress, having no strength to hold them up anymore. Matt moved his arms to accommodate her and collapsed on top of her, holding her tightly to him, still throbbing inside her heat.

Nicki felt them coming as she came, the tears that seemed were inevitable when she was able to love him like this. She held him fiercely, her hands splayed across his back, feeling his jagged breaths, his lips on her neck, his hands in her hair. Their bodies were covered with moisture, and it sealed them together. She smiled into his shoulder and sang Bono's lyric in her head, "stuck together with God's glue." It made her smile, and she hugged him tighter, trying to keep him there, stuck to her, wanting every ounce of love she felt to flow right through his skin and into his heart.

"I feel you, Nicki," he whispered into her hair. "I feel your heart beating right against mine." It was now or never. If what they had just done didn't convince him, nothing ever would. Her chest was heaving beneath him, and he lifted his chest, thinking he was crushing her. When he looked down at her face, she was crying…really crying.

"Hey, beautiful," he said softly. "Why the tears?"

Nicki tried to wipe the stupid tears so she could see him clearly. He was so big and strong looming above her -- she'd never felt so safe in her life as she did in his arms. He had to know; she knew he must know. It might as well be stamped on her skin, but she had yet to say it out loud to him.

She brought her hands up to his face, and he kissed each palm, looking back in her eyes expectantly. "Matthew James Fuller," she whispered and saw him smile. He knew it was coming -- he wore that crooked grin that got her every time, and she laughed a little. "I love you with all my heart and soul, and I have for as long as I can remember." She laughed again, covering her eyes with her arms, feeling a wash of relief and just a little bit of fear.

"Ah, Nicki." Matt smiled down at her, tears threatening to well up in his own eyes at the sound and meaning of her words. He moved her arms so he could see her face and look her in the eye. "I love you, too," he said softly. "I am so damn crazy in love with you."

"You are?" she sniffled. Oh, thank you, God.

He kissed her softly, pulled back, and kissed her again. "Really, truly, madly, *deeply*." He moved inside her, eliciting a smile.

"Oh, I'm so glad!" Nicki kissed him, her tears finally subsiding. "I'm sorry about the crying. I just can't seem to help it."

He laughed. "If it makes you feel any better, I almost just cried, too."

Nicki laughed. "I never knew rock stars could cry." She was teasing him, but they had yet to talk about his performance.

Matt laughed and slowly pulled out of her. He got off the bed and cleaned up quickly, returning to her and pulling the sheet up over them. He pulled her in beside him and held her tight against him.

"Seriously, Matt, what you did tonight ...was incredible. I had no idea! You were awesome. I mean, the way you played that guitar, and you have an incredible voice!" And he loved her! "How long have you been doing that? And how come Ali didn't know?" Nicki sat up, her chest leaning over his, and he automatically reached for her breasts.

He grinned at her as he played with them. She was so beautiful. "I've been playing since I started taking lessons in high school. I told you I played, remember? I just keep it private. Maybe I'm a little shy." He grinned as he kneaded and fondled.

Nicki laughed at that. "You, shy? And yes, you told me, but I figured you just fooled around, maybe knew how to play a few campfire songs." She laughed. "And then Jason told me you played and weren't really any good, only *you* thought you were great, so when you went up on that stage, I was horrified for you!"

Matt howled with laugher. What an asshole! "He told you that? Oh, I so have to pay him back for that!" He was laughing hard, thinking what Nicki must have been going through. "You were scared for me, huh?" Oh, shit, that's funny. He caught his breath, calming down.

Nicki hit him playfully, "Yes! I was picturing you getting booed and everything. I wanted to murder Jason on the spot!"

He laughed again. His brother was so funny. "So it turned out okay, right? You liked it?"

"Matt, I *loved* it, when I heard you start on the guitar, I was floored, and then when you started singing! And that song, and those lyrics! I've always loved that song, and you sounded just like the guy -- what's his name?"

"Scott Stapp." Matt was grinning, enjoying the compliments.

"Yes, and the way you looked at me while you were singing? I just about melted on the spot. The words just fit, and I believed you when you sang them to me."

"Good, because I meant them. I heard that song a hundred times on my iPod working this week, and every time I heard it, I thought about you. So I was lucky the band knew it. I play it all the time at home -- Creed's a great band."

"So you can play it again for me sometime?"

"Anytime. I almost brought a guitar with me, too, but scratched the idea at the last minute."

"Why? That would have been great. You could have played for all of us."

"Too shy," he joked.

Nicki rolled her eyes. "You should be in a band. You're incredible." And she meant it. "I'll be your number-one groupie."

Matt moved her up to kiss her. Her chest now pressed to him, he reached between them and caressed her breasts again. "I love these, you know."

She laughed. "I kind of thought so -- you touch them a lot."

"They looked so good in that dress tonight. You had the attention of every guy in the room."

"I was trying to get your attention, make you want to stick around a little longer."

"I'm not going anywhere."

Her stomach fluttered. Except back to Boston in two weeks.

"I love you."

Hearing him say it was something that until tonight she'd only dreamt about. "Oh, God I love you, too," she breathed, and rested her head under his chin, doing her best not to cry again.

"I couldn't wait to get back here and tell you that, and hearing *you* say it was worth every agonizing minute I had to wait." He stroked her back and ran his hands through her hair.

"I can't believe you love me," she said softly.

"How could I not? You're a beautiful, intelligent, powerful woman."

"Powerful?"

"You're strong, inside and out. It's impressive -- *and* you have nice tits." He smiled as she slapped him, laughing.

"Those are nice compliments -- thank you. Even the last one." She grinned.

"I had a lot of time to think these past four days, *alone* at night."

"What did you think about?" She grinned.

"I thought about how I didn't like being away from you, and how no one has ever made me feel like that before."

"No one?" She knew he'd had girlfriends for long periods of time. She knew everything about them.

"Not one person, Nicki. I ached being without you."

She moved her hand down to touch him.

"Not just there Nicki." He guided her hand back to his chest and placed it over his heart. "Here, too."

Nicki felt the tears start to well up again. How did she get so lucky?

"I don't want to ever have another week like this again."

Nicki kept her head down on his chest, not daring to look at him. What was he saying? "No?"

Matt held her and shifted them so that she was on her back again beneath him. He rested on his arms, his hips and legs between hers. "Nicki, look in my eyes," he demanded.

She did, but hers were filled with tears again, and she had to use the backs of her hands to wipe them dry.

"I want you…" His voice was suddenly hoarse.

"I want you, too," she said quickly.

"No, ssh." He wiped a falling tear. "I want you to marry me and have my babies. That's how I want you."

Nicki's mouth opened to speak, but he kissed her so that she couldn't. Was he for real? Did he just say that? Her heart was pounding, and her nose was stuffed and she couldn't breathe. She pushed him away.

Matt moved back, thinking there was something wrong. Maybe he shouldn't have said that so soon.

"Matt, you don't have to say that. I love you, and knowing you love me is enough." Nicki reached over to the night stand for a tissue. He was caught up in the moment or something -- he'd lost his mind. Knowing that he loved her *was* enough. She would never expect his love to match the intensity to which she loved him this soon. She could wait and hopefully one day he would love her as much as she loved him, because she did want nothing more than to be his wife and have his babies -- lots of babies.

Matt got off her and knelt beside the bed, fumbling in his jeans, the slight light in the room shadowing his naked body. Nicki watched as he tried to find a condom. She smiled. "I put some in the top drawer." Except he didn't go for the drawer. He turned to face her, still kneeling, and reached for her hands. Nicki turned to her side, leaning up on one elbow, to face him.

"Nicki, I said those things because I really mean them." He brought her left hand to him and kissed it. "Will you marry me, Nicki?"

Nicki sat all the way up in a shot. "You're really asking me to marry you?" she asked incredulously.

Matt stared at her breasts again and her slender waist, and became instantly aroused. "I'm bare-assed naked in front of you, asking you to marry me. You don't get more real than this." He laughed.

She laughed, too, sucking in her lower lip, "Do you know how many times I've dreamt of this?" She was crying.

"No, I don't. Is that a yes?"

She let out a whoop. "That's a yes!" She hugged him and could see he was holding something in his other hand behind his back.

"What do you have?" She grinned through her tears.

Matt smiled and brought his hand around, holding out his palm.

Nicki's jaw dropped at the exquisite diamond that lay in it. "You had this planned?" She sobbed. It wasn't just the heat of the moment or the excitement of the night -- he'd planned it, he'd actually thought it through.

"I told you, I can't stop thinking about you, and I want us to be together -- forever."

"Oh, Matt." She gently picked the ring up and admired it. "It's beautiful."

"You're beautiful." He took the ring from her and placed it on her finger. It fit perfectly.

"How did you know if it would fit?" She held up her hand to admire it on her finger.

"I had some inside information," He grinned, getting up off the floor and sitting beside her.

"I can't believe this. I'm dreaming, I know I am." Nicki leaned into him.

Matt laughed. He was so happy she was happy. "You like the ring?"

"I love the ring, it's beyond beautiful. Who told you my ring size? And who else knows about this?" She laughed, still looking at her hand.

"I put in a call to Grace. She told me your size after giving me her blessing."

Nicki felt overcome and dropped her head to his shoulder. "I just can't believe this."

"I called her Tuesday..."

Tuesday? He knew he wanted to marry her on Tuesday? Nicki smiled widely and let him finish.

"...and asked her to explain things to your parents so when they get home they don't think this was all that crazy. I couldn't very well call your dad and ask for permission when he hasn't seen me in a few years and probably has no clue about us. Am I right?"

"Yes, that wouldn't have gone over too well," Nicki agreed. "But what did Nan think?"

"She was quite happy and said, 'What took you so long?'"

They both laughed.

"Oh, I am so deliriously happy." Nicki was truly overwhelmed.

"Good, me, too, and I'm also starved. Let's go raid the kitchen. If you want a rock star in the bedroom, I'm going to need fuel."

Nicki laughed, accepting the hand he held out, "Why come back to the bedroom? I'll take a rock star in the kitchen, over on the couch, maybe out by the pool," she teased him.

Matt bent to kiss her. "See, *that's* why I asked you to marry me."

Nicki followed him down the hall, "I knew it, just for my tits."

Matt stopped her in the hall and pressed her against the wall, his hands right on her tits. "I'm just lucky they're part of the package." He kissed her hard and decided to refuel later.

CHAPTER FORTY-ONE

"I could be convinced to leave now, too," Rafe told Ali.

"I'm ready." She smiled. She picked up her purse along with Nicki's, who had left it on her chair in her haste.

Jason was head to head with his new friend Katie when Ali and Rafe stood up from the table.

"Jason, we're heading back to the cottage. Are you going back to the house?"

Jason sat back in his chair. "There's not a chance in hell I'm going back there!"

Rafe laughed, understanding. "Yeah, probably not a good idea."

"I'll just get a room here. I'll see you guys tomorrow before I go."

"Can't you change your ticket so that you fly out of Fort Myers on Sunday instead?" Ali asked. She didn't want him to go.

"I don't know, I guess." Jason looked at his new friend and smiled. "Probably."

Ali and Rafe exchanged a knowing glance. "Let's meet up tomorrow, then. I'll call the rock star and his groupie in the morning." Ali smiled at Katie and gave Jason a kiss goodbye.

Jason laughed. "Sounds good. Goodnight, guys."

Rafe and Ali walked outside into the balmy air, leaving the air-conditioned bar behind.

"Umm, that feels so good, doesn't it?"

"It sure does." Rafe held her steady while she unstrapped her heels and took them off.

"Matt was incredible tonight. I'm blown away."

"How could I not know that he could do that? I feel kind of left out." Ali sulked.

"Oh, don't. I bet it's as Jason said -- Matt's just private about it, although he shouldn't be. Why don't you talk to him about it tomorrow? I'm sure he'll be honest with you." Rafe put his arm around her as they walked. "Right now, though, you should only be thinking about being naked underneath me."

Ali laughed. "You're right -- that's a much better thought. Race you to the door!" She took off with her heels swinging in her hand and her bare feet digging into the shelled parking lot, but the sudden pain in her shoulder slowed her down and brought her to a stop. She turned to face Rafe. "Hey, you didn't even try to run," she complained.

"Because I knew it would take you ten seconds before you realized your shoulder was hurting. What are you trying to do, open up the stitches?"

"I kind of forgot, actually," she said, embarrassed.

"C'mere." He scooped her up and brought her to the door.

Ali kicked the sand off her feet, rubbing them together, before Rafe put her down inside the cottage. She dropped her heels and put hers and Nicki's pocketbooks on a nearby table.

"Want a water?"

"Yes, please." Ali headed off to the bathroom.

Rafe grabbed two bottles from the fridge and followed Ali into the bedroom. He could hear the water running in the bathroom. When she finally came out, her face was freshly scrubbed, and she was no longer wearing her dress. She was completely naked.

Rafe put his water down on a nearby table and went to her. "You're beautiful."

"You make me feel that way."

He traced a finger from her throat down over her breast and down to her stomach.

"Did I shock you tonight?"

"Yes." She started to unbutton his shirt. "I still can't quite believe it." She used both hands to slide it off his shoulders, and once it was off, she slipped right into it, fastening a few buttons.

"What did you do that for?" he asked, placing his hands under the shirt to touch her again.

Ali's skin tingled with his light touch. "I want to ask you something. Let's go out on the porch."

She took Rafe's hand and led him out to the small love seat. The cottage was nestled neatly behind a bank of hibiscus and gardenia bushes, giving them a modicum of privacy and a heady scent to go along with it. The tall palms that framed the entrance swayed gently in the warm night breeze, and Ali felt so grateful just to enjoy the sight and be there with Rafe. "I'm going to miss your beach house, but this is so romantic and cozy."

Rafe sat and pulled Ali's legs on top of his as she leaned back on the opposite arm of the couch. "What did you want to ask me?" He moved his hands slowly up and down her smooth legs.

Ali settled back against the seat and relaxed, enjoying his touch. "It's so beautiful here," she sighed.

Rafe nodded, waiting.

Ali took a deep breath. "Something special definitely happened here this past week..." she paused, "...and as long as I live I'll never forget it." She laughed softly, looking at her shoulder. "I have a permanent reminder."

He could see the emotion running through her as she struggled somewhat to speak her words. He squeezed her leg in encouragement.

"I... just want you to know that I realize we may have both been overcome and caught up in...well, I'm not going to hold you to anything." Ali had been thinking about his words all night, and as much as she wanted everything he said, did he realize what he'd be giving up? "I mean, it's crazy, right?" Her laugh was tight in her throat. She swallowed hard, fighting back the emotion she felt threatening to spill over.

Rafe placed his hands under her thighs and scooted her over so he could bring her right up against him. Her head immediately went to his chest, and his fingers moved through her hair, massaging her scalp, and he felt her relax beside him. They sat there in silence for several minutes.

Ali took his silence for defeat. She knew he realized it, too. My God, he was an FBI agent in New York City! That was important. He was needed there -- it wasn't like any ordinary job. She couldn't ask him to give that up. As much as her heart would break, she would cherish any time they had left together. It would be even harder at the end, but she would survive, wouldn't she? Maybe they could try a long-distance thing, but could they make that last?

Rafe was her ultimate fantasy -- Beckham's great looks and body with the masculinity level jacked up to a 100. Tall, strong, and mysterious with eyes that stripped her naked, a man who could rock her world six ways to Sunday…*and* he carried a gun!

What she hadn't expected as she lived out her fantasy was that she would fall in love so hard and so fast. He was kind and sweet and thoughtful -- he was smart and loving and fun to hang out with. He made her feel safe, he made her heart race, and her stomach flip, and when she wasn't with him she counted every minute until she could be. How would she survive being apart from him?

"I'm going to tell you something." He broke the silence. "And I want you to listen carefully." He felt her nod against his bare chest.

"I'm thirty-three years old. I've been an FBI agent for the past ten years, I've been an uncle for nearly as long, and I've had a few girlfriends and lovers along the way. In all that time and in all that experience, I have never felt anything remotely close to what I feel like when I'm with you.

"When I saw you on the surveillance camera that night, yes, I was drawn to you sexually. Who wouldn't be? And then when I saw you in the bar up close and in person, my attraction to you hit a whole new level. I had to be with you. But it was when I actually met you out running that morning and looked into your eyes and heard your sweet voice that I was taken, and it only got better from there. You're beautiful, Ali, but you're funny and intelligent, too, and I respect you and your goals and aspirations. I want to help you achieve them."

"I love the way you look at me." He laughed. "Those eyes, oh, man, those eyes." He went on, "And you've definitely inflated my ego. I love that you're impressed with what I do and *that I carry a gun*." He laughed again and felt her do the same against him. "You make me feel like I can conquer the world when you look at me the way you do. You turn me on beyond belief, and when I see you, all I want to do is feel your naked body against mine. When I tell you that sex with you is like none I've ever had, I'm not lying or exaggerating. It's incredible -- you're incredible, and I honest to God am head-over-heels in love with you." He felt her arms tighten around his waist and the wetness from her tears on his skin.

"This is going to work, Ali. I've already put in some calls about transferring to Boston and..."

Ali lifted her head off his chest, and Rafe could see the steady stream of tears flowing from her eyes. She sniffled. "You did?"

He smiled, using his thumb to wipe them away. "Yes, and it looks like there's a job for me there if I want it. I obviously wanted to discuss it with you first, but I can start there pretty much when you go back."

Ali couldn't believe that he would do that for her. "Rafe, everything you just said," she cried. "How did I get so lucky?" She buried her face in his chest inhaling him, loving the sound of his beating heart beneath her head.

"It's not luck, Ali. Something brought us together because that's the way it was supposed to be."

She nodded against him again. She believed that, too.

"Are you going to cry all night?"

More nodding.

He laughed. “But I want to kiss you.”

Ali got up off the little couch and motioned for him to follow her.

She was so sexy in just his shirt, and he was reminded that she wore nothing underneath it when she reached up for a tissue on a nearby shelf. He followed, fully aroused, as she walked into the small bedroom. She pulled back the covers on the bed and got in.

Rafe sat down on the edge of the bed next to her. “I was thinking about another idea, too.”

Ali smiled playfully. “I’m listening.”

He grinned, “I was thinking that maybe the last two weeks of my vacation we could drive up to New York. We could stop along the way anywhere you wanted, and you could shop for things for your store. We’ll just ship anything that doesn’t fit in my truck. We can hit all the antique shops through the Carolinas, or any state you want. We’ll map it out, and then when we get to New York, I’ll introduce you to my family.”

Ali was sitting up now and hugging him tight. “Rafe, that sounds so good! So good! But you’re giving up so much for me. You know, I thought about it too, and I could just as easily move to New York.” She looked at him, her heart so filled.

“I want to do this, Ali. I want to go to Boston. I’m ready for a change, and I want you to have your shop right where you envision it. I want to make all your dreams come true. I want to make you happy, Ali.” He bent to kiss her, and she pulled him down on top of her playfully.

He pulled back, laughing. “Besides, New York is only three hours from Boston. We’ll be able to visit my family on long weekends and some holidays.

“What about your friends and colleagues? Won’t there be people you miss? Like Mike?”

“I actually have some friends in Boston who work for the Bureau, and my friends are always traveling. Mike especially -- he's actually worked in Boston before." Rafe fingered the buttons on the shirt. "I'm looking forward to this, Ali."

"Oh, God, this is really going to happen?"

"Yup." He grinned. "Now I'd like my shirt back."

She smirked. "Okay, but I'm going to need those jeans."

Rafe stood to accommodate her, and she sat up to do likewise. When he reached in the nightstand, he turned to look at her, and he shook his head when she saw the gun.

Ali couldn't help it -- it gave her a jolt every time. God, the thought of him with it was so damn sexy.

"You're twisted, you know that?" He laughed, taking what he needed and shutting the drawer. "I'm going to have to keep my eyes on you."

"It just reminds me how powerful you are," she said, kneeling on the bed, his shirt in a circle around her legs.

He grinned. "The gun doesn't make me powerful, babe -- this does," he said, proceeding to show her with a grin.

CHAPTER FORTY-TWO

Nicki woke up to a warm breeze on her skin and the unmistakable sound of splashing in the pool. She turned her head lazily and found the source. Her bedroom sliders were wide open, the drapes drawn back and flowing with the light breeze, and she could see Matt doing cannonballs in the pool. She started laughing and sat up on her elbows to watch him. He got out of the pool, dripping wet, sneaked a peak into the room, and jumped back in, creating a noisy splash. Nicki was still laughing as she got up and crossed the room. She leaned on the door frame, waiting for him to surface.

"Hey gorgeous." He broke the surface and leaned over the edge. "Did I wake you?"

She laughed and folded her arms. "Wasn't that your intention?" Matt was looking at her hungrily, and Nicki unfolded her arms and walked over to the low end of the pool, stark naked.

Matt watched her slowly enter the water, bristle at the chill, and descend up to her waist. There is a Santa Claus. He covered the distance and wrapped his wet body around her. "Good morning."

"Good morning." She kissed his bronzed chest.

"We've come a long way since a week ago."

She laughed. "Yes, you went from having me topless in the pool to completely naked. What's your trick?"

"I showed you last night."

"Umm, show me again."

"Right here? Right now?"

"Is that a problem?" She peeled his shorts off under the water and threw them to the side of the pool deck.

Matt looked down. "I guess it's not a problem. Did I tell you I'm getting a pool when we go back to Boston?"

She laughed. "No, but that sounds nice." She jumped up, surprising him, and wrapped her legs around his waist. He held her by her bottom and laughed.

"What, no waffles first?" he teased.

"Did someone say waffles?"

"AAHHH!" Nicki screamed as she looked left over Matt's shoulder to see Jason standing at the pool gate, grinning widely. She released her leg hold on Matt, found her footing, and pressed herself tightly to him. Matt turned them quickly so that his full back was to Jason and his arms came around Nicki' protectively as he laughed at their predicament.

"Matt, this is so not funny!" she said, her head bowed against his chest in mortification.

"I guess I don't have to say good morning." Jason laughed as he walked over to a lounge chair.

Matt laughed into Nicki's hair. "You're up early," he called out.

"No, I'm out late."

Matt peered over his shoulder, taking in Jason's sunglasses, unruly hair, and clothes from the previous night. "Ouch!"

"Yeah, ouch," Jason agreed.

"Uh, Matt," Nicki reminded him, "a little help here."

"Okay," he said, chuckling. "Jay, go in the house a minute will you?"

"I'd be in there now if I had a key. Do you really think I'm comfortable out here staring at your ass?"

Nicki couldn't help but laugh. "But it's a fine one, ain't it?" she yelled over.

"Oh, is there someone there with you, Matt? Turn around, introduce me." Jason teased.

Matt was laughing.

"Ha-ha, very funny. You can get in through my bedroom sliders, and if you forget you ever saw this, I'll make you breakfast." God, had he seen *her* ass?

"Unfortunately for you, this little scene is forever embedded in my memory, but I'm only looking for a cup of coffee, so I won't be much trouble. I'm getting up now and going in. Make sure you count to twenty before you get out -- give me time to get down the hall." He was having too much fun with this.

Nicki peeked over Matt's shoulder. "Oh, my God! Do you think he saw anything?"

"Yup." Matt grinned, still chuckling.

Nicki stuck to him as he maneuvered them out of the pool. "Get a towel, quick!" She grabbed it out of his hands as soon as he picked one up and wrapped herself in it. She watched as he sauntered over to the side of the pool to pick up his bathing suit, all muscle and male, not one bit embarrassed.

Matt pulled his shorts back on and laughed at Nicki's expression. "What? You wanted this for breakfast didn't 'cha?"

Nicki squealed as Matt chased her back into the bedroom.

Jason went right into the guest bathroom and took a shower, hoping it would make him feel less like death. He had continued drinking with Katie, her friend Sam, and Rafe's friend Mike, who was a real funny bastard, late into the night. They had all closed the bar around two a.m., then went back to Katie's and Sam's room to continue the party. When Mike and Sam left, the party hadn't stopped. The alcohol had run out, which was probably a blessing, but Katie's energy had not. Jason had a new respect for the stamina of a ballet dancer.

As he stepped out of the shower, he was grateful she had had to leave the resort early to head back to Miami. She was starring in a show tonight, God bless her. He'd had a great time, but he was looking forward to some rest. He did have her number and address, though, in case he was ever in Miami, and he had received strict instructions to look her up, which of course if he was ever there, he would -- he wasn't a complete idiot.

When he emerged, dressed and somewhat revived, Matt and Nicki were nowhere in sight. He grinned and went to put the coffee on himself. He picked up his phone from the counter and dialed Ali's cell, not surprised when Rafe answered.

"Hey, man, sorry to call so early."

"No problem. I had an early phone call; I've been up for awhile." Rafe sat on the porch enjoying the morning air, letting Ali sleep. He had taken a phone call from Daniels out on the porch.

"Are you guys up for breakfast at the house?" Jason asked as Matt and Nicki appeared at the kitchen stools looking like two cats that swallowed an aviary. "Nicki's cooking." He winked.

"Sounds good to me. Let me go ask Ali." Rafe went into the bedroom and sat on the edge of the bed by Ali's side. He stroked her good arm, and she opened her eyes.

"Hi." She smiled at him, and his heart thumped in his chest. Why had he said breakfast sounded good?

"Jason's on your phone, wanting to know if we want to come to breakfast at the house. Nicki's cooking." He smiled.

Ali laughed softly. "Fruit and eggbeaters? Count me in."

Jason laughed and said to Rafe, "Tell her I heard that, and no, Nicki will be cooking a full breakfast with the works." Jason looked at her playfully, threatening her with his eyes.

Nicki threw a dishtowel that had been sitting on the counter at Jason and stuck her tongue out at him. It was then that he saw it. It had caught the sun coming in from the back sliders just so. His eyes went wide, and he looked at the both of them. Nicki had turned back to Matt, and she was smiling up at him and he was lost in her gaze. Holy crap!

"Rafe, tell Ali that she doesn't want to miss *this* breakfast." Jason ended the call and stared at his brother and apparently his future sister-in-law. They in turn were now staring back at him, no doubt having heard the tone in his voice at the end of the call.

Nobody said anything. Nicki and Matt just stared at him, hopeful but unsure looks in their eyes, as if he might not approve, and Jason found himself all choked up. He had listened to Nicki's heartsick tale of her nearly decade-long love for Matt, and it had made him sad to hear it, but it was such a great love story, Matt finally noticing her years later when it was actually possible for them to be together. When Jason had finally seen them together as a couple last night, he had been so happy for the both of them.

He came around out of the kitchen purposefully and stood in front of them. He grabbed his little brother and pulled him in for a bear hug. "Holy shit, man, congratulations." Jason spoke softly, conveying to Matt how truly happy he was for him.

Matt coughed, clearing his throat and patting his brother on the back. "Thanks, Jay."

Jason pulled away and looked at Nicki. He could see tears brimming at her lashes. They had become friends the day before at that little outside bar, and he loved her. She was perfect for Matt. He gave her a great big hug and said, "I couldn't be happier about this."

Nicki swallowed back her tears and looked at Matt with a big smile.

Jason smiled and walked back into the kitchen. "Of course, if I had known an hour ago that you were going to be my sister- in-law, I wouldn't have stood at the pool gate for so long."

"Jason!" Nicki shrieked and looked at Matt, horrified, as if it were his fault.

Jason was cracking up. "I'm kidding, I'm kidding. You can't possibly think that you're ever going to live that down?"

Matt was laughing hard, too. "Are you sure you want to marry into this family, Nick?"

Nicki smirked. "And here all these years I thought Matt was the only wise-ass." She turned to Matt. "Of course I'm sure. You and I can surely come up with some way to get him back over the next fifty years."

Matt smiled; he liked the sound of that. He took her in his arms and kissed her.

"I guess I'm cooking again," Jason muttered, getting out the eggs.

"I wonder why I'm not going to want to miss this breakfast?" Ali sat beside Rafe in the truck, Nicki's purse in her lap. The morning was beautiful, all blue sky and sunshine. The Gulf was as flat as a pancake and looked irresistible. "Maybe we could all beach it today. We'll come back up here so we can keep the drinks coming from the pool bar."

"Whatever you want to do sounds good to me. I love hanging out with your family."

Ali smiled. "My mom is going to love you."

Rafe smiled back. "And your dad?"

"He's going to love you, too. I should have said my mom is going to *fall* in love with you." She laughed.

"Is she hot like you?"

"Hey!" Ali laughed. "And yes, she is, by the way."

Rafe laughed. "My family is going to love you, too. I can't wait to bring you to New York."

"I can't wait to go." Ali couldn't wait for any of it: their road trip, his family, getting back to Boston, and starting a full-blown relationship with him. "Are you okay with me telling these guys that you're moving to Boston?"

Rafe took her hand. "Of course. I've already told your brothers I was in love with you."

Ali looked at him, shocked. "You did?"

"Yesterday, at the cottage. They were pretty cool about it."

"They're going to be really happy for us, I think."

Rafe pulled into the driveway, cut the engine, and helped Ali out of the truck. They went into the house through the front door and were swiftly blasted with the aroma of breakfast cooking in the kitchen. Nicki and Matt sat at the counter stools while Jason tended to the food.

"Wow, Jay, you sure you can't stick around? We could get used to this treatment." Ali smiled and greeted hello to everybody. She went to a cabinet and pulled down a mug. As she poured Rafe some coffee, she noticed Jason, Matt, and Nicki were rather quiet. She looked from one to the other as she handed Rafe the cup.

"Thanks." Rafe took the coffee and noticed what Ali noticed. They had clearly walked in on something.

Ali went to sit with Rafe on the sofa, snuggling up close. "So did everyone have fun last night?"

Jason spoke first. "I had a great night. I haven't been to bed yet, by the way, so if I disappear after breakfast, you'll know why." He turned from the stove to address Rafe. "I was hanging out with your friend Mike most of the night, Sam and Katie, too."

"No shit?" Rafe grinned. "Then I know you must be hurtin'."

"It could be worse -- we ran out of alcohol around three."

"Wow, Katie the ballerina is a boozer?" Ali kidded.

"No, actually me, Mike, and Sam did most of the damage. Katie, the poor girl, had to get up early this morning and drive back to Miami for a performance tonight."

"You're kidding! That's got to be tough -- she must feel like hell," Ali commented.

"Hey, what about me?" Jason winked at Matt. "I starred in her own personal version of The Nutcracker last night. I'm exhausted, too."

"Oh, my God, Jason!" Ali yelled, scrunching her face. "*Way* too much information."

Rafe, Matt, and Nicki couldn't stop laughing.

"I told you she couldn't take it," Nicki laughed.

Matt was doubled over, laughing so hard.

"I'm never going to be able to see that ballet again without thinking of you, Jason. Thanks for the visual." Ali shook her head trying to suppress her laughter.

Jason turned back to the stovetop to finish cooking, all the while whistling The Nutcracker Suite.

Rafe was laughing as hard as Matt, and Ali gave in. She met Nicki's eyes across the room as they laughed and saw something in them. Nicki smiled at her, and Ali figured it out. Matt had finally told her he loved her, and Nicki had obviously told him, too. She could see it now -- the way they were sitting next to each other, the way they kept stealing glances at one another, the way he held her hand. Whoa -- her hand. Ali stared at Nicki's hand, which held a huge mother of a diamond on it. Ali felt the emotion tighten in her chest as she looked at Nicki's face and then to Matt's. He was grinning at her.

"Oh, my God," she said quietly.

Rafe looked down at her. "What is it?"

Ali's squeezed his hand and got up and went to Nicki. Tears were streaming down both their cheeks. She hugged her fiercely, so happy that her dream had come true, and so happy that Nicki would not only be her best friend but the sister she never had as well. "Congratulations," she whispered. "I told you he was crazy about you."

Nicki nodded, holding her tight and sniffling against her.

Rafe watched the embrace and saw the ring on Nicki's finger as she embraced Ali's back. He got up as well to shake Matt's hand. "Wow. Congratulations, man, that's fantastic."

"Thanks, Rafe." Matt smiled and accepted a warm embrace from Ali.

"This makes me so happy," she told him.

Rafe gave Nicki a congratulatory hug and kiss as well. "I knew this would have a happy ending." He winked. She smiled gratefully at him.

"Breakfast!" Jason yelled, breaking the moment. Rafe offered his hands, and Jason placed two plates in them. "We'll eat outside."

Everyone grabbed something and brought it to the table. Nicki poured coffee and juice for everyone and sat down.

"I'd like to propose a toast to the happy couple," Jason started, "and to my brother, who deserves all the happiness in the world. You're blessed with an unbelievable talent and now with an unbelievable woman, both of which are going to keep your life fulfilled for a very long time. Congratulations, Matt and Nicki."

Ali shared a smile with Rafe. "Matt, you were unbelievable last night. I was blown away -- you have to keep playing for people, a lot of people. You should start a band."

Matt actually felt himself blush. "Thanks, Al, I had a blast last night." He grinned at Nicki and laughed, getting himself a playful slap under the table. "I could see myself doing it again."

"You absolutely should. It was incredible," Rafe added and laughed, too, picturing Matt carrying Nicki out of the bar.

Matt thanked him. "And how 'bout my girl here? Front page!" Matt hugged her shoulders to him.

Nicki smiled. "I couldn't have done it if I hadn't had an inside source with the Feebies." Nicki grinned at Rafe.

"Anytime. Hey, I got a bit of news this morning. Scintillo, you know, the Miami nightclub owner? The tobacco plant he owns with D'nafrio in Pinar Del Rio burnt to the ground this morning."

Nicki's jaw dropped. "Where the meth lab was located?"

Rafe nodded.

"Where's Pinar Del Rio?" Jason asked.

"Cuba. It's a small town. Scintillo bought the plant back in 2000.

D'nafrio became an investor only last year, just about the time we started seeing an influx of Ecstasy in the Miami clubs."

"Obviously not a coincidence. Was anyone hurt?" Ali asked.

"No, it happened just after midnight. The plant was closed." Rafe draped an arm around Ali's chair.

"Has Scintillo been arrested?" Nicki asked.

"Nobody can seem to find him." Rafe agreed with Daniels' guess that Scintillo had moved his operation to Mexico. "It's just a matter of time, though. We'll watch where the money from the clubs is being filtered. He can't function without that revenue."

"Will you have to go back to working the case?" Nicki asked and shot a look to Ali.

Rafe shook his head and put his empty coffee cup down on the table. "Actually, no, they've got a whole new team assembled already, my friend Mike's heading it up."

"So what will you do after vacation, Rafe?" Nicki pressed.

Ali saw the look pass between Matt and Jason. They were clearly uncomfortable, thinking Nicki had put Rafe on the spot.

Rafe smiled at the three of them and then at Ali, who gave him a look of encouragement.

"I've actually put in for a transfer to the Boston field office, and it's been accepted." Rafe waited as they all seem to process it.

"That's fucking great, dude!" Matt said with genuine enthusiasm. He and Rafe had become pretty good friends.

Nicki looked at Ali, a big grin forming on her face.

"So your going to move to Boston? You're not going back to New York?" Jason asked.

"Yes, and no." Rafe laughed softly, sensing Jason's trepidation.

"Because of Ali?" Jason ignored the incredulous look Ali gave him. He wanted to be sure.

"One hundred percent," he answered, and saw Matt smile.

Jason reached across the table and held out his hand. "We'll look forward to having you there, man. That's great news."

"Thanks." Rafe shook his hand. "I'm really looking forward to the change." And to starting a life with Ali.

Matt kidded him. "We of course can't guarantee your safety at Fenway if you're wearing a Yankees hat, but that's where your gun might come in handy." They all laughed.

"I'll try to be discreet in my support of them. Maybe only the hat and T-shirts inside the house with the shades drawn." More laughter.

"Hey, the beach is gorgeous today. Let's go camp out in front of the resort and drink 'frozens' all day." Ali stood up to clear some plates.

Everyone agreed but Jason. "I need a serious nap. I'll meet you later. I'm going to go online and change my flight, then go to bed."

"Don't sweat it, bro. Just leave your credit card on the counter -- I'll change your flight for you. I've got some emails to send anyway," Matt offered.

"Thanks, anytime tomorrow is fine." He got up from the table and yawned.

"Goodnight, all." He walked back into the house, whistling The Nutcracker Suite once again, emitting a wave of laughter.

When he was gone, Nicki turned to Matt. "You're totally going to screw with him, aren't you?"

"Oh, yeah, he's going back to Boston by way of Timbuktu."

"That's so mean!" Ali laughed.

"Between last night and this morning, he's two up on us." Matt grinned and winked at Nicki. "Lucky for him it turned out all right, but he still needs a payback."

Nicki reddened with a look of apology to Ali and Rafe.

The four of them cleared the table and gathered in the kitchen.

"I don't want to know about this morning, do I?" Ali asked.

"Not unless you want to hear about the sexual escapades of your best friend and your brother." Matt grinned.

"Is that like the Ice Capades?" Ali teased him back.

Nicki smirked shaking her head.

"Whoa!" Matt looked at Nicki in feigned shock. "I do believe she's coming around, Nick. I mentioned sex with you, and she made a joke."

Rafe laughed.

"Seriously, you two, I'm overjoyed with your news. Both our families are going to be so thrilled, and it's just going to be so much fun!"

Nicki smiled. "Thanks, Al, and we're happy for the both of you." She looked at Matt. "Now that we're engaged, I can speak for you, right?" she teased.

"You can do anything you want for me, and to me." He gave her the crooked grin, and Nicki slapped him playfully.

"See, it's that right there. I can't handle that." Ali grabbed Rafe's hand, laughing. "We'll see you at the beach."

"Yeah, we might be awhile," Matt called out, and Nicki giggled.

"I'm not listening, la, la, la, la…" Ali sang on her way out the door.

They had had a long, fun day at the beach, and even Mike and Sam had joined them, and Jason -- after a four-hour nap. Ali couldn't remember a happier time. They had all celebrated and discussed an actual date for the wedding and possibly a honeymoon right back here on Captiva. Nicki was bursting at the seams with excitement. She and Matt even planned a weekend back home to announce their engagement and show off her ring.

They had come to the solution that Matt would fly to the islands every Thursday night and leave Sunday night until the end of the summer, when Nicki would come back home. Matt assured her that it wasn't an issue monetarily at all, and in fact surprised everyone telling them that he was building a summer cottage on Cape Cod. Nicki was ecstatic, and Ali couldn't have been happier for them.

They had spent the following couple of weeks doing much of the same: beaching, biking, and finally getting out on that fishing boat. The guys had had fun catching their share of fish, and Ali and Nicki had enjoyed just getting to see the dolphins up close, frolicking and riding in the boat's wake. They picnicked in Ding Darling and took picture after picture of the beautiful birds and wildlife they found there, and Ali even got her first picture with Rafe, which she emailed straight to her mom, who proudly displayed it as her screen saver.

After Ali had gone back to the doctor at Healthpark and had her stitches and staples checked and to see that she was healing nicely, Rafe had taken her on a long motorcycle ride to Pine Island. They had had a nice lunch by the water and then got right back on the bike at Ali's request. She just wanted to ride with him -- the freedom was exhilarating, and she couldn't wait until fall when Rafe promised a trip to upstate New York.

They enjoyed reading Nicki's small articles and interviews in the Beach News each week and had laughed hysterically when Matt landed his picture on the front page of the paper for finding a junonia shell. Of course it had been on a day Nicki was working, so he had marched right down there to see her, demanding his fifteen minutes of fame.

Ali had even had a day just with Nicki when Rafe and Matt had gone to Miami for a golf outing at Mike Caplan's invitation. The guys had gone and even spent the night and the whole next day, while Ali and Nicki spent the night at Nan's house together, watching scary movies and staying up late into the night talking about their futures and laughing about their pasts. It had been the kind of night they had envisioned having when they first arrived on the island, before their lives turned blissfully upside down.

And naturally just one night away from their men was one night too many, so they both plotted a welcome back. Ali, of course, didn't want to know Nicki's plans, but her own had included Rafe walking into the cottage to the sound of the Foo Fighters reverberating through the CD player while she showered.

She and Rafe had watched sunset after sunset and swore that one morning they would get up for a sunrise, but sleeping in always won out until the morning they were to set out on their drive for New York.

"Wake up, sleepy head."

Ali had started running again just days before and thought Rafe was being a real taskmaster getting her up at the ungodly hour for a run. "The sun's not even up yet," she complained.

"Exactly. C'mon, we'll drive to the lighthouse, watch the sunrise, and go out for breakfast."

Ali opened her eyes. "That does sounds nice," she relented. She had thrown on some shorts, flip flops, and a hoodie, and they had taken the Ducati, which Rafe had decided to trailer back north rather than ship in case they wanted to explore by bike along the way.

Ali loved riding behind him on the motorcycle. It was such an intimate experience, her arms around him, her breasts pressed to his back, her legs against his, which he would inevitably caress at some point in their ride. The experience always left her completely turned on. So by the time they reached the lighthouse that morning and spread a blanket out on the sand, she was longing for him.

It was just at first light, and they lay on the blanket, kissing and holding each other close. They were the only two on the beach save for a dozen sandpipers digging for breakfast.

"Are you excited about leaving today?" he asked her.

"I am, but a little sad, too," she admitted.

"Why sad?" He moved a lone piece of hair away from her eye.

"I'm going to miss it here, miss *us* here. I only know us *here*." Ali sat up and hugged her knees.

"Are you afraid for us in the real world?" He laughed softly.

"Kind of." She looked at him. "For a few reasons."

"Like what?" Rafe sat up, too.

"Like you going to work in a new place and meeting new people --specifically women." She looked away, slightly embarrassed. "Like, where are you going to live? We never talked about it. I live in the suburbs. Will you want to live right in the city to be close to work? And if you do, realistically, how often would we see each other? I'd miss you like crazy, and then you might feel smothered." She leaned her head on his shoulder, wanting the closeness. "And I worry about you seeing me in work mode, either in real estate or setting up shop. I've been in vacation mode for so long here. Will you love that me? The one who might be stressed sometimes and not that happy when winter rolls around, when it's too cold to get out of bed in the morning, and who might gain five pounds from baking and eating lots of chocolate chip cookies over said winter. Will we argue? Will you regret moving? Will we ever not want to have sex? I'm scared about those things."

Rafe sighed and looked out at the placid Gulf. The sun was just starting to make its way to the horizon. "Ali, I am going to meet lots of new people, men and women, but I'm going to come home to you. I want to live with you, Ali. I want to live wherever you live. If you think it's too soon to be in the same place, then I'll buy a place next door."

She laughed and hugged him. "I don't want you next door. I want to live with you, too. I just assumed you'd get your own place -- I don't know why. My apartment is small, but we could look for a bigger one."

"Ali, I don't want to live in an apartment. I want to buy us a house where you can sit in your favorite chair and I can massage your neck and shoulders when you've had a lousy day at work, where I can light you a fire and keep you warm in my arms each winter night, where I can feed you those chocolate chip cookies and help you gain that five pounds in 'said winter' and where I can argue with you about how you were wrong to worry, I never regretted it a day moving to Boston, and also where I can make love to you in every room of that house, in every position, with clothes on and clothes off, in minutes and in hours proving to you that I will *never not want to have sex with you."*

Ali wiped the tears and watched the sun slowly rise, her head resting comfortably still on his shoulder, her arms still around his waist. She loved him so much, and her heart swelled at his words.

"Remember on the porch at Tween Waters, and I said that I wanted you to be my wife someday and that I wanted us to have babies and for our babies to give us grandchildren that we could one day tell this story to?"

"Yeah, that's kind of etched in my mind quite vividly." She laughed, sniffling, still wiping tears away.

"And remember I said I wouldn't rush you?"

Ali nodded, and he was moving to face her. He was kneeling in front of her, taking one hand, bringing it to his lips.

"I changed my mind, Ali." He'd done so in Miami.

Huh? She looked at him. The intensity of his eyes was softened by the love she saw there.

He bent to kiss her, just a tender, soft kiss. "I love you, green eyes, and I want to rush you. Will you marry me?" Rafe turned her hand palm up and placed a ring inside of it. Ali picked it up slowly and stared at Rafe. The ring actually looked like the sun -- its center stone was a brilliant round yellow diamond with white baguette diamonds encircling it, like a sunburst.

She didn't wipe the tears, just let them fall, her heart never more full. "Oh, Rafe, yes I will marry you." She smiled. "I love you. I love you so much." He slid the ring on her finger, and she kissed him with all the love she felt. "Look," she whispered.

Rafe hugged her close, thanking God for her, then turned to watch with her in his arms as the sun burst up over the Gulf in all its glory -- an infusion of pinks, oranges, yellows, and golds starting a new day.

A SPECIAL THANKS TO YOU THE READER-

Thank you so much for reading the first book in my island series. I'm having so much fun with these characters and it's only going to get more exciting!If you enjoyed The Three Sunrises please post a review on Amazon.com and feel free to email me from the guest page of my website www.kristenhartmanbooks.com or like me on Facebook-KristenHartmanbooks

Thank You!!!!!

NOW AVAILABLE

SIGNS OF FATE

SECOND IN THE ISLAND SERIES

BY

KRISTEN HARTMAN

VISIT

www.kristenhartmanbooks.com

When Jenna Thompson arrives at The Three Sunrises on Captiva Island, she isn't expecting to have to share her grandmother's vacation house. But the fridge is already stocked, there's a big black duffel bag in one of the spare rooms, and it all belongs to one man, Special Agent, Mike Caplan. Jenna's unexpected roommate is larger than life with the size, attitude and damnable good looks to back up the 'special'. She is entranced at once but this FBI agent's bewildering, cocky and dismissive attitude sets Jenna's pride and stubbornness in motion. She refuses to let him get under her skin. She's had it with men! Until, that is, her intended vacation is suddenly swept into a dark and erotic underworld complete with bad men straight out of central casting. Then she suddenly needs Special Agent Mike Caplan—in more ways than one!

FBI Special Agent, Mike Caplan is on Captiva Island for two reasons only—to end a year-long investigation and to get some R&R. He'll seize and arrest a wanted fugitive and then start his well-deserved vacation… simple. Except he un-expectantly meets Jenna Thompson, a gorgeous little spitfire who unwittingly puts his vacation on hold and catapults Mike into yet another investigation with familial ties to the last; it will put both his and Jenna's lives on the line. And while trying to save an innocent Jenna from the drug entrenched clutches of a Miami nightclub, Mike finds his defenses crumbling. He's falling fast for the strong, stubborn, and oh so vulnerable Jenna Thompson.